Saddled with Trouble

This is a work of fiction. Names, characters, places, and incidents either are the product of the author's imagination or are used fictitiously, and any resemblance to actual persons, living or dead, business establishments, events, or locales is entirely coincidental. The publisher does not have any control over and does not assume any responsibility for author or third-party websites or their content.

SADDLED WITH TROUBLE

Copyright © 2011 by Michele Scott.

All rights reserved.

No part of this book may be reproduced, scanned, or distributed in any printed or electronic form without permission. Please do not participate in or encourage piracy of copyrighted materials in violation of the author's rights. Purchase only authorized editions.

To Mom and Dad,
who nurtured my love of horses

ACKNOWLEDGMENTS

I want to thank my cousin and lifelong horse enthusiast Jessica Hanson for helping me with the research on this book; my friend and horse expert Nikki Shea for being a first reader; Bob Avila and Dana for allowing me to come up to their amazing facility and meet some gorgeous animals (Rocky included); Brian Davis of the Santa Rosa Police Department; Mike Sirota for his continued dedication to me and my writing; my agent, Jessica Faust; and my editor, Samantha Mandor.

ONE

MICHAELA BANCROFT DIDN'T HEAR HER SWORN enemy walking up behind her until it was too late.

"Working overtime?" Kirsten Redmond said.

Michaela whipped around in her desk chair, where she'd been sitting for thirty minutes going over finances. She immediately stood up. "What do you want, Kirsten?"

"I know you received some very important papers early this afternoon from our attorney, and I'd like them signed, sealed, and delivered as soon as possible, so that Brad and I can get on with our lives."

Michaela brushed a patch of dirt off her Wrangler Jeans. She'd been working with the horses and out in the barn all day and knew that her appearance wasn't remotely close to Miss Glamour Puss's here. The thought caused a flutter of discomfort. "You amaze me. What, do you have your little hair-sprayed, fake-bake, plastic Barbie doll-looking friends spying on me? Because it truly is a wonder how you know every little detail of my life. Or maybe you're screwing the mailman, too. Does his wife know? What, did he give you a call as soon as he delivered the papers?" She hated sounding so bitchy. God, why couldn't she just turn her back and ignore Kirsten?

"You're such a bitch."

That was why. Not that she *was* a bitch, but Kirsten and Brad had sort of pushed her into that category and she was living up to it, at least at that moment. "Yeah, well, it takes one to know one. Now, be a good girl and run along and play dress up or paint-your-nails with your girlfriends. Okay?"

"At least I *have* friends."

"Oh, that hurt. And, you probably have some real quality conversations with them. You know, about important subjects like what color hat and boots you'll wear to this year's Miss Rodeo Pageant. C'mon, Kirsten, give up the dream. You're a bit too old for the crown and from what I know of rodeo queens, they have a lot more class, know how to ride a horse, and have a brain. Oh yeah, and they're what, usually about five years younger than you are?"

Kirsten frowned. "I was Miss Rodeo of Indio, you know."

"Yeah, five years ago. I think I do remember. Wasn't there some article about the Coachilla Valley being desperate for entrants?" Michaela smiled sweetly, knowing she was getting the best of Kirsten.

Kirsten stomped her foot. "At least I've got Brad and you don't, and as soon as you get those papers taken care of we can start planning our future and I can start thinking about what color to paint our nursery. We want *lots* of children."

"I feel sorry for those kids." Michaela's stomach tightened and she clenched her fists.

"Just sign the papers."

"Just go away. Bye, bye." She waved at her. "Some of us have important things to do."

Kirsten stood her ground, planting her light pink Justin boots into the dirt. Her long blonde hair hung loose down her back, and her overly made-up face caused her to look aged and brittle for someone who couldn't be over twenty-five. She shoved her hands into her plastered-on jeans, belted in by a bright silver belt buckle— her Miss Rodeo Indio silver belt buckle.

"Listen. I've asked you to leave nicely. I don't have time for your games. Trust me, I don't want Brad within fifty feet of me. Why you feel the need to annoy me like this is very confusing. *I've* moved on."

"Great, so you'll sign the papers?"

Michaela sighed and forced a smile. "The papers. Yeah, well see, those divorce papers aren't your concern. It's really between Brad and me."

"Not really. We want to get married. Brad just got a new truck. A Ford F-350. It has a backseat. We got the backseat for when we start having babies. And, trust me, it won't be long."

Anger rose from Michaela's gut and rushed straight to her brain. "As I told you, I don't want Brad back at all. Here's the problem, though: Brad owes me a lot of money from debts incurred by him, and I want that money. When I get it, I will sign the papers. Maybe he should think about returning the truck."

"*I* bought the truck. And, Brad would be able to pay you off on *your* debt if your uncle hadn't fired him."

"That debt is *our* debt, not just mine. And, as for my uncle Lou firing Brad, that was cut and dry: Brad wasn't showing up for work even before Lou discovered what was going on between you two, but once he did and showed me the proof, Brad never even phoned Lou. I don't think my uncle had much of a choice, other than to let him go."

"Whatever. You are so gonna be s.o.l. if you don't make a move quick and sign the paperwork." Kirsten did the hair flick thing, a sign of her disdain for Michaela.

All it did was make Michaela want to laugh. "Let me give it to you in simple speak. Brad is an adulterer, so I will sue him to my heart's content until he pays me back every dime, and something tells me that the judge is going to be on my side. Or, how about this? I just won't sign the papers *ever* and all those babies you're talking about having will automatically have a stepmommy."

"You can't do that!" Kirsten whined.

"Watch me." Michaela was aware that she really couldn't. After all, it was California, and she knew she only had thirty days to sign the papers or contest the decree before she defaulted. She was banking on Little Miss Hot Pants not being exactly well-versed in California state divorce law. But, surely Brad's lawyer was, and no matter how Michaela tried to play it, she'd likely be *forced* to sign those papers. She also knew that she would probably have to sue Brad for what he owed her in medical bills, and rumor had it he was going to file bankruptcy, which meant that she wouldn't ever see a penny from him. The lawyer fees alone in taking Brad to court would put her out of business. She knew Brad was living off Kirsten, so why not sign the papers and be free of him, her, and the whole mess? Because *they'd* stuck it to her and she wasn't about to let them get the best of her. Not yet, anyway.

Kirsten turned on her heel in a huff and marched out. Michaela walked out of her office and peered outside the breezeway, watching Kirsten roar away in her red convertible Mustang GT, kicking up dust all the way along Michaela's drive. Talk about trouble. Michaela shook her head and let out a long sigh. What she'd ever seen in Brad Warren was beyond her, because anyone who could fall for a tramp like Kirsten was not a man she would ever want to be involved with. But she had been, and as Mom always liked to spout the age-old adage, "You made your bed," now she'd have to lie in it.

She turned and headed back to the barn to say her goodnights to all the horses down the row. She stopped at the end— at Leo's stall. Her ten-month-old colt glanced out, then returned to his dinner. Michaela had big plans for the little guy. She'd nurtured him from the night he'd been born last March and for a time it had been touch and go. She hadn't known if he'd make it . . .

* * *

THE EARLY SPRING NIGHT STILL HAD A CHILL IN the air. Michaela held a thermos of coffee in her hand as she curled up on a cot inside her office, checking on her mare every hour or so and listening intently for any sounds that might echo down the breezeway, alerting her that the time had come. Cocoa, her brown Lab, lay at her feet, snoring. Michaela had put a blanket over the aging dog. Usually by this time of night the two of them would be sound asleep in the house.

Her mother, after calling earlier, stopped by and brought her some homemade chicken noodle soup and coffee, aware that Michaela would be keeping vigil into the wee hours. It didn't matter how many foals Michaela had seen born in her thirty-two years. It never ceased to amaze her.

Around 1 A.M., as she drifted off to sleep, a thud woke her. She hurried into the stall. The mare eyed her from her straw bed.

Michaela went inside and knelt down beside her, stroking her face. "I know, girl. It's okay. You're all right. You're all right."

Little Bit let out a groan and lifted her head, groaned again, and laid it back down.

"Easy, easy. You're doing good. Good girl."

The mare's water broke and wet her underside. This was it. Michaela went around to Little Bit's backside. The front hooves came first, and then the long spindly legs, revealing black legs like Little Bit's. Next, a tiny face with a small star on it poked through, and with one final push the foal slid out, slippery and covered in the birthing sac, which with Michaela's assistance came right off. She took a hand towel from her jacket pocket and wiped the foal's nostrils and eyes. The foal struggled, laid back down and struggled again. Michaela wiped the tears from her face. The miracle of life.

Little Bit groaned again and Michaela noticed that she was having a hard time lifting her head to look at her baby. She watched for seconds before she realized what was happening with her mare. A lot of blood— everywhere. Oh God. Wait! This was all wrong. Oh God, no! She was hemorrhaging. Somehow she'd been torn inside during the birth. Michaela pulled her cell from her coat pocket and called Ethan Slater, her vet— and longtime friend. Growing up around horses and being a rancher's daughter, she knew that there wasn't a whole lot she could do, and it was unlikely the vet could either. She was losing too much blood, too fast to get her into surgery, and Michaela cried as she gently stroked Little Bit's face, willing her to live and in some way hoping she was alleviating any pain the old girl felt.

Ethan pulled in fifteen minutes later. But it was too late. Little Bit had died, quietly bleeding out as Michaela held her head and whispered to her. When he opened the stall door, he reached his hand out to Michaela and she took it. He pulled her up and hugged her. "I'm sorry, kid. I'm really sorry." He let go after a minute and looked at her with his intense green eyes. "We've got work to do now. She's gone, but *he* has a chance. C'mon. Go to the truck and in the right side of my vet box are packages of Foalac. You'll find a bottle there, too. Get them out and follow the mixing directions. I'm going to move him, so you don't have to see her like this. Okay? Now, go unlock one of the open stalls and slide the door for me."

Michaela knew that the timeline they had to get the colt to feed was about one to two hours, but the sooner they could get a grip on things the better, just in case there were further complications where he was concerned. She was so grateful for Ethan's no-nonsense, methodical ways. She wanted to fall apart. She loved that mare. Hell. Thank god, Ethan knew exactly how to handle the situation *and* her.

She nodded and followed his orders, leaving the stall as he went to pick up the colt, who weighed about seventy pounds. Michaela had lost animals before, but the pain was always just as intense. But she'd never lost a mare this way, and of all her horses, she'd had a real connection with Little Bit. She had an inside joke with herself about how she'd wished for years she was more like her mare, who had no problem at all getting pregnant.

    She took the supplemental food and mixed it as Ethan tended to the colt. She brought it back in the large bottle he'd told her to grab. Ethan asked her to set it to the side. "Let's get him up to drink. We don't want him choking." Together they helped the colt get to his feet. Michaela grabbed the bottle and handed it to Ethan, who took it from her and stuck it into the colt's mouth, teasing him a bit at first with it, allowing him to get used to the feeling of the rubber nipple. The baby gummed it, but soon his pink fleshy tongue wrapped around it, and as sucking noises escaped from his mouth, Michaela felt her body relax. She stood on the other side of the colt in case he lost his balance on still-wobbly legs. That night, she resolved to see him through, to see him grow strong and healthy. She'd named him Peppy Leo after his great-grandsire Mr. San Peppy and great-great-grandsire Leo San, both of whom had been huge cutting horse champions, and because her colt was as strong as a lion. And he had *survived.*

* * *

"GOOD NIGHT, CHAMP," MICHAELA SAID TO HIM. She turned out the breezeway lights and headed toward the house, knowing that in a little more than two years her colt would indeed be a champion. As resolved as she'd been to save him that night ten months earlier, she was just as committed to her vision for him— and herself— now. Kirsten might have taken Brad from her, and the bank might come after her, and who knew what else might happen, but no one could steal her dream from her— the dream she knew would become a reality.

TWO

MICHAELA OPENED THE BACK DOOR TO HER ranch-style house, which led into the laundry room. The house, located in Indio, California, amid the Coachella Valley, had been built in the early 80's and was badly in need of an update. Michaela and Brad had bought it with the horse facilities in place a couple of years after they were married, almost a decade ago. Her plans to bring it into the twenty-first century would have to wait until the debts were paid off.

She breathed in deeply. The smell of fabric softener and detergent filled the air. Unbelievable. Camden had actually been doing laundry. Huh. Surprise, surprise. She had come to believe that Camden simply went through clothes until she didn't have any left and then went out and bought more.

Michaela pulled her boots off, not wanting to track mud through the house. Shania Twain's "Whose Bed Have Your Boots Been Under?" blared from the family room. God, why *that* song?

A little farther away the blender in the kitchen whirled at full throttle, probably mixing the contents of a powerful concoction— tequila, lime-aid, and more tequila. Michaela shook her head as she headed to her room to shower.

Cocoa, who recently had made it to her tenth birthday, lifted her head off her doggie bed and wagged her tail. Michaela bent down and patted the dog's head. "Hey you, you lazy girl. I see how it is, as soon as the sun goes down you hightail it back inside. By the looks of it, I'd say Miss Camden has been letting you dig into the doggie treats again. I'm going to have to scold her." Cocoa just kept on wagging her tail.

Michaela checked her voice mail:

"Hi, sweetpea, it's Uncle Lou. Give me a call back. I was wondering if we could have breakfast in the morning."

She smiled. Uncle Lou was definitely one of her most favorite people.

But the smile faded when the next message came on. "Michaela, it's Kirsten. You better sign those papers, or else we're gonna have big problems."

Michaela flipped a finger at the machine. Why did she let that little hooker get to her? "Ooh look at me, I have fake boobs, collagen lips, lipo on my ass, and I'm Miss Rodeo America," she said out loud, her head bobbing from side to side in an exaggerated fashion.

"News to me."

Michaela spun around to see her best friend and newly acquired roommate, Camden standing, in the doorway, margarita in hand. She tossed back her latest colored locks— flame red— and held out a glass of the concoction. "I gotta tell you that if those are fake boobs, your plastic surgeon did a shitty job, because girlfriend, you're about a B cup. And, for God's sakes who would pay five thou for a measly B cup?"

They both laughed.

"Let me guess: The evil babe who the *shithead* robbed from the cradle has been bugging you again."

"Yep."

Camden held out the margarita. "Drink on me?"

"Nah. Thanks, though. It's been a rough day. The evil babe came by and gave me a piece of her mind. I don't think a margarita will cure this girl's blues."

"No. But a shot will, and I am not taking no for an answer. Now, c'mon." Camden grabbed her hand.

"I need a shower."

"Ten minutes more won't hurt. If I can stand you smelling like a horse, then you can wait. Live a little, and don't let this stuff get you down. You'll be old before you know it and then you'll be dead and you'll be saying, 'Damn I should have had more tequila shots with my best friend.' "

She held up her hands, palms out. "Fine, I give up. I know better than to argue with you. Besides, maybe you do have a point." She followed Camden into the kitchen. "But don't you have a date with Kevin tonight?"

"Nope. He's taking clients to dinner. I'll be seeing him tomorrow. He's taking the day off and we're going to spend it together." Michaela frowned, and Camden added, "I know you don't care for him."

"It's not that. I don't know him that well, really. I just didn't like that he was kind of a jerk to my uncle when he wouldn't sell him his property."

"He can be pushy, I admit that, but he backed off when Lou told him he wasn't interested. He's moved on to other projects."

"I know, but be careful, okay? Get to know this one a bit better than the last one before he slips a ring on your finger." Michaela had a right to be concerned that her friend would rush into another relationship. Her recent split from her third husband, Charlie Dawson— a big-time financial advisor— had left her in a lurch. Seems Charlie knew exactly how to work the financials to his benefit and Camden was out on her butt and wound up at Michaela's front door needing a place to stay, until she could find a place of her own to rent or buy. That had been six months ago, and as far as Michaela knew, Camden hadn't done any house shopping as of yet, only man hunting. She kept insisting to Michaela that Charlie would settle with her, because she hadn't signed a prenup, and then she'd get into a new house. But Michaela really didn't care. She enjoyed her friend's company and wild ways, so far removed from her own behavior, but entertaining nonetheless.

"What, you afraid you're gonna be stuck with me forever? That you'll have to install a revolving door for your divorcée friend? Won't happen, worrywart. I'm gonna find me a real man who can take good care of me and me of him. Who knows, it might be Kevin, it might not." She shrugged. "Now, let's have that drink."

Ten minutes turned into twenty and before long an hour had passed and Michaela had filled up on two of Camden's cure-alls, though refusing to down the shot. She didn't think she could handle the booze straight. "You know that SOB has a new truck," Michaela said. "A Ford F-350." She shook her head. "Kirsten tried to tell me that she bought him the truck. Please. Does it say sucker somewhere on my forehead? Jerk probably hid some money away that I didn't know about— maybe he hid some cash in a safety deposit box or under the mattress, or better yet under, his *girlfriend's* mattress. He's such a jerk, and that little trophy he hangs out with is a piece of work." Oh boy, the alcohol was certainly going to her head.

"You know." Camden pointed at her. "It's not like you aren't gorgeous. I don't know why you always say *she's* the trophy. She's no prize. Brad lost the prize and I bet he knows it. Look at you. Oh, and I might add that you have a brain, too. A commodity Kirsten definitely lacks."

They were sitting on the couch in the family room. Camden took her by the shoulders and turned her to face the mirrored wall behind them. "Just *look* at you."

"Oh yeah, look at me. Real prize. I've got horse crap on my jeans, and my hair is pasted to my head from sweat. Yep. I'm a real prize."

"Shut up." Camden stood with her empty margarita glass. "Want another?"

"Nope. I think I've had enough."

As her friend walked into the kitchen to pour herself a refill, Michaela turned back to the mirror. She pulled the rubber band from her blond hair, letting it down, and studied her reflection. Twenty-two was ages ago; well, ten years to be exact. Although her boobs were small, they were still perky, and her hair wasn't bleached blond like a *Playboy* model— or Kirsten the rodeo queen— more of a sandy color, long and thick, too. That was a good thing. But, those damn freckles that the sun liked to exaggerate still gave her that "I'm the cute girl next door" look. At least her eyes were something; she really liked her eyes. They were nice— warm, hazel, garnered-lots-of-compliments eyes. Who needed fake anything, anyway? Botox was rat poison! And plastic boobs could rupture. Yep, *natural* worked just fine. A little more sunscreen and a Miracle Bra, maybe, but the other stuff— forget it, and who could afford it anyway? Damn if she could.

Michaela moved to a barstool at the counter, watching Camden pour some more margarita.

"It would be kind of fun to do something nasty to him, wouldn't it?" Camden asked.

"Who? Brad?" Michaela shrugged. "Yeah, I suppose it would. I'd love to do something to that stupid new truck of his. I'm sure he loves the thing."

"Ooh, like key it?"

Michaela gave her a look. "Nasty and mean are two different things. I don't know if I could go that far."

"You're a prude."

"Are you calling me a goody two-shoes?"

"If the shoe fits."

"Shut up. Pour me one more of those. Tell you what. Since we're in no shape to drive, I'll carry out a dirty deed to give Brad a nightmare to contend with." Camden rubbed her hands together. "On one condition." Michaela shot her index finger up.

"This is going to be good, isn't it?"

"We've gotta do this on horseback."

"Oh, sister, you expect a lot from a friend. You want me to get up on one of those filthy beasts?"

"Um, Camden, I doubt it would be the first filthy beast you've gotten up on top of."

Camden started to protest, then said, "Okay, you may have a point. So, you're willing to take a chance on putting my drunk ass on one of those animals and venture out in the dark?"

"Yep. Besides, I know you. You're barely buzzed. Me, on the other hand . . . phew, you make a strong drink. I'll put you on Booger. He's push button. I'd put a baby on him and trust him."

"Great. I get to ride a horse named Booger. The fact that I am even doing this is *so* not me."

"Who knows, you may like it."

They took their drinks out to the barn, where Michaela saddled up the horses. "Okay now, come here and give me your left foot." She clasped her hands together.

"What?"

"Put your foot in the stirrup here. Grab the saddle horn here with your left hand, and the back of the seat of the saddle with your right hand and step up in the stirrup and swing your right leg over the rear end of the horse and sit in the saddle."

"God, Michaela, I had no idea I'd have to do a flipping gymnastic stunt."

"Aren't you the girl always bragging about her flexibility?"

Camden sighed. "Fine. Let's do this before I change my mind." Michaela got next to her and helped to give her a boost up. Camden squealed as she swung her leg over and nearly came off on the other side. Michaela helped her get adjusted. "Oh shit, shit, shit. Get me off. Get me off now!"

"No. Now trust me. Hang on. That's all you have to do. Hang on."

"No shit, Dick Tracy, you think I'm about to let go?"

Michaela grabbed a trash bag filled with the *contents* they needed and put them inside a saddlebag. The saddlebags tied on, Michaela put her left foot in the stirrup and swung her right leg over the mare.

"Showoff," Camden muttered.

They headed over to Brad and Kirsten's place, which was only a couple of miles away. It took some time because Michaela had to keep in mind that Camden hadn't been on a horse more than three or four times in her life. Every time she glanced back to see how she was doing, she could see by the light of the full moon that Camden wore a mask of fear. She tried to make small talk, but Camden was hanging onto poor Booger for dear life. Her hands were both around the reins and saddle horn so tight and from what she could tell it also looked like Camden had poor Booger's girth or mid-section in a vice. It was lucky Booger was exactly what she'd said he was— one mellow fellow— because a horse who wasn't so well broke would have been having a fit with Camden on board.

The lights were on inside Kirsten's house. Was that laughter? Yes it was. Oh, how nice for them. They were having a grand old time.

Kirsten's place was a modest ranch-style home with a few acres of land. There were a couple of horses out in a small pasture. One whinnied at the sight of newcomers.

"Shhh. Shut up," Camden whispered.

Michaela pulled slightly on Macey, her mare's, reins. The mare stopped, as did Booger. "Uh, Cam, they don't understand shut up. Besides, horses whinny at times. They won't think anything of it, even if they can hear what's going on out here. Sounds to me like they're having a party."

"Hmmm. I think you're right. Well, good, because we *are* the party crashers. Still want to go though with it?"

Someone inside cranked the stereo up another notch. It was playing Faith Hill and Tim McGraw singing "It's Your Love." Michaela peered through the front window and saw what looked to be Brad and Kirsten dancing. He had *never* danced with her. Jerk. "Oh yeah, I am so ready." Michaela dismounted and led Macey over to a hitching post next to the pasture. The other horses trotted over. The same noisemaker let out another "How do you do," and Michaela realized that time could be of the essence if he didn't pipe down. After enough whinnies someone would surely take a peek, and she wanted to be certain they were long gone before that happened. She wrapped Macey's reins around the post, and walked over to Camden.

"Okay, you always want to get on and off on the left side, so bring your right foot out and back around, then kick your left foot out of the stirrup— kind of lean over the saddle with your body and basically step down and off."

Camden did as instructed and landed on her butt. "Like that?" she asked, a smirk on her face.

"Not quite. You'll have a second shot at it later though, when we get back home. Now come on, get off your ass. We've got a treasure for Brad."

Michaela retrieved the trash bag and the two of them, quietly and quickly, all the while trying not to giggle at their immature antics, snuck up on Brad's brand-new red Ford F-350. She opened the driver's side door, knowing the moron wouldn't have locked it, sliced open the bag with her pocketknife, and shoved the contents under his seat. Boy, was it was going to be a real pain getting it cleaned out. "Nothing like the aroma of fresh manure to take away from that new car smell."

She tossed the bag down and grabbed Camden's hand as they ran back to their horses. She quickly boosted her friend up, who this time managed much better, and then she got back up on Macey. They rode off, cracking up the whole way home, making Camden loosen up, and actually enjoy riding Booger. Their laughter didn't stop even after they'd put the horses away, got cleaned up, and wound up on the couch with a bag of popcorn in front of the boob tube. "What I wouldn't give to see the look on his face."

"Oh God, I'd love to see him get in that truck and start smelling the smell and then he'll have to get out and when he looks under the seat, he's gonna die," Camden said.

This put them into another fit of gut-wrenching laughter. Yes, as childish as it had been, it did feel really, really good. Facts were that Brad had left for the much younger Kirsten after Michaela had spent the last few years trying to get pregnant. With Brad's support they'd sought out fertility specialists and Michaela had given herself shots daily in the abdomen in hopes of conceiving. She'd gone through the expensive in vitro process twice, and the day she was prepared to go through it again for the third time, Brad's infidelities had been brought to light. Now, there were a stack of bills from doctors on her desk and every time she looked at them, she couldn't help but be reminded of what Brad had done to her. Worse than sticking her with the bills, was his total deceit. But tonight was the first time she didn't feel a ton of anger toward her ex. Funny how a stupid teenage-type prank made her feel a bit better.

Michaela finally made it off the couch and into the shower she hadn't taken all evening. Then, finding Camden sound asleep on the sofa, Cocoa curled up on the floor next to her. Michaela decided to leave the two of them there, covering Camden with a blanket and patting her old dog on her head a good night. As she settled into bed, exhausted, her phone rang. She looked at the clock on her nightstand: a little after eleven. Her stomach sank. What if it was Brad or Kirsten and they'd seen her and Camden? No, caller ID said that it was her uncle.

"Hi, Uncle Lou."

"Hi. I didn't hear back from you tonight. Did you get my message? I thought I'd better check in and make sure you're okay."

"I'm fine. I did get your message. Sorry. I was a little busy."

"No problem, sweet pea. I was only concerned because I know that you've had some rough times this past year."

"Thanks. But I'm fine. Really. In fact, I'm doing, uh, really well." She loved the way he'd called her sweet pea ever since she could remember. Her father always called her pumpkin, and that made her feel good, too, but Daddy also knew how to spank and send her to her room, or ground her when she needed it. She loved him for his sense of fairness. But Uncle Lou was the spoiler. He'd never had any kids of his own, so spoiling Michaela was one of his favorite things. "You want to grab breakfast in the morning with me, right?"

"I do. There are some things I need to talk about with you." He cleared his throat.

"Uncle Lou? Are you okay? You sound . . . I don't know. Tired?"

"I'm fine. Working a lot, that's all. I'm having a hard time unwinding these days for some reason. I'm getting old, and riding the animals every day is starting to wear on me."

"You are not getting old," she said. "Sixty-one is a spring chicken."

They both laughed. "I don't know about that. I'm feeling like a cooked goose. You get to bed now, and I'll see you about seven-thirty over at The Dakota House."

"Ooh, sounds good." Her stomach rumbled just thinking about the yummy breakfasts The Dakota House specialized in, especially considering that all she'd had tonight was a liquid diet. "I can't wait. Sleep well."

"You too, sweet pea."

Michaela hung up the phone. Something in Uncle Lou's voice bothered her. What was it? The sound of exhaustion? At first she thought maybe that was it, but, no. Resignation? Maybe. Defeat? Yeah, it did sound like that, but about what? She yawned. Whatever was eating at Uncle Lou, she resolved to get to the bottom of it tomorrow over a ham and cheese omelet.

THREE

THE NEXT DAY MICHAELA ROSE EARLY AND HANDLED all of her morning chores before going to meet her uncle for breakfast. She suffered a bit of a headache from last night's fun, but it didn't take long to wear off as she went about feeding the horses and cleaning out the stalls.

Leo came up and nudged her while she changed his bedding, replacing the day-old shavings that had begun to smell like urine with fresh ones that made the air smell like sawdust. "Hi, you," she said. "What's wrong? You're not hungry this morning? You want to play?" She rubbed him on top of his forelock— the piece of mane hanging between his ears and down onto his face. He was such a beautiful animal— bay in color, a dark reddish brown with jet-black stockings going up past his knees, and an almost black mane and tail. He had a smidge of a star, almost like a crescent moon on his face, and his large brown eyes reflected an intelligence Michaela knew was indicative of a winner.

Leo turned back toward his food. She finished up his stall, and went into the office to see what was on tap for the day, after breakfast with Uncle Lou. It looked as if the vet was scheduled to come out and do some routine checks. She wondered if it would be Ethan or his partner. Had Ethan returned from his rafting trip? He'd suddenly taken off over two weeks ago without telling her he was leaving, and she'd been angry with him for it since. Ethan had been staying at her uncle Lou's place for a few months because his fiancé, Summer MacTavish, had broken off their engagement the night before their wedding. After Ethan left on his sudden trip, Michaela's mother mentioned to her that she'd heard he and Lou had had an argument. Michaela asked her uncle about it, but he wouldn't say much, just that they'd had a difference of opinion. It had bugged her since her mother had told her, and she planned to ask him about it if he was back today. She couldn't help but wonder if the argument had been over Summer herself, because Summer was Uncle Lou's accountant. And frankly, Michaela was a bit surprised that Lou had kept Summer working for him. Especially considering the way Summer left Ethan. Lou had been close with Ethan since Ethan was a kid, and Michaela figured that it probably hurt her friend that the man who really had been the closest thing to a father Ethan had ever known had kept Summer on.

After doing her chores she checked the clock: past seven. Time to go and meet her uncle. Camden wasn't on the couch when she went back inside to change. She must have moved in the middle of the night and made her way to her bed. She decided not to bother her. Camden drank twice as much than Michaela had last night and would probably feel much more the worse for wear this morning.

She beat Uncle Lou to The Dakota House and ordered a cup of coffee. The place smelled so good— a mixture of cinnamon, coffee, and bacon filled the air. She melted back into the vinyl booth and watched people come and go from the restaurant, which was decorated with various Indian "artifacts." Twenty minutes later she started to fidget as there was no sign of her uncle. It wasn't like him to keep her, or anyone for that matter, waiting.

She dialed his cell phone. It went straight to voice mail. She called the house phone. No answer, only a machine. She waited another fifteen minutes and tried again. Same thing. This was just plain screwy. She paid for her coffee and decided to drive over to her uncle's place to see what was up. He couldn't have forgotten. But maybe he'd simply slept in after his late night. It wasn't like him, but *that* tone in his voice last night hadn't sounded like him either. Had he been drinking? No. He hadn't come off like that. Granted, he liked a drink in the evening, but he was not known to booze it up.

A few minutes later she pulled into the luxury-style Diamond Bar Z, Lou and Cynthia's ranch. There wasn't much activity. Usually Dwayne, their assistant trainer, or Dwayne's cousin Sam, who also helped train, would be out working horses, and their ranch hand Bean— his nickname, because he was as skinny and lanky as a green bean— might be around. That was doubtful though, as Bean was notorious for being late. He was a bit slow. injury. Lou had taken him in years ago and given him a job.

Lou's truck was there. Cynthia's Mercedes wasn't. Strange. The big truck and trailer were both gone. Then Michaela remembered that Dwayne and Sam were probably hauling horses out to Vegas for the National Finals Rodeo. If she remembered correctly Uncle Lou said they were planning on pulling out for the rodeo yesterday, around noon. Dwayne competed in calf roping. Her uncle used to be involved in team roping, but with age had slowed down and now busied himself with the training and his responsibilities as the breeding manager. Michaela had made plans to trek over and see the rodeo over the weekend. Dwayne had given her free tickets, which were hard to come by, and Camden, who was going with her, had some connections at The Bellagio, so they were set with a nice room at a great rate. Michaela liked to watch the events; her friend liked to watch the cowboys. It was sure to be an entertaining weekend.

She got out of the truck and was greeted by her uncle's golden retriever, Barn Dog. "Hey, boy. Where is everyone?" She patted the dog, which licked her hand. "Some help you are." She laughed. "What's this? Paint?" She probed Barn Dog's fur near his collar. Maybe creosote. Lou used it to keep some of the horses from chewing on the wood pasture fence.

She headed toward the barn expecting to find her uncle there. Maybe one of the horses was sick. "Uncle Lou?" Her voice echoed through the breezeway. No Lou, but she did get a few whinnies as horses popped their heads out. None of them were eating. She looked at her watch. After eight. They hadn't been fed? Lou always fed them. Even though he had hired help, it was something he'd done for years. "Lou? It's me, Mickey."

She heard Loco pawing the ground in the last stall. Uncle Lou kept his multichampion cutting stallion a few stalls away from the other animals. Although a good stallion, he was still a stud, and he did have a mind of his own. A gorgeous blue roan in color, Loco came from great bloodlines and had earned almost almost three hundred thousand dollars in winnings. The horse was truly her uncle's joy in life.

"Hi, big guy," she said as she approached the stall. He lifted his head and snorted, his eyes wild. "Hey. What's wrong?" He was acting really off. His coat gleamed with sweat. And . . . what was that smell? Not horse sweat, but rather coppery. What the *hell* was that? She wrinkled up her nose. Was one of the mares in season? She doubted it. Lou knew better than to keep a mare in season in the same corridor as the stud. "Loco, what is . . ." Her voice faded as she peered into his stall. She stumbled back and grabbed hold of the stall's bars to keep from falling. Bile burned her throat. She swallowed hard and blinked several times. *"No, no, no!"*

The latch on Loco's door was undone; she whipped it open. The stallion bolted past her and out of the breezeway. She ran over to her uncle, who lay facedown in the straw— impaled on a broken pitchfork sticking through his back. She lifted his hand— cold. Her own hands shook uncontrollably as she dropped his to the ground. A scream caught in the back of her throat. She gasped and fell into the straw, pushing herself away from Lou. She brought her hands to her face, her voice catching up with her anguish as her horrified scream echoed through the breezeway.

FOUR

UNCLE LOU WAS DEAD. MICHAELA'S HANDS hadn't stopped shaking over the last hour since finding him, and the trembling had spread through her body. Even though the morning sun hit her face, she'd never felt so cold in her life. Would she ever be warm again? Would her stomach, all knotted, ever stop feeling like she wanted to throw up? Doubtful, after what she'd seen. She figured that her eyes were red and swollen from crying so hard.

This could not be happening. It could not be true. Why would someone do this?

She wiped the tears from her face and watched from the porch as more police pulled into the ranch. After she'd made the 911 call, a cruiser showed up, and within minutes was followed by detectives. A CSI team was now there, and the coroner was on the way. All sorts of people swarmed the property, taking photos, collecting evidence.

She'd been instructed by one of the officers to wait on the porch; someone would be over to speak with her. The poor horses in the barn were going nuts with all the commotion. Their whinnies resounded across the ranch, and they had to be starving. Michaela cringed listening to their distress, rested her face in her palms and sobbed. Again, the thoughts of who could've done something like this—*and, furthermore, why?*— raced through her mind.

"Miss Bancroft, would you like some coffee?"

Michaela looked up and squinted, blinded by the sunlight, to see one of the officers standing over her. He held out a foam cup. She took it from him, nearly spilling it, wrapping both hands around it to try and stop them from shaking.

The cop sat down next to her. "I'm Detective Jude Davis. I'd like to ask you a few questions."

She nodded.

He pulled out a small notepad and pen from inside his tweed sports jacket. "Your call came in around quarter after eight this morning. What time would you say you got here?"

"About five minutes before that."

"Did you notice anything unusual?"

"I noticed it was quiet." She set the coffee next to her on the step and took a tissue from her pocket. "I'm sorry," she said and sniffled, trying hard to keep from crying again.

"I understand. You say it was *quiet*." The sunlight caught his blue eyes, causing him to squint. He took a pair of sunglasses from his pocket. "Can you tell me what you mean by that?"

"Yes . . ." She paused. "Okay." She was having a difficult time finding words. This wasn't a conversation she could accept, much less even believe she was part of. "Usually in the morning there's a lot of activity with animals being fed. Sometimes my uncle might be on the tractor cutting grass or in the arena working with a horse."

"That's not what you found this morning?"

"No."

"What brought you here in the first place?" He raked his hand through his wavy blond hair.

She explained what led up to her finding Uncle Lou.

"Do you know anything yet? What happened?" she asked, as he continued writing in his notepad.

"We don't."

She shook her head. "I can't believe it. I don't know why . . ." She raised her soggy tissue. He pulled a clean one from his khaki slacks. She tried to force a smile, but instead broke down again. She realized Cynthia was not there and through her sobs she asked, "Do you know where his wife is?"

"Yes. We were able to locate her at the gym. She's on her way back here now."

"God, poor Cyn."

"You were close with your aunt and uncle?"

"I see them all the time. I'm usually over once a week for dinner. I help Cynthia prepare it and my folks join us, too. Uncle Lou stops by my place quite a bit." Michaela took a hasty sip from the coffee.

"And his wife . . . Cynthia? I take it since you don't refer to her as your aunt that she is a second wife?"

"Yes. They've been married for several years now. My aunt Rose died over ten years ago from breast cancer and my uncle met Cynthia a year or so later."

"Uh-huh. Were they having any problems that you knew about?"

"Oh, no. Cyn loved my uncle, and he worshiped her."

"Is this Mrs. Bancroft? Your aunt, or I mean, Cynthia?" He pulled a small photo inside a small plastic bag, marked EVIDENCE.

"Yes, it is. Where did you get that picture?"

"It was in your uncle's wallet, which we found in the corner of the stall near him."

"Oh." Michaela didn't know what else to say. "Do you know if there is anything missing? Maybe someone was trying to rob him and it went bad?"

"I can't determine that as of yet. I'm not certain what all he carried in his wallet. I can say it does look fairly intact, though. There was some cash and credit cards. We won't rule out anything, though."

She nodded. It would be difficult to believe that someone would try and rob Uncle Lou while working on his ranch. A random robbery didn't fit well for her either, and she could sense that Detective Davis reflected that thought.

"She's much younger than your uncle, isn't she? Your aunt? Cynthia Bancroft."

Michaela hesitated before answering. She could see where Detective Davis might be headed with this line of questioning, but he had it all wrong. Cyn really *did* love

Uncle Lou. Sure, her own family had wondered when Lou had introduced all of them to her and learned that she was twenty-five years younger, but over time it was easy to see that she loved him dearly, that she was good-hearted and down to earth. "Yes, that's true. She's only a few years older than me. Why? What does that have to do with anything?" She set her cup down and crossed her arms.

"Ms. Bancroft, I have a job to do. I have to ask these questions. I know the timing isn't great, but it's necessary."

Michaela shrugged. "They didn't have any problems that I knew of." She thought briefly about the conversation she'd had the night before with Uncle Lou— the way he'd sounded

She'd meant to get to the bottom of it today. Were he and Cyn having some type of problem, or did he *know* that someone wanted him dead?

"Are there others who work here?"

She nodded. "Dwayne Yamaguchi is the head trainer and is assisted by his cousin Sam, but the truck and trailer are gone. I assume they took horses over to Las Vegas, probably yesterday."

"Why would he do that?"

"The National Finals Rodeo begins this weekend and Dwayne will be competing. I think the guys planned on heading out yesterday, and Bean would be the one sort of running things here with my uncle."

"Bean?"

"I don't know his real name. He's a tall skinny guy."

"What does he do here?"

"He's kind of a caretaker and ranch hand, helps out where he's needed."

"You haven't seen him around this morning?"

"No. I'm not surprised though. He's, um, well, he has some mental problems."

"What do you mean mental problems, exactly?"

"Well, it's not like he's crazed or dangerous. He's a bit slow. He had a head injury as a kid. In fact, he really acts like a child in a lot of ways."

"Why did your uncle keep him around then?"

"Bean is good with the animals. He's very conscientious about them and he looked up to my uncle, kind of like an older brother. I think he's probably not too much younger than my uncle."

"Do you know where he lives?"

"No. I don't. Cynthia might know."

"All right. Thanks. Anyone else work here that you can give me some information on?"

Michaela sighed. "Well, Summer MacTavish does the books for my uncle. She's the ranch accountant, but she's not here daily. I believe she comes in once a week to do payroll and accounts receivable. I'm really not certain of her schedule."

Another cruiser pulled up. Michaela saw Cynthia in the back.

When it stopped she got out and came running to Michaela. "What happened? They said . . . they said that it's Lou. That he's . . . Is he, Michaela? *Is Lou . . . ?* Did someone . . ." she cried. Her taut face lacked its usual olive glow, now appearing almost alabaster against her brunette hair.

Michaela's stomach twisted and she closed her eyes, hoping the words would come. Instead, she wrapped her arms around Cynthia. "I'm sorry, I'm so sorry," she whispered.

Wracking sobs overtook Cynthia and Michaela couldn't contain her sadness any longer. They held each other for long moments and cried. Michaela didn't want to let go. Maybe if they stayed like this, she'd wake up and it would all turn out to be a nightmare. It had to be that— some horrible dream— or a joke. She felt Cyn waver and start to lose ground. The detective took her elbow.

"Mrs. Bancroft, why don't you come sit down inside the house and we can talk."

A shrill whinny sailed through the wind. "Oh, God. Loco," Michaela said.

"Loco?" Davis asked.

"My husband's stallion. He's out? Oh no! You have to get him!" Cyn wailed.

"He ran out when I opened the stall, when I saw . . ."

"You found him? *You* found Lou?" Cyn stared at Michaela in disbelief.

"Ms. Bancroft, why don't you see if you can find the horse? I'm going to take Mrs. Bancroft inside. There are a few more questions I need to ask."

"No. I'm going with her. I have to go with you, Cyn. You can't be alone right now."

Cynthia shook her head. "Go, please. Lou would be . . ." She sucked in a deep breath. "He'd be devastated if something happened to Loco. Please Mick, find the horse."

She could see the pleading in Cyn's brown eyes and knew she was right about Lou. He'd loved that animal probably as much as he loved anything in the world. Still, it tore at her heart to leave Cyn in the hands of the police, with no one to comfort her. Loco whinnied again in the distance. She had to go and find him. He might hurt himself.

The detective escorted Cyn into the house. Michaela turned and set out to find the horse, avoiding the many officers doing their job. She started for the tack room but thought twice. She didn't want to disturb what the officers were doing, and more than that she couldn't bear to see Uncle Lou again. She doubted that the police would allow her through anyway.

She went to her truck, knowing she had a halter and lead rope in the back, one of those things she always carried. She then approached the house, realizing there was no way she'd be able to capture Loco without some type of handout. She opened the front door. How many days had she entered this house and found Uncle Lou in his den reading the paper or having a whiskey sour, his favorite drink? Today, even though she knew that Detective Davis and Cyn were inside, an eerie silence and a pressure pervaded the air. A heaviness that she'd never sensed before. This place had always felt like a second home to her. Today it just felt empty— a balloon filled with sadness, ready to burst.

She found the cop seated at the kitchen table and saw Cynthia standing over the sink, vomiting. She placed a hand on Cyn's back, rubbing it. After a minute, the woman splashed water on her face, then turned and faced her. "Did you find Loco?"

"I haven't had a chance yet."

"You have to find him. You know that Lou would be beside himself."

"I know. I came in to get some carrots and see if I couldn't lure him back."

"In the fridge."

Michaela went to the crisper and took out a bag of carrots. She turned again to find Cyn back over the sink.

Davis motioned for her to follow him to the front door, where he said, "She's very distraught, obviously. I'll be here for a bit and I still have some more questions to ask you. We have a lot of work to do. I've got all of your information I think, so if it's fine by you, I'll come by your home so we can talk."

"Of course." She left the house and went to track Loco.

She spied him near the back pasture. He stood outside the fence with a mare butted up to him. Both horses were going crazy, stomping their feet, pawing at the ground and squealing at each other. Loco put all his weight into the fence, trying to break through. This was not going to be easy.

She held out a carrot to him. He sniffed it, snorted, and tossed his head about. The mare arched her neck, reaching for the carrot. Michaela waved her arms at the mare and made a hissing sound to chase her off. If she could get her out of the picture it might be easier to get Loco. The mare pranced about five steps away, tail in the air, and then came back. She flung her arms again. This time the horse took off down the fence, Loco close behind. The scenario went on for several more minutes until Michaela got smart, caught the mare first and led her back to the breeding arena.

She then put to practice the technique she'd learned from both her dad and uncle— called patience. For several minutes she stood ten or so feet away from the stud. He finally became curious about the handout she had offered and slowly came toward her until he got close enough for her to slide the halter over his face. Patience and persistence paid off— virtues both Dad and Uncle Lou repeated to her time and again.

It was difficult to lead Loco because he knew the mare wasn't too far away. She could've used a chain right about then, to have laced through the halter— it would've helped to control his unruliness. He pulled on Michaela, who felt as if all the strength had gone out of her: despair taking hold and not letting go.

They made it down to a set of corrals, but a mare and foal were too close by and she knew they'd have to be moved. She released Loco into the corral, not having any other choice, then went about maneuvering the mare and foal out into the pasture. She hoped she'd be able to get a hold of Bean and tell him to get to the ranch ASAP, because Cyn couldn't take care of the horses. If she couldn't reach him, she'd have to come back over that evening, put all of the horses back where they belonged and feed them.

After making sure the animals were okay, she walked to her truck. Bean stood there leaning against Uncle Lou's old green Chevy work truck, which she knew he allowed Bean to drive just around the ranch. He didn't look well at all.

"Um, hello, Miss Michaela. A policeman told me I had to stay right here because something bad happened to Mr. Lou. What happened? Do you know what happened?" He wrung his hands. "Why are the policemans here? What happened to Mr. Lou? I got here and they were here. The police. They would not tell me where Mr. Lou is and they won't tell me where Mrs. Lou is either. Do you hear that?" He pointed to the barn. "The horses keep crying and they sound hungry. I want to feed them. Where is Mr. Lou?"

She reached out and touched his shoulder. He shrank away from the contact. "Bean, Lou had to go to Heaven today and he's not coming back." She nearly choked on her own words.

"Why did he go there?"

"Listen, I know this will be hard for you to understand, but Lou won't be back. Heaven isn't a place where we go on vacation. It's a place where we go when . . ." She bit the side of her lip, then sighed and finished what she was saying, "We die. Heaven is a place where we go when we die, and Lou died this morning."

"I don't believe you." Tears sprung up in Bean's eyes as Michaela recognized that he realized she was telling him the truth.

"I want him to come back."

"I know. Me, too."

He wiped sweat from his graying brow. Bean was probably about fifty but looked a lot older. Hard years in the sun had weathered him with deep crevices on his face, and what hair was left on his head was completely gray.

Someone cleared his throat behind her. "Ms. Bancroft?" She turned around to see Detective Davis. "Yes?"

"I need to speak with Bean here, now. I'll be in touch shortly. You can go on home. Mrs. Bancroft is resting, so

I'll be stopping by your place or giving you a call in the next few hours."

"Sure. Okay. Bean if you need anything, please ask me."

Bean didn't respond, but rather stared blankly, tears still streaming down his face. She didn't know if he was going to be all right.

As she pulled out of the ranch she looked in her rearview mirror to see a distraught-looking Bean talking with the cop. She prayed Davis would go easy on him.

By the time she made it out onto the road, her tears flowed freely again. She sucked in a breath and drove to her parents' house. They had to be told.

FIVE

MICHAELA'S PARENTS LIVED FIFTEEN MINUTES away. She drove down the long gravel road bordered by barbed wire fence on either side, and overgrown grass and weeds swaying in the early winter breeze. Everything had begun to turn the color of straw, giving it an almost cold, desolate feel. The house she'd grown up in came into view— a cozy stone cottage style— nothing special to most, but to her it was still home. She noticed a piece of the fence was down and figured her dad must have been out mending it earlier because his materials lay across the driveway.

She stepped out of her truck and wrapped her arms tighter around herself as the wind picked up and bit through her, bringing with it the smells of fresh-cut hay and earth, chilling her further with the reality setting in that she was alive and Uncle Lou was not.

Her folks obviously hadn't heard her coming, because as she neared the house she could hear them through the kitchen screen. Her father was yelling, something he didn't do often. Michaela's body tensed. She couldn't hear what they were saying. Could the police have already called? No, her father was definitely hollering at her mother.

". . . dammit, Janie. My holier than thou brother is not always right, you know." She heard her dad say as she opened the door. They stood in the circa 1975 family room with flowered velvet sofas and oversized table lamps on oak end tables set on avocado green shag carpet. Mom with her hands on her hips, Dad with his arms locked across his chest. They turned when they saw her.

"Michaela?" her mother said concern in her voice. She always knew when something wasn't right with her daughter. "What is it?"

Her father, Benjamin Bancroft, uncrossed his arms, the angry flush of red draining from his face, and hurried to her. "You've been crying. What in the world is wrong?"

"I need to talk to both of you. Sit down, please."

Dad's eyes widened. Michaela noticed that his hand was bandaged. "What happened?"

"Oh, I hurt it this morning, working on a section of the fence. It needed new barbed wire."

"Looks bad," she replied, seeing some blood stain the bandage.

"No. I'm fine."

"What is it, honey?" her mother asked. "What's troubling you?"

"Sit down, please." Taking a deep breath, she told her parents everything. Apparently the police had not yet informed them. Her mother cried in disbelief. Her dad just sat there, stunned. No tears, nothing.

Finally he asked, "What about Cynthia? How is she?"

"Not well."

"I'm going over there."

"Maybe you should wait, Dad. The police are investigating and to be honest, I don't think us being around is such a good idea."

He looked down at his injured hand and rubbed it. "No matter. I'm going."

"I am, too," Janie Bancroft sobbed.

"No. Wait here," her husband said.

"Benjamin, you won't tell me what to do."

"I'm going, too," Michaela insisted. She looked at her father's hand again. "Dad, that thing is pretty bloody. You sure you're okay?"

He nodded, looked down at his hand and back up at her.

"Go change the bandages, Benjamin. A few minutes won't matter," his wife said.

That was Mom— practical, devoted, and deeply religious. Michaela knew how her mother would get through this: the way she did with every upheaval in her life, through her faith. It always awed Michaela, but Janie Bancroft had to be the strongest woman she knew, and this family would need that strength right now.

Michaela watched her father disappear down the hall to do as he'd been told.

Her cell phone rang. Janie was grabbing her sweater from the front hall closet. Michaela was shocked to hear Ethan Slater's voice on the other end. She'd forgotten that a vet was coming to her place that morning for a routine visit. Ethan had obviously returned from his trip and was on call.

"I know you're obviously out and about, but I think you may want to get back over here, Mick."

"What? Why?"

"It's Leo, kid. He's colicing and I need some help with him. I've shot him with Banamine and now I need to oil him."

"Oh, no. I'll be right there." She hung up and told her mother what had happened.

"Go, honey. There's nothing you can do right now. Your father and I need time anyway, and we need to get ourselves over to Lou's, see what happened, what we can do. I think it best if you take care of the colt."

"Oh, Mom."

"Go. I'll call you if we need anything."

Michaela hugged her and headed home. God only knew what else might be in store. She was all cried out at this point. Her mind whirled in a mixture of total confusion: her beloved uncle lay dead— murdered— in his prize stallion's stall, Ethan was keeping something from her— she knew that because of his abrupt disappearance on his rafting trip— her parents were fighting, and if she didn't know better, her dad seemingly *also* had something to hide. She could have sworn he'd been lying about how he'd hurt his hand. Benjamin Bancroft never was a good liar, and her intuition said that he hadn't told her the truth about his injury. *Why?*

And now Leo was colicing. This could be bad. Michaela knew that colic was one of the leading causes of premature deaths in domesticated horses. It presented itself as abdominal pain and usually manifested from some type of impaction in the intestine. If Ethan hadn't come by, then chances were that Leo would be gone now. Catching colic in the early stages was one of the only chances for a horse to survive. Hopefully Ethan had caught it soon enough. She didn't want to think about losing her baby right now.

* * *

ETHAN HAD ALREADY STARTED MEDICATING him, but oiling the colt would not be pleasant. Michaela knew she'd have to help Ethan get a tube down into Leo's stomach. Hopefully the oil would cause the impaction to move through his intestines.

She pulled up next to Ethan's truck and got out. He was in the stall with the colt. "Hi," he said. "I'm sorry to have to track you down. I've kept him on his feet and had him walking. I don't think he's been down too much."

That was a relief. If Leo had had much of a chance to lie down, he probably would have started rolling, twisting his intestine, and that would mean a costly surgery that was not always very successful.

"The Banamine should be kicking in," he said. Michaela knew from growing up with Ethan— who'd always wanted to be a vet— and helping him study for his finals during vet school, that Banamine was used to help alleviate the pain. "I was thinking I could give him a little ACE to ease him further while we tube him, but he's got a good nature about him and I don't think he'll give us too much grief."

Michaela nodded and took the lead line. She faced Leo, holding the rope tightly under his chin, lifting his nose in the air. Ethan began to slide the plastic tube up into one of his nostrils and down his throat. Leo stomped the ground and tried to shake his head, but Michaela kept a tight grip on him. Once the tube was down into his intestinal track, Ethan was able to pump the oil through. Leo didn't put up much of a stink. After finishing with the tube, they took him out of the stall and walked him around for some time to keep him from lying down to roll.

"I think we caught it in time. Good thing. He's a beautiful animal, Mick, and I know what he means to you." She nodded; her face grew taut and she felt the tears starting again. "Hey, hey, it's going to be okay. He'll be fine. We just have to keep a watch on him, but like I said, it looks like we caught it just in time. So relax now, okay? Let's get him in the stall and see if he'll eat some bran."

Michaela couldn't respond. Ethan put Leo back as she got a small bucket of bran for him. She poured it into his feeder; he started to eat it.

"See, look at that."

Michaela choked back the grief tightening her chest. Ethan put a hand on her shoulder. For the first time since she'd arrived back at her place, she really looked at him. Green eyes, sun-kissed, sculpted cheekbones, a crooked nose— due to a kick from an angry horse— faced her.

"What is it, Mick? What's wrong?"

She covered her eyes. Her body started that uncontrollable shaking again.

"Mick, you're scaring me. What the hell is it? Is it your dad?" She shook her head. "Brad? Is he giving you grief again? I can talk to him and make him leave you alone. Believe *me*, I'd get some pleasure out of doing that."

"Lou was . . . murdered this morning!" She blurted it out and as she did, the impact of the reality hit her hard. Her knees buckled.

Ethan held onto her. "Oh, my God. Oh, my *God.* Mick, no, no . . . Jesus, how, who . . . what in the hell?"

Sobs wracked her body as she shook in his arms, unable to speak. When she finally did she could only tell him what little facts she knew.

"*You* found him?" he asked, stunned.

"Ah, Mick. God, I wish I could do something. I'm sorry. I'm really sorry. I don't know what to say. Is there *anything* I can do?"

"No." She pulled away from him. "There's not."

"I can't believe it. Oh, man." He shook his head. "I was by there yesterday to talk to him."

"You were? Why?"

"I needed to talk to him about something."

Tears running down her face, she crossed her arms. "Ethan, why did you go on the rafting trip without saying anything to me? Why did you leave Lou's ranch? Did he kick you off?"

Ethan sighed. "Let's not go into this now. You need me, I'm here, and learning this is like getting sucker-punched."

She saw his eyes water. He turned away. "I'm sorry. The last thing I want to know is that you two had a fight, but you have to tell me. What was going on between you and my uncle? I asked him after you left and he wouldn't tell me either. When I spoke with him last night, something seemed to be troubling him, and now, knowing you went there, I have to wonder if it was *you* on his mind, and if so, why."

"Wait a minute, you think I could have something to do with this? With Lou being killed?"

"Of . . . course not."

"Why the interrogation, then? I didn't hurt Lou. He treated me like a son and I loved him." Emotion caught in his throat. "I would've never hurt that man, and just because we had differences between us doesn't mean a damn thing." His voice rose. "It's true we've been best friends since we were kids, Michaela, but I don't tell you *everything*. What Lou and I had between us needs to be kept there for now. Leave it alone and trust me. I wouldn't hurt him *or* you. For God's sake, don't you know me better than that?"

Michaela took another step back. She *thought* she knew him, but there was a rage combined now with a pain in his eyes she'd never seen before. Her body ached. She closed her eyes. He pulled her into him again. "Trust me, *please*. I can't tell you what happened. Not yet. When I can, I will."

She shrugged him off. "Fine."

Ethan's pager beeped. He read the number. "It's the hospital." He went to his truck and called in. A minute later he came back. "I've gotta head over there. I did emergency surgery on a mare this morning and now there's a problem. I'll be back to check on Leo . . . and *you*."

"We'll be fine."

Michaela went back into Leo's stall and stayed with him long after she'd heard Ethan drive away. She wondered where he was staying these days.

She finally made it inside the house. Camden wasn't home. No telling when she'd left or where she'd gone. Probably a spa day or shopping spree. In a way it was good she wasn't around. Michaela wanted some solitude. When Camden did show up, she knew she'd have to relay the horrific events all over again, and she wasn't sure if she was up to it. At the moment numbness had set in—thinking or feeling just seemed too damn hard. The energy to retell the events of this morning would be too much to bear right now.

She took a long hot shower, pulled on a sweater, and as the sun began to set she poured herself a glass of wine. She turned on the TV to try and take her mind off of what had happened, but it was all right there on the news. An attractive local newscaster relayed the story of how Lou

Bancroft, well-known rancher, had been found murdered at his ranch that morning. A pitchfork stabbed through his back. Oh no. That was the last thing she wanted to hear or see. She turned the TV off and tossed the remote.

Those were not the images she wanted to remember her uncle by. What she wanted was to hold his hand again, like she had so many times when she was a child. He had great hands— tough, strong, dependable. When she'd been little and he'd taken her to horse shows or the county fair he'd held her hand tight, letting her know that he was going to make sure she remained at his side. Aunt Rose would tell him to relax, that no one was gonna steal little Mickey, but Uncle Lou would guffaw at that remark and he'd say, "You're right, Rose, because I'm hanging onto the kid!"

She wiped her tears away and finished off the wine. Time to head back out and check on Leo. She urged Cocoa to come along with her.

At the barn, Michaela peered in on the horses before going to get another bucket of bran for Leo. She unlocked the tack room door and stopped. Leaning against the frame was the pitchfork she used for changing straw. She gasped when she saw it, her mind flashing back to Lou, the broken-off pitchfork sticking out of his back. It was like a stab in her heart. The tightness in her stomach came back and she felt woozy, her thoughts spinning with the memory.

Her stallion Rocky whinnied and brought her back to reality. Thank God. *Don't think about that, not now. Stay focused. Do what you need to do.* She went inside the tack and feed room. Scents of grain, saddle soap, and leather wafted through the air, and she breathed them in. She opened the can where she kept the bran. *Dammit.* Empty. She'd made a mental note earlier when she and Ethan had given Leo some, to go down to the feed store and get another bag of it. Maybe there was some in the trailer.

"Come on, Cocoa." Her dog stood her ground. The hair on Cocoa's neck rose as she seemed fixated on something at the other end of the breezeway. "You are such a silly old girl," Michaela told her. At times Cocoa could behave like an old woman who has had too much gin— brave and stupid, as if she needed to pick a fight with someone. "It's probably a rabbit. Let's go. C'mon." Cocoa growled. "For God's sake, come on." She patted the side of her leg, and the dog finally fell in line as they walked over to the garage, where she'd parked the horse trailer. She found a half a bag of bran up in the storage area. Good. She'd drag it over to the barn in the morning. For now she scooped out a half a bucket's worth and walked back to the barn.

She poured it into Leo's feeder and watched him eat. After he finished she took him for a short walk. She headed back to the tack room to get the blankets out and put them on the horses for the evening.

At the door of the tack room, she stopped. Something was wrong here. She stepped back. Her pulse raced and her heart beat madly against her chest as she realized that the pitchfork, which had been there only an hour earlier, was now gone.

SIX

THE BARN SPUN IN A MIXTURE OF BROWNS AND beiges. Michaela braced herself against the tack room door and tried to regain her composure. Think, *think.* Her hands shaking, she reached for the phone and started to dial 911, but what the hell would she say? *"My pitchfork has been moved?"* Maybe she could tell them someone broke into her place. *No.* That wasn't necessarily true, but someone *had* moved the pitchfork. She hung up the phone, yelled for Cocoa who dragged herself in, closed and locked the tack room door, then dialed the number to the police station and asked for Detective Davis. When she told him what had happened, he assured her he'd be right over, and to stay put. She hung up the phone and waited, looking at Cocoa, and for a brief moment she wished she had a Doberman instead of a Lab. Especially when she thought she heard something. There it was again. *Shit.* Someone was walking down the breezeway. One of the horses whinnied. Michaela looked around for a weapon. Nothing. Shit, shit, shit. Oh jeez, whoever was there was probably here to, to . . .

"Mick, are you in here?"

She threw open the tack room door and yelled, "Dammit, Ethan, don't you ever do that to me again!"

He stopped. "What are you carrying on about?"

"The pitchfork . . . and then walking down the breezeway. What were you thinking? Are you trying to scare me?" She trembled and her face burned. Here she'd gone and called the cops, and it had only been Ethan all along.

"The pitch . . . Girl, I have no earthly idea what you're talking about. What have you been smoking? I just got here. And since when did bumps in the barn ever put the hairs up on the back of your neck?"

She glared at him. "What do you mean you just got here?"

He looked at his watch. "Uh, well, pretty much just that. I pulled up a few minutes ago. I was coming to check on Leo, the next thing I know you're going psycho chick on me." He put an arm around her. "You okay? I'm sorry, dumb question. Of course you're not okay. You're shaking like a leaf, kid. What is going on?"

She told him what had happened.

"Are you sure?"

"Yes I'm sure. I know what I saw." She backed away and studied him for a second. "You don't believe me."

"No, it's not that. I think you've had a real difficult day and our minds can play all sorts of tricks on us when we're dealing with stressful events."

"Bullshit! It isn't stress. It wasn't my mind playing tricks on me. *That pitchfork was moved.* It was right here"— she smacked the wall—"and now it's not."

"Look, I apologize. I believe you, okay? And, because of that, I'm not letting you stay here alone."

"I'm not alone. I've got Camden."

He shook his head. "She'll do you a helluva lot a good now, won't she? What's she going to do if some maniac comes through your door? Throw a pair of stilettos at him?"

Michaela couldn't help but smile. He had a point. "I got Cocoa here."

"Uh-huh. You'd have better luck with your margarita-drinking, high-heeled, society-wannabe pal at your side than that old girl."

"That's not nice."

He shrugged.

"I don't need you staying here. You'd drive me crazy and Camden would drive you crazy and the next thing you know we'll all be snapping at each other. Not a good idea."

"Stubborn and foolish. That's the way you've always been."

"Look who's talking."

"I'll stay out here in the tack room, keep an eye on the colt, and if any trouble happens to come your way, I'll be within screaming distance. Just be sure to do one of those horror film-types, you know, a Fay Wray scream, and that way I'll know you're not joking."

She had to admit that having Ethan close by would be a comfort. No. She wavered for a second. She'd learned the hard way that men were not dependable. But, Ethan was different. They'd known each other since before they could each ride a bike, much less a horse. Was he really different, though? He was the same man— supposedly her closest pal— who'd taken off less than a month ago on a river-rafting trip without telling her or calling her while away. What had he been up to, alone on that trip?

"You can't sleep in the tack room. It's not exactly comfortable."

"In case you hadn't noticed, I don't need a five-star hotel. I just slept on the ground in a pitched tent for weeks, Mick. I think a cot in the tack room would suffice. Besides, half the time I'm woken up in the middle of the night to take calls."

She started to reply, but the sound of a car door closing sounded outside the barn. Detective Davis entered the breezeway. "Ms. Bancroft?"

"Hello, Detective."

He walked toward them. "Good evening, Mr. Slater."

Michaela glanced at Ethan. Davis must've already spoken with him. Was he a suspect?

Ethan nodded. "Evening." He turned to Michaela. "I'm going to grab a few things, and I'll be back."

"Don't worry about it. You needn't come back. We'll be fine."

"Stubborn." He shook a finger at her. "I *will* be back. If for nothing other than to make sure Leo is doing okay."

"Where is your stuff anyway?" Michaela asked, curious about where Ethan had been staying since he'd returned.

He hesitated. "Summer's place."

Before she could respond, Ethan hurried out. *Summer's place? His ex-fiancé? The same Summer who stood him up at the altar a few months ago? The one he'd been loyal to and had even gotten her the job at Uncle Lou's as his accountant? Oh boy, did they have something to discuss when he returned!* She'd surely give him a piece of her mind.

"Ms. Bancroft," Davis said. "Do you want to tell me what happened here?"

"It's okay, you can call me Michaela. Why don't we go on into the house?" She rubbed her arms. "I'm cold. I can fix us some tea or coffee."

"That would be fine. But before we do that, you said something about a pitchfork being in one place and then not being there later?"

"That's right. Follow me." She led him to the tack room. "I needed to go over to the horse trailer and see if I had any more bran for my colt, and when I came back the pitchfork, which had been right here, was gone. I did notice my dog seemed to be bothered by something outside the barn. I figured it was a rabbit."

"But the dog didn't bark?"

"No."

Davis nodded. "Okay. Why don't you show me around and we'll see if anything else looks out of place. Let's retrace your path as far as when you first came in to the tack room and spotted the pitchfork."

"Sure." She walked him through everything from the moment she'd entered the barn.

"You've got quite a crew here." He nodded down the aisle of stalls at the horses. The more curious ones peeked their heads out at the newcomer.

"They're my life. Keep me sane. Horses are good for the soul, you know." She'd remembered Uncle Lou often telling her those exact words from the time she was a child. He'd been right. "They're constant. There for you. Always."

"I can see that."

"Do you ride?"

"Me?" He laughed. "Hardly. Once, actually."

"Where was that?"

He stopped for a minute and shoved his hands in his pockets, kind of looking away from her. "Uh, Barbados."

"Barbados?"

"Yeah. One of those expeditions, you know, trail rides."

"But in Barbados?"

He shifted his weight from one foot to the other.

"My . . . honeymoon. I was on my honeymoon."

"Oh, right. Honeymoon. How nice."

They walked outside and headed toward the horse trailer about fifty feet away. Michaela squinted her eyes as they neared, then gasped. "Do you see that?" She reached out to touch the pitchfork leaning against the horse trailer, its metal spikes shining reflectively from a beam of light showering down off the top of the barn.

Davis grabbed her hand. "No. Don't touch it. I need to have it dusted for fingerprints."

"Sorry." She pulled her hand away and for some odd reason felt heat rise to her face, obviously angry over her faux pas. Or was it? For a brief second she couldn't help feel Davis's grip sending something electric through her. She took a step back, suddenly a bit dizzy. Her feelings had nothing to do with Davis, she reassured herself. Instead, it was the realization that somebody had been on her property and had either been playing a cruel joke on her, or had intentionally planned to do her harm. Yeah, that's all it was.

Michaela sat down on the step. The sadness she'd felt earlier still lingered, but now shared space with an overwhelming sense of fear.

"You okay?" Davis asked, pulling a pair of latex gloves out of his coat pocket.

"Tired. That's all." Michaela noticed, as he slid the gloves over his hands, that he wasn't wearing a wedding ring. Huh? What about that honeymoon in Barbados . . . ? Lord! What was wrong with her? Why in the world did she care if this guy was married or not? He was the detective on her uncle's murder case, for heaven's sakes, and now he was checking out a threat on her property.

He bent down next to the pitchfork and picked up a wrapper, holding it up to the light.

"What is it?" Michaela asked.

"A wrapper for chewing tobacco," he replied.

"Chewing tobacco?"

"Yep." He took another small plastic bag from his coat pocket and placed the wrapper in it

"Anyone you know around here chew tobacco?"

"No."

"Maybe Dr. Slater?"

"Definitely not." She stood up.

"Okay. I'll take it with me, too. Doubt it will tell us much, but you never know."

"So where do you think it might have come from?"

She shook her head. "That I don't know. It makes sense that whoever moved the pitchfork might have been the one to leave the tobacco wrapper. But that doesn't seem too smart to throw it down."

"No." He sighed. "But it could have dropped out of someone's pocket and they might not have seen it."

"Makes sense." Michaela felt a shiver run down her spine with the repeat thought that someone might have been watching her from outside the barn while she fed and took care of the horses, waiting for a deliberate moment to do something to spook her. Or, what if that person had planned to do something more than spook her, but had gotten scared when Ethan pulled in? She didn't like this at all. "Do you think whoever was trying to frighten me— which, I assume, is what someone was trying to do— could also be my uncle's murderer?"

"I don't know. But can you think of anyone you and your uncle knew that might have some type of, uh . . . well, is there anyone out there who might want to get even with you for something?

She sighed and nodded."Maybe I do. Let me pour you that cup of tea. This might take a while."

SEVEN

MICHAELA HADN'T THOUGHT ABOUT IT UNTIL Detective Davis mentioned the possibility of revenge. And, it clicked that maybe there *was* one person out there who wanted to get even with both her and Uncle Lou. The thing was, she knew how this might sound, because she knew exactly how it sounded to herself— not good.

Davis sat at her kitchen table sipping his tea. Camden still wasn't home. Where the heck was she? Must still be out with Kevin Tanner. Hadn't she told her last night they were spending the day together? Looked like day had turned into night. Camden sure was spending a lot of time with him lately.

She sat down across from Davis. He twisted the mug back and forth between his hands. "Good tea."

"Thanks." She took a sip and it warmed her insides. "Here." She opened the top of the cookie jar that sat on the table. "They're not homemade— Oreos. Kind of a vice for me."

He smiled. It was a nice, warm smile. Comforting. "I have a sweet tooth, too. I better not, though. Ms. Bancroft, you said that there was someone who might have something against you and your uncle."

"Please, like I said, you can call me Michaela," she interrupted.

"Okay, Michaela, who are you thinking of?"

She leaned back in the wooden chair. "Possibly my soon-to-be ex-husband."

"Really? Why is that?"

"Brad is a cheat and a liar. Something my uncle Lou always knew and tried to warn me about. But, you know the saying: 'Love is . . . ' "

"Blind." He finished the sentence for her.

"Right. Brad and I were married for nine years. We married young. I was right out of college, and there were some good times— a few, maybe." She forced a smile, trying to convince herself of this as much as she was Davis. "But then Brad became really involved in the rodeo circuit."

"Aren't you as well?"

"No. When we were married, I would go to the rodeos, and I still like to go and watch the big National Finals Rodeo held out in Vegas each year. I did use to run barrels as a kid."

"Run barrels?"

"Sure. It's a blast. Your horse running all out and rounding the barrels in a cloverleaf pattern. You know, barrel racing."

"Oh yeah, yeah. I got it. I've seen that before on TV."

She smiled. "I'm sure you have. Anyway, it's my favorite event to watch at the rodeo. In fact, the NFR starts this weekend, and I'd planned to drive out with my roommate, but now that seems wrong to do, considering what's just happened with my uncle."

Davis shifted in the chair. "I understand. Why would your ex be seeking revenge?"

"Like I said, this might take some time to fill in all the holes."

"I've got time." He leaned back in his chair, his blue eyes trained on her.

"Brad rides bulls. Or he did, anyway."

"A bull rider?"

"Yeah, I know, don't say it. Everyone does; you don't look like the kind of girl who would marry a bull rider."

"The thought crossed my mind."

"Well, when we met, bull riding wasn't his thing. He was more into the working cow horse events. But he got the bug. Someone dared him and the fool took the dare. He started riding broncs, and then onto the bulls because the money was great and he got hooked on the adrenaline rush. It also didn't help that he was good at it. Then, he got hurt, broke his hip, and I nursed him back to health. He had a few surgeries, and although he couldn't compete any longer, because it was too painful, it didn't stop him from wanting to go out on the circuit."

"He enjoyed the lifestyle," Davis suggested.

Michaela nodded. "The problem was, or I should say, *is*, that the money he'd earned, he blew partying on the circuit with his pals. I tried to salvage the marriage. I wanted children."

"He didn't?"

"Brad said that he did, promised me he'd be around more and help me grow my business, and that we could start a family. He tried to convince me that it was good for him to be out and about with his buddies, that they were all spreading the word about what a great trainer I was. Even though I don't train horses for rodeo-type events other than some barrel racing, there is quite a bit of crossover communication in the horse world. Plenty, actually, especially because most of us in this part of the industry ride quarter horses." Davis raised his brow and shrugged, and Michaela continued. "A quarter horse is a really great breed— stocky, athletic, good-natured, they tend to be of sound mind, and intelligent. I guess you could say that they're kind of the Labradors of horses, if that makes sense to you." He nodded. "They're a versatile breed. I love working with them."

"Your ex didn't exactly go around touting you as the brilliant trainer, I take it?"

"No. He was too busy with other things."

"And, you put up with that?"

A wave of shame swept through her. She *had* put up with it. "I did, but in my defense as I said, love is blind, or in this case plain stupid. I wanted to believe him and I really wanted kids. He did get me a couple of clients, and that kept me hooked into thinking that he was sort of a manager— the good husband doing his part to bring in the business. Stupid, I know."

"We all want to believe the best in people, I don't think that's stupid at all." In spite of himself, he took a cookie from the jar, bit into it, and set it down. It left a crumb on the side of his mouth. "You don't have any kids, then?"

"No." She didn't want to go there. It wasn't necessary. He just needed to know the facts, and why Brad would have the need to see her uncle dead . . . maybe even her. She couldn't imagine him actually doing it, but one never really knew a person. And, after nine years with Brad, she'd discovered that she hadn't really known him at all. But Uncle Lou had him pegged from the get-go. Why hadn't she listened to him?

"With Brad out *promoting* me, and me supporting him, my uncle Lou became even more wary of him. He didn't trust him. He never thought he was good enough for me, but he'd kept that to himself after I finally told him to drop it." Michaela took a sip of her tea before going on. Cocoa padded over to her, her tail wagging. She reached down to scratch the dog's head.

"Beautiful dog."

"Thank you. She's an old girl, but like tonight, she's obviously still got it, still alert— sometimes."

"I've got a feeling that your uncle may have stopped talking about your ex, but he did something else to prove his point."

"He did. First, he decided to play by my rules and give Brad the benefit of the doubt. He gave him a job at his ranch, helping out with the artificial insemination program my uncle started a few years ago. But, Brad took advantage of the fact that Uncle Lou was *family*, and it didn't take long before he came and went as he pleased. He also thought the job was beneath him."

"Why is that?"

Michaela felt heat rise to her cheeks. "Well, even though the program Uncle Lou ran was a breeding program, as I said, it was artificial insemination, and someone needed to collect the . . ."

Davis held up his palms. "Say no more. Brad was the collector?"

"Yes, but it's not what you're thinking. It's quite technical. They use dummy mares. It's all very clean, but still," she said, not really wanting to continue.

Thankfully, Davis didn't seem to either. "Right."

"Anyway, Brad was blasé about the job. My uncle grew more suspicious of him and had him followed." Michaela stood, walked over to a drawer in the kitchen, and pulled out a large envelope, which contained photos. She handed them to Davis.

"Brad."

"Yes, and Kirsten Redmond."

Davis thumbed through the prints that Michaela had gone over countless times in the past until she'd finally accepted that it was true: Her husband had cheated on her with Miss Rodeo America. She shut her eyes tight for a second as Davis continued scanning the photos. "I'll burn those after we go to court."

"Your uncle Lou had him followed, this is what came of it, and you divorced Brad. I would assume that Brad also lost his job at the ranch?"

"Yes."

"Do you think Brad wanted to get even with Lou for having him followed, thus causing your breakup?"

"Partly. But Brad did plan to divorce me."

"Then what gives?" Davis patted his leg and Cocoa came over to him. "I like dogs. I've got a Lhaso Apso."

She laughed. "That's not a dog."

"Oh, so you're one of those people who believes a dog is only a dog if it's big and loud. He may not be big, but I assure you he's loud." He grinned.

"I'm kidding. I like all dogs."

"Right. So, what happened with you and your ex?"

"Brad and I had been married nine years like I said. We were three months short of our ten-year anniversary when I filed for divorce."

"Let me guess: You were the breadwinner, and he knew by waiting the full ten years it would make him eligible to receive spousal support for a very long time."

Michaela couldn't help but laugh at the way he'd put it, but yes, that was exactly how she'd felt when one of Brad's ex-cronies told her of his devious plan. The laughter felt good for a moment. How could she laugh today, or any day ever again, for that matter? She'd found Uncle Lou only that morning with a pitchfork through him. She shook her head, hoping to cast that image from her mind. Doubtful that could ever happen. "You know a bit about California divorce laws."

He nodded. "He was banking that he wouldn't get caught cheating, could divorce you after ten years, and you'd be stuck paying spousal support."

"Exactly. But he did get caught, thanks to my uncle, and now it's hopeful a judge will take a look at that and things will go in my favor. Now, he's making all sorts of claims that we were separated while he was out having the time of his life, and that I'd kicked him out. His girlfriend harasses me to no end. She enjoys calling me, insisting that I sign the papers he had some moronic attorney devise. I read over them last night. He wants to settle with me. I love that. Crazy. But the best is we have a pile of medical bills that our insurance refused to pay, and he's basically skipped out on his portion of the obligation. I've even heard he's going to file bankruptcy. So, I'm stuck with that. But, I will hold out signing any type of papers that benefits either one of them."

Davis shook his head. "Did he plan to marry this rodeo queen? If so, the gravy train would have come to a halt, even if he hadn't been caught in the act."

"I don't think so. Brad is greedy. He's the kind of guy who likes his cake and wants to eat it, too. My gut tells me that Kirsten was a fun fling and he never thought I would find out about it. I do think he planned to leave me though, after the ten years was up. Things with us had ceased to be fun, and Brad obviously isn't one with too much depth."

Davis nodded. "I went through a divorce a few years ago."

That explained the no ring on the finger. "Not fun. Do you have children?"

"One. She's nine. My ex and I have joint custody of her."

"That's great. I mean, not great you have to share your daughter like that, or that you're divorced, but that you have a child." She swallowed hard.

"You think that it's possible your ex blames your uncle for everything?"

"I think it's possible."

"I'm going to need to speak with your ex-husband. Can you give me his information?"

"Of course." Michaela stood and went into the kitchen. She took out a pen and paper from her odds-and-ends drawer and wrote down Brad's address and phone numbers, then handed it to Davis. His fingers brushed her hand. On purpose? She didn't think so, but oddly enough— and maybe because she didn't want to be alone— her stomach fluttered at his touch. She tried to ignore it as he stood and shook her hand.

"I know it's been a rough day for you. I'll have a cruiser come by. But you should be safe enough here, especially with Dr. Slater around."

"Oh, no. He's not my boyfriend, if that's what you're thinking. I've known Ethan forever." That sounded brilliant. Why did she feel the need to clarify their relationship to the detective?

Davis nodded. "I thought you'd like to know, we have an officer stationed at your uncle's ranch."

"That's good. Thanks. Um, how is Bean?"

"Mr. Chasen?"

"Is that his last name?"

Davis nodded. "Sylvester Chasen. He's fine. We questioned him and let him go on his way."

"Oh." She wanted to ask Davis more about Bean, but had the distinct feeling he wasn't going to tell her anything.

"I was also able to get a hold of Dwayne Yamaguchi. He's coming back from Vegas tonight to help Mrs. Bancroft out. And, uh, Sylvester, or I mean Bean will be back in the morning to work, I believe. Again, thank you for your time. I'll be in touch."

As he started out the door, Camden breezed in past him and said, "Hello."

He nodded and continued on his way, Camden's eyes following him like a cat toying with a mouse, as he closed the door. She turned and faced Michaela. "Hot damn, look at you, finally moving on. Tell me, I have got to know, who *is* the hottie?"

"You don't really want to know," Michaela replied and burst into tears.

EIGHT

CAMDEN LOANED HER SHOULDER TO MICHAELA and after a couple of hours she was all cried out— again. They now sat in silence on the couch.

"I'm sorry, sweetie. I can't imagine what you've been through today, and I'm sorry that I wasn't here for you. I wish you'd called me, I would have boogied back here."

"I know. The day has gone by in a blur. It all seems so surreal. There are moments when it feels like it *didn't* happen, and I actually smiled when that detective was here, but then the reality hits and I feel so horrible. I can't explain it." She lifted her head, and the room spun slightly— the combination of exhaustion and lack of any decent food.

"Who do you think could have done this?" Camden asked.

"I don't know, and I don't know why either. Lou was such a good man. He didn't have it in him to hurt anyone. His gentle hand with the horses, his demeanor . . . You knew him. He was solid, decent." She shook her head. "It makes no sense to me at all."

"He was one of the good guys, Mick. I feel lucky to have known him, although I don't think he ever had much tolerance for me." Camden laughed.

"That's not true. Uncle Lou liked you."

Camden waved a hand at her. "Please, we both know that I am not quite as down to earth as your uncle would have liked, especially for someone in your life."

"Okay, so maybe you were a bit flamboyant for him. But he appreciated you. I know that."

"No matter. I liked him and I know how much he loved you, so we were both on the same page there. But again, who do you think would want him dead?" At that moment a knock at the sliding glass door caused them both to turn.

"Ah, Dr. Slater is back in town, huh?" Camden asked. Michaela nodded. "When did he get back?" Michaela shrugged. "I see. Well, better get the door. I'll make myself scarce. You two probably have some talking to do."

Michaela opened the door.

"Hi, Ethan. How was your trip? We missed you around here," Camden said.

"Good. Thanks."

"Did you come to comfort our girl?"

"I did."

"Great. I think she's a bit better. You always seem to have a knack for putting a smile on her face. And, I've probably done all I can for the evening. I'll let you two talk. I think she could still use some company."

Michaela cleared her throat. "Hello, guys, I'm right here. I'm not a kid, you know. I love how much you care, but come on."

Camden rolled her eyes. "There she goes again with that 'I'm-so-tough' act. Don't let her fool you."

"I won't," Ethan replied.

"Night all, and Michaela, if you need me, I'm just down the hall."

"Sorry I'm late," Ethan said. "I checked on Leo a minute ago; looks like things are moving along fine in his gut. I'm pleased, because you know colic can be rough. I wish I could have helped you more today with him," he said, taking a seat in one of Michaela's leather chairs opposite her tan sofa.

"I told you that you didn't need to come back here."

"I know what you told me, but since when do I ever listen to you?"

"Good point." She plopped back down on the couch. "Are you gonna tell me why Detective Davis was by to talk to you and what had you so upset with Lou?"

"No. Not right now." Ethan rubbed his temples. "Honestly, I can't tell you anything until I find out a few more things myself."

"What the hell are you talking about? You're really starting to irritate me, Ethan."

"Well, you wouldn't be the only woman I've heard that from tonight."

"Oh, no, no, no, do not tell me," Michaela said. She took one look at him and knew. Dammit, the man was a glutton for punishment. "You and Summer?" It all came back to her, Ethan rushing off to his ex-fiancé's house.

He nodded.

She would've shaken him if she'd had the energy. "Tell me, please, that you and Summer are not getting back together. It is *not* what I want to hear. Do you know how bad she is for you? What a *bitch* she was to you? My God, Ethan, she left you the day before your wedding. What are you thinking?"

Ethan took her hand. "Mick, Summer is pregnant."

NINE

"YOU DUMBASS. TELL ME YOU'RE KIDDING." Michaela shook her head and stared at Ethan to see if he was telling the truth. This was not the time to joke. He looked down, and when he looked back up at her with those green eyes of his, she could see there wasn't any lying going on. Nope, he wasn't yanking her chain. "What were you thinking? Wait a minute, let me rephrase that: What were you thinking *with*? Hmmm? I'll say it again: You are a dumbass."

"I don't need a lecture. I know all of this already. I know everything you're going to say to me."

"Oh, really? What? Isn't Summer the woman who left you high and dry after you saved for a year to give the princess her perfect wedding? She's a user, a loser, and she'll do nothing but hurt you, Ethan . . . Hasn't she done enough already? For all you know she isn't even telling the truth. You know this woman's MO. She just loves to play you and when she thinks you're over her, she hooks you back like a dumb puppy dog."

"Michaela!"

When she looked at him this time, his eyes were moist. "Like I said, I know all of this. But it's true. She is pregnant. I went with her to the doctor, and I can't . . . I just can't abandon . . ."

She sucked in a breath of air, her mind clouded over with the events of the day, and now Ethan's revelation. She could strangle him. But she softened at the look in his eyes and the words she knew he couldn't express. She took his hand. "Ethan, I know what you were going to say. I do. But look, this isn't about your father. I know you, and if the kid is yours, you will be there and be a great dad. But you don't have to get sucked back into Summer's drama." Ethan had never known his father. His mother had told him that their relationship wasn't long lived and once he found out she was pregnant, he took off. Then, he died in a car accident shortly thereafter. He and Michaela rarely discussed it, but the few times they had, it was obvious the pain Ethan felt from it. He'd once told her that he'd be the kind of dad a kid could count on. He'd always be there for any child he had, and she believed him. But, why did he have to be having a baby with Summer? What a cruel joke.

"I have to stick by her. I would never abandon my child, or Summer in her condition."

Michaela shook her head again. She couldn't take much more of this. "You know, women raise babies on their own all of the time. You can still be the dad. But at least promise me something."

"What?"

"You won't marry her without really thinking about it."

"I agree, Mick. But, I feel like a kid deserves a family. A real family, with his mom and dad together." He put his face in his palms and sighed deeply. "I want to do the right thing, and I was going to marry her before she left me. I don't know. I really don't know right now. She's angry at me anyway for coming back over here to stay the night."

"I'm sure she is. We're not exactly bosom buddies. You need to remember, marriage is for life. At least for someone like you, and I don't want you to be miserable because you made the wrong choice. I . . . care about you." She felt herself slipping and simply didn't want to deal any longer with the horrors of the day. Standing, she brushed off her jeans. "I'm sorry if I was hard on you. It's been . . ."

He wrapped his arms around her. "I know it's been difficult and I'm sorry my timing isn't great. You've always been there for me. It was selfish of me to come to you with this right now."

"That's what friends are for. We have needs during the craziest of times. I suppose it's what makes us human." She glanced up at the clock. Almost ten. "I've got to go to bed. I'm beat."

"I'm going to crash in the tack room. I'd like to be able to keep an eye on Leo."

"You said that he's fine and I think he is. Why don't you head back to Summer's? You said that you were staying there again, right? I mean . . . when you left earlier, you inferred that anyway."

"I've got some stuff there and yes, I've been there off and on since I came home. I stayed at my office last night. But tonight, if it's all right with you, I'll stay here. I think Summer and I both need some space to try and figure things out."

"Of course, but take the couch at least."

"I'll be fine."

"So, at least you haven't set up house yet with her?"

"She wants me to."

I bet she does. Summer knows she had a good thing.
"Yeah, well, you can stay here as long as you need to, as long as you promise me you'll think about this thing with her. I'm begging you."

"I told you that I would. I promised. I'll pinky swear if you want."

She laughed, remembering how when they were kids they would always pinky swear on secrets of the utmost importance, like the time they were playing with Ethan's G.I. Joes in Ethan's backyard, and they'd taken a gas can from his mom's garage and dug a trench, placing the figures down in it, pouring the gas into the trench and lighting it on fire. What they hadn't realized was that their fun and games would "backfire," as they just about caused Ethan's house to burn as a *poof* of flame shot out from the fumes and caught one of the trees in the backyard on fire. It had been horrible at the time, and they were questioned by Ethan's mom and her parents but they'd pinky sworn never to tell, and to this day their parents figured they'd done it, but because there was room for doubt on their innocent-looking faces, they hadn't been punished.

"No need to pinky swear. I believe you."

"Thanks for the couch, but I think I'll camp in the tack room. That way I'll be close to Leo and you won't have to worry. Did that cop find out anything?"

"We found the pitchfork out by the bales of hay . . . and a chewing tobacco wrapper."

"That's odd. Have you hired any help lately? Someone who might chew?"

"Nope. I am an island unto myself. In other words, with the lawyers tying things up between Brad and me, I'm too broke to hire help."

"Well, you know that I'll be here if you need me."

She kissed him on the cheek. Tears stung her eyes as she walked down the hall. She didn't know if the tears were for Lou, the thought that Ethan was about to make the biggest mistake of his life, or for the fact that a manipulative woman like Summer was pregnant, and she was still paying bills to doctors who, no matter what they'd put her through, hadn't been able to make her fertile.

TEN

MICHAELA SLIPPED OUT OF HER JEANS AND donned a long T-shirt. She brushed her teeth and splashed her face. No time for nightly rituals. She could hear Camden's muffled voice on the phone in the next room.

She picked up her own phone and dialed Lou and Cynthia's number. A man answered. "Oh hi, Michaela. It's Dwayne. Sam and I pulled back onto the ranch not too long ago. I cannot believe this. I plan to stay here with Cynthia until she feels it is okay for me to leave and go back to the rodeo. Bean is here, too."

Dwayne Yamaguchi was one of the best working cow horse trainers around and he'd worked for Lou for almost eight years. He was also quite the calf roper. Not Michaela's favorite rodeo event— maybe it was something about running down the calf and flipping him over and tying his hooves. Although her dad and uncle always told her that it wasn't cruel. Ranchers did it all the time. And, Dwayne was one of the best at his sport.

His cousin Sam, a *paniolo*— a Hawaiian cowboy— had come over from the islands a couple years after Dwayne had joined on with her uncle, to help out temporarily, and wound up never going back. He wasn't the rider that Dwayne was. He carried quite a bit more weight on him than his younger cousin. But from everything Michaela knew about him, Sam did a good job with the horses.

"Thanks, Dwayne, for coming back. Is Cynthia okay?"

"As good as you might expect. You know, she had a terrible blow, losing a loved one. Lou was a good man. Did not deserve this fate. She is resting now."

Michaela could hear him choke back emotion as she felt it rise again in her own throat. "I was hoping to speak to her. But it's good she's sleeping."

"You going to come by in the morning for a coffee, right? Maybe she be up to talking then. I hope I can get back to the horses in a day or so. Lou would want that."

"You're still going to ride?"

There was a pause on the other end. "You know, Michaela, I run it through my brain the whole drive home about what is right thing to do, or how it looks if I am still in the rodeo. I talk about it with my cousin Sam on the drive and he say to me that Lou was a cowboy. He was a horseman. He did not raise the animals and make investment in them without want of an outcome. He raised champions and I have to go and get a championship again. You know that is what he would have me do. Sam be right. I have to ride."

Dwayne was correct: Uncle Lou had never been a glass-half-empty kind of guy. "You're probably right. Yes, I'll stop by in the morning."

"Good. Get some rest and we will talk tomorrow."

Michaela hung up and turned off the light. She sat in the dark for several minutes, trying to clear her mind of the image of Uncle Lou lying dead on Loco's stall floor. But she couldn't. After a few minutes she decided to get a glass of water.

She passed Camden's room and could hear her still talking. Probably to Kevin. She reached for the doorknob, thinking she'd say goodnight, but before she could turn it, her friend's words came through the door.

"... with him gone it will be a lot easier acquiring that land. I understand you don't want to look suspicious, but I seriously doubt it. You've been trying to get your hands on that property for a while now. Besides, you don't exactly have a killer instinct. You know how to get people eating out of your hands. It's one of the things I love about you. But we both know just what a killer you are, don't we?" Camden laughed. "Listen, I better go, I need to check on Michaela. Today has been rough on her. Tomorrow night?

Yeah. Sure. Well, maybe I should stay home and take care of her. No, she won't want to come. Even when she isn't down in the dumps she's not exactly a party girl. Okay, I'll try. You're right, maybe it would help. Yes, and it would be good if she had a different impression of you. I know. I won't. Okay, sweetie. I'll talk to you tomorrow."

Camden hung up the phone. Michaela hurried back to bed and slid under the covers. A few seconds later she heard her door open. Camden whispered her name and stood over her. She reached out and rubbed Michaela's arm. "Poor kid. Get some rest."

After Camden left she lay awake for quite some time, her friend's conversation playing over and over again in her mind. She *had* been talking to Kevin. The way it sounded, they were talking about it being much easier now for Kevin to get his grubby hands on her uncle's land. Granted, Camden hadn't mentioned her uncle's name, but it made sense. The scenario about the killer instinct, the land being easier to acquire, all of it. Her stomach took a turn for the worse as she couldn't help wondering: Did her best friend have something to do with her uncle's murder?

ELEVEN

ETHAN WAS GONE BY THE TIME MICHAELA MADE it out to the barn the next morning, but he'd fed the horses and left her a note that said he'd stop by later on or give her a call. She knew she'd been hard on him the night before, but she wanted to protect him from getting hurt again— if that was at all possible.

She decided to head over and check on Cynthia, but first she needed to stop by her parents' place. They hadn't called last night, and she'd figured that maybe they had been so caught up in their own grief that they couldn't muster the energy. Whatever it was, she needed to make sure they were all right. She also knew she had to work her horses. Dwayne had hit it on the nail last night: Lou would expect nothing less from her than to move on, take care of her animals and keep working toward her goals, which the two of them had discussed time and again. Still, she knew it would be painful.

Camden was making coffee as Michaela walked in from the barn.

"Want some?" she asked. Her naturally curly hair was frizzed out from sleeping on it, and she wore a pair of men's black silk boxers, which Michalea assumed belonged to Kevin, and a T-shirt that read MASTER OF MY DOMAIN.

Only Camden. "No," Michaela replied curtly. "I'm going over to see my folks and then Cynthia."

"Oh. You want me to come?"

Michaela shook her head. "I'm fine."

"Okay. Well if you need me, call. I think, I'm gonna stay around today. So I'm here for you." She paused. "You know, hon, I was talking to Kevin last night."

"Were you?"

"Yes, and we thought it might be good for you to come out with us tonight. We'll have some Mexican food, maybe a few drinks. Why don't you ask Ethan to come along?" Camden raised her brows. "If I didn't know better, I'd say the two of you could wind up together . . . but what do I know? Look at *my* last three marriages."

"Exactly." Michaela was about to say something even more smart-assy and bring up the fact that her new boyfriend looked like a pretty good suspect in her uncle's murder, especially since he'd tried to purchase Lou's land not too long ago and had received a big fat no from Lou. But something stopped her. "Maybe I will go out with you tonight."

"Good," Camden replied, wide-eyed. "That's . . . great. I'm telling you that getting out will be good medicine. It will. You'll see."

Michaela said goodbye and headed to her truck. Tonight wasn't going to be about good medicine, but rather about fishing for answers. Maybe she'd get into that brain of Kevin Tanner's and find some hint that he might have been behind Uncle Lou's murder, or— and this was a thought she hated entertaining, but after last night had no choice— to see if she could also figure out whether or not Camden had somehow been involved.

* * *

ANOTHER CAR STOOD PARKED NEXT TO HER mom's Trail Blazer. It took her a minute to recognize it, but she quickly realized that it belonged to Detective Davis. Something made her uneasy about him being there. Though likely routine, she just didn't like the idea of her parents being questioned by the police. Stepping out of her own vehicle she could smell her mom's famous cinnamon rolls. Janie Bancroft enjoyed cooking and always made major meals for her family, but in times of stress she went into overdrive. Michaela was sure to find a kitchen filled with baked goods and casseroles. For all she knew, her mom had been up all night cooking.

She came into the kitchen through the back door. Her mother and Davis were seated at the table, each with a cinnamon roll and a glass of milk.

"Hi, honey. Good to see you. Get a roll and come sit with us. I understand you've met Detective Davis already," her mom said. She fiddled with the cross around her neck, a habit she had when she was nervous. "I insisted that Detective Davis have a cinnamon bun. I fixed a little bit of food, I guess." Her face appeared strained, as if she hadn't slept, and her eyes were bloodshot. She *had* been cooking. There were brownies, the rolls, cookies, and when Michaela opened the refrigerator door to get a glass of milk she found it filled with a fruit salad, two covered casseroles that, if she guessed correctly, were a taco casserole and a lasagna. Oh boy, Mom was taking this really hard. She'd expected that to happen with her dad, but her mom was always the grounded one.

"Mom, who's going to eat all of this?"

Her mother shrugged. "I'm sure Cynthia could use some, and after the funeral there will be plenty for all who come. People loved Lou, so I suspect there will be quite a large number of folks. I think we should have the reception here. I think it'd be too much right now for Cynthia to deal with. I told her that yesterday that we would take care of the arrangements for a reception, but I'm not certain she heard me. Poor girl. She's beside herself, as expected. So having people here after the funeral, I think would be a nice idea, and as you pointed out, we'll have plenty of food."

"It's a lovely gesture, Mama." Mom was acting nervous, but it wasn't every day that a detective sat in your kitchen, trying to solve the murder of a loved one. Michaela looked at Davis, who smiled. "Good morning, Detective."

It irked her to see him sitting in her mom's kitchen all warm and fuzzy like, kind of like a flipping cover of *Good Housekeeping*. Then again, she knew her mom, Janie Bancroft, was one woman who didn't take no for an answer. More than likely she'd practically shoved the roll down the poor man's throat.

He nodded. "Ms. Bancroft. How are you?"

"That's to be determined."

Davis stood. "Mrs. Bancroft, I should be going. Thank you for answering my questions. I may have more as the investigation progresses and as I said, I do need to speak with your husband again." He handed her his card. "Please have him call me."

"Certainly," Janie Bancroft replied.

Michaela noticed that her hands were trembling as she took the card from Davis.

"Thank you for the rolls and milk. It was completely unnecessary, but certainly delicious, and very kind of you."

"Oh, gosh," her mom said, a pink hue coloring her cheeks. "My pleasure, Detective."

"Thank you. And, I can not express how sorry I am for your loss." He turned to Michaela. "You, too."

She nodded. "I'll walk out with you, if that's okay?"

"Sure."

Michaela led him out the front door. "What did you need to talk to my parents about?"

"Some routine questions, similar to what I asked you." He reached into his jeans pocket for his keys to his charcoal Ford sedan. "When they were over at your uncle's place yesterday, we didn't get enough time to go over a few things."

"Right. And, my dad, you have to come back and talk to him some more?"

"Yes. He's not home right now."

"He comes and goes. Sometimes my mom and I can't keep track of him. Did you find anything out? About the pitchfork with the fingerprints, I mean?"

Maybe his green eyes, and his smile, and the gentle way when he talked with people had something to do with the way her stomach kept fluttering. He was an awfully good-looking man. As that thought came to mind, she immediately chastised herself for even thinking it. Here her uncle had just been murdered and she was noticing how handsome the detective working on his case was. Right now, she hated herself for that and decided the one and only reason she felt this way around him was that he was a police officer and that in itself can make a person nervous, cause a twitter in the gut.

"Not yet. It may take a day or two. Sometimes longer, depending on the lab. As soon as I know something, I'll call you."

"Thanks."

He placed a hand on her shoulder. "I promise I'm going to do what I can to see to it you and your family get some closure. I'll be in touch."

Michaela watched as he drove away. God, she hoped he was right. She rubbed her shoulder where Davis had touched her, and for a few seconds found herself lost in thought. Why had he done that? It wasn't like an intimate type of touch but one of comfort really, and honestly, she couldn't help feeling comforted by him in the brief second that he'd placed his hand on her. Dammit. She could not, *could not* have ridiculous fantasies about nice, good-looking detectives! She went back inside the house.

Sitting across from her mom, she picked at her roll. They were silent for long moments. Michaela finally reached across the table and took her mom's hand. "Are you really okay?"

"I think I'm better than your dad. He's a wreck. And, of course he won't talk about it with me. But that's the way he is. He gets quiet and goes within himself. He's been doing that more and more, even before this happened. Keeping to himself, leaving the place after he's done with chores and being away for a few hours at a time. Some things, like that fence he was mending the other morning when he got hurt, I've been on him to get done for weeks now, but he takes off and doesn't let me know where he's at. And you know I can't get him to carry a cell phone. When I ask him where he's been, he says that he was in town or running errands or visiting Lou or some of his cronies. I don't know, though. I'm worried, and I'm praying that he isn't gambling again."

"Oh, no, Mom. You don't really think that, do you?"

"I don't know, but if he is, Lou's death could send him into a spiral, and we don't have anything to pay back any more debt. All we have is this place, and we can't take a second on it. We did that last time this happened and now we simply can't go that route. With us only collecting Social Security and not being too smart about how we saved for retirement— I guess because we always figured we'd have this roof over our heads— we can't do that. If your father is back at it again, I don't know what we're going to do."

"But, it's been years since he's had a problem."

"It's an *addiction*. You know that."

"Where is Dad now? I'll go and talk to him."

"I don't know. I asked him to go to the store to get me some things and he said that he had a few errands to run before that. I didn't question him much. He's far too upset right now for me to go snooping, and for all I know he's being truthful. He has slowed down, and he does like to visit with some of the men he used to ride with. So, I may be pointing a finger where I shouldn't be."

"I'd still like to talk to him."

Her mom nodded. She stood and cleared the plates from the table, the scent of her strawberry lotion wafting through the air. "That Detective Davis is a nice man."

"I hope he finds out who killed Uncle Lou, and soon. What was he asking you?"

Her mom faced her, brushing off the front of her rose-colored knit sweater. "About Lou, and who he might have had any troubles with. He asked quite a bit about Bradley, too."

"Brad? What did you tell him?"

She pursed her lips. "I told him that . . . the boy is an ass."

Michaela couldn't help but laugh. "Oh, Mom." Her mother never swore, unless pushed hard and very angry. Brad seemed to have that knack with everyone in her family, though.

"It's true. And then he asked quite a bit about your marriage."

"What about it?" The muscles in her neck tightened.

"He asked if I thought that Kirsten was the only one I knew he'd been unfaithful with, and how you felt about Brad and what Lou had done when he had him followed."

"Really?" She didn't exactly care for Davis's line of questioning with her mom. She thought she'd told him everything he'd needed to know about Brad last night. Why had he grilled her mother? Of course, her mom was naïve and trusting, so she would have opened up to Davis.

"I got the feeling that he'll be having a talk with Bradley sometime soon."

"I'm sure he will. Well, I think I'm going to head over to see how Cynthia is doing. I'll call and see if Dad is home when I'm finished there. I want you to get some rest, Mama. No more cooking or baking. Got it?"

She smiled. "Can I knit?"

"Yes. But that's it." She kissed her on the cheek.

On the way to her uncle's ranch, she couldn't help thinking about her dad and what Mom was thinking. Was he gambling again? He'd always played cards, bet on races or sporting events when she was a kid— no big deal. Then, when Michaela was in high school, one of the local reservations had built a casino nearby and he started frequenting the place. It got out of control, from that point, as he began to miss work. At first she thought her mother suspected that there was another woman. Michaela had tried to steer clear from all of it. After all, she was a teenager, spreading her wings and doing things with friends, studying and just figuring out her own life. And, she definitely did not want to think about or know if her dad was having an affair. She remembered when her parents did tell her about his addiction. She almost thought it funny. Like, how could anyone become addicted to playing cards? But she soon learned it was no laughing matter when her mother grew tightfisted with money for her to go to the movies or to pay for horse show entries. Her sophomore year had been rough, as the year prior she'd started to make a name in the horse world with her barrel racing. Then, suddenly, it was yanked out from under her as the Bancrofts had to find ways to pay off her father's debts.

Along with trying to make ends meet, Ben started going to Gamblers Anonymous, which seemed to work. Eventually life settled back to normal in the Bancroft household.

Then, the bug bit Ben again when he'd been invited by some of his pals from the American Quarter Horse Association to the races at Los Alamitos. He hadn't told his wife about it. It was only months later when he was knee-deep in trouble again, and they couldn't afford Michaela's tuition, that he'd copped to his problem. Michaela had to take out a student loan and get two jobs to get through school. This time, Janie insisted he get help. They refinanced the ranch, took out all the equity, sent him to some high-priced rehabilitation center in Washington. He came home, went to meetings, and as far as Michaela knew hadn't been involved with his vice since then— over a dozen years ago.

She'd have to talk to her dad because she didn't want this weighing on her mother, or herself, for that matter.

The other thing twisting itself in her mind as she drove over to her uncle's ranch was Davis, and his line of questioning with her mom. He was obviously looking into her theory of Brad seeking revenge, and considering Brad a suspect. But she wondered if there was more to it.

It was a disturbing thought, but it still crossed her mind: Davis likely considered her a suspect, too. After all, she'd been the one to find her uncle's body. Her earlier feelings of warmth toward Davis dissipated some, realizing he was probably not being the nice guy to her because he was simply *a nice guy*. She was pretty sure it was a tactic to extract information from her, and it had worked.

TWELVE

PULLING INTO UNCLE LOU'S PLACE FELT DIFFERENT. It would never be the same again. It was as if his death darkened every corner of the ranch, for this morning nothing looked as green as it always did, or as bright. Even the smells were somehow different when she climbed out of her truck.

Usually there would be plenty of activity going on right about now, with Uncle Lou either in the arena working a horse or fixing something around the ranch. Horses being groomed, at least one in the wash rack after a morning workout, as well as a couple of horses going through their paces on the hot-walker. Not this morning. Her uncle's presence was definitely gone. The sadness filtered back into Michaela's heart and gripped it in a vise. Would she ever again laugh over a joke she and her uncle had shared? Or would this ache remain? How did people overcome death? Sure, it happened every day. People went on with their lives. They had no choice. But how? Now it was her turn to figure out how the process worked. The first thing she realized that morning was that there truly was no way to be prepared.

She tapped on the front door then let herself into the house. She went into the kitchen where she saw Dwayne Yamaguchi standing over Cynthia, who sat at the table looking as lost as Michaela felt. Dwayne's hand rested on her shoulder. He squeezed it as he swung around and spotted Michaela.

"Good morning," he said. He had dark Asian good looks with a blend of his native Hawaii thrown in. There was a scar underneath his right eye from what Michaela had heard was a barroom fight in which Dwayne hadn't fared well. He also sported a tattoo of a Polynesian dancer on his left shoulder. Dwayne was known to have been a bit of a womanizer and partier back in the day. But a bit of age and the horses he worked with seemed to have grounded him, as he spent most of his time working with them instead of drinking and carousing.

Michaela couldn't help wonder if the slight pain she noticed at times in Dwayne's eyes had something to do with the hula dancer on his arm.

"Hi," Michaela said, and walked over to Cynthia.

Dwayne moved away and went into the kitchen. "I'll get you a cup of coffee." He walked around the counter to get the carafe and pour their drinks.

Michaela sat down at the table and took Cynthia's hand. "How are you?"

Cynthia glanced up with her large brown eyes. "I don't know. I feel numb, like this isn't real."

"I know. I really do." They sat in silence for a moment.

Dwayne brought the coffee over to them. "I've gotta go out to the barn and check on a few things. Sam is out looking over one of the yearlings. Say he may want to buy one, ship it back to Hawaii for working the cows. Thinks he's ready to go on home now. Lou's death shook him up. When you're ready to head out, Michaela, why don't you come find me?"

"Sure." He obviously wanted to talk to her but she wasn't sure why. She turned back to Cyn

"You know, if you don't want to stay here, you can come and stay with me. Or, if you want, I can come over here. I hate the idea of your being alone."

Cynthia nodded. "Thank you, but I belong here and the police have been by. An officer stood guard last night, and then Dwayne came back. I think I'll be fine."

"Sure, okay, but when Dwayne heads back out to Vegas, I can come over."

"Dwayne says that Bean can stay here and take care of the animals."

"Is he responsible enough?" Michaela couldn't help asking. Bean was good with the animals, but could he do the entire job? He was such a naïve man. She recalled with anger how Brad had taken advantage of Bean when he'd worked for Lou. He'd "befriended" Bean, out of what Michaela had come to believe was for self-centered reasons. She figured that he used Bean to cover for him when he left the ranch to rendezvous with Kirsten, and that he also had him do much of the work Brad was supposed to do around the ranch. She found Bean in tears one afternoon when she'd stopped by to bring Brad lunch, and Bean told her that Brad had gone to the feed store for some supplies. She should've known then. When she asked why the tears, Bean had explained to her that he didn't think he could get all the chores done, because Brad had given him some new ones and he couldn't remember all of them. Boy, had she ever wound up with a jerk!

"I think he is. I know he has some problems, but he's conscientious and he loves the animals. He may not always show up for work on time, but you and I both know it's not going to kill the horses if they get fed an hour later than normal. Bean is loyal. Besides, there's no one else to do it right now, until Dwayne gets back. I'm not up to it, and you have your own place to take care of. I'll be fine."

"What about Sam? Can't he stay?"

"He probably could. But you know those two, they're peas in a pod and Sam is such a help to Dwayne when they're out on the road. It'll work out."

"Okay, but don't hesitate to ask. I don't mind helping around here."

Cynthia nodded. She stood and walked to the bay window that overlooked their patio and pool. She sighed. "Come with me. I want to show you something."

Michaela followed her into Uncle Lou's office. Cynthia went behind his desk and opened a drawer, pulling out a file. She handed it to Michaela. "Take a look."

She opened it. "What is this? Lawsuits?" Cynthia nodded. She glanced over the paperwork. "What's going on?"

"That is exactly what I asked Lou the night before he died when he showed them to me. There are six of them, all pertaining to the artificial insemination program. All of those people in the lawsuits are claiming that the foals born to their mares are not Loco's. They have DNA evidence to prove Loco is not the father."

"What? They're saying that Lou substituted another stallion's sperm to breed to their mares?"

"Yes. But it's worse than that. Lou has no recollection of ever sending product to any of these people."

"Then their claims are bogus."

Cynthia shook her head. "I don't think so. They all have signed breeding contracts. That's Lou's signature on the bottom of each, and look, the attorney included photocopies of the back of the checks. That's my husband's handwriting. The odd thing, though, is that Loco's stud fee is $3,500.00 and those checks are each for two grand."

"A bit of a deal." Michaela studied the papers. Cynthia was right. It did look as if Lou had signed the contracts with these people, as well as the back of the checks. "I don't understand."

"Neither do I. Lou swears he doesn't remember signing any of this stuff. And he claimed that he'd never given anyone that type of deal. I wanted to believe him, but how could I? The other part of it is that I can't trace the money to any one of our checking accounts. The numbers on the deposits don't match up. I can't even find a bank that they went into."

Michaela studied the photocopy of the back of one check to see if it listed the name of the bank where the deposits were made. It didn't, but it did have the bank's routing number and indicated that the deposits were made in Los Angeles. "We need to find out which bank uses this routing number here." Michaela pointed to the number. "Once you can find that out, we can locate the bank and branch where the account was open and maybe go from there."

"How do I do that?" Cynthia asked.

"Did you talk to Summer MacTavish about this? Is she still handling the books for the business?"

"She is, but Lou limited her responsibilities somewhat after she left Ethan. You know how he feels when somebody hurts someone he cares about."

"I do know that. What did he stop having her do?"

"Well, he told her that he'd take over running the books on the breeding program. He only left her in charge of accounts receivable and payroll. I haven't had a chance to speak to her yet, because like I said I just discovered all of this within the last forty-eight hours. But it's driving me crazy because I have no idea where these checks were deposited. I'm afraid to say anything to the police, because what if it's true? What if Lou was defrauding these people?"

"You think Uncle Lou would hide money from you and steal from people?" The words coming from Cynthia sounded completely incredulous.

"No. Not really. It sickens me to think about and now we can't figure it out together. The only other explanation that might make sense is that Lou was having memory problems."

"He was?"

"I noticed it about a month ago, and then when he showed me these papers the other night, he said that he'd been to see his doctor, because he felt like he was losing his mind. He was practically in tears."

Michaela took a deep breath, feeling like all the air had been sucked from her lungs. This was unbelievable. Could that have been why he didn't sound like himself the other night? "Are you talking something like Alzheimer's or senility?"

"I have no idea. I'm hoping his doctor will speak to me about it. I'm the one now who will have to deal with these suits, and they're asking for over a million dollars in damages, claiming that the foals they expected from Loco's bloodline could have profited them greatly."

"You think that any of these people who filed these suits could be responsible for Uncle Lou's murder?"

Cynthia shrugged. "It's a crazy world. After looking over all of this, and wondering what was going on with him, I don't know what to think. But they're all located in Ohio. So, if someone from this core group of people is behind it, they would have had to hire someone, and that really doesn't make a lot of sense, because with Lou gone a lawsuit such as this can become even more convoluted." Michaela put the papers back inside the folder. "I hate to ask you this because I know you're in pain, too, but would you mind taking these papers with you and seeing if you can't find out where the checks were deposited? And, what's going on? I don't think I have the strength right now."

Michaela hesitated for a minute. She wasn't sure she wanted to get herself involved in any of this. Seeing the sorrow in Cynthia's eyes and the grief tightening her face, she said, "I'll see what I can find out."

"Thank you."

"What about Dwayne? Doesn't he handle some of the AI transactions, or Sam?"

"No, not really. They're involved in the training and that's pretty much it. It's mainly been Lou. Of course they've helped at times. Everyone has, even me. And Ethan has also helped out when he was here. Lou was about ready to start looking for some more help, and then he received the lawsuits and thought he better wait until things were cleared up. But no one else handled the paperwork. Lou was the breeding manager, after all. I mentioned this all to Dwayne this morning and he was as floored about it as I was."

"Maybe these lawsuits do have something to do with his murder. Or maybe not. Say this is true. I mean . . . I can't believe that it could be, because Uncle Lou was so ethical in everything he did. But if by some chance there was a mix-up with the DNA?"

"I don't think that's likely. We're dealing in large amounts of cash. People want to be assured of protection in case this exact thing were to happen. I'm sure you're aware that the American Quarter Horse Association maintains DNA samples of all the stallions involved in AI, and for the foals to be registered they also have to be DNA typed, if they're bred via AI. And, the claim is the DNA doesn't match. The plaintiffs have all contacted the AQHA and they're backing these people, saying that their claims are valid. I think they could even force us to shut down the operation."

Michaela frowned. She didn't have a clue what to make of any of it. "Do you know if the owners know who the real stallion is to these foals? There were three other studs here at the time these people would have received the product and had their mares inseminated, weren't there?" It could be as simple, albeit, a horrific mixup if one of the other stallion's sperm was sent out to the mares' owners. Loco's fees were some of the more expensive stud fees out there. The other stallions on the ranch were all of excellent breeding, but they weren't Loco, and Michaela could not blame any of the owners for being upset over such a mixup. People wanted to get what they paid for.

"The documents are claiming that there is an ongoing investigation. They also say that in the breeding reports Lou had to file that none of these mares were included. This was supposedly how the owners were first alerted there might be a problem, when they discovered they couldn't register their foals because there was no breeding report on file with their mares' names."

"So, the plaintiffs here have not named the stallion they believe to be the stud horse of these foals?"

Cynthia shook her head. "You know, it may not even be a stud registered with the AQHA. It could be some random horse. I don't know. At this point I think the AQHA is still trying to track the DNA. I fear that on top of everything, we will lose our business and I'll have to pay all of these damages."

"Did Uncle Lou indicate anyone who he thought would intentionally switch containers to be shipped to the mares' owners?"

She sighed. "He did mention Brad. Brad was working here at the time and knew how the program worked."

"But why? Why would he do that, and how would he get a hold of contracts and checks?"

Cynthia shrugged. "Maybe it's as simple as Brad was being plain mean. We all know he's proven himself not to be the most upstanding individual. Maybe he wanted to sabotage Lou, you know, make sure he ruined Lou's reputation. And once this gets out, my husband's memory will be forever tainted in the horse world."

"I won't let that happen. I don't believe Lou could have done anything to hurt anyone. Not intentionally. I'll help you figure this out." Michaela sighed, trying to wrap her mind around all of this. "What about Bean? I know that everything is on a numbering system as far as which stud's sperm is which in the freezer, that kind of thing, and you keep records, but could Bean have somehow gotten things mixed up?"

"Lou didn't let Bean have anything at all to do with the program for that very reason. He could have easily mixed things up."

"Who was the person in charge of sending everything out?"

"At first it was Brad, then Summer on occasion as business picked up and Lou needed the extra help. I did it as well at times. But Lou was the main handler of all of it. We really should have put better strategies into play. That's obvious to me now. Because somewhere along the way, something got screwed up. And as far as the contracts and checks go, it could be as easy to explain that with age my husband could have signed them *and* been having problems with his memory."

"He wasn't old, though. Sixty-one is hardly an age these days where people begin losing it."

"Alzheimer's disease can begin in your fifties."

"You know, I wish I'd known he was having health problems. Maybe I could have helped."

"Your uncle was a proud man. I'm his wife and he didn't confide in me until the other night. But I should have paid more attention." Her eyes welled up with tears again. "I had noticed that there were little things he'd forgotten, like bills that didn't get paid, and one night when Dwayne was out and Bean had already gone home, he didn't feed the horses until I reminded him. But nothing too major. I thought maybe he was working too hard. Or, maybe the blowup with Ethan was eating at him."

"What do you know about what happened between them?" Michaela asked.

"All I know is that right before he left on that trip, he and Lou had a huge argument and it tormented Lou afterward."

"What was it all about?"

"I don't know. I could hear this commotion going on out in the barn. I walked out there and Dwayne was telling Ethan to get the hell off the property."

"What happened after that?"

"Lou followed him, tried to talk to him, but Ethan wouldn't have anything to do with it. He shrugged him off. Lou nearly lost his balance as Ethan pulled away. Lou wouldn't tell me what it was about, and ever since then he's seemed preoccupied, and sad. Something changed; something Ethan told him changed him, but I don't know what. I even tried to get a hold of Ethan to find out what it was, but he never called me back." The phone started ringing. "Excuse me, Mick. It might be that detective or the funeral home. I'm trying to make the arrangements." She started for the family room.

"Sure. Do you have some aspirin? I'm getting a vicious headache."

"In my bathroom upstairs. Oh, your uncle had some Ativan that he was taking for some headaches he was getting. You can try those, if you want. They seemed to help him."

"Ativan is not for headaches. At least I don't think so. I always thought it was for anxiety or panic attacks."

"I don't know. I don't take that stuff anyway, but the doctor gave it to Lou for the headaches. Sorry, I gotta get the phone."

It wasn't like Michaela was a doctor or anything, but she was sure Ativan was prescribed for agitation. Her doctor had recommended it to her when she was splitting from Brad but she'd decided against it. Like Cynthia, she tried to stay more on the holistic route, if possible. But right now, she needed a Tylenol. Why was her uncle taking Ativan? Well, agitation did cause headaches, so what did she know.

Michaela climbed up to the second floor. Their bedroom was very *Home and Garden.* Cynthia had given the place life when she'd married her uncle. She put colors together well and had a knack for making a house feel like a home with earthy warm tones and various floral and equestrian paintings around. It was pretty and inviting. But now the house, too, felt different, just as the ranch had when she'd arrived. She didn't know how Cynthia could stay here. She knew if it were her, she'd want to get away, but maybe it was a comfort thing. Maybe Cynthia needed to be here at the home she'd shared for the last decade with her husband.

In the bathroom, she found the bottle of aspirin tucked away inside the medicine cabinet, next to a bottle of Ativan. She picked it up. It was a refill prescribed to Lou only two weeks earlier. He had two more refills available. What in the world? Her uncle was never one to take drugs, especially not something like Ativan. His headaches must've been horrendous. What was going on in her uncle's life that he was so stressed-out about? She picked up the bottle and read it again. It was prescribed to Uncle Lou by a Dr. Verconti. Huh. She'd thought he'd gone to the same family doctor as her parents had— Dr. Sherman. He must have switched docs for some reason. Goodness, what had been going on here? And how had she not sensed until the night before her uncle was murdered that something was deeply troubling him? The lawsuits? His memory loss? Where was the money for the breedings? And, what stallion was used to impregnate those mares? Why hadn't she seen that her uncle was in crisis? Had she been so wrapped up in her own problems that she hadn't been available to the one person who had always, *always*, made himself available to her?

Starting to tear up again, she reached for a tissue, wiped her face and tossed it away. She missed the wastebasket and bent down to pick it up. Her eyes widened.

"Oh, my God," she muttered. There in the trash was a pregnancy test, and Michaela knew from all those she'd taken in the past that this one read positive. Cynthia was *pregnant*? But how? Uncle Lou . . .

From a conversation she'd overheard between her parents when Lou and Cynthia wed, she'd learned that Lou had had a vasectomy. Maybe he hadn't gone ahead with the procedure. *Maybe* she was jumping to conclusions. She heard the blood rushing through her ears. But, if it was

Cynthia— and it had to have been done that morning, because that blue line would have gone away after several hours— and if Uncle Lou had had a vasectomy; that meant . . . Michaela shook her head. No. It couldn't be, but she knew she would have to find out. Had Cynthia been cheating on her uncle?

THIRTEEN

CYNTHIA WAS STILL ON THE PHONE WHEN Michaela came down the stairs. The revelation that Lou's wife was pregnant, and the strong possibility that the baby was not her uncle's, continued to stun her. Again she thought, maybe he hadn't gone through with the vasectomy. That in itself was bad enough. Here Cynthia would be without Lou to help raise a child, though the alternative was worse: the possibility that Cynthia had been cheating. Michaela's mind wandered even further as another thought struck her— could *Cynthia* have killed Lou? If she was in love with someone else, maybe that *someone* else could have done it. No. No way. She would not believe that. She would stick to the hope that Lou had not gone through with the operation. But Michaela knew that to put her mind completely at ease, she would have to check around, and she didn't really want to ask the two people most likely to know: her parents. What a mess.

She left a note for Cynthia saying that she'd call her later. She really didn't want to be there when Cyn got off the phone. This one had to simmer for a while.

She walked out to the barn and spotted Dwayne down the breezeway, putting Loco back in his stall. He waved her over. "How Cynthia seem to you?"

"She actually seemed grounded," Michaela replied. "More so than I would've expected." Or, maybe Cynthia was in as much shock as Michaela was— not only over the murder of Lou, but also about her pregnancy.

"That's her. Strong woman. She get through this. She know that be the way your uncle would want it. But, I think she put up a front right now. I think inside her there's a big piece of her crumbling."

"You're probably right. How about him? How's he doing?" She pointed at Loco.

"Oh, he know something up. He skittish today. Missing his man, you know. Horses sense. They know when something is different. He know. Spiritual animal. Remind me of home. Too bad he can't talk, tell us who did this."

"Any ideas?" Michaela asked.

"Me? No."

"Were you here when my uncle had that fight with Ethan?"

"I was working in the arena. Heard them shouting. I came on down. Man, oh man." He shook his head. "Ethan real unhappy, you know. Your uncle trying hard to calm him down, but it not happening for him. Mad. Real mad." Dwayne's voice had the melodic lilt that could only come from the islands.

"Do you know what it was all about?"

"No. All I hear Ethan say before I told him to leave was that Lou was full of shit. A disgrace, he say. If everyone knew the truth about him, they'd think, so too. Don't know what that meant. Lou was good man, you know. You'd have to ask Ethan. Lou wouldn't talk about it with me."

The problem was, she had already asked Ethan . . . and he wasn't talking either. Dammit. "Right. Listen, besides this thing with Ethan, do you know anything about the lawsuits against Uncle Lou? Cynthia told me that she'd spoken to you about it."

"You know, that be none of my business. But could be that Lou got things mixed up. I don't like to say that, but he try to take on too much in the last few years with this program. I tell him to just ride and train. No need for all the science, breeding nonsense. He get real stressed-out lately, ask me or Sam to pick up a prescription for him. I see him taking the medicine for stress and I worry about him. I say, Boss, why you taking this stuff?"

"Was it Ativan?"

"Don't know the name. Sam picked up the stuff at the drugstore for him and ask him why he needs medicine. He tells us for stress, and we tell him he needs a vacation. Then Lou, says to me, maybe me and Sam be right about a vacation, 'cause he forgettin' all sorts of stuff lately and feeling confused sometimes."

Michaela's headache wasn't going away *at all*. Everything Dwayne was telling her was very disturbing. "I wish he had taken a break. I wish I'd known the pressure he was under with this program. You never had anything to do with the AI program, then?"

Dwayne chuckled. "Nah. Dealing with all that not my thing. Sure, a lot of money in it. A whole lot, but I'm not interested. I think what happened, you want to know, is that the containers got switched somehow. Honest mistake. That's what I think."

"What about the signed contracts and the checks? Do you think Lou really forgot about that money or where he put it? And if he was hiding money, why would he?"

Dwayne shifted from one foot to the other. Something appeared to be bothering him. After a few seconds he said, "Don't know. But, I think maybe I should talk to you 'bout something else you should know, before you find it out another way. Me, I don't plan to say nothing to no one. But someone else might. I have no control in case they go to the police."

"What are you talking about?" Michaela asked.

"Your father." He fiddled with Loco's halter. "Like I said, none of my business. Lou told me the other day after your dad been to see him, they didn't agree on some things. He said they had a falling-out."

"What do you mean? What kind of falling out? No one said anything to me." Michaela crossed her arms. She didn't care for the tone in Dwayne's voice or the evasive way he was getting to the point . . . or not getting to it.

"Your dad, he gambling again. He been borrowing money from Lou to pay off his debt. I'm not sure, but Cynthia say she don't know where the money is from the checks those people sent for artificial insemination. Maybe your uncle hang on to that money for your dad. Maybe he keep it aside for him. Lou asked me to see into what was going on with your father, how much he owe, and to who. It's not good."

"Oh, no." Michaela sighed. Her worst fear had been confirmed. For a few seconds she couldn't say anything else as a gamut of emotions ran through her. "What, the horses again?"

"Everything. Horse, dog, sport."

"How much is he in for?"

"Over a hundred grand."

Michaela's jaw dropped. *"A hundred thousand dollars?"*

Dwayne nodded.

"Did Lou give him any money?"

"I don't know. He told me to find out how deep your dad in first. I told him the other night before I left for Vegas. The night before . . ."

Michaela held up her hand. "I know."

"Anyway, he say that he'd call up Benjamin and have a heart-to-heart with him. He hope to get him over here the next day."

Michaela took a step back as it dawned on her why she'd first gotten the runaround from Dwayne. Why he'd told her up front that he wasn't going to tell anyone but that the word might get out anyway. She knew what it might look like, and obviously so did Dwayne. "My dad didn't murder Lou because he wouldn't give him the money to bail him out, if that's what you were thinking." She recalled the argument she overheard between her parents when she'd gone to their house yesterday. Her dad had mentioned something about his brother.

"Whoa, no, no, I know that. I don't think anything. I know you love your family and with Lou gone, I figure I need to tell you. Then you could go and talk to your dad. See if you can help him."

"Sorry." She swallowed hard. "But even considering the money my dad owes, that doesn't explain where the money went from the people who filed these lawsuits."

"No. It doesn't."

"Hey, Dwayne." A large man wearing a Hawaiian shirt walked down the breezeway toward them.

"Yeah, Sammy boy, right here. What you need?"

Sam wiped the back of his arm along his forehead, then slicked back his thick, dark hair with his palm. "Phew. Hot out there and I'm working hard. Need a break."

"You not working hard. You just big," Dwayne teased.

"You funny," Sam replied. "Don't go listening to him. Always thinking he the big shot." He smiled, showing a large gap between his teeth. "How you doing, Michaela? Sorry about Lou. Gonna miss him. Thinking I'm going back home. Too sad here, now. When we done at the finals, I'm getting on the plane and going back."

"Can't blame you. I'd go too, if I think I could make a living back home. You know, life much simpler on the islands," Dwayne said.

"And food is better, too." Sam laughed and rubbed his rotund belly, which moved in unison with his laughter. "You come to islands and see some day."

Michaela smiled. "I'd like that."

Sam nodded. He held up his hands. "Okay, cuz. What you need from me? Soon, I gotta go get some lunch."

"Why don't you take out Ginger."

"Ah, good name. Like to cook with it."

"You like to cook with anything."

Sam shook a finger at his cousin. "You watch yourself, little cousin. I take you down."

"Get the mare out. She only a few months from popping a new baby. Gonna be a good one out of her and Loco. That mare be of champion lines herself. Girl need some exercise, though. Too fat. Put her on the hot walker and let her work for twenty/thirty minute. Then, let her go in the pasture. Get some strength before that baby drop."

"Okay, cuz."

"Hey, Sam, where Bean?"

"Don't know. Last I see him, he tell me that he needed to get a soda. Shoot, I the one who needs the soda."

"Bean been acting strange. I think 'cause of Lou. I'll find him."

"If I see him, I'll send him to you. Nice to see you, Michaela. My condolences. I better go take care of Ginger and the baby she gonna pop." He clapped his hands together.

She nodded.

Sam ambled away. Michaela turned back to Dwayne. "Speaking of babies, did Lou or Cynthia ever mention to you about wanting kids?"

"No."

"Huh. Okay."

"Why you ask?"

"I don't know. Kind of random question, I suppose. I was uh, just thinking it's too bad they didn't have any."

He gave her an odd look and she took that as a cue to leave before he started putting anything together, because, Michaela now found herself on a quest to discover just who her uncle's killer was.

FOURTEEN

LEAVING THE BARN, MICHAELA FOUND BEAN SITTING in the passenger side of her truck. She opened her door and got in, looking over at him. He had a Coke in his hand.

He sat up straight. "Hi, Miss Michaela."

She noticed him tighten his grip around the soda can.

"Hello, Bean. What are you doing in my truck?"

"I think it is a pretty truck and you smell good and I wanted to know if the truck smelled like you do."

Michaela wasn't quite sure how to respond to that at first. She pushed some loose strands of hair back into her ponytail. "Thank you, but I don't think the truck smells like I do."

"No, it does not. It smells like a dog."

Michaela laughed, knowing he was right. Cocoa had spent quite a bit of time riding around in the truck with her over the years. It had only been in the past couple of weeks that she hadn't been able to jump into the front seat. "I suppose it does. So, how are you doing?"

He chewed on the side of his lip before answering. "I guess I am okay. Sorry I kind of got mad at you yesterday. I did not want to believe you when you said Mr. Lou was dead. It made me mad and sad, too."

"Oh, Bean, you didn't do anything wrong. My goodness, I certainly wasn't upset with you. It's understandable that you're upset. We all are. Dwayne's looking for you."

"Oh. I'm having a soda right now. And." He paused. "I wanted you to know that I don't like to be mean. I was mean to you and I am sorry, 'cause I know you loved Mr. Lou, too. He was a nice man to me. I miss him."

"I know. We all miss him."

Bean opened the door and got out of the truck. "I will see you soon, Miss Michaela. Okay?" He crumpled the can in his hand.

"Sure. Be careful and take care of yourself."

Bean spat a wad of chewing tobacco on the ground. She grimaced. "I didn't know you chewed tobacco."

"I don't."

"But . . . you just spit it out."

"I tried it. I do not like it. Especially don't like it with soda. Doesn't taste real good."

"I imagine that it wouldn't. Where did you get the chew from?"

"Found it."

"Where?"

He shrugged. "I can't remember."

Was he lying to her? She couldn't tell. "You don't remember?"

"No."

"Can I see the container it came in?"

He pulled it from his pocket. It wasn't the brand that Davis found outside her barn last night, but it still made her wonder if Bean had anything to do with scaring her. He acted like a child, but even children had the capacity to frighten people. Some even had it within them to kill. Bean may have been a child inside a man's body. Was he also a killer? "See you later, Bean."

"Sure." He slammed the door of the truck. She winced. *That was really odd.* Was Bean really as vulnerable and naïve as he seemed, or had he perfected an act that in many ways could have helped him cruise through life? The accident that he'd suffered happened when he was a kid. Could his injuries not be as serious as he'd presented? Was he someone who'd learned it was easier to get by, by victimizing himself more so than need be? It was hard to fathom anyone doing such a thing. An even more disturbing thought was, could Bean be off just enough to murder Uncle Lou? Could they have argued over something and Bean lost his temper, left the ranch, then came back after the police arrived and acted as if he had no idea what had occurred? She hated thinking these thoughts about him. But his behavior just now made her wonder. It also made her wonder if she wasn't simply being plain paranoid. She glanced out her window, seeing Bean wave at her as she drove off, more confused than ever.

Michaela checked her watch. No time to mull this over in her mind right now. There were horses that needed exercising and she was way off with her schedule. One point that Dwayne— and even Cynthia, in a sense— had made was that Uncle Lou would not want her to sink into the misery of the situation. Hard to do, but the reality was that animals in training had to be worked.

She used her cell to try and call her dad. Her mom informed her that he still hadn't returned home.

"Do you have any idea where he is, Mom?"

"No, honey, I don't. I'm hoping that he's only out for a drive."

Doubtful. Michaela had a sick feeling that her father was probably somewhere making a deal with the devil. If he was in as much trouble as Dwayne suggested, he was likely covering his rear. It was also possible that the same question that had crossed Michaela's mind, had crossed her father's: Could someone have murdered her uncle to get back at her father for not paying his debts?

Instead of going home as originally planned, she headed over to Joe Pellegrino's. Joe was a big, slick Italian guy she'd gone to high school with. Joe'd always had a crush on her, which she didn't reciprocate. However, they'd become fast friends after he'd moved from a school at the other end of the valley, where he'd been teased ruthlessly about his size, even though he really wasn't *that* big. A little pudgy, maybe. After all, Joe did like his pasta. Kids at her high school didn't treat Joe much better when he came over as the newcomer, but she'd befriended him because she was also a bit of an outcast. Riding horses was far more important to her during those years, and still was, than the latest designer jeans or hairdo. Ethan had, as always, been her pal as well at the time, but he'd been quite a bit more popular due to his success on the football field. Joe, though not popular at school, kept her in stitches. He knew how to make a girl laugh.

Her mother did not approve of their friendship or his family, meaning that they didn't see much of each other outside of school. Apparently, his family was noted to have Mafia ties around the country, especially a large connection out of Los Angeles. Supposedly Joe was on the up and up with the hardware store he owned, and Michaela wanted to believe that, but really didn't. If anyone had ideas about who her dad was dealing with, it would be Joe. Dad had to have a bookie, and hopefully Joe could help her find out who it was.

A buzzer sounded as she entered the store. The smell of paint, resins, and metal permeated the air. "Be right with you," a gruff voice from the back called out.

Michaela went to the hammer aisle and grabbed a new one. Last week, while changing out some of the nails that had deteriorated on the saddle racks, she'd snapped the old hammer in two when she'd smashed it down on her thumb and in a fit of pain and anger had thrown it against the wall.

"Well, look what the cat drug in."

Joe Pellegrino approached her. He was at least fifty pounds overweight. The pasta was treating Joe well, or maybe poorly, depending on how you looked at it. He had warm brown eyes with a twinkle in them when he smiled. His chubby, dimpled face made Michaela think of an Italian Pillsbury doughboy. Joe had thick lips, flushed cheeks, and a thick cap of wavy black hair, which always looked shiny and coiffed. All in all Joe looked like the nicest guy in the world. He wiped his hands on his jeans.

"Been mixing some paint back there. How you doing? You look as pretty as always. Sure is nice to see you."

"Thanks, Joe." She waved the hammer at him. "Need a new hammer."

"Came to the right place. You need anything else? Nails, paint, you know I've got all that stuff. Oh, and I've got a great power drill. You want to take a look?" He smiled at her. "Right. I'm sure you don't want to take a look. I get excited over the damndest things, my Marianne tells me, but it's a guy thing." He lowered his voice. "Speaking of men, I heard about you and Brad. That jerk. Sorry, but he is." Michaela nodded and didn't say anything. "We've known each other since we were what, fourteen? You're a good lady. I like you. But you know that. You know, I could make sure your ex gets a little pain in return for all he's caused you. Maybe a little smack upside the head would remind him how to treat a woman."

That did sound like an opportunity not to be passed up. But in all good conscience Michaela wasn't a vindictive woman. "No, Joe. But thank you. Something tells me he's got all the problems he can handle with his new girlfriend."

"Yeah, she's sure full of herself. Came in here the other day, bossing me around, needing a few things. Pain in the ass, that one. Brad deserves her."

"Listen, I don't need you to do any smacking around, but I do need a favor."

"You name it."

"Did you hear about my uncle? Lou Bancroft?"

"Yeah, my friend, sorry. Read about it in the paper. Was gonna send over some flowers and ring you when I got a chance. That's rough."

"Yeah, thanks. This is kind of personal so I'd appreciate it if you'd keep it between us."

"Discretion is my middle name. Whaddya need?"

"It's my dad. He's gambling big-time from what I've heard, and he's in for quite a bit of money. He's got to be working with a bookie. I need to know who the bookie is, and I need to know how much he owes."

Joe frowned. "That don't sound too good to me. You may want to let your pop handle his own problems."

"Joe, he's my father. Just get me a name, and . . ." She looked out the store window.

"And, what?"

"You don't think my uncle's murder could have anything to do with my dad's gambling?"

Joe waved his hands animatedly. He really could've landed an acting job on *The Sopranos*. He had the drama thing down. "Come on, you know that would not be a likely scenario. It wasn't your uncle dealing with the cash. Look, from what I know about the families— and I'm not saying I know anything, because I only know this stuff from the TV and movies— but, uh, you know the families, they don't do that kind of thing. You piss them off, they take care of *you*. Retaliation on a loved one, well, that's not what they do."

Michaela nodded. "Right." She touched Joe's shoulder. "Could you just ask a few questions, see if I can't help get my dad out of trouble and see if anyone knows anything about my uncle Lou?"

"I got some cousins who might be able to help me out. I'll do what I can. Give me a day. C'mon, let's go ring up your hammer. You still hanging out with that friend of your's, Camden?"

"She's living with me, believe it or not."

"She's a firecracker, that one. I remember meeting her with you, what was that 'bout a year ago at The Dakota House?"

"I think so." The mention of The Dakota House saddened her. She should've had breakfast with Uncle Lou there the day before.

"Hey, if she's not hooked up with anyone, I got a cousin who could use a date. He's a nut like she is. Think they'd have a good time together."

"I'll mention it to her. I better run." She thanked him, but before she could get out the door he stopped her, his large hand grabbing her by the arm. "You be careful, Michaela. You need someone to watch your back, you let me know. You know, old crushes die hard." He smiled and winked at her.

She stood on her tiptoes and kissed him on the cheek. His face turned the color of the red paint he'd been mixing.

She'd try to find her dad later, but for now she was thankful that Joe Pellegrino had never lost the ache in his heart for her.

FIFTEEN

MICHAELA TOOK LEO A HANDFUL OF SLICED APPLES. The other horses down the breezeway gave her a curious look, and she was sure if they could speak they'd be saying, *Um, excuse me, what about the rest of us?*

She knew she spoiled Leo, but she couldn't help it. He was her baby, and— if her gut was right— a future champion reining horse, a horse that would make her a household name in the industry. She planned to show him as a three-year-old in the National Reining Horse Association Futurity in Oklahoma City. Leo came from the perfect bloodlines suited for reining . . . an event designed to show the athletic ability of a ranch-type horse with a little added elegance and finesse. Michaela had not ridden in the futurity before and although she had a little over two years to go, she felt certain that Leo was destined to be a winner.

Training him, in and of itself, was a challenge she would relish. She would have to teach him to move in very unnatural ways and perform extremely challenging and controlled maneuvers with grace. They included small slow circles, large fast circles, and flying lead changes— meaning that as he galloped, he'd have to switch the leg leading with each stride— while maintaining the same speed. He'd also have to learn how to do rollbacks, or a 180-direction change turning around on the hind end and continuing motion in the opposite direction, 360-degree spins done by pivoting his body around one hind leg that stays in place and doing it at a high rate of speed, and finally very long, smooth, sliding stops. She patted his forehead. Dream big. That was always Uncle Lou's motto. Dad's was, "Be cautious." Funny how he hadn't listened to his own advice. At least right now it didn't appear so. Gambling, and owing the kind of money Dwayne suggested, was anything but cautious.

She walked to the other end of the barn, took out her seven-year-old stallion Rocky and groomed him. He was a big, beautiful sorrel. She'd taken him to a few events as a four-year-old and he'd shown great promise, earning out a decent amount for his first year on the circuit, but she'd been trying to get pregnant at the time and that's where her focus was. Then her world went to pot with the discovery of Brad's infidelity. Rocky was past his prime now as far as the show scene went. Since she hadn't shown him much over the years, it wasn't likely he could bring a lot of money in stud fees. However, like Loco and Leo, Rocky was from good lines— his full name was Rocky Chex, with his great-grandsire being Bueno Chex. Now her options were to geld him and make a pleasure riding horse out of him, or turn him out to stud and see if he could still help supplement her income. She had to decide soon what to do with him. But for now, Rocky needed his exercise. She threw the saddle on him; the animal shifted his weight and turned his head toward her with a look in his eye that said, *Can't I just go back and eat?*

"No. You can't, but if you're a good boy today, maybe there will be a treat in it for you."

She retrieved his bridle from its post in the tack room and brought it back, sliding the halter off and slipping the bit into his mouth and the headstall over his ears. She led him out of the breezeway, stepped up into the left stirrup, grabbed the saddle horn and reins with her left hand, and swung her right leg over and sat comfortably in the saddle. She adjusted her seat and slightly squeezed her calves into his rib area, cueing him to go forward. He responded accordingly, and headed toward the arena.

Rocky side-passed around to the gate. Michaela reached over and unlocked it, maneuvered him inside, backed him around and shut it. Moments later they were working on conditioning techniques to better their patterns— flying lead changes, circles, and spins. She then pushed him into a full canter with a strong squeeze of her legs, shifted her weight slightly forward and loosened up on the reins. Reining horses, which were typically of the Quarter horse breed, shorter and stockier than most of the other breeds— had good heads about them and maintained calm demeanors. But like the thoroughbred on the track, the quarter horse trained for reining was a fierce competitor inside the ring. There were no other horses in the ring at the same time as the reiner— only horse and rider. But it was as if the animal had a complete understanding of what he was bred for and what was at stake— for him— a bucket of grain and a lot of praise from his rider. For the rider, a wad of cash and some major recognition. For Michaela as a woman, that recognition meant more to her than most of the riders on the circuit, who were men. She wanted to be at the top of her game. She wanted to be the trainer that everyone looked up to: horseman— or in her case, horsewoman— of the year.

    The training that went into teaching the horse to turn on his haunches by coming to a sliding stop from a full run, and doing a 180 turnaround immediately taking off the opposite direction, more like an elegant dancer than a thousand-pound animal, made Michaela's adrenaline run at a rapid clip. There was no other high that could compare. To be able to control an amazing beast while at a high rate of speed and while doing such complicated maneuvers, with just slight touches of her legs, balancing shifts of her seat and soft movements from her hand, gave her the same kind of power that she often imagined was what it felt like for CEOs of huge corporations who went in and achieved *the kill*.

    "Wow! Nice riding."

    Michaela slid Rocky to a stop and turned to see Detective Jude Davis standing at the side of the arena. She wiped the back of her right arm across her forehead, the reins still in her left hand. Heat rose to her face. She worked almost as hard as the horses she rode, and today she'd been so focused on what she was doing that the sweat matted the strands of her blonde hair to the sides of her face.

"Hey, Detective." Rocky stomped his foot, impatient to get back to work. "Relax, boy." She patted his neck. "Surprised to see you again so soon. How long have you been there?"

"Long enough to be impressed."

Now she was definitely more than flushed. "Thanks. What can I do for you? Did you learn anything more about my uncle's murder?"

He crossed his arms across his dark sports coat, which he wore over a crisp white oxford that wouldn't stay too white if he hung around much longer. "No, sorry. We're still checking into several leads."

Michaela urged Rocky over to the side of the ring and dismounted. "Leads? What type of leads?"

He shook his head and his golden hair waved in the wind. "I can't divulge that information; it's an investigation."

She patted Rocky on the neck. He was soaked in sweat. "Then why are you here?" She didn't have time for small talk, and the way her stomach churned while watching Detective Davis's lips move when he spoke made her uneasy. Men should not have sexy lips, at least not the one investigating her uncle's murder. How could she even watch him speak, and then look into his blue eyes? Worse yet, how could she continue this way? Had grief driven her insane? It simply was not appropriate for her to think like this about Davis. Plus, she needed to keep in mind that his nice guy act, was just that—*an act*.

"Actually I wanted to stop by and see how you were doing."

Sure. "Oh? I just saw you this morning at my mom's, so not a lot has changed since then." She looked down at the ground. "I'm doing okay, I suppose. I figured I better work my horses and try to maintain some semblance of normalcy around here."

"I think that's good. I mean, trying to get back to daily life."

Michaela didn't respond, confused as to why he was there. She shifted her weight from one foot to the other. What did he want?

"Are you sure you're all right?" he asked.

"I'm sure." She wondered if she should mention anything about her dad and his gambling problem, and that maybe his problem had gotten so out of hand that someone sought retaliation by killing his brother. But almost instantly she had second thoughts. That was something she would trust Joe to follow up on, and she needed to see her father and ask him about it herself. "Well, I've got some more work to do."

He nodded and seemed uncomfortable. "You were close with your uncle."

"I told you that. Yes. He was like another father to me."

"He never gave you a reason to be upset with him?"

Where was this going? Her uneasiness about him being there grew. "Of course not."

"You didn't have any recent arguments with him or discussions that might have caused tension?"

Her grip on Rocky's reins tightened. "No. Why are you asking me this? You questioned me yesterday. I told you everything I could. Is there a problem?"

He shrugged. "Only doing my job. I . . . received some information that maybe you were upset with your uncle."

"What?" she gasped. "Absolutely not. Who told you this?"

"I can't divulge that. This is an ongoing investigation. I've explained that already."

She shook her head. "Wait a minute. You're asking me questions that don't make a whole lot of sense, based on what I can only speculate is some type of twisted gossip. I'd like to know what it is exactly that you were told."

"You told me yourself that your uncle had your ex-husband followed and that was how you found out about his affair."

"That's true."

"Were you happy in your marriage?"

"What? No! How could I have been happy? My husband was screwing around. And, I know my mom told you the same thing this morning. Why all the questions about my marriage all of a sudden?"

"I have to investigate all possibilities. Prior to discovering his infidelity, were you happy?"

"Again, I have to ask you, what is this all about?"

"I'm trying to establish if ignorance was bliss in your situation. Maybe you had what you thought was the perfect life, and it was suddenly shattered when your uncle exposed the truth."

She groaned. Oh, yeah, his nice-guy façade had definitely crumbled right in front of her. "You have got to be kidding me. Now I get it. You've concocted some type of theory, or someone has put it into your head that I was so distraught over Brad's infidelity, that after I had time to let it all settle, I realized how much happier I was with the loser when I didn't know he was getting it on with the rodeo queen. No, Detective, I was *not* happy in my marriage and I was *not* disillusioned, and I did *not* seek a vendetta against my uncle."

He nodded, and she heard him sigh loudly. "This is rather a sensitive topic, but I have to ask."

"Of course it's sensitive."

"No. Um, see, I understand that you and your husband were trying to have a baby."

Whoa! She felt like the air had been sucked out of her. It took her a second to register where he might be going with this. She closed her eyes and shook her head.

Narrowing her eyes at him, she said, "What does that have to do with who might have killed my uncle?"

"I have to look at every scenario, Ms. Bancroft."

"Uh-huh. What scenario are you getting at, Detective?" Rocky pawed at the ground and stomped his foot again, feeling as agitated as she did. She would have liked to turn him around and allow him to kick the crap out of Davis at that moment. "Wait a minute." She sat up straight on the horse. "You're thinking that I wanted a child so badly that I would have put up with Brad's bullshit. Aren't you? And that my uncle took that away from me." Davis didn't say a word. "Sorry, Detective. I may have been a blind fool with my ex, but I am not a sucker, and another thing, I'm not desperate either. I may not be Miss Rodeo America." She shook a finger at him. "But if I wanted a man to have a baby with, I think I could find one who wouldn't cheat on me, thank you very much. Now, if you have nothing more to ask me, I'd appreciate it if you'd leave. In fact, even if you have anything else to ask, I don't care. It's time for you to go."

"As I said, I'm simply doing my job."

Wait a minute. Was he smiling at her? Was that a slight grin on his condescending, smug face? She could have sworn it was! "Right. Well, you're not doing it too well, because I am the last person who would want to hurt my uncle. Goodbye, Detective." Michaela turned away from him and got back up on Rocky. She trotted him over to the side of the arena, hot tears stinging her eyes. Asshole! When she turned Rocky back around, Davis was gone. She tried to regain focus and run Rocky back through his maneuvers, but found herself growing angrier. The horse sensed her tension, and responded in kind, tossing his head in the air and losing his direction. It was time to put him away, and get a grip.

She dismounted Rocky and led him down to the cross ties, where she took his tack off. Then she guided him to the wash rack, where she rinsed him off and brushed him down. She was still reeling from the detective's comments, which felt like accusations.

She let Rocky dry off in the wash rack, while she went back into the tack room and retrieved his day sheet to keep the flies from bugging him and from getting himself too dirty if he rolled, which inevitably he would, like within five minutes or so of being back in his pen.

Michaela turned as she heard one of the mares whinny from her stall on the end, then the pounding of hooves from outside. She bolted out of the tack room to see Rocky loose and running free around the ranch. Dammit! He'd yanked himself free from his lead line on the wash rack. That wasn't like him. What had gotten into him? But worse yet, he was taking off over the hill behind her place.

She ran into her office and grabbed the keys to her quad. Normally she wouldn't go chasing after a loose horse on a four-wheeler, but he'd taken off and where he was headed and as fast as he was going, there was no way she'd catch him on foot.

She revved the engine, kicking up dust all around her as she raced over the embankment that separated her property from the dilapidated old dairy farm behind her ranch. She'd wanted to buy it few years back, in order to expand, but the money hadn't been there. And now it was possible a developer was going to come in and build a mini-mall. Once Rocky made it past there, he'd hit the road and she couldn't let that happen. Geesh! She'd had it up to there with chasing loose horses in the last day.

As she came over the hill she caught a glimpse of him. He was still galloping, but he looked to be slowing down, and he also looked to have a destination. He was running into the old barn.

Michaela slowed the quad down as she approached the building, not wanting to frighten him. She didn't have anything to lure him with. She shut the quad off and slowly and as quietly as possible, entered the barn. Rafters lay strewn across the ground. It was difficult to see due to the haze of dust, kicked up by Rocky. Dust particles sparkled in the beams of light shining through the cracks of the old building, casting shadows around and causing Michaela to feel uneasy.

Rocky whinnied down toward the end of the barn. She looked around to see if there was anything she could use to catch him with. Another whinny. Michaela stopped. That didn't sound like Rocky. Wait a minute. There were two horses at the end of the barn, and as she came closer she could see Rocky standing outside a makeshift stall, and inside was a mare. They were nuzzling each other and getting awfully cozy. Holy smokes! The horse Rocky was snuggling up to was a mare and she was obviously in season. But who did she belong to? Something was not right here. At all. First thing she'd have to do was get Rocky out of the old barn. Since someone was apparently using the old place to house the mare, they did have a bucket of feed to the side and a halter. She got a scoop together in an old coffee can someone had left inside the bag of grain, and after a few minutes of working at it, she had Rocky haltered and was leading him out of the barn with neither the mare nor Rocky too pleased about it.

"Oh brother, you wouldn't even know what to do with her." It took her almost thirty minutes to get him back over the hill and another thirty to clean him up, since he'd gotten himself filthy on his escapade.

When she was finished she went into the house and called for Camden.

"Hey honey, you're a mess. You better get in a shower if we're gonna head out tonight. I just got back from getting myself a stunner of an outfit. Went to The River over in Rancho Mirage today. I love it there. We should move there. Far more, you know, well-to-do. I had a mojito with lunch, too. Those are yummy. I'm thinking, instead of margis, I need to learn how to make mojitos. Wanna see my new outfit? I was just going to get my shower."

Camden came down the hallway toward Michaela, wearing nothing more than a hot pink silk bra and matching panties. Michaela eyed her. "What? I told you, I was getting in the shower when I heard you come in."

"Get dressed. I need your help."

Camden frowned but went back into her room and came back quickly in a pair of jeans and a T-shirt. She followed Michaela out and got into the truck with her, who explained everything to her as they drove the back way around to the old dairy farm. "So, someone's got a horse there? So what?" Camden asked. "Probably a temporary thing. Maybe whoever owns the place is letting a friend use it for their horse. I don't know, but I also don't see why you're so weirded out about it."

"You don't find it strange that someone is keeping a mare all by herself in a worn-down deserted barn?"

"No. Not really. I'm sure it's what I told you, basic. Someone needed a place to put their horse and they either own the barn or know someone who does. Do you know who owns the place?"

"No. I've heard all sorts of rumors from developers coming and building a minimall to condos, to even the city buying it and turning it into a horse park for kids. But I haven't heard anything in awhile. Of course, I don't keep much track on local current events."

"I'm telling you, I think you should relax."

Maybe Camden was right. It wasn't a big deal. The big deal was that Rocky had gotten loose and acted like a maniac and it was the last thing she needed today. She pulled up next to the quad. "I'll drive it home and meet you back there. I'm going to set her halter back and check on her. Make sure she didn't try and bust herself out of here after lover boy paid a visit."

"Okay."

Michaela got out of the truck, carrying the halter she'd borrowed and walked back into the barn. This time all was quiet. No dust, no noises, and as she came toward the stall— no horse either. Nothing. No feed. No sign that a horse had been in this very spot an hour earlier. As she started to back out and get the hell out of there, something caught her attention. There on the ground not too far from where the horse had been kept was a pile of clothes and a sleeping bag. What in the world? Who had been staying here? She bent down to look over the pile. There was a small radio, a bag of chips and bananas, and a book. A children's book. Interesting. The clothes were too large to belong to a child, yet the book, a copy of *Peter Pan*, appeared worn. It was obvious there was a guest here at the old farm, and whoever it was could be lurking nearby. It had to be the same person who had taken the mare out of here. Michaela knew she'd better get the hell out of this place.

She set the book down and quickly headed out of the barn, feeling spooked. She jumped on the quad, drove around the opposite side of where she'd been before and turned to head home the back way. That's when she noticed a paper taped to the side of the barn, and even though her adrenaline was running from fear, she had to see what the paper read. It was a permit to build. And, it was issued to Tanner Developments. Michaela's mouth dropped. Camden's boyfriend owned the land.

SIXTEEN

MICHAELA WENT TO HER OFFICE BEFORE GOING back to the house. She was shaken and she didn't want Camden to clue in. She needed to pull herself together, before heading out for their night on the town.

She had to find out who the barnyard resident was at Tanner's newly acquired piece of property and if he was aware that a pretty little mare had been holding down the fort. Who owned that horse? And where the hell was that person now? Michaela wanted to head back to the dairy farm and take another look around, but she wasn't about to go there alone. That would be plain stupid. She'd already accomplished the *stupid quota* for the day. Who could she trust right now to go back over there with her? A frightening thought crossed her mind: She didn't feel like she could really trust anyone at the moment. Everyone she cared for seemed to be hiding something from her.

"Michaela."

She jumped, nearly coming out of her skin as she turned and saw Summer, Ethan's *ex*-fiancé.

Summer was a pretty woman with cinnamon-colored hair, which she usually wore slicked back into a ponytail. Her eyes were an interesting green color, so light that they almost appeared clear. Each time Michaela saw her she was reminded of a Stepford wife. Her skin was dewy with the perfect amount of meticulously applied makeup and she always looked as if she'd just stepped out of a Ralph Lauren catalog.

"I didn't mean to frighten you," Summer said. She fiddled with the knot of a khaki-colored cashmere sweater around her shoulders.

"Oh, hi, Summer. I didn't hear you walk up." This was the last thing she needed right now. Hadn't she had enough for one day? Now, she'd have to listen to Summer's crap.

"Yes, well that's obvious. You've done some wonderful things to the place since I was last here. When was that? I think your Christmas party? God, a year ago—can you believe that? We really shouldn't let time go by without visiting. It's simply not neighborly."

What in the world did Ethan see in this woman? "Summer, why are you here? We both know that there isn't a lot of love lost between us, so don't carry on about how we should get together more often."

Summer shrugged. "I wanted to tell you how sorry I am about your uncle. I cared a lot for Lou and I wanted to extend my condolences because I know how close you were with him."

Michaela studied her. "Thank you. You didn't have to come out here to tell me that, though. You could have called, but I do appreciate it." She wondered if she should pursue asking Summer about Lou's books. "You were still working for my uncle?" She'd decided to go for it, although with trepidation.

"Some. Lou really wanted to have somebody come on full-time, and I can't do that. I have my own business to run. I did his books on the side to subsidize my own work."

Why was she lying? Michaela knew that Summer had been relieved of most of her duties because of the obscene way she'd left Ethan. And, Lou held a grudge, as Ethan should have as well! "Oh, so your business is taking off? You training a lot of jumpers these days?" Michaela tried to be nice. She knew that Summer had grown up riding warmbloods and thoroughbreds and had done well in the world of show jumping.

"Yes. It's going well, and now with things kind of changing in my world . . ." She ran a hand over her stomach and looked down. ". . . I'm thinking about expanding my business into a breeding program, kind of like what Lou had."

"Huh. You're multitalented." Michaela tilted her head to the side. "I didn't know you bred horses."

Summer let out an aggrieved sigh. "I don't. I would, of course, hire a breeding manager, but I think that Ethan can help me get it off the ground. He's a vet, after all. I'm sure that until I found the right person, he could do it for me."

"Right." Michaela nodded. "Well, good luck with that. Thanks for stopping by. Sorry to be short, but I have work to do."

Something not so deep down told Michaela that this conversation was far from over and that Summer hadn't only come here to pay her respects. She'd seen the woman work her "magic" on her friend, and she had the art of manipulation down to a science. Michaela felt sick to her stomach and decided not to pursue a line of questioning about Uncle Lou's books with Summer until she found out what institution the money from the owners of the mares had been deposited into.

"Michaela?"

"Yes?"

"I am aware that Ethan has confided in you about our . . . little surprise." Again she touched her stomach, and Michaela's did a flip.

"Yes."

"Well, I am very happy about the situation."

"I'm sure you are."

"And I am coming to you woman to woman and asking that you remain neutral. Ethan and I have many things to work out between us, and, I'm not sure how to say this, so I'm just going to."

"Please do."

"I'm asking you to stay out of Ethan's and my business."

Michaela folded her hands together, squeezing them—an attempt to keep from wrapping them around the woman's swanlike neck. "You know, Summer, I could actually do that if you hadn't taken Ethan's heart and ripped it into shreds. The man would have crawled across broken glass for you. Believe me, I don't know why, but regardless, he would have, and I supported his and your relationship because he loved you. But, I'm sorry, I can see right past those pretty green eyes and that Pilates body and the graceful airs that you put on. Ethan is a man, after all, and I think we . . ." She pointed to herself and then to Summer. ". . . both know they don't always think clearly."

Summer crossed her arms over her crisp button-down. "You have some gall. I may have made mistakes in the past where Ethan is concerned, and I am willing to admit that and make changes. He can see that and forgive me. And, do not forget that Ethan and I *are* having a baby together, whether you like it or not. If you want to stay in Ethan's life I would suggest you stay out of mine. In fact, I would go so far as to suggest you support me thoroughly, or you may be sorry. We both know how important family is to Ethan. He would never leave a child, not after what happened to him with his own father."

"Are you threatening me?"

"No. I'm not at all. I am only stating facts. You know, I find something fascinating about you." Summer shook a finger at her. "You're a very controlling woman. You don't want your closest friends to be happy because you've never been able to have that. It's not only Ethan I've watched you try and control. It's that ex of yours, and now your friend Camden. I know Kevin Tanner quite well, and he's told me that you're negative about your friend dating him. Why is that, Michaela? Maybe you should look at that. Maybe it's time you let people go, and have your own life. What's the saying? 'If you love something, set it free . . .' and you know what I think about your opinion of me? I think this has nothing to do with me, and everything to do with Ethan."

"What?"

"It's obvious, Michaela. You're in love with the father of my child. You've been pining for him for years, and it appears that you'll have to continue to pine. Give up the *best friends* act. Ethan is mine. Stay out of our lives."

Michaela's mouth opened to say something. But nothing came out as she watched the arrogant Summer MacTavish leave her barn. A few seconds later she bolted out of the tack room and yelled at Summer as she climbed into her Cadillac Escalade, which had a decal on the back window that read MACTAVISH SHOW JUMPERS. "I am not a control freak! You are! Look at you! You've even gone so far to get knocked up so you can manipulate Ethan! And, I do love him, because he's my friend, and I refuse to stand by and watch you destroy his life! You bitch!"

Summer slammed her car door and drove away. Michaela went back to her office and thought about the words they'd just exchanged. Why hadn't she been able to make a quick-witted retort? Comebacks were not usually a problem for her. Instead, her anger had gotten the best of her and the words came out sounding immature, like something from a seedy talk show. God, what had come over her? And now, she couldn't help wondering if there was any truth to what Summer had said. Was she the controlling type who drove people away? More than that, was there any truth to the idea that she was *in* love with Ethan?

SEVENTEEN

THERE WAS NO CHOICE FOR MICHAELA BUT TO forget the day. At least for now. She couldn't let Camden know that she had a gazillion things running through her mind, including thoughts that Camden or her love interest might have wanted to harm her uncle, or that her own father was gambling again and possibly in debt to the mob, or that she suspected someone was trying to frighten her for God only knew what reason, and that there was even a possibility that the person trying to scare her was also her uncle's killer. Even more than that, she couldn't confide in her friend that Summer MacTavish was pregnant with Ethan's baby and that the perfect princess had come by to tell her to buzz off. But worse was the fact that Michaela wasn't able to ask the woman she'd considered her best friend for a decade now if she did indeed have control issues, and if so, did she push the people she loved away? Normally questions such as these— and honestly, there had never been questions posed for her quite like these— she'd have opened up about them to Camden. For as light-hearted as her pal seemed to be, she also had a good ear and an available shoulder to cry on, plus she'd always been totally frank and honest with her. At least she'd always thought so, and Michaela despised this burning ache inside her that raised doubts about Camden. She hated the thought that all of this could be true, but she really hated that she could even *think* there was the possibility that any of these thoughts were true.

Michaela was applying some blush when Camden walked into her bathroom, a margarita in one hand and a bag from Saks in the other. She swung the bag back and forth. "Here you go. Let's get this party started." She handed the margarita to Michaela.

Michaela set it down on the sink counter. "I think I'll wait until we get to the bar."

Camden frowned. "It's one of my specials. The Cadillac— you know, with a Grand Marnier float on top. Smooth." She took a step back. "Honey, I know sometimes I can be crass and put on a good game face. I know you're hurting, and I'm sorry. I thought maybe a bit of devil's brew might help relax you. But if you're taking it easy, I understand."

"Thanks."

"Now give it back to me. Why let it go to waste?" She smiled, but Michaela knew she was only half kidding. "Okay, since you're not ready for the hard stuff, do me the favor of . . ." She pulled out a black lace camisole, ". . . wearing this. I saw it, and knew it would look absolutely hot on you with a cute pair of tight jeans. You'll have all eyes on you from the minute you walk in the bar. The men will be fighting over you and the women will want to fight you."

Michaela looked at the wannabe blouse. Yes, it was cute in a Frederick's of Hollywood kind of way, and surely it would attract attention, but not the kind she desired. "As pretty as it is, Camden, you know I wouldn't be comfortable in that. I just can't."

"For me? I thought it would be so gorgeous on you. Come on."

She shook her head. "I'm sorry. I wish I could, but you know how self-conscious I get. Look, I know what you're trying to do. You want to make me feel better and I am so grateful, but it's hard enough for me to go out tonight, much less wear something that should really be worn by Pamela Anderson."

Camden waved a hand at her. "Oh pooh, she's got nothing on you. But fine, all right. I understand. Maybe someday, my friend, you will realize just how beautiful you are and start dressing like it. Me? I already know I'm hot property and I ain't afraid to show it. Now, Kevin's driver will be by in about a half hour. I am so pleased you decided to go with us tonight. Where's the doc? Hell, he might as well come, too. I figure he's not going anywhere. I can see it now: You and me in rocking chairs with our margis or one of them mojitos, Ethan nursing sick horses while pushing a walker, while the two of you still try and reconcile the fact that you have feelings for one another."

"What?"

"I'm just kidding. But face it, Michaela, you two can't live with or without one another. You've both got a bad case of unrequited love gone wrong."

"That is not true. That is *so* not true. I've known Ethan since I was three years old. I don't love him and he doesn't love me, at least not in that way . . . and why do people keep suggesting that I have feelings for Ethan?"

"People?" Camden brought the margarita to her lips, taking a big drink.

Great. She wasn't going to let this go, was she? No. Not in a million years. But, Michaela knew she couldn't tell her about her run-in with Summer or that Summer was pregnant. Ethan had made her promise not to tell anyone, and she was going to prove Summer wrong. She could stay out of Ethan's business and allow him to make his own decisions . . . or in this case, mistakes. But she knew that once she told Camden, the cat would be out of the bag and there would be no going back. "You. I mean, you. This isn't the first time you've made remarks like that, and, well, it's annoying."

"Sorry. I didn't know I was *people*, and I will work hard to refrain from making any further remarks that simply happen to be *the truth*. I may be annoying, but I am always honest, and I would never hurt you." Camden took a step closer to Michaela and reached for her hand. "I love you and you're my friend. You can always count on me. I'll see about working on that annoying part of me, once I go and get dressed to the nines, 'cause honey, this lady is getting lucky tonight. Oh, and in case you change your mind about the blouse, I'll leave it with you." She winked, let go of her hand, and sauntered away.

Michaela didn't change her mind and wound up wearing a pair of jeans— comfortable, not tight— a white T-shirt, and a caramel-colored fitted jacket with a pair of high-heeled Charles David boots— one of the few extravagant items in her closet that were the same color as the jacket. She went to her jewelry box and took out a pair of diamond ring hoops. They were another extravagance— one her ex-husband had given her. One she simply could not see fit to toss or sell on eBay, and when it came down to it, she'd been the one to pick them out. Plus, the facts were that she'd footed the bill in the long run. Therefore, technically, the expensive earrings were not from Brad at all, but a self-deserving gift from her damn self!

But the night he'd given them to her— Christmas Eve three years ago, had been so romantic, so sweet— a memory that she wished she could forget because it reminded her that somewhere in Brad was a man who she'd thought had loved her.

That was history, and to learn the reality of what her life had been at that time nothing but a lie— had allowed her to look at herself and others in a different light. One that at this moment she wasn't too sure she cared for. She'd become calloused, or at least it felt like it, and there was a part of her that longed for the days when life felt and seemed more simple, when she still had dreams of a family, of the kind of love only seen in the movies or written about in books.

She slid the earrings through the holes in her lobes and stood back. She kind of liked the way she looked tonight. She could actually see the resemblance to Faith Hill that others often mentioned to her, and she was pleased she'd chosen to wear her hair down in loose waves rather than drawn back in her usual ponytail.

"Mick, the car is here," Camden yelled from the other room.

Car. Jeez. Who did this guy think he was, anyway? For goodness sakes, it wasn't as if they were all the rage in Beverly Hills headed to The Ivy. Sure there were places in Indio that had plenty of its well-to-do class but there weren't exactly the Lindsay Lohans and Eva Longorias of the world coming to hang out in their local digs. However, that was Camden. Find the flash and run with it. To Camden that obviously meant Kevin Tanner. Michaela would go along with it for the night, because she was determined to find answers. Answers she hoped Camden's latest flame would supply.

EIGHTEEN

KEVIN TANNER WAITED INSIDE THE CAR AS THE driver opened the door for the women.

"Oh, my, aren't you dressed to impress," Camden remarked.

"Well, you know what they say, when in Rome," Kevin replied.

Michaela bit her tongue. For a moment she felt like rolling on the ground in laughter, even after her bizarre day and the past forty-eight hours.

Kevin was somewhere between forty and fifty; hard to tell, really. There was a chance that the reason he didn't have any creases in his forehead was because he'd been to see the plastic surgeon. He had light brown hair that he had to have blow-dried, because the only men she knew with hair as perfect as Kevin were either gay or looked like Kevin did— a wannabe Rico Sauvay. That was Michaela's name for men who thought they had "it," but didn't.

This Mr. Sauvay had "dressed" for the occasion in a western-style maroon shirt with a small navy flower print and oyster-colored snap buttons, tight Wrangler jeans, and what Michaela figured had to be real alligator boots stained the same maroon as his shirt. Yep, if there ever was a cowboy pimp, she was looking right at him. He even had a gigantic silver belt buckle attached to his belt. John Wayne had to be rolling over in his grave. Tonight might actually turn out to be fun. If they did wind up going to Boots and Boogie, the real good old boys there might not welcome Kevin with open arms. In fact, it was quite possible that the contractor would be out on his painted-on Wrangler ass before the night was through.

That thought made Michaela smile. "Yes, exactly, Kevin. When in Rome."

"I knew this was going to be fun!" Camden squealed.

Kevin shifted in his seat, looking uncomfortable. Probably wishing he were in his suit slacks rather than a pair of jeans that appeared to be cutting off any circulation from the waist down. Goodness, what was Camden thinking?

Uh-oh, was Michaela doing it again? Were her reasons for not liking the partners her closest friends chose more about herself than Kevin or Summer? Then she watched as Kevin put his arm around Camden, gold rings with ruby jewels on two of his fingers and a diamond one on his pinky. Hmmm, in this case, she was pretty sure it had nothing to do with her wanting to control her friend and who she dated, but instead wanting to protect her friend, who actually didn't look like she wanted any protecting from the letch.

It didn't take long before they made it to the restaurant.

"I hear this place is great," Camden said as they pulled into the parking lot. "It got five stars in the paper. The chef comes from Guadalajara so it's not like real Mexican food."

"Excuse me?" Michaela said. "Last time I looked at an atlas Guadalajara was still located in Mexico."

Kevin patted Camden's knee. "That's why I love this woman. She says the cutest things."

He had to be kidding. Camden looked at him with these goo-goo eyes that stirred the stomach almost to the point of retching.

"Oh, you two. You know what I mean. It's not the typical taco and burrito menu. The food is gourmet Mexican. For example, I read that they have a dish where the pork is cooked in banana leaves. Pibil style or something like that. And, it is supposed to be the new hot spot. After we eat we can hang out at the bar and then there are two dance floors. One with pop and that rap stuff, the other a bit more down to earth with a live band. We don't even need to go over to Boots and Boogie, because this place has it all and is supposed to be all the rage."

"Fun," Michaela said, trying to keep the sarcasm out of her voice.

"Now, come on. We *will* have a good time tonight. I know there is a fun master inside of you just waiting to come out and play. It'll be like Mr. Rogers' Neighborhood for grown-ups."

"You're a disturbed woman."

"Yes, I am. But I have to tell you, it's a blast. Try it for a night, Michaela. Let down that guard of yours and kick up your heels. You just never know what destiny has in store for you."

"I didn't know destiny had anything to do with tonight."

"Destiny has everything to do with everything. Now let's go have some of that pibil pork or whatever and a Cadillac Margarita."

For someone who was such a maneater and who always tried to come off as a sophisticate, listening to Camden at that moment reminded her why they were friends. When it came down to it, Camden's dinginess *was* endearing and laughable, and she was able to laugh at herself.

"Okay, señoritas. Let's make it fiesta time." Kevin laughed. Michaela stepped out of the car. He was still laughing. "Get it? Like Miller Time, only fiesta time."

"I get it," Michaela replied, and walked ahead of the couple while she was sure they busied themselves with a game of grab-ass.

Once seated with margaritas at the table, which Michaela planned to nurse through the dinner, she reminded herself of her mission, and talk turned to Uncle Lou.

"Hey, Michaela I am so sorry about your uncle. He was a really good man. I liked him a lot."

Michaela had just taken a sip of her drink and nearly shot it back out as the lie poured from Kevin's mouth. She put on her game face. "Yes he was. It's horrible."

"Do they have any leads at all as to who murdered him?" Kevin asked.

Camden glanced at him. What kind of look was that? A warning? What was going on between these two that concerned Michaela's uncle? Or was she being paranoid? "No. At least they haven't said anything to me about a lead. I don't know. It's a bit strange, though, how one of the detectives has been behaving toward me."

"Really? How is that?" Kevin motioned for another round from the waiter.

Michaela hadn't taken but two sips. "Well, he was really nice to me right after I found my uncle."

"He better have been," Camden cut in.

"Then he came over that evening to question me further, and again he was gracious, understanding, and he listened without what I assumed was any judgment."

"Is this that cute detective?" Camden asked and smacked her lips together. "Sooo divine." Kevin shot her a nasty look. "Oh, but so not you."

That was true. Kevin Tanner was certainly no Detective Jude Davis. Not by a long shot. No doubt, the detective had never even received a traffic fine. Kevin on the other hand . . . well, she was sure he'd dabbled in his share of dirty secrets.

"Let her finish," Kevin said.

Michaela noted the agitation in his voice. She had him right where she wanted him. She was tossing out the bait. "Yes, it is the same detective. Anyway, earlier today I was working one of the horses and he came by. But he was no longer Mr. Congenial. He'd obviously done his share of interviewing and someone on his list apparently made a suggestion that I was unhappy my ex left me, and I could have blamed my uncle for it."

Kevin took a long pull from his drink. "That's ridiculous!" Camden exclaimed.

"That's what I told him. He made some further insinuations about it until I asked him to leave. I was pretty uncomfortable with the direction in which things were going."

"No doubt," Kevin said. "You don't think someone is setting you up to take the fall? I mean, God knows you would have never harmed your uncle."

"That's a good question, *Kev*. What do you think? I do suppose it's entirely possible. I heard or read somewhere that the first twenty-four hours of a murder investigation are the ones that yield the most important facts. So, maybe someone decided to divert the detective's attention by exaggerating my circumstances and embellishing quite a bit."

Kevin nodded. "That's too bad. It could be that. But I am sure the police will find out who did this and justice will be served for Lou."

Michaela took a sip from her margarita as the waiter set down their food. She wasn't terribly hungry. The talk had dulled any hunger she might have felt earlier. It still felt wrong to take pleasure in anything, even simple pleasures like good food. Setting her drink down and thanking the waiter, she turned back to Kevin. "I didn't realize you knew my uncle so well. I was under the impression that the two of you had a rather tense relationship. Isn't it true that you'd recently made an attempt to purchase his property and even after he told you *no*, you remained persistent? Apparently you don't like to take no for an answer."

Camden set her fork down, her mouth full of pork pibil. She did not appear especially happy. She glared at Michaela, who attempted to smile sweetly. Camden's eyes narrowed, making her look like a Cheshire cat who'd just shoved a canary in her mouth only to discover that she'd really bitten into a snake. Oh yeah, she was pissed off, but

Michaela knew she'd get over it, especially if she didn't have anything to do with killing her uncle, which she hoped was true. But this Kevin jerk, she had a feeling in her gut, was responsible in some way for her uncle Lou's murder.

Kevin let out a halfhearted laugh. "Don't be silly. That is crazy talk."

"Is it?" Michaela asked.

"Of course. I had nothing but respect for your uncle. Sure, I would have loved to acquire his land. After all, he owned some prime property. A resort hotel and golf course would be great and do a lot to help boost the local economy. But I understood Lou's position. He'd owned that land for years and loved it. I don't think he needed it all, but that was not my business."

"No, it wasn't, but you still persisted, didn't you? And, now that my uncle is gone, it might be easier for you to buy property from a grieving widow."

"Michaela, that is enough," Camden said. "Kevin is a businessman. He wouldn't harm anyone. Please stop. We came out to have a good time. Okay?"

Kevin shook his head. "No. It's okay. I understand. I do. You're sad and probably feel miserable, and I can't blame you for lashing out. You've been through hell. I'm sorry if I ever made Lou uncomfortable, or you for that matter. He was a good man. I'm sorry for your loss. I did respect him, and I don't take no easily. I wish I had. Please accept my apologies."

Michaela studied him. He did seem sincere. Strange. Really strange turn of events. How to handle this one? "Then you don't plan on pressuring his wife Cynthia to see if she has an interest in selling to you?"

He shook his head. "Uh, no. I've come across some other property that will work as well, if not better."

Oh yes, he had, hadn't he? Suddenly that act of sincerity he'd expressed became just that—*an act*. "You have, haven't you? The old dairy farm, right behind my place."

Kevin didn't reply right away. He took another drink. Camden looked at him. "That's correct. I did acquire that piece of property recently."

"I can't wait to have condos or a golf course right behind my property."

"Maybe you won't have to. I'm willing to make you a very nice offer for your place and that way any condos I might build behind your land won't offend you."

Michaela pressed her back into the booth. How did Camden not see this guy's transparency? "You want to purchase my property?" she asked, amused.

Kevin nodded. "I'm willing to pay you full market value for it, and it's my understanding that you could use the cash."

Michaela shot Camden a dirty look. Was Camden telling this jerk that Michaela was having financial problems? Camden tried to smile, looking like a deer caught in the headlights.

"Excuse me?" Michaela raised a brow. "I'm fine, and I'm not interested in selling."

"Fair enough. Can't hurt to ask," Kevin replied.

Michaela knew that this was far from over. Her gut nagged her. Kevin was like a fox that would lie in wait. She'd been married to one, and she'd learned to recognize the traits. What really disturbed her was that she couldn't help wondering if this guy hadn't been using Camden all along to get to her.

"It never hurts to ask. And, you did, and she said, 'No,' so, let's see if we can't lighten the subject around here. Please," Camden said, fidgeting nervously with her hands.

"Sure," Michaela said. For the remainder of their dinner, she tried to stay as involved as she could about topics as simple as the weather to as complicated as politics in the Middle East, but her mind kept wandering back to

Kevin Tanner's proposition and the fact that the man had a horse on his newly acquired property hours ago. She wanted to question him further and see if he could answer her question as to where the horse had disappeared to, but decided for now to wait for another opening. She also couldn't forget the conversation she'd overheard between Camden and Kevin just the night before. Were they two simply fantastic liars with a huge secret to hide?

As they finished dinner and moved over to the bar and club, Michaela had a thought. "So, Kevin, have you ever ridden or owned a horse before?"

He nodded. "Sure. My first wife owned Arabians. Pretty horses to look at, but gawd, what a pain in the ass. High strung."

"Maybe. I'm not completely convinced. Sure they can be a bit more squirrelly than some of the other breeds, but I was out at the Scottsdale Arabian Show a few years ago to watch the stock horses and I was impressed. They're beautiful and agile. I actually wouldn't mind having one of my own. So, you don't have a horse now?"

"No. I like to look at them, but riding is not for me."

"Huh. Did you know that there's a horse been taking up house in your old dairy barn?"

"What?"

Camden shifted in the booth. "Yeah. My stud, Rocky, got loose today and he charged right over to your place. He apparently found himself a girlfriend. There was a mare there. In a stall, flirting with him."

Kevin shook his head. "That's impossible. I was over there two days ago and there was nothing there. Nothing but a bunch of cobwebs and rotted wood. I don't know if you're playing a game with me, but it's making you look a bit foolish."

"Me? Playing a game? Tell him, Camden: There was a mare there earlier today and then when I went back, she was gone." Camden didn't say anything. "Camden, are you going to back me up on this?"

"Technically, I didn't see a horse. You told me there was a horse there."

"I don't believe this." Michaela stood and put her hands on her hips. "Someone *is* playing games here, but it isn't me." She started to leave.

Camden caught up to her as Michaela walked toward the bar. "I'm sorry, hon, but I didn't see a horse." Michaela kept walking. "I think you're tired and angry and—"

"And what? You think I'm losing it? That I didn't see a horse in *Kevin's* barn?"

"No. That's not what I'm saying."

Michaela stopped and faced her. "Really? Then, why didn't you defend me back there?"

"I'm sorry. I'll go tell him right now that I believe you. I *do* believe you."

"You can tell him whatever you want, but I know what I saw and I also think Kevin Tanner is hiding something. And, I think he's making a fool of you."

Camden looked like she'd been punched. "What?"

"I think the man is playing you to get to me so he can buy me out."

"I don't . . . think that's true." Camden stuttered on her words. "I think he . . . really likes me. Men do like me."

"Yes they do. They certainly do. But not always for the right reasons. I think that men tend to play you, Camden." Michaela walked away from her friend, leaving Camden stunned and hurt— her own stomach sank as despair blanketed her heart.

NINETEEN

MICHAELA SAT DOWN AT THE BAR, SHOVING down her emotion, trying hard to keep from crying. Had Camden's greed for the good life come before loyalty and friendship? Could money and Kevin's love be *that* important to her? Enough to betray? Enough to . . . kill?

"A Coke, please. Can you make sure no one takes my seat? I have to go to the restroom."

He winked at her. "You got it."

When she came back there was a glass of white wine waiting for her, not a Coke. She called the bartender back over and pointed at the wine. "I didn't order wine. I asked for a Coke."

"Yeah." He tossed a dish towel over his shoulder, and leaned against the bar, his dirty blonde, longish hair falling down in front of his eyes.

"Yeah. Can you take it back?"

The bartender lifted his head, tossed back the hair, and gazed past her. "That would be rude, don't you think," a voice from behind her said.

Her stomach dropped as she recognized the voice and turned to face her ex-husband. "Brad."

He looked at her with his light brown eyes, the kind that made you wonder if they were green, hazel, or brown. They were brown. Poop brown. He ran a hand through his hair, which she was glad to see was thinning. The hair was the same color as the poop-brown eyes. His other hand was wrapped around a drink. Surely a gin and tonic: a mean man's drink, as far as she was concerned.

"I can stand." He squeezed himself in between the chair, the bar and her.

She pulled as far from him as she could and crossed her arms. "What do you want?"

"I wanted to say hi. Is that a crime?"

She laughed. "It's all a crime when it comes to you."

"Now, now, sweetie, you know that's not true . . . or fair."

Michaela eyed the wine. Suddenly it looked good. She took a long sip from it. "I am not your sweetie." She poked him in the chest. "And, I would appreciate it if you would leave now. Don't you have your Barbie doll to keep you company? What's she doing? Making sure her lipstick is just so?"

"My, you have gotten nasty. I'm having a drink with Bean." He nodded at a table in the corner where Michaela spotted Bean, who looked shell-shocked while drinking what appeared to be a Shirley Temple.

"What are you doing with that poor man?"

"We're friends."

"Friends, my butt! You used Bean while you worked for my uncle and you're up to something now with him, aren't you?"

"God, Michaela, always so suspicious."

"Of you. Uh, yeah. With good reason, I might add."

"Bean called me. He said that he wanted someone to talk to about Lou. He's sad."

"I don't believe you."

He shrugged. "It's the truth. Guy needs a friend right now. He's all distraught and so I told him that I'd take him out for some dinner and we could talk. Honest."

"Great, now leave."

"Don't be like that. I wanted to come by and say hello, buy you a drink. We used to sleep together, after all."

"Don't remind me."

"Look Mick, I really just came over to tell you I was sorry to hear about Lou. I figured you're having a hard time. I know how close you were with the guy and Bean says that you've been pretty upset. So, I'm sorry. I am."

If she could have crawled inside the barstool she was seated on, she would have. She eyed him. Frankly she was getting sick and tired of people saying things she doubted they meant. "Sure. I bet you are."

"Why would you say that? Of course I'm sorry."

"Please, Brad. It's no secret that you weren't exactly pleased you got caught all tangled up with Miss Do-Si-Do. I think you had a plan from the get-go. You wanted to have your cake and eat it, too, but you choked on it, and it was my uncle who saw to it that you choked."

Brad rolled his eyes. "Is that what you told that cop who came around asking both me and Kirsten a ton of questions? Were you the one to tell him that I have some vendetta toward you? You know that's not true. I don't appreciate having police at my back door looking into my personal life."

"Oh, and like you didn't tell the detective that I was so in love with you and wanted a baby so much that I was happier being in the dark about your affair. That I was angry with my uncle for showing me the truth. I'm sure you don't appreciate the police having a peek at your personal life. It hasn't exactly been stellar. But, I'm also sure that you have *nothing* to hide either. God knows you've never kept any dirty little secrets from me."

"You will not let it go, will you?"

"Excuse me?"

"Me, you, this bitterness you feel over me and Kirsten. I know you pulled that little horseshit stunt on me the other night. I'm not too happy about it, but I'll let it go. See that's the kind of guy I am. I'm a good guy. You need to let it all go, too, sweetheart."

"Brad, trust me when I say that I have let it go, but it doesn't mean I have to associate with you at all . . . and why in the world would I ever believe anything you say is sincere and truthful?"

"Dammit, Michaela, it was one mistake. One little mistake. So, I fooled around. She came on to me, and damn . . . well, she threw herself at me, and most men I know would have done exactly the same thing that I did. I didn't mean for it to get out of hand. I didn't want to carry on with her. It just sort of happened. And yes, I was not happy that Lou got involved in it. He should have stayed out of it, but he didn't. I know he thought of you like his own daughter and that he was trying to protect you, but I would have come around and we could have worked it out, if he hadn't sent you those pictures. I don't love her. I never have and never will, not like I love you. Come on Mick, I *do*, I still love you. Give me another chance. Let's work it out. We can keep trying to have a baby and I'll be there this time for you. I know how bad I messed up. I miss you a lot." He touched her shoulder; she swatted his hand away.

Michaela could hardly find words. "How dare you!"

"What?"

"How in the hell did I ever marry someone like you? I must've been drugged or insane. I can't believe my ears. One *little* mistake? No, it was a giant mistake and not just one time either. She came on to you? Hmm, well I don't remember anywhere in the vows we took, it stating that it was okay to be unfaithful if the other party instigates it. Or that just because you can get it up when a hot girl struts by doesn't mean you have to say yes. And, as far as my uncle doing the right thing? You *bet* he did. I'm so grateful every day for what he did. Work it out? Now you want to come back to me? And, you even have the audacity to mention trying to have a child with me, when you damn well know that we, and let me state it again—*we*— owe thousands in medical bills to an infertility specialist, which you won't cough up. You have to send your girlfriend over to hound me to sign divorce papers and you won't even meet your obligations? My guess is the only reason you're even suggesting any kind of reconciliation is that Kirsten threw you out on your ass tonight for some reason and you need a place to go. I suspect that right about now, tucking your tail and trying to convince me to take you back is rather appealing. And as far as love . . . Well, I believe you don't love Kirsten, and know what, I believe you don't love me, because the only thing a selfish prick like you can love is *yourself.*"

"Why, you little—"

"Everything okay here?" Michaela turned to see Joey Pellegrino, beer in one hand, the other clenched. "Is he bothering you?"

"I am not bothering her," Brad spat back. "We're having a private conversation."

"Actually, he is bothering me."

"The lady says you are. It looks like your 'private conversation' is over. I think that if you want to wake up in the morning looking as you do tonight— uh, in one piece, that is— then I suggest you leave." Joey stared at him.

That stare alone would have done the job, but the words . . . oh they were great, too.

Brad started to say something, then walked away mumbling under his breath.

"Thank you," Michaela said. Her hands were shaking and she decided to finish off the wine in one fell swoop.

"Easy there. He really got to you, didn't he?"

"I guess. He knows how to get under my skin."

Joey sat down next to her. "My offer still stands. I know some people, a few friends of some of my cousins who could make his life fairly miserable."

"No. I'm fine. Don't do anything foolish. I appreciate the thought, though. Hey, where is Marianne?"

"She and the kids are in the restaurant. I came in here for a beer. She doesn't like me to drink in front of the kids."

"Oh, the boss, huh?"

"Yeah, you know, I gotta do the right thing for the kids, and honestly I had to get away from them for five minutes. Joey Jr. is a handful. Kid is practically climbing the walls, screaming in my ear. And, then the baby on top of it, I tell you, it's enough to make me crazy sometimes. Anyway, I don't have a lot of time, and it's good you're here. I found something out about who your dad owes, and how much."

"Who?"

"Danny Amalfi, my aunt Luisa's godmother's brother's son."

"Huh?"

"It don't matter. He's a lowlife bookie and low man on the totem pole in the family. But your pop is into him for a hundred grand and keeps coming back. Danny don't say no, he just keeps racking up the debt knowing that your pop has some land and his credit probably ain't so great, that's why he doesn't borrow on it to gamble with. Danny's thinking he can get himself a nice little ranch out of this deal, if he plays his cards right."

"My mother would have to sign any papers having to do with their home and property."

"Right. She's the boss, too. Women. But she may have no choice, if your pop keeps sinking the ship. Anyway, Danny tells my cousin Pauly that he can force your pop to give up his land if he hooks him for a few more grand."

"Oh, God, no. This is bad. Do you think Danny had anything to do with my uncle's murder?"

"No. Danny might be one to break a kneecap or two, but he's a wuss, and like I told you, it's code that you don't go after a guy's family."

"Okay. I suppose that's a positive," Michaela replied. "But what am I going to do about my dad?"

"You gotta talk to him."

"I know."

"Listen, you get your dad to stop this nonsense. I think I can handle Danny. He owes me a favor, a big one. I think I can maybe make this thing go away for your dad, or at least get it reduced."

Michaela was stunned. "You would do that?"

"We're friends. You're a good lady. You've had it rough lately, so let me see if I can help."

She threw her arms around him. "Thank you so much. Oh God, I'll pay you back when I can. I will."

He pulled away and was definitely blushing now. "It's nothing. You talk to your pop."

"I will, I promise. Thank you again. I won't forget it."

"I better head out. You got a ride home?"

"Don't worry about me. I'll get home."

"I don't think Mr. Shifty will bother you again."

They said goodbye. She decided it was time to get a cab home. She'd had just about enough, and tracking down Camden and Kevin wasn't an option. She was still pretty angry and she was sure Camden's feelings were mutual.

She headed out of the restaurant, careful not to be followed be Brad or Camden. She didn't see either of them. Good. It was brisk outside and she buttoned up her jacket.

"Michaela." Dwayne and Sam walked toward her. "What you doing?" Dwayne asked.

"I'm waiting for a cab."

"You have a bit of the drink, huh?" Sam asked. She nodded, not wanting to get into all of it. "Well, how far you live?"

"Ten minutes."

"Ah, ten minutes, cuz, let's give her a ride home," Sam said.

"Yeah, definitely. Come on."

Michaela shook her head. "No guys, that's okay. Looks like you just got here. Go on in. I'll be fine."

"Ah, c'mon." Dwayne put an arm around her. "Sam don't need to eat nuthin', anyway."

Sam rolled his eyes. "Why you always gotta do that?"

"What?"

"Insult me? Ever since we been kids, you talking about my eating and how big I am. Just 'cause you scrawny."

Dwayne laughed. At first Michaela wasn't sure Sam was kidding, but then he started laughing, too, and as the breeze picked up, and exhaustion began wearing on her mind and body, she agreed to a ride home.

Dwayne drove an older Bronco. The car smelled of horses and saddle soap, which was perfect as far as she was concerned. "You doing okay?" Dwayne asked.

"I guess. And you?"

"Me too. Sam and I been talking about it."

"Yeah, still can't believe it," Sam said. "But, let's talk about something else. We been through a lot."

Michaela nodded.

"How's Rocky?" Dwayne asked. "You still wanting to show him?"

"I don't know. I'm actually thinking that I need to geld him." She told him about Rocky's field day.

"He figure out that pastures *are* greener on the other side," Sam said.

Michaela laughed. "I guess so. But that old place isn't exactly next door. I mean, he really had to follow his nose."

"Acting like he had some loving before, by doing that," Sam replied.

"Nah, like Michaela said, he just following his nose," Dwayne said.

"Yeah, I s'pose. Stud horse been bred or not still got the instinct."

"Oh my God," Michaela blurted.

"What?" Dwayne asked.

"That's it. Oh, my God. How come I didn't think of it until now? That's it." Her mind reeled.

"What she talking about, cuz? What you talking about, girl—*shit. Goddammit! What the hell!*" Sam yelled. He kicked the back of Michaela's seat.

Michaela turned around to face Sam. His body stiffened, and his eyes rolled back into their sockets. "Dwayne? Dwayne!" Michaela cried.

Dwayne turned. "Oh no!" He pulled the off the road and braked.

"What is it? What's going on?" Michaela yelled.

"In the back. Lift the hatch, get his duffel out. Get it!" Dwayne ordered.

Michaela complied as Dwayne climbed into the back seat with Sam. She handed it to him. Dwayne opened the bag, pulled out a bottle of pills and shoved one down Sam's throat. He held his mouth shut. "Swallow. Swallow. Juice. There's juice in the front. In the glove compartment."

Michaela suddenly realized that Sam was having a diabetic seizure. She found the juice and gave it to Dwayne. A few minutes later, Sam seemed to be doing much better.

"Are you okay, Sam?" she asked. "I didn't know you're a diabetic."

"Oh yeah."

"That's why I tell him not to eat so much," Dwayne said, pulling back out onto the highway.

"That's why I tell you I needed to eat." Sam laughed, trying to make light of the situation. "Sorry about my cussin'. Happens sometimes when the blood sugar drops."

"Don't worry about it. I understand." They pulled into her place. "Do you want me to make you something to eat?"

"No. I think I should get him home. I'll take care of him," Dwayne replied. "You okay?"

"Sure. I'm fine."

"I walk her to the door," Dwayne told Sam.

Sam nodded and said goodnight. It was nice, especially after everything that had been happening, to have Dwayne make sure she got inside the house okay. When they reached her door, Dwayne turned to her. "You started to say something about you had it figured out, or something like that, right 'fore Sam had his seizure."

She waved a hand at him. "It's nothing. It's crazy, really."

"What?"

She didn't know if she could trust Dwayne, but he *had* been in Vegas the morning Uncle Lou was killed, so he hadn't killed him. That she was sure of; but could he be the one who'd been scamming breeders by selling off sperm that was not Loco's? Sure, he said that he didn't have any affiliation to the program, and he was a really nice guy, but she bit her tongue anyway. "Oh, I just figured out why Brad was hassling me back at the restaurant. You weren't there, but my ex was giving me a bad time."

"You need me to talk to him?"

She shook her head. "No. But thanks for the lift home. I really appreciate it." She got inside the door, locked it, and leaned against it. What she didn't want to tell Dwayne was her theory about who was the father to those foals— her very own Rocky.

TWENTY

MICHAELA WOKE UP THE NEXT MORNING KNOWING that before she could prove her theory about Rocky being the father to those foals, she would have to get his DNA sent over to the AQHA. As she headed out to the barn, she couldn't help thinking that by doing this she could be implicating herself in a crime that she didn't commit. Maybe she should speak to an attorney before going ahead with it. Maybe she should go to Ethan with this. She wished Uncle Lou were there. He'd know what to do.

She tossed in a flake of hay for each one of the horses, and when she came to Rocky's stall, she opened it up. "Hey big guy." He turned and looked at her. "This won't hurt. He bobbed his head up and down and then turned back to his breakfast. It was almost as if he knew what she'd said. She loved that horses, like dogs, are social and love to communicate. They like to be around other animals and people for the most part.

She pulled out several strands of Rocky's mane and placed them in a plastic baggie. Back at the house, she typed up a letter to the AQHA. It wasn't an easy letter because who in the world would believe it? God, she prayed that it wasn't true. But she made the decision to take a chance and send it in, along with Rocky's hair samples.

What had alerted her to the possibility that Rocky could be the father to the foals in Ohio was something Dwayne— or maybe it had been Sam?— had said last night, that the horse had followed his nose. The dairy farm was close by, but not so close that Rocky would have caught a whiff of the mare in season. Yet, he'd beelined it straight to her— as if he'd been there before.

It might seem crazy, but Michaela was inclined to believe that someone was bringing in a mare to the dairy farm while in season, then taking a back trail in to get Rocky out. The barn was far enough away from the house that someone could do this. Leading him to the barn, using him to "breed," and then returning him. If this were the case, there was quite a bit of nasty business going on. Not the least of which was that someone was stealing her animal time and again. Boy, if she got her hands on that person, she'd . . . well, she'd kill him! How dare someone do that to poor Rocky! Okay, so Rocky probably didn't mind too much. But, still, it was wrong. Very, very wrong!

Horse owners were being scammed into thinking that they were going to be getting foals with Loco's pedigree, not Rocky's. Now, Rocky was no dumpy animal. He boasted those great breeding lines, too. However, Loco had won several championships and earned a wad of cash, and the titles helped to drive his stud fees up.

The question was, if this were true, it had been going on for some time now. She would first have to find out if her theory was correct. Rocky had never been typed with the AQHA because he wasn't being used to stand stud. She took the letter and the hair specimen down to the Postal Annex and sent it via overnight mail. She'd gone online last night to find out who she should send it to, and she planned to make a follow-up call either later that afternoon or early tomorrow morning. She'd probably sound like a loon, but it made sense to her. Michaela's gut told her that this was a possibility, and she had to pursue it. Her gut also told her that Brad could very well be the one who had been working the scam. He would have still been living in the house when the initial contracts were signed with the breeders. He could have gotten Rocky in and out of the dairy farm in about two hours' time. But she would have woken up if he'd gotten out of bed. Maybe it all took place after she'd kicked him out. She'd have to go back and look at the dates. Plus, she wanted to go over the contracts and lawsuits to see if she could learn anything from them. She had a full plate waiting for her after working the horses.

By the time she returned from the Postal Annex, Rocky was finished with breakfast. She got him out and readied him for his morning workout.

The beauty of being in the arena with her horse during those forty minutes was that she forgot all her worries . . . everything. She only focused on what she and her horse were doing. They became one together.

"Poetry in motion."

She brought Rocky to a stop and looked up to see none other than Detective Jude Davis. Oh, no. What now? Why did this guy have the knack for showing up at the worst possible time? "Hello, Detective. What can I do for you? I believe we discussed all we needed to yesterday."

"Yeah, we did." He shoved his hands into his pockets and looked down at the ground, then back up at her. "I don't believe you had anything to do with your uncle's murder."

She patted Rocky's neck. "You don't?"

"No. And, well . . ." he paused, "I'm sorry about bringing up that you and your ex were trying to have a baby. I'm sure that hurt and it was why you were so resentful and defensive."

She stared at him, not knowing what to say. He did look apologetic, but he'd fooled her before when he'd been all nicey-nice while questioning her in her home and then "coming to the rescue," the other night. Then, he'd turned around and showed up at her folks' place asking all sorts of questions about her marriage. And yesterday? Well, that had blown her initial impression of him. Was he really sorry?

"Look, I'm going to do something way out of line here. So if you say no, it's fine, but . . . I was wondering if we could have coffee sometime."

She almost started laughing. "Coffee?"

"Uh-huh." He waved his arms in front of him. "I know I was tough on you yesterday. I was, but I'm a good judge of character and the way you reacted, in all honesty, put any doubts I had about you and what happened with your uncle to rest. Not that I ever really thought you might have murdered him, but I have to look at all the possibilities."

"So now you want to have coffee with me?"

"Okay and a muffin, too, or you know, a croissant."

Wait a minute. Was he asking her out? Wasn't there some policy within the police force that made that against the rules? He shouldn't be asking her out. Should he? Could he? Well, he did preface it by saying that he was out of line. And, he was. Wasn't he? Heat rose to her cheeks. "Detective, can you do that?"

"Do what?"

"Ask me for coffee?"

He smiled. "It's not like a date. It's more of an apology coffee meeting kind of thing. I told you that I feel badly that I was a bit rough on you yesterday. Granted I was doing my job."

She couldn't help but smile back at him. She sure did want him to be sorry. She'd been fooled before, but there was also a part of her that wanted to stay angry at him. "An apology coffee meeting thing? Hmmm. And, so what, we go out for coffee and you say that you're sorry, which you already did anyway, and there you go."

"Kind of."

"Kind of. Okay, Detective Davis, you know your apology, the one you just gave me is pretty sufficient. But I have to ask you, you seemed, uh, fairly suspect of me. Why the change of heart?"

"I told you, I can read people. Gut feeling. You know what I'm thinking, let's forget it. I'll be in touch about the case." He pulled a pair of sunglasses out of his front jacket pocket and all of a sudden looked very TV cop-like. And, it made him even more attractive.

"Coffee is good. When? Where?"

"Do you know the bakery on Third? The Honey Bear Cottage?"

"Know it well. Best lattes in town."

He pointed a finger at her. "Good. Then that's where, and why don't we say day after tomorrow? I know that tomorrow will be a rough one for you, so if you want to wait until next week, I understand." His voice turned far more serious than it had been.

"Tomorrow? What are you talking about? What's going on tomorrow?"

"Didn't your uncle's wife tell you? The coroner's office released his body and she's decided to have his services as soon as possible."

Michaela shook her head, totally confused. "No she didn't tell me. I assumed it would be the end of the week. Thank you for letting me know. I'll give her a call."

"I'm sure she's planning on letting everyone know today."

Michaela nodded.

"Would four o' clock work, then, on Thursday?"

"Four it is."

"Also, if you need anything tomorrow, please don't hesitate to let me know."

"Thanks."

She watched as he walked down the hill. Why was she feeling so weird about him? Okay, one minute he was nice, the next he was not, and then he was again. Did he really believe that she had nothing to do with her uncle's murder, or was this some ploy he used to get people "to talk?" Not like she had much to say. Okay, so she did have some interesting theories at this juncture, like someone had killed Uncle Lou because he discovered who was substituting Loco's sperm with another stud's— possibly Rocky's. And why, even with all this horrible business going on, did Michaela hope that his desire to meet her for coffee meant more than some simple apology or the need to drag further information from her? Men!

And, what was going on with Cynthia? Why hadn't she called to let her know about Uncle Lou's services, and why the rush? Sure, she could understand wanting to get it over with, let him rest in peace . . . but why hadn't she asked Michaela to help her with the plans?

She dismounted and led Rocky out of the arena and down to the crossties, where she was reminded of yesterday's incidents. Should she have told Davis about the mare and the dairy farm, and what she thought was going on? Probably. But he might think she was losing it, and she'd been so caught up in the moment when he'd been there. He had that knack about him. Mesmerizing. Sort of. Also, she needed confirmation from the AQHA before she went further with her hunch. She had a feeling the contracts, the AI program, and the missing money had something to do with her uncle's murder. She decided she would tell Davis over coffee.

After sponging Rocky down, she put him away. She worked two more horses and then headed to the house. Camden was out. She'd never come home last night. God, she hated distrusting her friend. It was so damn uncomfortable. But she couldn't help it.

She showered quickly and headed out. Since Joey ruled out the possibility of the mob putting a hit on Lou because of her dad, there were others she needed to talk to. People who may have had a reason to want her uncle gone. She needed to start by looking into the lawsuits filed against her uncle, and as much as she didn't want to, she needed to go see her father and call him on the floor about his gambling. She also had to go see Cynthia. Her uncle's wife owed her some answers. She would find out why Cynthia was in such a rush to bury Uncle Lou. Michaela also planned to tell Cynthia that she knew Cynthia was pregnant.

TWENTY-ONE

MICHAELA CALLED CYNTHIA'S HOUSE A COUPLE of times, with no luck. She didn't answer her cell phone either. Michaela had a sinking feeling in her gut, because the last time no one answered a phone at Lou's . . . well, she couldn't even think about it.

She decided to take care of her next item for the day and then find Cynthia. Calling her parents' house, she learned from her mom that her dad wasn't there.

After dropping by a few local spots where she thought he might be, she found her dad at Roger's Sports Bar. He wasn't there to drink. That wasn't his vice. In fact, she'd put money on it that he was drinking a seltzer with lime. He'd come to watch the football game he'd bet on; he'd done it for years. Old habits die hard.

She sat down across from him. He didn't even look at her, his eyes remaining on the screen. "I'm only watching, Mickey. That's all."

"Dad, you've never been able to lie well. Besides, I already know. I know how much you're in for, and to who."

"Oh." He still didn't look at her. "You going to tell your mom?"

"She also has a pretty good idea, Dad. She just doesn't know the amount."

Benjamin Bancroft finally gazed at his daughter. His eyes were the same hazel color as hers. But, she recognized the look of shame suddenly covering his. "How did you find out?"

"Does it matter? I did, and I know you're in trouble. Quite a bit."

"Did someone come to you? Were you threatened by anyone?" He reached for her hand.

"No, Dad, nothing like that." She noticed he wore a fresh bandage on his right hand.

"I'm sorry." He looked back at her, his eyes watering.

She squeezed his good hand. "Oh, Daddy." He nodded, reminding her of a scared child, not the disciplinarian she'd grown up with. "How long have you been into this again?"

"I don't know, a few months, maybe."

"A few months? And, you've gone through a *hundred thousand dollars*?"

He nodded. "I couldn't say anything. I don't know how it started. The way it always does. I get down about something, obsess about it, and then I make one small bet and that leads to another then another and it gets out of control before I know it. I kept thinking I can make it back. I can make it work."

Michaela could never really understand that thinking. To her it was insane. How do you *not* know when you're out of control? How does one bet lead to another and another? Her stomach churned. She wanted to scream these questions at him. But she'd done that years ago while home on spring break and exhausted from working and going to school— resentful that she had to go above and beyond most of the other kids at Cal Poly, where she studied animal husbandry. He'd just kept apologizing until *she* finally felt guilty for her own anger.

What she'd read and learned over the years did at least convince her that gambling was an addiction, like drugs or alcohol, and it wasn't about the gambling itself, *or* even the money. It was the momentary thrill, the possibilities. It took gamblers out of the realities of their world and placed them into a fantasy. Gambling gave them a high similar to drugs or alcohol and fed them tons of endorphins while in the process. But the crashes were huge, as harsh realities set in when these people lost their homes, their livelihoods, and ultimately their families.

"Okay, well, Dad, what's done is done. I'm going to help you, but you are going to have kick this thing for good. I know I'm enabling you by taking care of this debt, but I can't stand to see Mom hurt by this. It'll tear her up. And, you can't lose your place."

"I know. I need help."

"Fine."

"How are you dealing with the money? You don't have that kind of money."

"I know a relative of your bookie. He's looking into what he can do for me . . . I mean for you."

"Oh honey. No. I can't let you do that. I don't want you getting hurt because of me."

She squeezed his hand again. "You have to let me do it. And, I promise I won't get hurt, but here's the deal: You find a daily meeting with Gambler's Anonymous, get a sponsor again, and stay straight. In fact, for the next month or however long it takes, I am going to personally escort you to those meetings. I also will have my friend report in regularly to see if you've gone to borrow money from anyone, because this guy knows all the shady characters around. You're a good man, you're a great dad and husband; you can beat this thing. You are bigger than it is. Do it for me, for Mom, but really Dad, do it for yourself. Because I am certain you do not want to die a lonely old man. And, I can almost guarantee that if this continues, that is exactly what will happen. Mom will leave you, and I don't think I could stand by and watch you destroy yourself any more. It's too painful."

The tears were coming down his face now. God, she hated talking to him like that. But she had no choice. She had to have some kind of leverage over him, and when it came down to it, she knew that family meant everything to him.

"What do I tell your mom, about the meetings?"

"I think you have to tell her the truth. I know it's going to hurt her. I've got to leave that up to you. Tell her that you're going back to GA and you're turning the books over to either me or a bookkeeper. We both know that Mom doesn't like to handle the finances, but it's obviously not a good idea for you to run them. Not at this point."

He nodded. "I don't know what to say. I love you. That's pretty much all I can say, kid. And, I am sorry for putting you through this, especially now. I'm weak."

"No you're not."

He shook his head. "I feel rotten over this, over Lou. I didn't mean for any of it to happen."

She watched his face twist into anguish. "Dad, what do you mean?" She got the feeling by the way he was talking that it was more than the gambling, and more than her uncle dying.

"The police have been talking to me."

"Yeah, they've been talking to me, too."

"Honey, I think they have me listed as a suspect."

She squirmed in her chair. "Why?"

He held up his hand. "I went to see Lou the morning he was killed. My fingerprints . . . are on the pitchfork."

"What?"

He nodded.

"Dad, what are you saying?"

He sighed. "That morning, early, I went to Lou and Cynthia's place. I hadn't slept the night before because we'd talked and it didn't go well. I'd told him what was going on with me and the gambling, and he said that he'd think about helping me out. He said that I needed to talk with your mother, and I told him that I couldn't do that. He hung up on me." He took a sip of seltzer. "I couldn't sleep that night and I knew he'd be up by six, so I headed over to see him. I found him in Loco's stall. We . . . had words. He said that he wasn't going to bail me out. That he had his own problems to deal with and that I needed to come clean with you and your mother. He was right. But I reacted badly and I grabbed the pitchfork and threw it, then punched the wall. That's how I hurt my hand. Stupid, I know."

"Yes it was, Dad. What were you thinking? Don't you see how this addiction eats you up? You could have hurt Uncle Lou, and you did hurt yourself! Now, the police think you could have done this?" She paused and choked back emotion. "Your addiction turns you into someone you're not. Someone I don't know and don't want to know."

Where was the dad she grew up with? The one who'd take her on trail rides and play cowboys and cowgirls with her and her friends? Sometimes they'd pretend to be the posse after the bad guys, or sometimes they were the horse thieves trying to outrun the posse. Those were great days and good fun. *That* was the father she remembered. Not this man, reduced to heated arguments with a brother he adored— someone who hid from the world through an addiction that caused nothing but pain.

"You're right. I don't want to be this man any longer. I don't. I'll do whatever it takes. I'll tell your mom everything. I'll be honest and we'll get through it. But you should know that I think the police might arrest me. I think they're already looking into the gambling and they know I was at Lou's place the morning he died. You know, that was the last time I saw him. That morning." He choked on a sob and broke down.

She scooted her chair up and put an arm around him. She let her father cry for several minutes. She noticed a few people glancing over at them, but it didn't matter. He needed her and she would be there for him. "It's going to be all right, Daddy. It is. And, I know Uncle Lou is watching us, and he loves you. You have to forgive yourself. You *have* to. He would have. I'm sure he did. Do this for him. And, as far as the police go, I know you didn't kill him. I know it.

"And, Dad, I'm going to find out who did."

TWENTY-TWO

MICHAELA SAW HER DAD TO HIS CAR AND FOLLOWED him home. They walked into the house together. Her mom was in the kitchen. "Hi, you two. Oh, Michaela, I didn't know you were coming by. Good, good. I'm making a lasagna for tomorrow's service. You want to help?"

That was Mom, always doing, always one step ahead. "I would, Mom, but there's some things I need to take care of. I ran into Dad and thought I'd stop by and say hi."

"Oh, nice. Ben? Are you okay?" Her mom looked from Michaela to her dad and back again.

Michaela cut in before her dad could answer. "I think he's tired, right, Dad?" She knew he needed time to think about what he would say to her mother.

He nodded. "I'm going to lie down for a bit." He kissed her on the cheek and walked into the kitchen, where he gave his wife a hug.

Janie frowned. "Benjamin Bancroft, do you feel okay?" It wasn't often that he was outwardly affectionate.

"I'm fine. I love you." He headed back toward their bedroom.

Michaela's mom looked at her. "What was that all about?"

"I think you should let him rest right now. He's got quite a bit on his mind, but don't worry, Mom. Everything is going to be fine."

"Michaela?"

"Mom, please. It's not my place. Daddy will talk to you when he's ready. Trust me."

"I don't like the sound of this, but fine. It appears I don't have a choice."

Wanting to change the subject and needing to find out about Uncle Lou's funeral, Michaela asked, "Mom, when did Cynthia inform you about the services?"

"Last night."

"She didn't tell me. I was out for a bit anyway."

"I'm sure she's tried to call you. It's at one. Why don't you meet us here and we can all go together."

"Sure." She kissed her mom on the cheek. "See you tomorrow. I love you. Oh, what should I bring?"

"How about that pear tart you do so well?"

"You got it." She knew that she left her mother feeling a bit confused. For now, she had to not only see what she could find out in order to seek justice for her uncle, she also had to keep her dad from going to jail. Once her mom found out about the gambling it would be heartbreaking, but her father going to jail would be devastating.

On the drive to Cynthia's she recapped in her mind everything she'd learned over the past few days. First: Ethan had fought with her uncle and never explained why. She would get to the bottom of that, because she hated suspecting that he had anything at all to do with this. Then there was Camden and her boyfriend. Their phone conversation still had Michaela reeling. Not to mention that Kevin now owned the dairy farm and had a mare housed there that he claimed to know nothing about. There was the issue with the contracts and the breeding and her suspicions around that. She had a feeling Brad was responsible for that mess. But a killer? She wasn't sure.

Bean had been acting strangely toward her, but she didn't think he had the ability to pull off a breeding scam and she certainly didn't think he could become angry enough to kill. Anything was possible, though. Plus, what was his continuing friendship with Brad all about? Sam and Dwayne had been off to Vegas with the horses. Summer had worked for Uncle Lou and handled a lot of the paperwork in the past. Could she have killed Lou for some reason?

She'd pretty much ruled out the mob, but there were still those lawsuits against Lou that she had to get to the bottom of, which led her to ponder Cynthia. She was pregnant, and she was hiding something— like a lover, or possibly something more sinister.

After getting out of her truck at Uncle Lou's ranch, she walked through the breezeway and over to Loco's stall. He came to her, his hot breath pouring through his nostrils onto her hand as she rubbed his face. Neither Dwayne nor Sam looked to be around either. Dwayne's truck was gone and she wondered where they might have gone. "Too bad you can't talk," she said to Loco, who pulled his head away and shoved it in his feeder.

She called out for Bean. He should at least be around. Deciding to see if anyone was up at the house, she knocked on the back door. No one answered. She turned the knob; it turned easily. "Cynthia? You here?"

She walked in through the laundry room. Cynthia wouldn't get upset if Michaela waited for her in the house. She headed into the kitchen. From down the hall, she thought she heard someone crying. No, it was more than crying and as she got closer, she realized it was Cynthia and she was sobbing.

"Cynthia?"

Michaela saw her as she rounded the corner of the hall, slumped down against the wall, her face in her hands. "Cynthia? What is it? What's wrong?"

Cynthia didn't say anything. She didn't lift her head as she held out a note. It was stained. With what? Oh God, it looked like droplets of blood. Michaela took it from Cynthia's shaking hand. It read, I AM SORY I KILL MR. LOU.

"What? What is this?"

Cynthia looked up at Michaela. She uttered, "Kitchen."

Michaela stomach tightened as she entered the kitchen. Bean lay on the floor next to the table, a gun in his right hand, blood seeping from his temple.

TWENTY-THREE

SOMETHING WAS WRONG HERE. SO VERY wrong. Bean had killed Uncle Lou? Then, he'd committed suicide? Michaela's head filled with confusion as she struggled to wrap her brain around this.

The police showed up within minutes. Cynthia had called 911 immediately after finding Bean, and it was apparent that Michaela had come in right after that.

Detective Davis was there along with a team of other cops. He'd asked Michaela and Cynthia to wait for him in Uncle Lou's office, where they now sat on the couch. Michaela held Cynthia's ice-cold hand. "I don't understand why," Cynthia said.

"I don't know either."

"Bean loved Lou. He loved me. We helped take care of him. He was here because we had been meeting at this time of day for a few weeks now. I was teaching him to read." She choked back a sob. "He's come every day at the same time even the last few days, since Lou . . ." She shook her head. "I told him that he would have to wait a bit before I felt like teaching him again." A nervous laugh escaped her lips. "But, Bean didn't understand that. Obviously. That's why he's been showing up in the kitchen every day, waiting for me to teach him. Today I went out for a walk knowing he would show up here; I didn't want to face him. I didn't want to tell him to leave me alone. I knew it hurt his feelings, but I haven't been able to do anything like I used to." Cynthia couldn't speak anymore. She buried her head in her hands and sobbed.

Michaela rubbed her back, shoving down her own sorrow and disillusionment the best that she could. "I'm sorry, Cyn. I really am."

Davis entered the room, then stopped. He looked at both women with sympathy. Cynthia wiped her face. "Why did he do this?"

"Mrs. Bancroft, we don't know."

"Did he really kill himself?" Michaela asked.

"From what we can assess so far from the scene, I would have to say that he did."

Michaela nodded. "Do you think he killed my uncle?"

Davis sat down in the chair across from the women. "I don't know of any other reason for him to write that note and do what he did."

"I don't believe it." Michaela shook her head. "I'm sorry, but I don't. You met Bean. The man was like a six-year-old child. He couldn't have done this. He didn't have the wherewithal."

"Ms. Bancroft, I hear you, and we will investigate this situation completely. I did meet Bean and yes, he was very childlike. However, I have heard of some children gone very wrong who have done horrendous things to siblings, friends, even parents. There is not a lot of sense to be made out of a situation like this."

Michaela had had a similar reaction to Bean and his behavior just the other day. She'd even wondered if he somehow feigned much of who and what he really was. Had his behavior all been an act? But why? And for all those years? Or, was he like a child who had become angry at something Uncle Lou did and reacted in the heat of the moment before he'd realized what he'd done? If that were the case, then the morning that she'd discovered Lou's body, Bean likely would have reacted differently than he had. She couldn't help wondering if he would have even shown up. That is, if he truly had the mentality of a six-year-old, wouldn't it have been more likely that, after doing something so terrible, he'd run and hide? He'd seemed genuinely shocked over her uncle's death. She brought this up to Davis.

"Because of Bean's emotional immaturity and low IQ, it is possible that after killing your uncle, he blocked the memory due to the trauma it caused him. Then something might have sparked his memory, which upset him, causing him guilt, and he couldn't take it. I don't think he murdered Mr. Bancroft intentionally if he in fact did. I'm not a psychiatrist, so I can't say for certain. But believe me, we will continue to try and find out exactly what happened."

Michaela sighed. None of it sat well with her.

"I am going to need to take statements from both of you. Separately, of course. It's procedure."

"I need to use the bathroom," Cynthia said. "Is that okay, Michaela? Do you mind going first?"

"No. Go ahead."

Cynthia tried to smile, but it was forced and came out looking more like a frown.

After she left the room, Davis said, "I realize that this seems incomprehensible to you, but from everything I've seen so far, it appears that Bean committed your uncle's murder and killed himself."

"Yes, it's difficult to believe, but I guess so. I don't know what else to think. If the police are sure that's what happened . . ." She shrugged.

"The evidence points in that direction."

She nodded and looked down.

"I don't want to sound crass. You and your family have been through a rough time, but at least now you can bury your uncle with some sense of peace."

Her head jerked up. "Sense of *peace*? I'm not sure about that, Detective. I don't know how much peace can be found when you learn that a man with the mentality of a child has murdered someone you love dearly, then kills himself. There's no peace in that."

"I'm sorry."

Neither one said anything for several seconds. She felt like she was suffocating in that room with Davis, who stared at her. She needed to get out of there and think . . . or not even think, but just *be*.

"Why don't we go over what happened here today and how you found Mrs. Bancroft and Bean?" Davis finally asked.

Michaela told him everything from the time she arrived at the ranch. She didn't recognize her own voice as she relayed the story to him. It sounded far off, as if someone else was explaining to Davis what she'd encountered. But it was her. It had been her. Her neck and shoulders tightened with each word she spoke, and she knew that if she didn't get out of there soon, she would crack. Right there, in front of Davis, she would break down. Thankfully he finished his questions. He stood and held a hand out to help her up from the couch. His hand was warm. He squeezed hers and then let go. "I am sorry for all you've been through."

"Thank you." She saw Cynthia briefly and told her that she had to go. Cynthia seemed to understand.

Walking past the kitchen, she saw that Bean's body had already been covered with a tarp. She couldn't help but look. Was it morbid curiosity that made her do it? Or the fact that she still couldn't accept any of this? She heard herself say out loud, "Why?"

A police officer approached her. "Ms. Bancroft, you really shouldn't be here."

She turned to leave. Her eye caught the corner of the kitchen counter. On top of it sat a book. She walked over, ignoring the cop. She looked down at the book—*Peter Pan*. The same book that she had found yesterday in the stall at the old dairy farm.

TWENTY-FOUR

MICHAELA FELT IN HER GUT THAT BEAN HADN'T killed himself, and she doubted that he'd murdered Uncle Lou. He just didn't seem capable. How wrong could she have been about Bean? Had he really done it and fooled everyone? She needed a sounding board.

She walked into Joey Pellegrino's shop fueled by confusion and this strange twist of events, one that she didn't want to believe. "Hey, Mick. How's it . . . wait a minute, what is it? What's wrong?" Joey came out from behind his shop counter.

She tried hard to keep her emotions in check. "I need someone to talk to."

"Yeah, sure. Wait a sec, will ya? I gotta take care of a customer first." Joe walked over to help out some guy in the paint department. Once he'd finished, he locked the door behind him and turned the OPEN sign around to CLOSED. "Figure by the way you look and sound, you'z don't want no one buggin' us."

"Thanks. I appreciate it."

"C'mon. Follow me to my office."

They walked past aisles of nuts, bolts, and nails. He pushed away a pale blue curtain to reveal boxes upon boxes. He pointed to one of them. "My office. Take a seat. It ain't fancy, but it'll do." She smiled and was glad she'd come to see him as she sat down on the box. Joey sat down opposite her. "So, tell Joe what's goin' on." Oddly enough— or considering that it was Joe, maybe not so odd— opera music played from the radio in Joe's *office*. "Wait a minute." He got up and turned the radio down, then grinned and blushed as he turned around. Obviously he hadn't wanted her to see his *softer* side.

She started with how she'd found Lou dead in Loco's stall, how Ethan was keeping something from her that was related to an argument he'd had with her uncle; how

Camden and Kevin Tanner had joined forces and their intentions appeared dishonorable. Then, she told him about the cancelled checks and contracts and how Uncle Lou's memory was apparently fading on him, and how Dwayne and Sam both thought he could use a vacation. She filled him in on Cynthia's pregnancy, the horse at the dairy farm and what she figured had been going on there, and how she thought Brad was somehow connected. Finally she told him about Bean's apparent suicide and the doubts she'd had about him— whether or not he was just a really good actor, or someone who enjoyed playing the victim card.

"I mean, doesn't it seem odd to you?" she asked Joe. "Here's a guy with the emotional and probably the intellectual equivalent of a six- or seven-year-old and supposedly *he* did this? Why?"

"Maybe he got pissed at your uncle. You know, like you said, even the cop told you that he's seen it all. That there are some mean kids out there. And, this Bean guy was no kid, even if he acted like it."

"Yeah. But what about him sleeping at the old dairy farm with that mare? It had to be him taking care of the mare. I don't think he could have come up with some type of breeding scheme on his own."

He shook a finger at her. "You said so yourself that maybe you had some doubts about Bean, like maybe he was faking some of it. You know he's obviously been around horses, watched your uncle's operation. Maybe he saw a good thing as far as money and he thought he could get some of it. But once he realized that he wouldn't be able to get away with it . . . well, then it all soured on him. Then, maybe he figured, you know, like your uncle was gonna connect it all, or maybe your uncle *did* put the pieces together, and voilà! The guy goes all looney and stabs him with the pitchfork." Michaela winced. "Sorry."

"It's okay. No, Joe, it still doesn't ring true. Yes, it *does* look like Bean was involved in this somehow, at least the breeding scheme, which I'm still sure was going on."

"What about these two guys— Sam and Dwayne— who worked for your uncle? Bean worked with them, too."

"Yeah. Maybe." She shrugged. "They just don't seem like bad guys."

Joe laughed. "Oh my friend, things are never what they seem."

"The morning my uncle was killed though, they were in Vegas."

"Can you confirm that one?"

"Pretty sure. They were taking out a few horses. I'm certain there are hotel and restaurant receipts that can confirm their whereabouts. As soon as Dwayne heard about what happened he was on his way back."

Joey rubbed his chin. "I don't know. Sounds like one mess. I gotta tell you, Mick, why don't you let the police take care of it? They think they've got it all figured out, right?"

"I don't think they do. It's a gut feeling, but I really don't think they *do* have it figured out."

"But you ain't no detective, and I'm afraid you're gonna get hurt mixin' yourself up in this thing."

"All I'm doing here is talking with you, bouncing off ideas. I trust you, and you've got good instincts."

He smiled. "I do, don't I? Okay, since we're *just* bouncing out ideas here, you telling me about this wife of your uncle's gives me an idea. The lady is preggers, and you're thinking you heard somewhere in your family rumor mill that Uncle Lou didn't have the goods. You ever think that maybe she got knocked up by another dude, and then knocked off her hubby?"

"I did think of that, and I keep telling myself that maybe the pregnancy test I saw was wrong, or maybe Uncle Lou never *had* the vasectomy."

Joey shook his head. "You gotta tell the cops this. They need to know she's expectin', and you gotta find out if Lou was able to make that happen for her. Pretty big motive for murder, don't you think? And, if Lou's wifey was doing the deed with some other guy, well . . ." He shrugged, his large palms face up. "You know the guy bangin' her . . . oops sorry, sometimes I don't use the nicest language."

"No problem."

"Anyway, the guy sleeping with Lou's wife could have taken him out on account of her. Man gets all funny when he knows his seed's been planted. He might've gotten all possessive over Cynthia, with the kid comin' into the world. Or, it could have been a planned thing between them. They wanna get rid of Lou, so they can crawl off somewhere, start a new life as a family. Plus, your uncle wasn't exactly poor. Leave the money for the wife and she and her new family might be lookin' to have a *real* nice life together."

"True. I hate to think that, but of course, it *could* be true. You're right, I need to give the police this information, because I don't know who she might have been cheating on my uncle with. If she was, you're exactly right: it does make a motive for murder, doesn't it?"

"You bet. But don't you go looking into it. If Cynthia and her boyfriend— if she had one— took your uncle out, and you sniff around, it's possible you could be in danger too. You remember, we're just throwin' out ideas here."

"I got one more thing." She opened her purse and took out the cancelled checks and the contracts from the breedings. "Can you take a look at these?" She handed them to him.

"The contracts you was talkin' about?" She nodded. "What am I lookin' for?"

She started to tear up. This was all getting to her. "I wish I knew. Maybe where the checks were deposited? Maybe see if somehow Cynthia is connected, although if she is, I don't know why she'd ask me to look into it for her."

"Cover her tracks. Criminals know how to manipulate. I'll check into it. I got a second cousin who I think has a nephew in banking, maybe he can find something out."

"Thanks. I don't see Cynthia as a criminal, though."

"Maybe not her, but if she was cheating on your uncle, her lover might be *real* trouble, and people do insane things for love."

Michaela *could* buy that. Love did seem to make people crazy. That's why she was determined to tread carefully when it came to the romance department, especially after the way Brad had screwed her over. "Possible. I don't know. Look, I've got one more thing." As if he wasn't already doing enough for her.

"Name it."

"Can you see what you can find out about a Dr. Verconti? See when my uncle might have gone to see this guy. I always thought his doc was Dr. Sherman. The same doc my family has seen for years. Anyway, I found a prescription for Lou from this Dr. Verconti and I don't know if there's any way to find out why he prescribed Ativan for him, but if you could, I'd be grateful."

"Ativan, huh? For anxiety. Yeah, well, I gotta tell you, gettin' medical record info is tough, but I'll see what I can do. You say Verconti, huh? Italian. That might work in my favor. Who knows, I might have a cousin who knows somebody who knows someone who could get the lowdown from this doc." Michaela nodded and sniffled, tears again welling in her eyes. Joey was being so good to her with all of this, but talking about it, she couldn't stop the emotion rising in her again. "Hey, hey. C'mon now. It's gonna be okay. No more cryin'! Sure, I'll see what I can do for you. I told you I would."

"I know. It's hard, that's all. And you're being awfully kind to me, Joe. Whenever you want to bring your daughter by, I'll get her started on those riding lessons, and we'll see what we can do about finding her a horse. In fact, I've got one I can start her on," she said, thinking about Booger. He'd make a perfect kid's horse. If he could put up with Camden on his back flopping all around, he'd handle having a kid on him just fine.

"Maybe over Christmas break. That's in a coupla weeks, and by then the dust should have settled some for you. Look, why don't you go on home and get some rest. I'll check things out, see if there's more to any of this. Try not to worry your pretty head any longer."

She stood. "Thanks, Joe."

"Sure. I'll call you if I find somethin' out. And, well, anytime you need someone to talk to, I'm here for you." He thumped his chest and stood. "I'm glad you came to me."

"You're okay, Joe Pellegrino."

"You ain't too bad yourself. Be careful."

She was glad she'd gone to see Joe. The man was true blue. But she couldn't help feeling even more confused than ever. She knew what it was like to really want a child. There were times in the past when she thought she'd die if she didn't get pregnant, and as difficult as it was, she'd had to come to terms with it. Knowing that ache, she couldn't help wondering now if Cynthia could have wanted a baby and a life with a new man badly enough to kill for.

TWENTY-FIVE

MICHAELA LEFT JOE'S HARDWARE STORE AND suddenly felt famished. She knew there was nothing at home to eat. When was the last time she had eaten, anyway? The day had gone by in another blur— fast and furious and more confusing than ever. Joe was right: She needed to tell Davis that she thought Cynthia was pregnant and not likely by her uncle. Right now though, she had to eat, and she wasn't too sure what to say to the detective. She'd have to select her words carefully, especially since Davis seemed certain the case had been solved with Bean's *suicide*. And, what if that were all there was to it? She doubted it, but still, what if her theories were just her imagination gone wild? Michaela knew she'd wind up sounding like a complete lunatic to Davis, and she really didn't want that. Nah; she'd hold off calling him until maybe later, and if she didn't reach him, she'd leave a message. For all she knew he'd already packed it up for the day and gone home. He'd likely be out with some cop buddies having a beer . . . or maybe home with his daughter. The thought of Davis having a kid made her smile. She'd bet he was a great dad. Let calling him go until later. Plus, she promised her mom that she'd bake a pear tart for the reception. Couldn't let Mom down.

    Michaela picked up the ingredients she needed for the tart at the grocery store and thought about grabbing something to make for dinner, but didn't have the energy to cook for herself. And a microwave dinner didn't sound appealing. Before loading her groceries in the truck she called over to the China Lion down the street. She ordered some Kung pao chicken and an egg roll. That would do.

    When she walked into the restaurant the smells of ginger, garlic, and red pepper spice assailed her senses. Her stomach growled. Mmm. Good choice. The place didn't look to be too busy, which meant her order probably wouldn't take long. She walked up to the hostess booth and gave her name. The petite Chinese woman said, "One minute, please. I see if food ready." She nodded politely and disappeared behind a red drape.

Michaela heard someone call her name and saw Sam sitting alone in one of the booths. He motioned her over.

"Hi," she said. "How are you?"

He motioned at the spread of food in front of him. "Not too good. I eat even more when I'm upset. You know . . ." He shook his head. "Can't believe Bean would do this. Good man. A little slow, you know, but good. Just snapped in the head. Dunno. Don't understand, but it's terrible. Found out when we got back from the feed store, me and Dwayne. Bad dream, I tell you."

"More like a nightmare. I can't believe it. Do you really think Bean had the capacity to kill my uncle and then himself?"

"Dunno. Looks that way. That's what Mrs. Bancroft tell us. Who knows what goes on in the mind of a man? Maybe Bean be more of a thinker than we all figure. Maybe he have some anger stuff going on and Lou make him angry."

"Maybe." But it sure didn't sit well with Michaela. Bean might have been slow and even a bit odd . . . but angry? No. He was too kidlike to be *that* angry. However, she *had* been wrong about people before. Hell, look at what she'd been married to. "Where's Dwayne?"

"He back home. I eat. He don't eat when he upset. It be that way since we were kids. I can't help myself though. He real tore about all of this with Bean and Lou. Real sad and like all of us, mixed up 'bout it. Sit down." He sipped his beer. "Want one?"

"No. I ordered takeout. It should be ready in a minute. Uh, I hate to sound like a mother, but Sam, should you be drinking beer and eating like that with your diabetes?"

"Probably not. But I can handle it. Know how to take care of myself since I was a kid."

"You've been a diabetic since then?"

"Nah, been taking care of myself since I was a kid."

"Didn't you live with Dwayne's family growing up?"

"You got that one backward. He come to live with us when he was like fourteen, I think. Can't remember. My *makuakane* and *makuahine*— my dad and mom— always love him, you know. His parents drown in a boating accident off Oahu. Sad story. Dwayne come to live with us, but he fit right in. My family always love him."

"I thought you said that you've been taking care of yourself since you were a kid." She was starting to think that Sam had had too much to drink. "Sounds to me like you had a very loving family."

"Oh you know, all us kids grow up on the islands take care of ourselves. We learn from Mother Nature, you know. Just a figure of speech is all. Me taking care of myself, just the way it was, and Dwayne, too. We have a lot of fun together back on the island."

"That's really sad about Dwayne's parents. I had no idea." It did explain why she noticed that sad, faraway look in Dwayne's eyes at times.

"Yeah, bad stuff. Tough."

"But both of you are close with your parents?"

"Sure. Yeah. I want to go back home now, open a restaurant. Or go *somewhere*. Need to get off the mainland. Too crazy here."

"It does feel crazy right now, that's for sure. I had no idea that you wanted to own a restaurant."

"Oh sure. Been my dream for a long time now." He rubbed his thumb and middle finger together. "Need cash though, you know. I want more than a restaurant. Want to run a luau, or hotel, you know, think big. I almost went back a few years ago, had a buddy with an opportunity to open a place on Maui and we was gonna have us the best luau around."

"Sounds nice."

"Yeah well, didn't work out. Maybe now, I go home and find a job in a restaurant and try and work my way up. Being here for a while make me think I could go back and open a Mexican place. I make good tacos. I like them, too. Maybe Chinese." He smiled. "Like I say, I love food." He laughed and ordered another beer.

Sam was a talker, and since he was rambling on, she decided to do some more fishing. He might have answers to some of her questions related to the deaths, or on her theories about the breeding program and the lawsuits. "Hey Sam, did you know my ex-husband, Brad, very well when he worked for my uncle?"

He took a swig of his beer. "That guy? What a jerk."

"I know."

"Not just to you. He boss everyone around the ranch when he can, when Lou not around. He make Dwayne so pissed. Only one who like him was Bean, but that guy like everyone. Too bad he didn't take out your ex instead, huh?"

Michaela nodded, not exactly knowing how to respond to that. "Did Brad do a decent job at the ranch? I mean, when he was working."

"What? Handling the breeding?" He shrugged. "S'pose so. What's so hard? He gotta help the stud do his thing to collect the . . ."

She held up a hand. Might as well go for the jugular and see what Sam thought of her theory. "I know. He collected the semen. I guess what I'm getting at is, do you think Brad could have been involved in selling breedings to horse owners for a cheaper stud fees than Loco's, and substituting another horse's DNA in place of Loco's?"

"Semen? Sure. Don't think it would be too hard. Get into where the containers were and make a switch, yeah, not too hard. You know I even tol' Lou and Dwayne that with an animal like Loco on the place, we need better security. Horse worth $125,000, and his stud fees alone are $3,500, who knows someone figure out a way to work it?

Charge what, even half that and supplement the sperm, well, you send out say even one sample a day during breeding season and you could make some nice cash. I know Lou had a security company out not long ago after I talk to him, make him see he got a lot of money tied up in those animals. I know he planned to get some cameras set up around the place and some alarms real soon. Lou be too old-fashioned for too long. He still livin', well, *was* livin' in the dark ages. Bad people out there. Take your money. Steal your horse. You don't know. Just don't know."

She leaned into the table. "So, you *do* think it could have been possible for someone to be running this type of scam, and now the owners of these mares have caught on, and they've started suing the ranch." She sighed.

"It could have happened. Like I say, bad people out there. I don't know." He moved the food around on his plate. "You know, Dwayne mention to me something about Lou being sued by some people in Ohio. Dwayne think Lou just having memory trouble and accidentally shipped the wrong stuff out."

Michaela nodded as the hostess set her takeout down. "But you don't?"

"Like I say, don't know what to think. Crazy stuff."

"Wow, this could just be the beginning, then. If this were really happening, there could be hundreds of foals out there that aren't really Loco's, and owners will find out when they go to register them with the AQHA. This might only be the first batch of lawsuits. Not good." She shook her head as the reality of how severe this situation could be dawned on her. "We haven't even come into this year's foaling season. Oh, God. Wait until this batch of folks want to register their foals, if there is another group that was duped like the people who already filed lawsuits. It could be *a lot* of money."

"Anything possible." Sam took a bite of his egg roll.

"The AQHA has not found a match for those foals and all of Lou's studs are DNA typed and on file with AQHA."

"Yeah, tough. I *do* think there something fishy, too. Don't know what, but it don't smell right to me."

"Can I ask you something else?"

"Shoot."

"Do you think my ex could have been involved with this kind of a scam?"

"Your ex is one strange duck. He don't have the full deck, you know." He tapped the side of his head. "He know a lot about the animal and he a good lyin' man."

"I know. Thanks. Look, I better let you get back to your dinner."

"Anytime I can help." He downed the rest of his beer.

"Be careful, Sam. Go easy on the beers. Do you need a ride home? I owe you."

"Nah. I'm fine. I don't live far. I walked over and if I have to, I can call Dwayne."

She left Sam to eat and drink his sorrows away. So, Sam thought that Brad was more than capable of deceit. Duh! But was the man she was once married to also capable of stealing money, then murdering her uncle and now killing Bean and making it look like a suicide? She was beginning to think that Brad was capable of anything.

TWENTY-SIX

MICHAELA MADE A QUICK STOP AT THE BARN TO feed the horses. Even though she had food on the brain she tried to give each horse down the aisle some special attention with love pats. Most of them nudged her hand away and tossed their heads. Even Leo had no interest in making nice. She was late, so she couldn't blame them in the least. "I see how it is," she sang out, tossing flakes of hay onto her wheelbarrow to make her rounds. "All you guys want is your chow. What am I? Chopped liver?"

Finished, she went on up to the house to reheat her dinner. While she nuked it she played her messages. One was from her mom just checking up on her, another from Ethan with basically the same message. The last caught her interest: "Hello. This is a message for Michaela Bancroft. My name is Henry Stein and I'm an attorney with Goldbloom, Richards, and Stein. Please call me at your earliest convenience. It's in regard to your uncle's estate." Michaela jotted down the number. She tried to call, but no one was there. It was after hours. She'd try back tomorrow. Wonder what the attorney wanted?

The microwave buzzed. Ah yes. Food! She pretty much shoveled the Chinese food into her mouth, except for half the egg roll, which she shared with Cocoa, who was acting a bit neglected. She tossed the ball for her a few times and watched as her old dog jiggled across the family room to retrieve it, until finally deciding she'd had her fill. Game over, Michaela knew it was time to get to baking. As much as she didn't want to get up and make the tart, she'd promised her mom, so after cleaning up she went to work. She'd forgotten how therapeutic baking could be. No wonder when Mom was stressed-out she cooked and baked everything from one of Julia Child's cookbooks.

Putting the finishing touches on the pear tart, she wondered what was going on with Camden and if she'd show up back at the house. They needed to talk. Michaela was setting the tart in the oven just as the phone rang. It was Joe. "Hey, Mick, I got something for you."

"So soon?"

"What can I say? I got a cousin who's got a friend whose sister works as a nurse for that Dr. Verconti."

"You sure do have a lot of cousins."

"I know. Lots of aunts and uncles, too. You know, we're a good Catholic family. So, anyway, word is this Verconti is a pill pusher, you know. Hands out the Xanax, Prozac, Vicodin, and your uncle's Ativan like candy. Your uncle never did come in to see him."

"What?"

"According to the nurse, he called saying he was feeling all jittery and stuff, having panic attacks. The doc prescribed Ativan with a few refills."

"Was there anything she said about how he heard about the doctor?"

"I thought of that, too. Nuthin'."

"Weird."

"I got something else for you, too. This one is bigger."

"What do you mean?"

"You're right that there is some type of breeding scheme that's been going on and I think I found out who's behind it." Michaela sat down at the kitchen counter, knowing Joe was about to tell him that he found out it was Brad. She sighed. "Well, I called up the owners of the mares and played like I was an investigator for the AQHA, and asked if they remembered if it was Lou Bancroft they spoke to and who sold them the breedings."

"Yeah?" she asked with baited breath.

"They mostly said that he was the one, except two of them gave me a different name."

"Whose name did they give?"

"That horse trainer of your uncle's— Dwayne Yamiguchi."

Michaela about dropped the phone. "No."

"Yep. That's what they said. Told me that Dwayne was the one who sold them the breeding for a discount. They sent the check to Lou rather than making it out to the ranch, which they thought was odd, but Dwayne apparently told them that was because Lou was changing the name of his business."

"Wow, I hadn't even thought about the fact that the checks were made out to my uncle personally."

"Yeah. If you want my opinion, this guy Dwayne's been the one takin' your uncle for a ride and somehow wirin' money from an account he likely opened maybe via the Internet. Still checking on all that, though. Anyway, I think this guy was pretending to be Lou on the phone when he talked to these folks, but it looks like he wasn't as careful as he thought, and a couple of times he accidentally slipped his real name into the conversation. He probably got Lou's social security number and private information and opened the checking account I'm still tryin' to track for you, too. It ain't hard to get people's private info, and that guy was probably pretty tight with Lou, makin' it easy for him. Also ain't too hard to sign the checks and contracts in Lou's name. Maybe the guy been planning on making a run for it with the dough. Whether or not he killed your uncle . . . I don't know. Maybe he put Bean up to it and knew Bean wouldn't do too well taking the fall. You got me." Michaela didn't say anything. "You okay, Mick?"

"I guess. Thanks, Joey. I appreciate it."

"No problem."

Michaela hung up the phone, stunned. It took her a minute to decide how to tell Detective Davis, but she had to call him *now* and tell him what she'd learned— of course, keeping Joe's name out of it. To her dismay, she couldn't reach Davis and instead left him a message to call her back.

Dwayne, of all people? Why? But she didn't have time to think about it as Camden stormed into the house. She walked up to Michaela and waved a file folder in her face. "You were right. Okay? I give in. You were freaking right— again!"

"Whoa. Wait. What the hell is going on, Camden? What are you talking about?"

"Kevin Tanner. Look at this. Look at what I found on his desk." She tossed the file down onto the counter.

Michaela picked it up and thumbed through it. She had to sit down again. It was a set of plans. Her uncle's name written across the top: LOU BANCROFT. Flipping through it, she saw that Tanner had detailed *every* dealing, *every* phone call, all conversations with her uncle, and *then* all conversations and correspondence with anyone he was working with in trying to take over Uncle Lou's property. He included dates, too. The most disturbing date in the file was the day that her uncle was killed: four days earlier. Her uncle's name was written next to the date with a red line drawn through it. Below that was scrawled, *Deal is closed.* Right below that note was another that read, *Call Cynthia Bancroft to see about negotiations.*

Michaela's stomach twisted as she found sketches and drawings with plans as to what was to be done with the property. It included an eighteen-hole golf course, along with a spa and boutique hotel resort. She couldn't believe any of this. "Oh my God."

"You were right, and I feel like such an ass. The guy totally used me, and the worst part is, he plans to knock you off your property and spread his corporate crap everywhere. He bought that dairy farm with the intention of taking over this entire area."

Michaela put an arm around Camden, who had changed her hair color yet again— now it was chocolate brown. "I have to ask you something."

"What?" Camden looked at her, her lip quivering.

"I overheard a conversation you had the other night with Kevin about him being a 'killer,' and how easy it would be for him to take over the land since whoever it was you two were talking about was now gone."

Camden shrunk back from her. "Wait a minute, you don't think we were talking about Lou?"

"I hope not. But try and look at it from my perspective."

Camden sighed. "When I referred to a piece of property Kevin had his eye on I was talking about a chunk of land owned by a competitor of his. Some guy who was just arrested for embezzling and making illegal real estate agreements. Anyway, both Kevin and this man bid on the same property recently, and Kevin lost. I was telling him that it would be easier to acquire that property now. I'm such a jerk for falling for that moron!"

"But, I also heard you tell Kevin that he didn't have to worry about being a suspect."

"Kevin was the one who squealed on the guy. He was trying to involve Kevin in his illegal deals. He wouldn't do it, but that doesn't make him a nice guy. He's still a bastard."

"You don't think Kevin could have murdered my uncle since he wanted his property so badly? These plans indicate he had motive."

Camden laughed. "The guy is afraid of his shadow. He's an ass and made a fool out of me . . . but no, I don't think he killed Lou. I think he sees an opportunity now to try and go after Cynthia, though."

Michaela frowned. "I'm sorry I listened in on your phone conversation and that I ever doubted you."

"Yeah well, I'm sorry I didn't listen to *you*, and now we have the guy I was supposed to be in love with and vice versa trying to take over everyone's land."

"We'll figure it out." The timer went off on the oven. She took out the tart.

"Thanks for being a good friend."

"You, too."

"Listen, I need to go back over to Kevin's and get some of my stuff. I'm also going to tell him that we're onto him, and he doesn't have a prayer of getting Lou's land or yours!"

"Can't it wait?"

"No. I don't want anything left there."

"I'll come with you."

Camden shook her head. 'No, hon. You look tired."

"But what if he tries to hurt you?"

Camden smiled. "You don't know me as well as I thought you did. Tanner should be afraid I might hurt him."

Before Michaela could further protest her phone rang again. Davis was on the other end. She explained what she'd discovered about the breeding scheme, including what she'd found at the dairy farm— the same *Peter Pan* book that Bean had been reading right before he *supposedly* offed himself.

"How did you get this information about Mr. Yamiguchi?" Davis asked warily.

"I can't tell you that. But trust me, it's the truth. Will you at least look into it?"

"All right."

"I think that you should also know I suspect that my uncle's wife is pregnant, and . . . well, I don't think he was able to father children."

"Why do you think she's pregnant?"

"I saw a test in her wastebasket." She knew how that sounded, but it was the truth and Davis needed to know. "I think that there's more to my uncle's murder and Bean's suicide."

"You're a regular Miss Marple. Younger and uh, more attractive, but you certainly have done your share of detecting over the last few days, haven't you?"

"I guess you could say that."

"Maybe you should join the force. I have to tell you that I'm not pleased about your detecting. Murder is serious business. I don't want you getting hurt and I think I can do my job without you putting yourself in danger."

"I'm not in any danger."

She heard him sigh on the other end of the phone. "I have to tell you that you're making my job more difficult."

"Don't mean to, but I thought you should know all this."

"Thank you for the information."

"That's it? 'Thank you for the information?' " Michaela started pacing her kitchen floor.

"What do you want me to say?"

"I want you to go and question Cynthia Bancroft. I don't know, maybe ask her if she killed my uncle or if her *lover* did. I also want you to see what was going on at my uncle's ranch with the AI program. Also, there's a big-time developer who wanted to buy my uncle out. Kevin Tanner. Have you talked to that creep?"

"You *have* been busy."

Was he mocking her? Ooh, this guy knew how to get under her skin! "Obviously busier than you. You just want to sew this thing up, and I hate to tell you, Detective, I don't think it's as simple as it looks."

"Why don't you let me and my people decide that? I will look into everything you're telling me. I'm not discounting anything you've said. It's my job to try and take this type of information and sort through it. See where it all might fit. I am not putting you on the back burner. I promise."

"I sure hope not."

"I also have some news for you. About fingerprints on your pitchfork."

Michaela calmed herself. She wanted to hear this. "You do?"

"Yes. It seems a Ms. Kirsten Redmond's prints showed up along with yours."

"Kirsten?"

"Yes."

"Well, have you asked her about it?"

"I plan to. I can't arrest her on anything. Not yet, anyway."

"Not even for harassment?"

"She may have an explanation."

"What kind of explanation?"

"We'll have to wait and see. I haven't reached her yet, but I will keep trying until I do. And, I'll see what I can find out about Mr. Yamiguchi, as well as Mrs. Bancroft."

"Thanks," Michaela replied and hung up the phone.

Damn! Just when she thought she might have it all figured out, Davis sideswiped her with the news about Kirsten. None of it made any sense to her. None of it at all.

TWENTY-SEVEN

AFTER PERFORMING HER MORNING RITUALS, Michaela got ready for Uncle Lou's funeral and put on a simple black dress. After today, she'd likely burn it. The stupid dress would hold too much pain. Strange thing to think about, but it was a reminder, and reminders carried plenty of weight with them.

She slipped into a pair of classic black pumps. Her hands shook slightly as she tried to apply a little makeup. She pulled her hair back into a sleek, low ponytail and tied it up into a chignon. Today would be rough.

Ethan had offered to give her a ride, but she'd already planned on going to the service with her mom and dad. Camden didn't feel right about going with her family. "I'll be there," she said. "This day needs to be about your family and your uncle. I'm always running late, as you know, and I don't want to hold you back or be a pain. Not today anyway." She smiled, and Michaela was grateful that her friend knew how to act when the occasion called for it.

Michaela's parents were waiting out front when she drove up to get them. Good. She wanted to get through this day as quickly as possible. Their mood was solemn. She smiled at her mom, who looked as if she'd already been crying.

"Hi," her dad said. "You doing okay?"

She nodded her lie. "How about you?"

"Oh, you know. It isn't easy."

She believed there was a double entendre in his words. She knew that once they got past this, she would have to help her dad through what she figured would in some ways be more difficult for him to recover from than losing his brother. His addiction had been shrouded in secrets and lies. It was his vice, and allowing it to die and be buried would be something that he couldn't accomplish in a day.

Every day of his life, her dad would have to bury his gambling addiction. Michaela was determined to help him through it.

They shared small talk on the way to the funeral home, and her mom went over the day's schedule. After the services there would be the gathering at her parents' place.

A handful of people had already arrived at the funeral home. The director seated the family up front and off to the left, where they could look out and see others inside the home, and the guests could view them. It was almost like a separate room, but still open.

Her dad grabbed her hand and squeezed. She had the feeling he needed her more today than she needed him, and that was okay. Her mom took tissues from her purse and handed a couple to Michaela. She whispered, "Just in case."

Soon Cynthia came in, escorted by Dwayne. Sam waddled in behind them. Dwayne nodded toward them. Cynthia offered a weak smile. Then she looked right at Michaela, and her eyes, filled with anger, bore straight into her. Davis must've talked to her, because Michaela had never seen that look before. And, Cynthia had to have put two and two together. How? She wasn't sure, but that could be the only explanation as to why Cyn was looking at her that way. Interesting that she was on Dwayne's arm . . .

Oh, God. It struck Michaela like a horse kick in the face. Dwayne and Cynthia! Maybe he was her lover and he was the father of her baby and together they'd killed her uncle! But Dwayne had been in Vegas that morning. Still, Cynthia wasn't. Could she have taken Uncle Lou out before going off to the gym? And . . . oh, wow. Maybe Joey was right. Cyn had asked Michaela to look into the breeding scheme. Could it be to cover her own tracks? She didn't have time to let her mind run away with her. The room was filling up and she saw the pastor head toward the pulpit.

Out of the corner of her eye she caught another familiar face: Davis. He gave her a slight wave. She nodded and tried to smile in spite of everything. Why was he there? Out of respect? Doubtful. She'd heard somewhere before that killers often showed up at the funerals of their victims. Yes. That had to be why he was there. Watching people. Seeing their reactions. That meant he'd taken seriously what she'd told him the night before. Cynthia's anger toward her proved that. He wasn't blowing her off like she'd feared. Good man, she thought.

With her parents on either side of her, she almost felt like a child again. And on this surreal day that security flooded through her, as her six-year-old self returned momentarily, and she reveled in the comfort.

Once the pastor took the pulpit all was calm, actually peaceful. Michaela listened to his words of faith and an eternal afterlife. The scent from the roses covering the casket wafted throughout the room. She'd been raised Catholic, so she understood the meaning of the pastor's words. Lou had not been much of a churchgoer, but she knew that when he did attend, it was at the Presbyterian Church. She noticed that there were far less rituals than in the church she was accustomed to. The pastor spoke freely of Lou's love for his animals, his wife, and his family. *His wife. Traitor!* Her mind conjured up worse words, but she pushed them aside, as they felt blasphemous, considering. When the pastor ended with an invitation to accept Christ, he asked if anyone wanted to share a story or talk about Lou.

Ethan approached the pulpit first. With tears running down his face he said, "Lou Bancroft was the only father I ever really knew. He was my friend and an excellent man. I will miss him dearly as I know you all will, too." He started to choke on his words. After a pause, Ethan went on to tell a funny story about when he was a kid and Lou thought the best way to teach him to ride was to put him on an ornery pony that enjoyed bucking him off regularly. "Lou would tell me that I'd better get back up on that pony and ride him, or I'd never learn. So, I'd get back on him, and to this day I think it was the best thing anyone ever taught me. I learned to persist. Granted, Lou did give me a hard hat, so I wouldn't bash my head in." Quiet laughter sounded throughout the room. Ethan wiped away his tears. "Goodbye, my friend."

Michaela wanted to run to him, wrap her arms around him, and hug him tight— let him cry on her shoulder, like when they were kids, although it was usually her crying on *his* shoulder. He always teased her about being a big crybaby. She watched as he slid in next to Summer, who put her head on his shoulder. Talk about irony. She tried not to watch.

There were more stories from friends and people Lou had dealt with over the years about his honesty, his gentle touch with horses, his humor, and his love for life.

Finally, Michaela mustered the courage to go up. She shifted her weight back and forth, looking out at the sea of faces, not sure if she could go on. Then, she looked at her dad, who winked at her.

"My uncle Lou was the most decent person I have ever known. When I was a little kid he taught me the meaning of compassion by showing me an injured mare and how to take care of her. He taught me how to ride, and in many ways he is the reason that I train horses today. When I was a teenager I could go to him and tell him pretty much anything, and that lasted until only a few days ago.

"He knew what it meant to laugh and enjoy life. He wasn't a risk taker, but when he wanted something he went for it. He was the type of person who knew how to find balance, and stay balanced. We will miss his warm, easy smile and all that he had to give. For me, the one thing that seems to help the most is the idea that he is still close by.

He remains in our hearts, our souls, and memories, and no one can take that from us. Thank you."

She spotted Camden in the back, who smiled at her. Thank God she had her friend back. She also spotted Joey, True blue, that man. As she stepped down she glanced over at Davis again. He nodded and smiled at her, a look of sympathy in his eyes.

Michaela took her seat as the pastor announced the gathering that would take place at Ben and Janie Bancroft's place.

Moments later everyone filed out of the home, and because Lou had chosen to be cremated, there was no actual burial. Cynthia stood at the front and greeted guests. "I'm sorry for everything," Michaela told Cynthia.

Cynthia nodded. "Thank you," she replied coolly.

Dwayne stood next to Cynthia. It took everything she had not to say anything to the two of them. She wanted to scream at them both: "I know what you've done!" But soon enough Davis would solve this case. And, maybe that was why he was really there. Waiting for the services to be over. Shadowing Dwayne and Cynthia, preparing to arrest them. Had he found out something new? Something that revealed they were more than just lovers, that they were also killers?

Michaela's parents chose to stand with Cynthia at the front. Why wouldn't they? They had no idea what Michaela knew. She decided to head for the truck, not feeling like talking to anyone. She had to get out of there.

Davis grabbed her arm as she was walking out. "That was a beautiful eulogy you gave. Touching. I really thought you did a nice job."

"Thanks. I get the feeling you've spoken with my uncle's wife?"

He nodded. "Early this morning. You're right, she is pregnant."

"I knew it."

"But she wasn't keeping a lover. At least, I'm fairly satisfied with that."

Michaela put her hands on her hips. "What do you mean?"

"Mrs. Bancroft showed me appointment cards with a Dr. Collins."

"Dr. Collins?" Michaela knew him quite well. He'd been her doctor when she'd tried to conceive.

Davis nodded. "Yes, and it seems as though Mrs. Bancroft and your uncle were in to see him several times for consultation. They wanted to have a baby. I followed up with the doctor before heading over here. Mrs. Bancroft used a sperm donor. Her story checks out."

"Oh my God. I thought for sure . . . I thought she'd been unfaithful. I thought Dwayne and her had somehow planned this. No wonder she looked as if she hated me."

"It was an easy mistake to make, Michaela. I can see how you assumed what you did."

She was stunned. Wow. She'd really been off base there, now hadn't she? "Well, what about Dwayne, and what I told you about the breeding scheme?"

"We only spoke last night. I'm following up."

"Is that why you're here?"

"Among other things. I wanted to make sure you were all right."

"You did? I'm fine. Really. That was nice of you."

"Coffee tomorrow, right? The Honey Bear? Four?"

"I'll be there."

Davis's pager went off. "I've got to go."

"Everything okay?"

"Police work." He started to walk away quickly. That page must've been important.

TWENTY-EIGHT

MICHAELA WALKED TO HER TRUCK AND LEANED against it, looking out at the green rolling hills of the cemetery and the flowers that adorned various graves. The little chapel and funeral home were connected on one of the hills to the left of her. It was a crisp December day— typical Southern California weather— not overcast, but rather a blue sky filled the air with a handful of billowing clouds. Normally, she would have considered it a beautiful day— definitely a good day to get out and ride . . .

"Nice speech."

Michaela turned to see none other than Kirsten standing there, decked out in a black v-neck tight-fitting dress that left nothing to the imagination. "What are you doing here?"

"I came to pay my respects. Your uncle was a respected horseman and I felt I owed it to him to come by."

"God, can't you go crawl under a rock or something? You're not welcome here."

"I didn't know I needed to be invited. It was in the paper, and like I said, I'm only doing the right thing by paying respect to the consummate cowboy."

Oh brother. Michaela didn't have the strength for a go-around with her. "Thank you. That was kind of you." She figured if she stayed the course that Miss Rodeo America would be on her way. Kirsten was another one she'd like to question. She owed Michaela some answers, like why in the hell were her fingerprints on Michaela's pitchfork? And, hadn't Davis seen her in the funeral home? She knew he was trying to locate Kirsten. Come to think of it, Michaela hadn't spotted her either, and Kirsten was definitely one who made sure she was seen. That was strange in itself. But she had to have been in the home to have heard Michaela's eulogy.

"I know you ran into Brad the other night."

"I did." Nope. The bitch wasn't going to exit nicely.

"I would really like it if you could back off of him. I don't know when you're going to accept that he is gone out of your life. He ain't coming back." Michaela shook her head and sighed. "Oh, he told me all about how you bought him a drink and tried coming on to him, how you wanted him back and how you would forgive him."

Michaela didn't think her neck and shoulders could grow any tighter, but she was wrong. "Honestly, Kirsten, I don't know why we're having this conversation."

"Because you can't keep your hands off of *my* man."

Michaela laughed. She didn't want to go here, but she had no choice. "The last thing I want back in my life is Brad. Okay? Let me explain to you and hopefully you'll understand this, but Brad was the one who came on to *me* the other night. He begged me to forgive him and take him back. Once I told him, unequivocally, no, he had to be chased off by a friend of mine. He apparently crawled back home to you; I don't know why he fed you this ridiculous story. You two get off on the drama. You deserve each other, but the facts are, he's a creep and always will be. And, you, like me, will probably find out the hard way when he dumps your ass for a new model in a couple of years."

Kirsten pulled her arm back to swing. "Why, you bitch!" Her arm was caught in midair by none other than Summer.

"I don't think you want to do that, Kirsten. Why don't you try and show some class for once in your life and go home? Leave this family alone, especially Michaela."

Kirsten's face twisted in rage, but being outnumbered she did as she was told, and like the snake she was, slithered off.

Michaela faced Summer. "Thank you." Summer was the last person Michaela would have expected to do what she'd just done, but today was turning out to have quite a few surprises to it.

"Don't worry about it. I saw her accosting you and I figured she was the last person you needed today. For that matter I'm sure that I'm a close second, especially after our talk the other day."

Michaela smiled. "Normally I would say yes, but funny as it may seem, I don't feel that way. I'm glad you were there to stop her. I wasn't prepared for that at all."

"I'm sure you weren't." She shrugged. "I want to tell you again that I know I've made my share of mistakes in the past. I really want to make up for them now. I'm sorry if I came on strong the other day. I'd really like it if we could be friends."

Michaela bit her lip. "Friends." She reached her hand out and Summer shook it. That was a tall order, but why not? She could try, especially *if* Summer was having Ethan's child.

TWENTY-NINE

THE AFTERNOON WORE ON AT BEN AND JANIE Bancroft's house. Michaela tried to talk to Cynthia, but Cynthia was always engulfed by waves of people. Also, Michaela's mom kept her busy bringing food out to the table. Cynthia left early, before Michaela had a chance to speak with her. Her mom said that Cyn was tired and wanted to go home, so Dwayne and Sam drove her back to the ranch.

Camden lightened the mood with her crazy antics. She even got Michaela's mom to laugh. By the time the last guest left and Michaela and Camden finished helping with the dishes, all Michaela wanted to do was go home and climb in bed.

As she finished drying the dishes, her mom said, "Thank you girls for all your help today, and Michaela, for what you said about Lou. It was lovely." Her mother brushed a hand through her hair, which had recently begun to pale with age, going from golden blonde to blonde with some silver woven into it. She was still a beautiful woman and Michaela thought of her as someone who embodied the word *grace*, like Audrey Hepburn.

"You're welcome, Mom. It's how I felt, and as far as helping out, there's no question about it."

"Me, too, Mrs. Bancroft. I'm glad I could do it." Camden folded a dishtowel and set it down on the kitchen counter. She hugged Michaela and her mom. "Well, I hate to bug out on you, but I'm tired. Do you mind?"

"No. Go on home. I'll see you there. Thanks for your help."

Michaela went into the family room with her mom. Her dad sat in his easy chair. "Hi, pumpkin. You did good today. Lou would be proud of you." He looked at his wife. "You should know that I told your mom about my gambling."

Her mom shook a finger at her. "Don't you ever keep secrets from me again. I know you think I'm weak and that my heart is easily broken. But you're wrong. I'm tougher than the two of you think."

"Mom, I didn't think it was my place."

"Oh horse pucky." Michaela stifled her laughter.

"We're a family and when we have a problem, whether big or small, I'd better be told up front. Got it?"

Her dad winked at her. "Got it," Michaela said.

"Both of you got it?"

"Yes ma'am," her dad replied.

She turned back to her daughter. "I'm not going to leave your father. But I *am* dragging his rear to church from now on. I won't take no for an answer. And, I'm going with him to those Gamblers Anonymous meetings and watch him walk in, sit down, and I will take a book with me and wait for him in the car while he works out whatever it is he needs to work out."

Her dad turned red. "See why I love your mother?"

"Yes."

"I didn't take vows to break them. I knew when I married you, Benjamin Bancroft, that you were far from perfect. We'll get through this the way we do everything. *Together*. Now we'll let our daughter go home. She looks tired."

Michaela stood and hugged her mom, who whispered, "Thank you," in her ear.

Her drive home seemed longer than usual. She cranked up the radio and tried to sing along to Keith Urban's latest. Glancing in her rearview mirror, she noticed a set of high beams approaching . . . fast. What the . . . The truck was right on her tail, horn blaring at her. "Geez, buddy, back off." Michaela stepped on the gas; the truck stayed with her. Panic rose inside her. She went to reach for her phone, but it was in her purse on the floorboard and she needed both hands on the wheel to deal with this idiot behind her.

Again she sped up, but the other vehicle hung on her bumper, then passed her, cutting her off so close that she had to slam on her brakes, which sent her truck into a spin. Dizziness swirled in her brain. *Is this what it's like to have your life pass before your eyes?* she thought. Visions of her parents, Uncle Lou, Ethan, Camden, raced in front of her at gut-wrenching speed. She couldn't think or feel anything, other than her heart racing.

Then her world went black.

THIRTY

WHEN MICHAELA OPENED HER EYES, HER TRUCK was on the side of the road. She must have hit her head on the steering wheel, because it sure did hurt. She rubbed it and felt a knot. She couldn't have been out for too long, though, because no one had discovered her as yet. She leaned back against her seat. What in the world just happened? That certainly felt intentional, as if whoever drove that truck was *trying* to run her off the road. Still dizzy, she couldn't think straight, but didn't want to just sit there. What if the asshole came back? Her hands shaking, she used her cell phone to call Davis, who told her that he'd be there soon.

Waiting for him, she tried to make sense of what had occurred. Maybe it was high-school kids goofing around. She didn't *really* believe that. And why had she called Davis? Damn, she definitely was *not* thinking clearly.

When Davis pulled up next to her and got out she could see the look of concern on his face. "What happened?"

Yep, maybe she shouldn't have called him. Playing the damsel in distress wasn't her style. "I don't know, some kids or someone was driving on my tail and then raced around me and cut me off. I slammed on the brakes and maybe I hit something slick because I lost control and spun out."

He took out a small flashlight. "Did you hit your head?"

"Uh, yeah, but I'm okay."

He shone the light on her forehead. "That's quite a knot. Did you lose consciousness?"

Hmmm. How to answer this one? She knew he'd likely make her go to the hospital if she said yes, and okay, she probably should tell him the truth. But damn, she *was* okay, and all she wanted to do was go home and climb in bed. After some aspirin and a good night's rest, she'd feel a whole lot better. "No."

"You're lying." He pointed at her.

"What?"

"I said, you're lying. I didn't get to be a detective by not being able to spot liars and right now you're not telling me the truth. Come on, let's go see a doctor."

She sighed. "I don't want to. I'm so tired after today."

"No whining. You're going to the hospital."

"Hey, I'm not whiny. That's not nice. Can't I just go home? Please?"

"Nope. And, now you *are* whining." He reached his hand out. "Come on."

She decided to quit arguing, able to tell it was a battle she wouldn't win. She took his hand. He put his arm around her waist and led her to his car. "I just banged my head a little. I can walk."

"You certainly are hardheaded. No pun intended."

He opened the door and helped her in, then went back to lock up her truck. It was nice . . . well okay, maybe even more than nice. It felt good to have a man's arms around her, wanting to take care of her. There she was— doing it again. Fantasizing. Stupid. Is that why she'd called Davis, so she could continue to live out some bizarre romantic fantasy? He was only doing his job, what every police officer would've done in this situation. She didn't need a man. She was doing fine on her own. His arm around her still felt nice, though.

He stayed by her side as they walked into the hospital. Rubbing alcohol and cleaning agents smelled as offensive to Michaela as the gloomy interior of the aging facility. Ugh. She hated hospitals. Then again, who didn't? She waited to be seen by an ER doctor.

Davis was still concerned. "Did you get a good look at the truck? License plate? Make? Anything?"

She shook her head. "It was dark and it all happened so fast. The truck might have been blue or black, I don't know. It definitely wasn't white. I honestly don't know."

Something flashed through her mind: the moment when her truck was nearly clipped. Wait. There was something. "You know what, I don't think there was a plate on the back."

"Are you sure?"

"No. Like I said, it all happened so quickly. Do you think it was intentional?"

"Do you?"

She didn't answer right away. She had when it happened, but this week had been so filled with drama and trauma that her mind immediately assumed the worst. "Honestly, it felt that way, but again, it could have been kids being stupid."

"I don't like it."

"What are you thinking?"

"I probably shouldn't say anything to you, but I have to wonder, since we found Kirsten Redmond's fingerprints on your pitchfork, if she might not have anything to do with this."

Michaela recalled what had occurred between her and Kirsten earlier that day after her uncle's funeral. She told Davis about it.

"I didn't see her at the funeral. She must've been hiding in the back. I had to rush off."

"Kirsten drives a Mustang, but Brad drives a truck, and it's a *new* truck. Maybe that's why I didn't see plates."

"Maybe. I definitely plan to visit Ms. Redmond and your ex again."

"By the way, how were you able to match Kirsten's fingerprints on the pitchfork? DMV records?"

He laughed. "I wish. Believe it or not, the DMV won't let us use their records to track criminals. We found her prints because she worked for the county rec center some time back. Government agencies are required to take prints and they are managed by the State Department of Justice, who actually keeps track of arrest records and other sources in what's called AFIS or Automated Fingerprint Identification System."

"Oh." She didn't expect this lengthy answer, but something about him talking shop was endearing.

"I know that Ms. Redmond and your ex have given you a bad time. They both might be involved, or at least Ms. Redmond may be, in trying to scare or possibly harm you. If she caused this accident and I can prove it, this could be considered vehicular assault."

"Kirsten could go to jail?"

"If we can find enough evidence to arrest her, you bet."

Kirsten wearing an orange jumpsuit. That did sound appealing.

After another hour of being checked out, monitored, given some ice and Motrin for the pain, Michaela was finally released. Davis had her home in less than twenty minutes. They pulled up to her house. He stopped the car and turned to her.

"I need you to do me a favor and let me be the cop, okay? No more of this snooping around. You could get hurt. In fact, you did get hurt tonight."

"You think the accident is connected to my uncle's murder?"

"I'm not sure. I still have plenty of questions for some people. The evidence points to Bean, but I'm not willing to close this case yet. We're still waiting for handwriting analysis to come back on Bean's note, too. Now, let this go, and let me do my job."

"Fine."

He helped her inside. "I can stay the night— on the couch, you know— make sure that you're okay."

"No need. My roommate is home."

He brushed her bangs out of the way of her bump. "That looks pretty nasty to me. I know the doctor said that it would be fine, but I can hang out here, at least for a while."

"I'm okay."

"I know. I'm doing my job. That's all. I think it would be a good idea if I stayed."

Was he pushing so hard to stay simply out of concern? "Don't they have officers who do that? You know, to babysit those who may be in harm's way?" she joked.

"Sure, but look, I won't bother you, and I can do some work here and then take you to your truck in the morning."

"Suit yourself." She went to get him some blankets and a pillow. He *was* just doing his job after all.

Wasn't he?

THIRTY-ONE

THE NEXT MORNING MICHAELA WOKE TO THE sound of voices and remembered that Jude Davis had stayed the night. But wait. Who was he talking to? Camden surely wasn't up this early.

Rounding the corner into the kitchen, she could smell fresh coffee. She stopped short when she saw Ethan there with Davis. They each held a cup of coffee and looked to be hanging like good ol' boys together. Cocoa spotted her and began wagging her tail. Michaela started to back up, hoping they wouldn't see her. But she was spotted "Mick?" Ethan said.

"Hi guys," she said meekly. Dammit, here she was looking like the damsel in distress again. And why did Ethan insist on taking it upon himself to drop in whenever he damn well felt like it? Not that she hadn't appreciated it in the past, but what must it look like? Oh no. Prickly heat rose on the back of her neck. *What must it look like!* Davis was here before Ethan arrived. In fact, the guy had stayed the night. And what was Davis thinking, with Ethan barging in as the sun came up! Oh why did she care what either one thought anyway!

"Good morning," Davis said and went to pour her a cup of coffee.

Ethan wiggled his eyebrows at her, his expression reminding her of a Cheshire cat, confirming her worst fear: He assumed Davis spent the night because the two of them had slept together. The heat on her neck turned to perspiration. "I came by to check on you and Leo. From the looks of it though, you're doing a-okay."

She couldn't resist giving him a dirty look. "Thank you." What had Davis told him? Or *not* told him?

"I need to use your restroom," Davis said.

As he left, Ethan smiled at her. "You and the detective, huh?"

"No, Ethan, it's not like that. I can explain."

He held up a hand. "No need to explain. I don't care what you do. Actually I think it's good you're moving on with your life, and Davis seems like a nice guy."

She walked over to where Ethan was standing and put another scoop of sugar in her coffee. Her stomach tightened. "Yes, he is."

His eyes narrowed. "Mick? What's that bruise on your forehead from?"

Oh-oh. Well, she got her answer about what Davis had told Ethan: nothing. Good. Knowing Ethan, he'd be all up in arms about the accident and make a big deal, feeling the need to hover over her. And, Davis was doing that duty. She should never have called him last night. She would've been just fine. She touched her forehead. "Oh that. It's nothing. I banged it."

"I'll say you did. What do you mean it's nothing? How did you do it?"

She really did not want to go into it. "I . . . uh, I opened this cupboard here"— she pointed to the cupboard above her, where she kept her plates—"last night, and I guess I wasn't paying attention." She had actually hit her head on that damn cupboard quite a few times in the past. Lying to Ethan did not come easy, and she despised herself for doing it, but having him worried would make it worse, in her opinion.

"Okay. You better be more careful. You always have been a klutz." She smiled and sipped her coffee, silently thankful he'd believed her. "There's something I came by to tell you, and I need you to hear me out."

Oh brother. She definitely did not like the sound of this. She sipped her coffee and nodded.

"This weekend, while I'm on the vet staff in Vegas . . . well, I thought timingwise it would be a good thing because Summer isn't quite showing yet, and it really is the right thing to do. I know that it is."

"What are you trying to tell me?"

"We're . . . getting married this weekend, and I want you there."

Michaela about spit her coffee across the room. "What?"

"Y-yeah," Ethan stammered. "It's uh, really why I came here to see you."

"I think that's great," Jude Davis replied, walking back into the kitchen. "Sorry, I couldn't help overhearing. Congratulations."

"Thank you. Hey, why don't you join us? It's not a long drive over and we'd love to have you. I'm sure Michaela would want you there, too." He looked at her and winked.

She was going to kill him.

"I'd like to. But I'm working until five tomorrow, and then I have plans."

"Well it's not a long flight, in case you change your mind or your plans fall through—"

"No! He said that he had plans," Michaela interrupted. Both men looked at her. If looks could kill, she was doing her best to take Ethan out at that moment.

"Why don't I go out and take care of the horses for you? Relax for a change. Enjoy the morning," Ethan said.

Michaela wanted to make a smart-ass remark back, because he'd really done it to her this time. It would have felt good to say something about his being sure that his bride would show up this time, but she decided against it. It wouldn't do any good. How could he marry Summer? What the hell was he thinking! Why did he have to race to the altar? And after what Summer had put him through before. *"The best thing for everyone."* Stupid. That's what he was being— stupid. She had a good mind to go drag Camden's skinny ass out of bed and have her whip up several pitchers of her killer concoction. And what about Davis? Surely he'd picked up on Ethan's not-so-subtle hints that he thought they'd slept together. Men!

As Ethan left for the barn, Davis asked, "How's your head feel?"

"Fine. I guess we better go and get my truck." She looked out the window and watched Ethan heading out to the barn to feed the horses. She was done chasing fantasies.

On the way to her truck Davis said that he didn't mention to *Dr. Slater* about what had happened the night before. "I didn't feel it was my place. I know you two are close and I figured I'd let you be the one to tell him."

"We're not that close." Now, why did she say that?

"Really?"

"We grew up together, sure, and he's my vet and yeah, he's a friend, but that's it. He's getting married this weekend." Davis glanced at her. She needed to change the subject. "When do you get to see your little girl?" That was safe.

"Katie. This weekend. I can't wait. Those are the plans I have. I promised her dinner and we're going to see *The Nutcracker* in L.A."

Michaela sighed. Funny— she was relieved. She'd thought Davis's plans surely involved a woman. "That sounds fun."

"The kid is great. We have a great time together." He beamed, and his love for his daughter was almost infectious as Michaela felt herself smiling while he talked about her. "She's a bright kid. You know, she's doing sixth-grade math in fourth grade. Whoever said girls aren't good at math doesn't know what they're talking about. And she loves ballet. She started taking lessons a couple of years ago."

"Wow. I envy you. A daughter." Listening to him talk about her started a bit of that yearning again inside her. What it must be like to love someone so much. A child. She could only imagine.

"She's the best. Hey, do you give riding lessons?"

She thought about Joey and her promise to teach his daughter Genevieve how to ride. "Yes, I do."

"I bet you're wonderful with kids. My daughter would love to ride. Do you think maybe you could give her some lessons?"

Teaching Davis's kid to ride would mean that she would see him, maybe quite a bit. How did she feel about that? She flashed back to Ethan and his words about her moving on. "Sure. That sounds good."

"I can't wait to tell her. Of course, you probably want to wait until after the holidays. I know things aren't easy right now. And between you and me, I don't how this case is going to go."

"You have doubts, don't you, about Bean?"

"I think you know that I do. Technically I'm not supposed to talk to you about it, but since you're the one who opened some of these new doors, Miss Detective . . ." He pointed a finger at her. "There will be no more police work on your end. Agreed?"

"Agreed." She would try to let it all go and allow Davis to do his job, but it would be tough, because her uncle's murder and the surrounding circumstances troubled her. "I guess you'll be talking to Dwayne Yamiguchi today? And Kirsten? *And* Brad."

Davis didn't reply as he pulled up next to her truck. "Take care of that head, Miss Marple. See you this afternoon. The Honey Bear Cottage."

"Best lattes in town. Until then, Sherlock Holmes."

"Ah, but I have a license to investigate, *and* the training. You need to go train horses."

"I get it."

He waited until she drove off. What a gentleman Davis was. And, Ethan . . . well, he was one royal pain in the ass, and she'd had it up to there with his antics. First keeping secrets about what was going on between him and Uncle Lou, and now marrying Summer. Okay, so they were *supposedly* friends now, but Michaela still had reservations about the woman. She simply was not Ethan's type. Or, maybe she was. Who was she to determine Ethan's type when it came to women?

When she arrived home, Ethan was still there. "Just finished feeding everybody."

"Thanks."

"No problem."

"Ethan?"

"Yes?"

"What the hell are you thinking? I need to know. And I also need to know what happened between you and Lou."

He looked away for a second then back at her, his eyes filled with an intensity she didn't often see in him. But when she did, he meant business. Good, because so did she. "I suppose I owe you."

"You do."

He went around to the cab of his truck and opened the glove compartment. He handed her a photo, one of her uncle and another man, circa the late 1960s, she figured. "What's this?"

"That's Lou and . . . my dad."

"Your dad?"

He smiled sadly. "All my life, I wanted a dad. Right? Sure, I never verbalized those exact words to anyone, but you even once said to me when we were kids that if you could, you'd get me a dad for my birthday." He laughed. "I think we were like five or something. I don't know, but I never forgot you telling me that. And I knew that you would be my best friend for life, because anyone who wanted what I wanted so badly for myself without me having to say it was someone I would always be close to."

Where was he going with this? She *did* remember telling him that when they were kids, and he'd replied that it was impossible to give him a dad. That a dad wasn't someone you could go buy at a store. Ethan had told her that dads were men who *wanted* to be dads, that there was no one who wanted to be his. Michaela had always wished she could have changed that for him.

"Growing up, your family was like my family. Our mothers were like sisters. I know they still talk all the time, even though my mom is so far away." Ethan's mother had moved to Florida a few years back to be with a man she'd met on a cruise. The relationship hadn't worked out, but Ethan's mother found she liked living on the Florida coast. "Your father wasn't exactly like a dad to me, just because he keeps to himself, but Lou treated me like a son. Remember how he used to take us trail riding? And, he'd come watch my football games when we were in high school? He was even the one who advised me to become a vet. I looked up to him. I loved him, always wished he were my dad. Then, when Summer cancelled our wedding, he let me stay at the guest house and didn't expect a dime from me. Of course, I paid him. But my bank statements show he never cashed the checks."

He sighed. "Lou obviously knew my dad." He pointed to the photo. "He knew my dad and he knew he wasn't dead, like I'd been told by my mother. He'd known all these years, even knew where he lived. He *knew*."

"I'm sorry. I am so confused."

"Summer was the one who discovered it. While doing his books she saw checks for significant amounts written to a Tom Beckenhour. She asked Lou who the guy was. He told her that it was a buddy he'd bought some horses from. She asked him which horses so she'd know how to organize it on the books. He got a bit gruff with her. She mentioned something about looking at some of the previous years on the books and that this Tom received these checks on a regular basis. Lou told her to mind her own business. But it still bothered Summer because of the way Lou was acting. He even told her that he'd handle those transactions, and for her not to worry about it. Then, she found this photo while looking for some transactions from a few years back that the IRS asked for during that audit they did of the ranch last year."

Michaela remembered that well. Uncle Lou was angry about being audited, but Summer had done a decent job preparing for it, and the government found that all the deductions he'd taken on his taxes a few years back were legit.

"She noticed the resemblance to me." Michaela studied the picture, and it was true. The man in the photo with Uncle Lou did bear a striking resemblance to Ethan. "Well, she started looking into it, and she found out that Tom Beckenhour is some washed-up rodeo cowboy that Lou knew back in the '60s. They'd been buddies on the circuit. He introduced this guy to my mom one night and . . . well, *I'm* the product of that one night."

She shook her head. "Whoa."

"Right. It gets worse, though. Tom Beckenhour knew about me through Lou, who tried to get him to do the right thing. But this loser was a drunk and ran away from my mom and me."

"So, your mom and Lou *did* do the right thing not telling you about him. Did you ever think of that?"

Ethan shrugged. "No. I didn't, because I guess the guy did sober up when I was around ten years old and wanted to be a part of my life, but Lou has spent the last twenty years sending him cash to keep him away from me. That's why we had the falling-out. That's why I took off and was so angry and didn't tell you why I left to go rafting. I didn't say anything to you until now, because I had to make sure it was all the truth. Then on top of it, Summer tells me she's pregnant. I had to process it all, but now I feel like I have to tell you. I know you've been having doubts about me and my loyalty to Lou. I'm sure you've even wondered if I could have killed him."

"It'd be a waste of time to deny it."

"I loved Lou and I was hurt by the lies, but knowing him and knowing the extremes he went to, to shine the light on the *real* Brad for your sake, I understand why he did what he did for me. Lou wanted to protect the people he loved from being hurt. So he kept secrets, buried lies, and held on tight to all of us. Maybe too tight, and secrets and lies always catch up with you. The thing I don't get is why he continued to pay this guy off even when I got older. Why he didn't let me make my own judgments. Again, I've come to the conclusion that was him holding on as tight as he could, afraid of losing those close to him."

Michaela nodded. She took Ethan's hand and held it for a moment before saying anything. "Funny how you can love someone so much, you'll do almost anything to keep them from walking away, even if it means hiding behind a lie. Don't you wonder though, just what kind of man this guy who's supposedly your dad is? To continue to take money from Lou after all these years, and agree to stay away, does not bode well in my mind as to what your father would be like. I mean, if he really wanted to know you he would have told Lou to go to hell."

Ethan looked hurt by the words as he pulled his hand away from her. "I suppose that's true."

Why did she have to be so blunt? "What about your mother? Have you spoken with her about it?"

"No. I can't. Not yet anyway. I need to go and see her about this. I've been so angry though."

"She may be able to shed more light on it. I think you need to get to the bottom of it, Ethan, or you'll never be able to move on."

He nodded. "I did contact him. Tom. My father."

"You did?"

"Yep. He's married and has two kids. Weird, huh? I have two brothers."

"Are you going to meet him? Are you going to ask him why he did what he did?"

"I don't know if I want to or care to. But I want you to know that I forgive Lou. You know that the man was a father to me. Someone who loved me so much and wanted to protect me because he felt it was the right thing to do, even though it may not have been, proves to me that I *was* wrong to ever be angry with him. All he did was love me like a dad should, and now I feel horrible. The guilt is almost unbearable." He teared up.

Ethan rarely ever cried and her heart ached for him. "You and I both know that Lou would have understood. He loved you a lot. That's obvious. So please, don't do this to yourself. Promise me? Don't keep going down this road. Talk to your mother, maybe meet this man, but most of all forgive yourself. Lou did not take your anger to his grave."

Tears streamed down his face. "I hope not."

"He didn't."

"Yeah, well, I've done a lot of thinking about Lou, and you, and what you said about Summer over the past few days, and loving someone . . . and family. All of it. What I needed and *wanted* growing up was a dad. Sure, I had Lou, but there's a difference between someone who treats you like you're their kid and someone who *is* your dad. There just is. I can't explain it. Maybe I'm old school and believe that blood is thicker than water, though my heart knows it's ridiculous. You get love where you're supposed to. Right?" He wiped his face with the back of his hand. "Look at me, crying like a baby. Stupid."

"No. It's not."

"You're a good friend. I love you for that and more. Like I said, I've been doing a ton of thinking and through it all I've come to the conclusion that I have to be a father to this baby Summer and I are having. That's why I have to marry her, Michaela. I told you earlier, it's the right thing to do."

Michaela nodded. "Well, you have always been good about doing the right thing. But do you have to rush into it? It all seems so sudden."

"I know. I guess I'm just old-fashioned. I don't want Summer to have to walk down the aisle while seven or eight months pregnant, or after we have the baby."

"If you were so old-fashioned, you wouldn't have jumped in bed with her. Oops. That one kind of slipped out. I'm sorry, but it's how I feel. And another thing, how do you know this is your child?"

He looked wounded by the suggestion. "The timing is right. Of course it's my child." Oh God. Typical man. As if after sleeping with him a woman would never go to bed with another man. "Mick, it's my life. It's my child's life. I'm going to do this. With or without your support."

"So, it's this weekend, huh?" He wasn't going to listen to reason.

"Might as well be." He smiled.

"I guess there's nothing more that I can say, if this is what you want."

"Will you be there for me?"

"Oh Ethan. I don't know. I have tickets for the rodeo, but I don't think I can go. With Lou and everything . . . well, I don't think so."

"I need you there. You're my best friend. I can't imagine you not being there. Please."

She finally nodded, still not believing that she could agree to hand Ethan over to a woman who likely could never really love him. Not in the way he deserved.

THIRTY-TWO

AFTER ETHAN LEFT, MICHAELA NEEDED TO GET out and work the horses. She felt bad that none of them had received the attention they should have been getting over the past few days. A workout here and there simply was not enough; it was time to get back in the saddle, so to speak. She needed to. The revelation about Ethan and Summer's impending nuptials had her in a tailspin, not to mention last night's near-miss on her life, which she still was freaked about. Her head ached a bit, but she didn't know if it was from hitting it, or from everything else that filled her mind.

After lacing up her paddock boots, she again called the attorney who'd left her the message the day before. His secretary said that he was in court and that she'd have him return her call. As she put Leo out on a hot walker to give him some exercise, she couldn't help wondering what the lawyer wanted with her. It didn't take long for her to get involved in her work and thoughts of Ethan, Summer, attorneys, and even Jude Davis went away for the time being.

She worked Rocky and three more horses in the arena, finally winding up on a trail ride with Booger, giving him a chance to stretch his muscles. In between she gave the horses a quick rinse and let them stand in the sun to dry before putting them back in their stalls. She worked right through lunch, and damn, it felt good. Something about getting up on her animals and working them through their paces helped to heal her.

By the time she finished it was almost five. Where had the day gone? It almost felt like normal again. As difficult as it was, life did go on. She wondered if Davis had gotten anywhere with the information she'd given him about Dwayne. She still couldn't believe that Uncle Lou's right-hand man would have anything to do with this mess, but according to Joey, Dwayne had everything to do with it.

She got her answer when she made it back to the house and played her messages. Jude Davis had called. "Hi Michaela. It's Davis here." Oh no! She'd forgotten their coffee date. "Sorry I couldn't make it to The Honey Bear Cottage for our coffee. I tried to reach you on your cell." She sighed. Thank God. "But I was in the middle of an interrogation. I wanted to let you know that we arrested Dwayne Yamiguchi today on charges of fraud. I don't know if they'll stick, but I made calls to the owners of the mares you mentioned, and a couple of them gave me Dwayne's name as their contact. We don't know what he did with the money yet, and of course, he's denying everything. I've also called The American Quarter Horse Association and they received your letter and DNA samples. The results should be back tomorrow. Dwayne will be arraigned in the morning and the judge will set bail. You *do* make a fine detective."

So, Dwayne was behind bars for fraud. But it still didn't resolve who could have murdered her uncle. Dwayne might be a crook, but a killer? Plus, he wasn't even in town the morning Uncle Lou had been killed. Her mind wandered back to Cynthia: the anger in her eyes at the funeral service. But Davis said that her story checked out. Still, couldn't she have also had someone on the side that she was cheating with? Wasn't that a possibility?

She didn't have time to ponder these thoughts because her doorbell rang several times, insistently. "I'm coming. I'm coming." Patience. Whoever it was certainly had none. She flung the door open. "What in the world?"

There stood Brad, suitcase in hand. "Hi honey. I'm home."

"Like hell you are!"

He frowned and leaned against the doorjamb, preventing her from slamming it in his face. "Now, honey, let's get past all the bull between us. I'm here because I know we belong together. In fact, I found out that Kirsten was causing you some trouble and I told her exactly what I thought of her and that you were the best thing that ever happened to me."

"Get off my property."

He stuck his lower lip out. She thought about ripping it off his face. "Can't we just talk?"

She crossed her arms. "We have nothing to talk about. If you don't get off my property, I'll call the police."

He waved his hands in the air. "Women. Fine. Have it your way. I did a good thing for you, and you kick me like a dog." He pulled out a chewing tobacco tin and unwrapped it.

"You *are* a dog. No, actually you're a cretin. I would never put you in the same category as a dog. They're far better than you could even aspire to be. You are dog shit. That's what you are."

"You'll see what I did for you. I called the police about Kirsten. I think they'll be having a long talk with her and she's gonna be in some big trouble. And I did it for you."

"Okay, Brad, what the hell are you babbling about?"

"Let me in the house. We'll have a beer and talk about it."

"Bullshit! Tell me what you're talking about and then go away. Far away. Wait a minute: When did you start chewing?"

"Oh, that. I can stop that. Kirsten liked me to do it. Told me it was a man thing to do. Woman used to buy it for me."

"Really?" Now wasn't *that* interesting, considering that Davis had found the tobacco wrapper on the ground the other night after finding the pitchfork? "What are you up to?"

"You'll see the light after I tell you what I did. See that we belong together. That I still love you, and I know you still love me." She wanted to puke. "Kirsten knew it, and it's been killing her. She got pissed because she says I talk about you too much. But she's right. I can't stop thinking about you."

"You seemed to have no problem not thinking about me while you were screwing her."

"Dumb, I know. But I needed to sow my oats, stretch my wings a little." He tapped his chest. "But it's always been you, honey. Always."

"Right." She had to ask herself again: How in the hell had she ever wound up with this idiot?

"Anyway, I found a big-ass scratch on my new truck, and I asked Kirsten about it because she drove it to the store last night. First she tried to play all innocent. But she snapped and told me that she ran you off the road last night. That she was tired of you coming between us." *It was Kirsten last night.* "But, baby, I am back and I see the error of my ways, and I will never treat you badly again."

What an ass. "I appreciate that, Brad. And, thanks for doing the right thing by turning your bimbo in to the police. She could have killed me last night. But as far as you and me—"

"Yeah. You ready to make that baby we want so much?"

She shook her head. "Leave!"

"What did I say? I thought we were good."

"Leave.

Camden drove up and got out of her car. "What's the shithead doing here?" she asked as she approached the front door.

"You still friends with this dumb chick? Man." He shook his head.

"Dumb? Did you call me *dumb*?" Camden walked over and punched him in the nose. Hard. Nice right hook, too. "Don't *ever* call me dumb. I might be shallow. I might be a bitch. But I'm not dumb."

"Ouch. What the hell? You're freaking crazy. You're both crazy bitches!" He held his bloodied nose.

"I'll take crazy, but dumb? No," Camden replied. "Get out of here. I think you've already been asked nicely, and my left jab is even better than the right hook."

They both cracked up watching Brad hightail it off the property. "That was amazing," Michaela exclaimed. "Where did you learn to hit like that?"

"Kickboxing. You should come with me some time."

"You are full of surprises. How come you punched him, though? I could've taken care of him. He would've left. I don't think I've ever seen you so angry before."

"What can I say? I ran into Kevin earlier, and he called me dumb, too. I guess it got under my skin."

"I guess!"

Michaela told Camden about her day: Dwayne, Kirsten, and finally Ethan.

"He's really going to marry her? Why the rush? She couldn't even be showing yet."

"I know. I asked him about that. But you know Ethan, always the good guy, always wanting to do the right thing."

"The *stupid* thing this time. How are you?"

"What do you mean? I'm okay, I guess. Sure, I know he's making a mistake, but I'm not living his life."

"Look, it's no secret you love him. He loves you, too."

"He's my friend."

"Talk to him and tell him how you feel."

"I know you mean well, and want the best for me, but I am not in love with Ethan. And even if I was, he's having a baby with another woman. Who needs that kind of complication in their life? Ethan made his bed, he can lie in it."

"Yeah, well, I know you'd like to lie in it with him, and I only want that for you because I love you, too."

Michaela hugged her. "I know you do. But it wouldn't work between us. It just wouldn't."

Camden pulled away and looked at her, obviously deciding not to push the issue any further. "Well you can't go to that wedding alone. I'm coming with you."

"That would be great."

"Yeah. We can stay at the Bellagio. I've got an old boyfriend who works there as one of the managers. He likes me, and can get us a real good deal. Oh, shoot. Wait a minute. I have a job interview in the morning."

"A job interview?"

"Yes. Believe it or not, I think it's time I get off my ass and do something for a change."

"You're settlement isn't going to come through, is it?"

Camden shrugged. "That obvious?"

"Well, first off, I would never buy that you actually want to get off your butt and work."

She laughed. "Ah, you know me so well."

"Where's the interview?"

"Get this, the Chanel makeup counter at Nordstrom. Free samples. Huh? Beautiful, right? And, I know I'll get it. I can do it. I can sell makeup, girl."

"It's perfect for you. It really is." She gave Camden about a month . . . *if* she landed the job.

"But it's not a problem. I can book a flight and make it over there in time for the wedding. I'll call my pal and have him hook us up. Meet me there when you get to Vegas, or if you beat me, I'll make sure you have a key to the room. In fact, I'll see if I can't get a room for Ethan and the princess there, too."

"You'd do that?"

"Of course. I would do anything for you, and so would Ethan. Think about it, before you let him go and marry Summer. Think about talking to him."

"There's nothing more to say," Michaela said.

THIRTY-THREE

THE NEXT DAY AFTER WORKING THE HORSES, Michaela finally received a call from the attorney who'd been trying to get a hold of her— Henry Stein. "What's this all about?" she asked him.

"Ms. Bancroft, I have some news for you. Your uncle, Lou Bancroft, has left you the bulk of his estate." Michaela nearly dropped the phone. She couldn't say anything at first. "Ms. Bancroft?"

"Yes, I'm here. What do you mean, my uncle left me most of his estate?"

"Exactly that. According to his will, you receive his ranch, his home, three million dollars from various investment accounts, and his horses." Michaela was speechless. "I'll connect you back to my receptionist and you can make an appointment with her for next week to come in and work out all of the details."

She believed that she thanked him before speaking to the receptionist. After hanging up she just sat there, trying to let what she'd been told sink in. Uncle Lou had left almost all of it to her. Why? Why not Cynthia? She had to clear her mind. A trail ride. Yes. She'd take Booger out for a ride.

She went through the motions of taking her old gelding out, brushing him, throwing a pad and saddle up on him, sliding a bit into his mouth, and putting his ears through the headstall— trying only to focus on the task at hand. She got up on Booger and rode out to one of the back trails. Why would Uncle Lou leave all of his possessions to her? And then another thought— an ugly one. The lawsuits. Did this mean that the lawsuits were also hers to deal with? And if so, could Uncle Lou's ranch be lost? No. She couldn't allow that to happen.

Cynthia. She had to speak to her. Doubts or not about her, she had to find out if she knew that Lou had planned to do this. She put Booger into a lope. He reluctantly did as she asked, especially when she gave him a slap on the rear with the ends of her reins. That woke him up a bit.

She rode to Lou's ranch. What the hell? There was Dwayne. She saw him blanketing one of the horses. Unbelievable. He had to have made bail. She may have made a deal with Davis about no more detective work, but she certainly didn't agree *not* to confront people about their crimes

Although Booger wasn't off the track by any stretch of the imagination, being atop the horse strengthened her resolve while she rode on over to where Dwayne worked. She *could* get away quickly if he made a move.

Dwayne looked up at her and something about his expression caught her off guard. She saw sadness there. Despair. "I see you know," he said.

"Yes, I know. I know exactly what you've been doing for God knows how long to my uncle, and I want to know why. Why in the hell would you scam owners out of money and breed them to Rocky instead of Loco? I realize that hasn't been proven yet. But you and I both know that it will be."

He crossed the mare's blanket straps under her belly, fastened them, and stood up slowly, staring at her for long seconds before saying anything. Why was he looking at her like that? Booger lifted his back leg onto the front tip of his hoof, going into resting mode. She gave him a squeeze with her calf— enough to wake him. She wanted Booger on alert and ready to run if needed.

"I did not do what the police have accused me of."

"Really? How do you explain that your name came up when the owners of those mares were questioned?"

"I . . . don't know."

"That's a great defense, now isn't it? You don't know?" She shook her head. "You better hope you have a good lawyer, because I think the police also believe that you may have killed my uncle and Bean. And I think so, too. I'm not sure how you did it, but the police will figure it out. I believe that." As the words escaped her mouth, she again realized that she was possibly confronting a killer. Alone. What the devil was she thinking? She started to back Booger away.

Tears sprang to Dwayne's eyes. "Wait. I did not kill Lou. I did not kill Bean. I loved both of those men. I loved them like they were my own brothers! And I did not steal money from Lou or frame him, or steal money from anyone. I never posed as a breeder. If you look at all of this, I am the one who is being framed."

"Oh come on!"

"How is this not obvious? You think if I put together a con that the police say I did, that when I talk to horse owners, I give out my name? How dumb do you think I be?"

Michaela couldn't respond. Dwayne had never struck her as stupid, and the point he was making was a decent one. If he was trying to steal money, why *would* he give out his name? No. She wasn't going to buy into this. He was a liar. He had to be. It was the only thing that made sense.

"You have to believe me. I did not do this."

Now the tears flowed freely down Dwayne's face, and something inside of Michaela softened. Could he be telling the truth? Should she at least listen? "Then who? Who would have done this, and why?" She still made a point of keeping her distance. He didn't approach her, but instead put the mare back in her stall and returned with another one for the nightly ritual.

"I think a lot about this when the police ask questions, fingerprint me, and put me in the cell until I make bail." Ha! "Yeah, how did you make bail? It had to have been at least a few thousand dollars. I've never known you to be loaded. What did you do, use the stolen cash?"

He shook his head. "I tell you, I did not do this. I have a little savings. A little from my auntie who passed away a couple of years ago."

"Sam's mom? I didn't know she died."

He nodded. "Yeah. He don't talk about it much. Too hard for him. But it was that money I use."

She still didn't know what to think, but if he was lying, he sure was smooth. She sighed. "So who, Dwayne? Who do you think could have done this?"

He looked at her, his face taut. "Brad."

A flashback flooded her about Brad having dinner with Bean the other night, and how she'd wondered they were still so tight. Then, another thought came to her: Kirsten and the prints on the pitchfork. The fight with her at the funeral, and getting run off the road. And, Brad showing up at her place, trying to worm his way back into her life, pretending to be Mr. Nice Guy by tattling on his girlfriend. "Why do you say that?"

"You know what I think?"

"No, but I'm all ears."

"I think Brad find out that I be the one who Lou had follow him and his girl around to get pictures to prove to you he no good."

"*You* took the photos? *You* followed Brad?"

He nodded. "I agree with Lou, the man no good. He no good with the horses and he no good to you, so I follow him and take the photos and give them to Lou. Sam help me, too. I think when Brad find out I did that, he got mad, and he been planning on getting even ever since."

"Why?"

Dwayne laughed. "Why?'Cause Brad know that this place going to you."

"What? How did you know?"

"Lou talk to me about it. Tell me that if something happen to him, he gonna leave it to you because you good with the animals and he didn't want Cynthia to have to worry about it. He afraid it be too much for her. He ask me to stay on with you. Help you out, if he passed on."

"He did?"

"Yes."

"Okay, how about Brad? How did he know?"

"He know because he used to get the mail sometimes for the ranch and give it to Lou. Envelope came back from his attorney and Lou asked me who got the mail, 'cause it looked like someone had opened it and tried to reseal it. I knew it was Brad." He shrugged. "I got no proof. But my gut say so. The man already been cheatin' on you, and I had the pictures. Brad realize he lose out on big cash if something ever happen to your uncle."

Michaela thought back to the conversation at the bar with Brad— his pitiful apology and excuses— and his appearance at her house. Was that because he knew she was about to inherit her uncle's ranch? Had that also been a part of his plan? Kill Lou, and get back into her good graces? But why the breeding scam? Suddenly, it hit her. The scam was to set Dwayne up and get him out of the way. That bastard! But was Dwayne telling the truth? Again, she had to wonder. And the money? How did Brad gain access to the bank accounts? Did he have the breeders sending checks to another address— one he had set up just for this purpose? Could he have forged the checks? Shit, Brad could hardly write his name legibly, and Uncle Lou had fairly neat handwriting. Damn if she wasn't terribly confused.

"I know he's the one who do this to me, Michaela. I told the police. But I don't think that detective believed me. I tell you Brad hated me. Hated Lou, and Brad a bad man. He did this. I can prove I didn't kill anyone. For one thing, I was in Vegas. That I can prove. I can also prove that I . . ." He blushed. "I spent that night before and morning with a woman I met in the bar at the hotel. I still have her number. I gave it to the police. I didn't steal anything and I didn't kill no one. You have to believe me. You have to."

Michaela closed her eyes and uttered, "I believe you."

THIRTY-FOUR

MICHAELA *DID* BELIEVE DWAYNE, BUT IT WAS hard to swallow that Brad had put this thing together. Still, the man had lied to her more than once, cheated on her, manipulated her . . . and yes, she was starting to believe he was capable of stealing, and even murder, especially if he thought he might get some real money out of it. He must have figured that the owners of the mares would eventually be asked about their contact for the AI breedings. Brad had made sure he slipped both Lou's and Dwayne's names in, figuring that they'd both be caught. But why murder her uncle? Revenge? Or had Uncle Lou discovered the truth? Is that what he'd wanted to talk to her about the morning he was killed? Had he been about to blow the whistle on Brad? Her ex probably hadn't thought far enough ahead to take into account that, eventually, Lou would be able to put two and two together. The timing worked as far as Brad being one of the breeding handlers at the time the mares in the lawsuits were being bred. Brad never did think things through all the way, and this was case in point, assuming he was behind all of these events. Unless killing Lou was part of his evil plot.

Before she left Dwayne, he'd told her that the police were not allowing him to leave the state. Therefore he couldn't compete in the calf roping events at the NFR. "I can't believe it. First year in five I haven't competed. Me and Hobbit was gonna win, too. Just feel it in my blood, you know. Just know it." He wiped tears from his face. "Sam's driving there tomorrow to get the horses for me. But I worry about him with the seizures. Something happen to him on that drive, well . . ."

Michaela immediately volunteered to go with him. "I was heading there anyway. Ethan's getting married and wants me to come."

"What? Oh no. Not to that dipshit Summer?" She nodded. "Girl be trouble. I promise. That man have nuthin' but trouble for years to come with that one."

"I know. What can I do?"

"Tell him no piece of ass that good. None."

She couldn't help but laugh, and Dwayne smiled, too. She was going to help Dwayne out of this mess. She'd been partly responsible for getting him in trouble. Now, she'd do what she could to make sure Brad didn't get away with this. "So, I'll drive to Vegas with Sam. He can go to the wedding with me, and then we'll bring the horses home. We'll stay the night. Camden's flying over, later in the afternoon. She's getting us rooms at the Bellagio."

"Your crazy friend. I like her. She fun." He laughed. "But don't let Sam be staying there. He spend too much dough in a place like that. He need a cheap Motel Six. That work better for him. Not so good with money, my cousin."

"Not a problem. He can drop me and head to the other side of town."

"He good with food, though, so you watch him. Tell him to take his medicine."

"I will."

"Thanks for doing this. You a good friend. You didn't have to believe me, but you see people in the heart and that is good. You have a good faith. I like you for that and am grateful you trust me. If I can get that cop to believe me, then we all be good again."

They arranged for Sam to swing by her place in the morning. She asked Dwayne to take care of Cocoa and her horses while she was gone, and he said that he would.

She wanted to give Davis a call and meet with him. She needed to tell him that she believed what Dwayne was telling her about Brad, but first she needed to talk to Cynthia. She also couldn't help wondering if Kirsten was behind bars yet. She put Booger in one of the open stalls and asked Dwayne to feed him just a little, because she'd still have to ride him home.

"He can stay the night. It's getting dark and I can drive you home."

"No. A night ride won't be too bad and God knows he could use the exercise. Thanks anyway."

The house smelled like spaghetti and garlic bread. She walked into the kitchen and saw Cynthia standing over the stove. Cynthia turned, looking startled to see Michaela. "Hi. I didn't know you were coming by. I'm glad you did."

Something about her demeanor had changed. She didn't appear angry any longer with Michaela. Almost the opposite— happy to see her. "I came by to talk to Dwayne."

"He's had a bad couple of days. He told me everything."

"Do you believe him?"

Cynthia nodded. "The man wouldn't hurt Lou. Not in a million years."

"Then what do you think happened?"

"I think that Brad was involved."

'That's what Dwayne thinks," Michaela replied.

"And you? What do you think?"

"I don't think that Dwayne had anything to do with the scam. I have my doubts about Brad." She paused. "But I didn't come here to talk about that."

Cynthia turned back to stirring the spaghetti. "Finished. Will you join me? I couldn't eat all of it."

"I don't have a lot of time. I rode over here and I'm losing daylight."

"You sure?"

Michaela nodded. "Cynthia, I know you were upset with me the other day, at the funeral. Why?"

Cynthia sighed. "Sit down." Michaela joined her at the table. "You've spoken with the attorney? The wills and trusts guy?"

"Today."

"Well, I spoke with him the day before the funeral and he told me how Lou had adjusted his will."

She hadn't been angry over her telling Davis about the pregnancy.

"I had no idea that he'd changed it, and at first I was angry. Very angry."

"Understandable."

"I was angry at you. Him. If it had been up to me and I'd inherited this place, I would have probably sold it off in the future. It's a lot of a ranch for me, and that Kevin Tanner has already tried to call me to discuss the possibility of buying the ranch."

Bastard! "You wouldn't sell this place."

"I've got to think about me now, but you're right, I won't be selling the ranch, because it's all yours. I've had time to think about that. Lou did the right thing. He left me plenty of money. No, not the ranch, but I know and he knew that I can't handle this place and would likely sell. I don't love horses the way you do."

"You're really okay with all of this?" She couldn't help but feel a bit angry at the thought that Cynthia would even consider selling this ranch that her uncle had loved and devoted his life to.

She shrugged. "I have to be. I don't have a choice, and what good would it do me to be mad at you, or at Lou? He was only doing what he felt was right. Granted, I wish we could have discussed it, but maybe this place was never mine."

"What do you mean?"

"Your parents and Lou raised you to take on a ranch. I need to go home. My parents are in Seattle and I need to start over. I'm having a baby."

Michaela couldn't act surprised. "I know."

"You *know*?" Her eyes widened.

"I saw the pregnancy test in your trash the other day. I threw a tissue away and missed and . . . well, anyway, I saw it."

"And, you assumed the worst, didn't you?"

"Yes."

"That cop. Davis. You're the one who told him I was pregnant?"

There was no sense in denying it. "Yes."

"That explains it. He's a thorough detective. He's even gotten a court order that the baby have a DNA test when he or she is born to compare it with the donor we used. But I assure you, as I did him, that I don't have a problem with it. I never cheated on your uncle, and he wanted this baby as much as I did. We didn't tell anyone I was trying to conceive because we didn't know if I'd even get pregnant, and besides, we didn't want the criticism we thought we might receive. With Lou being sixty-one, it was a risky thing for us, but I knew he'd make a great father, and I knew that he would live to be a hundred. At least, I believe he would have."

"Cyn, I'm sorry."

"Don't be," she said. "It's better this way. Makes it easier to leave. You loved your uncle and he loved you. Why wouldn't you assume the worst of me?" Michaela tried to apologize again, but Cynthia shrugged her off. "I'll be fine. We'll be fine. I'm leaving next week."

Michaela nodded and left her uncle's home—*her* home, feeling like a real jerk and knowing she'd lost a friend.

THIRTY-FIVE

SAM SHOWED UP AT MICHAELA'S PLACE RIGHT AT seven A.M. She'd had enough time to feed and pack after getting up early. She hadn't slept well; the confrontation with Cynthia still weighed on her. She was just finishing out at the barn when Sam got out of his truck and asked to use her restroom. "I figure long ride, better go."

"No problem. It's the first left down the hall. Use the kitchen door. It's unlocked. In fact, do you mind grabbing my stuff? It's right there next to the door, and then lock the bottom lock? Camden might be up, but I doubt it, and I don't want to leave it unlocked."

She thought about Brad, and about Camden punching him. If he was the scumbag Michaela thought he was, then locking the door for her friend was prudent. After riding Booger home last night, she'd called Davis to tell him about her talk with Dwayne and what she thought Brad had done. She had to leave a message. Then, when she checked her messages on the house phone, he'd left her one saying that his daughter had broken her ankle at ballet class and that he was in the emergency room with her. She tried his cell, but it went to voicemail. She'd call again during the drive to Vegas and tell him about Brad, as well as check up on his daughter. Poor kid. What a bummer.

While Sam used the bathroom, Michaela locked up her office and then walked around the back of the trailer to make sure all the latches were securely locked down. She was sure Sam had already done so, but it was a habit. When she'd been a kid, her dad had forgotten to lock the latch on the trailer and it flew open while they were on the highway, nearly causing an accident. Thank God there weren't any horses on board. They were on their way to pick up a few, just as she and Sam were today. It turned out to be a good thing that she checked the latch, because she could see that one of them wasn't down all the way. She retrieved a hammer from her office and locked up again. Then she pounded the latch down. Once done, she climbed into the truck as Sam appeared. She put the hammer in the side pocket of the truck, figuring it would be good to have once they loaded the horses. The damn latch was tough to get down even with the hammer.

Sam handed her the overnight bag. "Thanks," she said.

"No problem. This is good of you to come out with me like this. I feel so bad for Dwayne, you know. Guy is heartbroken. Tol' me to go watch some of the events tonight. Gave me rodeo tickets. He's a good man. Don't deserve this. He did not do anything wrong."

"I'm glad and I can go with you and help out."

* * *

MICHAELA KNEW SAM WAS A TALKER. BUT GOODNESS, who knew he could carry on for hours! He talked about the rodeo, horses, Hawaii, girls he'd loved, and of course good food. He was still talking over halfway into their six-hour ride.

"Man, tough week, huh? Losing Lou and then Bean. It's hard to lose loved ones."

"It sure is. Dwayne mentioned that you lost your mother a couple years ago. The other night at the Chinese restaurant when you mentioned your folks, I guess I thought they were both still living."

"Nah. My mom died, but you know, I still sometimes think she's around. Too bad. She a good woman. She didn't have much love for me though."

His words caught her by surprise. "Why?"

"Oh you know, I be a big disappointment to my folks. Say I got no motivation. I got to follow my cousin and not be my own man."

"Ouch."

"Yeah. But I'm good. It's not true. I got plenty motivation. Like I say, I want to start my own luau now. I could have done it already, if my mom left me some money."

"She didn't leave you anything?"

"Nah. All go to Dwayne. But I get it. He a good guy and helps me out. He could have helped me out to get my restaurant back on Maui, but you know he believe my folks saying I no good with the green stuff. That's fine. I find a way. I think we gonna have to get some gas."

Sam pulled off at the next exit and filled the truck. "You need to go to the bathroom?"

"No. I'm good."

"Want a Coke or something?"

"Water. Thanks."

"Yep. You mind getting my meds out of the glove compartment? I gotta take some now."

"Sure."

She watched as Sam entered the convenience store. That must have been tough growing up in Dwayne's shadow. But Sam seemed to have a good attitude about it. Still, she could sense there was some pain. Maybe he'd stuffed it all down— literally. She was aware that eating the way Sam did could sometimes be due to painful emotions. Maybe she could get him to talk some more. It might make him feel better.

She opened the glove box and took out the pill container. "Topomax?" She'd never heard of the medication but then, she didn't have diabetes and didn't know anyone else who did. She read the label, which contained an alcohol warning, and she noticed that the prescription was from a Dr. Verconti. Wait. That was the same doctor who'd prescribed the Ativan for Uncle Lou. The pill pusher. Sam must have recommended him. She'd definitely be asking him what he knew about her uncle's anxiety issues again. Sam had told her that Lou needed a vacation, but it looked to her like he knew more, especially if he'd told Uncle Lou to call this doc.

Sam was walking back to the truck when her cell rang. Joey said, "I got some info for you. And you ain't gonna like it."

Sam climbed into the truck and she handed him the pills. He swallowed one and pulled back onto the highway. She smiled at him and pointed to the phone. He nodded. "What do you mean, I'm not going to like it?" she asked.

"Get this. The checks were all being transferred from a Washington Mutual account in your uncle's name into an account with The Los Angeles Grand Cayman Trust company. And, let me tell you, that place is hush-hush. All transfers were made online. But I got a cousin who has a friend who's married to the sister of one of the bigwigs at that trust company. That's how I got this info." Thank God for Joey and the million cousins. "The account at WAMU was set up online, like I suspected, but you can't do that with the trust company. They do banking in large sums. They have the L.A. branch, but all deposits wind up in the Caymans and it's under Cayman law once the money is out of the United States, which means no taxes and very difficult to trace."

"You say you can't open an account online with them?"

"Nope. You got to go in and do it. Your friend Dwayne may not be the one who put this thing together. Everything I've been able to find says his hands are clean on this. But his cousin, Sam, he's one bad dude. He's the one who opened the account. And get this: The guy did time a while back on the islands for forging bad checks and for identity theft. He knows what he's doing."

Michaela gasped. "Are you sure about this?" Sam glanced at her. She mustered a smile. Oh no, what if he could hear their conversation? She tried to adjust the volume on the phone.

"Positive. That guy has stolen over half a million dollars from your uncle. You better call the police and tell them, 'cause I'm betting he's planning to get the hell out of Dodge soon. Looks like he made another transfer yesterday, and he bought a ticket from Vegas to the Caymans. Know what else? That dude caught a flight from Vegas at 11:30 the night before your uncle was murdered. Got him into John Wayne Airport a little after midnight. Then he caught a flight back to Vegas the next morning. Early. At seven. He was back in Vegas before eight that morning."

"Oh my God."

"Yep. You better find that guy."

"Already have, Mom. Thanks for telling me. I'll take care of it when I get back. I'm actually on my way to Vegas to pick up some horses. You know Sam Yamiguchi, right?"

"Mick? Did you here what I just said. What the hell is wrong with you?" Joey asked.

"Yeah, *that* Sam. Anyway, I'm with him and I'll be back in town tomorrow, so maybe I can stop by and see you and Dad then."

"Oh, shit. You're with Sam right now?"

"I am. Yep. Like I said, be back tomorrow and I'll stop by. Maybe you can make some of those cookies I like. You know, the ones you gave to Detective Davis the other day."

"You want me to call this Davis?"

"That would be good. Well, I better go. We're traveling through the Mojave now."

"Got it. Be careful. I'm on it."

"Love you, too, Mom." She flipped the phone shut and sat back in the chair. Sam eyed her again and smiled. She smiled back, knowing she was stuck in a truck in the middle of the Mojave Desert with a killer.

THIRTY-SIX

KEEP HIM TALKING. THINK. GOT TO THINK AND act normal. Okay.

"Your ma, huh?"

"Yeah." She tried hard to sound light, but she could hear the strain in her voice. Did Sam wonder about it? Had he overheard Joey on the other end of the phone? "She's been trying to learn financial stuff, you know. With Uncle Lou dying, she figured it was time for her to get a grip, in case something happened to my dad. She doesn't know how to open an account, if you can believe that." *Keep it light.* "My dad and I told her she should learn how to do those things. Funny she had no clue that you can open bank accounts online."

Was he buying this? She sure hoped so. All she had to do was make it to Vegas. She didn't think he planned to kill her. Why do that? He only wanted to get out of town, and she probably made a good cover for him. Dwayne obviously had no clue what his cousin was capable of. Man, she was scared, because if Sam found out that she was on to him, all bets would be off. She eyed the hammer in the side pocket next to her seat.

"Oh, yeah? Huh."

"So, your luau idea sounds great. I was wondering why you didn't ask my uncle for a loan when the opportunity came about. He might have given it to you."

"I think that, too. But you know, I ask him and he tell me no. Say he like me and all, but Dwayne tell him I better off training horses than running a business. Lou tol' me that he not in the restaurant biz, but in the horse biz and a man got to make his own way."

"Yes, my uncle was a practical man." She was pretty sure now that she understood Sam's motive for killing her uncle and for setting up the breeding scheme— all in the name of revenge. The money didn't hurt either, especially since it looked as though Sam figured he was going to make his way to the Caymans or wherever and enjoy it. The guy did more than stuff his anger away. He'd let it stew, and he'd carefully planned this all out until the timing was right. "That was what, a couple of years ago, you could have bought into the luau?"

"Sure was. But like I said, no worries. I'll have my place."

She changed the subject. "My friend Camden is flying out today. Good thing it's a short flight to Vegas. She wanted to go to Ethan's wedding."

He shook his head. "Big mistake. Big one on Ethan's part."

She couldn't argue with that. Her stomach hurt badly, and she could feel her shirt sticking to her back from perspiration. *Keep him talking.* "You see Dr. Verconti? I saw it on the pills. I think my uncle was seeing him for his memory problems."

"I told him he was a good doc. His old doc say there was nuthin' wrong with his mind."

"What did you think?"

"I think you full of shit."

Her back stiffened. "What?"

He pressed down on the automatic locks. "Your mom got a deep voice."

So, her cell phone wasn't as good as she'd hoped. "My . . . dad got on the phone for a minute."

Sam pressed down on the gas. "You a poor liar. I notice the way you talk to whoever on the phone; it wasn't your mom. I listen, and I know I hear a man's voice. Then you try to turn down the volume. I'm not stupid."

"Sam, I have no idea what you're carrying on about." She shifted uncomfortably against the leather seats.

Sam took the next exit off the freeway. He barely slowed down on the exit ramp. She thought about trying to jump out. When he did slow down to turn the corner, heading south, he grabbed her arm, holding tight. His grip burned. He was strong. *Really strong.* Michaela's adrenaline pumped. She had to do something. "Sam? We're friends. We've been friends for a long time."

"We not friends. I don't have friends. I look out for me. It always be that way. I tried to make friends. Dwayne, Lou, Bean, even your jackass ex-husband. But no. No friends. People screw you. All the time."

"That's why you did it then, huh? Killed my uncle? Because you thought he screwed you out of having your own restaurant?" There was no use in faking it any longer. He knew and she knew that the truth had been exposed. How she'd missed it that Sam was the one all this time, she didn't know.

"Yeah. Your uncle, even Dwayne could've helped me out. But no. They like my parents: tight. Don't believe in me. I been planning this for some time. Ever since they both say no. I figure, fine. I get the money and start my place somehow. Then I learn how to do it. The breedings. I was in Ohio with Dwayne at the Quarter Horse Congress when I met some people looking for a good stud. I got their numbers. Told them I'd have Lou call. There's others, too." He paused. "Lot of money in good horses. I didn't want to kill Lou. I made more money stealing from him. I only want to frame him and Dwayne for fraud. Get them in trouble. Let them see how it feels to have people look at you with distrust. Lou would have lost his license. Dwayne would have never been able to show his face in the quarter horse world again, or Lou either."

"So why? Why did you kill him, then? If all you planned to do was frame him for stealing?"

He made another turn and drove down a narrow dirt road, heading straight into the desert. "Because Lou figure it out. When we got to Vegas with the horses, me and Dwayne, we unloaded them. We went to our hotel and the bar downstairs, had a few drinks. Some hooker came onto

Dwayne and he left with her. Good friend, huh? Good cousin! But he also forgot his cell phone, and it rang. I saw it was Lou. I answered and pretended I was Dwayne."

"How did my uncle not know that it was you?"

Sam suddenly changed dialect and voice. "I did not get to be who I am today, sweet pea, without studying." Oh my God. He sounded exactly like her uncle! Lou had always called her sweet pea. She closed her eyes tightly for a second, not wanting to believe any of this. He smiled wickedly at her. "I study people, voices, actions. I listen to everyone and everything. I am much smarter than anyone ever gives me credit for, and ambitious. I told you my parents were wrong about me."

"Where are you taking me?"

He didn't answer. "On the phone with your uncle, he told *Dwayne* that he knew who was running the breeding scam and that he thought he could prove it. He knew it was me. I was glad Dwayne went with the woman. I flew home that night, rented a car, killed Lou in the morning, got back to the airport, and made it back in time to meet my cousin for breakfast."

"You're really disturbed."

"No. I'm smart. You know what though, your uncle was a smart man, too. He also told me that he had found out the medication he was taking for headaches— the medicine I suggested and called in for him, and asked my doctor for— was for panic attacks and agitation, not so good for headaches. Old fool. I could've pulled anything over on him. What he didn't know was that I changed out his pills when I picked them up from the drugstore for him. I put my meds in his."

"Topomax?"

"Yes. You *know* what Topomax is for?"

"For diabetes, I assume."

He shook a finger at her. "No. Topomax is a drug for seizures, all right. But not diabetic seizures. I have what the doctors call a bipolar disorder."

No kidding.

"But give that medicine to someone who don't need it and it can cause memory loss and confusion."

Oh my God. Talk about twisted! "But what about Bean? Why did you kill him?"

"Bean not as retarded as we all thought. Yeah, he took care of that mare for me near your place. Good place to keep her. She get your stud, Rocky, all riled up when I needed him."

"You bastard!"

"Worked for me for a while. I tell Bean that the mare be his and he can live there at that dairy farm with her. But then Rocky get out the other day. Bean tol' me that he saw him there. He call me up right away, like I tell him he had to. I tell him that if he ever saw anyone or anything go on there without me knowing, that I'd take the mare away from him. I also say he couldn't tell no one about the mare. But after I got that mare out of there and had the horse killers come meet me with her. Bean learned what I did, and he said he was gonna tell on me. Ha! The retard was gonna tell on me!

"So, I know every day he go and read with Mrs. Bancroft. I saw her out walking before Dwayne and I went to get some feed the other day. I knew Bean was in the house. I thought, good timing. Tol' Dwayne I needed to check on one of the mares in the pasture I didn't put away. I went in, killed Bean, wrote the note, wiped it all clean, met Dwayne back out at the barn, and we take off for the feed store."

He stopped the truck. "Get out."

"What?"

He reached down into his boot, pulled out a gun, and unlocked the doors. "Get out!"

"You'll never get away with this. People know I'm traveling with you. They're looking for us right now. You can't kill me. The police know you have a ticket to the Caymans from Vegas tonight. Don't delude yourself." Michaela was sweating like crazy, her gut twisted in fear, her mind trying to grasp for words that might reach him. Maybe she could still reason with him.

"I didn't steal a half a million dollars to *not* get away with murder. I *will* get away with it. Now get out of the damn truck!"

She didn't move. He yanked her arm and started to pull her out of the truck on his side. Her hand folded around the hammer in the side pocket and as he started to pull her out of his door, she swung the hammer as hard as she could, hitting him on the side of his face. He yelled in pain. She opened up her door, jumped out, and started running. The sand slowed her down and she tripped. Sam was on her fast. She hadn't hurt him enough. She reached out and tried to poke him in the eyes. His breath was hot on her. He held her to the ground. She tried to knee him in the privates, but instead aimed too high and got his massive gut. He groaned. She won a little leverage as he gasped. He was wavering. What was going on? She squirmed out from underneath him, got to her feet, and started to run again. She was running as fast as she could when she heard the humming of what sounded like a helicopter overhead. Yes! She slowed and watched as the chopper flew lower. Emblazoned on the side of it were the words LAS VEGAS POLICE.

Michaela looked back to see Sam on the ground, convulsing in one of his seizures.

THIRTY-SEVEN

THANK GOD JOEY'S COUSIN'S BEST FRIEND'S uncle's daughter-in-law worked as a dispatcher for the Las Vegas Police Department. Between her and Davis, who didn't ask Joe how he'd gotten his information, they were able to get a chopper in the air and locate Michaela rather quickly, before she either died at the hands of Sam or was blown away by the Santa Ana winds out in the Mojave.

The police arrested Sam and took him under watch to a hospital in Vegas, where once released he would await trial for two murders and a whole lot more. Michaela was also taken to the hospital and released after being checked out. A police officer kindly drove her to the Bellagio, where she called Camden from the lobby of the hotel.

"You're late," Camden said.

"I have a good excuse."

"Come on up. I got us a suite."

"I take it you got the job."

"Nope. My lawyer called and my ex coughed up the money I was asking for. Suppose he figured I'd be a stiletto heel in his side forever. Now get your ass on up here. I've got something for you."

Michaela laughed and it felt *so* good. In the suite, Camden handed her a bag from Dolce & Gabbana. "What is this for?"

"Look, if I'm going to let you make the biggest mistake of your life along with Ethan, you might as well look damn good doing it . . . Oh my God! What in the hell happened to you? You look terrible. You already been out with the horses you were picking up? What, did one go crazy and throw you? I've warned you about those horses. And where's Sam? Thought he was coming with you. Wasn't that what you wrote in the note you left me in the kitchen?"

"Long story. Tell you over margaritas."

"You're on, sister. Now you better get your ass in gear if we're going to do this."

Michaela cleaned up and put on more makeup than usual with Camden's help to cover up the bruise on her forehead, as well as the scratches she'd suffered during the fight with Sam. She relayed as much of the story to Camden as she could while she did her face.

"I can't believe what you've been through," Camden said. "Murder— twice— buried your uncle, figured out the scam of the century, run off the road by a psycho bitch from hell, two trips to the hospital, about killed by the murderer, and now you're about to lose the love of your life. You're amazing."

"No. Now I'm depressed."

Camden laughed. "At least that detective was a positive, right? That man is *divine*. And, from what you've told me, he is into you."

"Davis, yeah. He is a great guy. I should call him." Michaela turned her cell on. There were a half a dozen messages from a worried and concerned Davis. He answered on the first ring.

"Are you okay? I just got off the phone with the Vegas PD. My God! I've been worried sick."

"You have?"

"Yes!"

"I'm sorry. It's just that with all that happened, I didn't really get much of a chance to call. I've kind of been . . . tied up. But I'm fine."

"You are?"

"Really, I am."

"I wish I could come on out there, but my little girl . . ."

"That's right, her ankle. How is she?"

"In a cast, but she'll be fine. But between the two of you, I think I've developed an ulcer."

Michaela laughed. This guy really cared. "I'll be back in a couple of days. I think I'll try and get some R&R.

Then, I have to figure out how to get Dwayne's horses home. The police impounded the truck and trailer. But that's the last of my worries."

"I'm working on getting Dwayne cleared of the charges. It doesn't look as if he had anything to do with his cousin's crimes."

She sighed. "Thank God."

"You *should* take some time out. See that rodeo you were talking about."

"The NFR isn't just some rodeo. It is *the* ultimate rodeo. You'd love it. Too bad you couldn't come."

"Yeah. How long you think you might stay?"

"I'll get things figured out by Sunday and leave here Monday morning."

"What are you doing on Tuesday?" he asked.

"Same old. Getting up, working horses."

"You need a coffee break?"

She smiled. "I just might. Know where I can get a good cup of Joe?"

"The Honey Bear Cottage. I like to go there around four."

"Funny. Me, too. I need a pick-me-up about that time."

"Maybe I'll see you there."

"Maybe you will." Michaela told him goodbye and donned the gorgeous, drop-dead-sexy rose-colored dress Camden had given her. She walked out into the front room of the suite. "Doesn't leave much to the imagination. Good thing I don't have big boobs, or I'd be falling out of this thing."

"For once, go with it. You look fabulous."

"I plan on it." Oddly enough she did want to look good, and although it had been one eventful day and she should be exhausted, a weight had been lifted. She knew that both Uncle Lou and Bean could now rest in peace.

They met Ethan in the lobby. Camden had done as she'd promised and arranged rooms for everyone. She had a date later on that evening with the manager.

Gosh, did Ethan look handsome in a light gray pin-striped suit and white shirt. Michaela's stomach sank.

"Look at you!" Camden said. "Didn't know you cleaned up so well."

"Thanks. I try."

"Where's the blushing bride?"

"She'll be down in a minute. Something about wanting to look perfect."

"Ah. I'm sure she will. I think I'll grab us some champagne before we head out." Camden winked at her.

Ethan smiled at Michaela and approached her.

"You okay?" she asked.

"Sure. Big step. A baby and everything."

"Yes it is."

"You do understand, don't you, Mick?"

No! she wanted to scream. *I don't understand why Summer is carrying your child and you're marrying her.* But the words that came out didn't match her feelings. "I do. You'll make a great daddy."

He hugged her. "Thanks." He kissed her on the top of her head. "You're my girl, you know."

She nodded. "I know."

"Always."

"Yep."

EPILOGUE

SAM WAS CONVICTED FOR THE MURDERS OF UNCLE Lou and Bean, as well as for fraud. Michaela received her inheritance and used some of it to pay back all of the owners of the mares who'd had foals that did prove to be out of her stallion, Rocky. The AQHA did not pursue the charges, and Michaela did move on to her uncle's ranch. Camden also moved in with Michaela and refuses to ever get involved with a man again, especially one like Kevin Tanner. Kirsten was convicted of vehicular assault, and on top of some jail time must do community service, which entails roadside litter cleanup. As far as Michaela and the rest of her family, friends, and foes, look for the next segment of The Horse Lover's Mysteries in *Death Reins In*.

AUTHOR'S NOTE

As a writer of fiction, at times for the story's sake, I might take a bit of literary license. I realize that in *Saddled with Trouble* that I did a bit of this with Dwayne Yamiguchi's character. I have been to the NFR in Las Vegas several times and have grown up around horses, so I know what it takes for the men and women of rodeo to qualify to compete at the NFR. With Dwayne's position at Uncle Lou's ranch, I realize that he probably would not, in the real world, be an NFR competitor. To compete at that level would mean a rider must be completely devoted to that task only. I completely respect the men and women of rodeo and hope you enjoy reading The Michaela Bancroft Series.

DEATH REINS IN

Death Reins In

Copyright © 2007 by Michele Scott.

All rights reserved. Except for use in any review, the reproduction or utilization of this work or in any part in any form by any electronic is forbidden without written permission of the publisher at DvinePress@gmail.com

All characters in this book have no existence outside the imagination of the author and have no relation whatsoever to anyone bearing the same name or names. They are not even distantly inspired by any individual known or unknown to the author, and all incidents are pure invention.

Printed in the U.S.A.

PROLOGUE

MEMORIES RACED THROUGH BOB PRATT'S MIND—both good and bad—as he lay gagged and bound in the trunk of the car. He hadn't seen the make or model, didn't even really know what had happened other than that he'd been ambushed from behind as he went to get into his truck at the end of the day. He'd worked late, jotting down his notes on one of Eq Tech's new supplements specifically designed for racehorses. Bob didn't even really feel it when he'd been slammed over the head—by *what* he didn't know, by whom, he could only guess at. There were a handful of enemies who'd want to see Bob in this state, and probably a few people he called *friend*. The trunk smelled like dirty socks and fast food. He could hear the faint thumpings of rap music, and he occasionally thought he might have recognized the sound of laughter coming from inside the car. Did that mean there was more than one person who'd taken him when he'd left work? Probably. At over six feet tall, he wasn't exactly a little guy. They knew he would've fought, so the sneak attack had to have been carefully planned.

His head ached as if it had been shoved into a vise, making it almost impossible to think but he wanted to try—try and play out what had happened. He needed to remember if he'd heard anyone say anything, if he'd noticed anything at all. Damn, he'd been so caught up in his findings on the new supplement that he simply had not been paying attention. He had to try though, in case he ever made it back alive. But the deep hole in his gut told him that wasn't going to happen, which led him to one continual thought streaming through his mind: his sister, Audrey, and what it would do to her if he didn't come back. Oh hell, what if his theories had been right? What if he had stumbled onto something sinister and revealed too much to her when they'd spoken the other night over dinner? He didn't think he had. As soon as she'd guessed something was wrong with him, which Audrey was so astute at, he'd tried hard to blow it off, said it was a little woman trouble, an issue at work here and there, that sort of thing. But he knew his sister well. He knew that nothing escaped her and if he'd said one wrong word, she might have picked up on it. He had to get out of this. He could feel his heart racing, beating hard against his chest, could smell the horse he'd been working with at the center on him, now mixed in with his own fear and angst.

Oh God, *what if?* What if he didn't get out of this? Poor Audrey. He'd given her problems all of their lives and now, finally, when the two of them had made amends over the past few years and grown close again, he was leaving her. All alone. He loved her. She was a good sister. She had a sweet smile, warmhearted nature, and a gentle touch with her animals that everyone who knew her admired. And she'd never given up on him. Never. She'd always believed in him and picked him up off the ground. Even when he'd turned his back on her, his sister had been right there with open arms, cheering him on. She was the reason he'd been able to not only maintain an equine veterinary practice, but also secure a position as a top researcher with Eq Tech in the very exciting fields of equine medicine and health.

The car slowed. What were they going over, an old bridge, a railroad crossing? A plume of exhaust wafted throughout the trunk, dizzying his already altered senses. Noises. More noise from outside. And the smell. It had changed, drastically. Petroleum; yes, that's what it was. And something else—food? Trash? Death? A mixture of all three. Then it hit him. They'd crossed the border. He was in Mexico. Oh Jesus, they were surely taking him there to kill him. He knew now that what he'd found out was the truth. And *they* knew he'd discovered it. A cold sweat broke out on the back of his neck.

The road wound around several curves, jostling him from side to side. Then, through the drone of the car and the grade of the trunk, he sensed they were going up a steep slope, maybe a mountain. And then he got it. He knew where they were going. Soon enough they'd be skirting the Baja coastline. He'd made this trip himself before. Would they kill him there along the highway down to Ensenada and dump his body in the ocean? Or would they take him east and leave him to rot in the desert? Either way, Bob realized he was totally screwed.

He should have lived differently. Should have made peace with the people he'd hurt. But it was too late for that, if he was right about who was behind this abduction. He would not be coming back. He'd been found out and would be dead before the sun came up. He was sure of it. Bob prayed his sister would accept that and drop it. Oh God, how he prayed for that.

ONE

MICHAELA BANCROFT SMILED AS SHE PLACED A hand over Genevieve Pellegrino's smaller one. Together they brushed the horse. Michaela spoke in calm hushed tones as the little girl's father, Joe, Michaela's good friend from childhood, had directed her. At first Michaela had been apprehensive about working with Gen. Until she started giving Gen riding lessons, Joe had never told her that Gen was autistic. She'd thought that maybe she was just quiet and a bit slow. Michaela hadn't been around Joe's family much after high school. Although they had always remained good friends, life seemed to get in the way. It was her uncle Lou's murder the previous year that had brought them back together.

"That's good. See how clean he's getting?" Michaela said. "What a good job you're doing, Gen. Look at how pretty you're making Booger. He likes that a lot." Working with the little girl was as therapeutic for Michaela as it was for Gen. Maybe even more so.

Once Booger had the saddle on him and Michaela slid a headstall over his ears, she kept him on a lead line and put Gen up, leading him to the arena. Over the course of half an hour she watched as the child relaxed into the saddle and seemed to almost become one with the horse, a smile appearing on her face as she asked him to trot. Booger performed his version, which was more of a very fast walk, semi-jog. But Gen didn't seem to care that Booger was lazy. An easy calm came over the little girl's face and she truly looked happy on the horse.

"Okay, Gen. It's time to get off now and we'll give him a brush-down. Are you ready?"

Gen nodded. Michaela helped her dismount. With a slight movement of the hand, Michaela pushed aside the strands of curly black hair that had fallen out from under Gen's helmet and into the girl's eyes. "You did a great job today. I am so proud of you." She removed the school saddle from Booger's back and set it inside the tack room, which was in serious need of an overhaul. She'd have to get on her assistant trainer, Dwayne, about that. He knew better than to keep things in such disarray.

She brought a soft bristle horse brush back to Gen and placed it into her hands. She knew to keep the barn quiet when the girl was there. No country western on the radio blaring through the breezeway, and she'd asked Dwayne to wait to turn any of the horses out. He also knew to keep his distance when Gen was there. She figured at this time, midmorning, he was likely making a feed run. They were getting low on grass hay.

As Gen slowly brushed Booger, Michaela stood back and watched her, knowing it gave the girl a sense of peace and accomplishment. There was a connection being forged between horse and child that could only benefit both of them. "Why don't we give him a treat?" she asked in a soothing tone.

She didn't get a response other than a slight glance from Gen. It was important though, she'd learned from Joe, that Gen be apprised of all that was going on. It helped her stay focused without overwhelming her. Gen handed her back the brush and followed her into the feed room; the smell of molasses and fresh-cut alfalfa perfumed the air. Michaela grabbed a blue bucket off one of the post nails and scooped it into a trashcan filled with oats. "Okay. I think he'll like this. What do you think?"

"Yes. I think so."

They gave the horse his oats, and after a good brush-down put him back in his stall. Taking him to the wash rack and bathing him would be too much for the child. She'd wait and let Katie, her afternoon student, wash him when she was finished riding.

After putting Booger away, Michaela was startled by the sound of a car horn. Oh no. She looked at Gen's face, which suddenly turned ashen. The car pulled to a stop outside the breezeway and Michaela heard Katie's voice. "Michaela, Michaela, my dad brought me early. I wanted to come help." The nine-year-old bounded down the breezeway.

Michaela started to bring a finger up to her lips to quiet the enthusiastic girl, but it was too late. Gen let out a horrible, almost primal scream. Her eyes widened with fear.

"What is it? What's wrong?" Katie yelled out, only exacerbating the problem.

Michaela was stuck between the two children and for a moment stood paralyzed, looking from one sobbing girl to the next. Regaining her wits, she went to Gen, wrapped her arms tightly around her, and in a low voice started reassuring the girl. "It's okay. It's okay. No one can hurt you. I'm here. You're safe. You're safe."

"Michaela?" Jude Davis appeared in the doorway. Katie got behind her father and peered around him, looking terrified.

"Call her parents, please, Joe and Marianne Pellegrino. Their number is on the schedule list in my office. I'm going to take her to the house." He nodded and Michaela picked Gen up, continuing to talk to her as the child began to calm down.

"Can I help you?" Jude asked.

"No, just please call her dad and ask him to come over."

Gen was a tiny girl for her age, but not so small that Michaela didn't feel her fifty-some-odd pounds in her lower back. Going through the back door, she took the girl into her family room, where she closed all of the curtains and sat the child down on the couch. Gen had stopped twisting around and now fell quiet. Ah, better; but Michaela felt horrible.

Minutes later, Joe and Marianne came through the door. "I am sorry," Michaela said.

Joe waved a beefy hand at her. "Happens." He looked like an Italian Pillsbury Doughboy, concern furrowing his bushy eyebrows. "I'm sorry we ran out on you like that." Rather than stay to watch her lesson as they usually did, Joe and Marianne had instead dropped Gen off earlier because they'd had some errands to run.

Michaela felt responsible because she'd insisted they go on ahead and take care of what they needed to with their other four kids. She'd assured them she could handle Gen. What had she been thinking?

Marianne contrasted Joe, being ramrod thin and almost frail looking. She headed straight to her daughter and turned back to Michaela as she sat down next to Gen, grappling for something in her purse, finally finding a medication bottle. "It's okay, Michaela. This happens from time to time. Do you have a glass of water? I'd like her to take this." Marianne was calm and collected. The premature lines on her face told Michaela that she shoved much of her worry into the recesses of her soul and likely dealt with them late at night, so as not to worry others in her family. She couldn't imagine what she went through day to day to manage her large brood, and Joe on top of it.

"Sure. No problem. I can't tell you how sorry I am, though." She quickly went to the kitchen for the water. Gen seemed much better when Michaela returned and handed the glass to Marianne. She watched as the woman continued to calm her child. Michaela asked Joey what the medicine was.

"Some herbal treatment. Marianne is all into these supplements and herbs and things. Next thing you know, we'll be having gurus by the house or she'll be taking the poor kid to yoga or something crazy like that." Marianne shot him a dirty look. "I'm sure they're good for her, but I'd feel better if they was FDA approved."

Marianne stood and took Gen's hand. "We better get going."

Michaela nodded.

"You did the right thing, Michaela. No sorries needed. I'd like to talk with you about what Joe and I have been up to, because it concerns you, but she gets tired after these bouts," Marianne said. "Maybe Joe can tell you while I put Genevieve in the car."

"Tell me what?"

"We've gone ahead and recommended you as a therapeutic riding instructor."

Michaela's jaw dropped.

Marianne whispered a good-bye as she walked out, and Michaela turned back to Joe. "What is she talking about? I told you I'd think about it. Why would you put in a recommendation without asking me?"

"We was thinking, Marianne and me, and we got to talking that you've been so good for Gen that we went to her therapist and the center she goes to for treatment and told them you would be perfect for the job. Therapeutic riding helps a lot of autistic kids and we don't have nothing like it out here in the desert. We think you'd be perfect for it."

"Oh no. No, I can't do that. Look what happened today. And"—She shook a finger at him—"you had no right to do that without running it by me."

"But you handled it the right way. The way you were supposed to. You love kids. You make my daughter happy. Give this a try. I see how much it does for you, too. After your divorce and then losing your uncle, I know what you've been through, and I see you smiling when you're teaching my daughter. Working with her makes you happy and you're damn good at it, and trust me, after all these years I've seen the good and the bad in this thing, and it takes quite a person to work with these kids. You got what it takes."

She shook her head vehemently. "Joe…Oh, man, I don't know." She knew that he was right about being happy when she worked with his little girl. But a center? A therapeutic center where she taught more kids? Granted, she now had the facilities to do it after inheriting her uncle's place, but could she do it? Really?

"Will you at least talk to the gal from the center?"

"I don't know, Joe. I don't think I'm cut out for it. I wouldn't want anyone to get hurt."

"No one's gonna get hurt." He raised an eyebrow, then wiggled the other. He knew how to work it. That always got her. For years she'd been trying to figure out how to wiggle just one eyebrow while keeping the other cocked.

Michaela had known Joey since junior high, when they'd bonded over pimiento loaf sandwiches, which everyone else thought were gross, and a mutual love for Billy Idol. Joe had been teased for his weight and Michaela had been on the shy side, so they'd formed a friendship that stuck over processed meat and eighties music. Joe was also known around town as the man with a million cousins. He came from a large Italian family whose ties were far reaching and, many suggested, of the unsavory nature. All Michaela knew was that Joe was a good guy with a lot of relatives, who knew how to find out information or get things done that other people seemed to have a problem doing. *And*, she was indebted to him. If not for him and the cousins, it was unlikely that the person who killed her uncle Lou last year would have been caught.

"Oh God, Joe, why do you do this stuff to me?"

"I think you should think about it," Jude said.

Michaela turned to see Jude and Katie standing in the doorway.

"Sorry," Jude said. "The door was cracked. You were talking. We didn't mean to interrupt."

Katie stood quietly next to her dad. Jude took her hand. The girl wiped her tears with her other hand. She was a petite thing with wavy, blond hair like her dad's and a splash of freckles across her nose that reminded Michaela of what she had looked like as a kid. Michaela had never lost the freckles across her nose and even sported a few more since childhood.

Joe went over to Katie. "It's okay, sweetie. She'll be fine."

Jude shook his hand. "She didn't mean to frighten her. She was excited and..."

"Hey, I got a handful of kids, and a lot of cousins." He laughed. "I know she didn't mean no harm and Michaela handled it. You talk to her, see if you can get her to agree to running a center.

"Think about it," he said as he walked out.

She walked over and pulled Katie into her. "You didn't mean to upset Gen. We all know that."

"Why did she scream like that?"

"She's autistic, honey, which means she doesn't react the same way you and I do. She actually hears and sees everything going on around her. Like, listen quietly for a minute. Really listen." They fell quiet. "Did you hear the birds outside? What about the pool running from out back? Can you hear the grandfather clock ticking from the library? And, if a horse got out, I bet we'd hear all the horses go crazy calling out to him. Gen doesn't filter out the noises in the way that we do. She hears all of them together at once and it's very loud to her. So, she kind of shuts down to keep the noises out as much as possible. To you, it probably seems like she's not friendly or she's weird. But to her, it's the only way she can handle life."

"So, when I started yelling, it scared her and on top of all the regular noises she hears it made her really scared, so she started screaming out."

"Exactly. You're a smart kid. What do we say we go have that lesson now? I didn't know you'd be early, but it works out great because I'm going to the horse races tomorrow in Orange County and I need to be at my friend Audrey's house early in the morning."

"Okay, let's go!"

Katie ran up ahead of them. Jude walked back to the barn with Michaela. "You're headed to the races tomorrow, huh? Sounds like fun," he said.

She sensed a slight hesitation in his voice. Detective Jude Davis and his daughter, Katie, had come into Michaela's life while the detective investigated her uncle's murder. Since that time they'd shared coffee dates, lots of phone calls, even a lunch and a glass of wine one night while Katie scoped out the trophies Michaela had won over the years showing horses. There was *something* between Michaela and Jude. That much she knew, but what it was exactly, she wasn't sure. "I am. My friend Audrey Pratt is taking me. We go every year. She used to work with racehorses and has a lot of friends in the industry, plus she manages a young woman who is an up-and-coming country western singer and the girl will be entertaining before the races start. I thought it would be a good time."

"Sounds like it." He cleared his throat. "Anyone else going with you?"

"Nope, just me and Audrey."

"Oh. Well, you'll be back tomorrow night, won't you?"

Michaela looked at him, her expression amused. His light blue eyes had darkened, and he palmed his hand through his hair, something he did whenever he seemed nervous. "Actually, no. I'm going on up to Malibu with Audrey to stay with the girl's mother, another friend of Audrey's. There are some horses we want to check out. I'm thinking about purchasing a few more, possibly a better lesson horse for Katie since Booger isn't much of a challenge for her. Audrey takes in animals off the track to let them retire in peace."

"Ah."

"Why do I get the feeling that you aren't too keen on me going?"

"Oh no. I think you'll have a great time."

She stopped and looked at him. "Jude? What's up?"

He sighed. "Actually...well, I wanted to ask you to dinner. That's all. I thought it was time we had dinner together. You and me. A real date. Candles, wine, flowers."

"Oh. A real date."

He nodded.

"That would be nice. Can you wait a few days?"

He smiled. "I think so." He squeezed her hand and then let it go.

Michaela's stomach dropped. She hadn't had a *real* date in years. Life was ever changing, though. She'd learned that for sure, and although she'd lost quite a bit in the past few years, it made her realize that maybe it was time to live again.

TWO

IT WAS DUSK WHEN MICHAELA WALKED BACK OUT to the barn. She figured that she'd run into Dwayne and give him a ration about the tack room. As she headed into the breezeway, she heard Hawaiian music echoing off the walls. Ah, yes, Dwayne was close by. One thing she loved about having a Hawaiian around was that he listened to such beautiful music. She closed her eyes and could almost smell plumeria instead of horse manure. Okay, so maybe not, but she wanted to.

"Michaela, Michaela!"

Her roommate, Camden, hurried toward her. Not Dwayne. Camden, in all her redheaded glory, wearing a too tight T-shirt and jeans. Wait a minute. Something was wrong with this picture. First off, Camden wasn't wearing expensive high heels. No. She was wearing boots. Cowboy boots. Working cowboy boots, and furthermore, she was in the barn. Michaela eyed her curiously.

"It's Rocky. Dwayne sent me to get you."

Rocky was Michaela's six-year-old stallion. "What's wrong?"

"I don't know," Camden said, a frantic edge to her tone.

Michaela didn't jump to any horrible conclusions, because she knew that Camden could be quite the drama queen. She hurried to the stallion's stall. Dwayne was inside. Rocky's sorrel coat gleamed with sweat. "What is it?" she asked.

"I don't know. He seem better now, but I work him on a lead line a bit ago. Didn't ride him because I notice yesterday when I did that he get tired too quick."

"He was worried about him last night," Camden interjected.

Michaela glanced from one to the other. "Last night?"

"I was coming back from shopping and saw Dwayne out here, so I stopped to say hi. He told me then that he was worried." Camden seemed flustered.

Michaela closed her eyes for a second, trying to wrap her mind around this. She held up a hand. "Okay, so Rocky was having problems last night?" She'd deal with the horse first, her friend's strange behavior later. "Why didn't anyone say anything to me?"

"No, it not like that, you know? I just thinking he be tired is all. I never say worry to her. He just being kinda slow for Rocky. Sluggish; but you know, they have moods and I figure he in one."

"Well, right now? What's going on?" Michaela placed a hand on Rocky's neck.

"His heart rate get up high and he seem...I don't know, different," Dwayne said.

"Antsy," Camden interrupted.

They both gave her a dirty look. As if the queen of Gucci and Charles David would know when a horse was *antsy*.

Camden seemed to get it. "You know, I think I'll go blend up some margaritas. Dwayne, you want to join us?"

He didn't answer. Michaela said, "We're going to take care of Rocky first. You do what you need to." She waved her off. For as much as she loved her longtime friend, she could be a royal pain in the ass.

Camden sulked away. Michaela asked Dwayne, "Did you call Ethan?"

"He be out of town."

"Oh," Michaela replied, surprised to hear that.

"The vet on call is gonna stop on by."

Michaela took the horse's pulse, which was normal. The sweat that had soaked him a few minutes earlier was beginning to dry. "He might have some kind of virus. Damn, I hate to leave him for a day."

"No. No. He be fine. I call you if there is a problem."

"No. I don't think it's a good idea. I can't leave him if he's sick. No way. I'll go crazy thinking about him. I better call Audrey and let her know that I won't make it."

"You being plain silly now, girl. You go, have fun with Audrey. Everything gonna be good. You see."

"I'll see what the vet has to say before I make a decision." She sighed and stroked the horse's neck. Looked into his eyes. "Hey, bud, what's wrong? You not feeling so good?"

The horse rubbed his face against her shoulder, wiping his wet mouth on her, smudging a mixture of dirt and hay across her navy blue T-shirt, already dirty from the day's work. She laughed. "Thanks."

"He love you. They all love you. He be fine. The vet gonna figure it out."

"Looks like the vet is here now." Michaela peered out the stall and could see a tall woman getting out of a truck.

She came over and introduced herself. "Dr. Burton," she said, hand outstretched. Michaela shook it. "Let's see what you got here." Dr. Burton certainly didn't have much of a bedside manner. She must've been new to the clinic, because Michaela had never met her before.

Dr. Burton had short brunette hair that skimmed her ears, and looked to be somewhere between forty and fifty. Hard to tell, because she had quite a bit of sun damage and deep crow's feet framing her light green eyes. She did seem to know what she was doing as she went about examining Rocky, going through every detail and checklist, after getting Dwayne's story. "I'd like to run a blood test on him."

Michaela nodded. "What are you thinking?"

"Don't know. No fever, pulse is fine, pressure is fine. Everything I'm looking at screams healthy horse. But I like to take precautions and it sounds to me like he had some type of episode. I think the best method here is to do some lab workups. I'll take a look or have Dr. Slater look and get back with you."

"Okay. Well..." She looked at Dwayne, "I think my plans for the races are a bust."

Dr. Burton looked up from her clipboard where she was making notes. "La Catalina races?"

Michaela nodded. La Catalina was a new track bordering Orange County and Los Angeles.

"No, you don't need to miss the races. The horse looks great. He might have had some kind of anxiety attack. He's fine. I won't have anything back for a day or two anyway, so if you have plans, go."

Dwayne agreed. "I tol' you, he be in good hands. Go to the races with Audrey."

"I need to draw some blood," Dr. Burton said, and walked to her truck.

"Friendly lady," Dwayne whispered.

Michaela smiled. "Listen, you really don't need to handle all of this. I'll just stay home."

"Jeez, woman, you be worse than a mother hen. No. You going. I be calling if he feeling bad. And that's that. You deserve some fun. You go, have fun. Done deal. Got it?"

She frowned. "Got it."

When Dr. Burton was finished, Michaela gave Rocky a last pat and headed down to the house. Dwayne walked toward the guest house where he resided. She called back to him, "Hey, you want that margarita?"

He jogged toward her. "You think she got them made?"

"Please. You obviously don't know Camden *that* well."

They walked into the two-story, stone-type cottage. It had been built English-country style, and that essence was captured throughout the house. Too much of a house for Michaela. She'd been grateful that Camden didn't have any plans of moving in with a new boyfriend or getting married to another rich guy who treated her like crap. Okay, she did wish that she shared the place with someone she loved. Not that she didn't love Camden, but a husband would be nice—one who didn't cheat on her, like her ex. What she really craved was to fill up the house with a bunch of children. She'd always wanted kids. But it did not look to be in her future. She hadn't been able to conceive during her marriage, even after several attempts at various fertility treatments. Now, there was no husband, no man even to be a dad to any kids, and there certainly was no sex going on in her house. At least, *she* wasn't having any. She eyed Camden standing in the huge kitchen with its dark cherrywood cabinets, oversized refrigerator with matching wood panels, a stove and oven fit for a chef, and a granite slab in the center where a pitcher held Camden's famous blended margaritas.

When Camden spotted them, she clapped her hands. "Oh goody, happy hour can commence. I am so excited. Oh, sorry. How's the horse? I didn't mean to be insensitive."

"We don't know," Michaela said. "Hopefully, it's a short-lived virus of some sort or an isolated case of anxiety that he'll work through."

Camden handed Dwayne and Michaela each a drink. They toasted. "To Rocky," Camden said.

Michaela nodded and silently prayed that her gorgeous stallion would be as fine as Dwayne had assured her.

THREE

THE NEXT MORNING MICHAELA PULLED INTO AUDREY'S ranch, Sampson's Corner, which was only ten minutes down the road. It was quite a bit smaller than her own place, but pristine. Audrey had worked alongside her husband, Charlie Sampson, for years, racing quarter horses. After Charlie died, Audrey ran the place on her own. Charlie had left her with a substantial insurance policy that kept her self-sufficient and able to take care of the horses. Money wasn't a problem, but time was. Audrey found herself needing to keep busy. That was when she'd gone back to her roots—music; she'd become a small-time entertainment manager and went back to using her maiden name, Pratt, for business purposes. She'd made a little here and there with new talent who usually wound up succeeding to a certain point with Audrey, then jumping ship to find someone bigger and better *and* located in Hollywood. The little money she made from her the management gig went back into her ranch and charity distributions. She took great pleasure in purchasing retired racehorses and providing them a home where they could live out their days in peace and solitude.

Michaela rapped on her door. Audrey appeared, smiling. "Hi honey," she said. "You ready?"

"You bet."

"Excellent." She picked up her overnight bag by the door. "I need to give Francisco some instructions. Come on out with me to the barn?"

"Sure."

They took a short walk outside to where Audrey housed her animals. She called out to her ranch hand. "Francisco?"

As they entered the breezeway, a thin, older Hispanic man appeared. *"Sí, Señora?"* He smiled and nodded at Michaela.

"I'm getting ready to head out. If you need anything, call my cell. Please feel free to eat anything you like, watch TV. The guest room is set up for you. The cat food is in the laundry room and you know what to do with the horses. My house is your house," she said in Spanish, which Michaela understood because she'd grown up on a ranch, too, often working with Hispanic grooms and ranch hands. Audrey struggled to take a key off her key ring. "Damn. Thing won't come off," she said. "It's the house key."

"I've got one," Michaela said. "From when I took care of your place a few months ago."

The key Audrey had been trying to get off came loose. "Oh no, you hang on to that just in case I'm ever in a bind and Francisco can't help out. Besides, I got it now." She handed the key to Francisco.

"Have a nice time," he said. "*Es bueno* here, okay."

Audrey smiled. "Okay. *Adios.*" They started back toward Michaela's truck. "I don't know what I'd do without him. He's been a godsend since Charlie's been gone. He takes care of everything around here for me. Even changes my car's oil when I need it."

"It's good you have him."

"It is. Oh, and it is grand to see you, Michaela. We always wait way too long to get together. For goodness sakes, you're only a few miles up the road. Life really has to stop getting in the way. I am so pleased you could join me today."

Michaela took Audrey's bag and put it in the back of the truck. Audrey, a pretty woman, looked to be aging well, with only fine lines around her lips and light green eyes, some freckles from the sun, and a hint of silver weaving through her light brown hair, which for as long as Michaela could remember had always been worn pulled straight back. When Audrey climbed into the truck, Michaela thought her thinner than usual. Though usually pleasant and generous, Audrey had a tendency to stress rather easily. Michaela hoped everything was okay with her friend.

They followed the circular drive in front of Audrey's ranch-style home. The early morning sun illuminated large paned windows that fronted the family room, a place where memories of hot chocolate with marshmallows warmed Michaela on crisp winter days after a riding lesson when she was a kid. The porch swing swayed as a slight breeze billowed down through the Coachella valley, only to be stalled by the rising dead heat of the Indio desert.

They headed down a dirt road. Beads of perspiration slid down Michaela's back as she leaned against the leather seat. She rolled down the window, the combined smell of hay, dirt, horse, and manure wafting in as they passed by Audrey's large pasture on the right, the springtime green grass beginning to yellow with the onslaught of the summer months. Rows of date palms lined the pasture fence, their olive-colored fronds casting shadows that one of the foals inside the pasture chased as he tossed his head and pawed at the ground, trying to make sense of the tricks his eyes were playing on him. All babies seemed to be ever curious of their shadows, human and horse alike. His mother and a few other horses spread out, enjoying their freedom and the grass, a couple of them hard at play, nipping at each other's rear ends, then whirling and racing down the side of the whitewashed fence, tails waving flaglike in the air, a look of wild instinct in their big brown eyes. God, they were beautiful to watch. Michaela couldn't help but smile.

They pulled out on to the highway, passing several ranches along the way, heading toward Orange County. The desert sky was cloudless, an azure blue that turned into a haze of light brown as they headed farther west. Ah, L.A.

"So, what's new? Catch me up," Michaela said.

"Good news. My brother, Bobby, is working for Eq Tech. He runs all of the research studies."

"That's great. I bet you're proud," Michaela said. She knew how close Audrey was to her only sibling and living relative. Bobby had been through a rough period over the last decade or so. He'd graduated with honors from the veterinarian school at UC Davis, but a broken heart combined with an accident where a horse had fallen on him, breaking both his hips, led him to pain medication and alcohol dependence. The addictions had consumed him for a time. But his sister never gave up on him, and about a year earlier, after paying for his treatment at the Betty Ford Center, saw him on his way to recovery. Hopefully, for both their sake, Bobby would stay clean and sober.

"I am. He's worked so hard, and they seem to be real happy with him there."

"I use some of Eq Tech's products. Good stuff. Seems to work well with my horses. Ethan recommends their products." Michaela glanced over at Audrey feeling her eyes on her.

"Ethan. Yes. Have you seen him lately?" Audrey asked, referring to Michaela's childhood friend and now veterinarian.

Michaela shrugged. "You know he comes by monthly to give Legend to one of my older mares."

"Really? I would think you could give that to her. You know how to do an IV injection."

Michaela sighed. She could see Audrey nodding and smiling from the corner of her eye. "I know what you're getting at. I like to have him out because I, well, because it's good to have him come by and I can ask hime questions about any other issues I might have with the horses."

"Uh huh. Keep telling yourself that."

"Audrey were friends. That's it. And I don't think his new wife thinks much of our friendship." Michaela waved her hand. "I don't want to go into it. Tell me more about this thing with Bob."

Audrey gave her a look that told her she'd drop the inquisition, *for now.* "Yes. Eq Tech...well, I don't use much of the supplements myself, though I have been giving some to that colt you just saw. Been awhile since I had a baby at home. Thought I might make sure he gets the best. The other horses I have are kind of pets, you know. And..." She smiled. "I suppose I pride myself in being budget-minded. Bob is good enough to give me Eq Tech samples from time to time. I just can't see spending that kind of money on vitamins."

Audrey had always been thrifty. But the woman was never cheap with her relationships. Once she made a connection it was a lifetime thing, as it had been between Michaela and her. Michaela had total respect and admiration for Audrey, who had taken her under her wing as a kid and introduced her to the show circuit. Michaela's dad and Uncle Lou had taught her the ways of the ranch and the ranch horse. She'd learned how to ride like a cowgirl. But it was Audrey who had recognized talent and put her through her paces in the show ring, until Michaela's family wound up having financial difficulties and could no longer pay the entry fees. "Yes, they are expensive vitamins."

"I'm just pleased Bob is working for them. I can't wait to get a look at his mug tonight. He had me a bit worried when I saw him recently."

"Really? Why?"

"I don't know. He seemed preoccupied. Edgy."

"Oh." Michaela didn't want to voice the question running through her mind, but Audrey answered it for her.

"No, I don't think he's using drugs again, or drinking. He just seemed distracted is all. He also gave me one of those large-sized envelopes to give to *your vet*, Ethan. I think there was a study in there he wanted Ethan to look at. He said that since we lived so close, it would be easier if I gave it to him this week because he knew that Ethan was going to be out of town for a few days and Bob was afraid he'd forget to get it to him. He knew he was going to be busy with the track and over at Eq Tech. Now, I've got that envelope out in my office in the barn, and I sure hope Ethan doesn't need it real bad. Anyway, Bob can be eccentric. When I pressed him on what was going on in his life, he told me it had to do with a woman, and some stuff going on at work. Jealousy in the company, that sort of thing. I tried to press him even more about it, but he insisted it was nothing. He clammed up and it bothered me, but I know my place, and I figured it was time for me to shut up, if you know what I mean. If you see *your vet* before I do, let him know that I have a file Bob thought he might want to look at. Some kind of research thing apparently."

"I'm sure Bob is fine, and it'll be great to see him. I think it's been a couple of years since I saw him last." And, Michaela recalled, it hadn't been pretty. A drunken Bob Pratt had made a scene at Audrey's Memorial Day party. She decided against bringing it up. "What do you think? Today's races going to be fun? It seems like every year, there's some type of craziness going on. If we don't hear about someone screwing someone over, or screwing someone else's wife, then it wouldn't be the races. What good dirt do you think we're in for today?"

"Oh, honey, today's races will be more than dirty. I am afraid the shit might fly. I got a feeling that today might prove to be downright…well, how do I put this? Different to say the least and sticky—even ugly—if I don't watch my step. I'm going to need your help to make it through."

Michaela stared at her, at first thinking she was kidding. But the strain in Audrey's face told Michaela that she was dead serious.

FOUR

"WHAT DO YOU MEAN?" MICHAELA'S STOMACH tightened. "I don't like the sound of that."

"You know, I realize that you've only met Kathleen Bowen a few times and she's even more high maintenance since the divorce." Audrey shook her head. "She's just not herself, and I need to ask a favor of you. It would be a good idea if you didn't mention that we're going over to Hugh's place tomorrow morning to look at horses."

"You mentioned to me that we were going to check out horses, but you didn't say anything about doing it at Hugh Bowen's place."

"I didn't?" Audrey asked, not convincingly.

"No. I think I'd remember that. It's not exactly every day that I visit the wealthiest and most famous racing quarter horse breeder in the country, not to mention restaurateur."

"Well, honey, it's not as if you haven't met Hugh before. We've known each other for years."

"I know, but, I haven't been to his place. It's kind of...I don't know, overwhelming. I understand it's the Taj Mahal of training facilities."

"True. Hugh, he's good man. Good natured. Even so, he's Kathleen's ex-husband, and she *is* my friend."

"Let me guess, she has that you-can't-talk-to-my-ex thing going on?"

"It goes a bit deeper," Audrey replied. "It has to do with Olivia."

"Their daughter is an adult; what's the deal?" Michaela asked. "Don't tell me they've pinned the kid between them. I hate when parents do that." In some ways, Michaela was happy she'd never been able to have a baby with her ex-husband. Surely she'd have figured him out at some point and wanted out of their marriage, and she'd never want to put a child through that. Her parents had been married for forty years and counting, and she was thankful they'd stayed together throughout the years, for better or worse.

"Kathleen has very high expectations for her daughter. She wants Olivia to be the next Carrie Underwood. And she could very well be on her way after tonight. Being a part of the opening entertainment is great for her. She's on right before Steve Benz."

"I've heard of him."

"He's moving his way up the charts; she's not yet. He's becoming quite the star, and Kathleen wants to see the same thing happen for her daughter. You know why I manage Olivia's career, don't you?"

"Because you're connected and you were in the business yourself for years," Michaela replied.

Audrey shook her head and frowned. "Sure, I thought I'd be the next Dolly Parton or Loretta Lynn. I started out my music career playing with Kathleen. It's how we became friends."

"I know."

"Anyway, Kathleen and I were wonderful together. We played some great gigs, then she met Hugh and got pregnant, and as Hugh's restaurant business took off, our career nose-dived. I don't know that many people in the biz anymore. As far as connections go, they're minimal at best. I've been able to get Olivia some decent gigs here and there, but nothing spectacular."

"Today's event is no small feat," Michaela said. "You should be proud of it. Olivia and her mom must be thrilled."

"I didn't land tonight's event for Olivia. Her father did it for me."

"Ah, now I'm catching on," Michaela said. "It's obvious that you and him have remained friends after the divorce. You've bought horses from him for quite some time, haven't you?"

Audrey nodded slowly. "True, but the divorce only happened a couple of years ago and..."

"And Kathleen doesn't know you still deal with Hugh. If she did, she wouldn't be too happy about it." Michaela knew of Audrey's long history with the Bowen family.

"Bingo. Hugh wasn't exactly graceful in his exit from Kathleen's life, but my friend was also no angel. No one was right in that mess, and I do agree with Kathleen on one thing: That new wife of Hugh's is no peach. She's a real pain and has driven quite a wedge between Olivia and her father. The only reason I'm managing Olivia's career is because Kathleen can't stand the idea of having her father involved in it. Olivia's dad can do things for her career that I can't. He's got the money and he *does* have connections. Today proves it, and Olivia has the talent to be a megastar, but I can't take her there. And honestly, I don't think the girl wants to be one. Olivia has her own dreams. She wants to be a jockey."

"Interesting," Michaela said. She could hear the tension in Audrey's voice. Audrey's own dreams hadn't panned out, and there were regrets. She'd always encouraged Michaela to go after her dreams, just like her uncle had. What she didn't understand was that if Olivia did have this dream of racing horses, then why was Audrey involved in the singing part? "She's certainly petite enough. And, I'm sure she's grown up riding. Why doesn't she pursue her dream? I admire it."

"It is quite a dream. You know it's not easy for a woman riding in your circuit. Racing is probably even more difficult. The sexism is ridiculous. A lot of owners don't think a woman can ride as well as a man, and I've heard stories where an owner will let a woman ride the worst of his horses. There are also some sleazy trainers and owners out there who will allow a woman to ride for certain...favors."

"But Olivia shouldn't have to deal with that, with her dad being an owner. She could ride one of his horses. Can't she talk to him about this?" Michaela felt terrible for the girl.

"It's complicated, like I said. Olivia is angry with her father over leaving her mom and remarrying. Kathleen is even more pissed at him and she'd come undone if Olivia started racing. Yes, Olivia can ride, but her mother won't hear of it. She is a complicated woman. She worries like crazy about Olivia but then pressures her into a business the girl doesn't want to be involved in. She's kind of pathetic. You'll see what I mean. I think Olivia somehow feels responsible for her mother's happiness since the divorce, so she keeps up the singing to please her."

"And you are caught in the middle." Michaela figured that, because Audrey had been friends with both Hugh and Kathleen for years and she adored Olivia, she felt totally stuck. "What are you going to do?"

"I don't know what I can do. I do love Olivia as if she were my own," Audrey replied. "But she isn't, and if I cause a rift, not only will I lose my friendships with Hugh and Kathleen, I may lose my connection with Olivia. So, you understand why when we see Kathleen this afternoon, we don't mention anything about Hugh? She would be horrified to learn we're going to his place, especially if the new wifey is around, and she very well could be. I don't think she goes too far from anything that glitters, and Hugh Bowen has plenty of glitter."

Michaela agreed that mum was the word. Audrey sighed heavily as they pulled in to the front gates at La Catalina, causing her to wonder if there was more on her friend's mind than what she'd revealed during the drive to the races.

FIVE

AS MICHAELA GOT OUT OF THE TRUCK WITH AUDREY, the sights and sounds instantly made her smile. The blurs of bright color, people chatting, laughing, the clip-clop of horses' hooves as they were lead into the paddock for the preview of things to come, the drone of tractors dragging the track, all of it spoke of great history and tradition. What was there not to love about a sunny Southern California Saturday at the races?

"I need to check in with Olivia. She should be getting ready for the show," Audrey said, taking Michaela's hand and leading her like a child, which had always been her way. Michaela had only met Olivia twice, but she'd heard quite a bit about her from Audrey over the years. Olivia was getting ready in a room off to the side of the racetrack restaurant, reserved for VIPs.

Michaela was a bit surprised to see a meek young woman putting her makeup on. She knew Olivia to be shy. But this woman—girl, really, from the looks of her—was pale and thin. Dark circles under her glassy blue eyes made her look gaunt. Her long blond hair hung loose down near her hips. Still, she was beautiful, with an almost haunting presence. "Hi," she said, spotting them, an edge of sadness in her tone.

"Hi, honey. You look wonderful."

"Thank you. My mom says I need some more shimmer and glimmer." She frowned. "She doesn't think jeans and this blouse are appropriate," she said sarcastically, holding the ends of a flowing-type blouse, which was white with a pattern of small red roses throughout. It was on the hippy side of apparel. But it worked well for what Olivia was about: a slightly artsy, folksy sort, like an Alanis Morissette meets Tori Amos. Man, did Michaela want to run out and get her a cheeseburger. No, make that a double double. The kid needed to put on some weight.

Audrey waved a hand at her. "What does she know, right? You look wonderful. You remember Michaela Bancroft? You met her at one of my Halloween parties."

Olivia nodded. "Oh, hey, hi." She reached her hand out and shook Michaela's with the grip of a child.

"Olivia," Audrey implored, "that's not the way you greet a guest."

"Sorry." Olivia rolled her eyes. "Good afternoon, Ms. Bancroft."

Maybe it wasn't sadness Michaela detected in her tone, but surliness. It had to be the fact that she was malnourished that made her come off as irritable. "Please, call me Michaela. I feel so old when someone calls me Ms. Bancroft. Plus, I feel like I've known you forever. Audrey talks about you all the time. She's very proud of you."

"At least someone is." Olivia turned back to face the mirror. She glanced back through it at Michaela.

"I'm looking forward to hearing you sing."

"Whatever."

"Olivia!" Audrey said. She led Michaela a few steps away and lowered her voice. "I apologize for her. She's not herself these days. I don't know what has gotten into her."

Michaela waved a hand. "No biggie. She's a kid. They have moods. Trust me, I'm not taking it personally."

"Hey, sweet thing." A young man who Michaela thought she recognized breezed into the room past Audrey and Michaela, and strode on over to Olivia. He held a large bouquet of red roses. "I wanted to give these to you personally. They are from me and Marshall, and we want to thank you for opening for me today. I know you'll be awesome," he said, a southern twang icing his words. Audrey stepped between Olivia and the man, her arms crossed. "Hey, mama, what you doing? I am trying to talk to the little sweet thing there and why are you getting in my way? Do you know who I am?"

"Steve Benz," Audrey answered, her lips pursed.

Michaela knew she'd seen him before, maybe in some ad or on TV. She wasn't sure. He looked like someone who should be on TV, with his long brown hair, sculpted face, and pretty hazel eyes. They were pretty. Hell, *he* was pretty. That much she was sure of. But his personality sucked. What a pompous jerk.

"That's right. That is who I am." He tried to step around Audrey.

"I'm Miss Bowen's manager, and I'll accept those for her. Thank you. She is not interested in speaking with your manager, Marshall Friedman, or you, for that matter. If you cannot leave respectfully, I will call security."

Benz laughed. "Security. You are funny, Audrey Pratt." He shook a finger at her. "Ah, you didn't think that I knew who you were. I do and so does Marshall, and let me just say that your days are numbered running this young lady's career. Like *sayonara*, mama. Marshall will have her under contract in a week. You'll see."

"Steve, I think you should go," Olivia quietly said.

"No problem, sweet thing. Knock 'em dead. See you soon." He winked at her. Then he turned his attention to Michaela and eyed her up and down. "Hmm, hey sugar, aren't you fine. Wanna ride in my limo later?"

Michaela was speechless for about three seconds. She shook her head, her eyes forming into slits as she eyed him back. "You're kidding me."

"Oh, sugar, I would never kid about a thing like that. We can go for a long ride around town. Maybe wind up in some swanky Beverly Hills bar, then who knows. You'd like that, wouldn't you? I can tell by the way you're looking at me."

Michaela cleared her throat. "You know, Steve, as appealing as that sounds, I actually think I'd rather have dinner with a horse." Okay, she knew it was probably one of the lamest comebacks in history, but at that moment she was at a loss for words; the man was so repulsive.

"You're into that, huh? I'm sure we could arrange it."

"Get the hell out of here!" Audrey yelled.

He set the roses down. "You'll be sorry you talked to me like that. And you"—he pointed at Olivia—"will want to jump on board. Trust me. Money is good, the gigs are good. We'll talk later. Don't forget your roses, sweet thing. Bye, sugar." He looked at Michaela, who scowled.

She couldn't help but feel the need to shower after meeting Steve Benz.

Audrey turned to Olivia. "Have you been talking with that guy or Marshall Friedman?"

Olivia shook her head.

"Olivia," Audrey implored.

"My mom did. Once. They've been trying to get ahold of me."

Michaela watched Audrey's face turn a shade of red. Anger didn't cross her friend's features often, but right now she was sufficiently pissed off. "Olivia, those assholes will ruin you. I plan to speak to your mother."

Yep, Audrey was mad.

"You think if you go and sign with Friedman and do a record with Steve Benz, which is what I'm sure they're trying to talk to you about, it will make your mother happy?" Olivia's eyes widened. "If you do that, they will ruin you. They are all about the money. The next thing you know you won't be able to live your own damn life. You have dreams that I'm trying to protect. Still trying to make happen for you."

"That will never happen," Olivia muttered. "You know it will never happen. God, I just wish everyone would leave me alone. Everyone always wants something from me. Leave me alone!" she yelled. "Nothing good will ever happen! My dreams are shit and you know it!"

"Olivia." Audrey stood over her. Both women were petite but Audrey's presence was strong and overpowered the girl. "Those dreams will happen for you. Give me time. I am doing everything I can."

"I want to be left alone. That's all I want."

"That's not true. You can't be left alone," Audrey replied. "Look what you've gotten yourself into already, and this Benz character and his manager will only make matters worse. They see dollar signs flashing in front of them and if you—if *we*—allow your mother to dictate what you're going to do with your life, you will be miserable. I am convinced of it."

Olivia shook her head, her eyes welling up. Tears snaked down her face. Hmm, weren't the races supposed to be fun?

Michaela felt like an intruder on a conversation that had likely gone rounds before. She decided to exit while Audrey and Olivia hashed this out. Before leaving, she told Audrey she needed to go to the rest room and asked her for her ticket. Audrey pulled it from her purse. "I'll see you in Kathleen's box," she said tersely.

Michaela stepped outside the dressing room and took a deep breath. The simple earthen smells of horse, dirt, and southern California smog invaded her senses. Maybe it was time for a glass of champagne. Not a usual indulgence for her, but wow, what a scene. She'd never seen Audrey so intense or protective over someone. Maybe that was because she'd never had children of her own. Michaela knew there was a strong bond between her and Olivia. There seemed to be more to it than that, though. Oh well, it really was none of her business. If Audrey wanted to share it with her, then she would.

She headed to the bar, feeling good that she looked fairly close to the part of wealthy racehorse owner, trainer, or something to do with racehorses, like the other ritzy patrons. She didn't necessarily enjoy the dress-up-and-toot-your-horn crowd, but she also found it worse to stand out in these groups. The more you fit in, the less chance you had of actually being noticed. No, she felt like she blended in. Thanks to Camden and her wardrobe and the fact that the two of them wore the same size. Camden had insisted she wear a pretty, flowing, Anne Taylor spaghetti-strap dress. It was a chiffon-type material with an empire waist, red on top and pale yellow on the bottom with a red flower pattern. She'd also borrowed a pair of red slingback sandals from Camden, but found them difficult to maneuver in. With the Chanel No. 5 she'd sprayed on and the reapplication of the blush-colored lipstick she wore for ventures out, Michaela couldn't help feeling like she belonged, until she saw all the diamonds and pearls in the line at the bar, not to mention the hats. Should have listened to Camden for once. She'd told her to wear a hat, even showed her a simple, lovely pale yellow hat that matched the dress perfectly. But Michaela wasn't a hat person, unless it was a helmet for riding or a cowboy hat in the show arena. She saw them as pretentious and…well, yep, pretentious. Hmm, maybe she should have worn a hat.

"Kir Royal?"

Michaela glanced behind her as she felt a whisper tickle her ear. "Excuse me?"

"You look like a Kir Royal. I mean, like the kind of woman who would order one."

The man speaking to her was beautiful. It was that simple. He had a Robert Redfordesque thing, circa 1980, going on. He was probably in his forties. Gorgeous blue eyes that took her breath away, blond hair that dipped into his eyes which he kept brushing back. Skin that looked as if he'd just come back from some island escape. Camden would definitely approve of his physique, and especially his attire—had to be Armani or some such designer. *Divine* was the only word that came to mind. Again she thought of Camden, who used that adjective on many occasions to describe men she met, but never had that word crossed Michaela's mind until now. Then, she caught herself, because that was not how she thought of men. No. She was not one of those women who went for looks and no substance. But, wait a minute, how did she know this man had no substance? Anyone who looked as handsome as he did couldn't have any substance. Obviously! She found herself coyly replying, "Really? And how does a woman who would order a Kir Royal look?" Now where in the world had that come from?

"I don't know. Sophisticated, educated, intelligent, good taste but not materialistic. A good woman. A beautiful woman."

Michaela couldn't help but laugh. "How often does that line work for you?"

He smiled. "Often."

"I'm sure."

"Hudson Drake." He shook her hand with a nice, strong handshake.

"Michaela Bancroft."

"Do you have a horse running?"

She laughed again. "No. I actually train reining horses. I'm here with a friend of mine."

"A gentleman, I take it."

The man was interested in her. Michaela felt heat throughout her body. She *was* just like Camden. Put a pretty face in front of her and it was as if the brain cells suddenly all died and she went all gaga. Memories of her ex-husband, Brad, ran through her mind. Another pretty boy—bad news. "No," she said, surprising herself. Why couldn't she lie, even to a stranger? He smelled good though. Maybe that was why? Oh boy, the brain cells had definitely exited the brain. His smell. Mmm. Like cedar and vanilla, maybe some musk thrown in. "An old friend. We're in Kathleen Bowen's box."

"Really? I'm good friends with her ex, Hugh."

"Huh," was all Michaela could utter. It was her turn to order a drink.

Hudson Drake stepped in front of her. "Kir Royal and a dirty martini, strong."

"Thank you," Michaela said as the bartender handed them their drinks and Hudson paid. "You didn't have to do that."

"I wanted to."

"So, you know Hugh?"

He nodded. "And Kathleen and their daughter, Olivia. The entire crew."

"How do you know them?"

He took a sip from his drink. "I'm the CEO at Eq Tech. Hugh is one of our major investors; we've been friends for some time."

"My friend, actually the woman I came here with, her brother works for you."

"Who is that?"

"Bob Pratt."

Something in Hudson's eyes darkened.

"What? Did I say something wrong?"

He didn't answer her right away, taking a sip from his drink and looking as if he were trying to carefully select his words. "It's...about Bob. I probably need to speak with your friend."

"What? Why?"

"I didn't know when or how long I should wait before I called her. I keep thinking that..." He took another sip. Worry wrinkled his forehead. "Really, I should speak with her."

Hudson Drake had her concerned now. "I've known Audrey for a long time. And, you are scaring me. I don't like your tone or what I'm reading from you. Can't you please tell me what's going on?"

He brought the drink to his lips again, taking a gulp. What in the hell was going on? After a few seconds he nodded. "Okay. Maybe I should tell you, and see what you think. I might be jumping the gun talking to his sister. At least that's what I want to believe. Bob hasn't shown up for work since Tuesday."

SIX

"THREE DAYS?" MICHAELA SAID. "YOU HAVEN'T SEEN Bob in three days?"

He nodded. "Yeah. Today being Saturday means it's been four days, but it is the weekend, so it's not as if he'd be at work anyway. I've called his house, his cell phone, even stopped by his place last night. No one there."

"Have you called the police?"

He sighed. "No. I...listen, how much do you know about Bob's past?"

"Enough to know that you might be thinking he fell off the wagon and is out on a bender, and you're trying to maintain status quo before rushing to the worst possible conclusion," Michaela replied.

He smiled. "I knew I liked you. That's exactly what I'm thinking. I like Bob. He's a good man, and sometimes things happen. He mentioned that a woman he was seeing was really sick—I think he said that she had cancer—and she didn't want to see him any longer. When he didn't show up on Wednesday, I thought that maybe he wasn't feeling well. I was in and out of meetings all day. Maybe I missed his call. I don't know. Then, on Thursday, I started to grow concerned. But I didn't want to alert his family—his sister—right away because what if all it turned out to be was that he was holed up somewhere with some booze? Once he came out of it, he'd realize what he'd done. He's a smart guy. He knows I won't can him over this. I am all about second chances, and trust me, Bob is a good enough vet and scientist that I don't want to lose him. I've gone back and forth on calling his sister. I didn't want to upset her or cause problems."

"I hear you...but he needs to be found. I think you're probably right. I know he's fought this battle off and on for some time, but still, he needs help."

"You think I should tell his sister, then?" Hudson asked.

Michaela shrugged. "Audrey needs to know. It's that simple. I think I should tell her, though. She doesn't know you, and it might be better coming from me."

"I agree. Whatever she'd like me to do; I can call the police or a private investigator if we need one. However she thinks it should be handled. I was thinking maybe I could visit some of the bars he used to go to, but I'm not sure what they would be."

"She might know."

"Thank you. You've been a godsend. I can't tell you how stressed I've been over this. Bob was supposed to vet here today and I'd hoped he would show up, but so far he hasn't. Maybe he'll come through. Come to his senses."

"I hope so." Michaela dreaded having to tell Audrey this news, but she really didn't have a choice. She needed to know what was going on, and together they could find out where Bob was and what had happened. She tried to keep thoughts of the worst at bay. She'd dealt with addictions in her own family with her dad, who had a gambling problem. She knew the strain it put on a family, and she knew how all-consuming it could be for the addict. So consuming, in fact, that it could cause someone to fall off the face of the world and not return for some time. She even doubted that the police would get too involved if they were aware of Bob's past and his struggles with alcohol and pills. Still, a nagging sensation in her gut made her wonder if there was something more to Bob's disappearance. She knew from Audrey how wonderful he'd been doing, how much he enjoyed his new job. But Audrey had mentioned to her this morning that she'd been concerned about Bob's behavior recently. Poor Audrey. On top of her issues with Olivia and the rest of the Bowen family, the woman didn't need any more stress.

Hudson reached into his coat pocket and pulled out a couple of business cards, handing them to her. "Those are my numbers. Maybe one of you could give me a call?"

"Sure."

"Well, I've got a box full of people, I better get back."

"Okay. It was nice to meet you, and thanks for the drink."

"I couldn't pass up an opportunity to meet a Kir Royal girl."

She laughed.

"Hey, would you like to join me in my box?" Hudson asked.

Her stomach sank again. "I can't. I'm with Audrey and as I said, we were invited to sit in Kathleen Bowen's box."

"I understand." He paused for a minute. "You know, I have this benefit to go to next weekend. I hate those things, but would you like to go with me? That would sure make it less unbearable. It's a good cause. Some of the same people here today will be there. We're raising money for handicapped riders."

"I don't live here. I'm from Indio." Now, why hadn't she simply responded with a *No, thank you*? Them dead brain cells again. She did like the sound of what the benefit was for, especially since she was working with Gen and thinking about running her own therapeutic riding program.

"That's not a problem." He pulled a handful of keys from his jacket pocket and took one off the ring. "This is to an apartment I own in Century City. Actually, the company owns it. We let associates or reps coming in for the weekend that kind of thing, stay there. Why don't you come and stay for the weekend, go to the benefit? You can do your own thing: shop, relax, whatever you want."

Michaela looked at the key, stunned. "I don't shop much. I don't know you. I like you fine. You seem nice and..." He certainly was handsome. "But, I can't do that."

"Why not?"

"I just can't." Okay, once again, a simple *No, thank you*, would have sufficed.

He frowned. "Are you seeing someone?"

A vision of Jude came to mind. "Sort of."

"In my book a sort of is not a yes or no. All I'm asking is for you to come to the benefit with me. Not a date. Join me, stay in the company apartment. We'll have fun and that'll be that. It's for a good cause."

She looked down at the key in her hand. She couldn't do that, could she? What about Jude? It *was* a good cause...and Jude and her weren't dating, not yet, not technically. "Okay. I'll go."

"Good." He wrote down the address on the back of his card. "Why don't you call me this week and I'll give you directions?" He winked at her and walked away.

Talk about blurred boundaries. Now why had she gone and done that? Here she'd had thoughts of staying far away from men, after what she'd been through with Brad. But she'd allowed Jude to get close to her, and now she was accepting a date from a stranger. And, not just a date, but to stay in his apartment? Well, his company's apartment. What had she just done? One thing was for certain: Camden would be proud. Yes, indeed, she'd for sure get the "You go, girl," from her pal. Maybe there *was* something to this blurred boundary thing. Certainty was comfortable. But at that moment she felt a sense of excitement that she hadn't experienced in quite some time. Yes, maybe it was time to blur the lines.

SEVEN

WHEN MICHAELA MADE IT TO THE BOX, SHE WAS relieved to find herself alone for a moment. She scanned the crowd, noticing all the usual suspects and many not-so-usual suspects. The quarter horse races at La Catalina were a little different than Thoroughbred racing. More cowboy hats and less suits, more down-home Americana and less celebrity fare, but still plenty of folks with champagne tastes, and they'd get what they'd come here for—a run for their money and *much* more. June, in what could be considered muggy for the OC; the quarter horses would be running today. Quarters ran shorter, faster races compared to the Thoroughbred, and "the quarter-mile race" was how the quarter got its name. Back in the day, the original cowboys enjoyed racing their ponies for quarter miles, discovering they were sprinters and had extreme speed from the get-go, but weren't endurance runners like the Thoroughbred—thus the quarter horse breed was born.

Michaela set down her Kir Royal, now nearly finished, and smiled. She dug through her purse, locating a rubber band to hold her blond hair. Thankfully, the box was in the shade.

"Not bad, huh?" Audrey walked into the box. "The seats. It pays to have friends in high places."

"I can see that. You okay? That scene with Olivia didn't seem too pleasant."

"Nothing I can't handle. She's having a rough patch of it right now. We'll get through it. I see you've been to the bar." She walked around the back of the row of seats and over to a table where a bottle of champagne chilled. "I don't think Kathleen will mind. It appears as if she's already begun." She held the bottle up, which was half empty. Audrey poured herself a glass and refreshed Michaela's. She nodded to her. "A toast to Olivia today…and

Kathleen's horse Halliday. He's a fine animal. Expected to win. We should definitely go and place a bet on him."

Michaela nodded. "To Olivia and Halliday it is."

"Here, here," another woman's voice from behind them rang out. Kathleen Bowen entered the box. "I will second that. To my daughter and my horse. Shall they both be winners today." She smiled brightly, her gray eyes—the same color as her pageboy-coiffed hair—lit up, emphasizing the deep lines around her eyes and mouth. Kathleen was a smoker and a sun lover, both of which had taken their toll on her face. "Nice to see you again, Michaela," Kathleen said, stubbing out her cigarette and blowing the smoke away from Audrey and Michaela. "Good of you to make it. Hope my horse wins and my daughter breaks a leg." She gave Audrey a hug. "And, how are you? You look great as always. Have you seen Olivia?" She asked, and took a sip of champagne from the flute she was holding.

"Just came from there," Audrey said. "You look great, too. Big day."

"Mmm, yes it is." Kathleen set her champagne down after taking another long sip.

"What time will Olivia go on?" Michaela asked.

"Soon." Audrey checked her watch. She glanced around.

"You sure you're okay?" Michaela asked. Poor Audrey. How was she going to tell her what Hudson Drake had related about Bob? She had to, though. It wasn't something that could wait.

"Sure. A bit nervous is all. You know, for Olivia."

"She'll be great," Kathleen said and tilted the light pink hat she wore with her matching Chanel suit. "I know it. My girl can sing. And, my horse can run. Going to kick Hugh's horse's ass. He'd better anyway. I'd love to see Hugh eat crow, along with that two-bit whore he married."

"Now Kathleen," Audrey said, "I thought you were past being bitter."

"Bitterness has nothing to do with the truth. And you know that I'm saying the truth. You know, I really don't want to be angry at Hugh or bitter about any of it. I wish I could let it all go. Wash my hands. It's crazy, but I still love him. He was the love of my life. How can you be married to someone for twenty-five years and then throw it away?"

Audrey sipped her champagne but didn't respond.

"Look ladies, I think the show is about to start. Audrey, would you mind pouring me another glass of champagne?" Kathleen handed her the glass. Michaela walked over to the champagne with Audrey, who leaned in and whispered in Michaela's ear as an announcer bellowed from the infield, "She gets tipsy easily, and then she gets on the Hugh kick and there's no stopping her. Be prepared. I can't tell you how many nights in recent months have started out with her in a great mood, only to turn dark as soon as she's knocked back a few and started walking down memory lane."

"I think I can handle it," Michaela said. "Look, there's something I have to tell you—"

"Hurry up, ladies. Sit, sit," Kathleen ordered.

"Can it wait? I think we better take a seat and prepare for the entertainment," Audrey replied.

Could it wait? Michaela struggled with that for a minute. She could tell Audrey about her brother now and have her fretting during Olivia's performance, possibly ruining the experience for her completely, or she could at least wait until Olivia was finished. It wasn't as if Audrey could do anything about her brother at that moment anyway. "Sure, it can wait."

"Good afternoon, ladies and gentleman. It's a great day for the races, isn't it?" The crowd's applause and cheers echoed through the stands at the announcer's intro.

Michaela noticed that Audrey took another sip of champagne but did not applaud, while Kathleen on the other hand was squealing with delight.

"You should be really proud of yourself," Michaela told Audrey, hoping to ease her nerves about Olivia's performance.

Before Audrey could reply, the announcer welcomed "Up-and-coming superstar Olivia Bowen," to the stage.

The crowd went nuts again, especially Kathleen, who cried, "That's my baby! That's my girl!"

Olivia appeared on stage, her ethereal beauty causing many to pause and study her. "Hi everyone," she said, seeming uncomfortable.

"Goodness. I told her not to wear that. She is such a beautiful girl. Why does she have to cover herself up in a frock?" Kathleen turned to Audrey.

"You know that Olivia is shy. It's her nature, Kathleen. You may have to accept that. It doesn't take away the fact that she has talent."

"You think that Simpson girl has any talent? Ha! My daughter is far prettier and more talented, but you know why that blondie is always topping the charts? It's because she knows how to work it." Kathleen muttered something under her breath. Michaela couldn't hear what she said, but it likely wasn't a pleasantry.

Michaela squeezed Audrey's arm as Kathleen turned back to watch Olivia sing her first song: a beautiful rendition of "Blue Moon." "Don't listen to her. You're doing everything right for Olivia and you know it. It's the way you've always been with us kids. Well, I guess I'm not a kid anymore."

"Oh, honey, you'll always be a kid to me. But what do you mean?"

"I mean, you've always let us be exactly who we wanted to be. You allowed me to explore various aspects of riding and I wound up finding my niche in reining. I'm sure you would have liked to see me go down the path of say, maybe hunter jumping, or even racing?"

Audrey smiled at her. "Hmm. That *is* what I had in mind."

"Right. But I would have been the tallest jockey in town. Granted I'm no giant, but not many are five foot six." Michaela pointed at her. "Regardless, you still let me go where I needed and wanted to, and that is what you're doing for Olivia."

"I don't know about that."

When Olivia finished with "Blue Moon," she played an original song of hers, which was more upbeat, and she had the crowd on their feet clapping. Kathleen turned. "Amazing. She is amazing. I know she's going to be a superstar."

Once Olivia was done with her set, Steve Benz came on and rocked the crowd with his mixture of good looks, rock 'n' roll moves, and sweet southern sound. Even so, Michaela's brief encounter with him had soured her on enjoying his performance.

"I can see why he's a star," Kathleen said as he left the stage. "I think I'll go and refresh my drink, maybe see if I can spot anyone I know before the race starts, and get a look at Halliday." She held up a pair of crossed fingers. "Come with me?"

Before Audrey could respond, Michaela said, "I think we have some bets to place, don't we, Audrey?" She wanted a chance to speak with her about Bob.

"We do."

"I'm sure you're betting on my horse, aren't you? The odds are in Halliday's favor."

"Of course," Audrey replied as they left the box.

They entered the betting lines. Standing in line, Michaela turned to her. "Audrey, when was the last time you spoke with—"

"Audrey!" an older man shouted out as he approached them. Michaela recognized Hugh Bowen. She glanced at Audrey and caught a genuine smile spreading across her friend's face. That was the first time today that Audrey had *really* smiled, and it lit her up.

Hugh leaned in and kissed Audrey's cheek, then Michaela's. His thick silver hair, dark brown eyes, and navy blazer paired with khakis gave him quite the distinguished look. He definitely appeared happier than his ex-wife. "Olivia was wonderful up there. I am so proud of her and everything you've done," he said.

"I haven't really done anything," she replied.

He waved a hand at her. "Nonsense. I take it you're in Kathleen's box?"

"We are." Audrey sighed.

Hugh placed a hand on Michaela's shoulder. "So, you two are coming by tomorrow to take a look at some of my retirees, huh? Audrey mentioned your new venture into giving riding lessons."

"I've got a couple of students right now, and may be taking on some more," Michaela replied.

"Sounds great. I think I have some horses that might work for you. So, Kathleen pressuring you to bet on Halliday, I suppose? It's not a bad bet. But you may want to put some money down on my guy—Flashing Chico. I've got a good feeling about him, and I've got one of the best jockeys around up on him—Enrique Perez. The man can ride. Plus, I've been watching this horse out on the track every morning this week and he has it. It's a gut thing. His times have been phenomenal. Since your brother had me put him on Eq Tech's new supplement, I think it really is improving this horse's speed. I'm a real believer in that stuff."

"Bobby is here today, isn't he?" Audrey asked. "He's vetting the track, right?" she asked, a note of apprehension to her voice.

Michaela looked at Hugh Bowen. Did he know that Bob hadn't shown up at work? Oh no. Maybe she should have told Audrey before now. She wanted to jump in and tell her what Hudson Drake had told her, but she couldn't find the words.

"Should be. I haven't seen him. I missed the vet check earlier, but I'm sure my trainer and jockey saw him. He's probably swamped. You know what it's like. He's probably busy testing and checking everything. Quit worrying about him. He's doing great. I saw him the other day and he's fine. Trust me, the man is back on his feet again."

Michaela swallowed hard. Hugh had seen Bob the other day? Which day? This was getting really complicated. How would she break it to Audrey that it wasn't looking as though her brother was really back on his feet, but had taken a step backward?

"I can thank you for that, too," Audrey replied.

"Audrey, I don't know why you won't ever take any credit. You do so much for everyone." He reached out and took her hand. The touch was somehow intimate, and the way they looked at each other further cemented that thought in Michaela's mind. She noticed Hugh squeeze Audrey's hand and then let it go, the two of them smiling at each other.

Okay, *something* was going on between these two. Michaela wasn't quite sure what it was, but her friend had some explaining to do about Hugh.

"Hughie, sweetie, c'mon. They're about to run. Let's go." They all turned around to see Bridgette Bowen, Hugh's trophy wife, hollering out to him—tall, voluptuous, blue-eyed and dark-haired, and about twenty years younger than him. She walked over to them. "Hi, ladies." She stretched out her hand to Michaela. "Bridgette Bowen. You must be a friend of Audrey's. Hello, Audrey."

"Bridgette."

Michaela shook her hand. "Hi, I am. Michaela Bancroft. Nice to meet you."

"Pleasure is mine. You two should come by after the races. We're having a get-together at the house."

"Thank you, Bridgette," Audrey said coolly, "but we have plans."

"If you change your mind, you are more than welcome." Bridgette started to walk away. "Come on, hon."

"Be right there. Get those bets in, ladies, and I will see you both in the morning. Wave to me in the winner's circle." He whispered something in Audrey's ear. Michaela thought about asking her what their secret was, but knew it would be rude, so she let it go as they placed a small bet on Halliday and a bigger one on Hugh's horse, Flashing Chico.

"We better hurry." Audrey grabbed Michaela's arm and they jogged back up to the box where Kathleen was already seated.

"Olivia should be here by now," Kathleen said. "I don't know what's taking the girl so long."

"She probably wanted to change, and I'm sure people are asking her to sign autographs," Michaela said.

"She should be here. This is an important race." Kathleen crossed her arms, frowning.

Michaela looked down at the track, watching the horses being led out by their handler horse. A couple were being squirrelly, tossing their heads about and letting out shrill whinnies, ready to race—do what they were born to do. But for the most part, the horses on the track remained calm; it was another wonderful quality about the quarter horse breed—they typically had good heads about them. The one horse that noticeably was the most amped was Halliday.

"What's wrong with him?" Kathleen said. "He doesn't get the jitters."

Again the well-muscled, sorrel-colored four-year-old stallion let out another shrill whinny. Kathleen stood up watching, strain tightening her face as the crew got him into the chute. "I don't understand. I've never seen him behave this way."

"Oh, Kathleen, horses have moods just like people do. Maybe he's in a funk," Audrey said.

"You know, Audrey, I wanted to talk to you about something earlier," Michaela said.

"Yes?"

"It's about Bob."

"My brother?"

"Yes. I ran into his boss at Eq Tech and—"

The chute buzzer rang out and the horses were off. "There they go," Kathleen said.

Audrey jumped to her feet. Michaela realized that she had to find the right words to say to her in the next couple of minutes, when the race would be over. Maybe she should have just waited until the end of the day. Too late now. Besides, Audrey really did need to know about Bob not showing up for work. It was the right thing to do.

The horses came down the straightaway, running at break-neck speed, jockeys vying for the best positions, a blur of browns, blacks, and grays intermingled with the bright colors of the jockeys' silks. Long tails flew in the air like flags as the pounding of hooves slammed hard against the ground, the rapid thud of their hooves kicking up soil. Halliday came around the bend and moved into the lead, Flashing Chico right on his tail. They were almost neck and neck, and then...It all happened so fast. A wrong cue, a bump from the other horse—the cause was not the issue. Michaela cringed as her stomach churned. The movement was so subtle, but Michaela knew what had happened immediately, and within seconds so did the crowd as Halliday's jockey pulled him up. The gorgeous animal had broken his leg.

EIGHT

"OH MY GOD, OH MY GOD!" KATHLEEN BROUGHT her hands up to her face as the reality of what they'd all just seen registered.

Audrey's jaw dropped. Michaela leaned forward in the box. Low murmurs rose from the crowd as they began to understand what they had witnessed. The pounding of hooves in the distance continued but soon stopped as the race ended. Hugh's horse won. Mixed cries sounded throughout the throng of spectators.

Audrey raised a pair of binoculars to see what was going on. A moment later, she put them down and started to run out of the box.

"Where are you going?" Michaela asked.

"Down to the track to find my brother. I'm going to see what I can find out."

"Wait," Michaela yelled as Audrey dashed away. "Audrey!" But her friend didn't stop.

Michaela started to go after her when Kathleen grabbed her arm. "Oh God, what are they doing? What's going on? I can't see!" She stood up on her tiptoes trying to get a better vantage point. Even though they had excellent seats, everyone else was also standing in an attempt to see what was going on.

Michaela stood a few inches taller than Kathleen. She didn't have time to look. She needed to go after Audrey and tell her about Bob—bad timing or not.

"Can you see what the hell is going on down there?" Kathleen exclaimed.

Michaela watched as several handlers tried to calm Halliday down. Soon an equine ambulance drove onto the track. Flashing Chico was being led into the winner's circle. Michaela saw Hugh and his wife entering the circle. A sense of helplessness and sadness came over her. This was not good.

She turned to see Kathleen slumped down in her seat. She needed to do her best to comfort the woman. Audrey would soon know the truth about Bob, and she was angry with herself for not telling her before. Michaela put a hand on Kathleen's shoulder. "I'm so sorry. It doesn't look good. They've got an ambulance on the track now."

Kathleen looked up at her, tears rolling down her face. "They have to save him. They have to save him!" she sobbed. "I love that horse. Oh dear God, I love that animal. Please help me. I can't go down there. I can't see him like that."

"Audrey is on her way."

"Can you go, too? I can't do it. I don't want to know how bad...Just tell them, tell the vets that whatever it takes, please try and save him."

Michaela nodded. "I'll be back." She would do what Kathleen wanted not only because she'd requested it, but also because she needed to reach Audrey first before someone else told her that her brother had not shown up at the track.

"Thank you," Kathleen whispered.

Michaela made her way through crowds of people, her stomach lurching. She didn't want to see Halliday in any pain either, but she understood Kathleen's heartache, and she definitely understood her love for the animal. Olivia's face flashed through her mind. Had Olivia seen the race? Wait a minute! She squinted as she caught a glimpse of what looked to be Olivia up ahead, and...oh no, she was with Steve Benz, holding his hand and weaving quickly through people. Another man walked alongside them. He appeared to also be escorting Olivia out at a rapid clip. She called to her, but Olivia didn't respond. Maybe they were also headed down to the track. She thought about following her, then realized that her obligations to Kathleen and to Audrey were more pressing.

When she reached ground level, she couldn't get past security. "I'm sorry miss, you're not allowed out there."

"You don't understand, I'm with Kathleen Bowen, the horse's owner. She asked me to speak with the vets." The guard eyed her up and down. "I'm not some gawker; I am with Mrs. Bowen and she has requested I speak with the veterinarian. Let me through or lose your job."

He asked for her name, then spoke into his walkie-talkie, muttering under his breath as if she were some kind of criminal. After about fifteen seconds of this bull, Michaela was ready to push him aside. He finally set the walkie-talkie back in its holder and motioned her on through. "You're lucky you know the vet. This isn't typical protocol, but he says you're his assistant," he snapped as she bolted past him.

She wanted to question him but didn't have time. Her heels caught on the divots of the track as she stumbled out to where the ambulance was parked. Damn, she should have worn paddock boots. Sure. To the races. This had been the last thing she expected. She rounded the ambulance, where the vets and handlers were with Halliday, and saw the reason she'd been allowed onto the track: Ethan Slater. He glanced in her direction, his blue eyes filled with an intensity she'd rarely seen in him. He was injecting something into Halliday's neck.

NINE

"NO!" MICHAELA CRIED OUT. THE GROUP, ALL MEN, turned and looked at her. Ethan motioned her over. "You can't put him down! You're not euthanizing him, are you?"

"No, I can't. I'm waiting to hear from the owner. Word is that you're representing her?" He looked confused.

She shot him an equally curious expression, not clear as to what he was doing at the track almost two hours from home and his own veterinary practice. "I'll explain later. I didn't know you were vetting here."

He shrugged. "No time for details. Guys, let's get him into the ambulance and off the track. The Sedivet is starting to work. Manny, you and Gordon stay with him. Give me a minute and then I'll be on board. Michaela, let me help these guys first, then I've only got about thirty seconds to fill you in on the situation."

She nodded and stood back as six men lifted the injured horse into the ambulance. The poor animal still wanted to get back on the track and run, his coat glistening from sweat and probably some pain as the initial injury was likely being felt by him right about now. Halliday tossed his head from side to side and let out a sharp whinny. Michaela's heart beat hard against her chest. She brought her hand up to her mouth to keep from crying as she watched the animal suffer.

Ethan came back out, sweat causing brown waves of hair to stick to the sides of his face. "Okay, so I've called ahead. If Mrs. Bowen wants us to try and save him we can take him to the Rocovich Center Center down in San Diego. If we can save him through surgery, then that's the best and closest facility to do it at."

"Yes, that's what she wants. Chances?"

"Right now, I'm not certain how bad the fracture is. I need to set the splint, get him on an IV for fluids, and shoot him full of some more painkillers. His head is still in the race. He's a strong animal. Once we get him down there, and get the X-rays on him, I'll have a better idea as to where things stand."

"Okay, thank you. Notify me as soon as you can."

"Mrs. Bowen needs to be aware that even if the break can be fixed, it'll be touch and go for a while, and after that a long period of rehab. There's the possibility of infection. It will be a long haul. I've already called in the best surgeon I know. I'll be in there with him, but Dr. Laube is top-notch."

Ethan started to climb in the ambulance.

"Hey, do you know where Dr. Pratt is?" She was hoping that Bob had at least communicated with the track vets.

Ethan shrugged. "Didn't show. Partly why I'm here."

"Call me?" Michaela asked.

Ethan nodded and closed the doors. The ambulance pulled away.

Michaela watched as they sped from the grounds. She felt on the verge of tears again. The poor animal…and Ethan. What was he really doing here? Ethan lived only miles from her in Indio. Memories of growing up with him interrupted her focus for a minute: hanging out with him as a teenager, holding his hand through his first heartbreak over Summer when she left him the day before their wedding, and then standing by as Summer worked her way back into Ethan's life. She couldn't help wondering if Ethan and Summer would wind up the way she and Brad had. But now Summer was due to have Ethan's baby soon. He wanted badly to be a father to the baby, insisting on solidifying his and Summer's relationship only days after she told him she was pregnant. That was eight months ago, and since then Summer had done her damndest—and had done it quite well—to purposely drive a wedge between Michaela and Ethan.

She shook off her thoughts, knowing she needed to find Audrey and tell her about Bob, and then they could go find Kathleen. The day at the races had turned quite horrible. She went looking for Audrey. Hadn't she headed down this way? Michaela glanced around, suddenly realizing she was still on the track. Turning to get off, she spotted Hugh and his trainer leading Flashing Chico back to the stalls. She called out to him.

"Michaela, I saw you on the track with the vet. What did he say?"

She briefly told him what she knew.

"Damn. He's a good horse. The last anniversary present I gave to Kathleen—for our twenty-fifth." He shook his head. "I know it won't mean anything to her, but when you see Kathleen, tell her how sorry I am."

"Sure. Congratulations." She nodded at the horse.

"Yes; bittersweet win, though. I would rather Chico had lost and have Halliday be okay than this."

She nodded. "By the way, have you seen Audrey? I thought she was going down to the track to check on Halliday, but I can't find her."

"No. Jeez, everyone seems to be disappearing. I hear Bobby didn't show up to vet today. I don't know what to think. The Eq Tech folks won't be happy about it. Hell, *I'm* not happy about it. I helped get him that job there as a favor to Audrey. He's a good man, but I sure in hell hope he hasn't gone off the wagon. I can't find my wife either. She was heading out to get a bottle of champagne. Took my jockey with her. And, I haven't seen my daughter since she was on stage."

Michaela remembered Olivia running out with Steve Benz and wondered if she should tell Hugh. Probably; but the girl was not a kid. She was an adult. Still, Hugh was her dad and she knew how much her own parents worried about her, and she was in her thirties. She'd already had misgivings about not telling Audrey about Bob, and knew it was a mistake not to have told her yet. "Uh, I saw Olivia."

"You did?"

"Yes. I saw her leaving with Steve Benz and another guy. Tall, bald, skinny."

"What?" both Hugh and his trainer said in unison.

Michaela caught the trainer's expression as his hazel eyes darkened. He was also tall; Michaela had noticed a slight limp in his left leg. He had shaggy brown hair, and some scars from the result of what had likely been aggravating acne during his teenage years. He brushed his hand through his hair and quickly introduced himself when he realized that Michaela was looking at him. "Josh Torrey. I train Mr. Bowen's horses."

"Right. Oh sorry, Josh," Hugh said. "What do you mean, Olivia was leaving with that Benz character? And who was the other man?"

"I have no idea."

"Marshall Friedman," Josh said. "I bet that's who it was. Benz's manager; they've been trying for weeks to track down Olivia. I told Audrey about it. They were really bothering her. They probably dragged her out of here to get her away from Audrey."

Michaela hadn't gotten the impression that Olivia was being dragged anywhere. Yes, they had seemed to be in a rush but it didn't look to be against anyone's will. Granted, she hadn't clearly seen Olivia's face.

"When did you see this?" Josh asked. Now he had Hugh's attention. 'I'm only asking for you, sir."

"Yes, when did you see her leaving?"

"When I was running down to the track, I'm pretty sure it was them."

"That Benz guy is such an ass," Josh said.

"He's not exactly who I want my daughter with. Let's get this fellow back to the stall." Hugh patted Flashing Chico's neck. "Then I'll try Olivia's cell phone."

They rounded the corner to the stalls. Grooms, trainers, and owners were busy with their horses. Horses' whinnies resounded, along with the strains of Spanish music being played in some of the tack rooms.

Josh handed Flashing Chico off to one of the grooms. He went inside the tack room and returned with cell phone in hand. "You can use my phone to call her," he said, handing it to Hugh.

"Thanks." He started to dial when a shrill scream rang out. The screaming didn't stop; it grew louder. "What the hell?" He handed the phone back to Josh and along with Michaela and a few other people, hurried toward the source, out past the stalls near where the massive horse trailers and semis were parked. Approaching the scene, Michaela gasped. Was that Bridgette, Hugh's wife? Yes. What was she standing over, screaming bloody murder about?

She walked closer, and...Oh, no! No! *No!* She started running. Hugh got there first. He knelt down while Bridgette continued to scream. A man stood next to her, his mouth agape. Hugh yelled at her to shut the hell up. She did. The other man stepped back. This could not be happening. Michaela stared as Hugh picked up the hand of her friend—Audrey's hand. Then pulled her body in close to him. *Blood everywhere.* Somewhere behind her she heard someone calling 911. She couldn't move. Paralysis shrouded her as reality hit. A pair of reins encircled Audrey's neck; her face was ashen, eyes bulging out in shock and pain. A terrified look on her face—again not real—like a mask. *Couldn't it just be a mask?* Please God.

But as Hugh looked back up, tears on his face, she knew it was no mask. Audrey had been strangled to death and the blood...the blood was coming from her head. She must have fought. That was who she was—a fighter—and, whoever had done this was evil, pure evil. The killer had finished her off with a deep blow to the head. Michaela knew her friend was dead.

TEN

AFTER AUDREY'S BODY WAS TAKEN AWAY, THE POLICE questioned the nearest group, particularly Bridgette and the man who had been standing next to her, Frederick Callahan. Michaela thought she'd recognized him, but in all the chaos had not been able to place him. The bad toupee should have tipped her off. It didn't even match the gray it was attached to: He'd chosen a golden blond. It was hard for people not to discuss his rug when talking about media mogul Callahan. Owner of *Pleasures* magazine for men, he was also an avid racehorse fan and owned several of them.

Michaela caught bits and pieces as to why he was with Bridgette Bowen and how they'd discovered Audrey. Callahan had been checking to see if his horse, which was running in the seventh race, had passed the vet check, claiming he was concerned about a leg. It had looked a bit lame to him that morning. He heard the scream first and ran to where Bridgette stood over Audrey.

"I-I was going to the limo." Bridgette glanced at Hugh.

Michaela studied her as she explained how she'd found Audrey. Still in shock, Michaela didn't know how to react. She wanted to fall apart, but knew this wasn't the place to do so with all the police around. She'd teared up a few times as reality came in waves. Focusing on the others around her helped keep the horrific reality at bay.

After the cops were done interviewing her, Bridgette continued explaining to her husband: "I really wanted some champagne. I decided to come out here and get it myself, what with you being busy with Flashing Chico and everything. I figured I'd make myself useful."

"Couldn't you have ordered champagne from your box?" Michaela asked, not able to help herself. She heard a tremor in Bridgette's voice; was the woman lying?

Bridgette glared at her. "I could have." She rubbed Hugh's arm. "But Hugh knew we would win today and I brought a special bottle for the occasion."

"Why not have it on ice in your box?" Michaela asked again, recalling the champagne that Kathleen had in hers.

"Who are you again? I know we met earlier and I know you're not the police. I've already answered these questions." Bridgette's eyes narrowed like a hawk readying for the kill.

"I'm not the police; I was Audrey's friend."

"I didn't kill her, if that's what you're insinuating. I found her is all. I think it's interesting, you being her friend that you weren't with her. If you had been, maybe she wouldn't have been killed…unless, of course you had a reason to see her dead."

Michaela took a step toward her. "Excuse me? What did you just say?" Rage boiled in her gut as tears stung her eyes. "How dare you! I would never harm Audrey!" Her entire body shook with gut-wrenching agony. "I loved her. She was my friend, you bitch!" Bridgette's eyes widened. "I want to know why in the hell you were standing over her…" Michaela put her face in her palms and sobbed.

Hugh put an arm around her. "I'm so sorry, honey. We're all shaken up. Bridgette didn't mean anything by it. We all need to cool off. This won't help bring Audrey back. Let's all settle down. I don't think the police would take kindly to a scene right now."

Michaela nodded and pulled away from Hugh. He was right. She didn't need one of the cops arresting her for assaulting Bridgette, though she still wanted to.

He whispered something in Bridgette's ear and then smiled sadly at Michaela. Taking Bridgette's arm, he led her over to their limousine. Her anger started to fade as sadness and shock continued to weave through her. She waited for the police to question the rest of the group. When they got to her, she told them that she and Audrey had driven there from Indio that morning. She went on to relate the events as she remembered them, from Steve Benz's subtle threat to Audrey in Olivia's dressing room, to the fact that she'd learned Audrey's brother had not shown up for work for the past three days, nor at the track that day to vet the horses. The officer in charge, Detective Merrill, asked her where Ms. Bowen was at that moment.

"Do you mean Olivia, or her mother, Kathleen?"

"I'll start with Kathleen Bowen. My partner is trying to track down the daughter," he said, his paper-thin lips tightening with each word he spoke. It made him look ghoulish. He jotted something down in his notebook. Michaela noticed the yellow on his fingers, probably from nicotine. As he stepped closer, she decided that it definitely was nicotine. Merrill smelled like one big, stale cigarette. He wore his dark hair slicked straight back, and from the lines on his face, she couldn't help the odd thought that maybe the man used Grecian Formula to keep his hair coal black. He looked back up at her with ice-blue eyes, as if expecting something. "Ms. Bowen? Where is she?"

"I left her in her box. Her horse sustained a major injury in the opening race and Audrey was going down to the track to talk to the vet. I followed, but when I reached the track I didn't see her anywhere." She told the rest of the story to the detective about walking back to the stalls with Hugh and Josh, and how it wasn't long before they'd heard Bridgette screaming. When he finished taking her statement, Merrill asked her if she had the vet's number. He wanted to find out if Audrey had ever made it to the track. Michaela wanted to know, too, but also knew that Ethan was tied up with Halliday.

Michaela watched as Audrey's body, now covered, was loaded into the back of the coroner's van. Her stomach ached and a lump caught in her throat. She couldn't speak or even cry. For a moment she wondered if she was even breathing as the pain in her chest tightened. How could this have happened? Why had Audrey charged out of the box? Dammit! She should have gone with her. If she had, maybe she'd be alive.

Merrill asked Michaela to show him to Mrs. Bowen's box. She agreed. She had to get out of there anyway; she didn't think she could watch as the van with Audrey's body drove away, or see the onlookers and the investigators. All she wanted to do was escape from there. It took about ten minutes to walk back to Kathleen's box. Merrill didn't say much. Michaela tried to ask him about his initial impressions, but all he did was nod occasionally, which made no sense to her. "Do you think it was someone she knew?" she asked.

The detective grunted. She gave up.

Kathleen sat in her box, staring off into space, her face stained with mascara. She looked up at them. "I know," she muttered.

"Know what?" Michaela asked.

"You're going to tell me they had to put him down, aren't you? That's why you and Audrey have been gone for so long," she said, slurring her words.

Kathleen appeared to have been drinking—heavily.

"I waited and I waited. Audrey didn't come back, my daughter never came to see me, and you didn't show up. I finally got up and had a drink. I was starting to think that maybe you all had left me here. I was going to call my driver. I didn't know what to do, who to call. I could see people on the track, people everywhere. They were running horses, even after Halliday, and then no one came to tell me what was going on. Who is that man?" She tried to stand.

Merrill stepped forward, steadied her, and helped her sit back down. "Ma'am, I'm Detective Tom Merrill and I need to ask you a few questions."

"About Halliday? Since when do they send in the police to ask about a racehorse breaking his leg?"

"It's not about your horse, ma'am. It's about Mrs. Pratt."

"Audrey? I don't understand."

Michaela looked at the detective. "Can I...?"

He nodded. Ah, he had a heart after all.

She sat down next to Kathleen and took her hands. Kathleen's eyes widened and she pulled back a bit, but Michaela didn't let go. "This is very difficult." She felt her throat tighten. "Um, it's Audrey. She...she was killed earlier." The words came out, but it didn't feel or even sound like she was saying them. She'd had to do it quickly, or she didn't think she could do it at all.

"What?" Kathleen pulled her hands away.

Merrill sat down on the other side of Kathleen. She turned to look at him. "Is this true?"

"I am afraid so, ma'am. Mrs. Pratt was found murdered."

Kathleen began to shake violently. "I don't believe this. I don't, *I don't!*"

"I need to ask you some questions." He glanced over at Michaela.

She took it as a suggestion for her to leave, and stood. "Where are you going?" Kathleen asked. "Stay. Please stay."

"Miss Bancroft, why don't you have the car brought around for Mrs. Bowen? I'll escort her down."

"She can't stay?"

"Police procedure, ma'am."

Kathleen nodded. "Use my cell phone to call the driver. All you have to do is press the number five and enter." Kathleen handed her the phone.

Michaela did as instructed. She didn't want to get into Merrill's way. He seemed pretty uptight. She had to wonder what types of questions he was asking Kathleen. She had a few herself. She wondered if she'd really remained inside her box the entire time, other than to get drinks. She'd insisted that Michaela go down to the track with Audrey, but it didn't look as if Audrey had gone down to the track at all. Could Kathleen have followed her? *Could she have actually killed her friend?* Is that what the detective was also thinking? Audrey had mentioned that Kathleen wasn't herself lately. And, she was insistent that Michaela not mention her continued friendship with Hugh, for fear of it troubling Kathleen. What if she found out that Audrey was still good pals with Hugh? Maybe she had even seen her chatting with him when she and Michaela went to place a bet. Could that have set the woman off? She didn't come across as the most stable of people. Then, when Halliday broke his leg, the crying jag: Had it been for real? Michaela didn't know. It seemed real. Of course it was real. She wouldn't have killed Audrey. No. That was ridiculous. Michaela knew she was being paranoid. The two women had been friends for years. This was ludicrous.

As she walked away she pressed the number five on Kathleen's cell. A man answered. "Kathleen?"

Michaela could hear loud music in the background. "No. This is a friend. Can you please bring the car around?"

"Excuse me?"

"Yes, the car?" she shouted into the phone. Maybe he couldn't hear her. He obviously had the stereo cranked. "Can you turn down the music? Ms. Bowen needs the car brought around."

"I have no idea what you're talking about."

"Aren't you the chauffeur?"

He laughed. "Hardly."

Michaela apologized and got off the phone. Why would Kathleen give her the wrong number? Must be stress. She hit the number five again out of curiosity to see if a name came up. The initials *MF* did. Hmm. She decided to try number six, and found the chauffeur. He told her that he'd be around momentarily.

When he pulled up, Michaela explained that Ms. Bowen would be there soon. "No problem," he said.

Several minutes later, as she stood lost in thought, Detective Merrill escorted Kathleen to the car. He told Michaela he'd be in touch with both of them soon. She thanked him.

Kathleen slid into the backseat and instructed the driver to take her home. "Get in," she told Michaela.

"My truck is here. I really should head out."

"No," she whined. "You can't go home. I need someone to stay with me tonight. I don't want to be alone. Please."

Michaela cringed. The last thing she wanted to do was stay with Kathleen. Granted, that had been the initial plan, but now everything had changed. After Audrey and Halliday, she couldn't help but want to return to her safe harbor. She wanted to see Rocky and her other animals, make sure they were all okay.

Kathleen poured herself a drink from the limo's bar. "Wait, please. Have a drink with me." She took something from her purse and put it in her mouth

"What was that?" Michaela asked.

"Valium, for my nerves."

"You've been drinking. You really shouldn't take that on top of alcohol. Put the drink down, Kathleen. It's not a good idea."

She waved a hand at her. "If I die, then so be it. Look at all that's happened today. My friend, my horse, and my child. Lord only knows where she is. You know that she never came to the box to see me. I doubt anyone would miss me."

Oh no. Michaela shut her eyes for a brief moment. *Think, think.* She sighed. "Okay, I'll follow you home."

"You will?" Kathleen looked at her through drunken eyes.

Michaela nodded.

"Thank you. You're a good person." She patted her hand. "I have to ask you first about my horse. Did he suffer?"

"He's alive. I told them to do whatever they needed to try and save him. Now, hand me the drink."

Her eyes brightened; she ignored Michaela's request. "Oh God, thank you. He's going to make it?"

"Hopefully.

She sighed. "I don't know what I was thinking, though. Trying to save him. I mean really, I can't afford to save him."

"Excuse me?" Michaela asked. How did she figure? The woman rolled in diamonds and spent cash like she'd picked it from trees.

She shook her head. "Nope. No money. I'm bankrupt."

"Bankrupt?"

"Yesiree. Broke." She leaned back and closed her eyes, her drink sliding from her hand. Michaela caught it before it hit the floorboard and set it aside. She started to ask Kathleen how that could be, but the woman had passed out.

ELEVEN

"MICHAELA, I CAN'T LET YOU DO IT! WHAT ARE YOU thinking, anyway? Kathleen Bowen can pay this horse's bill. She's got more money than she knows what to do with," Ethan said to her on the other end of the phone.

Michaela stood facing the bay windows watching the tide roll in. She'd been sitting on Kathleen's balcony outside her room, which overlooked the ocean, since before the sun came up. Listening to the ocean's sounds had likely been what kept her sane that morning, after seeing Audrey's body, dead—murdered—the day before. She'd hated coming to Kathleen's house, especially without Audrey, but the serenity of the Pacific gave her some sense of peace where she'd thought there would be none. "I don't know about that," she finally answered.

"Michaela, you are talking nonsense. Do you hear me? That's nuts. You may have inherited some money from Lou, but trust me, Mick, do not pay for this horse's surgery and medical care. It'll likely be in the hundreds of thousands. I can't believe that Kathleen doesn't have any kind of medical coverage on the horse. I'm sure the insurance company would keep this animal alive no matter what the diagnosis is, anyhow. They do their damndest to wait until the last straw. Too many of these animals suffer, all in the name of money, so the insurance companies want to hang on for as long as possible, hoping that they won't have to make a million-dollar payout."

"How is he, anyway?"

"The good news is, I wouldn't—and neither would the other vets—recommend putting him down. The break was a condylar fracture above the ankle. That is fairly easy to repair. The bad news is, he also has a fracture below the ankle in the pastern. Very similar to what happened with Barbaro at the Preakness Stakes a few years ago. It's not as bad, and with a lot of care, possibly more surgery, he'll likely grow old grazing in a pasture somewhere. I don't think he'll ever see a track again, though. He's been kept comfortable through the night, and now we're prepared to take him into surgery, but we need signed paperwork from Kathleen. Do you have the fax number there? She can sign it and fax it back to us."

"I don't know. Hang on. Actually, you know what, I'll see if I can find it and call you back." It was half past seven and she didn't know if she should wake Kathleen. She decided to check things out on her own first.

"Don't be too long. We'd like to get him into surgery before eight. The anesthesiologist is here and so is Dr. Laube and his team."

"I won't be long. I have to ask you though, how did you get involved in this? I mean, what were you doing vetting at the track?"

"It's a long story. I'll fill you in at the barbecue this weekend. You're still coming, aren't you? Friday night."

Oh no. She'd forgotten about the barbecue–baby shower thing that he and Summer were throwing. Summer had insisted on it being a get-together for everyone. Great. She sighed. How had Ethan wound up with someone like *her*?

"You're bringing that detective, right? Jude? Nice guy."

"Um, yeah. I mean, I'll be there. I don't know if Jude can make it,' she said, almost choking on her words and remembering Hudson Drake and the *date* she'd made with him for Saturday. That would be awkward, wouldn't it? Jude at Ethan and Summer's house with her, then the next night a date with a man she really didn't know at all. She'd have to call that one off, especially after everything that had happened. She'd mail him back his key. Surely he'd understand. And, she hadn't even asked Jude to go to Ethan and Summer's. Ethan was obviously assuming they were seeing each other.

"You have to be there. My wife and I are counting on you."

My wife. "Okay, well, I'll see what I can do about finding a fax machine and getting Kathleen up." If she found a fax, then she could wake Kathleen and have her fill out the paperwork after Ethan sent it. Poor woman was sleeping off a mixture of heartache, alcohol, and God only knew what else. Bad combination. A few times throughout the sleepless night, she'd gone in to check on Kathleen to make sure she was breathing. She tried to keep the images of Audrey at bay, and focus on Halliday and what needed to be done for him, but it was difficult.

She found Kathleen's office and went in. It was decorated like rest of the beach house—in white. There was a lot of it: bleached hardwood floors, antique white, modern white, white sofas, white chairs; different shades of white, but pretty much everything in white, except for the paintings on the wall, which were mainly watercolor seascapes.

Michaela found the fax machine next to Kathleen's computer and copied the number taped on it. Good. Okay, time to wake her up. First she'd call Ethan back.

She walked over to a white chaise lounge by the window; a phone sat on the table next to it. She called Ethan and gave him the number. Hanging up the phone, she noticed that the drawer on the table was askew. She bent down to fix it and place it back on the rollers. She tugged on it and the drawer came flying out, knocking her on her butt. Pens, a box of tacks and Post-its came flying out, along with a 5 x 7 envelope. "Oh shit," she muttered, hoping she hadn't woken Kathleen. She started to clean up the mess. She picked up the envelope, which had a photo partially sticking out of it. She pulled out the picture: Olivia on a racehorse…Flashing Chico. Hugh's horse. There were other photos in the envelope, which Michaela thumbed through. More of Olivia on the horse, Olivia with Audrey next to the horse, Olivia with Hugh's trainer, Josh, Olivia on the track running Chico in what looked like a practice session, then a lone picture of Audrey watching Olivia on Chico. All of the photos were candid. None of them looked as if Olivia, Audrey, or Josh knew they were being shot. In fact, they looked like the kind of photos a private investigator might take. Oh boy. Was Kathleen watching her daughter's every move? She turned around, thinking she heard someone in the kitchen. Shoving the photos back into the envelope, she quickly stuffed everything else back in the drawer and put the contents back together, then grabbed the faxed forms, which had just arrived, and joined Kathleen, who was pouring herself a cup of coffee.

"Good morning," she said to Michaela, her hands trembling.

She looked terrible and didn't appear to have heard the ruckus Michaela had caused back in the office. At least, she hoped that was the case. God forbid Kathleen find out she had snooped through photos of Olivia, Audrey, and the horse. She didn't know what it all meant, but she did know it wasn't good. Not at all. "Hi." Michaela tried to smile at her. "I hate to bother you with this right now, but the vets want to take Halliday in for surgery and they need your consent." She handed the forms to Kathleen. "I, uh, went into your office to see if you had a fax machine. Sorry. I didn't want to wake you."

"It's fine." She nodded. "I know what I said last night about saving him, but…"

"You have to try. I spoke with the vet and he said that it can be done, that he can survive this." She didn't want to go into the cost or rehabilitation time. Michaela's stomach knotted, feeling sick that Kathleen might change her mind.

"I know I told you last night about my financial situation. I said too much, I remember, and I don't have any insurance on him. I couldn't keep it up. I've been stupid with my money."

"I'll take care of the bill."

Kathleen looked at her. "What?"

"I'll loan you the money until you get back on your feet. Let me take care of the expenses for now. I can cover them."

"No. I can't let you do that."

"You have to. You can't let him go without giving this a try. I insist."

Kathleen walked over to the window. She stood, staring out at the expansive ocean in front of her. "Why would you do this for me?"

"Honestly, it's not for you. It's for the horse. He's an amazing animal. I've followed his career, seen the heart he has, and I can't bear to have him destroyed without giving him a chance. Don't have him put down. You can still stud him out with the use of AI," Michaela said, referring to artificial insemination, which was quite popular amongst quarter horse breeders, "You'll be happy you did it. Let me do this. You'll pay me back when you can."

Kathleen slowly nodded and signed the consent form. Michaela faxed the paperwork back to Ethan, and Halliday was on his way to surgery. When Michaela returned, Kathleen was crying again. "Thank you. Thank you so much. After Audrey's death last night, the thought of destroying Hal...I can't; as much as I feel ashamed about letting you front the cost, I agree with you."

"Can I ask you something?"

"Yes."

Michaela wanted to ask her why she was in a financial bind, even though part of her felt like it really wasn't her business. The flip side of her told her that at this stage of the game, with her paying the medical expenses on Hal, she did have a right to know why Kathleen was broke. Then, Olivia walked in.

"Mom! Mom!" Olivia cried out. "I heard about Audrey. I came right over. Oh God, how did this happen? I'm sorry I wasn't there." Olivia put her arms around her mother, who pulled away, her face drawn as she looked past Olivia. Josh Torrey stood behind her.

"Have you been with Josh at your father's place, celebrating the win? How could you? Do you even know what I've been through? What happened? I was worried about you. I didn't hear from you. I called your apartment, your cell phone. I had no idea where you were. Nothing. Dammit, Olivia. I am tired of this with you. It's time you move back home. I've let you play grown-up long enough, but it's obvious that you can't handle it." Kathleen's hands were on her hips, her face twisted in anger. Prior to Olivia's arrival, Kathleen had seemed so sad, desperate almost, but something about her daughter being with Josh set her off. Michaela remembered the photos in Kathleen's office.

"Josh picked me up and brought me home. I needed a ride. That's it. End of story." She looked at Michaela. "Hi."

"Hi," Michaela replied. Olivia looked as if she'd been through the wringer—makeup smeared across her usually flawless ivory face, long blond hair totally disheveled, and she wasn't wearing the cute blouse and jeans she'd had on for the concert the day before. She did have jeans on, and what looked to be a man's T-shirt.

"That is the truth," Josh replied. "She was not celebrating with us. In fact, we weren't exactly in a celebratory mood, Kathleen."

He didn't look as unkempt as Olivia. He looked ready to be out with the horses—breeches, paddock boots, and tucked-in T-shirt. He did, however, appear exhausted, with dark circles under his eyes and a lack of color in his face. Had he been as worried about Olivia as her mother claimed to be? He certainly seemed disturbed yesterday at the mention of Olivia sneaking off with Steve Benz and the mystery man. Benz was really the man toward whom Kathleen should be directing her anger.

"And, where did you pick her up *from*?" Kathleen squared up with Josh, who didn't answer. She stepped away from him and yelled at Olivia, "Where were you?"

"You know what, Mother? It's none of your business." She walked past Michaela and down the hall. "I'm going to have a smoke." A few seconds later a door slammed in the back of the house.

Kathleen fumed at Josh. "You had something to do with this. It's obvious, and I know—I know all about what you and Audrey have been up to with Olivia. Letting her ride those damn horses of Hugh's."

So, she *had* been spying on her daughter. What a tangled web of deceit. Who knew these people would have so much to hide. Why, *why* had Audrey gotten herself mixed up in all of this crazy business?

"I don't need this. I brought her home safely. I gave her a ride, and that's it. I don't believe you. Your horse is suffering, and now with Audrey? You're really disturbed."

"Stay away from my daughter. Do you hear me? Stay away from her!"

"You might be able to control Olivia, but you can't control me. Why don't you let her grow up and live the life she wants to live, not the life you want her to." Josh flicked back a lock of his brown hair that had fallen down over his eyes and walked out.

Kathleen stormed into the back of the house to find Olivia. Michaela heard them shouting back and forth. She couldn't make out exactly what they were saying, but she knew one thing for sure: She needed to get the hell out of there. Luckily because of last night's events, she hadn't even unpacked her overnight bag. When they'd arrived at Kathleen's place, Michaela had put the woman to bed with the help of the driver, then changed into a T-shirt and jeans and stayed awake through night.

She scribbled a note to Kathleen telling her that she'd be in touch, and then she hightailed it out of there. Before heading back to Indio, she decided to have a talk with Josh. She'd see if he was at Hugh's place. He'd been in those photos with Audrey, and they looked chummy. Audrey hadn't mentioned Josh to her, but that didn't mean anything. And, now he was closely linked to Olivia, whose unstable mother kept tabs on her as if she were five and not twenty. And, Josh had behaved oddly last night when he'd learned that Olivia was with Steve Benz. Had she really wound up with Josh? What was that all about?

Plus, what about Bob Pratt? Maybe Josh knew him. Hugh did. It was a small community within the horse-racing world and it was likely that Josh might have known him. Or maybe, just maybe, Audrey had mentioned something to Josh about Bob that, although it had seemed like nothing at the time, could lead to something. No matter what, Michaela couldn't shake the tug inside of her telling her that Bob Pratt's disappearance and his sister's murder were somehow linked. It made sense. But when she'd mentioned it to Detective Merrill last night, he didn't seem too concerned. Then again, the detective appeared to be holding his cards close. Maybe he also thought there was a link. What a mess.

Michaela knew she should just get on the freeway and head home, but someone had murdered her friend, and the ache she felt in her body every time she thought about what had happened to Audrey compelled her to find the answers. *And*, she had an inkling that the answers might lie somewhere amongst this strange crew of individuals Audrey had been associated with.

TWELVE

MICHAELA PULLED INTO HUGH BOWEN'S ESTATE and training facility up in the hills of Malibu. Although her ranch was not shabby in the least—her uncle had built up quite an estate—it paled in comparison to Hugh's place. After ringing the button on the security gate and responding to what she guessed had been Hugh's wife, Bridgette, on the other end, the gate opened. She wondered if Bridgette realized who she was. Doubtful.

The road up to the house, if it could be called a house—more of a mansion...no, a villa, actually—was cobblestone. Off to one side was a large pasture filled with grazing mares and their foals, the moms busy eating, their babies romping, some nursing. Pretty picture. Michaela sighed and rolled down her window, taking in the sweetness of the leftover marine layer wafting up from the coast only a few miles away. Off to the other side was a racetrack. Straight ahead she could see an indoor arena, and next to it, holding what she figured was up to a hundred horses, a large barn built of light wood and trimmed in teal and yellow—Bowen's ranch colors. All of his jockeys' silks were in these colors. Amazingly artistic looking. Farther back up on a hill stood the villa, replete with that old-world Italian look: arches and large paned windows, brightly boxed flowers hanging off balconies, and on one side of the house, ivy entwined from the ground on up. The place truly looked like it should be set amid the rolling hills of Tuscany.

She spotted Hugh as she got out of her truck, seated with another man on the first-floor balcony. Her initial plan had not been to see him, but maybe this was a good thing. She could find out if Josh was on the property, and maybe she'd ask Hugh a few questions about Audrey. It had been her impression when they'd run into him at the races that they were still quite close—more than simply a business relationship. Kathleen had obviously failed to come between the friendship that Hugh and Audrey shared.

Hugh waved to her. "Come on up. The front door is open. Go to your right and then out through the doors in the kitchen."

Entering the place, she decided the kitchen area could have filled the first floor of her home. Boy, the Venetian in Vegas had nothing on this place. Once she did find her way outside, Hugh ushered her over. "Good morning. I'm pleased you decided to come by today. I wasn't sure you'd make it, considering last night."

"Me either—" Michaela stopped short. The man with Hugh was Hudson Drake, looking as spectacular as she remembered. She quickly chastised herself for being so shallow, but dammit, the man was handsome and the human side of her told her that it was okay to think that. The friend of Audrey and Jude's—uh, sort of more than a friend—told her that it definitely was *not* okay. Being human right now was not an option.

Hudson extended a hand. "Nice to see you again, Michaela."

"You've met?" Hugh asked.

She nodded.

"Yesterday, as a matter of fact, at the races. We bumped into each other at the bar and discovered we have quite a bit in common," Hudson said.

"Actually, we realized that we both knew you."

"Oh," Hugh replied. "Good. Good."

"I came by, actually," Hudson said, "to talk with Hugh about Bob." He looked at the other man. "I had already told Michaela what I just told you about Bob. It came up in our conversation and we felt it was appropriate for Michaela to tell Audrey that Bob hadn't shown up for work, considering that she knew his sister, and I didn't. It is kind of…sensitive."

"No, no, I agree. Of course." Hugh sat back down in one of the wicker chairs and motioned for them to do the same. "Hudson was telling me that he's quite concerned Bob has not shown up at work, and now with Audrey..." He shook his head. "I don't know what to think. And, take a look at this." Hugh handed her the newspaper off the table.

It wasn't a front-page story but close enough. The headline read "Police Focus on Brother's Disappearance in Murder." The story went on to say that a source from the Orange County Sheriff's Department believed that Bob Pratt might be responsible for his sister's murder.

Michaela shifted uneasily in the chair.

"Would you like coffee, juice, water, anything?" Hugh asked.

"No thank you. I don't believe this. They're saying that they think Bob might have killed Audrey and skipped town? But you told me that you haven't seen Bob since Tuesday."

"I told the police that, too," Hudson replied. "The detective—Merrill—seemed to think that Bob not showing up for work since Tuesday was only a guise, possibly to make the police think that he'd been gone since then."

"They're thinking he planned this out, went into hiding, killed his sister, and then took off?" Michaela couldn't believe it. That didn't sound like the Bob Pratt she'd met or heard Audrey talk about.

"It's hard to say what the police think," Hugh said.

"What do you think? Michaela asked.

"I have my suspicions," Hugh said. "But I don't believe that Bob murdered Audrey."

"Hugh was thinking along the same vein as we were yesterday," Hudson added.

"That he's fallen off the wagon and hiding under a rock somewhere?" Michaela asked.

"It is a possibility," Hudson said.

"There's another one," Michaela replied. "What if Audrey's murder is connected to Bob's disappearance? Not that Bob killed Audrey, but..."

"You mean, whoever killed Audrey could have taken Bob? *Abducted* him?" Hugh finished her sentence.

"Yes. It does seem strange that Bob disappears, then his sister is murdered. I can understand why the police might target him, but I can't believe he would kill Audrey. What for? Why would he do it?"

Hudson sighed and crossed his arms, leaning back in the chair. "I hate to even think that the cops are right with their speculation, but what if they are? Maybe Bob did kill her for some reason, or had someone else do it."

Hugh shook his head. "No way. Bob and Audrey were close. They loved each other dearly. I can't believe that. Not for a minute. Sure, they had their problems when they were younger, but they'd worked them out, and Audrey always supported Bob. Hell, she came to me about helping him get the job with Eq Tech."

Hudson nodded. "I know. I interviewed Bob. He's great. He really is and I really don't believe that he would do something like that, but it is still difficult to ever really know people, and maybe there were underlying issues that none of us were aware of. It's only a theory and I doubt it's even close to the truth, but we all know that the cops may consider it because of Bob's past addictions."

Hugh fidgeted with one of the buttons on his shirt. "Addictions can destroy you."

Michaela agreed, thinking of her dad, who'd nearly lost his family and himself to his gambling addiction more than once over the years. She also thought she detected something in Hugh's voice that made her wonder if he might have also dealt firsthand with the issue of addiction, or if he'd had a loved one with a problem. She couldn't put her finger on it; maybe it was the tone of his voice or his distant gaze when he'd made the comment. For a second

Michaela thought of Olivia and her strange behavior and frazzled appearance that morning. Could Hugh's daughter have a problem with drugs or alcohol?

"Look, the police will be working on locating Bob, in connection with his sister's murder," Hudson said. "It doesn't look good. But we need to find him, to help him out and make sure that he really is all right. I'm planning on hiring a private investigator."

"I know someone. He's good, too," Michaela interjected. Both men looked at her. Hmm, maybe she shouldn't have said anything. Joe Pellegrino was not a PI...not technically, anyway. He just had all those cousins who seemed to have numerous ways of finding out information.

"I actually have someone in mind," Hudson said.

"Oh. Well, okay. I just thought that I could help in some way."

"Why don't you talk to your guy, then? I'll talk with this other man I've worked with in the past, and maybe we can come up with something between the two of them."

Hugh nodded. "How can I help?"

Hudson stood and clapped him on the shoulder. "I think you're doing all that you can. We just have to find him."

"Right."

"Didn't you say to Audrey yesterday that you saw him only a few days ago?" Michaela asked Hugh.

He nodded. "I did. He came by and did a vet check on a few of my horses. I talked with him for a few minutes. That was Monday. He didn't act strange or anything. Friendly as always. Pleasant. I only had a few minutes with him, though. I had a meeting to get to. Josh helped him with the horses."

"It makes no sense at all," Michaela said. The men agreed.

"I hate to run, but it's Sunday morning and I typically try and make it to mass. I'll be praying about this," Hudson said.

Michaela smiled. She liked the fact that Hudson had faith. She didn't attend church regularly herself, but her mother was a devout Catholic and she'd been raised Catholic, so her roots remained in the church.

"Michaela, I'll see you Saturday night," Hudson said. "I have to get to my office. I'm sorry about your loss. I know your friend meant a lot to you."

"Thank you."

"And Hugh, thank you." Hudson held up a check and waved it. "This will help us to keep up with the growth the company is experiencing."

"I believe in the product," Hugh replied.

Michaela started to bring up Saturday night and how it wasn't going to work out, but Hugh stood and walked Hudson to the door. The timing to bring up Saturday right now was awkward anyway. She'd have to call him about it. She'd also have to give Joe a call and see if he would help her find out what might have happened to Bob Pratt. She didn't like this one bit. She'd been sucked into what had happened to Bob and Audrey, and now a compulsion drove her to want to find out who had done this horrid thing to Audrey, and thus find justice for her friend.

THIRTEEN

WHEN HUGH RETURNED, MICHAELA DECIDED TO ask him some more questions. At this point she had nothing to lose. "I know it might be awkward, but I wanted to talk to you about Audrey and take a look at the horses we discussed. I know that she would have wanted me to do that anyway, and honestly I'm not sure it's sunk in for me yet that...she's really gone."

He nodded. "Nor me. Come on down to the barn. I've got to deliver these supplements that Hudson dropped off." He picked up a bucket of Eq Tech's all-around athlete vitamins and minerals. "Good stuff. I'm telling you; since putting my horses on it, I've seen a difference in their performances. I know I sound like a salesman, and sure, I've got plenty of cash tied up in that company, but I really do believe in the product. You using it?"

"Some," Michaela replied. "It's pretty expensive though. I've got a few of my horses on it."

"I'm sure Hudson would cut you a deal on it." He winked at her. "Did I notice a bit of an interest there?"

Michaela knew she was blushing. "No. As he said, we met yesterday and started talking, that kind of thing. Nice man. Really...nice."

Hugh raised his brows. "Uh-huh. Is that why you're going to see him on Saturday night? I imagine he's asked you to the Eq Tech charity event and auction. That's great. He's a good man, and I'll be there, too. I'm offering up two weeks at my vacation home in Capri for the auction. I'm certain we'll be seated at the same table. Josh and Olivia will be there...and word is, so will my ex-wife." His face darkened.

"Oh, that. No. Well, yes, he did ask me. Actually, agreeing was a rash decision on my part, and now the timing couldn't be worse. I won't be going. Speaking of Josh, is he around?" She wanted to change the subject.

"No. He's out right now. But we don't need him to show the horses. Back to Saturday night. I disagree with you. I think the timing is what we all need."

"What?"

"I know what Audrey would have told you. She would have wanted you to go out and live your life. Live it up."

"I'm sure that's what she'd say, too, but I don't feel right about it."

"Bull. I say think about it. Losing Audrey makes me realize a lot about the way I've been living my life, and I plan to make changes. Big changes."

Michaela thought she heard a catch in his throat. She wanted to ask him what he meant but didn't feel all that comfortable prying.

They started to walk out the massive front door, only to run into Bridgette, Hugh's wife, sauntering down the stairs and into the entryway dressed to the nines. She froze when she spotted Michaela. "Hello," she said curtly.

"Good morning," Michaela replied and decided it best to bury the hatchet with her, even though she didn't trust the woman as far as she could throw her. "I want to apologize for yesterday. It was an awful situation and I was pretty emotional."

"I understand and accept your apology." She looked at Hugh. "Honey, I have to go into L.A. for a lunch appointment, and I thought maybe I'd do some shopping on Rodeo Drive first." She ran her hands over her tight black pencil skirt—as if it needed any straightening—then fiddled with the waist of her white crepe low-cut blouse, which exposed cleavage and a very large diamond necklace matching the stones in her ears. She fluffed up her long brunette hair and smiled. "I shouldn't be too late."

"Considering what's happened, I'm not sure that going to Beverly Hills makes sense," he said.

"What? Why?"

He looked at her incredulously. "Bridgette, you found a friend of ours murdered yesterday. I would think that might affect you."

She nodded and frowned. "It was horrible. I liked Audrey."

Michaela watched her face. She was lying again. She had *not* liked Audrey. And Michaela did not like Bridgette Bowen any better today. She could even hear the lie in the woman's voice. But why lie? And why did she dislike Audrey? Because Audrey didn't care for her, or because of Audrey's relationship with Kathleen and Olivia? Or...was there another reason?

"I can't cancel my luncheon," Bridgette said. "It's for the charity event I'm doing with my Cedars-Sinai hospital group. We're trying to raise money for heart disease research. It's important and it will keep my mind off of yesterday's horrible events."

"I don't think it's a good idea. It feels insensitive to me," Hugh said.

"Honey, I am on the board and I can't bring Audrey back. I might as well raise money to help others."

"Fine. You go do what you need to do."

"Thank you." She nodded at Michaela. "Nice to see you again."

Oh, she was good with the lies. Actually she kind of sucked at them, but she sure dispensed plenty of them. "Nice to see you, too." Two could play that game.

"Ciao, honey. I'll be home in time for dinner. I've asked Lucita to make your favorite pork loin recipe. And her delicious crème brûlée. I thought a good meal would lift the gloom a bit."

Hugh opened the front door for Michaela. "Let's go see the horses." She followed him out and around the corner, where he climbed into a golf cart. "This driveway is a bitch to get around, and the older I get the less I want to make that trek down to the barn and back. Come on, hop in. Wanna drive it?"

"I think I'll let you do the honors." Michaela laughed as she got into the passenger seat.

"Can I ask if your ex-wife knew that you and Audrey had remained such close friends?"

"Oh, ha. No, she didn't. Kathleen has a horrid temper. Piss her off, she's like a rattlesnake. No one wants to get in the way of her wrath. I know, because I'm always in it. She is constantly taking me back to court for more money. Don't ask me what she spends it on, but the woman can go through cash faster than anyone I've ever known. Everything has to be first class. And now I've married her younger twin. Kathleen plays up the martyr act, but it's only an act. Trust me."

Michaela recalled Kathleen's anger toward Olivia that morning. "Did you see Audrey other than when she came to buy horses?"

"Now and again. She'd come up to take a look at horses, or we'd visit over lunch. We talked every week about Olivia or…you know, life, things." His voice trailed off. "I'll miss her."

Michaela noticed tears in his eyes. "Me, too."

"I can't believe she's gone. Nor why anyone would do this. Everyone loved Audrey. Dearly. How could you not? She was kind, generous, loving, and beautiful. I adored her."

"Sounds like you did."

His words again made Michaela think that there had been something going on between Audrey and Hugh. This was the second time she'd wondered about it. "You knew Audrey for a long time, didn't you?"

"More than twenty-five years."

"She worked for you?"

"She did."

"Waitress, wasn't she?"

"She was more than a *waitress*. She and Kathleen were the entertainment at the original Bowen's in Malibu. That's how we all met. They worked for me, and one night I overheard them talking about how they'd like to sing. I asked them if they had any talent and they said that they did. I told them to put something together and I'd listen, maybe let them sing at the restaurant. They did, and they were great. Packed them in. Audrey had a beautiful voice and could play the guitar. And Kathleen, she could sing, too, and play the harmonica."

Michaela laughed. That one was hard to imagine.

He looked at her with amusement as they entered the impressive barn, row upon row of horses—some sticking their heads outside their stalls to see the guests, a few nickers here and there, some pawing at the ground. "I know what you're thinking—Kathleen playing a harmonica."

"It doesn't quite fit with the picture of your ex."

He frowned. "Not today, anyway. But she wasn't always so uptight. She was a wild one. Audrey had a calming influence on her. Always the peaceful one, you know."

"I do. Audrey's nature was definitely gentle."

"I look back on those years and I know that she was the one I should have married. If I had, she might be alive today, and I know we would have lasted."

His words took her aback. She decided to take a chance: "You were in love with her, weren't you?"

Hugh didn't hold back his tears any longer. "I always was. Always."

"Did she know?"

"Yes. She knew. She definitely knew. I asked her to marry me last week."

FOURTEEN

"WH-WHAT?" MICHAELA ASKED, SPUTTERING ON the question.

Hugh nodded slowly, tears now streaming down his face. "I've made huge mistakes in my life, and letting Audrey slip through my fingers was the biggest. And now, she's gone."

"But you're married. I mean, I guess, um..." Michaela's head spun over this revelation. "Okay, I'm sorry, I know this is none of my business, but I have to ask: Were you and Audrey having an affair?"

"No. Audrey would never do that. Never. What we had was far more special than something as lurid as an affair. We had a *connection*. A real connection. We may not have ever had anything physical, but we did have an affair of the heart. In a sense, I suppose that's as bad. But I think it's worse for the two people who love each other not to figure it out than it is for the spouses. It's a travesty all the way around. I realized that last week after we had lunch, so I bought a ring and asked her to marry me."

"Did she say yes?"

"She did. And it was yesterday that I planned to tell Bridgette." He smiled, but his eyes betrayed his sadness.

Something told Michaela she'd found the reason why Bridgette didn't think highly of Audrey. Somehow, Bridgette knew about Audrey, or at least the love Hugh felt for her. How could a woman not sense that type of thing?

"And, now...now she's gone." He broke down.

Michaela put her arms around him. "I am so sorry."

He gently pulled away from her and wiped his face. "Please don't tell anyone. You're the only one who knows. I know what she meant to you and I had to tell someone. We were getting ready to tell everyone after I ended things between me and Bridgette. I wanted it to be as amicable as possible. I wasn't out to hurt anyone; I just didn't want to live a lie any longer. I've been doing it for years. And, even though she's gone and we won't ever be married, I have to divorce Bridgette. That's what I meant when I said that I needed to make changes. I also need to find out who murdered Audrey." The lines in his forehead creased deeply. "I'll kill whoever did this!" he exclaimed.

Michaela wanted to ask him why, if he'd loved Audrey for all these years, had this revelation not dawned on him earlier, causing him to pursue Audrey sooner than later. But he was so upset that she decided not to say anything further about their relationship for now. The man was distraught and it didn't feel right to delve into his or Audrey's personal life any more than she already had.

Hugh seemed to want to change the subject as he stopped in front of one of the horse's stalls. "Geyser. Good boy, he is. Audrey loved him. Wanted to take him to her place, but with the changes we were about to make that wouldn't have been necessary. She would have moved in here with me and sold her place in Indio." Geyser stuck his head out of the stall. Hugh patted the handsome dapple gray. "Hey, there." He looked back at Michaela. "Won a lot of races. And, he's sound."

"Rare," she replied, referring to the horse's legs. Soundness in a horse signified that they weren't lame, which was hard to come by, especially in a retired racehorse. These were animals that for a time in their life went at full speed, with all one thousand pounds or more beating down on their fine legs. "How old is he?"

"Eleven now. I've had him all his life, and he likes it here, but he's a real social guy. He'd love the attention that kids would shower on him."

"I can see that," Michaela said and laughed as the gelding nudged her hand, wanting a pat.

"But there are no kids around here, and when Audrey called me to ask if I might have a good horse for a kid, my first thought was Geyser. I have to tell you, he's not one I want to let go of. But when Audrey told me that he'd be for you, I knew he'd have a great home. Plus, she wanted you to have him."

"You know how I feel about my animals. They come to stay."

"That's a good thing. I don't know how profitable it is, but it's a good thing. You want to take him out, give him a go?"

"Yeah."

Hugh led Geyser from the stall. One of the grooms came by and offered to saddle him up. Hugh said that would be fine, and he finished showing Michaela around the barn.

When Geyser was ready, she put him first through some basic paces and then challenged him some. He still had his get up and go, but was responsive and definitely good natured. He'd be perfect for what she had in mind. "I love him. How much do you want for him?"

"He's yours."

"What?"

"Take him. My gift; but if you ever want to get rid of him, you bring him back here."

"But why? Why would you give him to me?"

"Because I know how much Audrey cared for you, and I want you to have him. And as I said, *she* wanted you to have him."

"I can't do that."

"Fine. Give me a dollar and we'll call it even." He smiled and it was warm, kind—just as Audrey had been.

God, she wished they could have been together.

"Please, Michaela. He's a good boy. He'll make the kids you're working with happy. I want you to have him."

The kids. Joe's proposition of working with his daughter and more autistic kids crossed her mind. Geyser would be perfect for the children. Was she really thinking about accepting the position? Maybe so. As Hugh had told her, Audrey would have wanted her to enjoy her life, and the joy she got out of working with Genevieve was evident.

She finally agreed. "I'll pick him up later this week, if that's okay. I need to get back home, check on things. And I don't have my trailer with me. Day after tomorrow work for you?"

"Works great."

"Good. But you have to promise me that you'll come out and visit. Watch him with the kids."

"You can count on it. Like I said, I hate to see him go, but know he'll be in a good place. I will be out to see him. He'll be great with the kids. Won't you?" Hugh rubbed Geyser's face.

Michaela hung his bridle back up in the tack room as Hugh put him back in his stall. Turning around, she bumped into a slightly built Mexican man. "Oh, excuse me. I didn't know anyone was there."

"Is okay," he replied curtly.

Hugh walked in. "Oh, I see you've met Enrique."

"Sort of," Michaela replied and laughed. Enrique didn't smile. *Jeez, lighten up.*

"Enrique Perez, this is Michaela Bancroft. Enrique is my jockey. The best around."

"Thank you, sir."

"It's true. Won the race on Chico yesterday."

"Good horse. Nice to meet you, *señorita*." He warmed slightly.

"You, too," she replied.

"*Señor*, I need to leave a bit early. It's my brother. I have something to take care of with him."

Hugh frowned. "Is he in trouble again?"

"No, no. He promise me no more problems especially now that you give him a job. He real happy about it, and me, too. No problems at all, just need to go with him to an appointment."

Hugh slapped Enrique on the back. As the jockey left the barn, they returned to the golf cart. "Man works so hard with these animals and he's got this brother—Juan—who has had some troubles with the law, but Enrique assures me the man is turning his life around. Sure hope so. I took a chance on him because of Enrique and hired him to take care of the mechanical stuff around here. So far so good. He does do a good job, but the jury is still out, if you know what I mean."

"I know what you mean. Family can be difficult."

"Yes, they can."

"Before I head out, do you think your trainer might be back?"

"Josh? I'm not sure. He may be with a horse on the exercise track. I know that he got a late start this morning. Why?"

"I...have some technical stuff to ask him." She didn't know if Hugh was aware that Josh had brought Olivia home, that the girl and her mother had already had quite an argument that morning. She decided to find out if he knew the answer to the burning question. "Hey, did you ever locate Olivia last night?"

"Yes. I sent Josh to pick her up. That idiot Steve Benz convinced her to go out with them."

"Them?"

"Him and his manager—Marshall Friedman. Don't trust either one of them as far as I can throw them. Friedman has been trying to get Olivia to sign with him and leave Audrey. Sure, the guy can boost her career, but I don't like it at all. The guy is a jerk."

"Was she here then, last night?"

"By the time I located her it was almost one in the morning. I told Josh to pick her up and take her to her mother's, who I figured would be worried sick to death about her. She's recently moved into her own apartment, but I knew with what had happened yesterday that Kathleen would've expected Olivia to come home."

Michaela decided not to tell him that Olivia hadn't made it to Kathleen's until after seven that morning. Where she'd been with Josh for those six hours was a question. Her mind wandered—could the two of them have simply been comforting each other all night?

Or did they have something to hide?

FIFTEEN

AFTER SAYING GOOD-BYE TO HUGH, MICHAELA found Josh down at the exercise track, dismounting a beautiful sorrel horse. She called to him. He waved at her. She walked up and the horse turned his head, taking curious note of the newcomer. "Gorgeous animal."

"Chapman's Lightning. We call him Chappy around here. A lot of heart, but not so fast on the track. The lightning part of the name is kind of a joke. He'd rather be back in his stall finishing his breakfast. But they all need their exercise. Personally, I think Hugh should sell him and a few others. Racing is a money-making business, but Hugh has a philosophy: Horses come here to stay and if they leave, he knows where they're going. It's either on their way to heaven or to the barn of someone he knows and trusts."

"Like Audrey."

Josh nodded and looked down at the ground, digging his paddock boots in. "Like Audrey. Can't believe what happened. She was a nice woman and good with horses."

"I know."

"I thought coming out here this morning that maybe I'd be able to erase some of yesterday from my mind, but it's not possible."

"For me either," Michaela replied.

"I'm guessing you're here to look at some of Hugh's old guys. He mentioned to me that you had an interest in lesson horses."

"I already had a look. I'll be picking up Geyser later this week. I wanted to talk to you before I left, though."

"Ah. Geyser, huh? Good boy. He'll be great with kids. Look, I can figure out why you wanted to talk to me. I'm sorry about that scene this morning with Kathleen and Olivia. I wish you hadn't seen that. Kathleen is difficult to deal with." He shoved a hand into a pocket of his breeches and pulled out a can of chew.

Michaela nodded. "She does come across as high-maintenance."

"You don't know the half of it. She wasn't so bad when she was married to Hugh. But after the divorce she wigged out. I think Audrey was probably one of the last ones to stand by her. The rest of her friends disappeared. And, Olivia...well, this thing is going to be hard for her to deal with. I think she loved Audrey more than her own mother. Not that anyone would blame her for that." He fiddled with the can and then shoved it back into his pocket. "Trying to quit."

"Kathleen does seem to keep a tight leash on Olivia."

"You saw it for yourself. The woman is a total control freak. Olivia has no desire to sing. She wants to be a jockey."

"And you've been letting her ride, haven't you?"

Josh didn't answer her right away. Her stomach sank as his eyes narrowed at her question. "Kathleen put you up to this? Are you here to grill me about Olivia because that old bag sent you? She's sicker than I thought."

Michaela shook her head. "No. That's not why I'm here. I'm trying to make some sense out of what happened to Audrey. There probably isn't any to be made, but I feel like I have to try. Olivia, Kathleen, and I were the last people to have any interaction with her before she died, and I thought that maybe Olivia said something to you about Audrey since you were with her last night. I already know that Hugh asked you to get her from Steve Benz's place around one this morning, and I also know that by the time she got home, it was after seven. I thought maybe you two would have talked."

"I told Olivia about Audrey on the drive back from Beverly Hills. She lost it, which I expected. I took her home with me because she asked me to. Said that she didn't want to be alone and she couldn't deal with her mother yet. I comforted a distraught friend. That's it." His anger was obvious. He started to lead the horse away from her toward the barn.

"Sorry, I didn't intend to upset you."

He stopped. "What do you want? Really?"

She sighed. "I want to know why Olivia went off with Benz in the first place. I want to know if she ever said anything to you about Audrey acting strange, especially lately."

"Olivia was shanghaied last night by Steve Benz and his ass of a manager, Marshall Friedman."

"How did that happen? I was with Olivia when she was getting ready to perform and he came by, hitting on her. She didn't seem interested in him." Michaela also recalled how rude Benz was to Audrey, who had tried keeping him away from her goddaughter.

"She's not interested in him. You can probably thank Kathleen for Benz dropping by to bug Olivia."

"What?"

"Sure, she played all innocent this morning. The *ever-*concerned parent. I'll tell you what she is: She's one of those psycho stage mothers. Olivia is a grown woman and her mother wants to make a superstar out of her…forget what her daughter wants."

That didn't make a lot of sense. Sure the control freak–psycho mother part sort of fit, but Kathleen's anger about Olivia's disappearance seemed real to her.

Chappy stomped his foot and pawed at the ground. "I've got to get this saddle off of him."

"Sure." Michaela followed him to the barn set up next to the track. This one was smaller than the other across the track and up the hill, where Hugh had taken her. It was obviously only used for the horses just after their exercise. Josh slid the horse's bridle off him and replaced it with a halter, securing both sides of it with cross ties to finish taking off his tack and get him over to the wash rack. As he scraped Chappy with a sweat scraper, she continued to probe. "Tell me how Olivia wound up with Benz and Friedman."

"Olivia was angry."

"About what?"

"No, angry with me."

"Why?"

"I wouldn't let her exercise Chico that morning."

"Does her dad know?"

"No. She asked me not to tell. She's afraid her mom would find out."

Michaela didn't tell him that Kathleen already knew. Those photos she'd found proved that much. She was afraid that if she revealed it to Josh, he'd go ballistic. Although he seemed like a nice guy, he'd also given her reason to believe he had a temper.

"Olivia is a good kid, but she does like to get her way. How could she not, being the only child in this clan? She doesn't like to hear the word *no*."

"From what I've heard so far, she does seem to have a problem saying it to her mother."

He agreed. "I don't get it. Kathleen has a hold on her. And she had one on Audrey. As much as I know Audrey loved Olivia, and she knew what Olivia's real dream in life is, but she'd never say a word to Kathleen about it. She'd never tell her to back off or leave her alone and let Olivia live her own life. I could never get that."

"It wasn't really Audrey's responsibility, do you think? To tell Kathleen to not interfere with her daughter?"

"I do think she was responsible in some way. Audrey knew Olivia better than her mother does, and they were tight. Do I think she should have told Kathleen to back off her daughter? Yeah, I do. I also think that she shouldn't have been a partner in Olivia's career. But even Audrey, who could see how happy Olivia was when she rode on the track, came to me and asked me to try and dissuade Olivia—that her parents wouldn't be happy about our morning sessions."

"Did Olivia exercise horses a lot?"

He shrugged. "When she could get away from Mama's clutches. Audrey brought her here when she was in town. Kathleen trusted Audrey with Olivia and would have never guessed she was bringing her to the track to ride. Since Olivia moved into her own place last month after a battle with her mother, she's been showing up here more often."

"You said that Olivia was angry with you yesterday, but what does that have to do with her going with Benz, and her mom setting it up?"

He unhooked Chappy from the cross ties and walked him over to the wash rack, Michaela in tow. She turned on the hose while he led the horse onto the concrete slab, then took the hose from her, rinsing him down. Water sprayed onto Michaela. "Sorry," Josh said.

"No biggie. I do it every day."

"You train reiners, don't you?"

"Yeah. It's a great sport."

"Fun to watch, kind of like the dressage of the western discipline, but for me, there's nothing better than the track."

"I can see that. For Olivia, too, obviously." Michaela was starting to wonder if Josh was deliberately trying to change the subject. "What do you think about this thing with Olivia and Benz?"

He turned off the hose and threw it to the ground. "The dickhead got Olivia plowed, probably spiked her drink. I don't know, because she told me that she didn't have any more than two drinks before leaving the track with them. They took his limo up to Beverly Hills, where they had dinner. She says that Benz and Friedman harangued her, promising her the good life and telling her they could make her a star and she should sign on with Friedman as her manager."

"Did she?"

"Nope. It was about that time when I found her. Her dad tracked her down and sent me to get her. They even had a contract already drawn up, and like I said, I would not be surprised if Kathleen was behind the whole thing. It'd be just like her."

"What about you and Olivia?"

He stopped grooming the horse and eyed her. "What about me and Olivia? There is no *me and Olivia*."

Michaela studied him, not knowing if she should believe him about what had happened with Olivia last night. Her gut, his actions and reactions to her questions, caused her to believe that, if there was not anything more going on between Josh and Olivia than just friendship, Josh would have liked there to be. "I better get going. I've got a long drive back to Indio."

He nodded. "Hey, I am really sorry about Audrey. It's a shame."

Michaela nodded and walked to her truck. She got the feeling after talking to Josh that he had some ill feelings toward Audrey. He felt that she needed to be the one to make Kathleen loosen the noose around her daughter's neck. And, there were feelings there. Michaela could tell that Josh cared for Olivia. He was far more defensive about her than he needed to be. She could not help wondering if Josh was so infatuated with Olivia and possibly so twisted in his thinking when it came to her, that he'd do anything to see the young woman get her way.

Even kill for her?

SIXTEEN

MICHAELA PLACED A CALL TO ETHAN AS SHE DROVE the 10 East back to Indio.

"Hey, you," he said, sounding more upbeat than he had early that morning.

"Hi. Well?" She sucked in a breath.

"He's out of surgery and in the recovery pool so that when he wakes up, he doesn't thrash about and reinjure himself. We were lucky this facility is so close to the track. They have an excellent team here."

"What can you tell me about the break? What are his chances?"

"I'd say they're good. As I explained, he has a condylar break. He broke it all the way through. It was clean. The break below the pastern is what could threaten him, but he didn't shatter it, so from this point on we're looking at a long haul. I'm optimistic, though. In a lot of ways, this will be up to Halliday. His attitude is going to be important, just like a human patient, and how well he reacts up in the hoist, off his feet for some time. It's vital that we keep his weight balanced and not put any undue pressure on the other three legs. We want to avoid laminitis at all costs because then we could have an entirely new problem on our hands. It'll really be his temperament that gets him through. If he can tolerate us and him babying that leg for the next several weeks, then he should come out of this."

"That's great."

"Yeah, and from everything I've seen so far, this animal has a good temperament. Sometimes in these cases, if a horse can't tolerate the treatment there's the risk of reinjuring the leg, and if that happens it can be many times worse than the initial break. So that's why we'll stay cautious, plus watch for infection. He should be coming out of the anesthesia soon and once that happens, I'm going to head back home. I'll make the commute over the next few weeks rather than stay here. With Summer only being a few weeks from delivering the baby, I'm trying to stay close to home."

Michaela cleared her throat. "That's probably a good idea. Can I ask how you got involved in this?"

He paused. "I wanted to wait and tell you at the barbecue, but considering this situation...I became certified as a state vet, Mick. That way I can vet at the track. I thought it might be an interesting challenge. Yesterday when Halliday sustained the injury, I happened to know the vets on the surgical team and was invited to take part in performing the surgery. Since I was with him for the ride down and saw the injury happen, I wanted to be here with him. The vets have been kind enough to allow me to be involved."

"Wow. I had no idea that you wanted to vet the track. That's great." She considered telling him about Audrey. It was obvious he didn't know. Sooner or later he would, but he seemed genuinely happy at that moment—he was pretty sure Halliday would recover and he and his wife had a baby on the way. He'd be upset over Audrey's death, and Michaela didn't want to put a damper on his day. She also did not want to go to the barbecue–baby shower deal.

"I've got some other good news: We found out the baby is a boy."

"Oh, Ethan, I think that's wonderful. You're going to be a great dad."

"I hope so. I'm looking forward to it. One of the other vets told me about this baby store close by the center. I thought I'd stop at on my way home and pick something up for him. Who would have ever known I'd get all mushy over a kid?"

"I knew you would."

"That's not saying much, you know me better than I know myself."

She laughed. "Probably so. Okay well, I'll see you Friday, then, if not before. And keep me posted on the horse. Hey, by the way, does Kathleen Bowen know about Halliday yet?"

"I've tried calling a few times and got no answer. I finally left a message on her answering machine to call the center for an update. It's surprising that she hasn't made the trip down here. Maybe she's on her way."

She doubted that. For all the concern Kathleen had portrayed about Halliday the day before, Michaela had to wonder if she was off taking care of what she considered more important matters, like delving into her daughter's affairs. "Maybe."

"Hey, Mick, you're not still planning on taking care of this horse's bill?"

"Yes, I am."

"I don't get that."

"Tell you what, I'll explain it all to you when I see you."

"You'd better."

* * *

MICHAELA TURNED INTO HER PLACE BEFORE 1 P.M. and found Joe and Genevieve standing out by the barn. Oh no, she'd forgotten that she was to give Gen a lesson that afternoon. Part of her wanted to cancel it, take time to think about Audrey. She hadn't mourned her loss; not really. But she couldn't do that to Gen, and working with the little girl would be therapeutic for her as well. It would be what Audrey would want her to do. She got out of the truck, spotted Audrey's overnight bag still in the backseat, and sighed. She'd deal with it later.

"Hey, I'm sorry. I forgot about today. I've been in L.A.... and oh God...anyway, I'm sorry."

Joe looked at his watch. "I was ready to send one of my cousins out after you." He laughed. "Never knew you to be fifteen minutes late for nuthin'. You okay?"

"Sure. A bit of traffic, that's all."

"And you couldn't pick up that cell phone you got glued to your ear half the time?"

"Joe. Stop it." She smiled at him. "Hey, by the way, I need to talk to you about your cousins."

"What you need?'

"Some information on a guy named Bob Pratt. He's a veterinarian. I thought one of your cousins might be able to find something out about him."

"What gives, Mick?" He bent down to Gen. "Go get the horse a carrot, sweetheart. Daddy and Miss Michaela are gonna talk for a minute, okay?"

Gen nodded and walked toward the feed room, where she knew Michaela kept the veggie drawer in the fridge stocked with carrots and apples.

She sighed. "His sister was a friend of mine and she was murdered yesterday. Bob is missing. Has been for the past four or five days."

"Oh no. I'm sorry about your friend, but you don't need to go messing into this. I'm smelling trouble here."

"Please. All I want to know is if the guy has fallen off the wagon. He's had a drinking problem in the past, and his sister helped him get back on his feet. I find it hard to think that he might be involved in her murder, but with him incognito it does not look good. The police seem to think he killed her and is on the run. I'm actually hoping he's on a bender somewhere. And, that's where you or one of your cousins might be able to help out. That's it. Just want to know if he is okay. That is all I need to know, and then I'll drop it. Promise." She crossed her heart.

"Where was he living? And, what about where he worked?"

"L.A."

"Okay, got some cousins in L.A. that might be able to help me out. We'll see. But that's it. *Capisce*? No more this crazy you-playing-Miss-P.I. business. Hear?"

"You got it. Thanks."

"Okay, so the guy lives in the City of Angels. You know any of his pals? Where he works? His address, phone number? I gotta have something to go on."

Michaela gave him the information that she had, which wasn't much, other than his employer, that he worked the track, and had been to rehab at Betty Ford within the last year.

"That's a start. Now you gotta do me a favor." She knew this was coming. "You gotta call that director over at Genevieve's school and tell her that you want to organize the riding program. I've done a lot for you, Michaela." He crossed his arms over his wide chest.

"You sure know how to guilt a girl, don't you?"

He smiled. "You know and I know that you are perfect for this." He took out his wallet and handed her a card. "Call this gal, tell her you'll set it up."

She sighed. "Okay, Joe, I'll give it a shot."

"Good woman. I knew you'd do it." He pointed a finger at her. "Now go and work with my kid. I'll see what I can find out about this Pratt dude."

Michaela looked at Gen walking back to them, carrot in hand, her dark, curly hair pulled into a low ponytail in order to fit her helmet over it, her big brown eyes staring straight ahead. She took the little girl's hand. "Thanks."

Joe bent down and gave his daughter a kiss on the cheek. "I'm proud of you, pretty girl. I know you're going to be great up there today. Miss Michaela will take good care of you. Daddy is gonna come up and watch soon. I have to make some phone calls." He winked at Michaela.

Michaela put a halter around Booger. He was perfect for Gen. Calm, well behaved, with no intention of moving any faster than a walk. The new horse she'd purchased from

Hugh that morning, Geyser, would be the right addition for Jude's daughter. Katie was up for the challenge of a horse that would eagerly move out.

Together they brushed the horse. Michaela placed a hand over Gen's on the brush and they stroked Booger's coat. She spoke in calm, hushed tones. "That's good. See how clean he's getting?" Michaela asked. "What a good job you're doing, Gen. Look at how pretty you're making Booger. He likes that a lot."

Once Booger had the therapeutic saddle on him and Michaela slid a headstall over his ears, she kept him on a lead line and, after putting Gen up on him, led him up to the arena. There, Booger did as Michaela asked him, and Gen finally smiled from ear to ear when Michaela put Booger into a jog on the lead line. "Look at you ride Booger. You have a great seat. Stay with the horse. Keep your bottom in the saddle. Wow. Nice job, Gen. Really good."

After they finished their lesson they headed back to the barn, where Michaela had Gen get the carrot out of the groom caddy. Michaela broke the carrot into threes and reminded Gen to hold her palm flat so the horse couldn't nip her fingers or hand. "He wouldn't mean to do it," Michaela said. "But it could happen. So, we hold our hand out like this." She held out her palm flat then, with the other hand she smoothed Gen's hand out, placing a carrot in her hand and putting her own hand underneath the child's to keep it stable. Booger took the carrot gently and Gen smiled again. Peace and a genuine feeling of happiness came over Michaela for those few minutes alone with the girl. This was what life was about. The moments where a real connection happened.

While Michaela put Booger back in his stall, she told Gen that there was a treat for her inside the tack room. The girl knew what that meant. It had become a ritual since she'd started working with her. Katie was also aware of the cookie jar. Michaela made sure that she baked a new batch every few days for the girls, and when they were done with a lesson they could have one.

Joe came into Michaela's office while Gen ate her cookie. "I'm still checking this dude out, seeing what I can get on him. I'll give you a call when I know something."

"Thanks," Michaela said, hoping inside that Joe and the cousins would find out what had happened to Bob Pratt.

SEVENTEEN

AFTER JOE AND GEN LEFT, DWAYNE SHOWED UP. He'd had Rocky, who appeared to have recovered from his bizarre "attack" the other day, out on the hot walker. Michaela kept her fingers crossed that it had been an isolated incident.

"You doing good with that kid," Dwayne said.

"Thank you. How is Rocky doing?"

"He be okay, you know. No more problems. The vet call me and say he had some higher testosterone levels than normal. She say that could be causing him a problem."

"Interesting. Did she know what might be causing it?"

"No. She ask if you give the horses any kind of bute or steroid."

Michaela laughed. "Oh, sure. I'm all about drugging these animals up. Why would she ask that?"

"Dunno. I think she trying to figure it all out. She say that she have Dr. Slater take a look when he get in tomorrow. She don't seem to know. Say maybe something with his pituitary gland."

"Hmm. Okay, well, I'm glad Ethan will be taking a look; if anyone can figure this out, it might be him."

"Michaela, you okay? You looking tired."

She sighed. "No. I'm not okay." She told him about Audrey.

"Oh, lady, you been through a lot these last coupla years. Losing Uncle Lou, then old Cocoa passing on," Dwayne said, mentioning her chocolate lab, who she'd lost in the spring to old age. "Now your friend." He shook his head. "Must be good things on the horizon for you. Hawaiian spirituality tell us that when there are tough times to be grateful, cause there are nothing but good things coming around the corner. Everything happen for a reason and it serve you."

She touched his shoulder. He was good to have around.

"Hey, hey! I'm ready for my riding lesson."

Michaela turned to see Camden bounding down the breezeway. Holy cow! Was she actually wearing Wranglers and a pair of riding boots? "Whoa! What is going on here?" Michaela stifled a laugh as she remembered the last time Camden got on a horse and nearly broke her tailbone falling off the other side.

"Oh, hey you. Didn't know you would be back so soon from L.A. Yeah, well I decided that if I'm going to live on a ranch, I might as well learn how to ride. And Dwayne is teaching me." Camden flashed a smile at him.

"Huh. Really?" She glanced at Dwayne, who had turned a shade darker than his native skin tone. He nodded. Okay, something was up between these two.

"Yes. Really."

Michaela bit her tongue and for some comic relief watched Camden in the arena while Dwayne gave her a riding lesson. To her surprise, Camden did well up on the horse. She'd been on a horse more than a few times of late, because there was no way that the Camden Michaela had out on a horse a while back was the same woman on her mare Macy right now. She shook her head, confused, and decided to let it go for now. But later, when Camden had filled up on margaritas, she planned to ask her what in the world was really going on. She'd never shown an interest in horses and she'd been living with Michaela for almost two years.

She let the two of them finish their lesson and went on down to the house where, to her surprise, she found a dozen pink roses in her kitchen. Camden and her admirers. She picked up the card and saw that they were for her: from Hudson Drake. *Looking forward to Saturday.* "Great," Michaela said out loud. "What the hell am I going to do?"

"About what?" She jumped and looked up to see Jude Davis leaning against the kitchen doorway. "Sorry, it was open and I saw you standing there. Didn't mean to frighten you. Who are the roses from?" He walked into the kitchen.

He smelled good—kind of tropical, coconut maybe. He looked good, too. He always looked good with his blue eyes and rugged features, and he dressed how she liked a man to dress—simple; jeans, nice shirt. No sport coat today. Sunday was his day off. She set down the card. "Oh, um, just this guy who...well, I met him at the races and he knew some of the same people that I know and I don't know, I gave him my card and I kind of offered to do him a favor."

"Favor? Must have been a pretty good one." Jude smiled and rocked back on his heels. It was a nervous habit that Michaela had noticed.

"Wait, no, it's nothing. I only told him that I'd relay a message for him." She thought back to the conversation she'd had with Hudson and her plans to inform Audrey about Bob. It was not something she wanted to get into with Jude, the cop.

"Must have been some message."

"Jude!" she implored.

"Hey, no big deal. So, some guy sent you a dozen roses. I'm not dumb. Men are going to pursue you. And I personally don't mind a bit of competition."

"You don't?" She wasn't sure how she felt about that. "Why?"

"Because I plan on coming out the winner."

"Really?"

"Really."

He walked over to her. His eyes reflected a bright intensity. "I think I can top the flowers." He pulled her into him and kissed her. The touch of his lips, his hands on her waist, all of it shocked her, but she didn't resist. The kiss was sweet, smooth, and really nice. It shot a surge of electricity through her as her heart raced and what felt like a thousand butterflies fluttered in her stomach. Wow. She hadn't been kissed like that in a very long time. In fact, she wasn't sure she'd ever been kissed like that at all. She pulled away from him. "Yeah."

"Yeah what?"

"That was better than roses."

He pointed at her and started to leave. "There is more where that came from."

"Wait. Where are you going? Why did you come by?"

He smiled. "Just to say hi. And see when you'd like to go out for dinner. How about Friday?"

"Friday? Oh, uh..."

"Oh no, no. You just told me that the kiss beat out the roses."

"It did. Definitely. Hands down. It's that, um, it's Summer and Ethan Slater's baby shower–barbecue thing on Friday. God, I don't even know exactly, but it's kind of this couples thing, and I thought..."

"Yes, I'll go."

"I didn't ask."

"You were going to though, weren't you?"

"Maybe."

"So we'll have dinner another night. Friday we'll go to a baby shower–barbecue instead." He laughed. "See you Friday."

"See you Friday," she uttered, bringing her fingers up to her lips, still burning from Jude's touch.

EIGHTEEN

MICHAELA TRIED TO MAKE LIGHT OF JUDE'S KISS, but it stuck with her for the rest of the day. Why did he have to go and do that? It only made everything that much more confusing. But confusing about what? she chided herself. He liked her, she liked him; maybe they could have something together. Why did that have to mean *confusion*? Why couldn't she be more like Camden and just go with it, and if it didn't work out...well, then it didn't. But she wasn't like that. As much as she thought she'd like to be, she simply wasn't, and therefore Jude's kiss caused her confusion, some stress, as well as a smile when she thought about it.

What wasn't making her smile and was also making her crazy was Audrey's murder, and she wondered if the police had made any headway at all in the investigation, other than focusing on Bob as the killer. She hesitated to pick up the phone and call Detective Merrill. What kind of questions could she ask him anyway? She did want to know if they had discovered anything new. It probably wasn't such a good idea to call Merrill, and she knew she should drop it anyway. She was doing what she could by asking Joe to help her out, and he'd promised to give her a call if he found out anything.

The sun was going down, which meant it was time to feed the animals and make herself some dinner. She'd let Dwayne have the night off since he'd covered for her while she was in L.A. Funny, she hadn't seen Camden *or* Dwayne since the riding lesson. She couldn't wait to quiz Camden about her newfound interest. Where had they disappeared to?

She filled the wheelbarrow with several flakes of hay and distributed it to her "kids." She then went back into the feed room and filled buckets with supplements for the handful she fed them to. Rocky nickered as she came to his stall with his bucket of treats. She dumped the contents into his feeder and he immediately dove in. "It's the good stuff you like, isn't it?" She laughed, and then stopped as she thought she heard someone else laugh. Where was that coming from? There it was again. Definitely laughter.

It was coming from the tack room.

Michaela walked into the tack room and the words slipped out at the spectacle she saw. "Oh, my God."

Camden immediately started buttoning her shirt. Dwayne pulled his shirt back over his head. He turned crimson. "Oh, oh. I'm sorry. We uh, well, we uh…"

Michaela held up a hand. "That's okay. I think I know what you were doing." She turned and started to walk away.

"Wait, Michaela. Stop," Camden called out. "You were going to find out one way or another. We planned to tell you."

"What in the hell is going on?" Michaela asked.

"We're in love," Camden said, beaming. "And I'm moving in with Dwayne. Look." She held out her left hand; on it she wore a ring with a small diamond.

"Is that what I think it is?"

Camden jumped up. Dwayne put his arm around her. "Cammy girl and I, we be gonna get married, island style, you know. We thinking a wedding on the big island. My home and all."

"It'll be beautiful," Camden gushed. "And, we're going to have a margarita bar, doesn't that sound great? And you have to be my maid of honor!"

"Cammy girl?" Oh boy, these two were intimate. "That's great. A real wedding, huh?" That would be a first for Camden, whose first three marriages were by elopement. She could not believe what she was hearing. Her friend and employee were not only getting it on together, they were getting married! "So, tell me, how long have you two been keeping this from me?"

Michaela looked at Dwayne. He smiled. "You know, it be like three or four months."

"Three or four months! Jeez, I must be blind."

"No. We were just good at hiding it," Camden said.

"We are in love. I feel it in my heart. Never met no one like my Cammy girl."

"Oh, I'm sure of that. I suppose that's what the riding lessons are all about. I figured you were dating someone new and didn't want to tell me because I'm always lecturing you on your poor choice in men, but I can't think of a bad thing to say about this guy." She pointed at Dwayne.

No, actually in this situation it was Dwayne who Michaela might have to worry about. Camden could be a heartbreaker when she wanted, and the last thing Michaela needed was a heartbroken horse trainer. Not to mention she wouldn't want to lose Dwayne. He was the best, and if it didn't work out between him and Camden he could very well quit his job. She cringed at the thought, but when she eyed the two of them, she could honestly say that she'd never seen Camden look at anyone the way she was looking at Dwayne, and vice versa. Maybe it was true love, and they'd gotten away with it right under her nose. She started to laugh.

"You aren't mad?" Dwayne asked.

"No, I'm not mad. I'm not your mother. You two are weird. Why would you think I'd be mad? I love you both. I want you to be happy and if you're happy together, I think it's great. A little strange, but great."

"I certainly never expected it," Camden said.

"You. What about me?" Dwayne laughed.

"Why don't you come have margaritas with us? We'll celebrate and make wedding plans."

"I've got to get the horses fed, so I'll take a rain check. Go back to what you were doing, but maybe take it over to Dwayne's—or can I now call it your place, too?"

"Not officially. We'll go the traditional route and I'll move in after the wedding. I mean if it's okay with you, considering it is your property."

"I may have to raise the rent, you know."

"You do that," Camden said.

"If it were anyone else but you, I would."

"Come on, honey, let's go to your place. Our place." Camden took Dwayne's hand.

"Have fun," Michaela yelled after them.

She watched them walk away hand in hand. She shook her head. Compatibility. Who knew those two would wind up together? Strange combination. Michaela prayed that it would work between them. She'd wondered how Summer and Ethan would work out, too. They didn't exactly seem compatible, but she was no one to judge. They were expecting their first child, and Michaela could not believe that she would be taking Jude with her to the baby shower. That thought reminded her that she needed to call Hudson Drake. She'd thank him for the roses but explain to him that Saturday was out. Maybe she could meet him for lunch when she went to Los Angeles tomorrow to pick up Geyser. No. That wasn't a good idea. Well, she would have to give him back the key. "Ugh," she said aloud as she went back to taking care of the horses. Now that was something she could do, do it well, and have it all make sense—take care of the animals.

Humans made no sense, while animals made perfect sense.

As she finished feeding and started back to the house, a horrible realization hit her. She could not believe that she hadn't thought of it earlier. Oh no. *Francisco.* Audrey's ranch hand. Had he heard what happened to Audrey? She knew how much Audrey thought of the man. He needed to be told.

Instead of going into the house, she got into her truck and drove to Audrey's place.

As she pulled in to the ranch, everything seemed quiet, until she got out of the truck and heard whinnies from the barn. She walked over to the stalls, which looked like they'd recently had a fresh coat of paint applied. The horses grew further agitated seeing her. She quickly realized that they hadn't been fed. She looked at her watch. It was past seven. Where was Francisco? She tossed them each a flake of hay, not knowing what else Audrey fed them. She walked over to the house and used the spare key that Audrey had given her to the back door. She stopped. There were voices. "Francisco?" she called out. She realized that the voices were coming from a TV upstairs. The guest room. Maybe Francisco had dozed off watching a show earlier. She'd better wake him and let him know about Audrey. Plans would have to be made for the animals. "Francisco?" she called out again as she climbed the stairs.

The door to the guest room was cracked. Francisco appeared to be asleep on the bed. "Francisco? Hello?" She went into the room, irritated that he hadn't woken up and bummed that he hadn't been taking care of the animals the way he was supposed to. "Francisco," she said, this time louder. She stepped toward the bed. *Paint. Next to the bed. Different color from the barn. Red paint, not beige.* Michaela touched Francisco's shoulder. *Cold. Really cold.* She shook it and realized, as his body turned and he stared blankly up at her, with dried blood on his chest, that he was dead. She backed out of the room and ran down the stairs, nearly stumbling at the bottom. As she picked herself up, someone reached out for her and she screamed.

NINETEEN

MICHAELA FELL BACK ONTO THE BOTTOM STAIR, terrified. She picked herself up, still screaming. "Michaela? It's me. It's me!"
"Olivia!" she yelled. "What the hell are you doing here?"
Olivia took a step back. "I...I came here to feel close to Audrey. I wanted to get away from my mom, too. I thought it would help me feel better."
Michaela grabbed her arm. "We have to get out of here now!"
"What?" Olivia shook her head. "What is wrong with you?"
She tugged on the girl's arm. "Come on. We have to call the police!"
"You're scaring me."
Michaela stopped, looked at her and said, "There is a dead man upstairs. I think he's been murdered and we have to get out of this house and call the police."
"Oh shit!"
They ran outside. "Get in," Michaela told Olivia as they approached her truck.
"You think that the killer is still here?" Olivia asked.
"I don't know what to think." Michaela grabbed her purse from the floorboard, retrieved her cell phone, and dialed 911.
The operator asked her some questions and told her to stay put and on the line as the police were dispatched to the ranch. In a matter of minutes the sheriffs' cars started pulling in.
Michaela and Olivia got out of the truck as men and women in uniform quickly swarmed the place. Two deputies approached them. One was a young, pretty woman, her dark hair pulled back, brown eyes trained on

them. The man next to her was older and stocky with a graying mustache. He looked as serious as the woman did.

"I'm Deputy Garcia," the woman said. "This is Deputy McDaniels. We're going to take your statements. We have officers securing the grounds."

Michaela introduced herself, then Olivia, who fidgeted nervously. The police had a way of amplifying an unnerving situation, but Michaela couldn't help wonder if there was more to Olivia's reaction than the situation at hand. Had she really come out to Audrey's ranch to *feel* close to her?

Garcia asked Michaela to come with her so she could take her statement. McDaniels stayed with Olivia. After half an hour of going over her story twice, Garcia looked up from her notes. Something caught her eye because her demeanor changed almost abruptly from questioning, hard-line cop to...mmm, what was that...womanly? Michaela turned around to see Jude approaching. *Oh no.*

"Detective Davis, this is Ms. Bancroft," Garcia said.

"Yes. I know, we've met." Jude crossed his arms.

Garcia looked from one to the other, then stepped aside. "Okay, well, I just finished taking her statement—"

Jude cut her off. "Thank you, Deputy. I'll take it from here."

"Of course." Garcia stepped away.

Wait a minute. She batted her eyelashes. No she did not. Oh yeah. Yeah, she did. Michaela stood up straighter. *What was that all about?*

Jude lowered his voice. "What is going on, Michaela? What are you doing here?"

She sighed. "It's not what you think."

"Oh, you don't know what I'm thinking."

"Okay, well you better not be thinking that I had anything to do with Francisco's death, murder, whatever."

"He was murdered, all right. A gunshot through the chest."

Michaela winced. "Oh no. He was a good guy. Audrey cared about him."

"Speaking of...you did not tell me that you knew Audrey Pratt."

"No, I guess I didn't. I know a lot of people."

"Michaela, I was just at your place earlier today. Why didn't you tell me about your friend being killed? I've only received sketchy details at this point, but what were you thinking?"

"Huh? What was I thinking? I don't know, Jude. You didn't give me a lot of time to think. If I remember right, you kind of took my breath away." She glanced behind him and noticed Garcia eyeing them. The deputy quickly went back to jotting something down in her notepad.

Jude blushed. "Took your breath away?"

"Jude!"

"Davis, need you in the house," one of the detectives called. "Looks like one of the rooms has been torn apart. May have been a robbery gone bad."

Michaela didn't buy that theory. It all seemed way too coincidental that Audrey had been killed the day before. *Someone had been looking for something.*

"We're not done with this. I know you. I know how you think, and I don't want you getting mixed up in this investigation. I don't want you hurt. Please."

She didn't comment.

"Davis!"

"I'm coming," he yelled back to the other detective. "I mean it, Michaela. We're not finished."

"Can I go now?"

He shook a finger at her. "Garcia, you finished with your statement?"

"Yes, sir."

He nodded and looked back at Michaela. "I'll see you later."

She found Olivia, who had just finished with McDaniels. "Oh my God, I was like totally bombarded by that cop. I told him like five hundred times that I just got here. I didn't even know there was anyone dead."

"Would you like to go have a cup of coffee or a bite to eat?" Michaela asked. She wasn't sure she felt like eating but she didn't feel like being alone either, and she had some questions she wanted to ask the girl.

Olivia looked down at her watch. "Uh, sure, okay. But I don't have a lot of time."

"Didn't you just drive a couple of hours to be around Audrey's things, her house?"

"Yeah. I did. But a friend just called me and wants to get together tonight, so I figured if I can't stay here, I might as well head back."

"It's almost nine."

"Right." She shrugged and didn't offer up any other answers. "So, coffee? Where?"

Michaela told her to follow her to the coffee hut she liked—The Honeybear. Once seated with a cup of decaf and Olivia fidgeting in front of her with some kind of fancy specialty coffee, she couldn't help herself any longer. She set her cup down and leaned in. "I'm kind of confused, Olivia. Maybe you can help me here. You drove out here to feel close to Audrey?"

"That's what I told you. Look, it may sound crazy to you. I know that cop was thinking I was full of crap, but I'm not." Tears filled her eyes. "I wanted to be here. I thought maybe if I drove out to her place that I'd feel close to her, like she was still here."

Michaela softened at the sight of Olivia crying. Maybe she was simply hurting over the loss of Audrey and was telling the truth. "Are you okay?"

"I don't know. No. Not really. My mom told me about Halliday, and with Audrey being killed..." She sobbed. "I can't believe it. I loved her so much and she would know what to do right now. I don't know what to do. I want everyone to leave me alone."

"To do about what, Olivia?"

"That stupid Callahan guy is leaving me messages on my voice mail."

"Frederick Callahan?"

"Yep."

"The guy who runs that men's magazine *Pleasures*?" Michaela recalled Callahan standing next to Bridgette Bowen, over Audrey's body. The thought caused a shiver to snake down her back.

"That's the one," Olivia replied.

"What does he want?"

"He's been bugging me to do a spread in his magazine. Says I can be dressed, just a transparent blouse. He wants me to wear a pair of breeches and—this is the best part..." She wiped her face. "He tells me a crop in my hand would look good, kind of do a jockey thing."

"Creep."

"I've told him no way, but he still keeps calling. Then Marshall Friedman, Steve Benz's manager, suggests I do the magazine and that Steve would like to do the photos with me, and together he thinks we would make a great pair."

"Jerks."

"Yep. But wait, the biggest jerk of all is my mother. I told her what they proposed and she said that I should do it. It would be good for my career. She says that as much as she loved Audrey and as hard as it is that she's gone, I have to think about moving on, and Audrey was holding me back. Can you believe that?"

"Oh my God. That is so cold. What the hell is wrong with your mother?" she blurted. "I'm sorry. I didn't mean to say that."

"No. You're right. My own mother wants to sell me out. Wants me to pose half naked with some asshole pop star in hopes of me making it huge for her."

It looked like Josh was right about Kathleen likely being the one to set up the meeting between Olivia, Friedman, and Benz after the races. She'd kept it from both Audrey and Olivia, maybe fearing that they would veto the queen and her ideas. "What did you tell her?"

Michaela also couldn't help wondering if Olivia was aware of her mother's financial troubles. Michaela had dealt with her own difficulties when it came to finances, but when it had happened in her life after her ex left and stuck her with thousands of dollars in medical bills incurred from failed in vitro fertilization attempts, Michaela had changed her lifestyle—slowed things way down. Not that she ever really lived beyond her means anyway, but she knew how to tighten up when necessary. That was clearly something Kathleen Bowen was unable to do, even while going down the tubes. Appearances meant more to her than honesty and reality.

"Nothing. I left. You don't tell my mom anything. It's not worth the fight. She'll wear you down."

"Is that why you haven't told her that you want to be a jockey?"

"You know about that?"

"I do. Audrey told me."

"Ah." Olivia crossed her arms. She looked paler tonight than she had the other day. Granted, she had ivory skin, but she appeared more gaunt and unhealthy. "That would be nice. Dreams are nice but they're bullshit."

"Is that why you left the races with Benz and Friedman? Why you were willing to discuss a contract with them?"

"Look, I did that because I was mad at Josh. He'd been a jerk to me earlier and I didn't want to be around him or my mom. Benz and Friedman came to see me after the show in my dressing room. We started talking and decided to go party somewhere else."

"Did you have anything to drink?" Michaela remembered Josh telling her that according to Olivia she'd only had a couple of drinks and they'd been before she'd left the races. He'd suspected that Benz might have spiked the drink.

"Yeah. I had a beer, maybe two. I don't know. It's kind of a blur now. We were talking and then Benz said he'd grab a few beers. Friedman hung with me while Benz got the drinks and then when he came back we downed them and took off."

Those moments that Benz went to get the drinks: He had the opportunity to spike Olivia's beer then. He also might have had opportunity to kill Audrey. He had threatened her only a couple of hours before with Olivia changing management camps. The timing seemed right to Michaela for Benz to have done it. Maybe Josh had good reason to distrust Benz. Not only was he trying to scam the girl he cared about, but could Josh have a gut feeling that Benz was even slimier than what he put out there. Could Josh suspect that the guy was evil enough to kill? "Josh seems to be pretty protective over you."

She nodded. "Yeah, so? He's cool. I know he has a thing for me." She shrugged. "I kind of like him, too, but my mom would freak, and I don't know what my dad would say."

"You are an adult."

"Right."

"You are, Olivia. Maybe you should try acting like one."

"What the hell does that mean? Oh forget it." She looked at her watch again. "I have to go. Thanks for the coffee."

"You hardly drank any."

"I know. But I need to get back." She stood, her demeanor changing.

Olivia obviously did not want to talk about the prospect of being a jockey, or acting like an adult, and she'd begun fidgeting again. Her cell rang. She took it out of her purse and answered, waving good-bye to Michaela as she walked out. Michaela shook her head in bewilderment. The young woman certainly was confused, and confusing. She sat there and sipped her coffee. The waitress came over with her bill.

"Oh, hon, looks like your friend forgot something; maybe it dropped out of her purse." The waitress reached across the booth and handed her a tiny envelope, the kind that typically holds a card attached to flowers.

"Thank you." Michaela took the envelope and couldn't help but look inside. No card, but there was something. Crushed chalk? No. Flour? Powder? *Oh damn.* A sickened feeling struck Michaela, for she doubted that the substance was anything of a legal nature. She felt pretty sure that what was inside the tiny envelope was cocaine.

TWENTY

"YOU LOOK LIKE HELL," CAMDEN SAID WHEN SHE walked into the kitchen the following morning and found Michaela trying to jump-start herself with a strong cup of coffee.

She hadn't been able to get to sleep until the wee hours of the morning and then it wasn't exactly restful, as nightmares invaded her dreams. "Thanks. Not all of us get to sleep in the arms of a loved one, all warm and cozy. I am still mad at you, you know." Michaela poured herself another cup from the carafe. She had to hit the road if she wanted to reach Los Angeles early and get out before the late afternoon traffic kicked in. She took a bag of bread from the cupboard. "Toast?"

"No. I'll have some cereal, though."

Michaela served up her friend's favorite cereal—Fruit Loops. *How fitting.* By the time she finished waiting on Camden, her toast was ready. She slathered it with peanut butter and sat down. "Aren't you going to say anything?"

Camden set her spoon down and shrugged. "Look, I knew that you would discourage me from a relationship with Dwayne. And I know what you're thinking, that I'll dump him, leave him brokenhearted and he'll hightail it back to the islands."

"You got it," Michaela replied.

Camden reached across the table and took Michaela's hand. "I know I've been a flake. I know I've been unlucky in love and that's why I'm here with you. You always warned me with each guy I've brought around that it wouldn't work, that he wasn't good enough. That he was some superficial moron. And that's what's different this time. You know as well as I do that *superficial* is the last thing Dwayne is. He's unlike all the men I've fallen for in the past. There isn't a phony thing about him, and material gain isn't what he wants."

"You're right. And that's what worries me. I don't want Dwayne to be the flavor of the month or year because he is different. Camden, you like material things, and you can be phony." At that comment, her friend scowled. "You can and you know it."

Camden nodded. "I love him." She looked up at Michaela, tears in her eyes. "I can honestly say for the first time in my life that I am in love with a man and he loves me. It's not about anything else but that, and I want your blessing. Please."

Michaela squeezed her hand. "Okay then. But don't ever keep something like that from me again. I feel like an idiot. I can't believe that I didn't notice."

"I won't. Thank you. It's not hard to believe that you didn't notice, though. You've been busy with the horses, running this place, Joe's kid, and that hot detective's daughter. Hell, I feel like I haven't seen you much these past few months."

Camden was right. She had been busy. They hadn't spent much time together lately like they used to. "We need to change that, don't we?"

"We'd better, considering we'll be planning a wedding together."

Michaela smiled. "Should be a good distraction for me."

"What do you mean?" Camden asked between bites of cereal.

Michaela sighed. "Dwayne didn't tell you about Audrey?"

"No."

She began the sordid tale. "Oh my God." Camden brought her hand up to her mouth. She stood and wrapped her arms around Michaela. "I am so sorry. Is there anything I can do?"

"I don't know. Last night after finding Francisco, I asked Olivia to have coffee. She was acting really strange.

Then she took off and left something behind. It must've fallen out of her purse."

"What?"

"A small envelope of cocaine."

"Ah, jeez. Not good."

"Poor Hugh. I should tell him."

"Oh no. You need to stay out of this. None of this sounds good at all. I know how obsessed you became when Lou was murdered, and you almost got yourself killed. Promise me you're not off trying to piece it together. Let that family unravel without you being stuck in the middle. You're a good person, you don't need outside hassles getting in the way of running your life. That's your problem: you're always trying to solve everyone *else's* problems. Take care of yourself for a change."

"All I'm doing is trying to find some answers."

"Michaela," Camden implored. "Run as far away as you can from those people."

"Joe is checking into a few things for me and that's it. Then I'll drop it. I even promised him."

Camden shook her head. "Stubborn. Very stubborn. Now you got Joey Pellegrino involved. I knew it, and I bet your cute detective is aware of your activities and he probably is not too happy about it."

Michaela looked up at the clock. "Oh, would you look at that, gotta run. I have a horse to pick up."

"Michaela."

"I'll be back tonight."

"Michaela!" Camden yelled. "Stay out of it. Please. You have a lot of people who love you."

"I love you, too. Thanks for caring. Have a good day."

With that she shut the door behind her. Camden was right. Leave all the dysfunctionals back in Hollywood. She'd do that tomorrow, she promised herself. Today she had to go and pick up Geyser. So asking a few more questions couldn't hurt, now could it?

TWENTY-ONE

BEFORE HEADING OUT, MICHAELA STOPPED OFF AT Audrey's place to make sure the animals were all okay. Jude had left a message to call him. She was going to give that some time. She wasn't ready for the third degree. At Audrey's, she found Deputy Garcia holding down the fort. She sat on her porch swing looking beat tired and bored out of her mind. She eyed Michaela up and down.

"You know, technically you're not supposed to be here. I do know that Ms. Pratt was a friend, but I have my orders, straight from Detective Davis," she said as she glared at Michaela. Maybe it was her imagination, but did Garcia have a bone to pick?

"I understand. I only came by to feed the animals."

"The animals will be fine. Arrangements have been made for the Humane Society to pick them up. That's why I'm still here. I was off two hours ago, but they send in the rookie to do this shit."

"Oh, no! Not the Humane Society. I have room for the horses. Please give me a day."

"You'll have to take it up with the Humane Society. Or maybe your boyfriend." Garcia stood up from the porch swing and crossed her arms.

Something about her intimidated Michaela. Maybe it was the fact that she carried a gun. That might have been it. But her comment was way off base. "I don't know what you mean."

"You and Detective Davis. I saw the way you were looking at him. You two *do* know each other."

"Yes, but we don't have anything going on."

"Can't blame you. He's a hottie. That's for sure. More power to you, girl. But let me just say that you've got all the women around the station a little peeved at you. They've all been competing to spend some time with Davis."

"Peeved about *me*?"

"Word is that you and Davis have a thing. It's the gossip around the station. I'd be careful if I were you. He's got the womanizer thing down. You can ask anyone in a skirt back at the station. He and I have even spent some time together." Garcia winked at her.

"You can go back to the station and tell the ladies there that Detective Davis is more than available," Michaela said.

"You sure about that?"

"I'm sure. Now, can I go and check on the animals? Feed them? They have to be hungry and it's best if I turn some of them out to pasture."

"Why not?"

"Thanks." Michaela stormed off and could have sworn she heard Garcia chuckle under her breath. What was that all about? She did not like being the subject of gossip. And to even have become that subject, Jude must've told someone that they were seeing each other, or something like that. *Whatever.* And what was that comment that he and Garcia had spent time together? Was Jude different from what she'd thought? Could he be another womanizer? God knew she had a knack for picking them, and then getting blindsided like a deer caught up in headlights. Had she fallen into another man's trap? No, she had not. She wouldn't let Jude get the best of her. If he wanted to chase the skirts back at the station that was just fine. But she wasn't about to allow him to get under her skin and feed her lies. No way.

She made her way to the barn and started feeding the horses. Then she went out to the pasture and brought the roving ones to their stalls and fed them. Audrey had about twenty head. By the time she was finished, it had taken nearly forty-five minutes. As she was locking up, her cell phone rang.

"Mick, it's me, Joe. I got some info for you on that Bob Pratt dude. Seems he had a girlfriend named Cara Klein. She lives in San Diego. That's all I've been able to get so far. I'm still working that angle." Michaela made a mental note of the information. "Also, he liked to hang at this bar up in Malibu. Place serves good fish and chips, my cousin told me. Anyhow, he was in there a couple of weeks ago."

"Drinking?"

"Only Cokes, according to the bartender."

"Was he by himself?"

"No. Says he was with a couple of younger men, both Hispanic. He said that one didn't seem as friendly as the other, was kind of an ass to the bartender and it made Pratt nervous. The other guy seemed okay. The bartender also said that guy was a short dude."

"Interesting. We've got to find out who those men were that he was talking to. Can you do that?"

"You're getting sucked into this, Mick."

"Joe, do it. And I know you will. You know why?"

"Cause you're working with my kid."

"Nope. Well, maybe that, but it's also because you love this cloak-and-dagger stuff."

He didn't comment for a few seconds. "I'll call you back. Be careful."

"Always."

Michaela went into Audrey's office to see if she could find a pen and something to write on. She wanted to jot down Cara Klein's name. She doubted she'd forget it, but she wanted to be certain.

She opened the top drawer and found a pen but no paper. The third drawer down, she located a stack of legal pads as well as an 8×10 envelope addressed to Audrey. But what caught her eye was the return address: that of her brother, Bob.

TWENTY-TWO

OKAY, SO SHE SHOULDN'T HAVE DONE IT. IT WAS impulsive. Michaela knew she should not have done it. But she had. She'd walked out of the barn with the large envelope, keeping an eye out for Garcia, hoping the deputy wouldn't spot her and ask her what the envelope was about. She knew she was taking something that didn't belong to her. Maybe she should've passed it on to Garcia. Heck no. Why do *her* any favors? She set the envelope in the backseat and headed west. Besides she had a feeling that this was the envelope Audrey had mentioned the other day. The one that she was to give to Ethan. It didn't belong to the police or her. It belonged to Ethan. Right? That is, if it was the right envelope. Michaela could not be sure about that without opening it. And, she didn't know how she felt about opening it. But she certainly couldn't give it to Ethan to open and then have it be something he would have no clue about. She'd have to ask him if he'd gotten Audrey's message about it. She'd also have to tell him about Audrey, if he hadn't already heard. Detective Merrill had told her that he would be needing to speak with Ethan and ask if he'd spotted Audrey on the track after Halliday had broken his leg.

Over lunch: Maybe that's when she'd take a look at what was in the envelope. She would have to eat lunch today. And she'd be in Los Angeles at lunchtime. Hudson Drake came to mind. But she was pulling a horse trailer. It might be nice to have lunch with him, her treat. Ah, who was she kidding? She was irritated that Jude might be talking about the two of them as if they were a thing. They were *not* a thing. And she didn't like feeling suspicious that he might be playing her and another woman, or women. That she did not like at all. She recalled his almost egotistical attitude about coming out the winner yesterday when he'd kissed her. Was he like that with all women?

She'd discovered that the kind of man who exuded the kind of self-confidence Jude did around women indicated he'd traveled the path to a woman's heart or bed more than a few times. But did she have a right to feel that way?

She picked through her wallet where she'd put Hudson's card and gave him a call. He told her that he'd love to have lunch with her, and since she was pulling a trailer they could meet at Duke's, a nearby restaurant. "It's laid-back there. Not the jet set in and out, and the parking lot is huge. They've seen trailers come in there before," he said.

"Great. Noon work for you?"

"Sure does."

She wondered if he'd had any luck with the private investigator he'd said that he hired to look into Bob's disappearance and intended to ask him about it. Lost in thought, Michaela at first didn't see the flashing lights in her rearview mirror. When she did, it took her another second to realize that she was being pulled over. What had she done? She wasn't speeding. She hadn't cut anyone off, had she? Oh brother! She didn't have time for this right now. She pulled off to the side of the road and cut the engine. A highway patrolman approached the truck. "Hi, Officer," Michaela said. "I'm not certain why you pulled me over."

He faced her, eyes covered in dark sunglasses, a serious expression on his face. This could not be good. "Can I see your driver's license, ma'am?"

She removed her wallet from her purse. "Sure, but can you tell me what I did wrong?"

He opened up his ticket pad and took the license from her. "I'm going to have to write you a fix-it ticket. Did you know that the lights are out on your trailer?"

"Oh no." She sighed, relived that it wasn't anything more than that. That sounded like an easy fix. "Are you sure?" He frowned. *Stupid question.* "I will definitely have that fixed." He finished writing the ticket and tore it off.

"Have a nice day," she said taking the ticket. He walked back to his car. Damn. She was only thirty minutes from Hugh Bowen's place. She'd have to get the trailer fixed. There wasn't a way out of it. She couldn't haul a horse back without those brake lights working.

She called ahead to the Bowen ranch. Hugh told her that someone should be around who could fix them, that she should just pull on in and either find Josh or Enrique. "I have some errands to take care of. I don't think I'll be around by the time you get here. Hopefully you can get the trailer fixed quickly and be back on your way. I know it's quite a drive."

"True. I'm sorry that I won't see you."

"Me, too, but you'll be at the charity event on Saturday. We'll catch up there. I'd actually stay and wait here for you, but I need to find out when Audrey's body might be released. We have to plan a proper service for her."

Michaela recognized the emotion in his voice. How had she not thought of a service for her friend? Of course, something needed to be arranged. She thanked Hugh for his willingness to take care of it and offered her help in any way that she could.

When she pulled into the ranch, the gate was open. She parked the truck and trailer near the main stables. She looked around but didn't see anyone at first. Then a Hispanic man in jeans, T-shirt, and leather gloves came toward her. "Hey," he said. "I'm Juan Perez. You Ms. Bancroft?"

"Yes."

"Yeah. Okay, Mr. Bowen said you would be by. He said that your trailer's light are out."

"They are." She frowned.

"I'll unhook it for you and see what's going on, okay?"

"Thank you. That would be great. Quiet around here this morning?" she said as Juan started unhooking the trailer.

He nodded. "Josh and my brother, Enrique, had to take care of some business with the American Quarter Horse Association. I think they're in the office on the phone or something."

"Oh."

"And most of the grooms are on break, but I'm trying to get ahead, you know. Mr. Bowen, he just give me this job, so I'm doing the best I can."

Michaela couldn't help but remember what Hugh had said about Juan—something to the effect of him having been in some trouble. She also couldn't help wondering who it was that Bobby Pratt had been talking to at the fish and chips bar in Malibu a few weeks ago. She suddenly wondered if it was possible that the two Hispanic men he'd been hanging out with were Juan and Enrique Perez.

"Hey, Juan, do you know Bob Pratt?"

He stood up. "Who?"

"The vet. I know that Mr. Bowen uses him at times, and that they're friends. I'm sure you heard about the murder at the races."

"Sure, yeah." He nodded emphatically. "I heard 'bout that. No good, you know. My brother tol' me, and he say it was real bad. Mr. Bowen pretty upset 'bout it."

"Me too. The lady who was killed was a good friend of mine."

"Oh no. I'm real sorry."

"And, her brother is Bob Pratt. He's been missing for several days now."

Juan clucked his tongue. "That's too bad."

"So, you don't know him? Never met him?"

He shook his head again. "I don't think so. I only work here on and off, you know. I haven't been here for about three months, maybe. My brother got my job back though. Mr. Bowen is a good man. He's helping me out. I don't want to mess up, you know? But the vet, no. I wouldn't know if I did see him because a lot of people come here and look at horses. I just fix stuff."

"Right. Thanks. Hey, is there any water down here? I'd like something to drink."

"You know, I gotta fix that, too. The faucet in the tack room got all messed up. You can maybe go in the office where Josh and Enrique are. There's a refrigerator there."

"No, I don't want to bother them if they're on the phone."

"You can take the golf cart up to the house. Mr. Bowen, he has a fountain in the garden."

"That's okay. I can just get a drink out of the hose. I was only looking to quench my thirst a bit. No biggie."

"Might as well go up to the gardens and see it anyway. It's gonna take me some time to find the problem here. And it's real pretty up there. Take a cruise around the place. It's nice. And the water is much better than from the hose." He laughed.

"Okay. Thanks." She really didn't have time to kill, but she also had no choice. She climbed into the golf cart and cruised around the ranch. Either Juan Perez was lying or he really had no clue who Bob Pratt was, and the men he'd been with at the place in Malibu were two different people than she'd guessed at for a second. Another thought struck her: What if it had been Francisco, Audrey's ranch hand? He'd met a horrible, untimely demise as well. Michaela could not believe that his murder was not somehow connected to Audrey's, and she was also pretty sure that Bob's disappearance was what tied everything together. She realized that both thoughts were kind of out there. After all, there were quite a few Hispanics living in Los Angeles. What type of business would Bob Pratt have had with Juan or Enrique or Francisco? Just because they were all Latino didn't mean anything. She realized that she was grasping at straws here.

As she jetted around on the cart, she took in the opulence of the place. She passed the practice track, the stables, and palm tree–lined pasture, which had a beautiful pond in the center of it where ducks lazed through the water. The facility was magnificent and seeing it all made Michaela sad, knowing that Audrey would have enjoyed living here. She would have appreciated the ranch and she would have been happy with Hugh. "Oh, Audrey," she whispered as tears stung her eyes.

She approached the garden, complete with the English hedge maze that Juan had mentioned. Unsure exactly where the water fountain was located, she got out of the cart and took a walk through the garden. Various rosebushes gave off their soft floral scent as hummingbirds dipped in and out of water feeders. A large fountain, with a statue of an angel atop a horse, sat in the middle of the garden. The artwork was gorgeous. She finally found the fountain off to the side of a path that led into the hedge maze. She took a long drink. She decided it might be fun to take a walk through the maze. Apparently there was time to spare. Why not?

Michaela started in through the maze, taking in the sounds and smells. It really was like an English garden. As she wound herself farther into the maze though, some anxiety came over her when she'd heard something—a rustling in the maze. Probably birds. No need to get spooked. She glanced around. She wanted out of there. Her nerves buzzed with the idea that if someone were inside the hedge watching her, she certainly wouldn't be heard if she screamed. She backed away. She had to get out of there. Her brow started to perspire as she tried to wind her way back through the route she'd come in. A few minutes later she was at the entrance of the maze. Thank God. Then she heard the rustling noise again. She inched toward one of the Spanish moss trees that lined the gardens. There it was again—only now, she also heard a voice. A woman's voice.

She stayed close to the shadows and tried to make out where it was coming from and who was talking. She caught a glimpse of blond hair as a person walked through the hedge and then out of the maze. Bridgette. Had she spotted Michaela? She'd been walking the maze at the same time? She must have been on the other end, because she didn't seem concerned, or to be looking for anyone herself. It was obvious to Michaela that Bridgette did not know that she was there.

Michaela watched, intrigued, as Bridgette headed toward the rosebushes, cell phone to her ear, and then sat down on the bench. Michaela kept out of sight, and she could now hear the woman quite a bit better.

"I have to see you." She smelled one of the roses. "No. Look, I know it's not a good idea, but please. I need you right now. If Hugh knew what was going on…What we did. Oh God, I could lose everything. Everything. Dammit." She paused. "No! I need to see you now. This is a big deal. It's a huge deal. What we've done, well…if anyone knew. Please, lover. Please. We can just have lunch. That's all I'm asking. Okay. I'll meet you at the restaurant then. Shutters. Half an hour. Thank you, love." She turned off her cell.

Michaela moved even closer to the tree. Bridgette glanced in her direction. Oh no. Don't see me. *Don't see me.* Bridgette stood up and started walking toward the house. Oh God, what about the cart? Michaela had parked it off to the side, but if she saw it, she'd wonder who had driven it up here. She might look around. Michaela watched as she veered off to the other side of the garden. She finally dared to breathe, knowing that Bridgette hadn't discovered her.

So, who was the good Mrs. Bowen off to meet? And what was this business about losing everything? And who was she calling *lover*? Furthermore, what had they done that Bridgette seemed to want covered up? Did it involve

Audrey? Michaela jumped back in the cart after waiting a few minutes to be sure Bridgette didn't spot her. She knew what Shutters was: a luxury hotel down in Santa Monica, about thirty minutes away if the traffic was working with her.

She found Juan. "I need to take my truck and run some errands while you're working on the trailer. When do you think it'll be ready?"

He laughed and held up a handful of shredded wires. "Something tells me you got a rat problem at your place. Not so good. They chewed through a bunch of the wires. I think it's gonna take me a while. Why don't you call the ranch around four? I'll see what I can do."

She nodded and started her truck. She didn't have time to wait around Los Angeles all day hoping her trailer would be fixed, but it appeared she didn't have a choice. And since she didn't, she made her way down the Pacific Coast Highway to see if she could find out exactly who Bridgette had been speaking to on the phone in the garden.

TWENTY-THREE

MICHAELA FELT LIKE SHE COULDN'T BREATHE AS she headed down the 101 toward Santa Monica. A ton of thoughts rushed through her mind, and her anxiety levels soared—Audrey, Francisco, Hugh, Olivia, Kathleen, Bridgette—all of them blurred in her mind.

She reached the luxury hotel shortly after Bridgette pulled in, noticing that the valet was parking the woman's Mercedes. Michaela parked her own truck, not wanting to be seen. She counted on the fact that Bridgette Bowen would not exactly be looking for her. What was Michaela's goal here anyway? How had she become some real-life Jessica Fletcher? She didn't have time to ponder that thought, as she noticed Frederick Callahan climbing out of a white Rolls-Royce. Now, wasn't that interesting? He was an easy one to spot, with that bad toupee. Her mind churned. She pondered what to do as she watched Callahan go through the front doors of the hotel. What in the heck was she doing? Jeez—spying, that's what! As the thought crossed her mind, an eerie feeling swept over her: The kind that says you, too, are being watched. She glanced to her left and caught a very tall man with a large build—almost like a football player—dark hair, and olive skin, eyeing her with deep-set brown eyes. His eyes turned away when she made contact with him. He glanced back as he headed for the front of the hotel. He smiled slightly, then picked up his pace. That was odd.

Okay, if she was going to play this out like one of her old favorite TV detectives, she knew she'd have to go in.

The valet greeted her as she breezed past him; she asked him where the restaurant was. The conversation Bridgette had had with Callahan—assuming it was Callahan she'd been speaking with—was about having lunch. Interesting that they also chose a high-end hotel to have lunch in. Michaela guessed that there was more than just lunch plans on the agenda. The valet told Michaela that there were two restaurants inside, one a more upscale place, the other an al fresco café out near the bike path. She first looked inside the formal restaurant, spotting only an older couple and a younger man. The al fresco café held quite a few people, and she spotted Callahan and Bridgette in a corner, tucked in tightly near a large potted plant. So, it *was* Callahan that she'd been talking to! Mmm, she would love to be a fly on a leaf of that potted plant.

"May I help you?" the maitre d' asked. She didn't answer right away, and he persisted. "You are here for lunch?"

"Damn!" She clapped her hand over her mouth. The maitre d's eyes widened. "Oh, I'm so sorry, I..." She held up her hand. "I'll be right back." Surely the man thought she was crazy, and as she started to flip around she spotted the same tall, intense guy she'd seen out in the parking lot. He was seated at the opposite end of the café, but in sight of Bridgette and Callahan, and he was watching them. Yep, he definitely was studying them. He held a pen, an expensive ballpoint, which he clicked off and on. Now, her mind reeled. This spy thing was getting to her. Was that guy using one of those pen cameras to take photos of Callahan and Bridgette? Oh, boy! Could it be? Was there even such a thing as a pen camera? Michaela shook her head and hurried into the lobby, where she quickly called Hudson, hoping he had not already left his office. She was supposed to meet him for lunch in only half an hour. She quickly explained to him that her problems with the trailer were worse than she expected. She didn't go into any details but said that she'd have to postpone the lunch. He sounded disappointed. "Are you sure?" he asked. "You can't make it?"

"No." She could. She knew she could. But something was going on inside that café and she wanted the skinny on it, if there was any way to get it. Then on impulse she said, "You know, it does look as though I'll be here for the afternoon. How about an early dinner?"

"That would be great. Let's do five. Duke's still?"

"Perfect." And, it was, because if the trailer was fixed, then she'd have time to load Geyser and get down to Duke's. The horse wouldn't mind waiting for an hour. She'd be sure to give him some extra feed, and she'd pay the parking attendant a bonus to keep an eye on him.

After hanging up, she sat in the lobby for a few moments, not sure what to do. She was kind of hungry. She went back to the maitre d' and asked for an inside table. She wanted to position herself to see both Bridgette and Callahan, but she could only see his face and her back. She ordered a bowl of soup and tried to be inconspicuous. She could not see the weird guy, who sat to her left and behind her on the patio. Callahan's facial expressions at first showed concern, maybe even anger, but then they mellowed as he picked up his phone. Who was he calling? She also noticed after he hung up that he moved from his chair to the other side and sat next to Bridgette, where he put an arm around her. The around-the-arm thing could just mean he was comforting her about something. No, that didn't fit. There was something going on between these two. That much was obvious.

They finished their meal. She waited a couple of minutes after they paid their bill and left before following suit. She didn't want to lose them, but if Bridgette spotted and recognized her, what was she going to tell them—that this was where all the horse trainers went to lunch when in town?

Outside the restaurant, she spotted the couple going up in an elevator. So, they *had* gotten a room. Sneaky snakes. Poor Hugh! After losing Audrey, his problems with his daughter…now a cheating wife? She wasn't sure what to do. Some of her questions had been answered. Maybe it was time to quit the spying act. She started to walk out of the hotel when she spotted Steve Benz walking in. Now what the hell was *he* doing here? Coincidence? Before he could see her, she ducked behind the large floral arrangement in the lobby and opened her purse, pretending to be looking for something. *Please don't see me.* Would he remember her anyway? She heard Benz say, "Hey." Oh no, had he seen her? She glanced up. No. He stood near the elevators, on his cell. "It's me, Cal, what room you two in?"

Cal? This was getting shadier by the minute. Was Benz going to pay a visit to Callahan and Bridgette? Michaela didn't know what else to think, but she decided it best to go and wait in her truck. What if someone else who might recognize her showed up for this little get-together?

Almost to her truck, she heard footsteps at her heels. Oh no. She spun around and stood face-to-face with the weird guy. That dark look he'd had when he'd eyed her earlier? Well, it was much darker now.

TWENTY-FOUR

"HEY!" MICHAELA YELLED AS THE GUY GRABBED HER arm. "What the hell are you doing? Let go!" She pulled free of the strong man's hold.

"I could ask you the same thing. Would you mind lowering your voice?"

"What? You're lucky I don't scream." She noticed the valet watching and was relieved. Who was this nutcase?

He quickly pulled a card from his wallet and handed it to her. "Dennis Smith? Private investigator?" she read.

"Exactly. What I want to know is why you're so interested in Bridgette Bowen and Frederick Callahan."

She shrugged. "I'm not."

He rolled his eyes. "Lady, I am a trained investigator."

"And why do *you* want to know? You investigating one of them?" He didn't respond. She clapped a hand over her mouth and then pointed at him. "Holy…You *are* investigating one of them." A warm ocean breeze blew across the parking lot. "Wait a minute, wait a minute…Hudson! Did he hire you? Hudson Drake?" That made sense to her because of the conversation she'd had with him at Hugh's ranch the other day. Smith said nothing, just eyed her. She pulled herself up tall. "Listen, I don't know you, and you haven't told me jack about why you noticed me supposedly watching those two, but I'm not saying another word until you start talking, too." She crossed her arms as he took a step back. Then she gasped as her focus turned to the front of the hotel.

Smith turned to see what she was looking at. He grabbed her arm again. "Get against the truck, as if we're talking."

"We *are* talking. Well, I'm talking anyway, and you're still a freaking stranger. A tall freaking stranger!"

"I'm not a threat. Hugh Bowen hired me. Now do what I say," he said in a rush. "We are having a nice chat with each other, as if we're lovers."

"I don't think so."

"Okay, friends."

Steve Benz had just emerged from the hotel and sauntered toward his Lexus, which the valet had brought around. She watched Smith. He took a tiny camera from his coat pocket—definitely one of those devices that only a private investigator or someone in law enforcement would use—and started taking covert shots of Steve Benz. "Hugh hired you?"

"Yes," he said, still snapping.

"What are you doing? Why are you following Bridgette and Callahan?"

"I could ask you the same thing," he replied. "You know my name, now who in the hell are you, lady?"

"Wait a minute. Does this involve Audrey's murder?"

He stopped taking photos as Benz got in his car. "Murder? What are you talking about?"

"My friend. She was murdered the other day, and she was close with Hugh."

"Oh." He stuffed the camera back into his pocket as Benz pulled out of the lot and sped away.

He studied her. "Go on...Wait." He held up his palm. "Can I get a name?"

"Michaela Bancroft."

He shook her hand. "Sorry for earlier. It's my business to be perceptive, and you were far more than just curious about those two. You were definitely searching for some kind of answer."

She nodded; emotion rose in her throat, as his question conjured up her last memory of Audrey. He raised his eyebrows. "Well?"

She sighed. "Audrey was a good friend. She was killed at the races the other day, and like I said, she and Hugh were close. This morning I was up at the Bowen ranch and overheard Bridgette having a conversation that sounded suspicious, as if she had something to hide. Obviously, it was Callahan. She mentioned meeting at Shutters. I followed. I wanted to know who she'd been talking to, and what it was they were trying to hide."

"You thought they might have had something to do with your friend's murder."

She nodded. "Hugh didn't tell you about Audrey?"

He shook his head. "He hired me three weeks ago to follow his wife. He suspected that she was having an affair. I haven't spoken with him in days. I am supposed to report to him tomorrow."

Michaela didn't quite know what to make of this. Why would Hugh care if Bridgette were cheating? He was getting ready to leave her and marry Audrey. Unless, of course, it would make him look better to a judge during court proceedings. That made sense. But, what it didn't do was prove that Bridgette or Callahan had anything to do with Audrey's murder. It only cemented the fact that they were messing around. And how did Benz fit into this thing? Why had he shown up at the hotel? He certainly hadn't stuck around for long. If the three of them had some weird sex thing going on, someone must've changed their mind. "What about Benz, how do you figure he's involved?"

Smith didn't have time to reply as the sound of sirens drowned out their conversation. An ambulance pulled into the front entrance of the hotel. They turned to see what was going on.

"What do you think that's all about?"

"I don't know. But here's our girl," Smith said.

Bridgette walked out the front door, looking dazed and quite pale. Her demeanor certainly was different from when she'd gone into the elevator with Callahan. Something was wrong. She handed the valet her parking stub. Smith started in again with the photos.

"Callahan should be right behind her," he remarked. "Typical." He shook his head. "I've seen this kind of thing go down way too many times. The woman leaves first and then a few minutes later, the man follows. But man, they were quick. Guess that happens when you're with a woman who looks like her." Smith chuckled.

Michaela didn't find his comment amusing. But Smith was right. Callahan did exit a few minutes later, only he was on the EMTs' stretcher. She turned to the private investigator. "You see that very often?"

TWENTY-FIVE

"CAN'T SAY THAT I HAVE," SMITH REPLIED.

Michaela remained fixated on the scene as she watched the paramedics load Callahan into the ambulance. What was going on? Why had Benz taken off so suddenly, and then Bridgette? Had they killed Callahan, or tried to? He looked to be alive. In fact, from where she and Smith stood, the paramedics appeared to be speaking to him before closing the back doors and speeding off.

"What in the hell?" Smith muttered.

"I've got the same question."

"Look, it's obvious that Callahan is on the way to the hospital. What those two did to him is a mystery. It's also obvious that you have a stake in finding out who killed your friend. I have a stake in getting paid by Bowen, but this little scenario ups the ante quite a bit. Do you know what a scandal like this is worth in this town? I could sell these photos to the tabloids and take a five-star vacation in the tropics." He paused. "Want to get some coffee? Maybe share some thoughts on this?"

She considered it. "Yeah. Maybe so."

"Good. Let me make a phone call and see if I can find out where they're taking Callahan and how bad off he is. We'll start there. I know this place probably costs ten bucks a cup, but…"

"My treat," she interjected.

They walked back into the café and ordered coffees. Smith made a call, inquiring about Callahan. "He's headed to Cedars-Sinai. No word yet on his condition, but I'll get it. So…"

"So?" Michaela said, still shaken by what she'd witnessed.

"Your friend who was murdered…"

"Audrey."

He nodded. "You mentioned that Benz threatened her."

Michaela told him about the races the other day and what had occurred inside Olivia's dressing room.

"That guy is an ass."

"Do you think the three of them could be involved in Audrey's murder? Why else would they be meeting? Maybe to talk business, I suppose."

"There are other possibilities. A hotel room? One woman, two guys...although typically, it's usually the other way around—two women."

Michaela brought her hand up to her mouth. "No. Don't even go there. That's disgusting. The three of them...together?"

"It's possible. I doubt Benz came here for a drink. But there is another possibility. Maybe I know the reason Benz paid a visit to the lovebirds. And if my guess is correct, it might have caused the old geezer to have a problem with the ticker."

"What's that?

"What if I told you that Steve Benz has been known to supply Mrs. Bowen with some good old-fashioned cocaine?"

"Oh." Michaela thought about Olivia and what had fallen from her purse at the coffee shop the night before. This was twisted. Olivia using drugs, Bridgette using drugs, Callahan trying to get Olivia to pose for his magazine, Benz possibly the supplier and maybe—just maybe—Audrey somehow got caught up in the middle of it all, and they'd killed her. Or one of them might have killed her. But Benz was a real up-and-comer on the country western scene. What about his career? Why would he jeopardize what he'd worked so hard at? "How do you know this?"

"It's the nature of the business. When things get slow, I start snooping and I sell some of my information to the tabloids. This situation here might have taken on an entirely different angle for me, and an added bonus. I know a guy at one of these rags who has it in for Benz. Says he had a one-night stand with his girlfriend after some bigwig Hollywood party. He's asked me to pass any information about Benz on to him. He knows that I work for the people who run in fast circles."

"What about Hugh Bowen? Would you exploit him if you found out that his wife is not only cheating on him, but might be linked to the murder?"

"If that's the truth, someone will discover it and put it out there. Besides, if that *is* the situation, he's a victim here. And so is Audrey. What was her last name?" She hesitated. "I won't lie to you, I will be checking into this thing. If Callahan, Benz, and the latest Mrs. Bowen are up to no good, I will exploit it. You want justice, don't you?"

"What if it's the wrong path?"

He shrugged. "It's a starting point."

"Okay, I'll tell you what I know, but you need to give me some of your insight. About Benz."

Dennis produced a notepad and repeated Audrey's name as he wrote it down. "Okay. Steve Benz is a party boy who started out in this town as a pool boy."

"Pool boy?"

"Yeah, you know, cleaning pools for the rich and famous. He met Bridgette on the party circuit before she hooked up with Bowen. They liked to hang together. Then, Bowen and Bridgette hooked up and he put her in rehab, right after the two of them got married. They tried real hard to keep that hush-hush, and for the most part Bowen's money did a good job of it. Money can pretty much buy you anything in this town. But people *do* talk. So, Mrs. Bowen's stint in rehab was one of those unspoken things amongst the rich and spoiled."

Michaela thought about Bob Pratt, his stint at Betty Ford, and a possible link between him and Bridgette Bowen, as well as the fact that Bob was now missing in action. Could it be coincidence, or was it linked to what had happened to Audrey? Was it possible that Bridgette and Bob had been in rehab at the same time? "Tell me then, or at least confirm if I'm on the right track."

"Go on."

Michaela's theory came from the center of her gut. "Bridgette went through rehab, tried to stay straight. That didn't happen. She's back at it with Benz as the supplier, because she trusts him and she knows that with him in the limelight, he'll keep things quiet. She likes rich and powerful men, thus her rendezvous with Callahan. Benz brings the party favors for the two of them, and in return uses Callahan and Mrs. Bowen to become a superstar. Because from what I hear, Benz is looking to do a magazine spread with Olivia Bowen for *Pleasures* magazine. He thinks that Callahan can help put him on the map. Maybe he also thinks that Bridgette has some kind of in with her stepdaughter. Although, that's the furthest thing from the truth from what I understand."

"What did you say you do?" Dennis asked, placing his elbows on the table.

"I didn't. Why?"

"Because I think you'd make one hell of an investigator."

"Not everyone would agree with that," she replied, thinking of Jude. "I'm a horse trainer."

"Horse trainer? Really? Nah."

She didn't reply.

"Oh, shit. You're serious. You're really a fucking horse trainer? Sorry for my trash mouth. I pegged you for a bored, rich housewife, or maybe a mistress."

"Oh. Thanks, asshole. Pardon me for my trash mouth; I'm not used to being insulted."

He laughed. "I gotta say, you are a breath of fresh air. You are in a town knee-deep in bullshit, and here you are going around just trying to get the truth by telling the truth. You may have to change your ways to ever really find the truth. Nothing wrong with a bit of whitewash to get what you need."

"Sorry, lying isn't my style."

"Did I say lie? I said whitewash."

She couldn't help but smile. As offensive as this Dennis Smith seemed to be, there was something about him she was warming up to. Maybe the no-nonsense part appealed to her. Whatever it was, she wasn't in that fear-for-her-life mode around him any longer.

"Where did you hear about Olivia Bowen posing for Callahan's magazine?" he asked.

"The horse's mouth."

"Is she going to do it?"

Michaela shrugged and decided to go ahead and tell him about Kathleen Bowen's possessiveness over her daughter, and how she seemed to be the one behind the girl's career. Michaela decided to hold one piece of information back from Smith, not certain if it was important and not completely trusting him yet.

"They are a strange bunch. You see it all in this town."

"Looks like it. What do you think happened to Callahan in the room?"

"Possibly a heart attack, or maybe Bowen's wife and Benz had it in for him and it backfired. But *someone* called the paramedics. I can't imagine that if either one of them were up to no good where Callahan was concerned, they would've placed that call. He might have been able to do it himself, but the timing of Bridgette leaving the room doesn't work for me. I'm not sure, but trust me, I will find out."

"She seemed different when she left. Kind of like she'd had the wind knocked out of her. But why leave behind Callahan when something bad had obviously happened?" Michaela asked.

"That might have been a necessity. You said that she was jumpy on the phone earlier with Callahan. Maybe after whatever happened up there, she figured to save her own skin, she'd have to pull herself together. I'm sure she didn't want to have a chat with the paramedics or the hotel management. That would certainly get back to her husband."

"Yeah, but what she doesn't know is that it's already going to get back to her husband."

Dennis held up the camera. "Yep. Listen, you're a nice lady and I'm sorry for first scaring you in the parking lot, and then insulting you. My bad. But can I give you some advice?"

"Something tells me that you're going to give it to me anyway."

He ignored the comment. "This crew you're keeping tabs on, they've got a lot of cash, and if any one of them has something to hide and finds out that you're trying to uncover their dirty laundry, you could get hurt."

"Trust me, I've heard this before."

"Well, then...be careful. Here's my card. I'll see if I can't get anywhere with what happened to your friend, and not only because I want to sell a big enough story so I can head out on the next flight to Tahiti, but because I can tell you really cared about Audrey, and I think you deserve answers."

She took his card. "Yeah, Sorry about the asshole thing. I don't usually call people names."

He laughed. "Are you kidding? That's a compliment. Trust me, I've been called worse. By the way, do you need directions to Cedars-Sinai?"

"Why would I need that?" She tried to play dumb.

"Fresh air. That is what you are." He stood and shook a finger at her. "Just take my advice and watch your back, horse trainer. Watch your back."

TWENTY-SIX

MICHAELA HAD HAD ONE OF THOSE LUCID MOMENTS while speaking to Smith at Shutters, and because she still had plenty of time before dinner with Hudson Drake, she figured there was no better time to check her theory. Marshall Friedman had flown under the radar during this entire thing. But everyone knew him. Everyone involved had a connection to him. He sent Benz to make a nasty threat to Audrey at the races. He was using whatever tactic he could to pressure Olivia into signing with him as her manager. He obviously had business ties to Callahan. She didn't exactly know how Bridgette Bowen was connected to him, but she had a sense that Kathleen Bowen was somehow in his inner circle.

It was the last minutes of the day at the racetrack that hit her: minutes that at the time had gone by in a blur, and she hadn't stopped to really consider them. But now she had a hunch that she was right. Kathleen Bowen had asked her to call the chauffeur. She'd told her to press five. When Michaela had, she'd gotten a man, but not the driver. When she looked down at the call that had been made, the initials *MF* had come up. It had struck her as odd at the time, and she believed it had been just a mistake on Kathleen's part. It could be someone else with those initials. Michaela was aware that she was betting against the odds, but it made sense to her. The name *Marshall Friedman* had popped up in the course of conversations between her and Kathleen, her and Josh, her and Olivia, and her and Hugh. Marshall Friedman was lowlife Steve Benz's manager, and they were in cahoots over signing Olivia to a recording contract with them, and then some—like baring herself for Frederick Callahan's sleazy magazine. Who was this Friedman, anyway? How well had he known Audrey? As Michaela thought back to earlier that day at the races, she also recalled Benz's threat—or what had now, in retrospect, sounded like a threat. Weren't his exact words something like, *"Audrey's days are numbered and that Marshall Friedman will have Olivia under contract in a matter of a week."*? Interesting how things had gone down after that.

She dialed Information and was connected to Friedman's office. She made up a story that she was with one of the major hotel chains that she was in town on a quick trip and wanted to speak with Mr. Friedman about contracting some of his talent for entertainment in their larger hotels. "I don't have much time, and I promise I won't take much of his. I need ten minutes. I'd really like to speak to him. This is a major opportunity." She was told that he was in a meeting for the next half hour. She asked where the office was located. It was off the I-10 in Century City.

The secretary hemmed and hawed for a second, then finally agreed to allow Michaela to meet with him. Okay, she'd taken Smith's suggestion of whitewashing to heart. And, she'd apparently learned a thing or two from Joe. What would he say? What was *she* going to say when she came face-to-face with Friedman? Oh well. She would come up with something. She had to give it a try. Audrey's murder wouldn't stop haunting her.

By the time she made it to Century City and got out of the truck, she was perspiring and her nerves were shot. Was she crazy? It sure felt like it at the moment. What the hell. She'd never have to see this man again, and if he gave her any answers to satisfy her curiosity, it would be worth it.

She started toward the building just as two familiar figures emerged: Kathleen and Olivia. She called out to them, but with the din of the traffic they didn't hear her. They slid into the back of a limo before she could reach them, and it pulled away. She felt relieved that Olivia was okay, relatively speaking. But what were they doing there? They must have been there to see Friedman. Had Kathleen convinced Olivia to sign an agreement with him?

Michaela found his office on the eleventh floor. The receptionist took her name and eyed her. She knew she didn't exactly look the part of a traveling businesswoman.

Michaela eyed her back. She was just a little slip of a thing and Michaela had no doubt she could take her if she wanted to. "I'll let him know that you're here," the girl said.

"Thank you."

She came back a moment later and said that Mr. Friedman would see her. She followed, and was led to a well-appointed office where Marshall Friedman sat behind a huge desk, one devoid of papers and files and the normal clutter of a busy man.

He stood. "Good afternoon, Ms. Bancroft."

"Good afternoon." Her stomach became one nauseating wave.

"Have a seat."

Michaela sat down in a plush leather chair opposite him.

"You're from Starwood Resorts, my secretary said. It's unusual to schedule an appointment on this short a notice. How can I help you?" Friedman was bald with a big nose and light blue eyes.

This was the tricky part. Michaela shifted in the chair and tried to sit as tall as she could. "I've heard quite a bit about you."

He gave her an odd look. "Many people have. Again, how is it that I can help you?"

Beating around the bush was going to get her nowhere. "I was with Audrey Pratt, Olivia Bowen's manager, at the races the other day. The day that Audrey was murdered."

He held a finger up. "Ah, yes. You mean former manager, don't you?" He smiled slightly...or maybe it was a smirk. "Is that what brought you to our fine city? The races? You knew Ms. Pratt, huh?"

What a jerk. "Excuse me? The *former* manager? That seems callous, considering what happened."

He held up what looked to be a contract. "I don't mean to be disrespectful. My apologies, if you knew the woman. However, I've recently acquired Ms. Bowen as a client."

"That's convenient, isn't it? Audrey Pratt is murdered and the singer you've been after to sign with you for some time now is suddenly available."

Friedman shifted in his chair. "What are you getting at, Ms. Bancroft? It's obvious that you didn't come here to speak about entertainment for the Starwood Resort chain. Why are you wasting my time?"

His asinine comment about Audrey and his overall pompous attitude pushed her buttons, pressing her to go for the jugular. "I'm here because you represent Steve Benz, who was one of the last people to see my friend before she died. He said something to her that I'll be sure to mention to the police—or maybe the tabloids—since you represent such an up-and-coming star." His face flushed. "It was something like a threat actually, about how Audrey didn't have much longer to manage Olivia, that she'd be signing a contract with you within the week. I'm also aware that when the two of you were with Olivia after the show, Mr. Benz stepped out to grab drinks. To me that feels like he had time and also motive. Maybe that motive is directly tied to you."

"I barely knew Ms. Pratt. Steve is full of hot air at times. Whatever he said to Ms. Pratt does not concern me. Steve is certainly no killer, and if you are implying that I would ask him to murder a woman because I have a business-related issue with her, or for any reason for that matter, I'd say you are full of shit, lady. Certainly the reason I am representing Miss Bowen now is because she is wise enough to make an intelligent career choice—"

"I'd like to know how and why you took Olivia Bowen from the races."

"I don't think that's any of your business. It's time for you to leave." His face flushed once again.

She stood. "I'm sure that the police will probably find it as interesting as I do that you now have Olivia as a client only a few days after Audrey was murdered."

He shrugged. "Business is business. I'm sorry about your friend, but you are delusional. Now get the hell out of my office before I call security. And if you ever bother me again with your bizarre accusations, I will have you arrested."

"On what grounds? I wasn't accusing you of anything."

"Trespassing and harassment. I have a lot of pull in this town."

"I'm shaking." Michaela walked out of his office, baffled and if she admitted it, a bit shaken. She didn't trust Friedman at all. She also found it awfully strange that Olivia, who had been disgusted by the prospect of being his client the night before, would have signed that contract.

TWENTY-SEVEN

MICHAELA HAD JUST ABOUT STOPPED SHAKING when she got into the truck and her cell phone rang. It was Joe.

"I got some more info on your friend Bob Pratt."

"What did you find out?"

"I worked the Betty Ford angle."

"The treatment center?"

"Yep, and it paid off. I got a list of people he spent time with there at the BFC."

"How did you do that?"

"I got a cousin who has a friend whose wife works in the cafeteria there."

"Of course. I should have known."

"I did some research on Bob and Audrey and who they are associated with. The name Bowen ring a bell?"

"It does."

"Uh-huh. We're gonna have to have a powwow, so I can learn what else you know about this guy, if you want me to help you the best that I can."

"I'll be home tonight. Late. Or you can come by tomorrow."

"I'll call you after I get the kids to bed. Maybe I can swing by; otherwise I'll stop by your place in the morning. You need to be thinking about everything that you know about this Pratt dude. Everything."

"I will. Promise." She sighed. What had she really gotten herself into?

"Deal. Check this out. What would you say if I told you that Bob Pratt and Mrs. Bowen spent some time together in rehab and they got pretty close there?"

"Bridgette?"

"The one and only."

A lightbulb moment happened as Michaela tied in the idea that Bob and Bridgette were in treatment at the same time. It could give Bridgette even more motive to want Audrey dead. Maybe she was afraid of what Bob might share with his sister. Not only that, what if she had done something to Bob? What if Bridgette was hiding something horrible that she'd confessed to Bob, and once out of rehab with some time to ponder, Bridgette knew she needed to get rid of them both? "What do you mean by close?"

"Hard to say. My cousin's friend's wife didn't know if there was any hanky-panky going on. Those types of places really frown on fraternization, plus Mrs. Bowen was already married."

"What was Bridgette Bowen in Betty Ford for? Alcohol, too?" She already knew the answer to that one, but wanted to see if Joe could confirm it.

"Nope. She had a problem with the white powder."

"Cocaine?"

"Yes, ma'am.

Michaela didn't respond.

"Mick? You there? You okay?"

"I'm here. Just thinking, is all."

"Want me to see if I can find out anything else about the little scenario at rehab?"

"Would you?"

"You know I will. You was right when you said that I loved this stuff. But have you called that gal over at the autism center?"

"No. I'm sorry. I will, though. I promise. I think I may have some new horses coming in soon for the center." She thought about Audrey's horses. It was likely there were a few in that group that might work for the kids. She'd have to make a call to the Humane Society, too.

"Get on it, Mick, or I'm gonna stop this Colombo business for you."

"Thanks, Joey, you're the best. I'm on it."

Michaela turned off her phone. Bridgette Bowen and Bob Pratt? Tight? Odd combo. Looked like Michaela would be having a discussion with Hugh's wife. Should she come right out and confront her about what she'd seen at Shutters? And then ask her about her time in rehab with Bob? What if the woman was a cold-blooded killer? Oh dammit. Then, there was Callahan to consider. He'd been with Bridgette when she *found* the body. Maybe the two of them had something to do with Audrey's murder. And what about Callahan anyway? She wondered if he was okay and if Bridgette was responsible for him being in the hospital.

It was after three and she wanted to know if her trailer was ready. Juan had suggested she call after four. She was already in Century City. Cedars-Sinai was within a couple of blocks. She'd never guessed when she started out that day that it would become a fact-finding and info-gathering trip. A part of her almost felt like she was being directed to do this. Was Audrey somehow guiding her through this maze of lunacy and lunatics? She'd always believed in angels. It somehow comforted her to think that Audrey might be one, and that she was watching over her, helping her to find the justice she so deserved. Maybe it was a silly notion, but it comforted her all the same. If only she could also find out what had happened to Audrey's brother.

Even with the hospital nearby, the afternoon Los Angeles traffic made it difficult to maneuver through the surface streets in her truck. She graciously received the middle-finger salute by some kid whipping around her in a battered Honda.

She was happy that she made it to the hospital in one piece, and although she didn't know Callahan from a hole in the wall, she was relieved to learn that he was in good condition and able to see visitors.

She walked into Callahan's hospital room; he looked half asleep, but sat up when he saw her. "Well, hello. And, who may I ask is calling?" he sputtered. "Do I know you?

Wait." He snapped a finger. "Miss April 2003? Great photo shoot, wasn't it, love. You were divine. Roses draped over you. Ah, what a dream. I am right, aren't I? I still have my memory intact."

She tried not to laugh as his toupee was askew and to the side of his head. "Keep dreaming. I am hardly Miss any month, nor do I intend to be."

"You break an old man's heart."

"Looks like someone else already took care of that."

He shook a finger at her. "She's funny, too. I should have had an affair with you. What are you, a reporter? I thought my assistant was keeping you fiends away."

"There was no one outside your room."

"I knew I should have fired that moron long ago. Doesn't do a damn bit of good to have an assistant if they can't even keep the vultures at bay. But you're so lovely, I may talk to you. Maybe when I get out of this place we can have dinner together or something."

"I'm not your type. Trust me."

"Oh, baby, you're all my type."

Michaela moved the newspaper that had been left on the chair next to Callahan's bed. She handed him water from his tray.

"Why are you being so nice? I already told you that you could be in my magazine. Give up the tabloid reporter gig and make some real money. Come pose for *Pleasures*. I can make you a star."

Michaela sighed and took a seat. "Listen, I'd love to tell you that I'm here as a reporter, but I'm not, and I'm not here to land my ass in your magazine. I feel terrible about what's happened to you though, and I want you to know that." Maybe a little sympathy would go a long way with him.

"Gee thanks, sweet cheeks, I think." He laughed. "Can I ask you, if you're not with the paper and you aren't a nurse, then what are you doing here? And, how did you find out I was here? News couldn't have spread that fast."

Another sticky situation. Hell with it. If she could get through the Marshall Friedman thing earlier, she could handle a sick old man lying in a hospital bed. "Don't ask how. But I saw you at lunch today with Bridgette Bowen. I saw you go up in an elevator with her at the hotel. I also saw Steve Benz come and go, and then I watched as the paramedics wheeled you out shortly after Bridgette Bowen took off, which wasn't too long after Benz made his getaway."

"Not with the tabloids, huh? Because I could sell you the story for a ton of money. You do seem to know all the players."

"I don't want money. I don't plan to take your story and sell it or anything. I want answers. I was a good friend of Audrey Pratt. Does that help make my reasons for being here any clearer?"

"Audrey?"

Michaela nodded. "I think there is a lot more to what happened to her than that her brother may have killed her after drinking too much over some sibling issue, and made his way out of town. I knew Bob Pratt and he and Audrey might have had issues like most siblings, but they loved each other. And I don't know what to think after what I saw today. I had to wonder if Benz and Bridgette hadn't poisoned you."

He laughed, then placed a hand on his chest. "Oh dear, no. It was nothing like that. Bridgette didn't try to kill me and neither did Steve. I was being a foolish old man, doing things I have no right to be doing at my age. Then I felt a burning in my chest. Thought I was having a damn heart attack. Turns out I shouldn't have eaten the Mexican shrimp dish I had for lunch. Just some acid reflux is all. At the time I didn't know what the hell it was. Bridge called the emergency crew and I told her to get out of there before her presence raised any questions."

Smith had been right about that observation. He'd mentioned that might have been the case. Callahan obviously had a soft spot for Bridgette. "And Benz. Why did he pay you a visit?"

He clucked his tongue. "You are an inquisitive one. I think we should let it all die down."

Michaela shook her head. "I wish I could. But my friend is dead on a cold slab at the morgue waiting to be buried properly, her brother is missing, and there are a lot of people around her who I simply find crazy. Sorry to say, but you're one of them."

He smiled. "I like you. You've got spunk. Are you sure we can't just do some test photos? Being a *Pleasures* girl can do a lot for you."

"Mr. Callahan—"

"Frederick, please."

"Fine. Frederick, I don't want to go to the police with what I saw, because I seriously doubt that you are a killer. I do wonder if you know who killed Audrey, though."

He took another sip of water. "Benz came to our room to give us some party favors."

"Drugs."

"Yes. I know, it's very stupid to do, and I do know better, but Bridgette can be quite persuasive and she was feeling upset, so I indulged her."

Another point for Smith. He'd been right about Benz being a supplier. "Why was she upset?"

"Isn't it obvious? She and I have been fooling around. It's what we were doing at the races, out in one of the stalls, way on the back forty. Afterward, she left first and came upon Audrey. I ran when I heard her scream and soon after a crowd formed...Wait a minute, you were there. That's where I saw you."

She nodded. "So Bridgette was upset that the two of you might get caught. Don't you think that this will all come out? I'm sure that I'm not the only one who saw you two at the hotel. You weren't exactly discreet. And it's possible you were spotted at the races."

He laughed. "I suppose we weren't too careful. Sometimes that's a part of the thrill. I probably do owe Hugh a phone call, before the shit really hits the fan."

"Probably so. He's been through a lot. Can I ask you, why Bridgette? You have lots of women in your life. Why choose Bridgette Bowen?"

"You've seen her. She's damn gorgeous, and for the record, I didn't choose her, she got her hooks in me and wouldn't let go."

"She pursued you?"

"Does that surprise you? Look, I've seen Bridgette's type around and if you ask me, I did Hugh a favor and in time he'll see that. Bridgette is one of those women who are opportunists to the nth degree. She had a wealthy, wonderful husband in Hugh, but when he started paying more attention to other things, she became angry or sullen like a spoiled child. Men like us are busy people. To get his attention back, or to get any attention at all, she looked to another man. These women typically look to other men who have more money or power than the one they're with. I happened to be that man."

"Looks are one thing, but aren't you and Hugh friends?"

"Men like us don't have friends. It's healthy competition."

Michaela raised a brow. "Healthy, huh?" She scanned him up and down.

"Not this go-around, I suppose. And, maybe I deserved it. Little scare to knock some sense into me, I suppose."

"No comment. You mentioned that Hugh had other interests besides his wife. Do you mean the horses and his businesses?"

He laughed. "You are such a treat. Is that naïve streak in you for real? Or do you like to play coy?"

She rolled her eyes at him. "I actually like to think the best of people. See, in my world, it's not totally common for people to go around screwing other people's spouses behind their backs." Okay, so that wasn't completely true. Her own ex-husband had played around on her, but Callahan did not need to know that. Maybe she *was* naïve. Hell, she'd rather live in a rose-colored-glasses world than this seedy place she found herself in currently.

"It's in everyone's world."

She felt her face heat up. "What is this about Hugh and other interests?"

"Hughie boy had his own love on the side, but his was a bit more serious than just a fling."

Michaela uncrossed her legs and leaned in.

He nodded and for a second, as he gazed outside his hospital window, his face took on a faraway look. "I was in love once. Beautiful emotion."

Okay, there was no time to go down memory lane with Mr. Pleasures. "Who was he in love with? Who was Hugh seeing?" Michaela knew the answer, but wanted to confirm it with Callahan. If he said who she thought he would say, then that meant there were more people who were aware of Hugh's real feelings. Could Hugh's feelings for Audrey have caused someone else to murder Audrey other than Bridgette?

"The woman he's always been in love with. The one he should have married. Audrey."

She still couldn't find any words for a while. "How do you know this?"

"I think almost everyone knew. Back in the day when Hugh opened his place in Malibu and we would all hang out, I'd see the way Audrey would look at Hugh, but he missed the signals. Everyone knew they should have been together. Everyone but Kathleen…or if she did, she would make certain it didn't happen for them. Kathleen Bowen gets what she wants, and she wanted Hugh. And Kathleen was a gorgeous woman, too, back then, before the bitterness set in. She came on to Hugh like a mare in season and didn't let go. Audrey, being as gracious as she could, stepped away. But that love never died and when Hugh realized the mistake he'd made, he tried to set it right."

"What did he do?"

Callahan started to cough. Michaela stood and gave him a sip of water. "Thank you. How would you like to be my personal nurse?" he asked and winked at her.

"You are bad."

"So they say."

"How did Hugh try to make things right?"

"Recently Bridgette came to me in tears. Said that she'd found a ring."

"A ring?"

"She found it in Hugh's private safe. The naughty vixen got into the safe. Don't know how she did that. But there are many things she does that I haven't been able to figure out how." He smiled.

Michaela wished he'd stop with the innuendos and memories of his sexual escapades with Bridgette Bowen. It was pretty disgusting.

"The ring wasn't just any ring. It was a princess-cut diamond and on the inside of the band it was inscribed *To Audrey, my forever love.*"

"Oh."

"Oh, ho!"

"An engagement ring?" The ring that Hugh had mentioned to her. It was all true, then. Hugh and Audrey had been deeply in love for years.

"It does look that way now, doesn't it?"

Michaela took a minute to absorb what Callahan was telling her. "Do you think Bridgette would have killed Audrey out of jealousy, or worry that she wasn't going to get the payday I'm sure she'd expected from Hugh?"

"No. Bridgette may have a naughty streak, but she's no killer. A killer in the sack, sure, but no. She may not have had a prenup, but if Hugh had left her, he would have treated her right. She was dumb to keep pursuing me, but maybe she saw a bigger payday where I was concerned. Hell, though, I wouldn't have married her. She is what she is—an expensive whore, plain and simple. She was playing all the angles. Crapshoot if you ask me, and the stakes were high. I'm pretty sure Bridge has lost it all by now. If Hugh doesn't know what was going on yet, he will. Sad thing is Hugh would have treated her right, though, if she'd just kept her cards a bit closer to her chest or not even ventured outside the house. Like I've already told you, I'm never one to turn away a hot piece of ass. But Bridge didn't off Audrey. No, if anyone killed Audrey out of jealousy it wouldn't have been Bridgette. It would have been Kathleen."

"What?"

He waved a hand at her. "You bet. The woman always had this competition thing going with Audrey."

"They were friends."

"Friends! That's a joke. Maybe Audrey *thought* they were friends, but Kathleen espoused the idea of keeping your friends close but your enemies closer."

"Okay, say that's so, then why bother after Hugh left Kathleen for Bridgette and not Audrey. Why keep up the charade then?"

"Control and power."

"Excuse me?"

"Oh, that damn Kathleen is a control freak. She likes to have control over anyone she knows, and she lost it with Hugh. Look at the way she treats her daughter. The kid doesn't blink an eye without asking Mama, and I think Audrey was the same way. And Kathleen enjoyed that. Kathleen plays the beaten mouse, but trust me, there is a monster lurking inside and if she winds up being arrested for killing Audrey, I won't be a bit surprised."

"That's horrible."

"Life isn't always nice, sweet thing."

"You're saying then that it's possible Kathleen killed Audrey because she was jealous that Hugh was always in love with her."

But if Kathleen murdered Audrey, could there be other reasons for the savage brutality? Could it have been more about Olivia than anything else? Maybe Audrey did know about her drug problem and wanted to help Olivia. Maybe Kathleen didn't want to take the risk of having Hugh involved, and silenced Audrey before she had a chance to go to him.

He nodded. "There's that fine line between love and hate. For Kathleen, I think that means something."

"You're filled with all sorts of clichés, aren't you?"

"I'm an old man. What do you expect?"

"I'm not sure what I expected. But for now, I think I've had more than I can take."

"Thanks for stopping by. Anytime you want to come on over to my mansion in Bel-Air, give a ring. We all have a swell time there."

Michaela didn't even acknowledge the comment and left the perverted old fart behind.

TWENTY-EIGHT

MICHAELA CALLED THE BOWEN RANCH AND GOT a recording. She decided to drive over there. Someone should be around. Hopefully, the trailer would be ready to go; she could load Geyser and meet Hudson for that quick dinner without any more bizarre turn of events. She didn't know if she could handle anything else for the day.

It was half past four when she pulled into the ranch. Climbing out, she heard hooves from the practice track. She noticed a bay coming around the backside, tail in the air, looking like a fierce machine. It seemed late in the day to be running.

She stood against the rail watching as the horse opened up into full stride. What a spectacular animal. Quite an athlete. The rider knew how to handle him, and Michaela wondered who it was. It didn't appear to be Josh. She jumped when she heard a voice behind her. "Hey!"

She turned to see Josh, hands on hips, staring at her. "Oh, hi. So, it's not you up on the horse."

"No. It's Olivia."

"Oh!" Michaela was a bit shocked by this revelation. She wondered if Josh was aware that Olivia had been using drugs.

"I know what you're thinking."

"I'm not thinking anything," Michaela said.

"Really? So, you aren't wondering why she's riding with the knowledge that her mom would freak out?"

"Okay, maybe."

Josh faced her. "Olivia needs help. I know it, Audrey knew it, and her mother is in denial about it."

"I don't know what you mean." Maybe he was aware of the drugs. She was waiting to see if he'd spell it out for her.

He ignored her reply. "My way of helping Olivia is by seeing that she gets to do what she wants with her life, and that's riding."

"Okay."

"Okay," he repeated.

What was it with Josh? Why was he acting so pissy toward her, like he had a bone to pick? Maybe he did that with anyone connected to Olivia. Not that hers was a huge connection, but the trainer appeared awfully protective over the young woman, always prepared to come to her defense.

"Hey, can I ask you something?" At this point Michaela had lost her inhibitions about asking questions. She done it with the slick, asshole entertainment manager, Smith the asshole—sort of—and Callahan the dirty old man, so it certainly couldn't hurt to talk to the horse trainer. They at least had something in common.

"What about?" His tone had a definite edge to it.

"Bob Pratt. You knew him, right? He came here to vet last Monday, Hugh said, and that you helped with the horses. What do you think of him taking off and the police saying he's their prime suspect in his sister's murder?"

He shrugged. "Not sure what I can tell you. I don't know Bob all that well. Yeah, I helped him out last week with the horses. That's not unusual. We might have had an occasional drink in the past. It's the horse business. You know, birds of a feather and all. He's a good vet. I like him. He doesn't drink anymore, and I'm not a big drinker so yeah, we'd grab a Coke once in a blue moon and shoot the shit."

"What do you think about his disappearance?"

"I don't know what to think. Didn't know him well; I already told you that."

"Obviously you knew him well enough to grab a Coke and 'shoot the shit,' as you put it."

"Come on. I'm a guy, so is Bob. We don't do deep-therapy types of discussions like you women do."

Michaela took a step back to blow off his pissy attitude. "Did Bob ever talk to you about his sister?"

"Not a lot. I know he thought a lot of her, but he was busy with his new job at Eq Tech and with his new girlfriend."

"Girlfriend?" She wondered if this was the same woman that Joe had gotten a bead on.

"I didn't stutter."

"I'm sorry." Michaela decided to placate the man. Maybe being sweet would get him to open up. She had a feeling that Josh Torrey was hiding something about Bob, maybe Audrey, too. Or, if he wasn't hiding anything, the information he might have, which he didn't know he had, could lead her down a path that could help her figure out who had murdered her friend and why. "I wasn't aware that Bob had a girlfriend." Michaela thought it best to hold her cards close. The less that anyone knew she was putting her nose into places that she probably should not be, the better off she figured she was. "Audrey and I had a lot of those womanly talks, you know, about relationships, that sort of thing, and she mentioned Bob quite a bit. This is the first I've heard anything about him having a girlfriend." She was getting good at this whitewashing tactic Smith suggested.

"I don't know. I think she was a girlfriend. I know they worked together at Eq Tech. She was one of the chemists there. At least I know they hung out. I met her one night when he made a vet call at the ranch. Pretty lady. Nice, too. Bob seemed into her and vice versa."

"You don't know what to make of him just not showing up for work, or that no one can find him?"

"No, I don't. I know what the papers are reporting and that everyone is thinking he fell off the wagon and had something to do with his sister's murder. But I don't believe any of that shit. Bob might have had problems in the past, but from what I know of him, he's solid and was headed in the right direction. He also mentioned to me that he was going to go see his girlfriend for the weekend, that she wasn't feeling too well. I don't know, maybe he took off early to be with her."

"He would've been in touch with someone, contacted somebody, if that was the case. Don't you think?"

"Yeah. I'd think so." Josh raked his hand through his hair.

"Then maybe it's foul play."

"Maybe it is."

"Do you know of anyone who would want to hurt Bob or Audrey?"

"No."

"What about his girlfriend? Do you remember her name?"

"Carla, something." He snapped his fingers. "No. Cara. I didn't catch her last name."

"She still working for Eq Tech?" It looked to be that the woman Joe had discovered and the one Josh was referring to were one and the same.

"I don't know. When I met her, she mentioned something about the commute and how she hated it; even took the train pretty often, she said."

"Where was she commuting from?"

"Down near San Diego, if I remember right. Maybe Del Mar? I honestly don't know. I really don't know what to tell you, but it sucks. The whole thing does. Wish I had some insight. But I don't, and I hate to cut this short, but I've got work to do."

"I understand."

Michaela needed to call Joe and give him this information, see what he could find out before they hooked up. Maybe this Cara had heard from Bob. She watched as Olivia dismounted. When the girl spotted Michaela, she turned away. Maybe she'd figured out that her drugs had been found. Michaela approached her, but Olivia abruptly turned to Josh. "I've got to go. Sorry."

Michaela thought about confronting her but changed her mind. She would be talking to Olivia or her dad about discovering the cocaine, but not now. There were still some parts of this puzzle in regard to little Miss Olivia that she wanted to put together.

Josh looked baffled as Olivia ran off. He turned back to Michaela, leading the horse in her direction. "Look, I'm sorry about Audrey and I don't know what to think about Bob. It's a shame, that's what it is. A damn shame."

Michaela nodded. "Is Hugh around?"

"No. He's not. I don't know what happened up at the house a little while ago, but there was some shouting going on and then Bridgette took off with Hugh speeding down the drive behind her."

Looked like the cat was out of the bag.

"Hey, aren't you here to pick up Geyser? Juan told me about your trailer." Josh pointed at it in the distance.

"Yeah, is he around? I've got to get on the road."

"You're not going anywhere with the trailer."

"What?"

He frowned. "Sorry. Juan told me that he had to get some more parts to fix it, and what he needed he wasn't able to find at the hardware store in Malibu."

"When did he say it would be ready?"

"He didn't. He's gone for the day. I'm sure he'll have it taken care of in the next few days."

"Few days. Damn. It's not like I live down the road, you know."

"Tell you what, I'll find out for you, and once it's fixed, I'll get someone to transport the horse out there for you."

Now he was being Mr. Nice Guy. What was it with these people that Audrey hung out with? They were cold one minute, warm the next.

She gave Josh her number and looked at her watch, Happy hour with Hudson was fast approaching, and if she didn't head out now, she'd be late.

TWENTY-NINE

HUDSON DRAKE TURNED OUT TO BE AS DELIGHTFUL as Michaela remembered. She also discovered that they had a lot in common.

"Grew up on a ranch, too," he said. "My dad taught me how to ride. I don't ride like I used to, what with work. It ties me up quite a bit," he said, the candlelight bouncing off the sparkle in his blue eyes.

They'd started with a glass of wine and appetizers during happy hour and their conversation carried them through dinner. Michaela decided against any more wine, knowing she had more than a two-hour drive home. But his company made her feel giddy, almost as if she'd drank more than she really had. He looked as handsome as he had the other day, only toned down now in a gray V-neck sweater and jeans. She'd thought about telling him about her ridiculous day, but decided against it. His conversation was far more upbeat. She had mentioned the horse trailer fiasco and he'd laughed heartily, then apologized.

"I'm not laughing at your expense. Okay, maybe I am. That stinks. What did you do all day? Why did you have to cancel lunch?"

"I had to take care of some business." She'd leave it at that. "And, no offense taken. Come to think of it, it is kind of funny. Stupid rats. I'll have to set some traps."

He didn't make any moves on her, which was nice. No flirtation, just nice conversation. She felt oddly at ease with him. Jude made her kind of nervous, left those butterfly feelings in her stomach. Now she was just plain angry and irritated with him. Ethan…well, he was another story. He was her best friend and that was all, and she wanted nothing but the best for him. Their relationship was comfortable, almost too much so for friends at times. She knew it had to bother Summer that they were as intimate as they were, what with all they'd shared growing up over the years. Those childhood ties could never be broken, and Michaela comforted herself with that thought quite often.

Hudson was interesting and fun. "How are you doing? After everything that's happened?" he asked.

"It hasn't really sunk in; I can't believe that my friend was murdered. But I'm keeping busy. That's all I know to do. Damn!"

"What?"

"I forgot to call the Humane Society. I wanted to talk to them about taking in some of Audrey's horses."

"That's nice of you."

"She would have done it for me. She was like that. A really kind, good-hearted woman. I hope they find who did this to her."

"Me, too." He picked up her hand and squeezed it. "I have a guy working on finding Bob."

"You do? So, you called in the private investigator that you were talking about?"

"I did, but so far, he's got nothing."

"Nothing at all?" Hmm, maybe Joe's cousins were better at this than any private eye.

"No, nothing. You better get on the road if you're going to make it home at a halfway decent hour. It's already past eight."

"You're right."

"By the way, you did get my roses, didn't you?" he asked.

"Oh, my gosh, I'm sorry, I meant to thank you. Yes. They were beautiful. I loved them. Um, but about that..."

"Oh no, you are not going to back out on me now."

She sighed. "It's just the timing and all the driving I've been doing and I really need to get back into the swing of things."

"Do it next week. We'll have a great time, forget your worries for a night. I won't take no for an answer. Besides, all the 'in' crowd will be there." He rolled his eyes. "The

Bowens, Fredrick Callahan, who owns *Pleasures* magazine and several winner's circle horses, and just about anyone who is a player in the racing arena."

She might have had enough of all of them, but she thought about Jude and how angry she was with him and she agreed that she would see Hudson on Saturday.

He walked her to her truck, gave her a peck on the cheek, and held the door open for her. "I had a nice time this evening and I'm looking forward to Saturday night."

"Me, too. But, I have a question: What do I wear?"

"Dress to the nines. This thing is quite an event."

"The nines, huh?" He nodded. She knew she'd have to raid Camden's closet to find something. When she looked in her rearview mirror, she saw Hudson waving. She smiled and headed home.

THIRTY

THE NEXT DAY MICHAELA PLAYED PHONE TAG with Joe, who hadn't been able to make it by between the hardware store, one kid's doctor's appointment, another one's soccer game, and some other event. She did leave him the message about this Cara person who had worked at Eq Tech with Bob Pratt. She wanted to know if he'd been able to find out anything more on that front.

She'd also placed a call to the vet who had seen Rocky over the weekend. It was already Tuesday and she didn't understand why it was so difficult to get any answers. Granted he appeared to be fine, but she was still concerned and wanted to know what his labs reported. She would have to track Ethan down; the last she'd heard, he was still in San Diego with Halliday. She was planning on stopping by his and Summer's house that evening. She needed to tell them she was not going to attend Friday night's baby shower. As for Jude, Michaela planned to leave him a message through the receptionist at the station, because she didn't want to talk to him yet. The last thing she wanted to do was show up sans half of a couple at a couples' baby shower. Not that she and Jude were a couple anyway. Sheesh! Who ever heard of a couples baby shower? That had to be Summer's idea. Sure they were in vogue now, but *come on*, as if the men really enjoyed sitting around with a group of women oohing and aahing over baby clothes and toys. That was a scene she wanted to miss. She already had a gift for the baby—a bath set and a teddy bear. Generic, but useful.

Since neither the other vet nor Ethan had called, Michaela decided to speak to Dwayne about Rocky. It was feeding time and Dwayne was mixing the grains and supplements for the horses. Camden hung at his heels, which was kind of annoying, because it wasn't as if Camden knew a damn thing about horses. However, being around Dwayne, maybe she thought that she'd gained a master's of equine through osmosis.

"Maybe he needs to be turned out more. You know, he is a stud and they need to roam, feel like they're in charge of their brood," Camden said, winking at Dwayne. "Didn't the vet say that Rocky's testosterone levels were high? Maybe he just needs to get out and about more. Burn off some steam."

"From what I understand, this is a medical situation and not so much about lifestyle," Michaela shot back as she walked up. Her friend looked genuinely hurt, which made her feel bad. Camden was trying, and the bottom line was that she'd been her friend for years. So why was she feeling so irritated by her? Did it really have to do with Camden trying to express her limited knowledge about horses? Or, did it have more to do with the fact that Camden seemed to have found true love, and Michaela...Well, she was still struggling with the idea of whether or not such a concept even existed.

"Michaela is right, Cammy girl, Rocky not too worried about running with mares right now. He be a happy boy, but this thing he got going on has something to do with his insides."

Camden nodded. "You know what, why don't you two talk about it while I go and make some dinner?"

Dinner? Now that was a first indeed. Michaela might have expected Camden to say she would be going to make margaritas. But dinner? Michaela had been the cook over the last couple of years. Sure, Camden might have popped in a Lean Cuisine once in a blue moon, but dinner? That sounded fishy. She eyed Dwayne as Camden walked away. "Dinner?"

He shrugged and grinned. "She's taking cooking classes. She not so bad, you know. A little bland, but she be trying."

"You two are really in love, aren't you?"

He nodded. "She want your approval. She want you to be happy. She worry about you so much."

Michaela nodded, feeling the back of her throat swell with emotion. "I am happy. I'm just shocked. Surprised, you know. I already told her that I'm happy for the both of you."

"I know."

Michaela took a deep breath and asked, "So what do you think could be going on with Rocky?"

He shook his head and scratched the toe of one of his boots into the dirt. "I thinking about it a lot, and I don't know. Really don't. I seen lots of problems in horses over the years, but not like this. I been taking his vital signs and writing them down because the vet asked me to, and I see nothing crazy. I think we be worrying 'bout a onetime thing, until last night and again this morning." He walked into the office, brought out a sheet of paper with Rocky's vitals, and handed it to Michaela.

She didn't like the sound of that. "Why didn't you say anything if you thought there was a problem?"

"I wasn't so sure at first and didn't want to scare you. You been going through a lot, and I think I better be real sure before we go and get worried again, plus he didn't have no more spells like the other day."

"Dwayne! This is my horse. My kid. You can't keep anything from me. I don't care if it'll cause me worry. I love this animal. Dammit, don't try and protect me."

"Thought I was doing right."

"No. You weren't." She looked at the sheet where Dwayne had recorded Rocky's vitals, blood rushing through her, angry with her assistant. From the records Rocky's heart rate and blood pressure looked like they elevated at about eight in the morning and eight at night. "This looks like it happens about two hours after feeding," Michaela said, tucking away her anger.

"Right," Dwayne said.

"I don't get it. And I'm irritated that I can't get a hold of this vet. I'm going to see if Ethan is back from San Diego." She used the office phone to call Ethan's cell, but it went straight to his voice mail. She hesitated but decided to call his house. Summer answered.

"Oh, hi, Michaela. Are you calling about Friday?"

"I am. Um, something has come up. I'm terribly sorry, a commitment I forgot about. But I was wondering if I could stop by and drop off a gift for the baby."

"Sure," Summer replied, and Michaela could have sworn that the woman sounded as relieved as she felt about her nonappearance at the baby shower.

"Is Ethan going to be home? I need to talk to him about one of my horses the on-call vet saw on Saturday."

"He should be. He's on his way home from San Diego now. I'm expecting him any time."

"Okay, I won't be long." Michaela hung up the phone and sighed.

"You going to see Ethan?" Dwayne said standing in the doorway. Michaela nodded. "That's good. Call me tonight at home if you get an answer. I got to go and check on my girl. I am sorry about Rocky. I'll never do something like that again."

Michaela hugged him. "It's okay. I understand and I do appreciate it, but I'm a big girl." She pulled away and socked him lightly on the shoulder. "And as far as you and Camden go, I am happy for the two of you. I really am. You're good for her."

"Thanks. She good for me, too."

Michaela grabbed the gift for the baby and was heading out the door when the phone rang. She should let it go. She wanted to get over to Ethan's, talk to him about her horse and get home quickly. Maybe it was Joey though, with some word on Bob Pratt. Her caller ID didn't register. Probably a damn solicitor. She grabbed it anyway. The phone crackled loudly. No one seemed to be on the other end, as she didn't get a response when she first answered. She started to hang up, when a man's voice on the other end said, "Is it true?"

"Is what true? Who is this?"

"About Audrey?" His voice sounded distant.

"Who the hell is this? What do you know about Audrey?"

Again, no answer. "I said, what do you know about Audrey?" she yelled.

Finally the man said, "Terrell Jardinière." Then the line went dead.

THIRTY-ONE

"OH, MICHAELA, WE'RE SO GLAD YOU COULD COME by," Summer said, a little too unconvincingly as she opened her front door in all her pregnant glory. She still had her perfect ivory skin and shiny red hair sleeked back in a ponytail. On top of all her perfectness she had that pregnancy glow, and she hadn't gained a ton of weight, except for her tummy. It seemed as if there were a perfect basketball resting inside her. "I'm only sorry that you won't be able to make it Friday night. Why don't you stay for dinner this evening?"

"That sounds lovely, but really I can't."

Ethan appeared next to Summer, his rugged, chiseled features quite the contrast to his wife's delicacy. "Hey Mick, what's this I hear you can't come on Friday?"

"I'm sorry, it's, well, I have to…"

Ethan interrupted her, sensing her panic. "I know, if I remember right, I think you said you were doing something with Joe Pellegrino's little girl."

She nodded. "Yes. Gen. It's a party at Joe's and since I'm her riding instructor and am going to be working with more of the kids in her group, I thought I'd better go."

She smiled at him, secretly thanking him. He'd saved her. That was Ethan. She knew he understood that it was not easy for her to be at a baby shower. She was sure he didn't quite grasp the fact that it also had a lot to do with the fact that it was *his and Summer's* baby shower, but that was okay. He understood enough. He'd been there through the years when she'd tried to get pregnant to no avail while married to Brad, and he knew how badly she wanted a child.

"That's great," Summer said. "Ethan mentioned that you were working with her. She's autistic, right?"

Michaela nodded. "Yes, and Joe and his wife, Marianne, have asked me to run a riding program for other autistic children. I plan to take that on soon. I'm getting a great horse from Hugh Bowen—should be here in a day or two—and I placed a call to the Humane Society today. They picked up Audrey's animals, and I'd like to adopt the horses. I think she had quite a few that would work out well for this program."

"That's terrific, Mick. Man, I am so sorry about Audrey. I just can't believe it."

"Me either."

Summer smiled. "Oh, I'm sorry, can you excuse me for a minute?" She glanced at Ethan. "I'm making one of Ethan's favorite's—veal cutlets in a lemon caper sauce and au gratin potatoes."

"Sounds and smells delicious," Michaela said, somewhat jealous, knowing that her culinary expertise didn't extend much past barbequed chicken on the grill—with sauce from a jar. She could make a mean hamburger, too, though.

"Thank you. I'll be back in a jiff." She scurried into the kitchen.

"Oh, here," Michaela said when Summer walked away, and handed Ethan the baby gift.

"Thanks."

"No, thank you, for covering for me."

"That's what friends are for. I know it isn't easy for you, and as much as I want you to be here on Friday, I understand why it's hard."

"You're not upset?"

"No. I am kind of upset that you didn't tell me about Audrey. I know what she meant to you. I had some cop call me—a Detective Merrill—and ask me if she'd been down on the track right after Halliday had the break. I was in shock to hear the news, but no, I didn't see her on the track."

"I'm sorry that I didn't tell you. I wanted to, but I knew—know—that you have a lot on your plate right now.

With Summer getting ready to have the baby, and your new job, all of that has to be on your mind. The last thing I wanted was to burden you."

He took both of her hands. "Shut up. You've been my friend for what? Almost thirty years? And you think by telling me about what is going on in your life and the pain you're dealing with is a burden?"

She shrugged. It might not be a burden to him. She knew that. But what she didn't want to do was come between him and his wife. He was married to Summer and she respected that his wife was not super keen on their friendship, even though it had been one from childhood.

"You or what you're going through is never a burden. Got it?"

She nodded. "Got it."

"Now, Summer said that you needed to talk to me about a horse. What's up? Come on in and sit down."

She followed him into the family room, which was floral, feminine, and delicate in pastel shades of green, rose, and yellow. Michaela almost laughed seeing Ethan plunk down on the rose-patterned sofa. To recall what his bachelor pad had looked like! This was all *so* Summer.

"Talk to me," Ethan said.

Michaela explained to him about the vet coming out to see Rocky, what the labs had shown, and how she'd been having difficulty getting a hold of Dr. Burton for further explanation.

"She's new. A little overwhelmed. I'm trying to get her to take on more, since I've taken on the track appointment, but it's been difficult being in San Diego so much. I'm going back down on Thursday morning to check on Halliday when they change his cast and then hurry home to help with the preparations for the shower. I'm sorry to say that I have not seen Rocky's labs, but when I get into the office tomorrow, I'll take a look."

"Do you have any idea by what I'm saying as to what it might be?" Michaela asked.

"Not without examining him. He's six now, and it's possible that he could have some type of degenerative heart thing going on. The one thing I do find kind of interesting is that from what you're telling me, the initial labs that were reported are sounding similar to Halliday's labs."

"What do you mean?"

"Come on. I'll show you what I have in his file. I brought it home with me to go over again. It's up in my office. First, I want to show you the baby's room. I finished painting it a few days ago."

"Sure." They walked up the stairs of the very formal, almost museum-like home, passing his and Summer's bedroom, all done up in peach and gold. Puke. But when she took a second look, it really wasn't barf material at all. It was as tasteful and beautiful as Michaela figured it would be, though she didn't get a sense that it would be easy to relax in all that perfection.

Next door was the baby's room. "Oh my gosh! This is amazing! You did all this?" she asked. He nodded, a huge grin across his face. Was he blushing, too? Ethan was obviously proud of all he'd done.

"I didn't paint the horses. Summer had a pro do that. But I set up the crib, and painted the background colors. I even helped sew the curtains."

Michaela crossed her arms. "Look at you."

"I know. I can't wait for this kid to be born."

Michaela gave him a hug. "I'm so happy for you. And for Summer. You two will make great parents." She *was* happy for him. She knew how much Ethan wanted to be a father. His own dad had abandoned him before he was born and only recently had he even discovered the true identity of his father. She knew that he felt a certain obligation to be the best father ever, and she was sure he'd live up to that. The room was painted a light tan with an amazing mural of wild horses running through the desert; the ceiling was a blue sky with billowy clouds, and the drapes and baby's comforter were red with a cowboy pattern on them.

"Thanks. We're excited."

She followed him to another museum-quality room with some of his degrees up on the wall. He went up to an ornate mahogany desk, grabbed a file, and handed it to her. "Look at this and tell me what you think."

She opened the file. "I'm not a vet, Ethan."

"No, but you know quite a bit. Remember all the times you've helped me study? And it's not like you haven't had your fair share of illnesses on the ranch. Plus, I'm looking to see if any of this sounds like what you or Dwayne has seen going on in Rocky."

"I'll try." She studied the results. "His testosterone and cortisol levels are high, like what we're seeing with Rocky, and it looks like he has a spike in blood pressure after meals. Might be a thyroid problem. I meant to bring you a sheet that Dwayne has been keeping on Rocky. It resembles this almost to a tee, with his pressure rising after meals. Do you think it could be steroids in Halliday? I know it isn't in my horse, but it's a possibility with a racehorse."

"He was tested prior to the race and he didn't have any steroid, bute, *nada*, in his system."

"Maybe they were masking it somehow."

"Maybe. I am concerned though. I noticed this afternoon that his heart rate and blood pressure were up again, this time not after eating. First we suspected an infection. I don't know. I had him started on a course of antibiotics because you can't be too cautious after a leg break like the one he's suffered."

"Could this diminish his chances for survival?"

"It might."

"Oh no."

"Ethan?" Summer yelled from downstairs.

"We better go down. She hates to climb stairs if she doesn't have to these days. I'll let you know what happens."

"Okay. Did Kathleen Bowen ever turn up at the center?"

"Nope." He shrugged. "Maybe she figures since you're footing the bill that she can ignore him. I still think you need to reconsider that."

"I know you do."

"You know what, I almost forgot." Michaela smacked herself on the forehead. "Did Audrey call you and leave you a message about a file that Bob asked her to give to you?"

"Yeah, she did. She called me last week. I called her back and we played phone tag. Then I got busy and forgot about it. Now that you mention it though, I remember. I have no clue why she would have one of his files. Especially one that he thought I might need. I have to think about and look at some of my cases. I know that we've conferred on some things together, but I can't recall anything lately. But I've had a lot on my mind. How did you know about it?"

"Audrey mentioned it to me the other day. She thought it was strange that he asked her to give it to you, but apparently he said that it was because the two of you were in close vicinity and he thought you might get it faster from her. They'd had dinner last week together."

"Huh. I still don't know what it's about."

"I have the file."

"You do?"

"I think I do, anyway."

"Michaela?"

"I took something from Audrey's desk that was in an envelope that came from Bob."

"You did what?"

"I figured that it was for you."

He rubbed his chin. "Okay. Where is it?"

Thank goodness he didn't press her on it. She didn't want to admit that she'd left Audrey's ranch with the file right underneath the nose of one Officer Garcia. "I left it at home. I meant to bring it with me tonight, but was kind of in a rush to get over here." She didn't want to tell him that the reason she'd lost her focus was the mysterious phone call she'd received before leaving. "I'll get it to you."

"Ethan," Summer called again.

"Come on."

They walked down together. Summer stood at the bottom of the landing, frowning. "What were you two doing?"

"I was showing Mick the baby's room."

"It's gorgeous. You two have done a wonderful job," Michaela said.

"Thank you," Summer replied. "It's time to eat. Are you sure you can't stay?" She smiled sweetly at Michaela, but there were daggers in Summer's eyes aimed right at her heart.

"No, but thank you."

Michaela left their place with a ton on her mind, from Halliday's and Rocky's conditions to Audrey's murder, and of course, to the very strange phone call she'd received before heading over to Ethan and Summer's house. Had it been a prank call from someone who knew that she and Audrey were close? If so, that was sick. Terrell Jardinière. That's the name the caller had said. Who in the hell was Terrell Jardinière? Michaela didn't have a clue, but she knew she'd be up late into the night trying to figure out who this guy was, or if he was anyone at all.

THIRTY-TWO

EVEN THOUGH SLEEP HAD ELUDED HER MUCH OF the night, Michaela rose early the next morning. She'd worked the Internet for about an hour after getting home from Ethan's and found out a little about Terrell Jardinière, a guy living in Los Angeles—a boxer who'd had a stroke but had survived. It wasn't much, and it felt like a dead end, but when she and Joe finally hooked up after Gen rode that afternoon she passed on that information, plus everything else she'd learned about Bob Pratt.

"Getting info can take some time," Joe said as they sat on Michaela's porch watching Gen hold Booger's lead line while he chewed on a patch of grass.

"I understand. I feel like there is no way Bob did this horrible thing." She felt her throat tighten. "Even if something bad has happened to him, I want to know. It seems as if Audrey wants me to get to the truth and vindicate him, find justice for her."

Joe patted her on the back. "You may have to accept that it might not happen. The cops seem focused on Bob, and you vindicating him might not be in the cards."

"You're going to keep helping me though, aren't you?"

He nodded.

She had told Joe about discovering Francisco, and then the story about Olivia and her odd behavior afterward at the coffeehouse. "There is more to this than that Bob went nutso. And how would it tie into Francisco being killed at Audrey's? Doesn't it make sense that both of the murders have some kind of connection?"

"It does seem like that."

"Can you do something for me?"

He laughed. "Mick, if I had a dollar every time you asked me that question, I'd be able to send all my kids to private school."

She went inside and brought out the envelope she'd found in Audrey's office when she'd gone back the day after Francisco had been killed. "I've had this for two days now. I think it's something that was meant for Ethan, but I'm not sure. I don't know what's inside, or if it's even important, but it does have Bob's address on the return."

"And you want me to open it."

"Would you?"

"Girl!"

"I know, Joe. Please."

"Mail fraud. Or tampering or something like that. What the hell." He tore it open.

Michaela had not been able to bring herself to do it, and with everything else that had been going on, she'd left it in the truck, but now she knew she needed to find out what was in the envelope. She wouldn't give it to Ethan until she knew it was meant for him.

Joe pulled out a file, opened it. "Don't know what it is. Here's a note on it though." He handed her the file.

She read the note. *Dear Sis, Please give this to Dr. Ethan Slater, as I asked. Love, Bobby.* Michaela studied the sheet on the inside. Names that appeared to belong to horses, and all sorts of numbers, percentages. They were labs. Huh. No big deal. It made sense that they would be sharing lab information. "I'll get these to him. He did say that they conferred on cases from time to time."

"Okay. I'll keep on seeing what I can learn. Get some rest. You look tired."

"Thanks."

After Joe left and Michaela finished up for the day, she sat down at the kitchen table and looked over the labs again. The phone rang. She could see from her caller ID that it was from Jude. She'd let it go.

The machine came on. "Michaela? Where are you? I've been calling and you're not returning my calls, then I got this message that we're not on for Friday. What is up?

Please call me. And how about Katie? She's asking to come for a lesson. Can you at least call me about that?"

She reached for the phone, but he'd hung up. She knew it wasn't right to treat him this way. But what if he was playing her? What if Garcia was right about Jude being a womanizer? She'd been down that path with her ex-husband. She hadn't seen the signs at all. She didn't want to make that same mistake. But she did owe Katie her time. Definitely. She'd call tomorrow, after the girl was home from school.

She put her dinner in the microwave and the labs on her kitchen counter. Okay, so it was normal for vets to pass information, especially because they were both track vets. But why would Bob have sent the labs to Ethan?

Without taking her food out of the oven, she grabbed the files and once again drove to Ethan's place.

Luckily he was the only one home. Summer was out shopping for the shower. She explained to him how she'd come into possession of the file.

"Thank you," he said. "I thought about it after you left last night. The only thing I can think of is the information in here is about a case that we worked on together a few months ago with a horse at the track." He looked them over. "I'll see if I can't figure them out." He closed the file. "Listen, I want to take Rocky down to theRocovich Center with me tomorrow. I called you earlier but didn't get you, so I'm glad you came by."

She sat down. "What do you mean? Why do you want to take him?"

"I want to run some more tests, and there isn't a better facility around than that."

"Ethan, you're scaring me."

He placed his hands on her shoulders. The familiar warmth that came from him traveled through her for a second.

"I'm not trying to scare you. I don't know that there is a real problem, but I don't like the labs that I've seen with Halliday, and I don't like the comparison with Rocky's. I know how much you love the boy, so let me take him down tomorrow and see if we can't get to the bottom of it."

"I'm coming with you."

"No. You're better off running your day. Let me do my job and if there is anything significant I'll call you and you can come then."

"Like hell. I'm going. I want to be with him. You obviously think there is a problem. I need to be there."

"Please, Michaela, you know that I wouldn't do anything to hurt Rocky or you. You're going to worry yourself sick while we do an exam and run more tests. Tell you what, if you'd like to come on down in the afternoon, fine. But while the vets are taking care of him and doing what they need to, just trust me on this."

With tears in her eyes, she agreed to let him take Rocky. "You better call me if there's a problem."

He wiped her tears. "You know I will. I don't anticipate one."

She nodded, silently praying that he was right.

THIRTY-THREE

ETHAN ARRIVED EARLY THE NEXT MORNING WITH his truck and trailer. It took everything Michaela had in her not to get in that truck with him.

"Promise me he'll be okay," she said, after they'd loaded Rocky into the trailer.

Ethan hugged her. "I'm only taking precautions here, Mick. It's a few tests, that's all, and I'll call you the minute I know anything."

She smiled through her tears. Silly really, she knew that. She didn't need to cry. Rocky was in good hands. The best. He'd be fine. But dammit, he was like a kid to her. All of her horses were.

Before leaving, Ethan said, "Stop worrying your pretty head. Do your thing. You've got other animals that need you. I'll call."

She nodded and watched as he drove down the dirt road until the trailer was no longer in sight. He was right. She'd work hard today and before long she'd know what was going on with Rocky. There was plenty to do after her trip to Los Angeles. Work would keep her mind off of Rocky and Audrey. She planned to give Hugh a call today to see what he'd learned about the coroner releasing Audrey's body, and when they might have a service for her. She also needed to find out the status of her trailer. First she needed to work Leo, her two-year-old. He'd just been started under saddle and she expected a champion reiner out of him. Reining was a real art form as far as she was concerned, where horses performed routines with various elements including spins, sliding stops, turns, and a gamut of difficult feats. It was her goal to win the big futurity held in Columbus, Ohio, annually. Leo had it in him to be a winner. Working with him did take her mind off of everything for a bit, as she had to place all of her focus on the young horse.

As she was putting Leo up, she heard a car coming down the road. She peered out of the breezeway and spotted Joe's minivan. He drove fast. After pulling up he rushed over to Michaela. "What are you doing today?" he asked.

"Um, what I usually do. I'm working the horses. Why? What's up? You're acting like you got a bug up—"

"No horses today. Get your purse. We're taking a trip."

"Joe! What is going on?"

"I got a lead on Bob Pratt and I knew you'd want to be in on it. You coming or what?"

"Hell yes." She jotted down a note for Dwayne that she'd be gone for a while. He was out running errands with Camden. "We'll take my truck." Joe frowned. "Come on, minivan is not my style."

"You're no fun. I thought you liked to live on the wild side," Joe replied.

"Guess I'm not quite that wild."

"You're a snob. Okay, but I'm driving," Joe said, and she tossed him the keys.

"What's this all about?" Michaela asked as they headed onto the highway. "And where are we going?"

"Malibu."

"Ugh," she replied. "Maybe I should rent a place in L.A.; I've been there, what, twice already this week. Want to fill me in?"

"Bob hung out sometimes at that fish and chips biker place up there in Malibu, right?"

"Yeah."

"The manager who was working the last time Bob was in is there today. He told one of my cousins that he thought Bob was acting strange that day he saw him with a couple of other guys. He didn't say anything else but my cousin got the feeling the bartender knew more than what he was saying. I figured that maybe I ought to go and see this guy.

I figured you'd want to go, too. I know what it means to you to find out what happened with Audrey."

"Thanks, and you're right. I definitely want to find the truth. Since we're headed there anyway, maybe we could also check into this Terrell Jardinière." She'd left him a voice message yesterday about the mysterious phone call she'd received.

"Yeah. I got an address where he used to box. It's a gym in Venice. We can head there, too."

"One more thing."

"Now what!"

She laughed. At least she'd be able to take her mind off her worries around Joe. "Right. My trailer is at the Bowen ranch, plus a horse that was going to be delivered to me. Maybe if my trailer is fixed we can grab them, too."

"Whatever."

The traffic was miserable, but the company good as she and Joe chatted about his kids, her horses, his wife, politics, and his cousins. The lively conversation filled the three hours it took to finally get through the traffic, into Los Angeles, and up the PCH.

They parked in front of Mermaids. Michaela took Joe's arm and they walked into the place. Greasy, divey, with a slight musty smell, Michaela mused over the thought that this was where Bob liked to hang out. Maybe the food was good.

A handful of patrons already in various states of drunkenness at a little after twelve noon sat at the bar partaking of their choice of poisons. A couple of them looked at Joe and Michaela when they entered. The others didn't bother. The bartender, a man with long hair pulled back into a ponytail asked them what they wanted to drink. Joe ordered two beers.

They waited until the bartender put their drinks in front of them. After a few sips and some small talk between him and the bartender, Joe asked, "Is Pete around?"

"I'm Pete."

"The manager?"

"Yep."

Joe reached across the bar and shook the man's hand; he looked bewildered or irritated, maybe both. "Joe Pellegrino. You talked to my cousin Anthony. He said that you was here when Bob Pratt came in last." Joe produced a small photo of Bob.

Michaela looked at Joe. He was good.

"Yeah, so?"

"Yeah, so. My cousin says that you said Bob was acting kinda weird that day."

"Oh, you know, that just might have been him having an off day. We all have 'em."

"Right." Joe leaned back and laced his fingers together, stretching them out and cracking his knuckles. "I'm thinking that you might know if there was another reason for Bob to be acting *off*."

Pete hesitated. "You know I don't like to talk about people."

"Sure, sure. I understand." Joe stared him down.

The bartender caved. Michaela figured she would have, too. Joe had one piercing, mean look. "Bob was saying some weird shit, you know?"

"No. I don't. Was he drunk?"

"Nope. Not as far as I could tell. He was drinking a Coke, eating fish and chips, hanging out, but he got on this kick about his girlfriend—"

"Cara," Michaela interrupted. Both men looked at her. "Sorry."

"I think that was her name. Anyway, he was saying that she's got cancer and how he knew it was all a conspiracy. That someone gave her the cancer."

"Cancer's not contagious," Joe said.

"Right. See why I didn't want to say anything? The man was talking crazy and he seemed really upset. My shift was over before he left."

"And that's it?" Joe asked.

"That's it." The bartender turned. "Hang on, someone else needs a drink." He pointed to the end of the bar, where a man and woman had just sat down. Joe nodded.

"Odd," Michaela said.

"You guys talking about Bobby Pratt? The vet?"

Michaela and Joe turned to see an older man looking at them—silver haired, dark brown eyes, lines on his face that made him look far older than his years. He reminded Michaela of an ancient-looking medicine man. "You know Bob Pratt?" Joey asked.

"Maybe. Who wants to know?"

Joe lowered his voice. "You ever hear of the Pellegrino and Torrino families?"

The man's face turned white. He wrapped his hand tightly around whatever it was he was drinking—whiskey, maybe some kind of rotgut. "Yeah, I heard of them."

"Thought you might have. Anyway, they wanna know."

"Oh," the man whispered.

"Well?"

"Let's get a booth."

They followed him to a corner booth across the room, where the vinyl seats were torn and cracked. Michaela slid in next to Joe, opposite the old man. "Well?" Joe said again.

"I heard that some not so good things happened to Bob."

"Do you want to elaborate?" Joe asked.

The man glanced around nervously. "I heard that some dudes took him down to Mexico and sort of…dumped him."

"Sort of dumped him. I don't know what that means."

"You know, I think they hurt him pretty bad like."

"You know who these guys were?"

He shook his head. "No, sir. Don't know."

"I don't believe you."

The man's eyes widened more. Michaela shifted uncomfortably in her seat. She hadn't witnessed Joe playing the heavy before, and it made her nervous, but she trusted that he knew what he was doing.

"I swear. That's all I heard."

"Right. Let's try something different. Where did you hear this—or wait, who did you hear it from?"

"Some guy. I don't know him. Swear I don't. Look, I'll tell you what I know, okay, but don't hurt me."

"I wasn't planning on hurting you, but I got a lot of cousins."

"That's true," Michaela said before she could catch herself, then decided to sink back into the booth as Joe glared at her.

"I get the point," the old man said. "There's this place up in the hills here. You go up a few miles. Street is called Vista Cielo, go right. It's the only way you can go or you take a trip into the drink."

"I got that," Joey replied. "Go on. What's this place?"

The man lowered his voice. "It's a barn, a place where...things go on."

"What kind of things? I'm losing my patience."

The man cleared his throat. "Cockfighting. They got cockfights up there."

Michaela gasped. "What? Roosters? There are people who really do that?"

The man nodded, his craggy lips formed in a slight smile. She wanted to reach across and wring his scumbag neck. So much for the medicine man impression.

"That's sick."

Joe shot her a look that told her to shut up, and she figured that was probably a good idea right about then.

What she wanted to do was *throw* up. The thought of that kind of cruelty nauseated her.

"Go on. Tell me where this place is and who you talked to."

The man finished the directions. "But, like I said, I don't know the guy. Some Mexican dude. There was a lot of tequila going around. Lots of people there, and I really don't know him."

"What exactly did he say?"

"I ain't so sure what he said, but know it was sumthin' like Bobby Pratt got dropped off outside of TJ and he wasn't coming back."

Now Michaela was sure she'd vomit.

Joey grabbed her hand. "Come on."

"Where are we going?" she asked as they exited the bar, leaving the man sitting there in shock.

"We're going to the cockfights, babe. We are gonna get some answers about what happened to your friend's brother. Cause that guy knows more than he's telling us."

"How do you know he's hiding something?"

He rolled his eyes at her.

"Dumb question?"

"Yeah. Wish I had a cousin close by."

"You don't?"

"Closest one is in Venice Beach. Might have him send someone out to have a talk with the geezer. But something tells me he'll be long gone the minute he sees us pull out of here. I would have shaped him up if I had it in me. But I don't believe in violence."

Michaela started to laugh.

"I don't, but even more than that, I can't stand when someone hurts an animal. I don't care if it's just a rooster. That's plain wrong."

She patted his shoulder. "And, that's exactly why we're friends."

"Let's go see if we can save some roosters."

"Let's," she replied.

THIRTY-FOUR

"I LIKED THE TOUGH GUY ACT IN THERE," MICHAELA remarked on the way to the rooster ranch or whatever the place they were headed was called.

Joey blushed. He definitely was a good guy, connected cousins notwithstanding. And, as far as she knew they weren't really *connected*, they just knew a lot of people. "Yeah, well."

She scowled. "What kind of person operates a cockfighting ring?"

"That's no person. It's savage. That's what it is. Man, I hate to see anyone hurtin' animals. Since having Gen, I guess I have softened a bit. And you know she loves animals, and I love watching her with them. Hey, did you call that gal yet at the autism center?"

"I've had a lot on my plate this week. You know that. And honestly, I still don't know that I'm the right person for the job. I appreciate your faith in me, but I'm so afraid I might damage one of the kids."

"Bullshit. You're afraid of how much you'll grow."

She was taken back by his words. "What do you mean by that?"

"Mickey, we've always been honest with each other. I like you. You're a good woman. But since your ex-husband made off with the rodeo queen and you weren't able to have a baby, you've been living half-assed. I know it's been a rough few years. I do. But the Michaela I remember growing up with was balls out. Pardon my mouth, but it's the truth. And lately, I've watched you let life kind of go on automatic. Start living again. Try this. You can do it. Gen loves you and the horses are good for her. They'll be good for other kids, too."

"Talk about not holding back." She looked out the window. Was he right? Had she been in auto-pilot mode?

She didn't say anything for a few seconds. "Since you know how to lay down the perfect guilt trip, I suppose I could give it a try. Maybe it is time to *grow*, as you put it. Time to live."

"Damn straight. Hey, here's our turn."

The place was hard to find after they made the initial turn, because the road they were traveling up wound in and around with various dirt road offshoots. She wasn't sure they were even on the right road, but Joe seemed certain. Michaela started to think that the old man back at the bar had led them on a wild goose chase. Then again, he did seem to know exactly who Joey's "cousins," were, and he'd either have to be stupid or ballsy to lie.

"There it is." Joe pointed out a dilapidated house, and off to the right of it a large, but mostly rotted-out barn.

"You sure?" Michaela asked.

He nodded. "I'm sure."

They drove on past and parked. "We'll walk down and see what we can find out." It didn't look like anyone was there. No lights. No cars that she could see. Nothing. But as they neared, Joey led them off the road. "We'll go in this way."

She wanted to laugh seeing Joe all Ramboed out, as he'd even seemed dressed for the occasion in a pair of combat boots, black T-shirt, and army pants, but she knew that they could be in real danger. Maybe she should pretend that she was a secret agent spy. One who was going to rescue a bunch of roosters.

They came up behind the house. As they did, Michaela squinted her eyes to see because of all the trees, which thankfully shadowed their movements and much of the property. "Get down," Joey said. "There's a car in the drive."

"There is?"

"Yup. Nice one, too. Lexus, I think."

"Lexus?" It was getting weirder. What kind of freakazoid drove a Lexus and ran a cockfighting operation? "Let's go over to the barn."

They rounded the back side and went in through an area that had rotted out.

"Oh no," Michaela said, looking around. Feathers were strewn everywhere and several crates were crammed full of the poor roosters.

"Assholes," Joey muttered.

They started toward the cages when they heard voices.

"Get down, Mick. They're coming in here." Joe took her hand and they hid behind some crates. He held a finger to his lips. She rolled her eyes at him. She wasn't so stupid as to alert whoever it was coming into the barn.

Through the dim light, she could barely make out two figures. "I don't like it, man. We ain't been paid for taking care of jack. You know that job wasn't easy. You need to go and see the boss man this time. You got more pull than I do with him," one of the men said in Spanish. She thought that she recognized the accented voice—Juan Perez?

Joe looked at her and shrugged. He obviously didn't understand Spanish. She was thankful that she'd picked it up so easily as a kid.

"You know, you think I got a better connection with him, but I can't make him pay me, or you. He knows he got us, man. We the ones doing the dirty work. And what about your deal you got us into with *pinche vato* Benz." It was Enrique Perez. Michaela was shocked. Wasn't he supposed to be the good brother? Hugh had told her of his doubts about Juan but praised Enrique. Why would a jockey of Enrique's stature go and get involved in something so seedy?

"He's good for the *dinero*. He don' want no trouble. He got a lot to lose, man. I not worried 'bout him. He easy, we give him drugs, he pays us, and that's it. He don't want me to beat his ass and he don't want me to go tell the news he really a loser druggie. No man, he's no big deal. What I don't like is the boss is loaded and we been doin' a lot of bad shit, you know, for him, and he don' give us nuthin' yet."

"He'll pay. He gonna pay us, bro. I know the man real good. He good to me and the money is on the way. He promise me," Enrique said.

Michaela squinted to get a better view. Juan went over to one of the cages and took out a rooster. "You know what's gonna happen if we don't get paid. You know what, lil' bro. I gonna be real mad and the shit will fly. I tell everyone it was you who did that guy in."

"What?"

"Yeah. You better take care of it, or else."

Joe covered Michaela's eyes as she heard a loud crack. Her stomach flipped. The men left the barn a minute later, still arguing. They heard the sound of an engine, and figured they were leaving.

"You didn't want to see that," Joe said as they stood up.

"Right." Michaela glanced at the dead rooster and thought that she and Joe just might have stumbled onto the largest piece in this mystery yet. Her gut told her that not only was Benz more of a lowlife than she'd figured, but that Juan and Enrique Perez had something to do with Bob's disappearance and Audrey's murder. However, they obviously weren't the only ones involved. The sick feeling in her stomach worsened, as she had to consider that the boss they were referring to was none other than Hugh Bowen.

THIRTY-FIVE

"MICK, THOSE ARE NOT GOOD GUYS BACK THERE," Joe said after she told him what the Perez brothers had discussed. They were making it back to the highway, winding down along the coastline. "So, you know them?"

"Sort of. I've met them." She explained to Joe how Enrique was Hugh's jockey and Juan, his brother, worked around the ranch.

He shook his head. "You gotta tell Hugh Bowen about this."

"I can't."

"Why?"

"They were rambling on about a boss man. It just might be that the boss man...is Hugh. I hate to think it, but it adds up. What doesn't add up is his sincerity over being in love with Audrey. I really believed that he loved her. I can't imagine why he would kill her. It makes no sense."

Joe shrugged. "None of this is making sense. The only thing that does is you heading back to Indio with me now, and forgettin' this whole mess."

"Can't do that. We're close. I can feel it. Maybe it is Hugh who caused Bob's disappearance and killed Audrey. I just don't know anymore. I have no clue what to think. But those two bastards back there *do* know who it is, or at the very least they're up to no good, and I suspect that it all ties in to what happened to Audrey. And Benz? He might be a part of this after all."

Joe asked her about Steve Benz and how he played into everything. She shared her thoughts on him and what a creep he was, how he also connected to Olivia, Callahan, and Bridgette, not to mention the weirdo Friedman. There were too many paths she could wind her mind down, and she had no clue which one to take.

Joe's cell rang. "Hang on. Yep." Michaela could hear the high pitch of a frantic woman on the other end. "Now calm down, Marianne. It's okay." He held the phone away from his ear.

"It's *not* okay!" Marianne yelled. "Get your ass back here now before we have a lawsuit on our hands."

"You gonna have to take it down a notch, hon, and explain to me what this is all about." The shrillness in Marianne's voice did not subside, although Michaela couldn't make out what she was saying. "Uh-huh," Joe said. "Dammit! What in the hell! That's it. He's grounded forever. Tell him that. I'm in L.A. No, I can't get back right now! I told you I was gonna be gone all day, that I had business in the city to take care of. No I didn't mean Riverside. C'mon, honey. Can't you take care of this? Marianne?" More yelling from the other end. "Okay, okay. I'll be there as soon as I can. Tell them four o'clock. Now honey, calm down, please. It don't do any good to get so upset." He shut off his phone. "Little shit!"

Michaela cringed. "Do I dare ask?"

He sighed. "Little Joe has a bit of a temper and if someone looks at him cross-eyed he takes it upon himself to kick the crap out of that kid. I've tried everything from taking away the PlayStation to making him clean the toilets. Don't know what to do."

"I don't like the sound of this."

"Today, he went too far, broke a kid's nose on the playground. The parents are threatening a lawsuit, and the principal wants all the parents in his office as soon as possible."

"Guess we'd better head back, huh."

Joe nodded and grew silent for a minute. "No. Take me to my cousin's place down in Venice. It's not that far. I can borrow one of his cars. Won't be a problem. I know you want to go and handle a few more things. I shouldn't let you. But my gut tells me that as soon as you took me back home, you'd be back here to see what more you can find out."

"Joe."

"Michaela? Am I wrong?"

"Okay. Maybe, I would like to figure a few of these angles out. Like I said, I think we're close and I do want to hunt down that boxer. Terrell Jardinière."

"What if I send a cousin to talk to him?"

"No. Audrey was my friend. I need to do this."

He nodded, gave her directions to his cousin's place, and then handed her a Post-it with the address of the gym where Jardinière supposedly worked out. "Careful. Call me when you get back?"

"Thanks, Joe. You know I will. I'm sorry about the kid."

"Nothing we can't handle." He shook a finger at her. "Be careful. And here, take this." He reached into a backpack he had with him and took out a small can.

"What's this?"

"Some mace, Mick. I make Marianne carry it, and my sisters. Don't know why I hadn't thought to give this to you 'til now, but I want you to have it. Use it if you need to. Even if you aren't sure if you need to but feel scared or threatened by someone, pull it out, keep your hand on the trigger."

She smiled. "Thanks, Joe." He was the closest she'd ever come to having a brother. Michaela watched him as he ran up the front steps of a condo on the beach. Apparently the cousin wasn't hurting for cash. Out of curiosity, she wanted to see what one of Joe's cousins was like, but decided against it. Maybe she wasn't ready for that part of Joe's world.

She took her Thomas Bros. map out of her glove box and thumbed through it to get directions to the gym where Terrell Jardinière worked out. Down near Muscle Beach. Then she was on her way, in hopes of putting one or more of the pieces to this puzzle together.

THIRTY-SIX

THE ARTICLES MICHAELA HAD FOUND BY SEARCHING Google for Terrell's name, along with what Joe had discovered about him, gave her the same information. Terrell Jardinière was once an up-and-coming boxer out of Los Angeles in the late nineties. He'd apparently had a stroke and, although he survived, he'd retired from boxing.

The gym near Muscle Beach occupied a two-story building a block from the water. She could hear and smell the gym before she even opened the door. Nothing like the odor of sweat and the sounds of groans and grunts to make a woman's heart go pitter-patter. Inside, the gym turned out to be pretty much what she expected of a gym in Venice: from muscle men obviously on boatloads of steroids, to serious boxers in the ring, dodging and punching each other out. Who actually considered boxing a sport? The idea of two men going rounds in attempts to beat the crap out of each other made her queasy, and seeing it in action even more so.

"Can I help you?"

Michaela turned to see an older, rail-thin black man. At first she didn't respond, because she hadn't planned this thing out very well. Here she was, one of maybe three women in the gym, and the other two were working out— boxing, actually. The man stuck out his hand. "Brian Dell. I own this place. And you are?"

"Hi. Sorry. Just kind of watching." She'd have to wing it, which she was getting good at anyway. Brian Dell seemed like an okay guy. "Michaela Bancroft."

"Morning, Ms. Bancroft. Are you here to find out about our self-defense class, or are you interested in taking up boxing?"

She started to laugh when she realized he was serious.

"Neither, actually. I'm looking for someone and I think he used to train here."

"You the ex-wife looking for back child support or something? Cause if that's the case, I hate to tell you, I won't be giving out any details."

"No. I think this man knew a friend of mine who was killed."

"You the police?"

"No. I'm only trying to find answers concerning my friend's murder."

"Murder, huh? Well, if one of the boys here gone and killed someone, I certainly don't want them in my place. Who we talking about?"

"I don't think this man killed my friend. I think he knew her. That's all."

"Alrighty then, like I said, who we talking about?"

"Terrell Jardinière," Michaela said and brushed her hair back behind her ears.

Dell glanced at the fighters in the ring. He didn't answer her for a few seconds, his face taut and filled with what appeared to be sadness. "No, Terrell certainly could not have killed your friend. Terrell had a stroke a few years ago. I used to train him."

"I know about the stroke. I'd like to talk to him."

Dell shook his head. "You can't. Terrell's been living in a home for the last few years. He can't do a lot for himself anymore. Such a shame. I go to see him occasionally. Good guy. Good fighter."

"He lives in a nursing home?"

"Yep." Dell's expression changed from one of sadness to what Michaela thought was anger. His eyes darkened, and the brow on his forehead creased. "State takes care of him now. Man, it's not good, you know."

"I'm sorry. It sounds like you're close. He must be a good man."

He nodded. "The best. Terrell was always good to everyone he knew. He lived in South Central all his life. He started boxing and I discovered him, got him set up in a place here in Venice. I wanted him away from some of those guys he grew up around. You know, he didn't need any bad influences. He was winning fights and making money. He don't deserve to rot in that nursing home."

"Can I ask what kind of money Terrell was bringing in?"

"You could, but let me ask you, why all the questions about Terrell? What's this story you got going with your murdered friend?"

Michaela sighed. Truth time. She told him about Audrey and the phone call.

"Sounds like a mystery to me," he said. "No way Terrell could've called you. The man can't eat on his own. No way on God's green earth that he could have picked up a phone. You would have known something was wrong with him by his speech. To answer your question about how much Terrell pulled in, it was getting close to six figures. And, everyone knew he was a rising star, destined to make millions. He had an aunt who kinda raised him, and she blew all of it away once he wasn't able to control it."

She shrugged. "That's horrible."

"The world can be a cruel place. Man like Terrell doesn't deserve what happened to him. He did do a few print ads for some vitamin company and a boxing glove outfit. But he didn't make a wad of cash doing that. Maybe a couple thousand bucks or so."

"Hey, Brian," one of the boxers in the ring called out.

"Yeah. Be right there." He told Michaela, "Wish I could help you out and I'm sorry to hear about your friend, but there's no way in hell Terrell made that call to you. No way. I better get back at it."

"No problem. Just one more thing: You have an address for the nursing home where he lives?"

"It's called Sheltered Palms. It's in the mid-Wilshire district. Don't bother going to see him though. Like I said, he can't tell you anything."

"Thanks."

Michaela left the gym. The same question kept playing out over and over in her mind: If it wasn't Terrell Jardinière who'd called her last night, then who was it, and why? Furthermore, why had he used this poor ex-boxer's name?

THIRTY-SEVEN

SHELTERED PALMS WAS A CONCRETE INSTITUTIONAL building with a decent-sized water fountain out front and a handful of palm trees that weren't exactly sheltering. The grounds were nice, though, in a park-like setting of grass and flowerbeds. A dozen or so patients lounged outside by the water fountain and another half dozen were either walking on the lawn or sitting in wheelchairs, some accompanied by caretakers.

Michaela figured she might not have an easy time getting in to see Terrell. She was already running a story in her head. Once inside the building, which smelled of disinfectant and age, she found the front desk, where an older nurse sat behind a glass partition. Nurse Ratched came to mind, the scowling woman's eyes boring into Michaela as if to say *What the hell do you want?*

"Yes?" was what she actually said as she slid the window open.

"Hi," She gave the biddy her best smile. Not even a flicker of pleasantry emanated from the woman. "Um, I'm here to see an old friend. I'm from out of town, and it's important that I see him."

"Did you make an appointment?"

"No. I didn't know that was necessary."

"It's necessary." The nurse slid the window shut and looked down at her paperwork.

Michaela rapped on the glass. The nurse frowned. "Please," Michaela said.

The woman slid the window open. "What?"

"This is important. I've traveled a long way and I'm only here for the day. I really need to see my friend."

The nurse sighed. "Name?"

"Michaela Bancroft."

"There's no one here by that name." She started to shut the window again.

Michaela stopped it with her hand. "No, that's *my*...Do you have a manager? Someone who is in charge?" She was pissed now.

"What's your friend's name?" she asked, ignoring Michaela's question.

"Terrell Jardinière."

The woman looked up at her and smirked, shaking her head. She handed her a badge. "Put this on. He's in room 306. Third floor. But if he's a friend from the past, he won't remember you. Elevator doesn't go to the top anymore, if you get my drift."

"I'll take my chances."

Michaela rode the real elevator to the third floor, passed a nursing station and walked down a long, dingy hall. Entering room 306, she saw a man in a wheelchair, his back to her, looking out barred windows. "Mr. Jardinière?" He didn't respond. She came around, letting him see her. "Mr. Jardinière?" His fingers moved slightly and he seemed to be trying to focus his gaze on her. "Can I talk to you?" No response. Maybe Brian Dell and the nurse were right: This was probably a waste of time. But still, she was here and she had to try and see if he could communicate in some way. She turned his wheelchair slightly so that she could sit in a chair opposite him and hopefully be able to decipher any body language or sounds he might make. This was definitely not the man who had called her. He was still a big man; He had on a tentlike patient gown and a pair of sweatpants. His brown eyes, although distant, expressed sadness.

"My name is Michaela Bancroft. I know that you used to be a great boxer. I spoke with your trainer, Brian, today." Terrell tilted his head slightly and his eyes seemed to light up. "Yes. He says that you were great." Michaela sighed. Why in the heck was she here? Whoever had called had only used this man's name for some reason. None of it made sense. She decided to tell him her story. She found herself crying again when she talked about Audrey and everything that she'd gone through in the last few days. Terrell didn't respond, but she believed that he was listening, and it felt good to let it all out; then, she felt ridiculous to do so in front of a stranger. A man who was ill, at that. "I'm sorry, Mr. Jardinière. I thought you could help me. Someone called me the other night claiming to be you, and asking about Audrey. But it obviously wasn't you. I wish I could figure this all out. Who murdered Audrey and why her brother, Bob, disappeared."

Terrell made a noise. She looked at him. He was trying to say something. It was difficult for him. Michaela couldn't make sense of the sounds he uttered. "Did you know Audrey? Did you call me?" Terrell shook his head…barely. "No. What is it? What is…?" Here she'd told him the whole story, but he hadn't reacted until that moment. What had she said that triggered him? Wait a minute. "Bob? Did you know Bob Pratt, Mr. Jardinière?" He became further agitated, trying hard to speak. "You did, didn't you?"

At that point a caretaker who looked like a linebacker walked into the room. "Hey, Terrell, pretty visitor today." He smiled at Michaela, who smiled back. 'What is it, T? You lookin' a little off. Time for your meds." He glanced back at Michaela and then at Terrell. "What's going on in here? He's usually very subdued."

"We were just talking."

"Uh-huh. I'm going to have to ask you to leave. It's time for his medications."

"Oh no, please."

"Are you a relative, Blondie?" She frowned. "Yeah, don't look like you two are cousins. I need you to leave."

"One more thing." She looked at Terrell. "Do you know what happened to Bob?"

Terrell became extremely agitated this time and was trying hard to say something. But all he could get out was the word *Bob*.

"You need to leave, miss, or I'll call security."

"I'm going. I'm so sorry. I really am." She reached out to touch Terrell on the shoulder. The caretaker pushed her hand away.

She walked to her truck, upset and baffled, but convinced that somehow Terrell Jardinière knew what had happened to Bob Pratt.

THIRTY-EIGHT

MICHAELA HEADED TOWARD THE FREEWAY AFTER leaving Sheltered Palms, almost in tears again, thoroughly frustrated and not knowing where to turn or what to do next. It was peak traffic time, and the last thing she felt like doing was trying to make her way home amid the sea of cars and smog. She pulled over and called Ethan to check on Rocky. Although she'd kept busy, he'd been on her mind and it had taken all of this craziness to keep her from losing it.

She was relieved to hear Ethan's voice. He sounded upbeat. "Hey, Mick. I told you that I'd call as soon as I knew something."

"I know. I'm just checking in."

"I don't have any answers so far, but he's happy and comfortable."

"That's good."

"I guess you've taken my advice," he said.

"What do you mean?"

"About Halliday."

"I'm confused. I don't know what you're talking about."

"I received a message from Kathleen Bowen today that she would be taking care of the expenses."

Michaela didn't know what to say. The woman had said she was bankrupt. "This is the first I've heard about it."

"I don't know. You may want to give her a call and find out. She's a strange one."

"I'm aware. Thanks. Call me, okay?"

"Sure. Are you okay? You sound upset."

"No. I'm fine. Worried. That's all."

"Quit worrying. He's fine. Now, go rest or take a ride, or do something to get rid of that anxiety."

"Right. Bye." She didn't divulge that she was well over a hundred miles from home.

She sat back in the seat, traffic whizzing past her, somewhat relieved to hear that Rocky was doing well. But she wouldn't feel completely at ease until he was back home in his stall with a clean bill of health. She also knew that she wouldn't truly be able to relax until Audrey's killer was caught, which made her wonder about Kathleen.

What was it with Kathleen Bowen? How had she come up with the cash to pay for Halliday's bills, and why hadn't she contacted her? Michaela didn't bother trying to answer the question herself. She got back on the road; what was a few more miles? She wanted to hear the answer straight from the horse's mouth.

The sun had started to set, casting a rose-colored haze across the sky, but she couldn't revel in the beauty of it, because the traffic was migraine worthy. Her blood boiled by the time she made it back up the PCH. She'd been cut off, flipped off, and nearly run off the road. There was a reason she lived out in the middle of nowhere: It was called serenity.

A silver BMW Roadster stood parked outside Kathleen's beach house. Michaela rapped hard on the front door. She was tired of the games these people played, and she wanted some answers. Kathleen Bowen came across as a victim in her bizarre world, but Michaela had her doubts. Kathleen didn't come to the door; rather, Olivia opened it. Her nose was red and running, her eyes bulging. She tried to slam the door when she saw who it was, but Michaela pushed it open and walked inside. "Where's your mother?"

"I don't know. She said that she was going out of town for a few days. Why? What do you want?"

"What do you mean, she's out of town?"

"Duh. She's gone. Like I don't know where. Maybe Italy, Paris. Beats me."

Michaela trembled inside. "You're high, Olivia. You need some serious help."

"And you, babe, need to seriously mind your own damn business," Steve Benz said as he appeared from another room.

Michaela crossed her arms. "Figures. You know, your name keeps coming up in all the wrong places, and now you are actually *in* the wrong place." She looked back at Olivia. "Can't you see what this guy is? He's no megastar. He's a lowlife drug dealer, and he's got you hooked. And if I were to bet on it, I would say that your mom has been crying poor to you. You did the good daughter thing, and agreed to sign with Marshall Friedman and pose with this creep here for Callahan's magazine to help her out of debt. My guess is she's just come into some cash, and that cash is yours. Now, I don't know if she's aware that you are doing cocaine. She's likely stuck her head in the sand due to her selfishness. But trust me, this scumbag and his no-good manager knew exactly what they were up to; you sign with Friedman, and you do their bidding, and they keep you high."

Olivia stared blankly at her. Was any of this getting through?

"Hey babe, you're ruining a good time here. You really are. Why don't you just leave?" Benz said.

Michaela ignored him. "Does Josh know this guy is with you? Does he know about the drugs? Would he let you get back up on a horse knowing you're stoned out of your mind? No, I don't think he would. I believe he cares about you. What are you thinking, Olivia? You have dreams to be a jockey. You can't do this to yourself. Come with me, okay? We'll find you some help."

Olivia shook her head. "I think you better go. Please."

"No. I'm not leaving."

Benz walked over and got in her face. "She asked you to leave. You deaf, bitch?"

Michaela knew she shouldn't be messing with this crazed, drugged-out rocker, but she also knew the right thing to do when it came to Olivia—what Audrey would have wanted her to try and do. "Let me tell you something, jerkoff, I've found out quite a bit about you and what you do to make extra cash. Oh, and I also know who you visited at Shutters the other day. Bridgette Bowen ring a bell? How about Frederick Callahan? Freddie boy told me that you deliver party favors for friends in need. I'm sure that Callahan wouldn't think twice, if it came down to causing him a problem or ruining your career, as to what he might tell the media—or the police for that matter. I wasn't the only one who witnessed your visit with Bridgette and Callahan. Let's just say, you look good on camera."

"What the..."

"Right. Here's the deal. You're going to leave now if you don't want those pictures to surface." Michaela knew she was telling him something she had no control over. She was pretty sure that Smith was at work offering the photos to the highest bidder in the tabloid realm. "So, you go on your way, while Olivia and I stay here." Michaela stood her ground. "Oh, and come to think of it, I've also heard your name mentioned in regard to Audrey's murder." She was stretching that one, too, and she knew it, but this asshole had it coming. She had not forgotten though, what Olivia told her about the fact that Benz had gone to retrieve beers while at the races, and the timing looked to coincide with Audrey's murder. She knew she might push him over the edge with her comments, but she needed to see his reaction. As far as Michaela figured, Benz might have killed Audrey for his own needs—to boost his career by having Olivia away from Audrey and under his manager's wings, which would mean a profit all the way around—or he might have murdered Audrey at Friedman's behest. She still didn't know where or how Francisco's death played into it, but right now she only wanted to get Benz out of the house. She knew she was taking a huge risk, but if he was a killer, she was prepared. She had her hand stuck down into her purse, wrapped around the vial of mace Joe had given her earlier, and she'd use it if need be.

"You are freaking psycho. I didn't kill anyone, and what's the big deal? If people want to party once in a while, how does that hurt you?" He looked at Olivia and shook a finger at her. "This is your mother's fault if you don't succeed. I had nothing to do with any of this. She's the one taking all your cash, babe. Call me when this bitch leaves!" He grabbed his wallet off a side table and walked out, slamming the front door.

Yep. Michaela was not making any friends in this neck of the woods. She had to wonder what Benz's comments meant about Kathleen. But before she could question what he'd said, she needed to try and help Olivia.

She turned back to see Olivia still staring at her. "Why are you doing this?" Olivia snapped. "Go away."

"Because you need help. And because Audrey loved you and I loved her. These people are ruining you. They're taking away your dreams. Are you going to allow your mother and her lackeys to control your life? Is that what you want? You can ride, Olivia. You're good. I watched you on the track, and you can do it, but not like this. Not wasted. I think we should call your father."

Michaela didn't know if she trusted Hugh any longer, but she believed that the man loved his daughter. That was a strange thought, especially since she figured that he could also be a killer. This was not good.

"No. I can't call my dad!" Olivia started to cry. "I don't want him to know. He's already been through this with Bridgette. I'm fine. I don't need help. Go away."

"You *do* need help. Do this for Audrey." Olivia wiped her face. "You have a long life ahead of you. Don't ruin it because you didn't follow your own dreams, or because someone took advantage of you."

"I do have dreams," she sobbed.

"I know. Now get smart. You can get help for this, and you'll be fine. You'll get better and then you can pursue your dreams."

Olivia's lower lip trembled like a child. Damn that Benz. "I don't know. I just don't know."

"Why don't we call Josh? Okay? I think he would want to help. One phone call, okay? That's it. We only have to start there."

Olivia didn't respond for a while; finally, she nodded. Michaela took her over to the couch and sat down with her. "This will be good. You'll see. You're strong." She shook her head. "I can't understand your mother. Where did she go, and why?"

"I don't know. I really don't."

"Do you know what Benz meant when he said that your mother was taking all of your cash?"

Olivia looked away ashamed. "You were right. I signed that contract for her. Callahan is going to pay me a lot of money to do the photos and Friedman gave my mother some money up front."

Michaela wrapped her arms around Olivia. She couldn't help wonder if Kathleen had taken Olivia's money and skipped town. Maybe Callahan had been right. Kathleen's jealousy took over where Audrey was concerned and she'd killed her. Now she was running. She'd used her daughter and was trying to cover her tracks. Michaela squeezed Olivia tighter. She couldn't avoid the possibility that the girl's mother had not only used and abandoned her, but might also be a murderess.

THIRTY-NINE

THE SUN FINISHED SETTING OVER THE PACIFIC AS Olivia paced back and forth on the oceanfront deck of her mother's beach house, chain smoking, while they waited for Josh to show up. She talked nonstop to Michaela, who sat in a lounge chair, continuously waving away the toxic nicotine plume as she listened to the young woman ramble on. Now that Olivia had admitted to her drug use, she was like a well sprung open, and although Michaela had her own set of concerns, she listened to her talk. There was no alternative.

"Funny thing is, you know who got me to even try this shit?" Olivia said. "Bridgette."

"Your stepmother?"

"Oh yeah. My dad thinks she's all better because he hooked her up at Betty Ford, but she was back using a few months later. She does a good job of hiding it from him. But I know all about it. Tons of people do. Benz gives it to her."

No surprise there.

"Last year at my dad's Christmas party? She gave me some. Told me that she wanted to be friends. That kind of thing. My mom had been driving me crazy. She'd pushed me into these recording sessions where she'd hang out half the time, or make Audrey stay with me for hours. I was wiped out. Bridgette said that the coke would pick me up, and it did."

"Did Audrey know about it?"

Olivia shrugged. "Maybe she suspected something. I don't know. She kept trying to convince my mom that I needed a rest. Audrey said that she wanted to take me to Hawaii or something, just to have a break. I wanted to do that. Last month I was feeling rotten because the drugs keep me up. You know? At first you think they're going to help you get through the day. But they don't. They just make it worse."

"Do you know Audrey's brother, Bob?"

"I met him a few times. He took care of my dad's horses, and also Halliday for my mom. He seemed like a nice guy. He didn't like Bridgette, though. But who does, really?"

"Why do you say that he didn't like her?"

"One time he was over at my dad's and my dad wasn't there. I was down at the barn. The vet was there—Audrey's brother. And Bridgette was there, which was weird because she doesn't have a lot to do with the horses. She didn't realize I was down there, but she was whispering and I heard her ask him if he'd told anyone."

"Told anyone what?"

"I don't know. That's all I heard her say, because then he turned on her and told her to leave him *effing* alone. She kept trying to ask him stuff, until she saw me there. Then she left. He didn't say anything to me, and I didn't ask. He seemed pretty pissed off though."

Interesting. Maybe Michaela was on the right track where Bridgette was concerned. Maybe she and Bob had had an affair. From everything she'd learned about Bridgette, honoring her vows wasn't high on her priority list. Or maybe she'd shared a secret with him at Betty Ford and she was afraid that he'd tell Hugh what it was. She wanted to believe the latter, as she didn't want to think Bob would mess around with a married woman. This was a piece of information she'd have to mull over a bit.

"Your mom told me that she was bankrupt. So, now she's taken money owed to you from this contract that you signed. Want to fill me in?"

Olivia took a long drag on her cigarette. "My mom is not so great with money. She's great at spending it, but it's my dad who knows how to handle it. Mom has made poor investments, and she spends cash as soon as it's in her hands. She was near declaring bankruptcy when she came to me and begged me to help her. She told me that she knew about me wanting to be a jockey and that if I did this for her just for a few years that she wouldn't ever ask me to do anything else for her again and that she'd let me ride and not bother me about it.

"I agreed."

"Why?"

"She's my mom."

"She has a problem. She's an addict, too. She spends money. Do you think signing away the next few years to Friedman and posing for Callahan with Benz will be the end of it? Come on. You know better than that. I've heard you sing. Your mother is right: You could be a huge star. But if that's not what you want, don't do it so that she can temporarily get out of the hole she's dug herself into and then watch her piss it away again. You'll constantly be supporting her."

"Have you ever said no to your mom or dad?"

Michaela thought about it. She nodded. "You know, I guess I have. My dad is an addict. He's a gambler. And, the last time he wound up doing it, I told him that I couldn't support his habit. I knew that my mom would leave, and I could not stand by and watch him destroy himself. He listened and now he's in a program, which is what you'll have to do. And you'll also have to be tough with your mother. I realize that you love her, but you're not doing either one of you any favors."

"Maybe you're right," Olivia replied and finally stopped pacing. She stood facing the ocean.

Michaela heard the doorbell ring and went inside. It was Josh. "Got here as soon as I could. She okay?" he asked.

"Yes. She's outside, thinking. Might want to give her a few minutes before you go out there."

"Thanks for calling me," he said. "Boy, you have been through it this week, haven't you?"

"We all have, but yes, I will agree that this has not been the best week. I still don't know what to think about who murdered Audrey, and I'm really confused about Bob's disappearance."

"I saw Hugh earlier and he said that the police are releasing Audrey's body tomorrow. He's started making plans for a funeral service next week."

"Oh. Good. I'll let him know again that if he needs anything, I can help."

"I'm sure he'd appreciate it. You know he was in love with her, don't you?"

Michaela slowly nodded. "Did he tell you that?"

Josh shrugged. "No. Bridgette moved out today. I told you about the yelling and her tearing down the drive the other day?"

"Yes."

"Today, she was back and she had movers picking up her things. I came up to the house to tell Hugh something and she was screaming at him that she knew about Audrey. After Bridgette took off again, he told me that he had loved Audrey and they'd planned to get married."

Michaela didn't know what to say. She already knew this, but she still had doubts that Hugh's love was sincere. But what would be his motive to kill Audrey, who everyone claimed he loved? Even Callahan said that Hugh had been in love with her for two decades.

"Josh?" They both turned to see Olivia standing in between the French doors that led to the balcony.

"Hey." He walked over and hugged her.

"I'll let you two talk. Would it be okay if I used your mom's computer, Olivia? I need to check my e-mail."

"Sure."

Josh put an arm around Olivia and they walked back outside. Michaela beelined it for Kathleen's office. She had a few things to check before they came back inside.

FORTY

THE FIRST THING MICHAELA DID ONCE SHE SAT down at Kathleen's computer was to Google Cara Klein's name. It had been bugging her for a day that she hadn't had the opportunity to look into the woman. Joe also hadn't called her with any new information. She seized opportunities whenever they presented themselves. Now looked as good a time as any.

At first she came across the typical ads for finding someone by that name, but as she scrolled down to the bottom of the page she found an article about a woman named Cara Klein who had been the president of a company called Strong X. The company had filed for Chapter 11 over five years ago, and Cara had stepped down as president and CEO. The company closed its doors within six months after she'd left. The article went on to report that a handful of lawsuits had been filed against Strong X, which was the maker of muscle-and endurance-type supplements for athletes, including runners, gymnasts, and boxers. *Boxers!* Michaela picked up the phone on Kathleen's desk and called Joe.

"You home now?" he asked.

"No."

"What?"

"I don't have a lot of time." She quickly filled him in and he immediately ran with her thoughts.

"Somehow this Cara Klein is linked to Terrell Jardinière. Sorry I hadn't had a chance to follow up on that lead yet with her."

"It's okay," she replied and then told Joe about her encounter with Terrell.

"Oh shit. I follow, Mick. Let me see what I can come up with. Be careful…and get your ass home!"

"As soon as I can."

She had a strong gut feeling that she was onto something here. She wasn't sure what it was, but if two and two added up, and this Cara Klein was the same one that Bob had been dating, there was a link of some sort. She knew she couldn't go back to see Terrell; there was no way anyone would let her in. Had Terrell known Cara? Was Cara the missing link to Bob's disappearance and Audrey's murder?

She went to log off her search and accidentally hit the back menu button. What she saw made her suck in a deep breath of air. There on the screen was a copy of Kathleen's itinerary for today. She was headed to New York City and would be back on Saturday morning. Whirlwind trip. So maybe she wasn't on the run after all. But that wasn't what had taken Michaela's breath away. It was who Kathleen was traveling with—Marshall Friedman. Marshall Friedman's name was on the itinerary. She scowled. In hiding or not, they were up to no good. Had to be.

Her curiosity aroused, she figured it couldn't hurt to do a bit of snooping around Kathleen's office. She first checked to make sure that Josh and Olivia were still out on the deck. They were. Then she rummaged through a few drawers. The photos she'd discovered had been moved. What she was looking for, she didn't know.

But she didn't expect what she did find tucked in with some files inside a leather ottoman that also served as a space saver. She pulled out a file marked "CHARLIE SAMPSON." The Sampson ranch! Charlie Sampson had been Audrey's husband. Michaela opened it up and found an old insurance policy, one that Audrey had taken out on herself with her late husband as beneficiary. An addendum had changed the beneficiaries to Bob Pratt and Kathleen Bowen. The policy's face value was three million dollars. Good grief! With Bob out of the picture, Kathleen stood to inherit a ton of money.

Michaela heard the sliders close, and she quickly put the file back inside the ottoman. As she closed the lid, Josh said, "Looking for something?" He stood in the doorway.

"No. I had seen one of these ottomans in the Pottery Barn catalogue and just wondered how they worked. Great idea. Space saver thing, you know." She yawned. "I am beat. Everything good with Olivia?"

"I think so. She's agreed to go with me and talk to her dad. He'll want to help. It's the right thing to do. Thanks for calling me."

"Not a problem."

"Hey, I know it's getting late, but I think your trailer is ready. Juan mentioned it to me today."

"I need to get back home." The last thing she wanted to do was drive to the Bowen Ranch, even if it meant getting her trailer back and picking up Geyser. "I'll be here Saturday for the Eq Tech Gala."

"Oh good. I'm going."

She nodded. "I'll either pick it up Sunday morning, or I may send my assistant to do it."

"Sure."

Michaela left, sighing as she closed the front door behind her. Josh had eyed her suspiciously a minute ago, and she wasn't sure she trusted him. Hell, she wasn't sure *who* she trusted. She had run the idea of Hugh murdering Audrey over again and again in her head, and it didn't sit right. She couldn't fathom it. But the *boss man* she'd heard Juan and Enrique referring to still had her wondering who that might be. Was it Josh? They all worked at the same place, and Josh held a higher position than either one of the Perez brothers. But now she had all of these other pieces not adding up. Terrell, Cara Klein, Kathleen, and Marshall Friedman. She had a long drive ahead of her. Maybe she'd be able to flesh out her thoughts.

But her thoughts were cut off when she received a call from Ethan. "You'd better come," he said. "It's Rocky."

FORTY-ONE

MICHAELA BARELY REMEMBERED THE DRIVE DOWN to San Diego. She was a mess. Thank God the traffic was moving and a California Highway Patrol guy didn't spot her speeding, because she probably wouldn't have stopped until she made it to the center.

The grounds of the Rocovich Center were well lit. She told the guard at the kiosk who she was, and he waved her through. Ethan was waiting for her.

"What is it? What happened?"

Ethan shook his head and placed a hand on her shoulder. "I don't know. We've got him stable now. He's comfortable. I've sedated him some, and we're going through the paces again with the labs. His pressure went up after he ate, along with his cortisol and other hormone levels. He had a seizure, Mick."

"Oh no." Her stomach sank as a wave of horror made her feel dizzy.

"We're testing him for Cushing's disease, which typically doesn't occur in a horse as young as he is, but we need to rule it out. He doesn't look like he has it. He doesn't have the potbelly, or lethargy and a thick crusty neck. Those are symptoms we would likely see with that disease. So, I'm also looking into hypothyroidism, which is pretty rare. It's hard to differentiate between the two though, because with either illness we're going to see the rise in cortisol levels and other hormones. Now his glucose levels aren't way off, and he does not seem excessively thirsty, so I don't think we're looking at diabetes. There are a handful of other possibilities I'm checking into. He could have a tumor on his pituitary gland, either benign or malignant. I just don't know yet. What I need you to do is detail his history for me. Obviously I know what his environment is like, but I want you to write out his daily schedule:

workouts, feedings, all of it. I have his medical history. And, we have to look at his entire system: cardiac, respiratory, everything. The thing is, seizures are fairly uncommon in horses. They can be difficult to diagnose. I've ruled out liver or renal disease. I've also been able to rule out hyperkalemia, which is a muscle disorder found in certain lines of quarter horses that can be confused with seizure activity. I've had a CT scan and MRI done on him and neither shows any type of cerebral edema. And, I'm running an EEG. He's been started on Diazepam to control any recurrence of a seizure tonight."

Michaela held up her hand. She'd had enough vet talk. "Can I see him?"

"Of course. We have him in a padded stall, and we've considered putting a padded helmet on him, just in case he goes down again. Right now though, his levels have started dropping and the Diazepam appears to be doing the job. I'm sorry, Mick. We'll find out what's wrong, and take care of him."

She followed Ethan through large steel double doors, where the mixture of antiseptic and familiar horse smells wafted through the air. They passed a surgical suite and walked through another set of doors. Once past them, Michaela spotted Rocky and tears sprung to her eyes. He was inside a stall with his head hung low.

She slid through the stall door and wrapped her arms around Rocky's neck, stroking him underneath his mane. "Hey guy. I'm sorry. I'm so sorry. They're going to make you better, okay? I promise. Then, I'm going to take you home and spoil you with carrots and molasses and a handful of mares." She smiled through her tears, knowing that if he could really understand her, he would've liked the sound of all that. He was such a great animal. She hated seeing him like this. It tore at her heart, her core. God, she loved him. She stayed in his stall for over an hour like that, talking to him and stroking him, while Ethan left them alone. Rocky did seem to perk up, knowing that she was there.

When Ethan came back it was past eleven and her body and mind felt exhausted. "Listen," he said, "I know you won't want to check into a hotel; we have beds here. They aren't great, but you can get some sleep, and that way we can be close by and check on him through the night."

"I don't want to leave him."

"You won't be. We'll be right through those doors, and you can come in anytime and see how he is. He looks pretty happy right now. Once he knew you were here, I noticed he relaxed even more. Come on, I've made you some tea."

She sighed and squeezed Rocky's neck. "I'll be back. Okay. I suppose I could use something to drink.

"And eat? I had a pizza delivered."

"I don't know if I can eat much."

"Give it a try. You won't be doing him any good by starving yourself. Now come on."

She followed Ethan into a break room, where he had the pizza set out. She'd noticed a few other techs and vets in and out since she'd been there, but as the night wore on it grew quiet, which was good. She didn't feel like talking to anyone she didn't know.

They sat down and started in on their late dinner, eating in peace for a few minutes. She decided maybe it was time to lighten the mood. "Won't be long until you'll be a dad."

He smiled. "Yeah, I know. Cool. Some day, it'll be you. You'll be a mom."

"Maybe."

"I'm worried about you, Mick. You look tired to me. Exhausted, actually."

"Well, you look like you're having sympathy for your pregnant wife, or are you trying to match her on the weight gain?" she chided.

"Hey!"

"You told me that I looked exhausted. I can't jab you back a little?"

"It's only a few pounds. Maybe five."

"Or ten."

"You're a pain in the ass."

"So are you. You really ready to be a dad?"

"You know what? I am. I can't wait for this kid to be here. We are going to do everything together."

"I bet you will."

"Summer and I may have had a rough start, but things have calmed down a lot, and I know she isn't the perfect wife, or...Wait, let me rephrase that: She actually *is* the perfect wife; she just may not always be my perfect fit. She's a bit too perfect. Hell, who am I kidding? I know I should be home with her right now, but she's just so moody, almost angry all the time." Michaela listened and decided not to put in her two cents. "But she loves me, and I do love her. I really do." Michaela wondered who he was trying to convince of that—her or himself. "I know in my gut that we'll make great parents together. And, I can't wait to be a dad."

"I think that's wonderful."

"It is. Hey, while you're here, do you want to take a look at Halliday?"

"Yeah." She followed him through two large steel doors that led into the intensive care area. It was as sterile as any human hospital. Classical music played softly over the speakers.

"Over here is the hydrotherapy pool." They walked into a separate room with a large pool and a sling off to the side with a lift and pulley setup. Ethan said, "Halliday has spent quite a bit of time in this already, and throughout his rehab he'll spend more time. We get him into the sling and pull him into the water, where he is able to move freely, to help keep his muscles from deteriorating. And also to keep his spirits up. Horses want to move, so the hard part for these guys when they break a leg is making sure they don't lose it mentally. It's a shame that he has to go through this. Come on, he's over here."

They walked through another set of double doors. The new area wasn't quite as antiseptic smelling, but there still was that faint scent of alcohol. Michaela took in more of the normal horse-related smells that she was used to—straw, hay, manure, and horse. There were four stalls in the area. Two were occupied, one with Halliday.

"That's Rosa in there. Came in here for colic surgery yesterday. She's doing much better. Here he is."

Halliday looked up from his feeder. He was in a sling, which held his feet slightly off the ground, but he nickered as they said hello to him. "Poor guy," Michaela said.

"No doubt, but see how bright his eyes are? He's going to make it, Mick, I feel it. And when he does, I'm sure he'll command quite a stud fee."

"Doesn't bode well for the racing industry, does it?"

"What do you mean? Halliday injuring himself?"

"No, what I'm talking about is all that goes into the racehorse and then when he's injured, possibly even a fatal injury, human greed takes over. What do you think of racing in general?"

"You know, people have been racing horses for centuries, and tons of different breeds. Yes, you see some greed out there. You'll see track owners get their dirt padding down to next to nothing hoping to increase speed and get a record time on their track. It happens, and there are a lot of owners who are against those types of practices. Many of them will pull their horses out of those races. Many won't because of the fines that are put into place by doing so, and by the bureaucratic crap that goes along with it. A lot of owners don't want to make waves. They love their animals, but this can be a money-making business and there is a lot of power and control that goes into it. That said, am I against racing horses? Not really. These animals are built to do this. It's what they're bred for. Now, get Halliday out into a pasture and he'll be a happy retired animal. But, there will still be that thread inside of him that pushes him to want to run, and get him on a track when all of this is said and done, and he'll feel compelled to break out. What I don't like about racing—or any type of event for that matter when it comes to animals—is exploitation of animals of any kind. Racing tends to have gotten that bad rap over the years, because in many cases it fits."

They gave Halliday some attention and then headed to where the cots were set up. Ethan gave her a pair of sweats and a clean T-shirt from his bag. "I know they'll be huge on you, but at least they're clean."

"Thanks."

"Well, I'll let you get some rest."

"Ethan?"

"Yes?"

"Will you stay me with me? I don't want to be alone."

He studied her for a few seconds. "Yeah. I'll stay."

FORTY-TWO

MICHAELA AND ETHAN TALKED INTO THE WEE hours and took turns checking on Rocky, who remained stable throughout the night. It felt like old times between them. They talked about horses, his unborn son, a bit more about Summer. Ethan brought up Jude, but Michaela quickly changed the subject. She also let him in on what she'd been up to over the past week concerning Audrey and Francisco's murders and Bob's disappearance,

"Mick, I've got to agree with your detective boyfriend on this one. Don't mess with it," Ethan said.

"First off, I don't have a boyfriend and second, I feel like I'm close to figuring this out. I'm pretty certain that I have all of the pieces. I'm just not sure how they fit together. Like this thing with Kathleen and Halliday. I know how she can cover his expenses now."

"Oh, yeah. How?"

Michaela explained to Ethan about Olivia and the contract she'd signed with Friedman and Callahan, as well as the old insurance policy.

"She sure sounds like a suspect," Ethan said.

"I know. But so does everyone else."

Ethan agreed with that assessment after she'd finished detailing the week's dramas. "Hey, Ethan?"

"Hmmm?" he asked, sounding like sleep was ready to take over.

"Thank you."

He propped himself up onto his elbow. A night-light that he'd turned on so she'd know how to maneuver if she needed to get up in the middle of the night cast shadows across his face. "For what?"

"For taking care of Rocky, and for listening to me. I've missed you."

"I've missed you, too, Mick." He lay back down.

Michaela rolled over onto her side and surprisingly, fell asleep after a few moments. Even though it had been a late night, she woke up before seven the next morning, as the center came to life. Ethan showed her where she could shower.

"I put your clothes in the wash last night, while you changed into my sweats. By the way, they look good on you, even if they're a size too big."

"A size? Try a few sizes."

He winked at her. "I got up early and put them in the dryer. There they are." He pointed to a desk in the room where they'd slept. He'd even folded them for her.

"Thanks. I think I will take that shower, after I check my horse."

Rocky appeared to be fine. Ethan had changed up his diet, so he was being fed in smaller increments and more than twice a day. He checked all of his levels after each feeding.

After getting dressed, Michaela poured herself a cup of coffee in the break room, and waited around for the rest of Rocky's test results. She checked her messages. Joe called and told her it was important to call him back.

"I got an address for Cara Klein. And she *is* the same woman who was dating Bob Pratt, and she did work for both Strong X and Eq Tech, but she was in their marketing departments."

"I thought that she owned Strong X."

"Don't know about that."

"Where is she?"

"She's in a hospice facility in San Diego. She has cancer." Michaela did remember Josh telling her that the woman Bob had been seeing was sick. Cancer? He gave her the address. "That is all we can get on her. Other than that, she was clean. That's all I know. But I did learn something else: There is a connection between Strong X and Terrell Jardinière."

"What's that?"

"Terrell was a spokesman for the company. Rumor has it that the supplements he was taking from them were what caused his stroke. Kind of similar to that company that gave Barry Bonds those supplements that supposedly don't have no connection with steroids." Joe snorted.

"Oh my God. I've got to go, Joe. I'll call you later." Michaela went searching for Ethan.

"What is it?" he asked. One look at her face must have told him that something was wrong.

"That file that I gave you from Bob. The one Audrey had…"

"Yeah?"

"Have you looked at it yet?"

"No. I meant to, but then Rocky took that turn and—"

"You need to. When I looked at it, it looked to me like a grouping of horses, not just one case. You need to look at which of those horses were on Eq Tech supplements. I think that something in those supplements could be hurting the horses. It's what's making them sick."

"What?"

"Can you break down the chemical components in the supplements?"

"Someone here can."

"Do it. I've got to see someone. I'll be back."

"Mick, where are you going?"

"Just trust me. It's in the supplements."

She left to speak with Cara Klein, who she knew would provide the missing link.

FORTY-THREE

MICHAELA DROVE TO AN AREA CALLED MISSION Valley, northeast of downtown San Diego. The hospice sat high up on a hill overlooking the valley and the many freeways that crisscrossed the area.

Entering, Michaela felt a bit nervous not knowing what she would learn, if anything, that might help find Audrey's killer. A nurse greeted her. "May I help you?"

"I'm here to see Cara Klein. I'm Michaela Bancroft." This woman was way friendlier than the nurse at the home that Terrell was in.

She checked a roster. "I'm sorry, but I don't see you on the list of visitors. I can ask if she'd like to see you."

Michaela nodded. "Tell her that it's about Bob Pratt."

The nurse looked at her oddly, but nodded and walked down the hall. She returned a minute later and told Michaela that Cara was in room 219 and would see her. She walked to the room, where she found a tiny woman lying in bed. She couldn't have been over thirty-five; she had no hair, her face was pulled taut, and her hazel eyes seemed glossed over. She smiled weakly at Michaela and said, "Hi."

"Hello." Michaela closed the door and walked over to the bed. "I'm Michaela Bancroft."

"The nurse told me." Cara slurred her words a little, likely from the pain medications. "You know Bob?"

"Yes." Michaela wasn't sure how to start this conversation. It would be awkward, to say the least. "I was a friend of Audrey, Bob's sister. I don't know if you're aware, but Audrey was murdered a week ago and Bob has disappeared. I was hoping you could help me piece some missing links together."

Cara frowned; her eyes widened. "I'm sorry. I don't think...I can help you."

Michaela could hear a tremor in the woman's voice, and she wasn't very convincing. "Please." Dammit. She felt that Cara Klein might actually have some answers. Why did the woman sound scared?

"Cara," she continued, "there are horses being hurt, maybe even dying. I think you know why and I think that whatever is going on with these animals might have something to do with Bob's disappearance and Audrey's murder."

"Yes," she whispered.

"So you do know about this?"

Tears came to Cara's eyes. She sighed. "I do."

Michaela sat down and scooted the chair close to Cara's bed in order to better hear her. "Last weekend at the races was where Audrey was killed. We'd gone together to see Olivia Bowen perform and were watching the races from Kathleen Bowen's box."

"I know them."

"You do?"

Cara nodded and started coughing. The horrid barklike cough lasted a while. Cara placed an oxygen mask over her face for a minute. "Sorry," she said, once the coughing was under control.

"You don't need to apologize."

"I know the Bowens and that entire circle."

Michaela wasn't sure what she meant by that. "Entire circle?"

"The racing scene."

"Do you mean Frederick Callahan, Marshall Friedman?" Michaela knew that each of them owned racehorses. They also knew the Bowens.

"I'd say they're...part of that group." She started coughing again. Michaela saw a bottle of water on the table next to her and reached across to give it to her.

Cara shook her head and put the oxygen back on. After another minute and some deep breaths, she closed her eyes. Michaela's stomach sank. "Cara?"

The woman opened her eyes. Thank God. "You'll have to…bear with me. It might take some time, but there are some things I…need to tell you."

FORTY-FOUR

MICHAELA HAD BEEN RIGHT: CARA KLEIN HAD ANSWERS. At first there were parts to her story that she doubted. But the woman had been very convincing, and the more she thought about it, and allowed the information to settle in, the more she realized that what Cara told her had been the truth. She now knew what had happened to Bob, and had a good idea as to what went down with Audrey. And she was ready to catch a killer, but she would need some help.

She called Joe and told him what she'd learned. They devised a plan on how she'd trap the killer.

"It's good, Michaela...but why not just bring in the cops?" Joe asked.

"The woman who gave me this information made me promise not to go to the police."

"Why?"

"She's afraid. She's been burned a few times and doesn't trust many people."

"She trusted you."

"I'll fill you in when I see you. Now, can I count on you?"

"When have you not been able to count on me?" She laughed. "I'm in," he said.

Michaela spent Friday night at theRocovich Center again, and to everyone's relief Rocky was doing great. Trusting her instincts, the vets had altered his course of treatment and he was perking up nicely. The chemicals in the supplements were still being broken down. The vets had to send them out to a separate group of chemists, who would be able to better determine what compounds made up the product. They wouldn't have results for a couple of days, but Michaela felt that she was right. And now that Rocky looked better, she also felt better. Ethan did not stay the night again as Summer called, full of complaints. Guilt-ridden for leaving her alone for a few days, he went home.

Saturday morning, Michaela gave Rocky a hug, "You'll be coming home in a couple of days, bud. You're going to get better now." She left her horse behind again, only this time certain that he would make a full recovery.

She got to Los Angeles late in the afternoon and found the Eq Tech apartment. She called Joe one more time. "We're on it," he reassured her.

"Good."

She called Hudson Drake to let him know that she'd made it. "Hey, do you still want that date for tonight?"

"You know it. I take it you're on your way now."

"I just pulled into the parking garage, so I'll see you soon. I'm looking forward to it."

He laughed. "We're going to have a great time. Did you get a gown?"

"I have one." She'd stopped at one of the million malls along Interstate 5, quickly deciding on a simple long silk lavender gown, one of the classic types. Nothing fancy in the least, but she figured it would be appropriate.

"I have a surprise waiting for you inside the apartment," he said.

"You do? What is it?"

"I can't tell you, or it wouldn't be a surprise. I'll pick you up at six."

Michaela unlocked the door to the apartment and was stunned by its opulence. She knew walking through the front courtyard with its water fountains and immaculate garden that it would be nice, but this surpassed *nice*. Her nerves were buzzing. A decorator had done the apartment up beautifully. It was about 1,500 square feet of amazing views of Century City from all angles. The living room area was done in metallic colors of gold, bronze, and olive, with the sofa done in a gold-and-bronze damask pattern. Two matching leather chairs faced a fireplace in front of ceiling-high windows. A vase with a dozen red roses stood on the long mahogany dining room table with a card attached that had her name on it. The flowers were beautiful.

She opened the card. It was from Drake, saying that there would be many surprises tonight.

Michaela headed to the bedroom. She walked with trepidation; what she found sitting on the gold sateen bedspread of a four-poster bed was an amazing gown, its color a perfect shade of pink rose, with a long V down the back outlined with small beads and sequins. The front was a scoop neck with folds of silk that looked as though they would lie delicately across a woman's chest. Michaela picked it up. It was the right size—a six. On the bed next to the dress was a pair of shoes the same color of the dress with thin straps and high heels. Looked like Hudson Drake was out to romance her.

Michaela showered, and then slipped the gorgeous gown over her head, smiling as the fabric fell gracefully along the still-youthful curves of her body. After stepping into the heels and adjusting the straps, she arranged her hair into a sleek chignon at the nape of her neck, and applied more makeup than usual, going dramatic on the eyes and trying hard not to mess up. She was looking at herself in the mirror, applying the last touches of her makeup, adding the simple gold earrings she'd brought with her, when the doorbell rang. Her hands shook.

She opened it to see Hudson standing there. "Amazing," he said. "I knew it would be, though."

"Thank you...for all of it. You didn't have to buy a dress for me or the shoes, or even the roses. You've been way too kind."

"All for a beautiful woman. I have one more gift."

"Oh no. I couldn't accept anything else."

He smiled as he brought a small bag out from behind his back and handed it to her. "Open it," he said.

She took out a small handbag, silver with pink roses appliquéd onto it. "This is beautiful. It matches perfectly."

"That was the plan. Now, put whatever you need in it and let's get going. The limo is waiting and I have a bottle of champagne chilling."

The event was held at the Beverly Hills Hotel, the utmost in old Hollywood prestige and money. The red carpet was laid out for all attending. Once inside they saw about three hundred guests milling around, drinking champagne and chatting each other up, all in their diamonds and pearls.

Michaela spotted Olivia walk in, Hugh on one side of her and Josh on the other. She looked sober. She approached them as Hudson was busy speaking with some business associates. Hugh smiled at her. "I heard about what you did for my daughter."

Michaela didn't know what to say.

"I told my dad. Josh convinced me that it was a good idea."

"We're here for you." Josh rubbed Olivia's arm. "I want to thank you, too," he told Michaela.

"I'm going to rehab next week," Olivia said.

"That's good to hear. How about your riding?"

"One day at a time," Hugh said. "But I want her to pursue her dreams. Audrey wanted that for her, too."

Michaela nodded. "She did."

"I've arranged for her service to be next Wednesday. It'll be in Indio."

"Thank you. I wish you would've leaned on me for some help," Michaela said.

"I think it would be appropriate for you to speak."

"I'd love to do that. Oh, about my trailer and Geyser: I told Josh that I would have my assistant, Dwayne, take care of it."

"Of course."

"Well, I should probably get back to my date," she said.

Hugh kissed her on the cheek. "Thank you again," he whispered in her ear.

Michaela smiled and started to return to Hudson, when she spotted none less than the spectacle of Bridgette Bowen sauntering up to the bar flanked by Frederick Callahan, who wore a second ornament on his other arm—a striking, tall blonde. Michaela shook her head. *Some people never learn.* She buzzed by the spectacle, saying, "Bridgette, how are you? I heard about your split from Hugh. It's terrible. So sorry."

Bridgette scooted in tighter next to Callahan. "Some moves are strategic. Some just smart. You think I didn't plan my most recent maneuver?"

Callahan rolled his eyes and grinned.

"I think that you plan everything out very carefully," Michaela said. "Nice to see you, Freddie. How's your heart?"

She left knowing that her slight would make Bridgette's blood boil.

Steve Benz was setting up on the stage. Michaela walked up to him. "Hey Steve, how's it going?"

Benz glared at her. "Great. The psycho-bitch is here."

"Right. Takes one to know one." She smiled, knowing it was a childish remark, but wanting to continue getting under his skin, which she obviously did. He was such an ass. She really hoped that Smith had sold those photos of Benz and Bridgette to a rag magazine.

Oh yes, all the usual suspects were here, including Kathleen Bowen, who sat next to Marshall Friedman, lots of bling around her neck. Hmmm. Michaela sat down next to them. "How was New York? Nice shopping spree?"

"What? I don't know what you're talking about," Kathleen said aghast.

"Really?"

"What kind of question is that? You know this wacko?" Friedman asked Kathleen.

"I'd rather be a wacko than a jackass," she told him and got up from the table.

"Well, I never," she heard Kathleen say as she walked to her own table.

Sitting down, she heard someone behind her say, "Champagne?" She turned around and smiled.

"Don't mind if I do."

Joe smiled and winked at her. "Told you we had your back," he said in a low voice. "This place is crawling with cousins."

As the evening wore on and patrons went through the scrumptious buffet line, Michaela grew nervous. She knew that the time was fast approaching when their plan would go down. Could she really do it? Maybe she should have another glass of champagne. No, she needed to think clearly.

"Are you all right?" Hudson asked. "You've gotten kind of quiet in the last half hour."

"I'm fine. Tired. That's all." She looked around the table. Hugh, Olivia, and Josh sat at their table along with another couple that Michaela didn't know but who apparently owned a slew of racehorses. Mr. and Mrs. Black—older, sophisticated, and obviously quite wealthy.

Michaela turned to Mr. Black. "Do you use Eq Tech supplements on your racehorses?"

"Of course," he said. "It's a great product. I'm thinking of investing some money in the company." He smiled at Hudson.

"I'm looking forward to it," Hudson said. "I think we can grow this company tenfold and really make a difference around the world in the performance of athletic equines."

The waitstaff was walking around, changing out the cutlery in preparations for the filet mignon about to be served.

"Here, here," Mr. Black said, raising his glass to toast.

Everyone around the table raised their glasses in response. Michaela was slow on the uptake. When they finished, Hudson stood. "I better get up to the microphone and get this auction rolling."

Michaela grabbed his arm. "Wait. I'm sorry, but could I say something? Can I make an announcement?"

Hudson sat back down. "What is it?"

"I think I told you that I'm planning to open up a therapeutic riding center for autistic kids."

"Yes."

"Well," she lowered her voice as the others at the table began talking amongst themselves, "there are a lot of wealthy people here who might be interested in contributing to the center for autism. It's a worthy charity. But I don't want to steal your thunder."

"Oh no, not at all. Please, make your announcement." Hudson stood up with Michaela and escorted her to the stage.

Her hands trembled when she took the microphone. "Good evening, ladies and gentlemen. I'm Michaela Bancroft and I'm here to make a very important announcement." She paused. The crowd's eyes were on her, and once again she didn't know if she could go through with this, until she spotted Joe in the corner. "You see, I lost a very dear friend this week to the hands of a killer."

She spotted Hudson, who had been walking back to their table, stop and turn around, a smile still on his face, but looking at her oddly.

"And the killer is here, in this room."

"She's a nut," Marshall Friedman shouted. "Get her off the stage."

"Michaela? What's this about?" Hugh said, standing.

"Trust me, Hugh; you will want to hear what I have to say. I couldn't figure out why anyone would kill my friend Audrey Pratt. She was one of the sweetest people that I've ever known. The tragedy about the way she lost her life is that she probably had no idea why she was being murdered when it happened. She was killed because someone wanted to hide something. Something he thought that she knew about. But she didn't."

"What are you doing, Michaela?" Hudson asked,

"Good question. I've had an interesting conversation with the Blacks this evening about how highly they value Eq Tech supplements." She eyed the Blacks. "I'm sure many of you here use the product and think it's wonderful. But what would you say if I told you that those supplements can kill your horses?"

The room, which had grown silent now, made a collective gasping sound.

"I told you that she was crazy," Friedman said.

"Psycho-bitch!" Benz yelled out.

"Michaela, maybe you need to have a seat." Callahan stood and started walking toward her. She spotted Joe moving.

"I guess I didn't realize that my date was also the entertainment for the evening. She's had too much to drink. Michaela, come down from there," Hudson said.

She pointed at him. "You orchestrated Bob Pratt's disappearance because he knew the chemicals in your supplements could be deadly. He reported his findings to you and told you that if you didn't take the product off the market, he'd reveal what you were doing." Her words came out in rapid fire now.

"This is insane." Hudson moved closer to the stage.

"No. *You're* insane. When you hired Enrique and Juan Perez to kidnap Bob and take him to Mexico to kill him, you had already learned that Bob had sent a file to his sister that you didn't want anyone to see. A file that proved his findings about the supplements. You stalked her at the races and murdered her when the opportunity was there. You murdered her hired hand Francisco, too, when you surprised him at her ranch while searching for the file. The thing is, what you didn't know is that I ultimately wound up with the file."

"Get down from there! This is all bullshit." Hudson's face was turning red.

Joe made his way to the front of the room. He set a tray down on one of the tables.

"She's telling the truth." The crowd turned to see a man hobbling in, his right eye heavily bandaged. He'd been badly beat up.

"Bob!" Bridgette Bowen exclaimed.

"Oh my God," Hugh said.

A murmur floated through the banquet room. With all eyes on Bob Pratt, Michaela and the rest of the crowd failed to see Hudson grab a steak knife from one of the server's trays. Moving quickly, he lunged at her. She felt the knife strike her leg as she stumbled. Joe and the cousins hadn't been able to move fast enough and Michaela found herself being dragged down off the stage by Hudson, the knife to her throat, blood seeping from her leg.

"You blew it," Hudson said into her ear. "You're coming with me."

She watched Joe and a half dozen other men approaching them.

"Get the fuck back!" Hudson yelled. "I will kill her. I will! Let us walk out of here and she might have a chance to live. Anyone else comes any closer and she dies. Her blood will be on all of your hands."

The men froze as Hudson, his arm still around her neck, backed out of the banquet room. Blood rushed through Michaela's insides, turning them ice cold as she realized these were likely her last moments alive.

FORTY-FIVE

HUDSON DRAGGED MICHAELA UP ONTO THE HOTEL roof. The knife had sliced through her skin on her throat, and she noticed a trickle of blood falling onto her bare arm. He'd manhandled her up the stairs and she'd torn the dress. When she'd spoken with him earlier, then seen the dress and all of the gifts he'd left for her in the apartment, it had taken everything she had to muster up the courage to play out the role of his happy date. The last thing she wanted to do was alert him that she knew Bob Pratt was alive, and that the truth about everything was about to come out.

"I'm telling you, if you want something done right, you have to do it yourself," he hissed. "Those morons, Juan and Enrique, if they'd done the job right, Bob would be dead, and you and I would be on our way to my bedroom."

"I would *never* go to bed with you!" Michaela spat.

He tightened his grip. "You would have. I saw it in your eyes the day that we met. You wanted me. And we could've had a great time together. What a waste. I can't believe Pratt is alive."

It had been Bob who'd made the call to her the other day claiming to be Terrell Jardinière, too afraid to alert anyone other than Cara that he was alive. But he'd heard through Audrey that it had been Michaela who was ultimately responsible for discovering who had murdered her uncle Lou the previous year, and he'd hoped that she would do the same thing for Audrey. And she had.

"You've been doing this for years. Didn't you think that you would eventually get caught? You're a chemist. You know that these supplements that you've been producing, first with Strong X and now Eq Tech, can hurt the user. Why not make a product that doesn't?" She hoped to bide time. Keep him talking and maybe someone would save her. She prayed that a SWAT team was surrounding the area now. She had no other idea how she was going to get out of this alive. Even though it was chilly outside on the roof, she felt perspiration trickling down her back. How could she get this maniac to let her go? He had an ego. Keep him talking. That was all she could think to do until a better plan hopefully worked its way inside her head.

"Are you kidding? My products have proven successful. They make people and horses stronger, faster, and sharper minded. It's proven."

"It's also proven that they do harm. Look at Terrell Jardinière."

"Some people had reactions," he growled.

"He is completely incapacitated."

"It can't be proven that Strong X caused it."

"What about the horses? That *can* be proven."

"You should have minded your own business."

"You shouldn't have murdered my friend. And I know you not only killed Audrey, but Francisco, too. How did you do it anyway? How did you lure Audrey onto the back forty and kill her?"

"I saw it as opportunity. I'd tapped Bob's phone, knew he'd had dinner with her and that he planned to tell her something. I was afraid he told her what he'd found out. So, when I spotted her heading to the track, I called her over. Told her that they wouldn't let her out onto the track. That I'd tried. Then I told her that Bob was missing. I suggested we take a walk and discuss the options. At that point I didn't realize she was clueless, but I couldn't take the chance."

"You killed an innocent woman! You're really sick, Hudson. What about Francisco? Why did you kill him?"

"I didn't. That was something Juan Perez took care of for me. I sent him out to Audrey's ranch to locate that file and lo and behold he ran into Francisco. Casualty of circumstance, so to speak."

Michaela felt her throat tighten. "Why do you want all this blood on your hands? Don't you care at all? Is money and power all that you want? I also know all about Cara's husband, Shawn Klein."

"Oh please. Cara Klein is an idiot and Shawn was a loser. If you ask me, I did her a favor." He grabbed her arm tightly and dragged her to the side of the building. She looked down. It was a long way. Lights from the hotel gardens reflected off the hotel pool. She doubted she could survive a fall.

Michaela flashed back to her conversation with Cara as Hudson pulled her closer to the edge. "Hudson Drake killed my husband, Shawn," Cara told her. "Supposedly Shawn died in a boating accident, but I know that it was Hudson who killed him. My husband was a sailor. He'd been on the seas since he was a kid. It was a clear day, and all he was doing was sailing out to the end of Point Loma, which isn't far."

"Why did he do it?" Michaela had asked her.

"We were both working for Strong X. I was in the marketing department and Shawn was the head chemist. Drake asked Shawn to add a drug called diazepethicone to the recipe, saying that some of the athletes they'd been in discussions with had heard of the drug and how it made athletes in Russia stronger, more vital. The problem is, it's a steroid derivative and as you know, steroid use in most sports is completely banned. Hudson's request of Shawn was to find a way to hide the drug within the supplement so that when athletes were tested it would not show up."

"Did your husband do it, put that drug into the Strong X supplements?"

"He did, and he paid the ultimate price for it. Shawn had a bad feeling that what the supplement was comprised of could cause serious damage to athletes, to people in general, but he did what he did because we needed the money and were desperate at the time. I know that sounds horrible, and I won't bore you with the details, but we went through with it. Shawn tucked his ethics way down and became one of Drake's henchmen. Then, Terrell collapsed, and so did a track runner. A kid really, only nineteen, up and coming. His family didn't pursue anything because they didn't put it all together. But Terrell Jardinière's aunt had her suspicions and she started asking questions. Drake agreed to pay her a lot of money to keep her quiet, as well as pay for his medical expenses.

"When Terrell had the stroke, Shawn became scared. He had a bad feeling that eventually it would all blow up in their faces and he'd be the fall guy because he was the head chemist. He decided to deal with it before that happened. He began taking files and copying them, keeping them in a safe-deposit box. He wanted to collect all the evidence he could before he went to the authorities."

"Were you aware of this?"

"No. Not until after he was killed. He made me a video. On it he told me everything that he suspected and what he'd been up to. He also told me where the safe-deposit key was and how to get into it. When I went to the bank, the box was empty. I don't know if he emptied it before he died for some reason, or if they did. Maybe Drake and his crew learned about it and found the key. My guess is someone got on that boat that day with my husband and tortured him or threatened him until he told them where he was keeping the files he'd copied. Shawn was afraid that our phones were tapped and that they were watching him."

"You continued working for them, though, for Hudson Drake."

"I felt I had to. I was too scared that if I stopped working for him that he would become more suspicious of me and kill me. I thought that maybe I could continue putting a case against him together. That was my hope."

"What happened?"

"After Shawn, they started to phase out Strong X and that part of their human line. They began to go into the equine division claiming they wanted to diversify, and after doing a lot of research they also said the equine market could produce millions of dollars, which it's doing. I also think that they figured they were taking less of a risk by dealing with equine athletes like racehorses."

"How did you meet Bob?"

"Once Drake started to phase out Strong X and change direction, Bob was brought on as the research vet. I met him and thought he was a nice man. We had lunches together. He confided in me about his alcoholism. I got sick last year and was diagnosed with stage IV cancer. I only worked another two months before I had to leave."

Cara continued. "Bob came to me, actually. He said that he didn't like the way some of the test results were turning out with some of the horses he'd been giving the supplements to and that it bothered him. He said that when he went to Drake, he was told that the studies looked great, and for him not to be troubled and just keep doing his work. Bob got scared. He said that Drake used a threatening tone with him when they discussed this. That was only a few weeks ago, before I entered hospice care. I became really worried about Bob. We were still seeing each other on occasion. I even went up to Los Angeles a couple of times in the last few months. He knew that I was concerned and I told him what I thought they'd done to Shawn. He then told me that he was also trying to collect evidence against Eq Tech. I begged him to stop, but I don't think he did. That was the last time I heard from him. Until now. Just yesterday."

Michaela had left the hospital knowing that she had some work ahead of her to get Hudson to confess. She thought that if she accused him in front of a roomful of guests and presented the evidence she'd discovered, he'd crack. Oh, he'd cracked all right. Being taken hostage had not been part of the plan.

"Why don't you just let me go?" Michaela pleaded. "You can get away and no one will find you. I'm sure you've got money in offshore accounts. Do you really want another murder on your hands?"

"I've got plenty of money...and as far as killing you? It won't bother me a bit, sweetheart." Still standing behind her, knife at her throat, he kissed her on the cheek. "You've got your choice though: I can either push you off or slice your throat."

"Great options."

"You should have minded your own business."

Michaela knew she didn't have much more than a few seconds. As her brain scrambled for a way out, she heard a loud bang. Hudson's arm fell from her neck and he grabbed at his leg, the knife falling to the ground. "Fuck!" he screamed. Realizing that he'd let her go, he lunged for her, his leg seeping blood.

Michaela, stunned, didn't think, just reacted, picking up the knife. "Get away, Hudson! Stay away from me!"

He kept stumbling forward. "You're not going to kill me."

Tears stung her eyes. "Get away! I *will* kill you!"

"No you won't—"

Another shot rang out as he again lunged for her. An anguished scream rose from Hudson as he fell against Michaela, the knife piercing his stomach. He stumbled backward, trying to pull the knife out. He stared at her, shocked. Then his body swayed as he took one too many steps backward and, leaning to the side, his body fell off the roof. She backed away and felt arms wrap tightly around her. She turned and cried on Joe's chest.

"I'm sorry, Mick. Sorry we couldn't get to you in time."

"It's okay. I'm okay," she sobbed. "Did you shoot him?"

"No." Dennis Smith, dressed in a tuxedo, came forward.

"Smith? You were here?" She pulled away from Joe to see a smiling Smith standing there, gun in hand.

"Yep. Had to keep tabs on Benz and the rest of the shysters. Made myself a nice deal with one of the tabloids. Looks like I'll get my Tahitian vacation after all. And this tops it off."

She couldn't help but smile. Although her leg hurt, she was thankful Smith had been there. "You saved my life. I can't believe that I didn't spot you in there."

He shrugged. "I'm a private investigator. You weren't supposed to see me."

She thanked him and Joe, happy to be alive.

FORTY-SIX

SUNDAY, THE DAY AFTER HUDSON DRAKE'S DEATH, Michaela was back at home with her animals. Ethan had called and found a link between the chemicals and the damage it was causing to the horses; along with Bob they reported their findings to the *Los Angeles Times*. The story would be a huge one by the following day.

Bob was back at home with Cara; he wanted to care for her during her last days. He'd explained how he'd reached Cara the day before Michaela came to see her, but he'd asked her not to tell anyone that he was still alive, afraid that Drake would find out and finish him off before he could discover a way to put him behind bars. Cara had contacted him after Michaela left, and told him about her visit. They had then contacted Michaela, who with Joe and Bob's help devised what they thought was a foolproof plan to catch Hudson Drake. What they had not expected was the actual turn of events. However, it had all paid off in the end, as Hudson Drake suffered his own horrible death, thanks to Dennis Smith—a memory Michaela would not soon forget.

After the chaos that had taken place at the hotel, Bob further explained about his connection with Bridgette Bowen—indeed, she had a secret to keep and did not want Bob to expose her. When they were at Betty Ford together, Bridgette had come to Bob's room and tried to seduce him, but he'd wanted no part of it, and she hadn't forgotten the incident. Michaela was sure that Bridgette would recover just fine from her divorce and bounce right back, be it with Callahan or some other rich old geezer.

When the Perez brothers learned what had happened to Drake, they'd made a run for the border, only to be caught by the police and placed in jail.

Olivia was apparently on her way to rehab, and Hugh was shocked and dismayed but relieved that the lies had been exposed.

Kathleen and Marshall Friedman were indeed an item. She would get her half of Audrey's insurance policy. Michaela hoped she would use the money wisely, but doubted it.

Hugh had done his best to put the fear of God into Friedman and Callahan to let his daughter out of the contracts with them. Callahan graciously agreed and Friedman threatened suit, but Hugh was confident he'd back down. He wanted his daughter to pursue her dream of becoming a jockey.

Joe was back with his wife and kids preparing for a Sunday feast and had invited Michaela to join them, but she asked for a rain check, needing a day of rest. She did, however, call the woman from the autism center at home and told her that she would take the job. Dwayne was on his way to get her trailer back and bring Geyser home. She planned to head down to the Humane Society first thing Monday morning and claim Audrey's animals.

And with her brother now home, Audrey could truly rest in peace. Although Michaela was still saddened by her tragic death, she knew that Audrey had not died in vain. No more people—or animals—would suffer at the hands of Hudson Drake ever again, and she knew that Audrey would be proud of that.

As for Camden, Michaela located her in the kitchen preparing dinner. When Camden spotted her, she gave her a hug. "You are one crazy bitch, you know that?"

That morning, Joe had come over and they replayed everything for Camden and Dwayne. "I know."

"You have got to stop tracking down killers. It's not healthy for you."

Michaela laughed. "I guess not."

"Jude has been calling here all day. All week in fact. He knows about what happened and he's worried. The guy really cares about you. You need to call him."

Michaela nodded. She supposed that she would have to do that, but not now.

The doorbell rang and Michaela looked at Camden. "I have no clue," her friend said.

Michaela opened the door; Ethan stood on the other side. "Hey, what's up?"

He beamed. "I was on my way here to tell you some great news, but I have to rush, because I just got more great news."

"What's going on?"

"Real quick. First of all, Halliday looks to be out of the woods. It'll be some time yet before you can bring him home."

"What do you mean, before I can bring him home?"

"He's yours. Kathleen Bowen called the center and said that she was giving the horse to you. That you should have him. Gratis. She said that she felt she had a lot to make amends for. I didn't ask."

"No kidding? What about his expenses?"

"No kidding. Yeah that part, well she did say that she'd cover half, if you would pay the other half."

Michaela laughed. "Of course she did. I'll take the horse." Maybe Kathleen would make wiser decisions when it came to money after all.

"And guess what else?" Ethan said.

"What?"

"I just got a call from Summer. She's been out shopping and she started contractions. Our baby is going to be born today!" he practically yelped. "I'm on my way to the hospital."

"That's great, Ethan. Really great."

"I can't wait."

"Well, what are you doing waiting around here then? You better get going."

"Right." He gave her a quick hug. "I'll call you later."

"You better," she yelled after him.

Camden came up beside Michaela and put an arm around her as she watched Ethan drive away, tears in her eyes. "Let him go, honey. Let him go. It's time." Michaela nodded.

The phone rang. "Will you get that?" she said.

A few seconds later, as Michaela still stood in the doorway; dust from Ethan's truck settling back down onto the ground, Camden reappeared and handed the phone to her. "For you."

She brought it up to her ear. "Please don't hang up." It was Jude. "Look, I'm not calling to lecture or anything like that. I'm calling to apologize. I know what Garcia told you. After your message canceling our date, I started investigating. I knew Garcia was up to no good. She's tried to get me to go out with her since she started here, even accused me of sexual harassment when I told her no thank you. She found another way to get at me, though: through you. That's it. That's all. I swear."

Michaela didn't respond.

"Michaela?"

"Yes."

"You have to believe me."

She sighed and leaned against the doorway. "You know what, I do believe you."

"Good, so can we have dinner together?"

She paused. "Yes." She remembered what Joe had told her about living half-assed and decided that he was right.

"Yes? Thank you. I am sorry..." Michaela heard him talking to someone else. "She said yes." Michaela heard Katie whoop in the background. "Sorry, but my daughter has missed you, too."

Michaela couldn't help but smile as she heard the joy in Jude's voice, recalled his kiss, and listened to Katie's laughter. Her bittersweet tears dried on her face.

Author's Note

I hope you've enjoyed "Death Reins In," as much as I enjoyed writing it. I have a passion for horses and since I was five-years-old they've been a huge part of my life. My other passion in life (besides my wonderful family) is my writing. As an author of fiction works, I am fortunate to be able to take fictional liberties. For instance, it's not every day that someone stumbles onto a dead body (at least, I hope not), and for poor Michaela this is now becoming a frequent situation. I am also aware that jockeys and horse trainers are professionals and passionate about the animals. Therefore, it is my desire that no one in the professional equine trade was offended by the fictional liberties that I took with this book. It is my hope that all who read the book had a good time with it and were entertained. Any and all mistakes, I take full responsibility for.

Thank You and Happy Trails!

A.K. Alexander

Tacked to Death

D'Vine Press San Diego, Ca U.S.A.

This is a work of fiction. Names, characters, places, and incidents either are the product of the author's imagination or are used fictitiously, and any resemblance to actual persons, living or dead, business establishments, events, or locales is entirely coincidental. The publisher does not have any control over and does not assume any responsibility for author or third-party websites or their content.
Copyright © 2008 by Michele Scott.

All rights reserved.
No part of this book may be reproduced, scanned, or distributed in any printed or electronic form without permission. Please do not participate in or encourage piracy of copyrighted materials in violation of the author's rights.

ONE

THE MAN STANDING ACROSS FROM MICHAELA Bancroft gave her the creeps. Sterling Taber was handsome by most women's standards: He had that tall-and-dark thing going on with brooding brown—almost black—eyes, his cheekbones were something Michelangelo would have been proud to sculpt, and his longish black hair hung slightly in front of his eyes. He'd been voted Coachella Valley's most eligible bachelor and Michaela had heard the word *mysterious* used in regard to him. Her word was *repulsive*.

Sterling set the ropes on the glass-topped case, which inside held equestrian-related jewelry and various sets of spurs and silver belt buckles. Michaela and her friend Camden had recently delved into the venture of owning and running a tack store. Today was not only opening day, but Camden had convinced Michaela that an accompanying fashion show and charity polo match would make this an opening to remember, an *event* even.

"So, isn't it true that you rope?" Sterling asked.

"No. I rein." If he'd listened at all to her in the past few months, he would've known exactly what Michaela did. She'd spent plenty of time around Sterling as of late. He was one of the bigwigs on the polo team, and in less than an hour she'd be on the field playing against him in the charity event.

"That's right. Reiner. You look pretty good up on a polo pony. Good technique." He fiddled with the ropes. "I like watching the ropers. Real cowboys, those guys."

"Yes, they have great technique." Michaela narrowed her eyes, wishing he'd buy the ropes and get on with it.

"You plan on continuing with polo when this thing is over?"

She almost laughed at the thought. "No. It's been fun and hopefully we raise a lot of money for the autistic riding center, but I don't plan to continue."

He snapped his fingers and pointed at her. "Right. You run that place. That handicapped riding place."

She nodded. "It's for kids with autism."

"Handicapped" was not really how she saw the kids with whom she worked. They had special needs, sure, but they were capable, loving children, and just the way he'd said the word *handicapped*, as if it were a bad one, bothered her. Again, if he'd taken the time to listen when they'd had meetings regarding today's event he'd be on top of it, but she got the feeling that he knew all this already. If anything, he enjoyed this head game she felt he was playing with her. She sighed.

"You sure do look good up there on those ponies," he said again.

"Thanks. But I can't afford polo and it's pretty rough." Granted, Michaela had inherited a large sum of money and her uncle's ranch when he was killed, but much of it was tied up in the ranch, establishing her center for the kids, and now in the tack shop that Camden promised she'd run, since Michaela was already busy with plenty of commitments. "Speaking of polo, we should probably hurry up. You want to buy these?" She wasn't sure what Sterling needed a set of ropes for. He wasn't exactly the rugged cowboy type. She was trying hard to be nice, silently reminding herself that this was a business she and Camden were running and he was a paying customer.

Sterling leaned against the counter and folded his arms. A large diamond in a ring on his finger caught her eye. It was on his right hand, and for some reason it only annoyed Michaela even further that he was there. Show-off. He winked at her. "You bet. I've got some plans with these. You know that there are other things that ropes can be used for besides steers." He winked at her, held up the ropes, and set them back down.

She didn't comment. She picked the ropes up off the counter and scanned the price into the computer. Sterling handed her a credit card and she slid it through. It came back denied. She put it through again—still denied.

"Is there a problem?" he asked.

"Do you have another card?"

"Why?"

She felt her face flush. "This one's been denied."

"That couldn't be. Put it through again."

"I put it through twice already."

"You did it wrong then."

"No, I didn't."

"The card is fine. I own nine polo ponies; I think my card works. It's your machine."

From the back room, where the office and kitchen were located, Michaela heard raised voices. She recognized them immediately and knew she needed to put out a fire, because the two who were arguing were not exactly the most amicable of personalities. She tossed Sterling the ropes. "Here, take them. They're yours." She was done dealing with him.

She started out from behind the counter as a smug smile spread across his face. "See you on the field. I'm looking forward to it."

She walked quickly past him feeling like she'd just seen a cockroach crawl across the floor.

Michaela found the cause of the commotion in the kitchen.

"Oh no, no, no! I don't want spaghetti, Pepe. You can't do this to me!" Camden tossed her copper-colored tresses behind her shoulders and screamed at the rotund, older Italian man. He appeared to be matching her temper for temper, with his arms crossed and a look on his face that said he didn't care one iota about Camden's complaints

"You promised me that we would have veal scaloppine and chicken parmigiana. You said it wouldn't be a problem. I could kill you for this! Do you know how many people are coming to this event? I can't believe I already paid you up front!"

Michaela watched Camden's face contort with rage. Next to Pepe Sorvino stood his twenty-year-old daughter, Lucia. It was hard not to notice that Lucia turned heads when she entered a room with her pale green eyes, long, wavy dark hair and voluptuous body—a young Sophia Loren in the making. She stood about Michaela's height at five feet six inches and she could see by the fire in the young woman's eyes that she was about to explode, along with her father.

"You didn't pay my father enough. Not for all these people."

"Wait a minute," Michaela interrupted. "What's the problem?" They would need to get it solved sooner rather than later. Sorvino's was catering the Sunday afternoon event, and people would be arriving shortly expecting hors d'oeuvres and champagne while they watched the polo match and a catered lunch during the fashion show.

"The problem is," Camden shouted, "these two are trying to rip us off."

Lucia took an aggressive step toward Camden. "Whatever. I don't think so. You're a cheap ass. That's the problem."

Camden pulled an arm back. Michaela grabbed it before she had a chance to swing.

"Did you see that?" Pepe said, his Italian accent growing thicker in line with his anger.

Michaela placed a hand on Camden's shoulder. "Why don't you take a breather? Let me work this out."

Camden held up a finger, her face the color of her hair. Michaela shook her head at her best friend, and then nodded her toward the front door. Camden glared at Pepe

and his daughter, but heeded Michaela's advice and left.
"Go see Dwayne," Michaela suggested, knowing that her assistant trainer and Camden's fiancé was helping set up the tables for the lunch outside. If anyone could calm her down it would be him, with his Hawaiian philosophy and mellow attitude.

"I cannot work with her. She's crazy. You see how she yelling at me, and swearing at me, she saying she gonna kill me!" Pepe took his index finger and made the loopy sign around the side of his head. "Crazy!"

Michaela took a step back. "Listen, Pepe, I agree that my friend can be a bit temperamental—"

"A bit temperamental?" Lucia said. "She's a bitch. We're not doing this thing, and we're keeping your deposit money."

"Wait a minute," Michaela said.

"What's going on?" Mario Sorvino, Pepe's son, walked in with a boxful of tomatoes in his arms. "Oh great. My sister and father giving you a hard time?"

Michaela mustered a smile. Could it be there was a levelheaded individual amongst this clan? Mario set the box down on the counter and put an arm around Lucia, whom he towered over. He was definitely one of the tallest Italian guys Michaela had ever seen—long but muscular, his dark hair slicked back into a ponytail, and an apron covering his barrel chest. "Bella, run along and be a good kid. Leave Michaela alone. We'll work this out."

Lucia opened her mouth to say something, but Mario cut her off. "Go. There're tables to be set." She stood her ground a second longer. "Now!"

Pepe watched as his daughter skulked away. Mario looked at his dad and shook his head. "Papa, she doesn't need to be trying to run things. She's a stupid kid, and you give her too much freedom. Now, what's the issue here?"

Pepe frowned at his son but didn't retort. It appeared as if Mario Sorvino pulled the strings in the family.

"That other lady, that Camden, she's a hothead and she doesn't want to pay what they owe us." He pointed at Michaela. "We gonna make spaghetti and that's it."

"Yes, well, you see, we do have a contract." She directed her reply to Mario. "Your father agreed to make chicken parmigiana and veal along with spaghetti, so I'm confused as to why there's a mix-up."

He crossed his arms. "You not pay me enough, that's the mix-up."

"No, that's not true. We paid you exactly the amount you quoted us." He was beginning to try her patience. No wonder Camden had lost it on him. Everyone knew Pepe had a tendency to be cheap.

"It's not enough."

Mario held up a hand. "Okay, Dad, if there's a contract and you didn't estimate properly, it's not Michaela's problem."

She sighed. "No, it's not our fault if you miscalculated the price."

"Not gonna do it."

She looked at Pepe. "I don't have time for this. I have to be on a horse in an hour, swinging a mallet in front of a hundred or so people, who afterward expect to have a gourmet Italian meal while they watch a fashion show. I know that you would not want those *influential* people to walk away hungry, thinking poorly of Sorvino's, now would you? Those are well-to-do folks out there." She rubbed her finger and thumb together. "Cha-ching. *Capisce?* I'm certain that a man with your business sense and your talent will want to impress the people and have them come back to dine at your divine restaurant." Yeah, so she was pouring it on, but she could tell she was getting to him as the downturn at the corners of his lips started to relax. If his son couldn't convince him, she'd give it her all. "I mean, after all, you do make the best veal I have ever had. Really." She leaned in closer. "And, I heard that a food critic from the *L.A. Times* may join us today. Oh, and I believe *my friend* Joe Pellegrino and some of his cousins might be around, too."

She knew it was not very nice of her to mention Joe. He'd been a friend of hers since childhood and he owned the local hardware store. It was rumored he had some unsavory *family* ties. She had made a conscious decision not to ask him about those rumors. Joe was a good friend, and he'd saved her butt on more than one occasion.

At the mention of Joe, Mario shot her a dirty look. "You'll get your veal and chicken. The Sorvinos don't go back on their word. Right, Papa?" He said it so that his father didn't have much choice but to agree; however, Michaela got the distinct feeling that tossing out Joe's name helped.

"Hmph. *Capisce*."

Pepe stormed out of the kitchen and Mario said, "Sorry about that. My family can be overbearing sometimes. I'll make sure they stay in line for the rest of the day." He took a tomato from the box he'd brought in.

"Thank you." She started to walk out.

"Michaela?"

She stopped. "Yes?"

"One thing about my family though, is that threats, subtle or not, don't usually sit well with us."

"What?"

"I don't miss much, in case you hadn't noticed." He smiled. "Mentioning Joe Pellegrino was unnecessary. I know why you did it, but I didn't like it."

"I'm sorry."

"We're even then. You'll get your food and you now understand how I operate." He picked up a sharp knife and sliced through the tomato. For some reason Michaela felt like he was taking his time cutting that damn tomato and it sent a chill down her spine. He eyed her. "I think you should be careful the names you toss around and threaten people with. It could get you into some trouble."

Michaela winced. "What is that supposed to mean?"

"Take it as you like," Mario said and slammed the knife directly through the tomato, squirting seeds and liquid onto the wall. He looked at her and then at the mess he'd made. "Sorry about that. I'll get it cleaned up."

Michaela walked away shaken and unsettled, with the definite decision to never again hire the Sorvinos for a damn thing.

TWO

HOPEFULLY MICHAELA HAD REALLY DOUSED THE fire in the kitchen. Between Sterling Taber, Camden, and the Sorvinos, she was already exhausted; now she had to go and get on a horse, run it full speed with balls flying this way and that, and pray to God she didn't somehow get clobbered with a mallet. Sure, she could ride. She'd ridden horses all her life; but the sport of polo was a whole 'nother ball game altogether—literally.

She took a few minutes to splash water on her face and pull her long blonde hair back into a low ponytail in order for her helmet to fit over it. She slathered on a good-sized dollop of sunscreen across her already sun-kissed, freckled face. She didn't have freckles like many redheads did, but enough years in the sun on horseback had dotted them across her nose, giving her a somewhat younger appearance than her thirty-three years. After a few more minutes of pulling on her boots and breeches and changing into the light yellow polo T-shirt her team had chosen to wear for the event, she figured she was as ready as she'd ever be to play the match.

She spotted Camden as she was leaving the shop, which wasn't exactly a tack shop in the true sense; rather, it was like a department store with equine-related equipment for sale. Her friend had gone over the top, like she did with everything in her life. The place had hardwood floors and faux cream and butter yellow paint on the walls, which gave it an almost marblelike look. The tack was organized by event, announcing the section with wooden engraved signs: hunter jumper gear here, dressage over there, western upstairs. Yes, there were two stories to the place—and the apparel section, which Camden definitely enjoyed best, was displayed in a large section in the back of the store. At first Michaela found it ostentatious, but she was proud of Camden for putting it together. Only five months earlier Camden could barely bring herself to go out to the horses' stalls. But since becoming engaged to Dwayne, she'd taken it upon herself to learn everything she could about horses and the lifestyle. To her credit, she was doing a good job.

Still, Michaela pondered on a regular basis—especially after the way her morning had gone—as to how in the world had she been roped into this idea with Camden. She should've known better, even in her buzzed state that night over margaritas, four months earlier. She really should have known better when she committed to the two-thousand-square-foot place that Camden had turned into the Saks Fifth Avenue of tack stores. Everything from jazzy jeans to highly polished leather saddles, stationery and art featuring the beautiful animals, to protective leg wraps for equines was available at Round the Bend, and lately Michaela found herself hoping that the opening day would be as lucrative as Camden promised. Having so much cash tied up in inventory was extremely uncomfortable for her.

She knew they'd need to turn a profit quickly, so she'd thrown herself full throttle into helping put the event together. But the kicker was this charity polo event. Camden had come up with the idea to get some of the team players to mix it up with some of the locals. But the prerequisite of being a local was that you did have to know how to ride; thus, Camden had hit Michaela and Dwayne up to be involved, and Michaela had turned around and hit up her childhood friend and veterinarian, Ethan Slater. Ethan did have an advantage: He'd played a bit of polo in his younger years. He was playing against her on that jerk Sterling's team.

Because she didn't want to make a complete fool of herself, Michaela had been taking lessons from the polo team's coach for the past three months. She'd played with the other members, like Sterling and her coach, Robert Nightingale, but she still felt like she didn't have a clue as to what in the world she was doing. What she did know after a few experiences with being hit by a mallet was that it was definitely a rough sport. At least she had convinced the polo team and the other riders that, instead of having a match of polo players against other types of riders, each team should be evenly mixed. She was afraid some of the macho cowboy types who had never before swung a mallet in their lives just might wind up seriously injuring someone in the knee, or worse, the face.

She located Camden and told her, "The Sorvino thing is handled. I've got to get over to the field. Are you coming?"

"Yes. Thank you. I owe you."

"Yes you do."

Michaela walked outside, breathing in the faint smells of orange blossom and honeysuckle that hung on into the Indian summer, even in early November. This was the desert, and thankfully today it was tolerable—beautiful actually, reaching only eighty degrees. Rolling hills and peaks surrounded the valley, hued in golds and a rustic claylike color she found stunning against the manicured kelly green of the polo fields.

Having been cooped up inside the tack shop for most of the morning, she hadn't witnessed the festivities' setup progression. A large white tent was in place in the parking lot for the fashion show. She peeked inside and took a step back. Everything was gorgeous. Camden would be pleased. There were about a hundred tables topped with cream-colored tablecloths, with vases of pink bud roses placed on them for the centerpieces, and a catwalk and stage lined with clusters of more roses, spread out in front of where the guests would be seated. A crew worked with the sound system. No doubt that this would be some event.

She saw Dwayne plugging in the stereo system. He glanced up and immediately smiled and waved at her. He wore his breeches and polo T-shirt. The number on the back of his shirt was 2. She sported 1. He was the other amateur rider on her team. Each team consisted of four members, two who had been at it for some time. She couldn't believe that Camden had been able to talk both her and Dwayne into playing the charity match. Like her, Dwayne trained reiners and working cow horses. It wasn't that either one of them had to learn much in the way of riding per se—both sports required agility and a good seat in the saddle. And both of them were fast. The difference all came down to that ball flying through the air, and the mallet with a bamboo shaft and hardwood head. If that sucker connected with any body part, it hurt like hell.

Michaela still found it pretty unbelievable that her assistant trainer and Camden were planning their wedding. They definitely fit the old adage that opposites attract.

Dwayne came over to her. "Got my girl calmed down a bit."

"I appreciate that." Michaela enjoyed hearing the melodic sound of his voice, accentuated by his native Hawaiian tongue.

"Sorvino sounds like he be difficult to deal with."

"Yes." She didn't add that although Pepe was difficult, his son kind of frightened her.

"You heading to the field?" he asked.

"Yes."

"Me, too, in a minute. I got to help one of the guys move a speaker first. I be right over."

"See you in a few." Even though the field was just across the street from the tack shop, it entailed a bit of a walk because the grounds were so large. She decided to drive her truck over. As soon as the match was finished, she'd have to get back in a hurry to help with the last-minute touches before everyone made their way over for the fashion show and lunch.

She pulled up, and parked under a row of trees that shadowed the unmarked dirt parking lot. She knew that she'd already find the ponies she was to ride saddled up and ready to go. Technically, the horses weren't really ponies; they were horses that averaged fifteen hands. A "hand" is a four-inch measurement used to determine the horse's height. Michaela had learned from her coach that when the British discovered polo in Persia, the average polo pony stood only about twelve hands high, which is the customary size for an actual pony today. Contrary to the thinking many nonequestrians share, ponies are not baby horses. The first height limit for polo ponies was set in 1876 at fourteen hands. In 1896 the limit was raised to fourteen hands two inches. Limits were abolished in 1919. Polo ponies were not actually a breed but a crossbreed. Players looked for agility, speed, and intelligence. Many times the cross they'd found to fit their criteria was between a Thoroughbred and quarter horse. The Thoroughbred had the stamina and speed to last, and the quarter horse maintained the agility and intelligence.

But real-world players didn't own just one polo pony; they owned several because of the wear and tear on the animals. Michaela would ride three different ponies today, but she knew that Sterling would ride six and she was pretty sure that one of the pros on her team, Zach Holden, would also use six horses. They would be exchanged between chukkers, which lasted seven minutes. There were always six chukkers to a game, with three-minute breaks between chukkers and a halftime where spectators would rush out to stomp down the divots. The rules stated that no horse could be played for more than two chukkers, thus Michaela's three school horses.

She got out of her truck and looked around the parking area—Sterling's Porsche was there as well as a few other cars. It didn't look like she was either the first or last one to arrive. She grabbed her gloves and mallet from the backseat. She'd pick up one of the school's helmets from the office. The helmet she used at her place was different than what they used in polo. It reminded her of one of those safari hats that elephant tamers sometimes wear. She turned around to head over to the stable and heard a car door slam, then another. An engine roared and the next thing she knew a car raced past her and down the gravel road. What in the world? She squinted to get a better look. She could've sworn the BMW that sped down the road belonged to the polo coach's wife, Paige Nightingale. Then she saw Sterling climbing out of his Porsche. Had Paige been in the car with him? She didn't see anyone else around. It struck her as odd. What reason would Paige have to be in Sterling's car? And what were the slamming doors and screeching tires all about? She wondered where Robert was.

She certainly didn't want Sterling to spot her. He was the last person she wanted to talk to, so she picked up her pace and headed to where the horses awaited. Who really cared what that had been about? She'd met her stress quota for the day.

The three horses were lined up at a long hitching post. Her favorite was a bay mare named Rebel. The mare had the kind of eyes that Michaela liked on a horse: intelligent.

"Hey, Rebel," she said, patting her on her rump. "You look good." The horse glanced at her with a baleful eye, and then turned back around. "Uh-huh. That's what I like about you. Not one for small talk." Michaela laughed. She knew the horse had no clue what she was saying—for the mare it was probably like a Charlie Brown cartoon where the kids listen to the teacher and all they hear is "Waa, waa, waa, waa, waa, waa." But she did know that horses liked to be talked to. They were social animals, and the sound of their rider's voice could put them at ease, or wind them tight—depending on the person and the tone.

She gave the other two horses a pat and a few words of encouragement—again knowing they could care less what she had to say. She headed over to the office on the grounds—a decent-sized trailer—needing to get her helmet.

Robert sat inside the trailer on a tattered, blue velour couch, pulling on his boots. "Oh hey, Michaela. You ready for this?" He pulled up his other boot and sat back, running his hand through his light brown hair, which appeared to be thinning on top. Michaela guessed him to be somewhere in his mid to late fifties. He was known for his intensity on and off the polo field but he'd been nothing but nice to her, and she found the rumors of his brusqueness to be just that so far. She'd had a soft spot for Robert and Paige ever since she'd learned that their only son had been killed in a car accident a few years earlier. She couldn't imagine ever enduring that type of pain. Although she tried not to let it bother her, she still wondered why Paige had left the grounds in such a hurry, either trying to get away or leaving Sterling Taber behind. Again, Michaela reminded herself that it was none of her business.

"Uh, no. I doubt I'll ever be ready." She laughed.

"You're a good rider. You'll be fine up there. Don't let any of my guys intimidate you. Plus, you got a couple of your buddies out there, too."

"Yeah, but I'm the only woman."

He waved a hand at her. "You'll be fine. Got your helmet?"

She picked through the bin where the school helmets were kept, and held one up after making sure it was the right size. "I do now."

They walked out of the trailer together and back over to the horses. Dwayne had shown up and she saw Ethan pulling into the parking area.

She wondered if his wife, Summer, was with him and breathed an audible sigh when she didn't see anyone else get out of his truck. Michaela loved Ethan. They'd known each other since they were little kids. Camden insisted Michaela was *in* love with him, but that wasn't true. It *couldn't* be true, because Ethan was a married man. Married against Michaela's wishes, but that was only because she knew Summer was not right for him. The woman had strung him along, left him at the altar where Michaela picked up the pieces left behind, and then had the audacity to strut back into his life, get pregnant, and manipulate him into marriage. Now Ethan was the proud daddy of little Joshua, who was also her godson, most certainly against Summer's wishes.

"Hey, Mick, Robert," he said.

Robert shook his hand. "Good to see you, Ethan. I'm going to make sure everything is a go. Looks like all the riders are here. I don't see one of the umpires, though."

"Sure. Do your thing. This is gonna be fun," Ethan said, "even for an old guy."

"Old guy? Please." Ethan was only a couple of years older than her. Michaela had noticed him aging a little in the last year, but he was far from old—a wrinkle here and there above the forehead, a few around his eyes. She liked it. It added character. Not that he needed any. Ethan had plenty of character with a slightly crooked nose from a pony kicking him in the face, but he was still a good-looking man.

He looked at her with his dark green eyes. "I don't know about going against you, Bancroft. You might kick my ass."

"Sure." She laughed. "Who else is on your team? I know Sterling Taber is, and Tommy Liggett is the other pro rider, right?"

Ethan nodded. "Yeah, and I got a buddy of mine…do you know Lance Watkins?"

"Sure. He trains show jumpers. Wow. He's going to ride today?"

"He is."

"Impressive."

"What do you say we get on the field? Looks like the grooms have everyone ready," Ethan said.

"Ah, the luxury of playing polo."

"Yeah, really. Good luck."

They both laughed, knowing that because of the wealth surrounding the sport, it was a rarity that any of the players ever actually groomed and tacked up their horses. Today, even the locals like herself and Ethan were being treated like kings—and supposedly polo had been dubbed the sport of kings.

Michaela mounted Rebel and they headed onto the polo field, which was three hundred yards long and one hundred and fifty yards wide. She would be playing the most conservative position as the number four, or back, player. Her job was to play defense and guard the goal to keep the opposition from scoring. Dwayne was playing first position, which was offensive, along with the number two position, played by a longtime pro in the sport and owner of the polo field, Ed Mitchell. He would have to play aggressively, his goal to break up the defensive plays of the opposition. In third position was Zach Holden, a young guy and good friend of Sterling's, but totally opposite from the pompous ass. Michaela liked Zach. He was congenial and generous—always giving her tips and advice. Zach would be the pivot man, kind of like the quarterback on a football team. He would be making the long-ball shots and be the key playmaker for the team. Michaela admired his playing ability. He was also the player who would most likely be hitting any penalty shots.

The two umpires and a referee, all on horseback, were ready to go, along with the scorekeeper and time recorder. Michaela's heart pounded as a wave of nervousness coursed through her. She looked out at the crowd, all in their designer outfits, champagne flutes in hand, and couldn't help but question her sanity.

Then, one of the umpires tossed the ball into the center, and everything began to move. Michaela forgot the crowd, the morning, what was on tap next, and just played the game. Once the ball was in play it traveled at speeds upward of one hundred miles per hour. The ball came flying toward her as she guarded the goal. Sterling had hurled it toward her, and when she stopped the ball with a forehand by swinging her mallet forward on Rebel's near side, she almost whooped out loud. The pounding of hooves drummed in her ears as clumps of dirt kicked up around them. She had just sent the ball back into play when it came back down the line, and before she could blink Sterling was next to her, his mallet hooked with hers. She got it undone in time to save another goal from being scored, this time on a shot from Ethan.

The ball had once again turned around and Dwayne had it down the line. Michaela squealed when Dwayne hit it past Ethan's pal Lance Watkins. She could have sworn she heard Sterling down at the other end scream an obscenity at Lance. How immature.

Before Michaela knew it, they were into the last chukker and she had changed to her third horse, a white speckled gelding named Snowman. Her team was ahead by two points and Zach yelled to her, "Nice work out there!"

"Thanks." She wiped the sweat off her brow and one of the grooms gave her a leg up onto Snowman. They were back in play, horses going at a full canter, well-toned athletes moving with grace and speed, carrying riders who depended on the sound mind of their animals to keep them in the game. The ball flew between thin, fine legs—riders bumping shoulder to shoulder, mallets hooking and clanking around one another, red nostrils of the horses flaring, and the smell of sweat and dirt and grass hanging in the air. Shouts from the crowd and curses from the riders who missed a goal contrasted the whoops of joy when one team scored. Michaela wasn't sure she even breathed the rest of the game, it was so intense. And in the end, her team won by one point after Lance Watkins fouled and Zach was allowed to take the penalty shot, zipping it past Dwayne.

The losing team congratulated Michaela and the others. Sterling rode up next to her on a beautiful black gelding. He had to have been from Argentina, where many of the best polo ponies came from. "Looks like lady luck was the key, huh? Or maybe the guys were just taking it easy on you. Granted, Watkins plays like a girl, but that's what I'd expect from some guy who trains jumpers."

Sterling didn't realize that Lance Watkins and Ethan were directly behind him and within earshot. Michaela didn't reply; she simply turned her horse, walking him over to Ethan and Lance. "That guy is an asshole," Lance said. "I'd like to bump him off his high horse. I'm sorry, Michaela. I don't mean to be rude. Nice to see you. Great playing out there."

"Thanks." She didn't know Lance well, but she couldn't blame him for being irritated with Sterling. "You guys played hard, too. I don't know about this polo thing."

"It's not for me," Lance replied. "I need to take off. See you two later."

"You going to the fashion show and lunch?" Michaela asked Ethan.

"I wish I could, but Summer has something she needs to do and I need to get home and be with the baby."

"Oh." She tried hard to keep the disappointment out of her voice.

They talked for a few more minutes, until Dwayne rode past and reminded her that they didn't have much time to get back over to the shop for the rest of the day's festivities. She said good-bye to Ethan and dismounted her horse, giving him a pat and handing him over to one of the grooms.

Zach Holden was over by the stalls with one of his horses. "Good game out there," he said.

"Thanks. You did a good job yourself." He couldn't have been over twenty-five and was from money, like most of the people on the pro team.

"She did do well." Sterling Taber approached them. "Lucky for her we had that pain-in-the-ass show jumper on our team." He laughed. "That guy is clueless. He wasn't on his game at all."

Michaela tried to maintain a smile, but Sterling was such a jerk. Lance Watkins had an excellent reputation in the show ring, and although she'd only met him a few times, he was always pleasant and, as Ethan had indicated, he was a good guy. She chose not to respond to Sterling's comment. Ignoring him was taking the higher road, by far.

Funny thing: Sterling did seem to have enough of something—be it charisma, charm, she didn't know exactly what—and whatever it was, he always appeared to have plenty of friends, like Zach.

Sterling swung his mallet back and forth. "Well, like I said, dumb luck or lady." He winked at her. "Just kidding. You did well out there. I gotta run." He pointed at her. "See you at the show. Hey, anyone seen Tommy? He was supposed to catch a ride with me over to the shop."

"Yeah, but I think he already went on ahead."

"Okay. Thanks."

There was another friend that Sterling had in his entourage—Tommy Liggett, who again, by all accounts, was a decent guy. And he hadn't been born with a silver spoon in his mouth like the rest of the crew.

Sterling waved at Michaela and Zach, as if they wouldn't see each other in only a manner of minutes. They watched as he slipped into his Porsche Carerra and zipped it around the gravel road that led to the tack shop. She noticed Zach staring after Sterling, a scowl on his face, and if she wasn't mistaken, she could've sworn she recognized hatred in his eyes.

THREE

"AREN'T YOU IN THE SHOW, TOO?" MICHAELA asked Zach.

His expression softened. "Uh, yeah. I just wanted to make sure the groom put this new liniment on my horse's right front suspensory. He's sore and favoring that side."

"I think Ethan already left. Do you need to call him back?"

"No. I don't think so, but I'll come back later and check. I should probably hurry, too. I'm sure Camden is beside herself. We shouldn't be standing around chitchatting."

She nodded. "Yep, you better go. The makeup lady should be ready for you guys."

"Makeup?" Zach said.

"Camden's idea."

"Okay, I'm gone. Sure you don't need a ride?"

"No. I'm good. I've got my truck. I'm going to drop off the school helmet to Robert and I'll be right over."

She headed to Robert's office. The door was propped open a crack, but she still went the customary route and announced herself before entering. When she didn't get a reply she figured that she'd go in and drop the helmet in the bin. The bin stood near Robert's desk, which was a mess. Piles of equine magazines and books filled one side of the desk, and papers were stacked high. She knew that Paige helped him with the business, but it looked as if they were getting behind. God, how she could relate.

Odd; a sharp letter opener was stuck right down the center of the papers. Why would Robert would do that? Maybe it was to keep the stack from blowing away as people walked in and out.

She put her helmet in the bin. Before leaving, she noticed that the paper on top on the stack was an invoice to Sterling. He owed quite a bit in board and training. In fact, it looked as if he were several months past due. But it wasn't the numbers that astounded her so much; it was the fact that across the statement someone had written *SCREW YOU!*

"Hey Michaela, what's up?"

Michaela spun around as Robert walked in. "Uh, I was just returning my helmet. You going to the fashion show? I know Paige was really excited about it."

Robert waved a hand as he sat on the sofa. "Nah. I think I've had my fill of charity for a while. Fashion shows are not my thing."

Michaela nodded, not sure what to say, still processing the scrawled message on Sterling's invoice.

"What about you? Don't you have to get over there?"

"I sure do." She checked her watch. "Definitely." She reached for the doorknob and turned to tell Robert goodbye.

"Hey, before you go, can I ask you something?" the older man said.

Uh-oh. Had he seen her peering at his paperwork? Before she could reply, her cell phone rang. She glanced at Robert.

"No problem. Answer it," he told her.

Saved by the bell. She flipped open the phone; Camden was in hysterics. "Where are you? I need you now. We've got a huge problem!"

Michaela started to ask her what it was, but Camden hung up. "I'm sorry," she said. "I've got to go. There seems to be a problem at the store."

"Go. It's no big thing."

She walked out of the trailer. Another problem; great.

FOUR

CAMDEN'S FACE WAS FLUSHED THE COLOR OF magenta; her arms flailed in obvious frustration as Michaela entered the back room of the tack shop. A handful of models clustered around, all eyes on a petite, dark-haired, gothic-looking young woman, her lips painted a purplish black. Michaela had an odd thought: dark fairy from beyond, or a woman trying hard to resurrect 1985.

Camden grabbed Michaela by the arm and pulled her aside. "That's Erin Hornersberg."

"Okay."

"She's our makeup artist and she's the best, but she is refusing to do the models' makeup. She's packing up her stuff. Do something!"

This was the crisis? Oh boy. "Camden, hold on. First of all, I am not a mediator to every little problem that springs up."

"Yes, but you have a way with people. Now go over there and convince her to stay."

Michaela sighed. "What, is she claiming that we didn't pay her enough, too?"

"No. It's about Sterling."

"Sterling?"

Camden nodded. "She won't say what, but within two minutes of him sitting down, she started screaming for him to get the you-know-what off her chair and the hell out of here. When he refused, she told me to forget it. She's saying that she's not about to do *anyone's* makeup for the show."

It was only makeup. Couldn't the models do their own? "Just ask Sterling to leave. I need a few minutes to shower and set my things in the office." She held up her mallet and purse. With so many people milling around she hadn't wanted to leave the polo mallet in her truck, and definitely not her purse. Although she had no intention to play the sport any longer, the mallet had been a gift from Ed Mitchell, and she wanted it as a keepsake.

"Are you kidding? You don't have time. You have to talk to her now! Sterling was voted the most eligible bachelor from Indio to Palm Springs and probably all the way to L.A. Most of the women here today came to see him. I can't do that."

"Right. Do you know what he might have said or done?"

Camden shrugged. "I don't have a clue. I wanted to put on the best show from here to flipping Timbuktu, and dammit, it's all falling apart."

Michaela turned back to see Erin locking up her makeup box. She walked over to the woman, still holding her mallet and purse, both starting to weigh on her. How was it that purses got so heavy? It needed a good dumping-out, and the mallet wasn't exactly light to begin with.

"Hi, I'm Michaela Bancroft, part owner of the store, and I'm sorry to hear there's a problem. Can we talk about it?"

"Nothing to talk about. He's an ass. I want him out of here." She pointed at Sterling, who stood drinking a Coke, seeming not to care at all about the drama swirling around him.

Michaela leaned in closer to her. "I agree with you. I think he's a pompous piece of you-know-what. Look, can you just come outside with me? We'll see if we can work something out."

Erin shook her head. "Nothing to work out. I want him out of here. It's simple."

"Okay, look, what if I make sure he's not anywhere near you and you won't have to do his makeup or even see him?"

Erin eyeballed her. "And you'll make it worth my while? You know, it's a pain in the ass to have to take all my stuff out and now I had to put it back, and then I'll have to take it back out again, and—"

Michaela held up a hand. "I'll see what I can do." Great. Erin and Pepe Sorvino must have gone to some sort of lecture on how to screw a client prior to an event. If her instincts were right, she'd be paying out more money than they'd planned to the makeup artist. But she was still curious about what Sterling had done to get under the woman's skin.

"I *could* use a smoke."

"I'm sure you could."

And right about now, she could use one of those shoulder massages Jude Davis was famous for. She wished he wasn't away for the week on a Caribbean cruise with his daughter, Katie. Michaela and the detective had been dating for a few months. It wasn't anything serious, not yet anyway, but she realized that she missed him. His calm demeanor in stressful situations like this would have been exactly what the doctor ordered. Needless to say, there wasn't much more she could do than play diplomat. Tonight though, when this thing was over—one long hot bath, oh yes.

She followed Erin to the door. Camden looked at her wide-eyed and tapped her wrist several times, indicating that the clock was ticking. "I'm doing what I can," Michaela muttered. Never again would she agree to something of this magnitude—for charity or not. She'd rather get smacked by a polo mallet than deal with this.

Erin pulled out a pack of Marlboros from the black apron holding a variety of makeup brushes in the front pockets. She lit one and took a deep drag. Michaela knew time was of the essence, but she also understood she was likely dealing with someone who, when push came to shove, could shove back pretty hard.

Michaela tried to subtly wave away the toxic plume. "So, Sterling was being an ass to you." She presented it more as a statement rather than a question, and decided to keep going along those lines. "He's a real jerk. You should see that guy up on a horse playing polo. He whoops and hollers when he scores, as if he's made the winning touchdown in the Super Bowl."

"Yeah, I bet, like his shit don't stink." Erin snorted.

"Exactly. He gets under my skin. Who would have ever voted him most eligible bachelor?"

"Eligible? Isn't he hooking up with that Juliet chick? The one whose folks own the club?"

"It looks like they're dating to me. But you know, I haven't seen them hanging out this past week at the field. They're usually all over each other. So, I don't really know. I'm not interested in his love life." She had to wonder though, if Juliet and Sterling were together, then how *did* Juliet feel about her boyfriend being considered an "eligible bachelor"? Juliet Mitchell was Ed's daughter. Michaela knew Juliet from the field because she also rode. She seemed like a nice girl. But it was a wonder how she tolerated Sterling. Juliet was from a priveleged family and Michaela doubted she would tolerate playing second fiddle.

"Yeah, probably her and about a hundred other stupid chicks are dating him."

Michaela nodded as she let Erin speak. She was pretty sure she'd won the woman's trust.

Erin continued: "I've seen him around, you know. At clubs. He works a room. Got all the girls after him. He *thinks* he does, anyway."

Michaela hoped this was going somewhere. "I'm sure he does. You've seen him out and around then?"

"Uh-huh. And he's seen me. He made a point of letting me know it, in there." She pointed to the tack shop.

"I take it he said something rude to you?"

Erin nodded. "About me and my girlfriend."

"Girlfriend?" Michaela tried not to allow shock to creep into her voice. Did Erin mean girlfriend or *girlfriend*?

Either way, it didn't really matter. She didn't know why, if Erin had a *girlfriend*, this would surprise her, but in a way it did. She would have pictured this woman having a tattooed, biker-type boyfriend. So much for stereotypes.

"Yes. Sheila. She's my girl." She arched her brows. "I'm gay."

"Oh."

"Don't tell me you're one of those redneck homophobes, too."

"No. Not at all. I just didn't expect that."

"Why not?"

Oh great, now *she* was making waves with the makeup artist. "I don't know. But it doesn't bother me. Look, I don't know what Sterling said to you. I can only imagine it was something nasty. But right now, we're running short on time. I promise that you won't have to deal with him again. The jerk can do his own makeup as far as I'm concerned."

Erin tossed down her cigarette, stubbing it out with her boot heel. "Double my pay."

"Double?"

Erin nodded. "I'm the best and, right now, the only one you have here. You're in a freaking bind, lady, and you know how life can be unfair sometimes. I think your friend Camden in there might have a nervous breakdown if I walk."

She had one thing right: Michaela *was* in a bind. She still felt the models could apply goop to their own faces, but she thought about Camden and how much this meant to her. "Fine. I'll double your pay."

"Give it to me now."

Michaela sighed. "Tell you what. I'll go back in and ask Sterling to dress elsewhere. You can get started on the next model and I'll write you a check."

"Fine. Here's my card. My last name can be hard to spell." She took a card out of her apron. "Oh sorry, there's an address on the back, but I don't need it anymore. Anyway, that's my last card."

"No problem." Michaela took the card and marched back in to confront Camden. "You need to get Sterling Taber out of here *now*."

"No! What? Why? I already told you that he's the star of the show."

"Here's the deal, sis. Your star said some disrespectful things to the makeup girl and she's ready to walk. I've convinced her to stay as long as she doesn't have to deal with him, along with some extra cash on top of it."

"Why, that little bitch," Camden replied.

"That little bitch is extremely offended by Mr. Taber. And, as you mentioned, she is the best and you seem to think we need her."

Camden looked mortified. "What am I supposed to do?"

"I don't know. You and Sterling seemed to be buddy-buddy. I think you can figure it out."

"What does that mean?"

"Nothing, really. I just noticed during the course of putting this thing together over the last few months that you got along well with him."

"Everyone gets along with him. He's a great guy."

"Whatever you say." From what she had seen, not everyone got along well with Sterling at all.

"Michaela, are you implying something? I'm engaged, for goodness' sakes. I would never cheat on Dwayne."

"I know that. You better not anyway. Why even say something like that?"

Camden's face softened. "I don't know why I'd say something like that. Of course you know that I would never cheat on Dwayne."

"Didn't cross my mind. For one thing, Sterling is just a kid, what twenty-five or something?"

"Twenty-six."

"Right. Get him out of here. I've done what I can to make this go smoothly. It's time for you to use your finesse."

Camden shrugged. "Okay, I'll get him out of here. Now, can you tell Erin to get in here and get the other models finished?"

Michaela watched as Camden approached Sterling, who was talking to Tommy Liggett. After a few minutes, Camden had succeeded in luring Sterling out of the area and Erin came back in to finish her work.

Michaela needed to grab a quick shower and wash the perfume à la equine off her. There wasn't much time, but it was necessary.

On her way to check on the silent auction items, she spotted Robert Nightingale and his wife, glass of wine in hand, engaged in conversation with Ed Mitchell. Robert must have changed his mind about coming to the event. Interesting. She'd be sure to avoid him. She didn't want to answer any questions about what she'd spotted on his desk. Facts were, it really was none of her business. Though she did wonder if it had been Sterling who'd written the unpleasantry across the invoice, or maybe Robert had written it in anger because the bill hadn't been paid.

She wound her way through the crowd and entered the back room of the tack shop. The storage area was a mess with discarded clothing, purses, and backpacks scattered all about, the remains of the flurry to dress the models and get them ready to strut their stuff up on the catwalk.

Michaela headed to the private office area that she shared with Camden and set her purse and mallet down. She'd already hung up the outfit she wanted to change into when she'd gotten there this morning—a teal-colored sheath dress, simple and casual but also classy. She brought it with her to the bathroom off to the side of the office and kitchen, and took a quick shower. Getting out, she thought she heard a door shut. There was no door to the kitchen, only swinging panels. The only doors were either the back one or the office. Must've been Camden grabbing something.

She dressed and headed back to the office to find her hairbrush and some lip gloss. Placing the key in the lock, she discovered that the door was already open. Hadn't she locked it when she showered? She didn't want anyone going in there, especially with her things around. Maybe in her haste she'd forgotten.

Michaela opened the door. It took a second to sink in that what she was looking at wasn't just a pile of discarded clothes…oh, she was looking at a pile of clothes, all right, but not just clothes—clothes with someone in them. Blue jeans, white T-shirt with red sprayed across it. Red. No. Blood! Everywhere. Michaela looked down again. A polo mallet. Next to the clothes. *Her* polo mallet. Oh no. Next to a body. Sterling Taber's body. And the back of his head all bashed in.

FIVE

MICHAELA KNEW THAT STERLING WAS DEAD AND all she wanted to do was get the hell out of there, but her conscience made her check just to be sure. She bent down next to his body. He was not breathing. His eyes were rolled back, showing the whites. She scrambled backward, ran out of the office and into the bathroom, where she threw up several times.

She faced the bathroom mirror, blinked her eyes repeatedly. Was this really happening? Then it hit her: What if whoever did this was still around? What if they were hiding in her office or just outside the bathroom door? She had to find Camden. No, she had to call the police. No, she had to find Camden. Hell. Security guards. Yes. They'd hired a couple to man the tent outside. Start there. No. The police. *Shit!* She stepped out of the bathroom hesitantly, then ran to the front of the store. They'd locked the doors when they'd started serving lunch, except the back door for the waitstaff going in and out of the kitchen. Dammit, why didn't she just go out the back door? Her mind raced with confusion. She turned and headed to the back of the store again, everything she passed a blur of colors.

"Michaela?"

Mario Sorvino was walking through the back door as she reached it. He looked at her oddly. "Is everything okay? You look a little pale."

"We have to call the police. St-Sterling Taber has been…murdered in my office."

"What? No." He shook his head.

She nodded.

"Stay here," he said. He headed toward her office.

Michaela suddenly realized that she wasn't too comfortable staying put. Mario Sorvino hadn't exactly proven to her that he was a good guy with his earlier remarks. No way. She was out of there.

Once out through the back door, she stopped the closest guest walking by. "Do you have a cell phone? I need to use it. It's an emergency."

The woman, dumbfounded, handed her a phone and Michaela dialed 911. "There's been a murder," she said, her voice shaking. The operator took down the details and told her that help would be on the way. She then went to find Camden, who was marching models onto the stage.

"Michaela! Have you seen Sterling? Jeez, I hope that little stunt the makeup girl pulled didn't chase him away. It's not good. See all those women out there? They are here to see *him*," she wailed.

In a sort of fast-forward daze, Michaela was aware that Camden had pulled back the drapes inside the tent where the show was going on and pointed to the crowd, but she couldn't see anything. It was all a blur. Oh God, she thought she might be sick again.

Camden turned to Juliet, who had just tripped over one of the acoustic cords, and said, "Hurry up, get out there. You need to be up there." Then she asked, "Have you seen Sterling?"

Juliet shook her head. "No, I haven't. I don't know if I can do this. I've never modeled before! There's a ton of people out there. I didn't know I'd get so nervous!"

Zach Holden was just coming off the stage. He looked at Juliet and asked her if she was okay. She nodded. "I'm fine."

Camden reached across a table for a large tequila bottle. She handed it to the girl. "Take a swig of this and get your ass out there. You'll do great."

Juliet shook her head. "No thanks. I'm good."

"Great. Never figured that one for nerves. I mean, hell, she comes from what, one of the wealthiest families around. She must have done this kind of stuff before. And I thought for sure that she and Sterling were doing a little…you know…in the back room, because I couldn't find her for a few minutes either. I've noticed those two flirting quite a bit."

Michaela listened to this as if she were outside of her body, as if time had stood still, and she wondered if this was what being in shock felt like. Then suddenly, as if someone slapped her, she blurted, "Sterling is dead!"

Camden shook her head. "What? What did you just say?"

She took a deep breath and felt emotion rise in her throat. Sure, she hadn't cared for Sterling Taber, but he'd been brutally murdered and no one, not even a jerk-hole deserved that. "Listen to me." She strained to get the words out. "The police are on the way. Sterling was murdered in our office. I found him."

Camden's face drained of color. She shook her head. "No. Oh no. No, no, no. That can't be. What? What the hell?" She nearly knocked Michaela down as she raced toward the tack store and into the back office. Michaela tried to catch up to her when she realized where Camden was headed and the horror she was about to see.

Mario, walking down the hallway, tried to block her, but as big as he was, Camden dodged past him. "Camden, please stop. It's awful! Don't go in there!" he yelled.

Camden was at the door, opening it, when Michaela grabbed her arm. Too late. The door had swung open. Camden's scream echoed throughout the tack store. She ran to where Sterling lay, kneeling down by him. Her eyes brimming with tears, she stroked Sterling's hair. "Oh, no, no, baby, I am so sorry."

Baby? Michaela placed a hand on her friend's shoulder. "I'm sorry. I know that you were friends. I wish you hadn't come in here."

Camden looked up at her, tears streaming down her face. "I've known him for years and we…we've been more than friends."

SIX

BEFORE A STUNNED MICHAELA HAD THE CHANCE to further question her distraught friend, the police arrived and asked them to wait outside the office. By this time word had gotten around, and Dwayne was now at Camden's side. Mario also lingered. He'd called the police from his cell phone just before Michaela did. His appearance, so soon after finding Sterling, bothered her.

Camden rested her head against Dwayne's chest. Michaela's stomach churned with confusion, shock, and horror, not only from finding Sterling's body, but from Camden's comment about her and Sterling being more than friends.

The police separated everyone, and no one was allowed off the grounds until each person had been questioned and their contact information recorded. The process lasted well into the evening, with many people becoming agitated over being detained for so long.

A forensics team was brought in, and Michaela was questioned a number of times in a grueling manner by a detective who was nothing short of a hard-ass. She recognized him from dropping off lunch to Jude at the station one day. The detective, Mike Peters, acted as if he'd never seen Michaela before, until he'd finally closed his notepad and looked at her with his dark brown eyes. The look in them was not friendly, and Michaela felt uneasy. He ran a hand through his thinning silver head of hair.

Cracking a grim smile, he shook his head. "Your boy won't be too happy about this, Ms. Bancroft."

"Excuse me? What? My *boy*?"

"Yeah. Davis. He isn't going to be too happy that you found yourself a dead man. Your reputation precedes you."

"If you're finished with me, I'd like to lock up when the forensics team is done. From the looks of it, your crew has pretty much allowed everyone else to go home."

"I'm done with you for now." He shook his head. "But don't it seem odd to you that you somehow stumble across dead carcasses a little too often for comfort?"

Michaela didn't reply. His insinuation was unsettling and insulting. "Again, if we're finished here, I'd like to start locking up."

He held the palms of his hands toward her. "Sure. For now."

She clenched her jaw. As the police left, she started to lock up. Camden and Dwayne had already gone home. Michaela really needed to talk with her friend.

A handful of police were wrapping things up outside as she headed toward her truck and unlocked the door. A crescent moon hung in the sky, surrounded by bright stars lighting up what on any other occasion would be a peaceful night. A cool breeze had dropped the evening temperature along the desert floor and Michaela wished she'd grabbed her poncho from the shop. Then she realized she'd left it in the office. Well, it wasn't really a poncho, the old-school kind with the drawstring around the neck. It had been a gift from Camden; it was cashmere and so soft, a pretty rose kind of beige color, and every time Michaela put it on, she felt good. But in all of the craziness, she'd left it in her office and she wasn't about to go back in there. Not right now anyway. She just wanted to get home. Then, just feet away from her maroon-colored truck, she heard someone approaching.

"Excuse me, Ms. Bancroft?"

She swung around to see a sullen Erin Hornersberg, makeup box in hand. Michaela brought her hands up to her neck in surprise. "You scared me!"

"Sorry. Hey look, I left some of my brushes in the back room where I was doing the makeup. Can you set them aside for me and I'll pick them up later?"

"I can just unlock the door and we can get them now."

"No. That's okay. I just want to get home and I have extras at the shop. I'll call you tomorrow and see when it's good to swing by."

Her attitude had softened in light of the events. "It's horrible about Sterling."

"Whatever. Good riddance," Erin said dismissively.

Michaela took a step back. "I know he wasn't the greatest guy in the world, but don't you have any feelings? I mean, at least show some respect. The man was brutally murdered."

"Like I said, whatever. I'll be by for my things."

Michaela watched Erin drive off. So much for a softer attitude.

* * *

MICHAELA MADE IT HOME AND RAN A TUB OF water for a hot bath. When she'd pulled in, the lights had been off in the guest house where Dwayne and Camden lived, and she decided that their conversation would have to wait until the morning. She contemplated walking out to the barn to say good night to her horses but found herself too tired. Dwayne would've fed them. Poor kids, though; they had to have been starving even by the time he got there, since the police had kept everyone for so long.

She lay in bed going back over the day, from Sterling acting so slimy when buying the ropes, which he really didn't buy since his card hadn't cleared; her confrontation with the Sorvinos; to Paige tearing off the grounds and then showing up later at the fashion show all smiles, with Robert on her arm. There was the polo match, where Sterling was more than rude to Lance Watkins, and also toward her. And what was the deal with the way Zach had looked at Sterling when the game was over? Had they had a falling-out? Then there was the invoice with the not-so-pleasant note written across it in Robert's office. Finally, the discovery of Sterling's body. Who had done that to him? And now Michaela could not help the guilt feelings welling inside her over her distaste for Sterling. Maybe she hadn't given him a chance. Was she simply too judgmental? What was it about Sterling that she hadn't liked? For one, it was his poor sense of sportsmanship. In the sport of reining and working cow horses, other riders were typically supportive of one another. Sure, men dominated the field and they had their own feelings about a woman doing well at the sport, but most of them had been taught respect for women while growing up. They typically kept their feelings either to themselves or within their tight circle of friends. Michaela had been able to gain a lot of respect from the men in her sport. But Sterling came across as a chauvinist with superiority issues.

She couldn't think on it any longer. Her head hurt from it all. She willed herself to sleep after a short prayer to help rid her of the day's trauma.

She didn't know what time it was when the banging woke her up. At first, she thought she was dreaming. But the banging grew louder, and then the doorbell rang. Michaela rolled out of bed, noticing that it was just past four in the morning. What in the world?

She pulled on her robe and tromped down the stairs. She really did need to get a new dog. She'd lost her old lab, Cocoa, a while back, and it was time to look into getting a puppy. She didn't like opening the door to someone at this hour, but because it was so late, she knew that whoever and for whatever reason they were on the other side of her door, it could not be good.

She peered through the peephole. Her stomach sank. Detective Peters stood there. What did he want? "Ms. Bancroft, open the door, please."

Michaela swung the door open. A uniformed cop, who Michaela recognized as Officer Garcia, stood behind him. "How can I help you? You do realize it is the middle of the night?"

"Turn around, Ms. Bancroft," he said, reaching behind him for his handcuffs. "You are under arrest for the murder of Sterling Taber."

SEVEN

"WAIT, *WAIT!*"

Garcia started reading Michaela her rights. Peters abruptly turned her around. "What are you doing? What is this about? I didn't kill Sterling Taber! You can't come into my home and do this."

"I'm afraid we can," Peters said.

"Can you tell me on what grounds you're arresting me?"

"Your polo mallet."

"My mallet? We went over this before."

"Yes we did, but your fingerprints are the only ones on it. And you *discovered* the victim and you had motive."

She shook her head. "Motive? What motive? I had no reason to murder Sterling Taber. This is insane! What motive are you talking about? And my fingerprints on my mallet—of course they were on my mallet. It's *my* mallet, for God's sakes! What about other prints? Weren't there any other prints? And again, what motive? It wouldn't be very smart of me to use my own mallet to murder someone."

"It might be smart for you to stop flapping your mouth, because I'm arresting you and, like Garcia said, you have the right to remain silent…"

This was no nightmare…well, not one she was sleeping through.

Camden raced through the door in a pair of short pajama bottoms and T-shirt, Dwayne at her heels. "What's going on?" she asked. "The flashing lights outside our window woke us up. What are you—? Wait a minute! What are you doing?" She looked at Peters.

"We are arresting Ms. Bancroft on suspicion of murdering Mr. Taber this afternoon."

"Oh no, no, man. You be wrong. This girl, she good people. She didn't kill nobody," Dwayne said.

"There has to be a mistake," Camden added.

"No mistake, ma'am. Now if you'll excuse us."

"Wait," Michaela said. "I'm in my robe. Can I at least change?"

Peters nodded. "Go on up with her, Garcia. You got three minutes."

"I didn't kill him," Michaela muttered as Garcia followed her up the stairs. There was no love lost between her and the officer. They'd dealt with each other in the past, when a good friend of hers had been murdered, and Garcia had caused some problems for her and Jude. It wasn't a secret that Garcia had a thing for Jude, who at that moment Michaela wished wasn't on vacation.

"That's for a court of law to decide," Garcia replied.

Michaela ignored her and quickly dressed, everything seeming so surreal at that moment. What in God's green earth was this all about? Someone had come into the office, picked up her mallet, and killed Sterling with it. Someone who had gloves on. Could it have been another player? They all wore riding gloves. But it could have also been a socialite with a pair of white gloves, showing herself off to the polo elite. Oh jeez, it could have even been a server. Didn't they all wear gloves?

Peters yelled up to them, "Let's go."

This could not be happening. But it was, and moments later Michaela found herself in the back of a squad car, Garcia at the wheel, surely with a satisfied look on her face. Camden and Dwayne followed them to the car. "We'll get you out. I'll call Ethan."

"No." She didn't want Ethan to find out about this. "Call Joe. He'll be able to help."

She thought about her parents for a minute and was thankful that the two of them had taken a well-earned vacation for their fortieth wedding anniversary. They were on an African safari—something her father had always wanted to do. She could straighten all this out by the time they returned. But it wasn't good that Jude was also gone. She needed him right now.

Emotion rose up in the back of her throat, making her feel like she was choking. She swallowed it, refusing to allow any of this to get to her. This was one big mistake. One helluva mistake, and she would find the answers, because she refused to be framed for murder and spend her life in jail.

* * *

THIS WAS LUDICROUS. PETERS AND SOME OTHER detective—a woman named Singer—had her inside an interrogation room. They were throwing questions at her right and left. She felt like a boxer inside a ring—right hook followed by a double left. If she could only pass out and then wake up to find them all gone.

"When did you meet Mr. Taber?" Peters asked.

"I don't know. I think four months ago. It was about the time I started taking polo lessons. Robert Nightingale introduced us."

"And what was your relationship like?"

"We didn't have one. We were acquaintances. That's it. I saw him at the polo grounds on occasion and we played polo together."

"So, you never spent any other time with Mr. Taber outside of the polo grounds?" Singer asked. She was an attractive, short-haired blonde who looked more like a soccer mom than a hard-nosed detective.

"Once, actually. A group of us went over to Sorvino's for dinner one night after practice. Ed Mitchell, the owner of the grounds, wanted to meet with us about the charity event."

Singer didn't respond. She left the room.

"Think about it, Ms. Bancroft, is there maybe another time or two that you *associated* with Mr. Taber?" Peters asked.

She tried to find the right answer to get him off her back. "You know what? No. What is this about?"

Singer came back in holding a set of ropes that looked like the one she'd given Sterling yesterday. "Do you recognize these?" she asked.

"Sure. I sell them at Round the Bend. They're roping ropes."

"Uh-huh, and did Mr. Taber get these from you?"

"He did."

"But I thought that you said that you didn't have a relationship outside the polo facility with Mr. Taber."

"I didn't."

"Do you want to explain the ropes?"

Michaela detailed the incident that had led Sterling Taber to walk out of her shop with the ropes.

Singer and Peters eyed each other. "You and Mr. Taber never used these ropes *together*?"

Michaela sat up straight, aghast at the question. "Are you kidding me? First, we could not have had time, considering he got them just before the polo match, and as far as spending any time with him, that wasn't going to happen. I didn't even like the man. He was repulsive to me…"

Oh how stupid. How could she have allowed herself to say such a stupid, stupid thing? Oh no, no, no. She could tell by the looks on the cops' faces that she'd helped put another nail into her coffin. Coffee! Maybe coffee would help her brain connect at this ungodly hour.

Singer and Peters looked at each other again. "Ms. Bancroft, we have it from a source close to Mr. Taber that the two of you had a sexual relationship and that Mr. Taber had certain fetishes." Singer held up the ropes.

Michaela's jaw dropped. Now not only was she as dumb as paint on a fence, she was speechless.

"Do you care to comment?" Singer asked.

It took her a few seconds. *Brain connect. Brain connect.* "What source? You are kidding me." She shook her head. "No, no. This is some kind of joke. Who told you that?"

"We can't reveal sources. But this person claims that Mr. Taber frequently discussed your relationship."

"Well, whoever it was is lying. That is not true. Not even close."

Peters sat down and pulled the chair up, his face now only inches from hers. Michaela could smell coffee on his breath. Her stomach soured as he spoke in an accusatory tone. "Is that why you killed him? Because he was spreading rumors that the two of you were sleeping together? Or did you kill him because you were having sex with him and he was dating another woman? Did you murder Sterling Taber because you were jealous? As I said, we have your fingerprints on the mallet. They match what's in the computer. Lucky for us when you applied for a license to teach autistic children, you were fingerprinted by the county."

"I did not kill him. I never slept with him. That's crazy. It's just not true!"

"Why would he say it then?"

"I don't know!" Michaela now knew what it must feel like to be a cornered dog—one being kicked and beaten for no reason. And, as her brain further connected, she realized that it looked like she needed a lawyer, and panic started to set in.

"Ms. Bancroft, you still have the right to contact an attorney."

"I think that would be a—"

Before she could finish there was a knock at the door. Singer opened it. On the other side stood a shorter version of her friend Joe. The man stretched out his hand. "I'm Anthony Pellegrino. I'm counselor for Ms. Bancroft here."

Yes, the man was definitely related to Joe. Same last name, same round stomach, wavy black hair slicked off his face, and warm brown eyes. A first cousin was her guess. It looked like Camden had called Joe, and he'd obviously gone to work rapidly, rounding up one of his cousins to save the day. Anthony looked to be doing well for himself. He wore a pinstriped silk navy suit, crisp white button-down shirt with a rose-colored tie—Italian, for sure. Joe had a barrage of cousins. He blamed it on his devoutly Catholic family. He claimed there were some he hadn't even met.

Michaela had learned over the years that Joe's many cousins worked at anything from garbage truck driver to chef...but an attorney? That was a new one on her. Still, at that moment she felt grateful, albeit a bit surprised, to see Mr. Anthony Pellegrino enter the room to represent her.

The attorney removed a handful of papers from a leather briefcase. He took his time—deliberate and slow, almost achingly so for Michaela. She wanted to get out of there. "It's my understanding that you've charged my client with murdering a Mr. Sterling Taber."

"That's correct," Peters said.

"On what grounds?"

"The murder weapon belongs to your client and her fingerprints were on the weapon."

"The murder weapon being the polo mallet I read about in your report," Pellegrino said.

"Yes."

"Of course her fingerprints are on the mallet. It's her freaking mallet. I don't see what that's got to do with anything." Pellegrino shook his head and looked as if he were about to laugh. Michaela wasn't sure how to take it, because she was about to cry. "You are so joking here. You do realize that it would take nothing for the real killer to slip on a pair of gloves and there you go? No wonder Ms. Bancroft's fingerprints are the only ones. Anyone can see that. You don't have to be detective to figure that one, eh, folks?" Pellegrino smiled. "You, my friends, have a weak case and I'm sure that you know it. I'd like to confer with my client alone."

Both detectives left the room. Pellegrino stuck out a hand. "Joe sent me over. I'm a cousin."

"I figured. I would normally say that it would be nice to meet you, but…"

He waved his hand at her. "I understand. So, did you off the guy?"

It took her a few seconds to process his question. "Of course not!"

"You can tell me, I'm your lawyer."

"No way. I didn't kill anyone."

"Yeah, Joe says you're a good lady. I think I did pretty good with them cops, huh?"

What did he mean by that? "Yes," she said. "I think so. Wouldn't *you* know? I, uh, have never been in a situation like this."

"Oh yeah, me either. Crazy, man. Kinda cool, like one of them cops-and-lawyer shows."

Michaela crossed her arms and stared at him. "What kind of law do you practice?"

"Who, me?" He pointed at himself and then flattened down his silk tie. "Yeah, well, I'm a tax attorney, you know."

"Perfect." She put her face in her hands.

"Don't cry on me. I don't do so good with tear jags."

"Out of all the cousins you guys seem to have, there's no criminal defense attorney?"

"Oh yeah, there is. That'd be Pauly, but he's out in Chicago, you know. But look, I can get you out of this. Like I said, it don't take a genius to see they got a weak case. We just gotta get your bail posted."

"Right." Anthony Pellegrino may not have been a criminal defense attorney, but he was all she had right now.

"Okay, so here's the deal. They got your prints on the murder weapon. But it was your mallet, so they gotta prove you had time. They got a motive with this thing, though."

"Uh-huh, me sleeping with Sterling. Do you know who told them such a thing?"

Pellegrino looked down at his notes. "Do you know a Lucia Sorvino?"

"What? Pepe's teenage daughter?"

"Says here she's twenty."

"I know who she is. We're not friends. But she's served me a platter of lasagna from time to time at her father's restaurant. I had a little disagreement yesterday morning with her father before the event. She was there and her brother showed up. I don't even really know the girl. Why would she say something like that?"

"I don't know, but the police have it on file."

"This is craziness!"

"I'm going to level with you. This Peters dude, he's a jerk, a real uptight cop, and I think he'd like to wrap this thing up because Taber was from a highfalutin family who lives up in Santa Barbara. He don't want no heat, so if you look like a good suspect, then that's the angle he's gonna pursue for now. But Joe says you got a friend here in the department."

She nodded. "Jude Davis. He's a homicide detective."

"He might be able to help us out. Have you spoken with him?"

"No. He's on a cruise with his daughter. He won't be back until Friday."

"Huh. Five days. Okay, so while we're waiting for your friend to come back from his vacation, there is a hearing arranged for first thing this morning. The judge will likely set bond, but it won't be cheap."

"How much?"

"Murder case? You're looking at a quarter mil."

"Two hundred fifty thousand dollars! I don't have that kind of cash right now."

"You only have to come up with ten percent of it."

Michaela sighed. She didn't even have *that* amount of liquid assets at the moment. She'd put most of her cash from her inheritance into building up the autism riding center and for the special equipment needed, along with the extra horses she'd bought. The money that hadn't gone into the center she'd invested in the tack shop, and she was working on just enough capital to keep her business running and pay her bills. Oh God, she couldn't turn back now. She'd been down the road toward bankruptcy a few short years ago, and she refused to go back there. "That's still a lot."

"What about your parents, friends, property?"

She cringed at any of those thoughts. Definitely not her parents. She couldn't ask any friends. She wouldn't do that to them. But her property? Uncle Lou's place. That was her only option. "My ranch. If I have to."

"Good. I talked with your friend Camden and had her pack an outfit for you for this morning. By the time they take you back to your cell, the clothes should be there."

Her eyes stung with tears. *Her cell*. The one hour she spent inside the jail cell in the wee hours she'd paced back and forth, her mind full of rage, fear, and shock. Then Peters had come for her and she'd been in the interrogation room ever since.

Pellegrino smiled warmly at her. "It's gonna be okay. We'll get through the morning. You'll be home by noon. That's my job, and after that we'll get to work on your defense and I will get to work on these clowns here and continue to remind them that everything they have is circumstantial and weak."

How was he going to work on anything? He was a *tax attorney*, for crying out loud, but she didn't have it in her to bring that up right now. All she wanted was to get the hell out of there. She nodded and tried to smile back in return, but she wasn't sure at all how she was going to make it through the morning.

EIGHT

IT WASN'T TWENTY-FIVE GRAND THAT GOT Michaela out of jail but rather fifty, and the thought of leveraging Uncle Lou's place made her ill. Apparently the judge thought she was a flight risk because she had the financial means to "get away." Please! Where would she go? She had a barn filled with horses that were family to her, a handful of children she gave riding lessons to whom she adored, parents who lived two miles from her that she saw at least once a week, and a circle of friends she couldn't live without. She almost laughed when the old curmudgeon of a judge brought up the idea that she might flee. It was as ridiculous as the notion that she had been sleeping with Sterling. She had every intention of speaking with Lucia Sorvino to find out why in the world she was spreading such vicious lies. That girl had some explaining to do. Didn't she know what rumors could do to a person's life? Try on *destroy it* for size!

Joe showed up at the courthouse to take her home, while her new attorney shook her hand and said he'd be in touch with her by the end of the day. "I'd go with you, but I want to see what I can line up for you before we talk again. Joey, take care of her."

"Always do." Joe opened the passenger door to his minivan. Once he was behind the wheel, he looked over at her. "What the hell happened, girl?"

"I wish I knew. One minute I'm riding in the match, the next I find Sterling dead in my store, then when it's all over with, I head home and just as I've finally fallen asleep, it sounds like a herd of my horses are trying to break the door down, and outside stand Starsky and Hutch."

"At least you haven't lost your sense of humor."

"I think I'm still in shock. Look, I'm in trouble, Joe. I can see it in Detective Peters's eyes. He thinks that I did this and so does that woman cop. I can't go to jail. I didn't kill anyone. And by the way, thanks for sending in Anthony...but a tax attorney?" Michaela felt something under her on the car seat and picked up a half-eaten cheeseburger, which she'd sat on. "What in the..."

"Sorry. I know, the kids. They got a problem picking up after themselves. We're working on it."

She spotted a few French fries on the floorboard and pointed. Joe glanced down. "Throw in a Coke and I might have a meal."

"That Joe Jr.! Anyway, of course you didn't kill no one. I've known you since we was kids, Mickey. I know Anthony isn't exactly what you need. But it was the best I could do on short notice, and he did get your bail posted."

"Yeah, he did do that."

"You could eat a little more these days. I'd tell you to eat that burger but I don't know how long it's been here. Why don't we stop and get a bite?"

"It does look partially dehydrated. Eating isn't always a priority for me. I've been busy. And right now I just want to get home and shower."

"Never too busy to eat." He rubbed his large belly. "I think you get overwhelmed with all you got going on and you are the last person you take care of. You handle the horses, the kids at the center, that crazy broad Camden you live with, and then some. You need some *you* time."

She smiled at his comment. Ah, the big bro she never had—technically, because Joe had become everything a big brother is for a sister. She knew it drove Jude nuts that they were such good friends. He liked Joe, but his family ties made Jude uncomfortable. They didn't bother Michaela, who had seen plenty of Joe's softer side. She'd seen him with his little girl, Gen, Michaela's first autistic student and the reason she'd agreed to open the riding center in the first place. She adored the little girl, who loved to be around horses. No, she was not about to lose any of it—her animals, her friends, the kids, her ranch. She'd fight whoever had set her up. "We've got to get a handle on this. You and I both know the cops won't help me."

"What about Jude? The guy is crazy for you."

"He's on a cruise with his little girl."

"Oh."

"Oh is right, and he won't be back for five days. I can't wait for five days while Peters attempts to burn me at the stake. I've got to find out who did this, who murdered Sterling Taber."

"Oh no. I see where this is going."

"It's not like we've never been down this road before. We make a good team. You know we do, and this time I *really* need your help."

He didn't comment for a second, just sort of frowned, then nodded. "Where do we start?"

She sighed. "By questioning that Sorvino brat. Pepe's daughter, Lucia." Joe turned the corner into Michaela's ranch. A slight sound escaped from her lips. "Oh my God."

"You can say that again. I don't think we start with Lucia."

NINE

A LOCAL TV NEWS VAN WAS PARKED OUT IN front, with a blonde-headed woman reporter all miked up and ready to interview, along with her cameraman. It looked as though Camden and Dwayne were trying to chase them off the property, but they were being completely ignored. Now they turned their attention to the oncoming minivan. "This isn't good," Joe said. "I can run them over."

"No!"

"Just kidding. Maybe I can flip a U-ee and we'll make a run for it."

"No, don't do that! What do they want?"

"I think we are about to find out. Keep your head down and walk to the house. I'll get rid of them." Joe parked the van and got out first, asking everyone to back away. He did his best to keep his hulking self in front of her while the reporter shouted obnoxious questions at her: "Did you kill Mr. Taber? Were you in love with Sterling Taber? What about your riding center?"

Michaela turned around and faced the reporter—a statuesque blonde with a crisp navy suit and heels.

"What are you doing?" Joe asked.

"I'm telling them the truth. For the record, I barely knew Mr. Taber. I did not kill him. My riding center will remain open. I ask that you respect my property and my privacy and please leave."

She turned around and headed toward her front door. The cameraman and reporter ran in front of her and were now in her face. The reporter shoved the microphone at her. "How did you meet Mr. Taber? Can you tell us about the mallet?" She tried to push the camera out of the way, which caused her to trip and nearly fall as she reached the front porch step.

Joe lost it at that point. "Get the hell out of here, or I will call the police. You are on private property and Ms. Bancroft will charge you with trespassing. She's made a statement, and has kindly asked you to leave. I won't be so kind. Get the *hell* out of here!" he bellowed.

One look at Joe and the newspeople understood he was serious. Michaela finally made it through her front door and heard her phone ringing. Joe eyed her as she reached for it. "Let me answer it." He grabbed the phone before she could. "No!" he yelled, slamming it down. He looked at Michaela, who set her purse on the kitchen counter. "Reporter."

"Ah. Great! As if I'm suddenly like Angelina Jolie adopting a new kid. At least instead of making *People* magazine's most beautiful list, I'll only have the honor of making Indio's most wanted list. Just what I need—star status. Yeah. Great. Why do they have any interest in me?"

Camden walked in with Dwayne like a lap dog at her heels. Michaela still needed to have that one-on-one with her, and the sooner the better. She had to get to the bottom of what Camden had said after finding Sterling's body.

"The media likes a juicy story, and you are apparently it," Camden said. "Remember that Sterling was voted most eligible bachelor by the women's league of social activities in the desert."

"Oh, what an honor. He was a regular Colin Farrell." Camden made a face at her. "I didn't do jack. I'm a horse trainer. I teach children how to ride. I barely knew that guy, and now this. And I plan to find out who did it. Speaking of that 'most eligible bachelor' thing, weren't he and Juliet Mitchell a couple?"

Camden shrugged. "I wouldn't know."

Sure.

The phone rang again and again Joe answered. "What? No, of course not. Now listen, Rhonda, you've got to be reasonable here. That's ludicrous. Yes." He paused.

Michaela turned her attention to Joe. Rhonda was the woman who headed up the autism society, had been the one to help Michaela get a license, and worked with her on teaching the kids. She had recommended many children to her, and Michaela was now working regularly with seven children, including Joe's daughter, Gen.

"Okay." Joe sighed. Oh, this could not be good. "Yes. No. I'm sure that she'll understand and we will get all of this worked out." He hung up.

Michaela crossed her arms. "Work out what? *What* will she understand?" Joe looked down. "What is it, Joe?"

"Rhonda received a call from channel 8 and they wanted a quote from her for tonight's six o'clock news about your arrest, whether or not you would still be working with the autistic society, and if they would still recommend children to ride with you."

"What? No! Oh no, no!"

Camden placed a hand on her shoulder. Michaela, near tears, shook it off and walked into the kitchen, where she took a pitcher of water from the fridge. She needed to think. "What did she say?"

"She wouldn't give them a quote. But..." He paused. "...she did ask that in light of the negative publicity that for a while, until everything is worked out, you not work with the kids. She's pretty sure that when the parents hear about this, there'll be some fallout to deal with."

Michaela slammed the pitcher onto the counter, spilling water on the floor. "Those are my kids! Those kids are everything to me, along with my horses. She can't do this! She has to know that I'm not guilty."

"Of course she knows, but look at it from her point of view, Mick. She's gotta cover her butt."

Michaela frowned as she said, "Unbelievable!" She grabbed her purse off the counter.

"Where are you going?" Camden shouted.

"To see Lucia Sorvino...but first, I want to talk to you. Upstairs. Now."

"Now?"

"Now." Michaela motioned for Camden to head up first. She wasn't about to let her get out of this.

Camden turned around to look at her. "What's this all about?" she asked when they'd closed the bedroom door.

"The comment you made yesterday about Sterling right after he was killed, about being more than friends. Do you want to elaborate?"

Camden sighed.

Michaela's stomach sank. "Please tell me that you weren't cheating on your fiancé!"

"No, no I wasn't."

"Thank God." Michaela plunked down on the end of her bed atop a coral tropical-flower print.

"But I did sleep with him." Camden tossed back her red hair.

"You better explain this one, my friend."

Camden sat down next to her. "Look, here's the deal. It was a long time ago. A very long time ago."

"Like how long ago?"

Camden scowled. "Do you remember George?"

"Your first husband?"

"Uh-huh."

"Yes. The golf pro."

She nodded. "Sterling was his caddy."

"Oh no. I can already tell that I am not going to like where this is going. Wait, George? That was what, eight years ago?"

"Nine."

"Nine, and Sterling was twenty-six when he died, which means that you and he...when he was seventeen!"

"He told me that he was nineteen."

"Oh my God! You...you're like a regular Mrs. Robinson. That is really disturbing!"

"Hey, I prefer more like an Eva Longoria on *Desperate Housewives* during that first season, when she was sleeping with the gardener kid. He was a senior in high school. Really good story line."

"I don't watch TV, and I don't care who you think you're like. That's just gross."

"He said he was a virgin and he wanted to know what it was like because he was going off to college. Kind of like a soldier going off to war."

"You've got to be kidding me. You're delirious, Cam. You believed him? Young guy like that waiting until he was nineteen? Even at seventeen, I'm pretty sure Sterling Taber did his share of the cheerleading squad long before he graduated. Wait. How did you even meet him?"

"Golfing one day with George. He had those dreamy eyes and his body, wow...And George was already messing around with Debbie, who became wife number four, so I figured, no harm, no foul—"

Michaela cut her off. "It doesn't matter. What I want to know is, were you sleeping with him again?"

"I told you that I wasn't. God, Mick. I just said that it was a long time ago. I'm engaged to Dwayne."

Michaela cocked an eyebrow. "Like that really stopped you in the past. I just want to be sure."

"This is different. I love Dwayne and you know that. I'd never do anything to hurt him."

"Then why even have Sterling close by? Why have him in the show? If you love Dwayne like you say that you do, then why tempt yourself?"

She sighed. "I'll tell you everything from the beginning."

"I wish you would. But, you can leave out any more details from your Mrs. Robinson days. I don't think I want to hear about any of that."

Camden took a sip of her tea before going into her saga. "I hadn't seen Sterling in years. He'd moved to L.A., then back home to Santa Barbara, and then I think he came back here, he said, when he was twenty, but I'd moved on and so had he. We only had a fling—"

Michaela held up her hands. "Forget that. What I want to know is what had been going on between you two as of late."

"I'm getting to it. His family is some well-to-do, high-society-type bunch."

"I thought you said he was seventeen when you met him, but his family lives in Santa Barbara."

She nodded. "He had some ups and downs with his parents. They tried military school and then finally agreed to let him move out here and live with an uncle, who got him the caddy job. If I remember right, the uncle passed away not long after Sterling turned eighteen, but I really don't know. I wasn't in his life at that point. I only caught bits through the grapevine of what was going on with him."

"Okay, and..." Michaela motioned for her to continue, finding herself growing impatient.

"I first saw him a few months back, when that spread ran about him being the most eligible bachelor in the desert and how he rode down at the polo fields. I went to visit him. I thought he'd be a great attraction for the fashion show. It was his idea to do the charity match in the first place."

"Sure, and you want me to believe that you just went over there for a howdy-do, and to ask him to be in the show." Michaela rolled her eyes. "I've known you for a very long time. You're not fooling me, and please don't try. This is my life on the line here."

"Okay, so maybe I was a little curious. We had some good times together. We were friends. But trust me, I had *no* plans to cross that line again, and I *didn't*."

Michaela studied her. She actually believed her. One thing that Michaela knew about her friendship with Camden was they were brutally honest with each other.

"You're telling me that Sterling came up with the idea for the charity match?"

"Yes. I don't understand why you didn't like him."

"He was a show-off, and he made me uncomfortable. I don't like overbearing men and he was one."

"He was just confident."

"We don't need to get into the reasons why I didn't care for your friend. The facts are he didn't deserve his fate, and I certainly don't deserve to be charged with his murder."

"No, you don't. I know you didn't do it."

"Did he talk to you at all about his personal life, anything that might have been going on?"

"He did. I told the police yesterday what he told me only a few weeks ago."

"What was that?"

"We met for lunch at the polo lounge. He called me, sounding upset and asked if I'd come and meet him. He said that he felt like someone was watching him. He thought someone wanted him dead."

"Did he say who?"

"Juliet's father."

"Ed Mitchell?" Michaela knew Ed fairly well after riding with him at the polo fields. He'd been the one to give Michaela her mallet. He'd told her it was a gift from the club. She couldn't see a man of Ed's prominence murdering anyone.

"Yes," Camden replied.

"Okay, wait, so he had this girlfriend, Juliet. But he was also considered an eligible bachelor. I've been wondering about that. Do you know what the deal is there?"

"That's why he thought her father might want him dead. He and Juliet started going out after he was voted most eligible. We talked. I even spoke with Juliet and she seemed okay with it at the time. We decided that it would bring in a larger crowd to the show if we promoted him that way. I think, though, that Juliet may have had second thoughts, and it upset her. Especially when Sterling was approached by one of those reality TV dating shows. He didn't agree to do it, but Sterling told me that Juliet freaked out about it. And Sterling told me that if Juliet is upset, her daddy becomes even more upset. And I guess Daddy Warbucks also has a bad temper. I told the cops all of this yesterday, too."

"What did they say?" Michaela had caught wind that Ed was protective of Juliet and that he occasionally lost his temper. But she still couldn't see him as a killer.

"All the detective said was thank you. I didn't know at the time that Peters was going to arrest you; if I had, I would've pushed the issue further."

Michaela stood up and paced across her bleached hardwood floors. She needed to think. "Can you do me a favor?"

"Sure. Anything."

"Can you see if you can locate any article, or whatever else you can on Sterling? I know he did some acting in L.A. and other modeling gigs. Maybe there's something there. Can you do that for me?"

"Why?"

"Please, can you just do it?"

"What are you looking for?"

"I'm not sure yet. But the mystery lies with the dead guy, and maybe we'll learn something about his past, his life, anything that will give us answers as to who really killed him, and why."

"Michaela, don't tangle yourself up in this."

She let out a sarcastic laugh. "I don't have a choice now, do I? Peters wants me behind bars. I'm in this mess whether I want to be or not, and this time I'm fighting to keep my sanity and my freedom."

TEN

MICHAELA PULLED UP IN FRONT OF SORVINO'S, which was on the hill overlooking the polo fields. To her dismay the restaurant appeared to be closed. Only one car stood in the parking lot—a silver convertible Mercedes. She was pretty sure Ed Mitchell drove a car like that. Maybe Sorvino's was open, but normally it was packed; one car in the parking lot didn't exactly constitute *busy*.

She didn't know where Lucia Sorvino lived and had hoped that she would be here at the restaurant. Maybe it was for the best if the girl wasn't around, at least for her sake, because Michaela's anger had only deepened as she'd wiped away angry tears on the drive over. How could anyone think she could have murdered Sterling? And now her students—*her kids*—not coming for lessons because of the negative press! It had been one thing that she owned the damn murder weapon and only her fingerprints were on it. But Lucia had sealed the coffin shut by making up the bizarre lie about her and Sterling. She would get to the bottom of it.

Even though Sorvino's might be closed, she decided to walk around the building. Maybe someone was there and she could ask them when Lucia might be in. Typically, a clear blue sky in November would have made her grateful to be alive. She'd have taken in the surrounding beauty of the grass field below and the majestic mountains in the background. But there was not a whole lot to appreciate at the moment. One minute it was Sunday afternoon and her team had won a polo match and raised a nice chunk of change for her riding center, then by Monday she'd been arrested for murder. All she wanted to do was be vindicated and get back her life—a life that seemed to have drastically changed in the last twenty-four hours.

She went up to the front doors and pulled on them but they were locked. She started to walk around to the back of the restaurant, passing some of the large picture windows, which allowed patrons to enjoy the view. Something caught her eye and she peered inside. Pepe Sorvino was talking to Ed Mitchell. So, it *was* Ed's car. They looked to be having a drink and laughing about something and did not notice her. Michaela continued around the back to knock on the door, but hesitated. Ed stood up from the bar and pulled something from his pocket. She squinted to see what it was. It looked to be a jewelry box. Pepe opened it, and took something out: a diamond ring. Michaela could tell by the way the light caught it. Why would Ed Mitchell be giving Pepe a diamond ring? Okay, jewelry was Ed's business, but wouldn't they conduct a transaction like this in *his* store?

She had to hustle as she saw the men make their way toward the back door. How would she explain being there? She didn't mind running into Ed, but she wasn't prepared to deal with Pepe again. She raced for a shed that stood behind the restaurant. It was open; she went inside and crouched down. From what she could tell, the shed was used to store catering needs like large platters, a cappuccino maker, extra plates and…a wig. What? A *wig*? Michaela picked up the long blonde wig. Strange. She set it back down again and listened as Ed and Pepe walked to the parking lot, still laughing.

"My wife and I loved what you did for our last party. You've got a knack for this, and when we open up the restaurant in Palm Springs, your business will only grow."

"I thank you for investing in this with me. This will be good, Ed. And I plan to have my daughter helping out in this restaurant here while Mario and I get the other one off the ground, now that she isn't so distracted by…other things. My apologies for that. I know Juliet was hurt by that incident with Sterling."

"The good news is that neither of us have to worry about Sterling Taber being a problem for us or our daughters again."

"This is true." Pepe laughed. "Is the Realtor meeting us at the restaurant?"

"Yes. She should be there before us. We better get a move on." With that, both men climbed inside Ed's Mercedes and zipped away as Michaela picked her jaw up off the ground.

ELEVEN

MICHAELA REMAINED IN HER STUPOR ON THE drive home. The question running through her mind was the obvious: Did Ed Mitchell and Pepe Sorvino have something to do with Sterling's murder? Neither one of them was upset by his death, that was for sure. What was the ring all about? And the restaurant in Palm Springs? Were they going into business together? It seemed like an odd pairing to her, but Ed was a good businessman and Sorvino's was a profitable restaurant. Oh boy, did she need to talk to Joe—someone whom she could tell everything she'd heard, seen, experienced. Maybe he could help her sort through this. She called his house and got voice mail, then tried his cell with the same result.

A wave of exhaustion hit her and she felt like she was on autopilot for the rest of the drive home. What she needed to do was think, and the best place to do that was on a trail ride.

She parked over by the barn and went into her office, where she kept an extra pair of riding jeans and boots. Moments later, she had Rocky hooked up to the cross-ties. She groomed him faster than usual, hoping not to have anyone notice that she was back. She needed a game plan and she didn't need anyone clouding her mind with their own thoughts.

Once up on her sorrel gelding, she and Rocky headed out onto the trails behind her ranch. Passing by the pasture that in the future she prayed would be home to champions, she sighed and breathed in the fresh air. The sun was beginning to set and its brightness cast shadows across the boulders on the mountainside. Rocky stepped out, seeming to appreciate being able to stretch his legs as much as she was to be free and away from the insanity. Much of the time her riding skills and that of her horses were expressed inside the arena, but there was nothing like getting out on the trail to remind a person exactly what the meaning of freedom was. *Freedom.* The clean, dry air perfumed by chaparral and the earthen floor. The sweet songs of larks here and there. She might even spot a predator bird looking for his prey; a hawk, or on occasion a golden eagle, soared on by. She sighed and gave Rocky a pat as she leaned slightly out of the saddle and forward while he worked to climb up the mountain's crest.

But what if her freedom were suddenly ripped out from underneath her? It had been, briefly…and what if it got worse? What if Joe's cousin couldn't remedy things as he'd insisted he could? She didn't see how any of this was simply going to resolve itself. She had to tell Peters what she'd overheard while in the shed behind Sorvino's. But what did it mean? She again analyzed what she'd seen and heard. Neither one had actually said that they'd done away with Sterling. They were pleased he wouldn't be a problem anymore. So, if she went and explained this to Peters, what would his likely reaction be? Probably the detective would do nothing. Ed Mitchell was well known and a bigwig in town, one of the wealthiest. The last thing the police would want to do would be to rock the boat with one of the movers and shakers. And Michaela still couldn't see Ed as a murderer…still, what about what Sterling had told Camden, about being afraid of Ed? That was weird, too, because Michaela couldn't see Sterling being intimidated by anyone.

She knew she still needed more information, and talking to Lucia was a must. She decided to make a mental list of all the players and see what her brain could turn up. She knew that Robert might have a motive and it was possible that he'd had time, unless he'd been with his wife when Sterling was killed. Then there was Zach and the way he'd looked after Sterling; the vibes coming from him were nothing short of hatred. Oh, and Lance Watkins. Sterling had been rude and disrespectful to Lance. And, Erin

Hornersberg—the makeup artist with an attitude—who definitely was not happy with Sterling. Her strange behavior last night in the parking lot bothered Michaela. What about Sterling's pal Tommy Liggett? She knew Tommy, but not well. What was the old saying—keep your friends close and your enemies closer. Right now it looked as if that was what Zach was doing—for what reason she didn't know, but what if Tommy had a reason, too? They always hung out together. At the very least, she'd need to talk to Tommy since he was Sterling's best friend. Maybe he'd know what had been going on with Lucia and why she would lie about Michaela and Sterling.

And Camden: She hadn't killed Sterling; she'd only slept with him. Michaela squeezed her hands tight around the reins. Rocky sensed her stress and sped up due to her shift in the saddle. "I'm sorry, bud. It's not you. Definitely not you."

They reached the top of the mountain and stopped. Michaela got off the horse to let him rest. She rubbed his face and he nuzzled her shoulder, his weight nearly throwing her off balance. "Hey, easy buddy."

She looked down across the vista spread below her, peppered with small ranches and homes—some plush and green with horses in their pastures. A few were weathered, aged, and in need of attention, but the landscape gave her a sense of security. This was her home—where she'd grown up, and knew people. It was where she belonged. She lingered there, taking it in, but knowing she should get back. She realized that to get through this she was going to need to suck it up and move forward. Typically, moving forward would've meant that she would work with her students, exercise her horses, and manage her ranch. Now, *forward* meant unraveling a murder mystery.

Another thought weighing her down was Jude. She didn't want him to come home to this mess. She should've gone with him and Katie on this cruise. He'd asked, but the timing had not been good.

Only a few days earlier—last Friday—Jude had taken her to dinner. They'd sat out on the patio at the restaurant eating shrimp cocktails and each having a glass of wine. The sun was setting, reflecting a myriad of colors across the desert sky, and candlelight flickered in the tea lights on the table.

The evening had been romantic from the get-go. Jude had shown up with a dozen red roses in one hand and a dozen pink ones in the other. Then he'd taken her to a gourmet restaurant, and she'd figured that she was pretty much being swept off her feet.

He had leaned across the table and taken her hand. "I wish you could go with me and Katie on this cruise."

"I wish I could go, too."

"Then come with us. Please. I'll pay for everything. Come on. You deserve a break. And Katie would love it. This is her week off with year-round school, and we've been looking forward to this for months. It would be over the top for her if you came along."

He smiled his devilish smile, which made her heart skip a beat. His smile and the way his skin around his blue eyes crinkled got under *her* skin in a very good way. She sighed. "You know I can't. I have the charity match and we're opening the store. I couldn't skip out on all of that. Plus I have kids to teach. It would be irresponsible."

"For once in your life, you should try on irresponsibility for size."

She laughed. "Sure. Come on, you know I would go if I could."

"I know. I understand. Next time though." He shook his head.

Jude had been right, because if she'd for once hadn't been so responsible she wouldn't be in this mess. She climbed back up on Rocky and they eased on down the mountain. She didn't know where things were headed with Jude, and now she was more uncertain than ever. Not because she didn't have feelings for him, but because she was in a hell of a lot of trouble, and she was concerned how he might react. Maybe that was the real reason she wasn't picking up the phone to call him. This wasn't her first rodeo. She'd found herself in the midst of murder and mayhem in the past and she really wished she could lead a quiet, simple life.

Ah, so much for simple. As she rode onto her property she knew simple didn't exist. Ethan's truck stood out front, and the last thing he represented in her life was simple.

TWELVE

NORMALLY MICHAELA WOULD BE HAPPY TO SEE his truck parked in front of her house. But not this evening. Ethan was waiting for her in the stable office, and he had Josh with him. Michaela spotted him before he saw her. He'd set Josh down on a blanket with some toys and was bending down, wiping something off the baby's face.

She decided to bite the bullet. Ethan never stopped by without a reason any longer. Michaela was pretty sure that Summer was behind that. Back in the day, Ethan would pop in after a long day of work and they'd have a beer together. They'd talk about his cases for the day and how her training sessions had gone. They'd known each other since they were three, and the comfort level between them was both intimate and special. Not many people had the kind of friendship that she and Ethan did. "Hey look, it's my favorite boys."

"Mick, what is going on?"

"You've heard."

"Heard? It's all over the news. You and Sterling Taber? I thought you were dating that detective—Jude."

"I am! You don't believe that crap? What, do you think I killed him, too?"

"No, of course not." He walked over and put his arms around her. She sank into him, leaning her head on his chest. "What are we going to do?" he asked.

"We? *We* don't have to do anything. I have to find out who killed him."

"That's the cops' job."

"You would think, but I am apparently the prime suspect and from everything I can tell, the cops have zeroed in on me and think they have the killer."

"Oh come on, that's absurd. They can't believe that, and you can't go around trying to figure this out, Mick. The last time you got yourself involved in something like this, you nearly got yourself killed."

She pulled away from him and threw her arms in the air. "I don't know what else to do."

He shook his head. "The police have to be looking at other folks. I know that guy was popular with the women, but he also seemed to have enemies, or at least I know that there were some people who didn't care much for him."

"Did you know him?"

"No. Other than playing that match with him. I met him a few times before that and never thought much of him. He was an ass; you know that and so do I. Look at the way he acted out on the field with the other players."

"What do you mean though, about enemies?"

"I don't know if you'd actually call them enemies, but the day I was out there I overheard some of the grooms grumbling about him, and we both know that Lance couldn't stand him. Remember yesterday after the match the way Sterling was talking trash about him?"

"I couldn't blame Lance for saying what he did about him."

"Yeah, well, before the match I was talking with Lance and he said that he couldn't wait until the charity event was over. He said that Taber was a miserable SOB to ride with. That the guy was always doing stupid stuff on the field, like cutting him off when it was unnecessary and just being a real ass to him. Then he caught him trying to flirt with his wife, who Lance said blew him off, but he wasn't real happy about it. The wife was pretty offended, too."

"I imagine. I think their dislike for one another went both ways."

"Right, no love lost there, huh? But that's what I mean; this Taber guy wasn't well loved by everyone."

"Do you think Lance Watkins might have killed him?"

Ethan shook his head. "You know, I've known Lance for a long time. The guy doesn't strike me as having an evil bone in him. He's always low-key. He's kind to his animals. His wife and daughter are really sweet people. I can't see it. But you never really know someone enough, do you? People will surprise you. I only know him through treating his horses and we've had a few beers together over the years, but no, I don't think so. Lance is a good guy. I'm only telling you this because if Taber could've gotten under someone's skin like Lance's, who knows who else he's pissed off. I think the police have their heads up their asses."

"Join the club."

"Tell me what you need, anything."

She smiled. "I appreciate it, but your plate is full." She pointed to Josh and bent down. "Hey, bubba, what you doing besides growing?" She picked him up and kissed the top of his head. "I've missed you. Ethan, why don't you take Summer out for dinner this weekend and I'll watch him." She wanted to try and divert him. She knew that his desire to help her would probably cause a rift between him and Summer, and she didn't want that for the baby's sake…or Ethan's. He'd made a commitment to Summer, and Michaela wouldn't come between that.

"No. You've got plenty going on. You don't need to be babysitting for me. That's the thing with you: You always try and help other people out and all it does is add more pressure for you. You've got to stop it."

"It'll help me take my mind off of everything." But she knew the real reason Ethan wouldn't have her watch Josh likely had more to do with Summer's feelings toward her than anything else.

"Maybe. But you do have to start thinking about yourself."

"I am. Honestly. I'm thinking about how in the heck I'm going to prove that I didn't kill Sterling Taber."

"And I want to help. I want you to keep me in the loop and tell me what I can do." He rubbed his eye. "Damn. Something in there. Been bugging me all afternoon."

"Let me see. Sit down on the couch, and I'll take a look." She set Josh back down on his blanket and handed him a set of plastic baby keys, which he eagerly went back to playing with. She leaned over Ethan, who lay his head back on the couch. "Whoop, yep, there it is. Eyelash." She gently removed the lash and then brushed it off his face. She went to back away but nearly tripped over the baby, who had rolled over next to them.

To avoid hurting Josh, she fell forward onto Ethan. Right into his lap. "Oops. Sorry." She scrambled to get up, her face burning. Ethan was looking at her in a way that he hadn't before. At first there was a slight curve on his lips and then as a second passed, the look in his eyes became one of intensity, almost as if were looking directly into her heart and soul, as if he knew her at her very core. Another second slipped by. Michaela shifted uncomfortably. She lifted herself and braced her hands against the couch trying to get all the way back up. They both started to laugh. The tension eased.

Ethan quickly reached down and picked up the baby. "That's okay. Better than falling on you." He poked Josh's chest and tickled him. The baby giggled. Ethan stood. "Promise you'll keep me in the loop."

Uh-huh. She believed that Ethan was there to support her, but Summer might not have too much of a problem with her being locked away. "I will. Thank you." She kissed both of them on the cheek and helped Ethan put the baby toys back in the bag.

Once they were gone, she went back out to the barn to take care of Rocky. Now, here was a male who understood her. She leaned her head against his neck and sighed, her mind spinning at not only the prospect of being a murder suspect, but also at the fact that something had just happened between her and Ethan. She couldn't deny it. It was something that had never happened before. When they'd looked into each other's eyes for that second, a powerful surge of electricity had shot through her—straight to her heart. It had been nothing like she'd ever felt before, and she knew Ethan had felt it, too.

THIRTEEN

MICHAELA WENT TO BED WITH HER MIND IN A jumbled mess. Between Sterling's murder and her confused feelings over Jude...And then—dammit—Ethan had once again messed up her head. That slight but intense moment they'd shared had her wondering about her feelings for him. They were feelings she could never act on, and she knew they were futile. It was silly, really. So, she'd kind of fallen on him and he'd looked at her in the way a man looks at a woman he wants to touch, to kiss—to love—but none of that mattered. She wiped the thoughts from her mind.

Not unhappy to see the sun rise, she made an organized list in her mind as to the order in which she planned to see people today. She figured that no one would be at Sorvino's until closer to the lunch hour, so Lance Watkins was up first. Even though she'd overheard that odd conversation between Ed Mitchell and Pepe, she couldn't get out of her mind the animosity that existed between Lance and Sterling. Ethan's conversation with her yesterday had only disturbed her further and made her more curious as to what the real situation between the two of them had been.

Michaela pulled up to the exquisite facility that Lance Watkins owned and operated. She got out and looked around. There was a dressage ring to her left, marked in the shape of a square and surrounded by trimmed date palms. Beyond that was a large green pasture where a handful of horses grazed and soaked up the sun, not to mention eating plenty of grass. She watched one lie down and roll. It was always a sight to see such large beasts rolling around in the grass, maybe scratching their backs, but more than likely doing it because it felt good. Not all horses took the pleasure in rolling, but many did and it brought a smile to her face to see a horse just being a horse.

There was a row of stalls and a barn to her right, painted a traditional brick red and trimmed in white.

Adjacent to them were sets of pipe corrals, likely for people who boarded their horses. Michaela knew that Lance earned a nice income by simply setting up a boarding facility. As far as training with him, that was expensive and only the cream of the crop fit into that category. His facility was traditional and well kept.

She walked up a small embankment to the jumping arena and saw that Lance was working a strong and forward-looking Hanoverian over a 3'6" grid. The horse stood over seventeen hands high and was a gorgeous dapple gray. Lance handled him beautifully, his patience and connection with the animal obvious. Together the horse and trainer moved elegantly, with the rider in perfect balance as the animal bent and worked his way through the training session, seemingly to want to please his rider, which is what every trainer desires.

Lance worked the gray a few times over the grid and then did some flat work to finish him out. He gave him a pat on his neck and let his reins hang loose, allowing him to stretch his neck after working those muscles so intensely.

Lance spotted Michaela. "Hey, to what do I owe this pleasure?" he asked.

"Thought I'd pay a visit. Great horse."

He rode the gray over to the side of the arena. "He's a sweetheart." Lance nodded. "Hey, sorry I was so rude at the polo field, then after what happened to that guy I felt really bad. I also heard about the cops arresting you. What a crock."

"Yeah, well." She shoved her hand into her jeans pockets. "About those ruffians and the polo grounds..."

"Uh-oh. I don't like the sound of that." He slid his right leg over the horse, dropped lightly to the ground, and loosened the buckle on his Charles Owen helmet.

She mustered a smile. "Sterling didn't make it easy for many people to like him."

"Ah. No, he didn't."

She noticed he wore the polo shirt from the event. She squinted. There was a dark reddish-brown spot on the sleeve. Before she thought, she blurted out, "Is that blood on your shirt?"

Lance pulled the sleeve up slightly off his arm and looked to where she was pointing. "Yeah, it is. How the hell did that get there? Oh, yeah." He bent down and undid a wrap around his horse's front leg. "He's got a nasty gash here, which I cleaned earlier. He clipped himself yesterday on something, I'm not sure what. I must've smeared some of the blood on my shirt when I was cleaning his wound."

"Oh." The cut was clean but it could have bled quite a bit. Michaela still couldn't help but notice that her mind was heading down a track she didn't like. She was here, so she needed to do what she came for. "Hey, so I wanted to ask you about Sunday. As you said, I'm no killer and I'm trying to see what I can find out. Not to put you on the spot, but I got the sense from Sterling that there was an issue between the two of you."

He chuckled again. "I didn't care for him, no. But, if you drove out here to ask me if I killed him, I can tell you that I didn't."

"No. That's not what I'm implying at all. I'm only trying to gather information. You were there. I wanted to know if you saw or heard anything."

"I wasn't at the show when he was killed. I'd taken off right after the match. Actually the guy pissed me off even more so after I rode away from you and Ethan. I won't deny that. He came right up to me afterward and told me that I played like a girl with my hands tied behind my back."

"Ouch."

"Yes. Ouch. You know, it irked me, but the thing that really bugged me was that it wasn't like we were playing some huge tournament for cash and prizes. We were playing for charity. A charity I believe in." He twirled his horse's mane around his fingers, his other hand holding the reins loosely. "You know, I hope the police find who did this. It's not fair that you've had to close your center. That money could do a lot of good. My wife's good friend's son is autistic. I know that he's involved with horses down in San Diego and it's been great for him."

"Don't worry, we'll be up and running again. I am sure of it. If the police don't find out who did it, then I will."

"Like I said, I'm not your man. In fact, if it would make you feel better you can ask my wife and daughter. They were both there on Sunday and once I was done the three of us took off, right after the confrontation with Sterling. My family was standing there when he went off on me like that, which I thought was classless. Hell, my eleven-year-old daughter was standing right there listening to this guy rag on me. I've got to tell you, I'm not surprised he's six feet under. Not that anyone deserves that kind of death. But I heard him being horrible to Juliet Mitchell right before the match."

"You did?"

"Oh yeah. He was giving her a hard time. Something about how she needed to listen to him because she was wrong and didn't know what the hell she was talking about. She kept insisting that her dad was going to find out about it and she told him to leave her alone. He grabbed her then, and I started toward them. So did Zach, who pushed Sterling off of her."

"No kidding?"

Lance nodded.

"What happened after that?"

"Juliet walked away and went back to her horse. Zach started talking real low to Sterling and didn't look too happy with him. I thought I heard him say that he didn't want anything more to do with him. That he was only playing nice for the day because of the event, but when it was all said and done they'd need to talk some more."

"Wow."

Lance shook his head. "Make anything of that?"

"Maybe. I thought those three were good friends."

"Yeah, well, one never knows what goes on behind closed doors. Juliet Mitchell seemed to know something ugly about her boyfriend and she knew her father would go nuts when he found out about it. Whatever it was, it was enough to make Juliet walk away from him, and from what I could tell, Zach, too."

"Okay. That's food for fodder, isn't it?"

He nodded. "I wish I could be more help. You know I'm in your corner. Whatever you need."

"Thanks. One more thing: Tommy Liggett was also on your team. Do you know him at all?"

"He's okay. Kind of walks in Sterling's shadow. You know the type—not as good-looking as his friend, not as rich, not all the girls hanging on him, so he's kind of the wing man. But the guy is nice enough. I never had an issue with him. I know he doesn't come from money and he puts most of what he makes into his horse and his lessons with Robert, so he's really into the polo. That's about it."

Michaela thanked Lance and walked back down the hill to her truck. She'd doubted he had anything to do with killing Sterling. It didn't fit. But she couldn't shake having seen the spot of blood on his shirt. Was it Sterling's blood? It was the same shirt he'd worn at the event. It was light colored, so even if he'd washed it, blood would've stained. But why would a killer be wearing the same shirt he'd killed someone in? And he was adamant about his wife and daughter being with him afterward. The only hole she could see with Lance was his *alibi*: Was it for real? Would his wife lie for him, and could his daughter not have a concept of the timing, being fairly young? She hoped not.

An altercation between Lance and Sterling had been something that Lance supposedly had been able to laugh off and then go home with his family. She really wanted to believe him. She liked Lance Watkins, and Ethan had told her that he couldn't see Lance hurting anyone. It was all super damn confusing.

On top of it, what Lance had told her about Juliet and Zach added to the mix that they could somehow be involved with Sterling's murder. Whatever they had argued about with Sterling seemed far more emotionally charged than the issue between Sterling and Lance, and Michaela aimed to find out if it had driven one of the two of them to murder.

FOURTEEN

LUNCHTIME: ABOUT TIME TO LOCATE ONE LUCIA Sorvino. Michaela was suddenly famous, but not with the kind of fame that anyone cares to have. As she walked down the steps into Sorvino's, all eyes fell on her. The women with their glasses of white wine, rows of pearls across their necks, and fine designer wear scowled at her. The men, on the other hand, seemed to be looking at her with a sort of awe. She wanted to scream, "I didn't kill him!" but decided that would garner even more attention, and the last thing she wanted was any more of that. This was either the ballsiest thing she'd ever done or one of the stupidest. But dammit, she was innocent.

Sorvino's at the polo lounge had a classic Italian feel, with crystal chandeliers, hunter green and cream décor, and photos from a bygone era of Palm Springs and the surrounding desert. It was kind of Frank Sinatra-ish, which fit, since Frank liked to hang out thirty minutes away in Palm Springs back in the Rat Pack days.

Michaela asked a busboy where Lucia Sorvino might be. He told her in the office. She asked him to show her the way. He did, also wearing that expression of awe. Michaela's stomach clenched. The busboy tapped on the door.

"Who's there?" a woman's voice asked.

"Uh, Miss Sorvino, there is someone here to see you."

"Yeah? Who?"

Michaela held a finger to her lips and shook her head, then shooed the busboy away. His eyes grew wide, as if she scared the hell out of him.

"Gino? Who is it?" Lucia demanded and swung open the door. She gasped when she saw who stood on the other side. Michaela quickly shoved her foot in the door and held her hand out to prevent Lucia from shutting it. It didn't stop her from trying, and they played push and shove for a few seconds until Michaela's strength won out and she was able to open the door all the way, storm inside the small office, and shut it behind her.

"I'm gonna scream!" Lucia said. "You better get out of here now, or I'll scream."

"I wouldn't do that if I were you." Michaela took a threatening step toward her. "You lied about me and I want to know why."

"Get out! Get out!"

"Why did you tell the police that I was sleeping with Sterling? That's a bald-faced lie."

"You killed Sterling. Everyone knows you did it. You need to get outta here because my papa will come in here and have a heart attack if he sees you."

Michaela took another step forward. "Spare me the drama. Someone told you to say that. You're just a stupid kid, and if I had to guess, I'd say you were sleeping with Sterling and you don't want your papa to find out about it. What do you think your brother would say? Or wait, maybe they already knew and killed him themselves for *tainting* you! You know that I didn't kill Sterling. What I want to know is why did you tell the police that I was sleeping with him?"

"Get the hell out of here, you screwed-up bitch!"

Michaela was getting right under the girl's skin. She could see panic in her eyes and felt pretty sure she was on the right track as far as something going on between her and Sterling.

"I'm only curious as to what a twenty-six-year-old hotshot polo player has in common with a what, twenty-year-old chef's daughter? Wait, maybe Sterling started to feel the same way and blew you off, so *you* killed him. Now you're trying to cover your tracks by making up stories about me. Maybe you're not as dumb as you look. You got into my office, you used my mallet, and now you can tell everyone I was sleeping with him. I think you need to start talking."

"Get out! I told you to get the hell out of here! Papa! Mario!" she screamed.

"The cops may be fooled by your big green eyes and crazy lies, but I'm no fool. And when your family sees you for who you are…well, I think you've got yourself in some hot water."

The door flew open and Pepe Sorvino thundered into the office, nearly knocking Michaela over. "You get outta here. We don't want you here."

"Thank you, Papa, she was harassing me. She scared me."

"*Harassing* you? Oh my God. You are one lying little—" Michaela blurted.

"Out!" Pepe screamed.

"Fine. I'll leave, but I am going to find out why you're lying about me, Lucia. And if it's what I think the reason is, your life will be turned upside down like you've done to mine."

"Go!"

"I will find out what you're hiding." Michaela turned on her heel, nearly running into Mario Sorvino.

Mario followed Michaela to the front door until she turned to him and said, "I'm leaving."

"Hey, between you and me, that prick deserved what he got."

"What?"

"Yeah. Taber. Man was nothing but trouble," Mario said.

"Really? And you knew him?" Her hands shook.

"Who didn't know him? Hotshot dude, come in here and never pay his tab. I wasn't surprised that someone killed him." Mario crossed his arms. "I want to give you some advice. You may want to be careful around my sister and my father. They got hot tempers. I'm only letting you know."

"Mario!" Pepe approached the front door.

He winked at her and retreated into the restaurant. "Be careful, Michaela. It's that simple. Be careful."

She got back into her truck feeling as if the Sorvino family had more ties to Sterling Taber than just Lucia Sorvino being his *friend*, and that Mario Sorvino was more than making small talk with her. If she was right, Mario had subtly threatened her with the "stay away from my father and sister" line. And he'd already warned her about making threats toward his family. She couldn't help wondering how Mario Sorvino tied into this and if she was spot-on when she'd told Lucia that maybe her big brother had done away with Sterling to protect her. He seemed the type to do something like that. And how about running into him right after finding Sterling dead on the office floor? He was on the kitchen staff. He had had the opportunity.

Did he also have motive?

FIFTEEN

WHY WOULD PEPE'S SON EVEN COME AFTER Michaela? What was his point? She would have to see what Joe might find out about the Sorvinos' ties with Sterling, but right now she had another stop to make. Her stomach sank as she parked her truck next to the stalls at the polo fields. This was not a conversation she wanted to have, but it was necessary. She had every intention to fess up to reading the invoice that had caught her eye and confront Robert Nightingale about it. This was her life she was dealing with and there were some obvious issues between him and Sterling.

She tapped on the office door, which swung open almost immediately. To Michaela's surprise Paige, Robert's sweet but eccentric wife, answered the door. Her eyes looked red, as if she'd been crying. Michaela noticed that the back of her hand had a smudge of black, likely from mascara that she'd wiped off her tearstained face. Paige tried to smile, her brown eyes taking Michaela in. She had cropped blonde hair, which framed her round face. She was on the heavy side and tended to wear drapey, flowy kinds of clothing. Today she had on a purple billowy blouse and black pants.

"Oh, Michaela, hello. Did you come for a lesson?"

Had Paige been the only one to not hear that Michaela was a murder suspect? "No. I wanted to talk to Robert. About Sterling."

"He's not here." She sniffled. "I don't know where he is or when he'll be back. I don't know if he's coming back." She started to cry. "Oh yes, Sterling. Oh dear, I'm sorry that you're having so many troubles over his murder. Goodness knows you would never do such a thing. It's just so horrible. An outrage."

Michaela took a step back. Whoa, this was unexpected. "I'm okay. I'm sure that this will all work out and the police will get to the bottom of it."

"It's not that. It's not you."

Now Michaela was really confused. "Oh, okay. Um…"

"Oh no, I don't mean to sound insensitive, but of course the police will exonerate you, it's not that, it's…" She wiped her tears and sat down on the sofa. "Nothing. Nothing at all. How selfish of me to carry on when you're obviously having problems of your own. Forgive me."

"You don't need to apologize, Paige. What's wrong?"

"Nothing. Nothing." Paige looked up at her, the tears starting again.

"People don't cry over nothing." Michaela reached into her purse and dug through it. She knew she had tissues somewhere in her bag. She found a packet and handed one to Paige.

The woman blew her nose. "Robert is leaving me. Actually, he's left me."

"What?"

Paige shrugged. "I don't know. I really don't know."

Michaela sat down next to her. "Do you want to talk?" She didn't know Paige all that well, but she couldn't leave her here like this.

Paige put her face in her hands. "I've lost so much in the last few years. First Justin, and now this with Robert, and of course Sterling."

"Sterling? You were close with him?" Michaela now felt certain by the way Paige was talking that it had been her who'd hurried away from the polo field grounds after getting out of Sterling's car.

"Oh, yes. He was Justin's best friend."

"Justin? I'm sorry, Paige; I don't know what you're talking about."

"We don't talk about it much. Only people in our small circle ever even whisper about it. I hear them sometimes and see the looks on their faces. The ones that say they feel sorry for me."

Michaela suddenly understood. Paige was talking about her son, who'd been killed in a car accident. She'd never known his name, but she'd heard about the tragedy.

Paige blew her nose. "Justin was our son. I'm sure you know that he died five years ago in a drunk-driving accident after a party. He'd had too much to drink and hit a tree. He was twenty."

"Oh, I am so sorry. I had heard, but I knew it wasn't something to ever discuss with you."

"I know, dear. It's kind of an unspoken rule that no one talks about it, but it's not my rule. Robert won't talk about it. People tiptoe around him all the time. I think he's lost it. He left me a note this morning that said we were through and he was leaving."

"And you don't know why?"

"I have an idea. It has to do with Sterling." She started to cry again.

Michaela waited patiently for a few seconds and then asked her, "What about Sterling?"

"Robert found out that I have been giving him money."

She would have to be careful here. Paige was giving Sterling money? Odd. From everything that she had ascertained about the man, he appeared to have plenty of money of his own and he was doing just fine with that, along with the money he earned with his modeling gigs. "Um, I hate to pry, but why would you give Sterling money?"

Paige smiled, her eyes reflecting nothing but sadness. "I told you that Sterling had been Justin's best friend. It was how Sterling started riding polo. Justin got him into it. And yes, he does come from a wealthy family in Santa Barbara, but they recently stopped providing him with money. Not the kind of money he needed to live on, anyway. I think he'd gotten himself into debt by overextending. He had been receiving twenty thousand dollars a month from his family and then they cut that in half. You can imagine how difficult that would be if you're used to having more."

How much did he need? Ten thousand dollars a month for a single guy sure sounded like plenty. "Why did the family decide to do that? Do you know?"

Paige shook her head. "He wouldn't talk about it. He said that it was too painful. All I know is that last summer he went back home, then he returned, and within a few months his family had sort of disowned him. And, because he was a link to my son, I didn't want him to suffer."

"You became a mother to him."

"Yes. He filled the gap in my heart that was missing my son...and now they're both gone!"

"Robert didn't feel the same way about Sterling as you did?" Michaela assumed this.

"No. He liked Sterling fine, but I think he might've blamed him for Justin's death. They were at the party together and Robert feels that Sterling should have stopped him from driving home that night. But Sterling was with a date and claims he didn't realize that Justin was intoxicated."

"Did Robert tell you that he blamed Sterling?"

"No."

"Oh. So you were giving Sterling money? I assume that Robert didn't know about it?"

"Not until Sterling told him."

"He told him?"

"Yes. Sterling was not paying Robert for the training and boarding bills here. I went to talk with him about it. I explained that the money I'd been giving him was from an insurance policy that we had on Justin and that he needed to use the money to pay Robert, and for his rent and education."

That must have been what Michaela witnessed between the two of them the other day. Paige had tried talking to Sterling about this. "I didn't know he was going to school."

"He was taking acting classes. It was his dream to be an actor and he would've been wonderful at it. He promised me that he'd get caught up with his bills with Robert. He went to talk to Robert. Things heated up, I guess, and Sterling lost it and told him that it didn't matter that he owed him money. Sterling laughed at Robert and told him where the money was coming from. Robert was so upset. He came to me and asked me what I'd been doing. I told him. I explained that Sterling was like a son to me and that I was trying to help him. I got him to calm down after a bit. Sterling had auditioned for a play and had promised to pay me back because he'd gotten the part. Robert was still angry, but not as much. Then this morning I found the letter. I guess he changed his mind."

Michaela was more than confused. This would take some time to digest. Sterling had played poor Paige. He *was* an actor. She felt sorry for the woman on so many levels.

She stood and tried to see if the invoice she'd spotted on Robert's desk was still there. It wasn't. She sighed.

"I'm sorry to have rambled on. I shouldn't have troubled you," Paige said.

"No. Not at all. I'm glad I was here for you." She put a hand on Paige's shoulder.

Paige nodded. Michaela said that she had to go, as she had a riding lesson to give. She walked out of the office, her brain twisted in frustration, for she had no real clue as to what had just taken place, or the significance of any of it. But if working around animals had taught her one thing, it was that trusting your intuition usually meant that you were on the right track. *Her* intuition told her that Sterling Taber had maintained some interesting and complicated relationships, and that more than one person had reasons to want him dead.

SIXTEEN

MICHAELA NEEDED A BREATHER AND HAD ABOUT an hour before she had to be back home to give a riding lesson to Joe's little girl. Thank God that Joey believed in her innocence and had no plans of removing Gen from the riding center.

She walked down the stalls at the polo field to say hi to Rebel. Someone had moved the horse and at first she couldn't find her. She'd been moved all the way down to the end of the row. The bay mare walked over to her as soon as she called to her from the other side of the barred stall. "Hi, gorgeous, how are you today? Tell you what, I've been better. Why'd they move you down here?"

The horse's ears popped forward and she stared at Michaela as if she were listening intently. The beautiful thing about these animals was that they provided total and complete therapy, and all for no money down. Well, that wasn't entirely true when you broke down board, feed, and training, not to mention show fees, vet bills, horseshoeing bills, etc. No, hardly free, but they were really good listeners.

Michaela opened Rebel's stall door and slid through. She stroked the mare's neck and scratched under her chin, which made her toss her head about. The chin was typically sensitive and the scratching caused Rebel to bare her teeth with her top lip turned up, as if she were smiling or laughing at Michaela. "Oh, so you find my woes amusing. Wish you could talk; bet you know something about all the strangeness that goes on around here."

She continued to pet the horse. She rounded behind the animal and saw that her back leg had been wrapped. That was not unusual. Horses acquired cuts and scrapes at times that caused the grooms to have to treat the superficial wounds and then wrap them to keep the flies away and prevent the area from getting infected.

Michaela noticed that the wrap was partially off. She bent down and rewrapped it, uncovering a fairly deep cut. Looked as if maybe she'd rubbed up against something sharp. Kind of like what had happened with Lance Watkins's dapple gray gelding. Rebel had probably gotten the scrape in the other stall and that was why she'd been moved. Michaela retightened the binding. As she started to stand, something shiny caught her eye. She bent back down and brushed away the shavings to get a better look. She stared for a moment as her mind registered what it was. Then she picked it up. Oh, wow! Someone would be looking for this: a tennis bracelet. Each diamond had to be a carat and had obviously cost someone a lot of money. She started to stand when she heard voices in the corridor.

Juliet Mitchell sat astride her chestnut gelding, and Zach Holden walked next to them. Neither noticed Michaela. "You did good out there," Zach said. "All you need is to relax. He can tell that you're tense." He gave the horse a firm pat on the neck. Michaela was about to step out of the stall and say hello.

"Tense! Of course I'm tense! How the hell could I not be stressed out?"

Michaela shrank back inside the stall. Maybe now wasn't the best time to reveal herself. She'd never heard Juliet so…edgy. The girl was always well mannered, typically soft-spoken, definitely upper crest. It was possible that, like her father, the young woman had a hot temper hidden beneath her polished exterior.

"Think about it, Zach." She slid off her horse. "We have to get that letter out of Sterling's apartment. Do you know if the crime scene tape has come down?"

Oh boy. This was mighty interesting. No way was Michaela going to announce her presence now. What were these two talking about? A letter? What letter? She ducked back down, the bracelet gripped in her hand.

"I don't know why you even sent him that. What was the purpose?"

"Look, I know it was stupid. Really stupid." She started to cry. "I don't even know if it's there anymore. I had to send it to him. I was scared of him and I thought that was the best way to get him to leave me alone. I tried to send an e-mail but I thought a letter would be more final, more to the point. I had no idea it would wind up like this."

"It's okay. I understand. It has to still be at his place. You mailed it on Friday? Maybe he hadn't gotten it by Saturday. Or maybe he didn't read the letter. It might still be in his mailbox."

Michaela watched the two through the stall bars.

"What if the police find it? The things that I wrote in there...it was bad, Zach."

"The police are focused on Michaela Bancroft."

Michaela bit down hard on her lip.

"We both know she didn't do it," Juliet replied.

"But until we get that letter, we have to let the police think what they want. We can't tell them anything. It will ruin your life, *our* life, and so many others in your family."

"It feels wrong."

"I know," Zach said. "But we can't afford not to be protective right now. Not until we know for sure. And then we can decide what to do."

Michaela watched as he pulled Juliet into him. "You didn't do anything wrong."

Juliet nodded. Zach lifted her face up and kissed her. "We'll get through this together."

Get through what *together?* Michaela had no idea what they were up to. She started to sink down lower in the stall as she saw Zach turn her way.

"I promise it's going to be okay, Jules. Trust me." He smiled and brushed a piece of hair out of her face. She smiled back at him and nodded. "Look, I've got to check on

Rebel. One of the grooms said she had a cut on her leg. Hang on. I know she likes to try and pull her wraps off."

Rebel. *Rebel! Oh shit, he was coming into Rebel's stall.* As he approached, Michaela lifted her head. Zach jumped back.

"Oh hey," she said. "Didn't know anyone was here." She knew she didn't sound very convincing. "I came to visit Rebel and saw that she had a gash on her leg. Silly mare had her wrap off. I redid it."

"Oh. Yeah, I was going to check on her. Gosh, we've been here for a little bit." Zach glanced back at Juliet, who had a wide-eyed look on her. "You didn't hear us?"

"No. I didn't. I was bent over treating the horse, and you know, I've been having sinus problems lately. My ears seem clogged. I don't know…" She shrugged. "Maybe allergies." Michaela was fairly certain that neither Zach nor Juliet were buying her story. "I'd better go." She slipped out the stall door. "I've got a lot going on, you know."

"Yeah, sorry about all that. We heard. We know you're not a killer." He frowned.

"No I'm not. You two have a good day." Michaela walked quickly out of there. She knew she wasn't a killer, but after overhearing those two chat, she wasn't so sure that either one of them couldn't have murdered Sterling.

SEVENTEEN

MICHAELA DIDN'T KNOW WHAT TO MAKE OF Zach and Juliet's conversation. What were those two hiding? Of all the gall for Zach to say that it was okay for the cops to focus on Michaela when they both knew she hadn't killed Sterling. They were so certain about it, too, and yet they didn't really know her all that well. She was pretty sure that, upon first impression, she didn't come across as a homicidal maniac. But, were they so certain for some *other* reason that she hadn't killed Sterling? Was it because one of *them* had done it? She recalled Juliet stumbling out onto the stage and appearing flushed at the time and apparently not knowing where Sterling was. It had surprised Camden. What did they not know for sure? What did those two have to make decisions about?

One thing was for certain, there was a letter that Juliet Mitchell had written to Sterling Taber and it was damning to her in some way—which meant that Michaela had to find the letter before they did.

She needed to make a stop at the tack shop and see if a new helmet she'd ordered for Gen had arrived. The girl's birthday was only four days away, on Saturday, and she'd promised to get some things together for Joe and Marianne to give Gen. She couldn't let them down. As much as Joe and Marianne had done for her, she had to come through for them. They were like family.

Camden was helping a customer with a pair of boots. Boy, she'd come a long way form the hopeless shopaholic who didn't care much for anything other than designer clothes and cocktails shared with a good-looking guy. She'd always been a good friend to Michaela though, and it was a delight to see her making such positive changes.

She checked the back room and found that the helmet had been delivered, but not the charm that Marianne had asked her to get for Gen. When Camden was finished with her customer, Michaela asked her if she'd signed for any jewelry that might have come in.

"No jewelry. Some clothes, a box of horse wraps, those leg wraps."

"Sports medicine boots?"

"Yeah, the Professional's Choice ones everyone's asking for. How are you today? I tried to get online this morning to see what I could find out about Sterling, but the Internet is down. I called the cable people."

"Thanks. I'm okay. I'm trying to get through this, figure it out. So far, all I can determine is that I'm not the only one who didn't think much of Sterling."

Camden frowned.

"I'm sorry. I don't want to speak badly of him, especially considering the circumstances, and I know you didn't feel that way about him, but try to understand where I'm coming from."

"I know. I do. I'll get online as soon as I can. I've got several things to do around here as well."

"You do what you need to here first. I'm weeding through what I've found out."

She didn't go into what she'd overheard and seen in the past couple of days, because Camden had a propensity to worry, and she had enough on her plate in trying to manage the new store. They'd made the decision to go ahead and open their doors on Monday once the crime scene investigators had cleared the scene, because they didn't really see another option. "How's business so far?"

"Not too bad. I didn't know what to expect after what happened. I think there are some people who have stopped by just to see where a murder took place, but most of the people coming in are buying things. You know who did stop by?"

"Who?"

"That Erin Hornersberg, still as rude as ever. She said that she wanted her makeup brushes. I didn't know what she was talking about. She insisted they were in the storage room, but I checked and didn't see anything. Then she wanted to go back and look herself. At first I wouldn't let her, but finally I went back there with her and stood over her shoulder, but we still didn't find them. She says we'll have to pay for them. She wrote down her address for us to send her a check." Camden handed it to her. "I told her she had to be joking. She says she left four brushes here and she wants more than two hundred dollars for them."

"I don't think so. Give me a break! Since when did makeup brushes cost fifty bucks each?"

"Actually, if you buy the good ones, like the professional ones, they can be expensive."

"Fifty bucks?" Camden nodded. "Like I said, I don't think so. I'll stop by her place and see if we can't work this out. I have a few things to ask her about anyway. Maybe her brushes will turn up."

"She's weird."

Michaela nodded. "Oh, speaking of *lost*. Look what I found in one of the stalls at the polo field." She took the bracelet she'd picked out of Rebel's shavings from her purse.

"Oh my God."

"I know. Someone has to be missing this. Can you post a sign up about it, and place a classified ad or something, maybe even call the police and see if anything like this has been reported missing?"

"Sure. Someone has to be missing it. One of my exes gave me one of those once. They cost thousands."

"That would bum me out, if it was mine. I'll hang on to it, and if anyone calls about it, let me know."

"Well, how do we know if they're telling the truth?" Camden said.

"Good point." Michaela looked it over closely to see if there was any way someone could distinguish it. "The only thing I can think of is to take it down to Ed Mitchell's jewelry store and have them tell me what size the diamonds are, and the clarity. That kind of thing. I'll try and get by there and see what it's worth. Whoever owns it should have all of that information on hand, I would think."

"I'd think so, too."

"Good, then that's what we'll ask if anyone comes by or calls saying that it's theirs. And let me know when a box from Horse Jewels gets delivered. I need to get it to Joe for his daughter's birthday."

"Sure. I'll get that sign up and see you at home. I promise I haven't stopped thinking about how to help you out of this mess. As soon as I can get online, I'll start surfing around and see what I can find out."

Michaela needed to get back to her place for Gen's riding lesson. She hadn't cancelled it, because in addition to owing Joe a great deal, she also wanted to try and keep something normal in her life.

Michaela glanced in the rearview mirror to change lanes. An uneasiness floated over her. What was this? If she didn't know any better, she'd say that someone driving a black Ford Explorer was following her.

She had two choices: punch it and try and get away from the Explorer, or pull into a strip mall and see if she was right. *Was* someone watching her, and if so, who? The *whys* she could kind of assume. She'd take her chances. She turned into the first Jamba Juice/Starbucks/drugstore parking lot she could find. Not too difficult. Even out here in the desert, they seemed to be going up on every corner. She dashed into the Starbucks and peered out the window. The black Explorer was there, parked down the way. From what she could tell, a woman sat inside. She ordered a coffee and then walked out; the SUV was still there. This was not the time to be anything less than ballsy, so she took a big drink of the coffee, hoping to get a good head of steam going. Maybe she'd go kung fu on her *friend.*

She walked briskly toward the car. The driver had sunk down in her seat, but Michaela could still see that someone was inside. Suddenly, whoever was behind the wheel figured out what her intentions were, and before she reached the Explorer the driver cranked the engine, backed out, and tore off. Michaela stood there, coffee in hand, bewildered.

EIGHTEEN

MICHAELA FELT PRETTY SHAKEN UP ON THE drive home. Why would anyone be following her? She couldn't see the person well enough to recognize who it was. Not all was lost though, because she'd been able read a part of the license plate. Maybe, with Joe's connections, he'd be able to find out who owned the SUV.

She sped home, certain that Joe and his daughter would be waiting for her. Relief swept through her when she saw him getting out of his minivan. After pulling up she walked over to the van and helped Gen out. The girl smiled slightly upon seeing Michaela. Through Gen, she had found many new reasons to see life in a different and special way. The girl's autism had taught Michaela to slow down and feel with all of her senses. And she knew from Joe's feedback and watching his daughter do a little better each week around the horses that she was teaching her something in return. She reveled in working with the ten-year-old.

"Hi. Are you ready to get Booger out and ride?"

"Yes. Yes. Ride Booger."

Michaela smiled. It came easy around this kid; even though things were crashing down around her, she couldn't help but see how precious life could be. When they'd first started working together, Gen rarely ever said a word. But she'd started talking a lot more in the last month, and Booger—Michaela's old gelding—brought the best out in Gen.

"Is she ready? I think she said his name fifty times on the way over." Joe laughed. "How you doin'? Things okay?" he asked.

"No, they're not okay. Now that you two are here though, it's a little better."

"Talk to me. Come on."

Michaela took Gen's hand and the three of them walked to the barn. She told Joe everything that had happened over the course of the last couple of hours.

"Not good. Okay, we put the Nightingales on the back burner. They're trouble soundin', but let's take care of this license plate you got first and then the letter you heard Juliet and Zach talking about. You got an address on this Sterling dude?"

"No."

"Okay, sit tight. I'm gonna see what I can do. It's probably gonna take some time before I can put the license plate thing together with the owner. A partial plate is a starting point. I'll see what I can do, and I'll locate an address on Taber. Right now, why don't you give my pumpkin here her lesson and I'll make some calls. I'm also working on the Sorvino chick. My cousin told me what she said. That was in confidence, you know, but when you took off after her yesterday, I figured I'd better check some things out myself. What I know so far is the girl is a clubber. Sneaks out past her pop and her brothers and heads into Palm Springs for the nightlife when she can. She's trouble."

"That much I am sure of," Michaela replied. She told him about her confrontation with Lucia and Pepe, and how Mario had followed her out of Sorvino's. She also brought up what she'd seen and heard with Ed Mitchell and Pepe.

"I don't like the sound of any of this. They're all trouble and you're wrapped up in it. We gotta take this thing step by step, 'cause one of these loony toons offed Sterling and they have an inkling that you're on the hunt, which you've made no bones about. Well, Mick, you're putting yourself in a risky situation. It's possible that whoever was following you is connected to Sterling's murder. I say you lay low a bit, let me see what I can find out, and then we'll go from there."

"That's easier said than done."

"I know you're antsy and I can't blame you, but you gotta listen to me."

He was probably right. "Deal."

Michaela spent the next hour with Gen and life suddenly felt normal again. The child smiled. The horse did everything asked of him and for a little while Michaela felt a semblance of balance. Then it was over.

With Booger put away and Gen feeding him his treats, Michaela found Joe inside her office on the phone. "Uh-huh. Interesting. Thanks." Joe hung up.

"What was that about?" she asked.

"I put in some calls about the license plate; nothing yet, but I'm not surprised. I'm working on Taber's address. But check this one out: I wrote down a list of all the people you mentioned to me, wanted to see what else I could find out about any of them, and I did."

"You did? What?"

"One of them killed somebody and spent some time in jail."

NINETEEN

"WHAT? WHO? HOW?"
"The makeup artist."
"Erin Hornersberg?"
Joe nodded and leaned back in Michaela's swivel chair, looking pretty darn proud of himself.
"What are the details?"
Michaela sat down slowly on her sofa, taking this new piece of information in. She didn't even bother to ask how he'd found it out. She knew his answer would be something like one of his cousins who works for the parole board or something like that. It didn't matter. Joe knew how to get information and, even better, how to process it.
"What I know so far is, the makeup girly was at a rock concert. A punk rock thing. Word is she was in the bathroom and another girl started giving her some problems, you know, makin' waves kinda thing, and this Hornersberg chick punched her so hard that she fell back and hit her head on the concrete wall and it killed her."
Michaela brought her hand to her mouth.
"She got time for manslaughter and assault and battery. She was supposed to do fifteen years, but her case went back on appeal and the defense was able to produce a couple of witnesses who said that the woman who died provoked Erin and hit her. Turned out it was a case of self-defense. The victim had a rap sheet, and Erin was out after spending nine months in the can."
"Provoked, huh? Self-defense? Even so, I don't know a lot of people who have it in them to kill anyone even in self-defense." Michaela let this jell in her brain. "If she's the kind of person who loses it easily, maybe she lost it just enough with Sterling the other day that she did him in. I need to talk to her. She came by the shop today looking for some makeup brushes she left. When Camden couldn't find

them, she said that we needed to pay for them. I've got her address in my purse."

"Hold off and we'll go there together. I can't today. My oldest, Joe, has a concert tonight. Lead saxophone. Kid is awesome." Joe beamed. "Otherwise, I'd say let's do it today. Maybe I could meet Marianne and the kids at the school."

"No way. You need to be with your family. I can drop in on Erin myself."

"Mickey, this is a woman who *does* seem like a loose cannon. We don't know all the details of what went on with her case, so you know, I think you better hold off on confronting her. You told me she was a strange bird. I don't want you going there alone."

"Fine."

Gen walked into the office and sat down next to Michaela, who said, "Did you like riding today? Did you have fun?"

The girl nodded. "Fun. I had fun. Booger is fun."

Michaela gently touched her shoulder. Gen tensed under her touch. "Good."

"Mick, I hate to go right now, but the family and all."

"Don't be silly." Michaela waved a hand at him. "You do what you need to do."

"I'll be calling in a bit and checkin' in with you."

"Thank you. And, thank *you*," she said to Gen.

She turned Rocky out into the pasture to play and get some exercise. Then she took out her two-year-old stallion, Leo, and led him up to the arena, where she attached a lunge line onto his halter. Letting the rope out as she trailed to the side of her horse with a long whip in her right hand and the line in her left, she asked him for the trot and then onto a canter, where he was able to get his energy out. She continued to lunge the young horse for several minutes and then she let him off the line so he could romp and play, tearing around the ring. After that she took her older mare,

Macy, out and worked her for a good forty minutes, putting her through her paces and enjoying riding an animal who knew how to move and seemed to almost anticipate every move right before Michaela asked her for them. God, it felt good just to get out and be with her horses again. For a while, she'd forgotten about Sterling and this big huge mess she'd become wrapped up in.

* * *

AFTER PUTTING THE HORSES UP, SHE WENT down the row of stalls, making sure that everything was locked up and then fed each one with care, measuring out needed vitamins and supplements and saying good night to each one—her kids.

It was nearly five, and what Joe had told her about Erin nagged at her. She knew what she'd promised him. Maybe she could get Camden to go with her. She'd seen Camden's BMW pull in during Gen's lesson. If she took Camden, she wouldn't be going alone. That made sense to her. What could happen with the two of them together? If Erin were trouble, they'd be double the trouble.

She knocked on the door of the guesthouse, where Camden and Dwayne lived. Her friend opened it. "Want to go see if we can get into some trouble?" Michaela asked.

Camden closed the door behind her. "Since when did you ever have to ask me that?"

A few minutes later, they were turning out onto the highway. "Can you get my purse? There's an address in it," Michaela said.

Camden found it; Michaela could see out of the corner of her eye that her friend was looking at her funny. "This is what you call going and getting into trouble? Come on. This is Erin Hornersberg's address."

"I know." Michaela gripped the steering wheel. "Hear me out." She filled her in on what Joe had told her about Erin.

"You need to turn around and go back home because Joe is right on this one! What are you thinking?"

"I'm thinking that Erin might slip up and say something about Sterling, and if you're with me, we can go to the police and tell them."

"No." Camden shook a finger at her. "You're *not* thinking. That is so stupid. Do you hear yourself?"

"Okay, I agree, it doesn't rank up there in the intellect department. But, come on, I don't know what else to do."

"Wait for Joe. His muscle is enough to make anyone quiver. Besides, think about it: Do you really think Erin is going to slip up and say, 'Oh yeah, I took the dude out'? I don't think so."

"All right." Maybe bringing Camden along wasn't such a good idea, but she wasn't convinced yet that going to see Erin was so dangerous. "Bear with me. We'll see if she's even home and if so, we'll handle the makeup brush thing. That's it. Let's go and see how she acts."

"Ridiculous, but you're not going to let me out of this, are you?"

"No."

"Fine. For this, I may pick one of those ugly bridesmaids' dresses."

"You wouldn't. And I thought I was the maid of honor."

"I would. Hot pink with frills and puffy sleeves à la 1990. And maybe I'll demote you."

"You're a bitch."

"Oh so true, so true."

They started laughing. "You know, I got some snooping done for you," Camden said.

"You did?"

"Told you I would. And I found out some interesting things about Sterling."

"Want to elaborate?"

"Looks like you were right and I am easily snowed. Sterling had some trouble with the law back home in Santa

Barbara. I found a newspaper clipping from last summer. All about big money, parties, and a dead girl. She supposedly was one of Sterling's girlfriends."

"Really?"

"Yeah. And there's more." Camden sucked in a deep breath. "Guess who's in the photo with Sterling? His polo mates—Zach Holden and Tommy Liggett."

"So, those guys went to Santa Barbara with Sterling last summer. I talked to Paige Nightingale earlier and she told me Sterling's family tightened up the purse strings with him last summer."

"That's about all I could find. The story seemed to die out. The articles were vague. The dead girl's name is Rebecca Woodson. She drowned after being at a party with Sterling; the article names him as her boyfriend. It also said that the two of them had been arguing and that this young gal left the party, while Sterling stayed and hung out there with his friends. There were conflicting reports. I guess that some partygoers said Sterling followed Rebecca out. Some said they saw him leave with a buddy."

"Wonder if that was Zach or Tommy? It only said *a* friend, or did it say *friends*?"

"I'll give you the articles when we get back, but I'm pretty sure it said *a* friend. Then I found an article from a few weeks after this girl's death; she drowned by falling off a nearby pier. Her family didn't buy it when Sterling was cleared of any wrongdoing, and they filed a civil suit. I can't find anything about it after that."

"Great. This is getting more twisted by the minute, Cam. As if having enemies in the desert wasn't enough for Sterling, the man had people in his hometown who might also have reasons to want him dead. I don't know what you think, but if the Woodsons think this guy killed their daughter, it seems reasonable to me that someone in her family might have wanted him dead."

"Sounds like a possibility."

"Here's our street," Michaela said. She parked the car in front of a decent-looking apartment complex with nice landscaping. "What number is her apartment?"
"Twenty-three."
"You ready?"
"No."
"Oh, what could happen? It's an apartment building, for crying out loud. There are people all over the place."
Camden gave her that funny look again. "Sure, what could happen, she asks. We're only going to talk to a psycho bitch capable of killing somebody. I don't know, what *could* happen?"

TWENTY

THEY STOOD OUTSIDE ERIN'S APARTMENT.
"Dammit, we're here, knock," Camden finally said.
"I know. I'm rethinking this."
Camden grabbed her arm. "Good, let's go."
Before she could pull her away, Michaela knocked. A few seconds later Erin opened it. "Oh. It's you. I take it that you brought my makeup brushes?"
"Actually, no, we didn't."
"You didn't? Okay, then you're writing me a check or handing me some cash for them?"
"Not exactly," Michaela replied.
"Not exactly? What does that mean? Why are you here then?"
Camden started to open her purse. "You know what? I do have some cash here and I know how important good brushes are, especially to a makeup artist—"
Michaela put a hand on her friend's shoulder. "Okay, before any money is exchanged here, I've got some questions for you."
"Questions for me? I don't know what you might need to ask me and I don't care. Red here wants to pay me for my brushes and that's what matters right now."
"No. What matters to me is that you spent time in jail and you had a beef the other day with Sterling Taber. And I'm sure that you know I've been arrested for his murder—a murder that I didn't commit."
"That's what they all say. My time in jail is none of your business, but if it makes you feel any better, I do understand your problems. I spent that time in jail for something that I didn't do. I sat there for nine freaking months until finally my lawyer, who I paid out the yin-yang, found a couple of chicks who really saw what went down in that bathroom. Maybe you'll get lucky and someone will come forward for you, too."

"I'm not counting on *luck* right now."

Erin postured herself in the doorway. She wasn't a big woman—not tall, anyway. But she was tough. The kind of girl in junior high who Michaela would have steered clear of. Right now, she wasn't even sure where she found her courage, but she was hell-bent on getting the truth.

"I think we should go," Camden said. "I can mail you the check. We'll get out of your hair."

"That's a good idea, Red."

"No. No it's not!" Michaela looked from her friend to Erin. "I know Sterling was a jerk to you, but I'm wondering if you knew him before Sunday."

"I told you, I saw him around. At clubs."

Michaela noticed the woman tightening her fists. Maybe it was a good time to leave. "At clubs. Right. Okay."

"That's it. Now, I'm going to be nice because you two paid me well the other day and you seem to be having a rough time." She nodded at Michaela. "Forget the check. I'll write it off, but also, don't bother me again." She slammed the door in their faces.

"That was a real party," Camden said. "Now can we please go?"

"Yeah, we can go. But she's lying to us."

"What do you mean?"

"I think she knew Sterling. I don't know how, I don't know what the deal is, but my gut says that she's full of it, and I want to know the truth."

"And I want a margarita."

They got back into the truck, Camden wishing for tequila, lime, and salt, Michaela determined to figure out what Erin Hornersberg hadn't told them.

TWENTY-ONE

WHEN THEY GOT BACK TO THE RANCH, CAMDEN gave Michaela the articles she'd printed up. Camden sipped a margarita while Michaela had a glass of wine.

"I still can't believe that you—I mean *we*—did that," Camden said. "Erin seems real shady to me. You need to be careful."

"Erin *is* shady and I know to be careful." She set the articles back down on the kitchen table. "This is it? This is all you found?"

"Yes. But I think it could be something. Sterling being in trouble with the law might have something to do with what happened to him."

"It might."

"Are you going to his funeral service tomorrow?"

"Sterling's funeral? It's tomorrow? That was fast. Wow. How did you know?"

"It's in the paper."

"I don't know. Maybe. Hey, where's Dwayne? I meant to ask you earlier, but we got *sidetracked*." She wanted to change the subject. Thinking about going to Sterling's funeral at that moment made her mind swirl with anxiety.

Camden brushed her hair back behind her ears. "He needed some time to think. I told him about me and Sterling."

"You did? How did he take it?"

She shrugged. "He's a quiet man. He's philosophical and he understands that I am a changed woman. I'm not the ditz who used to go around screwing anything that looked good in tight jeans. But I think he needed some time to let it settle and then move past it. I want this to be different between me and Dwayne. I love him and I believe that we are meant for each other. I couldn't keep this from him. I know it's my past, and he gets that…but my past isn't so great."

Michaela hugged her. "You did the right thing. You're a good person, okay? I love you and he loves you. And I know Dwayne; he's not a jealous type and he's not one to dwell in the past. You're right, he will recognize why you told him the truth and the two of you will be stronger for it."

"I know. I think he went to get something to eat and go a bookstore or the movies. He likes to do that once in a while."

"Yeah. It'll be okay. Well, it's getting cool and if he left earlier, I want to be sure that he blanketed the horses. Thanks for going with me tonight. You're a good friend."

As Michaela reached the barn, she saw Dwayne's truck pull in. Camden stood in the doorway of the guesthouse. She watched as Dwayne hurried to Camden, throwing his arms around her in a tight hug. She knew that Dwayne wouldn't hold Camden's past against her, and a knot of emotion tightened in the back of her throat. That was love.

An echo of whinnies traveled down the barn row when she entered. Dwayne hadn't blanketed the horses, so she went around to each one and took care of it. Leo, her two-year-old, turned and nibbled lovingly on her back as she buckled the straps underneath his belly. She stood up and scolded him. "No, no." He looked injured and went back to the few scraps he had left from his dinner. She knew that his nibble was harmless, but being mouthy like that was a bad habit to let him get into.

Once she'd blanketed the last of her animals, she hung out in Rocky's stall for a few extra minutes. So, Sterling's funeral was tomorrow. She knew it would be scandalous for her to go, considering the circumstances, but she really had to. She wanted to see the faces and reactions of everyone who knew Sterling, many of whom had been there the day he was murdered, particularly those guests she suspected might have had something to do with his death. She also wanted to see if a black Ford Explorer would be in the parking lot.

She turned off most of the lights in the barn and started back to the house as Joe's minivan barreled down her dirt road. He pulled up next to her and rolled down the window. "Go and put some black on—a sweatshirt if you got one, and some pants that you can get around in."

"What are you talking about?" Michaela asked.

"I'll explain after you get changed. Now hurry up."

"Okay." She rushed into the house, did as she was instructed, and met Joe outside.

"Where are we going?"

"First we're gonna drive through a Cotija's taco shop, because Marianne's put me on this diet and it's killing me. I'm wasting away."

"Joe, Marianne would not be happy about you having a burrito. You don't need to cheat."

"Once. Only once. I do a lot for you, Mick. All I want is a *carne asada* burrito. They can leave the cheese off. And I'll do a diet soda. But I need meat."

She frowned, but let him drive through the taco shop. While waiting for the order she said, "Okay, what is this all about?"

"The letter. The one that you heard Zach and Juliet talking about?"

"Yes."

"We are going to find it."

"Wait a minute. How do we plan on finding this letter?" She stared at him as he turned into a parking lot in front of a row of high-end townhomes. "Oh no, no. I see now. We can't. Is this where Sterling lived?"

"Follow my lead and keep your mouth shut."

"Oh no, we are not breaking into his place. I won't do it."

"You got a better idea?"

"Joe…" she implored.

"You coming or what, Mick?" Joe got out of the van and started walking.

Michaela found herself following him with the knowledge that she was about to become an everyday common criminal. But what the hell, she'd already been arrested for murder.

TWENTY-TWO

"JOE, I DON'T THINK THIS IS SUCH A GOOD IDEA," Michaela whispered as they stood outside the front door of Sterling's town house, while Joe took out a tool and jimmied the lock.

"And you think spending the rest of your days in jail is a better idea?"

"I didn't say that I *wasn't* going to do it, but—"

"But nothing, we're in." Joe opened the door and pulled out two small flashlights. "Here, take this one. We need to double-duty this. I'll check the front rooms. You find his bedroom, bathroom, and any other room up those stairs." He flashed his light toward a flight of stairs off to the right. "We gotta be quick, too. Not a lot of people out right now, but it's only eleven, so there may be some night owls coming and going. Lucky this place faces the way it does. No other residences looking in." Michaela took the light. Joe placed his hand around hers. "It's okay. It's gonna be okay. Right?"

"Right." She nodded. Joe had seen her hands shaking. It was *not* okay, but she was here, and his rationale made sense to her for now...if anything could make sense.

She took the flight of stairs and found what looked to be a guest room/office. Sterling had good taste, or else a decorator. He'd spared no expense, from little Limoges to elegant tapestries on the chairs and sofa in the office. The rooms had a traditional feel to them, all with a kind of horse/hunting theme. There were pictures of Sterling with just about everyone from the polo club; photos from his modeling and acting gigs; and one of him with Tommy and Zach, which had to have been taken last summer. The three of them were at the beach. It was the same photo that had been in the newspaper. Michaela took that one off the wall and shone the light on it. She studied it for a few seconds—three buddies, hanging out, having fun. Something about it, though. She knew there was more to the story of last summer than what Camden had uncovered. She placed the photo on the desk, hearing Joe downstairs. She ventured into Sterling's tidy bedroom. Sterling had been a neat freak, or else he had a maid—more likely, it had been the latter.

Michaela was curious about Sterling's expenditures. Here was a man who'd been used to living on twenty grand a month. Then last summer, according to Paige, he'd received the slap in the face when his allowance had been chopped in half. Then, he asked Paige for a loan and she'd taken money from her dead son's life insurance to give to him. Living "rich" meant something to Sterling. Was that why he had been dating Juliet? He didn't want to live a life less than he was used to, and Juliet's father was loaded.

She opened up the drawers on his nightstand and found a book, *The Kama Sutra*, as well as a list of acting jobs available in both Los Angeles and Palm Springs. He'd checked some off. There was a ticket stub from the club Sinners and Saints. From what Michaela had heard, this was the new hot spot for anyone who was anyone in the desert. But no letter.

She headed to a matching nightstand on the other side. This drawer was more interesting. In it she found a handful of videotapes. She pocketed them, knowing it was wrong. But Joe was right: What would Sterling care at this point? She walked over to his drawers, feeling creepy looking through his boxers and socks. *Really creepy*. But nothing was out of the ordinary. Next was his closet, and she even found herself digging into his pants pockets, where she found something interesting: an airline ticket. She looked at the date. Sterling had flown to Santa Barbara only two weeks earlier. Had he gone there for fun? Inside the folder was also his information for a rental car. Why hadn't he driven? It was only a half-day's drive. Had he gone to see his family? That had to be it. Had he gone to plead his case? And while there, had he sealed the deal on his fate?

The more she dug into Sterling Taber's life, the more twisted and strange it was becoming. Regardless, she had to find out why Sterling had gone home and what had happened there.

Michaela trekked downstairs with her new goodies. Joe stood at the bottom of the stairs. He waved an envelope at her. "Here it is. I read it and you should see what it says."

"Really? You found it?"

He nodded. "Right here in the 'to be filed' stack." He laughed.

"No kidding. What does it say?"

Before he could reply, a rustling noise came from outside the front door. "What was that?" Michaela whispered.

"I don't know." He grabbed her arm as they heard what sounded like a key being slid into the lock. "Come on."

They ran upstairs and into Sterling's bedroom. "Oh God, what if it's the police?" Michaela asked.

"I don't know. Let me think."

They heard the door shut, and then voices—a man and a woman's. Michaela strained to listen. Was it Peters and his sidekick, Singer?

Joe walked to the balcony off Sterling's bedroom. As quietly as he could he slid the door open.

"What was that?" the woman downstairs said.

"I don't know. Stay here and I'll check it out," the man replied.

They heard someone climbing the stairs. Joe motioned for Michaela to follow him onto the balcony. The area overlooked the community pool from two stories up. A palm tree swayed silently in the slight breeze, about two feet away from the balcony. "Hit it, Mick."

"What?"

"No time for questions. Jump onto the tree and shinny your ass on down."

"No way." The man on the stairs was almost to the top, Michaela figured.

"Do it, *now*."

Michaela knew Joe was right; they had no choice. Luckily for her she was athletic, so she took the chance and made the jump, then shinnied down the tree. She felt the pain in her hands and on her right knee. She leaped off the tree about five feet from the ground and looked up to see Joe attempting the jump. She closed her eyes. He might have been one savvy guy, but athleticism was not one of his attributes. Somehow, he made it.

They tore out of the parking lot in the minivan. "Shouldn't have had that burrito," he said. By the time they cleared the parking lot, they could not help but laugh. They roared for several minutes. For Michaela, part of the laughter was caused by the reality that she'd made it out of there without getting caught—well, basically—and the release of her pent-up stress.

"Oh my gosh, you should have seen yourself coming down off that tree," she said, tears streaming down her face. "I didn't know that you could move that fast, Joe."

"I didn't either. Yeah, that was classic."

"That wasn't Peters. Was it?" Michaela asked, already sure she knew the answer.

"Nope. I'd bet you it was Zach and Juliet."

"I'd bet you're right."

Joe reached into his back pocket and pulled out an envelope. She took the crumpled paper and turned on the overhead light in the minivan. "Do you mind? Will the light bother you?"

"Nah. I'm cool. Read it."

She read over the words that Juliet had written:

I know what you did. My father knows what you did, because I told him and for your sake, I would get out of town. You are disgusting and horrible and I will never trust you again. My father is out for blood. You've messed with the wrong family.

JM

"Whoa," Michaela finally uttered. "No wonder the two of them wanted the letter. Maybe they didn't murder Sterling, but what if they are protecting Juliet's dad?"

"Yep. It's a good theory, and we can't leave out Pepe Sorvino and his daughter."

"What do you think this all means? It's obvious Juliet wrote it. These are her initials, she and Zach were talking about it out at the barn, and those two are awfully friendly with each other these days. And all this stuff about her and her father knowing what he did...Wait a minute, I just had a thought about what Juliet might've told her father."

"What's that?"

Michaela quickly told Joe about the newspaper articles that Camden had found concerning Sterling Taber and Rebecca Woodson. "Follow me. The letter that Juliet wrote to Sterling may have to do with this girl."

"It might. But why wouldn't Juliet just break up with him?" Joe asked. "Why go through the whole deal of telling her dad and all? Sterling was never convicted of killing the girl. You said that the papers reported it to be an accident."

"I don't know. But Rebecca Woodson's family filed a wrongful death suit. They don't seem to think it was an accident."

"Okay. Keep talking. Go back to Sunday at the fashion show. Maybe you missed something."

"Juliet seemed flushed and hurried. Camden had thought she and Sterling were off together because she couldn't find either one of them. She offered Juliet a shot of tequila after she showed up, but she refused and got up on the stage."

Joe nodded. "But what about Zach? Where was he during all of this?"

"On the runway," Michaela replied. "I saw him up there, and then Juliet came rushing through because she was next. He asked her if she was okay when he saw her stepping up on the stage as he was getting down. She nodded and the show went on."

"One thing we know then is that Zach didn't kill Sterling, so we can cross him off the list, but what we don't know is if he's protecting Juliet. From the sound of it, he's protecting her from *something*. We can also guess they're protecting her father. Strange, though, I don't think Daddy would go and advertise to his little girl that he planned to knock off her boyfriend."

"No. I agree with that. Let's stay with this train of thought, that the murder has to do with Rebecca Woodson," Michaela said.

"Okay, we'll see if we can't peel this back a bit more and give each of them a motive. I know we can only theorize but it might help. Say Juliet felt threatened by Sterling. Maybe the dude did kill this Rebecca Woodson. He might have threatened Juliet for something; maybe she didn't want to see him anymore for another reason. Who knows if there was a lovers' quarrel? Say there was. Taber threatens Juliet Mitchell, who tells Zach, who is their buddy. Now, Juliet is a pretty girl, and Zach may have had a thing for her. You said they were all kinda lovey-dovey when you spotted them in the stall area?"

Michaela nodded. "Definitely. I would even go so far as to say that they looked to be more than friends."

"Okay. Zach sees an opening where Sterling screwed up with the girl. He's there for her to lean on and she tells him that Sterling threatened her. Zach was in Santa Barbara with Sterling when this Rebecca Woodson died?"

"Yes. And what if Zach knows that her death wasn't an accident and thinks that Sterling might have killed her? He decides to protect Juliet, and one or the other goes and tells her father about Sterling's threat and what happened in Santa Barbara."

"We're like a regular Holmes and Watson, girl."

She smiled. "Sort of, huh? Now, Ed Mitchell hears this and he's not happy. He kills Sterling. Zach and Juliet assume he did it because they told him about Sterling and maybe Ed went ballistic. Now Zach and Juliet feel the need to protect her father."

"Exactly. The kicker is, where does Pepe Sorvino and his clan come in and what's the deal with the ring that you saw Mitchell give to Pepe?"

"A payoff?"

Joe clucked his tongue. "Possible. I'm gonna call around to a few of my cousins and see if the Sorvinos have any ties with one of the families."

"Mafia?"

Joe shrugged and wheeled the van onto her property.

"Wouldn't you know that already? With your connections?"

"You've watched one too many *Sopranos*."

She shook her head. They pulled up in front of her house. Michaela extracted the videotapes from the backpack she'd taken into Sterling's place. "Wanna watch some movies?"

Joe looked at his watch. "Can't. What you got?"

"Compliments of Sterling."

"You little vixen."

"Never know what we might find. I figured I might as well grab them. We've already broken a hundred laws tonight."

"Report back. I told Marianne I'd be back before Conan. We like to watch it together."

"Deal."

Michaela went inside her house. A quiet staleness that she had never gotten used to since her old lab, Cocoa, passed away came over her. She sighed. What it must feel like to come home to a family. Lucky Joe.

She got her video camera out. These videos hadn't been transferred from the camera-type cassettes. She would have to put them through her camera to see, and then run it on her laptop. Maybe she'd make some popcorn for the evening's entertainment. Probably just shots of high-priced vacations that he'd taken. She put some popcorn in the microwave, grabbed a bottle of water, and started watching the first tape while it popped.

The bag remained in the microwave before she ever got to it, an hour later. What she saw on the tapes was not only startling, they also revealed someone who would have one helluva reason to put Sterling in the ground, where he couldn't speak a damn word.

TWENTY-THREE

WHAT MICHAELA VIEWED ON THOSE TAPES WAS completely scandalous. They were appalling, so much so that she had to fast-forward through quite a bit of it. All she could do was repeat the word *wow* over and over again, and shake her head.

All the tapes, except one, displayed a story of a love affair, if that's what it could be called. More of an *erotic* affair. The stars were Sterling and a woman she had never seen before, and they did things on those tapes together that she had no clue were even possible. One tape featured some other gal with Sterling. Probably a one-night stand. Is this what Juliet had discovered—that Sterling had this disgustingly perverted side to him? Had he taped *her*?

Michaela had never seen an X-rated movie—never had an inclination to—but what she saw on the tapes was likely way up there in that category. It was actually gross. The thing was, it became obvious to Michaela that the woman who was on most of the tapes had no clue she was starring in them. At the end of the last tape, which she assumed was the most recent one taken, Sterling sat by himself at the end of his bed. He slicked back his hair with his hands, sighed, and started speaking:

"As you can see, Carolyn, we've had quite a run, and I'm sure Charles will not be a happy man when he receives these tapes. Don't bother destroying them. I have a few copies in select places. You've been charming and fun and it is obvious that you make an excellent star, but you have not come through for me as you had promised." He raised his voice now, sounding like a madman. Ha! Michaela had always sensed there was something lurking underneath that suave, smooth exterior and here it was, coming out of him as a freakish pervert. "You, my dear, promised to get me back in good with the family and make sure my allowance not only matched what it once was, but was increased substantially. You've failed miserably. I am now giving you, as of today, one week to make good on your promises, or else something tells me that you won't be getting a dime of the Taber fortune once the family sees this. I don't have much more to lose, but you, my dear, have what, forty, fifty million that would slip out of your nasty little hands—which I love, by the way. One week, Carolyn. One week."

With that the tape finished up. The date flashed across the screen. It was almost a week to the day before Sterling was murdered.

Holy flying horse pucky. Who was the woman who had made promises to Sterling that she couldn't keep?

* * *

MICHAELA WRACKED HER BRAIN AND WENT OVER everything about three hundred times. At least it felt that way. Finally, at about 1:30 in the morning, she started to drift off to sleep, and that's when she heard it. At first it was like the moment when falling asleep as the body drifts into that next stage, almost as if the soul is being shaken loose—the body jerks and then a deep sleep follows. The jerk came, but not the sleep. A noise in the house. She sat up and listened. Had she started dreaming? No. There it was again—in the kitchen. What if someone was rummaging for a weapon—a knife? She quietly slid out of bed and tiptoed over to her bedroom door; she kept a baseball bat behind it. She now realized that she should've been keeping it next to her bed. What good would it have done her if whoever was down there had made it upstairs without her hearing? The phone. She needed to get to the phone and call 911. Dammit, she'd left the portable phone in her office. She wished for the day when phones couldn't travel all over the house, when they had cords on them and were stationary. Yes, that would've worked much better right about now.

She heard a creaking sound. Whoever was there now climbed the stairs. She gripped the bat tighter and hid behind the door. She stood still as she watched a figure enter the room. It was not a man, but a woman, and as Michaela switched on the light, she was stunned to see Juliet Mitchell spin around and point a gun at her.

TWENTY-FOUR

"JULIET! WHAT IN THE HELL ARE YOU DOING?" Michaela white-knuckled the baseball bat, poised and ready to swing. "Put the gun down."

"Give me the letter!" Juliet yelled. Her tearstained face was streaked in black from mascara. She did not look well, and if Michaela was right, she smelled of alcohol.

"Juliet, let's talk about this. Rationally. You put the gun down and I'll put the bat down and we can talk. Okay?"

"Give me the letter. I won't let you ruin my life!"

"I don't want to ruin your life. Let's talk."

"No. You don't understand."

"Tell me then, what don't I understand?"

"Juliet, put the gun down!" Zach Holden, standing behind the girl, looked as horrified as Michaela felt. "Please, Jules. This won't solve anything. Let's work together on this."

Michaela wasn't too sure she should be relieved to see Zach or not, but if he could get Juliet to put the gun down, she at least would still have the bat in her hands.

"Why should I? If anything happens to my dad, then what good is any of this? Especially after what you told me tonight!"

"Juliet, all I was trying to say is that we're young and we don't need to rush anything. This has nothing to do with your father."

"It has *everything* to do with my dad! Everything. You're just like Sterling. All you want is one thing." Positioned between Zach and Michaela, Juliet weaved a bit to the side. Michaela looked for the right moment to pounce. But she had no idea where Zach stood in all of this.

"My dad only wants to protect me and I thought that was what you wanted, too." She turned away from Michaela and pointed the gun at Zach.

"That's not true," Zach replied. "I'm sorry about tonight. You surprised me is all. I thought we agreed to take things slow. The marriage thing, it was out of the blue. You've got to admit that. But, I'm not opposed to getting married at some point."

Michaela saw that Zach was trying to save his skin, but she hoped it wasn't as obvious to the girl. "I believe him, Juliet. Give me the gun and you and Zach can go and work things out."

"Give me back the letter. We know you were at Sterling's tonight. It had to be you. You overheard us in the barn at the polo field." Juliet slumped to the floor, and Michaela and Zach both seized the opportunity. Zach wrapped his arms tightly around her, and shook the gun out of her hand, and Michaela quickly picked it up. She didn't want to aim it at anyone, but she needed the power right now. Still, instead of turning it on either one of them, she simply held it, while Zach wrestled with Juliet, who finally calmed down and began crying into his shoulder.

Michaela had a lot of questions and she was in no mood to not have them answered. "Okay, it's truth time for all of us. I know about the letter and what it says. What you wrote in there, Juliet, is disturbing to say the least. It's obvious to me that you and Zach are protecting your father because he murdered Sterling, and I have been made the fall guy. Frankly I don't care how it was done, but you two are going to tell the police. And—how in the hell did you get into my house?" Her body quickly filled with a heated rage. Tomorrow she planned to start looking for a new four-legged companion.

"The letter...yes, Juliet wrote it," Zach said.

"Got that much. Why don't we start with tonight, Juliet? How did you get in here?"

"Your kitchen window was cracked and I crawled through."

Here Michaela thought she'd been careful when she locked up each night. Living in the back forty wasn't apparently as safe as it once was. "Did you actually think you would find the letter and get out of here without me knowing? And you." She turned to Zach. "How did *you* get in, and how do you play into all of this other than wanting to protect Juliet and—from what I gather—keep on jumping her bones?"

Zach sighed. "We went out tonight. We figured that you'd overheard us in the barn talking about the letter and then when we got into Sterling's place, we knew it had to be you who was there. We tried to figure out how we could get the letter from you."

"How did you know that I even had it?"

"We didn't for sure, but we needed to know. Juliet drank more than usual and she was talking nonsense about coming here and confronting you and getting the letter back. I told her that we needed to wait until tomorrow and then we could all have a sensible discussion about it."

"I would've appreciated that, rather than having a gun pointed at me." Michaela wasn't completely buying their story. For all she knew they'd come here to kill her.

"I told her it was crazy, and we argued about other stuff."

"Uh-huh."

"When I dropped her off at home, I had a bad feeling that she might do something stupid, which she did. I called her a few times and when she finally answered she said that she was on her way to get the letter from you."

"So, you drove out here and obviously saw how she'd gotten in, made your way in as well, and here we all are—the three musketeers." She turned to the inebriated Juliet. "You're lucky you didn't kill yourself or someone else in your condition," Michaela snapped. "Okay, the letter. I'm not giving it back, and seeing how I now have the gun in my possession, we're going to call the police and the two of you are going to tell them everything that you know."

"We didn't do anything!" Juliet cried. "We didn't kill Sterling."

"I believe that. But you did break into my house and hold a gun on me, and I think you're protecting your dad, who may have killed him." Michaela tried to change her tone to one of empathy. She understood the need to protect a parent. Over the years she'd shielded her own father, who had fought his gambling addictions on and off, but this was far worse. Juliet was protecting her father from murder and had involved Zach to a point that the two of them could possibly be considered as accomplices.

"She's right, Juliet," Zach said.

"No. We don't know for sure it was my dad."

"Can I ask you what you told your father and why you think he might have killed Sterling?" She looked at Zach. "Does it have to do with Rebecca Woodson's death? I know about last summer."

Zach nodded. "I'm the one who told Juliet about that. I saw her getting serious over Sterling and I knew that his intentions weren't always honest. He was known for telling a woman one thing and then doing another. I thought he was stringing her along like he had Rebecca, and I didn't want her to get hurt."

"Do you believe that Sterling had something to do with Rebecca's death?"

He shrugged. "I don't know what to believe. I was driving home the night of the party. Sterling denies he had anything to do with Rebecca going off that pier, but Tommy Liggett was there and he confided in me that he saw Sterling follow Rebecca out on that deck. Look, Sterling was a complicated guy and I didn't know if Juliet could trust him."

"You and Sterling were friends, though."

He laughed. "Sterling had a lot of *friends*. He had friends out of convenience. When it worked for him, then it was all good. If there was someone better to hang out with, though, he'd leave you high and dry. People understood that about him. The only real buddy he ever had was Justin Nightingale. When Justin was alive those two were tight."

Robert and Paige's son. That part of the web had not been unraveled enough just yet, but she had to take it one step at a time. "And this didn't bother you? You went and hung out with him for a part of your summer."

"I was only in Santa Barbara for a weekend."

"I feel sick," Juliet said.

"Sit down," Michaela told her and pointed to her reading chair and ottoman in the corner of the room. The danger appeared to be over, and before she picked up the phone and called Peters she wanted to try and get as many answers as she could out of these two, although it looked as if Juliet was going to pass out.

She turned back to Zach. "Why did you go to the coast with Tommy and Sterling?"

"Why not? Tommy had been out there already with him for a month and said it was a blast. Sterling paid for everything. I thought it would be cool, so I went."

"And you met Rebecca Woodson."

Zach nodded. "Everyone met Rebecca. Total party girl, who wanted more from Sterling than he could give, but he fed her lines, you know—stuff like she could come visit him. He even told her he'd get her a place to stay in the desert. Stupid stuff for him to say, because we all knew that he wouldn't live up to it. I left because I was kind of over the scene and his bull."

"Do you think Ed Mitchell killed Sterling?"

"I don't know. I think he's very protective of Juliet and he'd do anything for her."

"And so would you."

"Yes," he replied quietly.

"Even if it meant sending an innocent woman to jail."
"I'm sorry. You have to understand—"
"No, I don't! And now you have to tell the police what you know. As far as the letter goes. I don't think it's necessary for us to tell the cops how either one of us might have it in our possession, but I'm giving it to them."
"You can't give them the letter." He pointed to Juliet, who had passed out in Michaela's chair.
"I don't care about your promises, Zach. I think you're a good man with ethics. I really do, and now is the time to live up to them. If Ed Mitchell is guilty and I go to jail for something that I didn't do, can you honestly live with yourself?"
Zach stood there for a moment, then pulled out his cell phone.
"Who are you calling?" Michaela asked.
"The police."

TWENTY-FIVE

DETECTIVE PETERS SEEMED TO BE AS THRILLED to see Michaela at three o' clock in the morning as she was to see him, which was not at all. But maybe they could get this mess straightened out and her life back to normal.

Peters questioned Zach over and over on his story. He stayed true to Michaela, but Juliet, when woken, freaked out and blabbed everything.

"She broke into Sterling's house." She pointed at Michaela. "And stole a letter that I'd written to him."

"Is that true, Ms. Bancroft?"

How was she going to get out of this? But Zach cut in. "That's not true. We went into Sterling's house. I found the letter and didn't tell Juliet. I told her that someone else had been there and taken it. I made up the story about seeing Ms. Bancroft there."

Juliet's jaw dropped. "What! I heard someone in his place, too. Why are you lying?"

"You came here in the middle of the night to tell Ms. Bancroft this?" Peters eyed them.

Michaela nodded and shot a warning glance at Juliet, figuring that Zach would possibly corroborate with her about Juliet breaking into her house and pointing a gun at her.

"Where is the letter now?"

Before the police arrived Michaela had taken it from her purse and brought it downstairs. She grabbed it off the coffee table and handed it to Peters.

"This all smells foul to me, Ms. Bancroft." He read it, then said, "If you think that this letter alone merits me waking up one of the most prominent men in this county to be questioned, then you are sorely mistaken."

"What? You're not going to question Ed Mitchell?"

"We've already questioned Mr. Mitchell and he has an airtight alibi during the time of death. He was with a group of people all day at the event and they have all checked out."

"You're not going to look into that then?" She pointed at the letter.

"I'll speak to him about it, but I don't think it has anything to do with Sterling Taber's murder."

Michaela had no response. If Ed had an alibi then the letter probably didn't mean a damn thing. "Don't you have any more to ask them?" Michaela looked at Zach and Juliet.

"Good night, Ms. Bancroft," Peters replied and opened the door, following Zach and Juliet out.

What a total mess. Had they screwed up by calling the police? At least Zach had defended her. He was a decent guy, or had possibly changed his mind about being head over heels for Juliet when she pointed the gun at him. God, how love was so very blind. Here a man was willing to protect the woman he thought he loved, and her father, and deny the truth, likely sending an innocent woman to jail. Crazy.

If Ed had an alibi, what did that mean for her? It meant that she's just wasted half a night of sleep and risked her freedom—and Joe's—at Sterling's place by breaking and entering. That's what it meant. It also meant that she hadn't figured things out yet.

There were still so many what-ifs, including the mystery woman on the videotapes that Sterling had made, the Sorvino clan, Robert Nightingale's vendetta toward Sterling, and, from Paige's account, his now supposed missing-in-action status. Lest Michaela forget, there was also Erin Hornersberg, who had already killed someone in the past, and who thought Sterling lower than a dust mote. She'd sure clammed up when Michaela and Camden had gone to talk to the makeup artist.

Then there was this bizarre situation with Sterling's old girlfriend Rebecca Woodson, the dead party girl. Michaela should've asked Zach about Sterling's family and what they were like. She would have to talk to Tommy Liggett about that. Tommy had spent more time last summer with Sterling than Zach had. Maybe he could shine some light on what had happened there. And there was the undercover blonde woman in the Ford Explorer who was keeping tabs on Michaela. It all seemed so strange; none of it made sense, but at that point her brain was fried from trying to piece any of it together. She decided to try and get some rest.

* * *

MICHAELA DIDN'T GET MUCH MORE SLEEP. AFTER tossing and turning for an hour, she got up and made a pot of strong coffee. She didn't know if she'd ever felt so exhausted before. Always an early riser, getting started in the morning wasn't typically a problem. Her life had been filled with plenty of ups and downs, like most people, but before this fiasco she'd finally settled into a peaceful place in her life. Her ranch was a wonderful place to live; she woke up and took care of her animals every day; she taught sweet and special children how to ride; and she thought that maybe there was a possibility with her and Jude. Only a week ago, she'd been able to wake up and be grateful for all that was right in her life. Today, it was hard to do, but she did it anyway, thankful that her animals were there waiting for her and happy to see her. And she was thankful for the caffeine. She was going to need it. Only two hours until Sterling's funeral service; she'd have to psych herself up for the appearance.

She weighed her options. None of them looked too great. Facts were that if she went, all eyes would likely be on her, including Detective Peters, who would surely show up. Wasn't that what investigators did while on a case? Show up at the funeral in case the perp made a wrong move? Oh goodness, she had watched one too many *Law & Orders*. Had Peters really questioned Ed Mitchell? What if

Juliet had convinced Peters that Michaela had stolen the letter? She knew she couldn't continue to lie to him. It wasn't who or what she was, and it could prove to be the final slice in cutting her own throat.

The downside of not going to the service was that she had a gut feeling whoever did kill Sterling *would* be there, and maybe, just maybe, she would pick up on something that the police had missed.

She slipped into a black dress, knowing that she had no choice but to make an appearance at that funeral. She would do her best to make herself nondescript. Maybe no one would notice her. Yeah, right.

Her plan didn't work. As expected, Detective Peters was at the church. He eyed her when she came in. Maybe she was being paranoid, but damned if a lot of people didn't stare at her when she walked in. So much for the nondescript, inconspicuous part. She tried to not allow him to unnerve her. Paranoid. That's all. She was being paranoid.

Then she spotted Robert and Paige Nightingale, which was odd to say the least. Hadn't Robert left Paige only two days before, his anger getting the best of him? And where was Camden? She had chutzpah when it came to the down and dirty questions. Robert's arm was wrapped protectively around Paige's shoulders. Quite a change of heart. Obviously they'd worked out their differences. Or not. Could it be that Paige knew something about Robert that he did not want the world to know? Maybe that he'd killed Sterling out of rage and now he needed her as an alibi? Was it possible that Robert had murdered Sterling over his grief and his belief that he was to blame for his son's death? Paige had replaced her child, in a sense, with Sterling. Loss of a loved one was the worst kind of grief. Michaela knew it firsthand. Maybe Paige couldn't take any more loss in her life, and had told Robert that she'd speak the truth if he tried to divorce her. Michaela had pegged Paige for an insecure woman. Would her sadness and insecurities force her to remain in a dead marriage? If Michaela had learned anything on this path called life, it was that everything was a possibility.

She decided to take a seat at the back of the church to be able to watch as people flowed quietly in and slipped into their seats. This way she'd be able to get a good look at everyone who showed up.

Watching the Nightingales seat themselves, she again thought about Robert's possible reason to want Sterling dead, and she understood it. She could not imagine what it would feel like to lose a child. If Robert truly blamed Sterling for the untimely and horrible death of his son, then she could almost understand his need for vengeance. But what about Paige? She'd been distraught the other day in Robert's office. Did *she* have anything to do with Sterling's murder? These questions needed answers. Michaela was still searching. But what reason would Paige have to kill Sterling? It didn't add up. So for now, she'd cross her off her list. She'd also been able to satisfy her mind that neither Zach nor Juliet had anything to do with Sterling's murder. True, they'd been up to no good, but she didn't think them responsible for killing him. Juliet's father didn't look as if he was a candidate any longer, but what about any one of the Sorvinos? She thought about the ring she saw Ed give Pepe. Had it been a payoff of some sort?

She watched as people continued coming into the church. Zach entered with Tommy Liggett, who Michaela felt could have some answers for her, at least about Sterling's family and Rebecca Woodson. Tommy worked for Juliet's father at the jewelry store. From all accounts, Tommy appeared to be a nice enough guy. But even nice people had skeletons to hide sometimes, and Michaela couldn't help but wonder if Tommy was one of those nice-guy-next-door types who one day went psycho on his good friend for a particular reason—or for no particular reason at all. Tommy had wavy light brown hair, sincere blue eyes, and dimples when he smiled. In a way he looked similar to Sterling, but was cuter, rather than handsome, like his pal had been.

Michaela turned as someone touched her shoulder. "I wasn't sure you'd be here, what with the bad press," Camden said.

"I had no choice but to come. Wish I hadn't though; everyone is looking at me."

"Relax. No one is looking at you. And if they do, I'll stick my tongue out at them."

Music began playing, an indicator that the services were about to start. As several latecomers filed in, Michaela's gaze fell on a man and whom she assumed to be his wife being escorted to the front row. "Are those Sterling's parents?" Michaela whispered in Camden's ear.

"I don't think so. He had told me that his folks were older. Those two look, what, in their forties. At least, the man looks like that. I can't tell with the woman."

Michaela nodded. The woman's head was down and it was difficult to get a good look at her face. "Well, they must be relatives."

"It would figure, but I'm not sure. I didn't know him that well to get his life story."

"You knew him pretty well."

Camden rolled her eyes. "You are mean sometimes."

"I know."

* * *

THE PARISHIONERS LISTENED TO THE HEARTFELT service given by the pastor, whom Michaela was pretty sure had never even met Sterling, as he spoke in generalities about the man. Something told her that Sterling didn't frequent church much.

When the pastor finished, he invited any attendees up to the podium who wished to eulogize him. It was strange, but no one took him up on the opportunity. Did *everyone* harbor ill will toward Sterling? After a minute, Tommy decided to go up. Michaela could tell by the way he moved back and forth from one foot to the other that he was nervous being in front of the crowd.

"Sterling was a good guy, a good friend, and all-around good man."

Michaela scanned the crowd and took note that Ed Mitchell had a protective arm around his daughter. Was he as uncomfortable as Tommy looked to be? Then she noticed Zach. He actually appeared almost bored. What a different crowd they all were.

Tommy went on to relate a humorous story about Sterling falling off one of his polo ponies and having to ice his rear. He got a few chuckles from that and then sat down.

Michaela figured they were about finished when the gentleman from the front row took his turn at the podium. All he said when he took the stand was, "On behalf of the Taber family, we thank you for coming today to honor my brother. Sterling's life was amongst his friends, and thus his family has made the decision to have him buried here, where he was loved by so many. Thank you again."

Hmmm. So the older, distinguished guy was Sterling's brother. Okay, so maybe, just maybe, there was an off chance that Sterling's family showed compassion for him by wanting to bury the man in Indio, but she doubted it. Here the brother was the only one making an appearance at the service and that was all he had to say about his sibling? Oh, that made her skin crawl. No, there was more to it. The Taber family wanted nothing at all to do with Sterling. Not in life or in death. That was as plain and simple as it seemed. It made her feel very sorry for Sterling, and actually she started to form a better picture of what appeared to be a lost soul. Not that she agreed with some of the things he'd apparently done or the way he'd conducted his life, but there may have been some deep, dark reasons for Sterling's actions and behavior. Michaela couldn't help wonder if the man's way of life had caused his own demise—a death that maybe his family was behind, wanting to rid themselves of any more scandal he might cause them.

TWENTY-SIX

MICHAELA'S STOMACH CHURNED AS SHE APPROACHED Sterling's brother and his wife. She had no clue what she would say. "Um, why is it that your family ostracized Sterling when he was never charged with or convicted of a crime?" No, that would probably not go over too well. She could not help thinking though that the Tabers had distanced themselves from Sterling because of what had happened to Rebecca Woodson.

She decided on the practical, caring approach. "Um, excuse me, Mr. Taber?"

Sterling's brother turned around. He had slicked-back silver hair and the same blue eyes that, for Sterling, had caused most women to melt. Granted, they hadn't done a damn thing for Michaela, but she appeared to be in the minority. Mr. Taber was of average height and looked to be physically fit underneath what was likely a silk Italian suit specially tailored for him.

Then his wife turned around and Michaela's blood ran cold.

"Yes?" Sterling's brother said.

Michaela tried not to stammer as she made every effort to take her eyes off his wife. She was as beautiful as the brother was handsome, albeit in a sort of "shiny and bright" high-society way. Her obscenely large diamond ring sparkled in the desert sun. But it wasn't the diamond that stunned Michaela, it was the fact that Mrs. Taber was the star of Sterling's videos.

"Yes?" Mr. Taber said again. "Can I help you, miss?"

Michaela reached out her hand, somehow finding a way to string words together. "I'm so sorry for your family's loss. I'm sure it was quite a blow."

"Ah, another girlfriend, I suppose," he replied hesitatingly. He shook her hand lightly, as if she might break.

"No. No, not at all. I hardly knew Sterling. I was on his polo team for a few matches and took lessons where he boarded his horses—"

"Charles, we need to go," the wife interrupted. She looked Michaela up and down.

"I apologize, miss, but our jet is waiting. What did you say your name was?" the brother asked.

Michaela hesitated.

"I know who she is," the wife said coldly. "I've seen her in the news. She's the woman who murdered Sterling."

"No. No, I didn't! I would never kill anyone."

"She's crazy, Charles. I've read the papers. Let's go now."

Charles Taber studied her, his lips turning up at the ends. It sent a shiver down Michaela's backside, as she thought it an evil look. Then he shook her hand again. "Well. If you did it, thank you very much, and if not, as you say, I'm sorry for your troubles."

"Charles, we have to go."

"Yes, Carolyn. Good day, and good luck with your legal woes." The Tabers picked up their pace.

Michaela went after them, all the knots in her stomach gone and replaced by rage. "Wait a minute, wait just a minute. I had nothing to do with your brother's death, and frankly, I find your callousness revolting."

"I knew she was one of his women," Charles said to his wife.

"Dammit, I never dated Sterling. I didn't even like the man, but I didn't kill him and I feel terrible that he's dead."

"That would make sense since you are charged with his murder."

Michaela stared at these two insolent jerks for a second in an attempt to regain her composure. "You know what, I have to wonder about the two of you. Why are you so relieved that your brother is dead? I know all about the controversy last year out in Santa Barbara. And Mrs. Taber,

I could have sworn that I've seen you before? Were you ever in any movies or any type of *film* projects?"

Carolyn's face went ashen. "No! Charles, come on. I told you she was insane! She's a lunatic."

"Maybe it was those home movies that Sterling showed to some of us. I think maybe you were on vacation. I should send you a copy. I'm certain that it was you. I don't remember your husband in them, but yes...looking at you now, I'm sure of it."

"We've never been on vacation with Sterling," Charles Taber replied. He looked at his wife.

"I have no idea what you're talking about," Carolyn Taber snapped. "They can't lock you up soon enough! Charles, we have to go."

Carolyn turned and marched away. Charles gave Michaela a nod and followed his wife, who turned around when she reached the car and glared at Michaela. The woman was chock full of secrets that she aimed to expose.

Camden caught up with Michaela, who stood there stunned, watching the Tabers' town car pull away. "What was that all about?" she asked.

Michaela shook her head. "Those people are strange. Really strange, and I have to tell you that Sterling's sister-in-law has some ugly skeletons in her closet."

"All super rich people have stuff to hide."

"No. There's something more here. I've got proof that Sterling and his sister-in-law were having an affair."

"No! Oh come on."

Michaela nodded. "Oh yeah."

"You've got to take it to the police. Michaela, you and your snooping are going to get yourself killed."

Now there was a thought to mull over. Spend fifty years to life in prison or take the chance that she might actually figure this all out and save herself. "You're probably right, I do need to hand the tapes over to the police."

But the other dilemma with that was explaining how she came into possession of the tapes in the first place. If she told the truth it would confirm Juliet's story to the police about breaking into Sterling's place. And once that was affirmed...well, it would likely plant further doubt in Peters' mind and could possibly cause her to wind up in jail on separate charges. Plus, would evidence that she'd stolen be allowed in a court of law? Oh jeez, what a mess.

"Yes, you do. Michaela, don't go delving into their lives. It'll be trouble. Look what they did to Sterling. They banned him from the family."

Michaela crossed her arms. "They didn't exactly ban him. They cut his allowance in half. And most of America wouldn't complain about Sterling's ten grand a month. I'm not sure what you don't get about the fact that I was arrested for Sterling's murder. If I don't find out who killed him, Mrs. Robinson..." Camden frowned. "Then I am screwed. Totally screwed. No more horse training, no more helping children, no more having margaritas with you as the sun goes down. Nothing, *nada, finito*. Get it?"

"I get it. Okay, let's figure this thing out. What do we need to do?"

"We need to find out exactly what happened last summer and how those two are connected. I want to know why his parents weren't here today, and see if we can find out who else knew about the affair."

"I'm on it. I've got some friends in the jet-set circle in Santa Barbara. Maybe I can call around, see what the gossip is. I need to head over to the shop. Are you going to the polo lounge?"

"I don't want to, but I think I will." The polo team had gotten together and planned a celebration of life after the service. Michaela thought it would be a decent idea to continue poking around.

* * *

THE EVENT LOOKED TO HAVE MORE PEOPLE AT IT than the actual funeral service. The Sorvinos were milling around, of course. Michaela caught Lucia's eye as she served slices of gourmet pizzas to guests and Mario poured drinks. Lucia shook her head at Michaela and rolled her eyes. If there weren't a hundred people milling around, she'd consider strangling the brat. Michaela didn't see Pepe but assumed he was in the kitchen.

Robert and Paige sat at one of the tables with their food and wine. Michaela was beyond caring much what they might think of her. She wanted to know about that invoice, and also how the two of them had made nice with each other. She walked over and sat down with them. No time to be shy. "Nice turnout."

"Yes," Paige said.

"It's also good to see that you two have obviously worked things out."

Robert looked at Paige and then Michaela.

Paige's eyed widened like a deer caught in the headlights. "I...told Michaela what was going on between us," she said.

"Oh," Robert muttered. He took a sip of his wine, then set it down as he searched for the right words. "I needed to blow off steam, that's all, and sometimes I lose my temper. I didn't think Paige would take it seriously. I sure didn't think she'd tell anyone."

"I was upset, honey—"

"Anyway, it is nice that you are working it out," Michaela interrupted. So, Paige had not told Robert that she'd been discussing the state of their marriage with anyone. "I can understand why you would have been upset, Robert."

Paige eyed her.

"I think that I would have been upset, too, if my spouse was secretly giving money to a man I thought responsible in some way for my own son's death."

"Michaela!" Paige exclaimed.

Michaela felt bad about saying it. It certainly wasn't her finest moment, but these two had been acting strange and, dammit, she needed to get to the truth here.

Robert sighed. "No, it's fine. I never talk about Justin. Ever. And today, burying Sterling, it has stirred up memories. I understand why my wife did what she did. At first when she told me, I struggled with it. But knowing Paige, she didn't do it out of maliciousness. She wanted to help Sterling and he'd been a link to Justin."

Michaela nodded, encouraging him to continue. God, she really did not enjoy taking Robert on a walk down memory lane. It had to be painful, but maybe through that pain the truth would be revealed.

"What Paige didn't understand was that I had seen the manipulative side of Sterling and, yes, I did blame him in part for Justin's death. But that wasn't Paige's fault, and I don't want to lose her now either."

"Oh honey." Paige took Robert's hand.

Michaela actually believed him. His emotion and sentiment were too real. He did love his wife, but that didn't mean he hadn't murdered Sterling. "I'm sorry to be so nosy, but I have to ask you something, Robert."

"Sure. I think you will anyway."

Michaela smiled. "The day that Sterling was killed and you went and got my mallet, did you see anyone else around your office?"

"There were a lot of people all over the grounds that day."

"I know, but can you think of anyone who stands out? I know that the mallet was wiped clean before I used it. If you didn't have your gloves on before you handed it to me, then your fingerprints would have been on there, too."

"You're not saying that Robert did this?" Paige asked.

"No. I'm asking him if he saw anyone around that might have stood out. That's what I'm thinking."

Robert swirled his wine around and frowned. "There was one gal who bumped into me and asked if I knew where to get a program. I thought it was kind of odd because they'd been handing them out as people came in. She didn't exactly fit the profile of somebody who would watch a polo match, if you know what I mean."

"No. What *do* you mean?" Michaela asked.

He shrugged. "She had tattoos and ears full of earrings, lots of dark makeup. That kind of thing."

"Purple, kind of magenta or hot pink–colored hair?" Michaela asked.

"Yes. You know her?"

"Erin Hornersberg."

"Who?"

"No one." She waved her hand dismissively. "Um, I don't know how to bring this up, so I am just going to do so. There was an invoice: one to Sterling, on your desk. I saw it. It was there that day, the day he was murdered. It had some not-so-nice words scrawled across it and a letter opener stabbed through it."

"Yes," Robert replied. "What about it?"

"Did you write 'Screw you' across it, or did Sterling?"

"I did," Paige replied.

"Why?" Michaela asked. She hadn't expected that answer.

"Robert and I had just had an argument about Sterling. He didn't know at that point that I was giving him any money."

Robert nodded. "I was upset because Sterling had come into the office and told me that he wasn't able to pay his bill for another week. He was already late. I felt he was taking my generosity for granted. I told him that since that was the case, the event that day would be his last. I didn't know that I was speaking the literal truth." Robert squeezed Paige's hand.

"When Robert told me what he'd said to Sterling, I became upset. In a way, I *did* see Sterling as a replacement for Justin, although now I see how crazy that was. I suppose I've never allowed myself to truly grieve over my son. Robert and I argued. He left and went to do something with the horses. I wrote it across the invoice and left."

"I found her at the charity event a little while later. Remember I told you that I didn't plan to go, but I changed my mind because I felt bad about our fight and I wanted to make it up to her. She told me that she was sorry for the note."

Michaela weighed their story. The two of them were looking at each other with tears in their eyes. She had the gut feeling that neither one had murdered Sterling. They were two sad and hurt people who truly needed each other and not any type of replacement to work through the void in their hearts.

She apologized for her questions and stood up. Turning, she saw Ed Mitchell walking toward her. He had two wineglasses in his hands. Giving one to Michaela, he said, "I understand that you think I'm a killer."

TWENTY-SEVEN

"I DON'T THINK YOU'RE A KILLER. I NEVER REALLY did, but...I had suspicions to go on." Michaela knew it sounded lame, but this was so awkward. Why didn't she just come right out and accuse him?

"Suspicions or not, you know me. If you had questions about me or my family, you should've come straight to me. I have nothing to hide. My daughter is distraught by your accusations and your sending the police my way. It's no trouble for me. I can handle Peters. However, Juliet is far more delicate and this situation is troubling her."

"Did Juliet tell you that she broke into my house?" Ed frowned.

Michaela glanced over Ed's shoulder and saw Juliet and Zach whispering at a table in the corner. She sighed. "Did Juliet tell you anything at all about last night? That she threatened me with a gun?" She noticed Ed flinch.

"I think that maybe we should discuss this outside."

She thought about this for a moment. "On the patio then."

Ed gestured for her to lead the way. Once outside they sat down at a small table. Ed leaned in. "Taber was a piece of shit and I don't care that he's dead." He shook a finger at her. "But I didn't kill the SOB. I didn't hire a hit man either, if that's what is going on in your curious mind. What I did was scare him away from my daughter. At least I tried to. Someone performed a service when they did away with him. Do I think you did it? No. I even told Peters that this morning when he rousted me at seven and quizzed me about that ridiculous letter my daughter wrote. Look, I had the guy followed. He was up to no good, screwing around on Juliet with anything that walked. Hell, Sorvino's little brat was on that list. I told Pepe he better keep an eye on his daughter, or else she could also wind up like that girl Juliet and Zach told me about in Santa Barbara."

"Rebecca Woodson."

"Yes. I know Taber got off on that rap, but he was one shady guy and I wouldn't doubt there was foul play involved. The last thing I wanted was to have Juliet carrying on with him."

Michaela didn't know what to say.

"My daughter doesn't always use common sense. I apologize for last night. I'm not pleased with what she and Zach did. I know you're no killer. My daughter should also know that I'm no killer. Saying that she was trying to protect me is ludicrous. I don't need any protection. I was with two other couples the day that Taber was murdered. She didn't know that because she was busy with the fashion show. But that is a fact."

"You say that you had Sterling followed?"

He nodded. "A private investigator."

"And Sterling and Lucia Sorvino were friends?"

"More than that. My guy followed them to the polo grounds, where they were messing around in a stall."

"Really? Do you know, then, why Lucia would finger me as someone who was screwing around with Sterling?"

"She did that?" He laughed. "She's a strange kid, and trouble, too. I have no idea."

"What about Pepe Sorvino?"

He shrugged. "What about him? Good man. Caters all of our parties. I respect his business and his family."

She nodded. "I see. Are you also friends?"

"We do business together."

"What kind of business?"

"You are one nosy woman. I'll indulge you, though, because I like your ambition. I told you that he caters my parties. He did such a wonderful job at our last party that I gave him a ring he wanted to give his wife for their thirtieth wedding anniversary."

That must have been what he'd been doing the day Michaela spotted them after Sterling had been murdered. Mitchell was paying Pepe in jewelry for a job he'd done.

"I certainly hope you get this straightened out, Michaela. If you need any help, let me know. Next time you think I might be involved in something sinister, communicate with me. It'll save you a lot of time and stress. Good to talk and air it out. I've got to go now. I need to see Tommy Liggett. We have a shipment due in this afternoon. I need to be sure that he's headed over there."

Michaela watched him saunter away, reminding her of a character Jack Nicholson might play.

She had pretty much reached the end of her rope and decided it was time to leave Sterling's memorial, maybe take another trail ride, or at the very least get out with the horses. Once again she needed to clear her mind, and the only way she knew how was by taking time out with her animals.

She didn't bother to say good-bye to anyone inside Sorvino's but instead walked to the parking lot. She did make a mental note that Tommy Liggett would be at Mitchell's jewelry store later in the day. She wanted to speak with him about last summer and hear his version of the Rebecca Woodson story.

As she wound down the hill from Sorvino's toward the main road, she spotted a black Ford Explorer at a stop sign in front of her. Sure there was more than one black Explorer around, but her gut told her that this was the same car that had followed her yesterday. She punched it and got right behind the vehicle, but then thought twice. It was the same car, and she knew it was because of the license plate. She'd been able to get the first three numbers and pass them on to Joe; now she read the other numbers and started repeating them out loud to memorize them. It looked to her like she'd found the driver who'd followed her into the shopping center.

She gave herself enough time to get behind a few cars after they turned out onto the main highway. She did note that whoever was driving did not appear to have long blonde hair. That made her wonder if she was on the right track, but intuition urged her on and she stuck with the car for about ten miles, until the driver turned into a residential area. Now she'd have to be more inconspicuous. She slowed her speed way down and figured that whoever was driving hadn't picked up on the fact that they were being followed, or else they would have made an attempt to lose her. At least that was her guess.

The vehicle finally stopped, and she pulled up in front of a house about a block away. Typical desert-style, flat-roofed homes lined the streets, their landscape a mixture of cactus, rock, and lawn. The area was a nice one, so people obviously made efforts to run their sprinkler systems and keep the greenery alive.

A man got out of the car—tall, dark-haired, wearing a suit. She squinted to get a better look at who it was. She knew him. He moved like a man on a mission, holding himself confidently and not really giving a damn what others thought. He shoved one hand into his pocket and headed toward the door. Yeah, she knew the guy—Mario Sorvino.

He walked up to the front door of the home, which was shrouded by bushes, and a woman came out to greet him. She had long dark hair—not blonde. Interesting. They hugged and kissed, then went inside the house. It had to be a girlfriend. It was the right Explorer, though. Those first three numbers gave it away.

After about ten minutes sitting in her truck and wondering what she should do, she decided to get out and search around the SUV. Sure it might be risky, but it was broad daylight and she'd scream bloody murder if Mario even came close to her. He was probably "busy" inside the house with the woman. She didn't know what she expected to find by peering into the back of the vehicle, or why she felt the need to do so. But she did, and what she saw on the backseat made her flinch: a blonde wig.

She hightailed it out of there, thinking, *Mario Sorvino with a blonde wig in the back of his car.* Mario Sorvino had followed her. Mario Sorvino said that Sterling got what he deserved, which appeared to be the consensus of many. But was Mario Sorvino the killer? Her jaw hurt as she realized she was clenching her teeth. Dammit, if she could tie things together and then take it all to the police, that's exactly what she would do. She needed Joe's help here. She tried to call him but didn't get an answer, so she left a voice mail.

Her phone rang and she immediately picked it up. It had to be Joe returning her call. To her surprise it was Ethan. "Hey, Mick. How are you?"

She didn't want to worry him, so she replied with the standard, "Fine. I'm fine."

"You don't sound fine," he replied. "You sound stressed. Why don't you come by and see your godson and get away for a bit?"

She sighed. "I would, but I'm just coming back from Sterling Taber's funeral and I'm not in the best of moods." She was trying to find some excuse. As much as Michaela would've loved to see Ethan and Josh, she doubted that Summer would welcome her with open arms. Whenever they did all get together there was a definite uneasiness between the two women.

"You went to the service? You are a glutton for punishment. All the more reason why you should stop by. Plus, I bought a new horse I want you to see."

"You did? That's great, but really, isn't Wednesday always your day off? You should hang out with your family."

"Mick, sometimes you can be so difficult. Stop acting like a pain in the ass and come see my new horse. I'd like to put him in training with you. He's a two-year-old, beautiful sorrel animal. Excellent bloodlines. Plenty of Peppy in him."

"Really?" She did like the sound of that. Okay, maybe she could deal with Summer for an hour.

"You're intrigued, I can tell. Come on over."

What was she thinking? She couldn't go to his place. She needed to track Joe down and find out what Mario Sorvino had been after and if he did Sterling in. Time was running out. Her parents would be returning from their vacation next week, and Jude was due back on Friday. She didn't want them to return home to this chaos that her life had rapidly become.

"You're coming, right? Only an hour. Come on, Joshy wants to see you. Me, too. I want to make sure you're as okay as you say you are."

She sighed. "Fine. But I don't have long."

Her stomach sank as she turned into the ranch where Ethan had moved only a little over a year ago. He'd gone from bachelor to husband and father in such a short time. The place belonged to Summer, who like Lance Watkins trained show jumpers. It was an interesting combination, with Ethan's reiners also lining the barn corridor.

Their place was large with both indoor and outdoor arenas, a small pasture, and several boxed stalls. A hot walker sat out behind the stalls, near a set of wash racks. It wasn't one of the larger facilities, but it compared with Michaela's. Summer had sold off quite a few of her horses since Josh had been born and she wasn't doing much training these days. Ethan had told Michaela that she didn't seem interested in the horses the way she used to be, and he'd wondered about it. Michaela figured that motherhood had replaced some of the need to be around the animals as much as before, but she didn't completely buy it. She'd been around the three of them from time to time and, as bad as it made her feel to think it, she didn't believe Summer was the most attentive and loving mother. From what she could tell, Ethan had taken on the brunt of the parenting. Then again, maybe she was simply judging with some jealousy mixed in there.

Summer answered the door in her typical state of perfection—long red hair curled at the ends, flawless ivory skin with makeup intact, a pair of navy slacks, and a pressed white blouse. Summer was so very Summer, and Michaela swallowed hard. "Hi, Michaela. Nice to see you." She fidgeted with her watch and checked the time. "Ethan has been talking nonstop about this horse and how great you'll be at working with him, so I suggested he call you and have you over." She touched her shoulder. "I'm sorry about what you've been going through lately."

Gag. Sure. "Thank you. I appreciate that."

"Come on in. Ethan is in the kitchen giving Josh his bottle." She grabbed a purse from the coat closet next to the front door. "I have to run out right now. Sorry I couldn't visit. Next time."

"Sure, no problem. Nice to see you, too."

Michaela felt relieved. It was so weird between them. Anyone who'd been watching the two of them exchange pleasantries could see that they were both being fake with each other. There was no love lost between them. She couldn't help wonder if Summer's exit had to do with her coming over.

"Mick? That you?" Ethan appeared from around the corner into the hallway of what Michaela referred to as the mini-manor, which was as perfect as Summer—decorated to a tee. Not a color mismatched, not a speck of dust anywhere.

"Hi."

Summer walked over to Ethan and the baby. "I have to go. See you later. Bye." She gave them each a peck on the cheek It seemed odd for a mother to be almost cold with her son, not to mention her husband. But again, none of her business. "Bye, Michaela." She waved and was out the door, a breeze blowing past as she shut it behind her.

Michaela turned to Ethan. "Everything okay?"

He shrugged. "Oh yeah, fine. Everything's great. How about you?"

"I already told you on the phone that I'm okay. I'm hanging in there." Josh's eyes were at half-mast as he sucked down a bottle. "He's getting so big."

"And heavy to lug around. Come on." He led her into their family room, painted in cream and a soft peach—once again, way too Summer for Michaela. He laid Josh down in his playpen. "Let's go see the horse real quick. He's asleep."

"Will Josh be okay?"

"Sure. I always lock everything up, and he can't get out of there."

She nodded and followed him out to the barn, feeling odd in her heels and black dress, but nevertheless wanting to see Ethan's new horse.

"Here's my boy." They stopped in front of one of the stalls. The horse padded over to them, his ears pricking forward, his eyes bright and intelligent. He stood about fifteen hands, sorrel in color with four perfect white socks and a blaze down the center of his face.

"He's beautiful, Ethan. Oh my God." Michaela brought a hand up to touch the soft nuzzle on the horse.

"He is. What do you think? Want to work with him?"

"Of course. I'd love to, but Ethan, I can't think much past tomorrow right now. Who knows what will happen with this Sterling Taber thing? I might be going to jail."

"No you won't. That won't happen." He shook his head. "It can't."

"But..."

She started to say that it could. He brought a finger to her lips. "No more of that bull about you going to jail. Life is just beginning for you, and this horse will be a part of it. Okay?"

"Okay," she uttered, and for the first time in several days she didn't feel afraid.

TWENTY-EIGHT

MICHAELA LEFT ETHAN'S PLACE FEELING ODDLY relieved. He was always the optimist, and spending time with him and Josh had rubbed some positive vibes her way. She hadn't killed Sterling Taber, and justice would prevail. It had to.

Dwayne's truck was gone. He must've driven to the tack shop to help Camden out. She was happy that the two of them had been able to move beyond Camden's past. Once this mess was behind her, she would have to start planning a bridal shower for her friend. She decided to take a break and sit outside with a glass of iced tea, put her head together, and then see about going over to Ed Mitchell's jewelry store to talk with Tommy Liggett.

She changed into a pair of jeans and light sweater. Thankfully the November days were growing cooler. In only a couple of weeks Thanksgiving would be upon them, and God, how she prayed this whole mess would be over by then. She would go to her parents, like she did every year. She and Mom would bake apple and pumpkin pies and have some of Mom's friends from church over. There would be the usual fare of garlic mashed potatoes, turkey, cranberry sauce, green beans, and what Michaela always made best: a black cherry Jell-O dish from a recipe her grandmother had passed down. Grandma had died a little over five years ago and was sorely missed; and then they'd spent the first holiday season without Uncle Lou last year, which had been real tough on all of them. But Camden and Dwayne would be there. Ethan wouldn't. Hell, maybe she should invite Ethan and Summer. She needed to get past the animosity. What about Jude and Katie? She would have to invite them. Why did even the holidays have to be stressful?

She knew Jude would be back tomorrow. How was he going to take all of this? It was strange, but she really hadn't had time to miss him. She'd been so wrapped up in this drama. She had missed the sense of security he provided, and she knew he might've been able to handle Peters's attitude toward her, but she didn't feel that deep sense of longing. It had to be because of the drama that had taken place over the course of the week.

She took a long drink of the tea and closed her eyes, then heard something behind her and sat up. Carolyn Taber stood a few feet away, her hand inside her purse. It took a second for Michaela to register who it was. The woman had raccoon eyes from mascara dripping down her face. "Why did you do it?" Carolyn sputtered.

"What are you doing here?" Michaela asked, standing slowly. Did Carolyn have a gun in her purse?

"Sterling!" she screamed. "Why did you kill him?"

Michaela shook her head. "I didn't kill him and I suggest you leave, Mrs. Taber. You're trespassing."

Why hadn't she gotten a new dog yet?

Carolyn's face turned a dark shade of red, her plastic-surgeoned nose pinching. "Yes, you did. Everyone knows you did. Why?"

"You're insane. You need to leave."

"Not until you tell me why you murdered him."

"Where's your husband, Mrs. Taber?"

"On his way home."

"Does he know about the affair you and Sterling were having? Weren't you supposed to be heading home with him? Is that why you're here? Did my comment about you starring in a film tip him off?"

"No. I told him that I wanted to stay and shop, then go to Los Angeles and do some more."

"Right. I didn't kill Sterling. I know about the affair. I have proof of it, and the police know about it, too." She was bluffing, but maybe by doing so she'd smoke out Carolyn Taber.

The woman looked ghastly, to say the least. "No, please tell me that you did not give those to the police!" She started to pull something from her purse.

"No!" Michaela yelled, but then realized that the woman was opening up a checkbook, her hands shaking.

"Tell me that you didn't give those to the police. I will pay you for them. How much do you want?"

"Yes, I did give them the tapes."

Carolyn's hands shook even more with this revelation. "You had the last set. I talked with Sterling and we worked things out. He said that he'd destroy the other tapes for me. He promised me. I know he did it. I believed him. He loved me! I can't believe that he gave a set of those tapes to you and you gave them to the police. What have you done to me? You've ruined me. You have completely destroyed me! You will pay for it."

Michaela wasn't about to tell her that she'd stolen the tapes from Sterling's house. She didn't figure that would be a good idea. Carolyn Taber spun around and stormed away. Somehow she was convinced that Sterling's sister-in-law would make good on her threat, and she also realized that she now had no choice but to turn those tapes over to Peters.

TWENTY-NINE

MICHAELA PUT IN A CALL TO PETERS, WHO wasn't at the station. She left a message. What to do? Well, she still wanted to talk with Tommy Liggett. She called the jewelry store, but the woman who answered said that Tommy was on a break and would be back in about half an hour. Frustrated, she slipped on a pair of riding boots and headed out to the barn, where she took Leo out and lunged him for a bit. Watching his smooth, clean lines, his taut muscles move through each pace diligently, was meditative in a sense. His hooves pounded repetitively against the dirt as he moved in a forward circle with each stride. He tossed his delicate head into the air and blew hard, his nostrils flaring as she pulled the lunge line taut and urged him to whoa. His long dark mane lay against his face and neck. She leaned her forehead on his and felt tears sting her eyes. She would get her life back, for her horses and for herself. As soon as she saw Jude she would hand over the tapes and plead for his help. He could help her with this. Thank God he would be home in the morning.

She cleaned Leo up and put him away. Her legs were like Jell-O, and it seemed as if she'd had the wind knocked out of her. This week had torn at a remote part of her soul—so much ugliness, seediness, scandal, and cruelty. If she put feelings on it, vocalized her thoughts, she'd knew she'd break down. Exhaustion engulfed her. She planned to take a shower and then talk to Tommy Liggett.

She stepped under the running water, and once again her mind traveled back to the events of the past few days. The polo mallet. Was the murder premeditated? Or was it a "heat of the moment" thing? Say it was premeditated. No, that didn't jive. Her mallet was a convenient weapon. A premeditated murder would've meant someone would have planned it, brought a weapon, and bam! But that's not what happened.

Who had been angry at Sterling that day? Then again, who hadn't? Juliet was angry. Did she know about Lucia? Oh, and what *about* Lucia? Here was a girl who'd told the cops that Michaela was sleeping with Sterling, which was so far from the truth it was laughable. And Mario's car...and the wig? What was that all about? Those two could have been in cahoots, or the three Sorvinos—Pepe included. Ed Mitchell told Pepe that his daughter and Sterling had been fooling around. Pepe would've gotten upset and maybe he went to Mario. What if Pepe confronted Sterling? Followed him into the back office where Sterling was going to change, things got out of hand, Pepe hit him with the mallet, then went to get Mario. Michaela didn't recall seeing Pepe around after she'd found Sterling, and in those few minutes when Mario went to see if Sterling was dead and Michaela called the cops, could Mario have wiped off the mallet? But her fingerprints had still been on the mallet. Pepe could've been wearing gloves. It was a good theory. It fit. The only thing that did not fit was, why would any of them follow Michaela around?

What about Erin Hornersberg? She'd gone looking for Sterling before the match, became angry with him before the show, and didn't care at all when he'd shown up dead. She'd been very uncomfortable with Camden and the women's visit. But this was a woman who did, in all respects, come across as slightly off. Maybe she should consider questioning Erin again, only this time she would take Joe with her.

And what about Carolyn Taber? She hadn't even been at the event. Or had she? Michaela wouldn't have known who she was at the time. There were a lot of people around that day, and if she'd been there she would've blended in with the rest of the crowd. Had she snapped over the videos? Sterling had said on the tape that she didn't need to bother destroying them, because he had more sets. Were the tapes that Michaela had the only ones left? Carolyn had been willing to pay for them. Had she also been willing to kill for them?

    These were all angles that she still needed to look into. She rinsed the shampoo out of her hair and turned off the water. Pulling back the curtain to grab her towel, she screamed and jumped back when she saw who was on the other side of the curtain, now staring at her buck naked.

THIRTY

"JUDE!" SHE PULLED THE TOWEL FROM THE RACK and quickly wrapped it around herself. "What in the hell are you doing?"

"I could ask you the same thing."

"Excuse me? You weren't supposed to be back until Friday."

"When Katie and I were in our last port, I called in to the office and heard about what happened. We flew straight home."

"Jude! Why did you do that? You didn't tell Katie, did you?"

"Of course not. She's a little angry with me, though. I told her that I had to get back for work."

"A *little* angry? I don't blame her. I'm angry, too."

"You're angry because I came back to try and help you?" He looked totally incredulous.

He also looked good. How she could think that just then, she wasn't sure, but she couldn't deny that the tan he'd gotten on the cruise highlighted his blue eyes, and his hair had bleached lighter in the sun. She wanted to reach out and touch the lightened waves. "I'm upset, that's all, that you would cut your trip short because of me."

"Come on, Michaela. The woman who I'm dating has been arrested for murder and I'm not supposed to get home as fast as I can to help? Why didn't you contact me?"

"You were in the Caribbean on a cruise."

"There are ways to get messages to passengers, you know. I wasn't off the planet."

"I know, but honestly, I didn't want to ruin your trip."

He sighed. "Why am I not surprised? And why am I also not surprised that this has happened to you?"

"What do you mean by that, 'not surprised that this happened to me'?"

She stormed past him, embarrassed and upset that he had the gall to enter her bedroom, then her bathroom, unannounced, and now he'd seen her in the buff. They'd shared some passionate moments together, sure, but they hadn't ever been naked together, and right now she felt like he had an unfair advantage, which she did not appreciate. And dammit, what *did* he mean that he wasn't surprised about her situation?

"It's not as if you run from murder. You're a modern-day Sherlock Holmes."

She turned on her heel and shook a finger at him, almost losing her towel. "That is so unfair, Jude. I don't go around looking for murder. I can't help what happened in the past and I certainly can't help this situation."

"You still should have called me."

"Oh please. That would've been selfish. You were on your vacation, for God's sake, and with Katie. I couldn't have done that to you, much less to your little girl. I had hoped that by the time you got home this would've all blown over and then we could've laughed about it. Besides, what would you have done if I got a hold of you in the middle of the ocean? You would've gotten on the first plane back home and stormed in here and tried to save me as if I'm a damsel in distress. Thank God you didn't find out until today. At least you had some of the week to enjoy yourself."

"Aren't you a damsel in distress, though?"

"No. I'm a very capable woman. I can take care of myself. I don't need rescuing. I don't need the white horse and Prince Charming. And honestly, that's been a problem for us all along. You seem to feel the need to take care of me."

"Maybe that's because you need a man to take care of you."

"What! Please. You don't know me that well, then."

"What I know is that there is some pretty incriminating evidence against you for a murder that, knowing you as I do, I can't believe you would have ever done. I don't plan to save you, Michaela. Why do you keep fighting me? Resisting me? All I want to do is help. That's what people who love each other do. They are there for each other. But I have to wonder if you even want my help. You're always pushing me away, and this is only the latest incident."

Wait a minute! Love! *Love?* When did that ever come into the picture? He'd let that one slip. Oops, and she decided that she'd let it fly by, pretending that she hadn't heard it, but dammit, why was there a lump of emotion tightening at the back of her throat? She was not ready for this.

He walked over to her. "Michaela, let me help you."

"I need to get dressed," she said.

"You do?" Jude traced the top of her towel with a finger.

"Yes. And we're arguing."

"No, we're not."

"Yes, we are."

"Can we go back to it later?" He kissed her neck.

"Jude, the timing is off. I don't want our first time to be...well, make-up sex."

"There is nothing wrong with make-up sex. And I may have been upset with you, but seeing you in the shower and having you yell at me kind of turns me on."

"Yeah, you shouldn't have seen me in the shower. How did you get in? You scared me."

"I'm a cop. I think I know how to get into a home. We need to get you an alarm system. You never know who will sneak in and suck the blood out of you." He sucked on her neck like a vampire. It tickled and Michaela couldn't help but laugh. "I can make you smile even more."

She sighed. He kissed her on her neck again, his fingers traced the edge of the towel wrapped around her. Feelings she hadn't been in touch with for a long time traveled through her, and she stopped thinking. She allowed Jude to keep kissing her as she dropped her towel.

THIRTY-ONE

"YOU DID WHAT?" JUDE ASKED. "OH THIS IS NOT good, Michaela! Damn! I could arrest you. I *should* arrest you. Breaking and entering? You stole the tapes? What were you thinking?"

They stood in her kitchen making sandwiches. The afternoon had turned into evening and they were both hungry.

"Arrest me? Please. I didn't want to keep it from you—and doesn't all of this show you that Peters is heading in the wrong direction with this investigation?"

"Maybe, but what you did by breaking into Taber's home was a crime. And you did this alone?" He raised his eyebrows.

That was the only part of the story that Michaela felt she had to omit. She could not expose Joe. He had gone out on a limb for her more than once. He'd given her the opportunity with the riding center and was always there when she needed a friend. No, she could not betray his trust.

"Yes," she replied. "I did it, and I'm not sorry either. What am I supposed to do, Jude? Stand by and let Peters see that I rot in jail? He's not doing anything as far as I know to find out who really killed Sterling. It's me he's after."

Jude stared at her. "This isn't the first time you've gone searching for answers where murder is concerned. The last time you almost got yourself killed."

"I know that. But this is the first time that my freedom is on the line and you and me…I mean, *us*…aren't we in a relationship? Because it sure felt like it over the last few hours. Like we'd taken that next step. We won't be taking any more steps if I'm in jail. You said that you came home to help me, and now you're thinking I should be arrested for trying to find out the truth."

"That's not fair. I haven't had a chance to speak with Peters yet, but I definitely intend to. I know that you didn't murder Taber. I won't let you go to jail, I promise you that."

"How do you plan to do that, Jude, with your boss so hot and heavy to seal my fate?"

He closed his eyes and shook his head. "I do. Just promise me that you'll stop playing detective for once."

"No. Not this time."

"I don't want you hurt. You have to stop this! It's ridiculous!" he shouted.

"Ironically, if I'm behind bars, who knows what could happen to me? It may be ridiculous, but I don't see another way out right now."

"That won't happen! Do what you do best: Work with kids, train horses, and I'll figure this out." He put his arms around her.

She tensed up. His words sounded good, but why didn't she completely believe him? Was there something in his voice that doubted he could help her? To her, he sounded almost helpless and she wasn't buying his pleas to drop her sleuthing.

"I'll take the tapes with me and get them into Peters's hands. I think you're right, Carolyn Taber seems a likely suspect."

"Peters hates me, Jude. You can't tell him how I got the tapes."

"I won't say how I got them. He doesn't hate you. It's his MO to be a hard-ass."

"MO or not, I'm afraid that Peters will ignore the tapes out of sheer laziness or the mere fact that he sees me as an easy target."

He cupped his hand under her chin. "Peters won't ignore them. God! I can't believe that you stole those tapes. Is there anything else you're not telling me?"

There was plenty, like Mario following her, Zach and Juliet breaking into her place, the threat from Carolyn, as well as the bizarre behavior of Paige and Robert Nightingale. And in the moment that he asked her the question, she wondered why she *didn't* tell him everything. The kitchen seemed to spin as she concluded that she'd made a mistake with Jude. She'd made love with a man whom she wanted badly to trust, to fall in love with, but who admittedly she didn't completely trust. And now she wasn't sure she *could* fall in love with him. Right now she felt weaker than ever before. She'd fallen into a man's arms because she'd wanted security.

"No. I've told you everything. You know, I'm feeling kind of tired and want to go to bed."

"We can do that. We can take our food back to bed with us, and forget all this other stuff for a while."

"No. I want to be alone."

"Michaela?"

"It's been a long week and honestly, I'm feeling overwhelmed."

He tried to hug her but she pulled away.

He looked wounded. "I don't understand."

"I...think we made a mistake," she said.

She couldn't believe what she was saying. She typically ran from her feelings. They were far easier to hide from rather than confront. And she had to wonder if by treating Jude like this, she was only doing exactly that. Maybe it was easier for her not to try and love and be loved than be willing to open up and take a chance.

"I'm only trying to protect you. I don't want you getting hurt and I am planning on taking all of what you've told me, plus the tapes, to Peters."

"I know. But I still need some time to be by myself."

"Okay." He nodded and tossed up his arms. "If that's what you want."

As Jude left, tapes in hand, Michaela stared out the front window for a long time, not knowing at all what she wanted.

THIRTY-TWO

MICHAELA DIDN'T SLEEP MUCH AFTER JUDE LEFT; the next morning, life seemed even more complicated than the day before. Being wishy-washy wasn't her style, but that's where she was in this game. Wishy-washy with Jude, her theories, everything but her horses. *Solid ground* would be nice.

She didn't trust that Peters would interview Carolyn Taber about the videotapes, and she had questions for Tommy Liggett, who might have met Carolyn and could enlighten her further. He might also know something about Sterling and Lucia. The brat certainly wasn't going to talk to Michaela. She needed to chat with Joe about the Sorvinos. Maybe one of his cousins had some information for her. Plus, Tommy could possibly fill her in on what happened in Santa Barbara to Rebecca Woodson.

She decided to head over to Ed Mitchell's jewelry store and have a talk with Tommy. First, she checked to make sure that the bracelet she'd found at the polo grounds was still in the zippered pouch in her purse. Maybe Tommy could take a look at it and tell her what it was worth and see if she couldn't get it back to the rightful owner. So far no one had called on it. The main reason for going to the jewelry store was because she needed answers; she headed over midmorning, hoping to find Tommy there. The buzzer rang, announcing her entry. The store was upscale, painted in a light gold, and several small love seats stood next to large windows, which looked out onto the main shopping district of Palm Springs. Classical music played through the surround sound. A couple looked at engagement rings, happily trying on possible contenders. Tommy was helping them.

"Be right with you." Tommy glanced up. "Oh hey, Michaela."

"Take your time. I'm not in a hurry."

He nodded. Michaela looked around at all of the beautiful trinkets, with their expensive price tags. There were gorgeous necklaces, bracelets, watches from the finest watchmakers in the world. This store was for the wealthy. She liked jewelry enough, but most of what she owned was simple. Fine pieces like these would never fit into her lifestyle.

Tommy handed the couple glasses of champagne, and they sat down on one of the sofas, continuing to admire a ring they obviously were considering. He walked over to Michaela.

"Hey, are you okay? I heard the news." He shook his head. "Everyone at the field knows you would never hurt anyone. One of the detectives questioned all of us, and I told him that there was no way you killed Sterling. I hope they catch the bastard who did it. You don't deserve this."

"Thank you," she said.

"What brings you in here?" He rubbed his palms together.

"I'm not here for jewelry."

He gave her an odd look. "Okay. How can I help then?"

"I appreciate you putting in a good word for me. Since you believe that I didn't kill Sterling, do you have any ideas as to who might have done it?"

He shrugged. "You know that people who met him either loved or hated him."

"How did you feel about him?"

A shocked expression came over Tommy's boyish features. "He was my friend. What do you think? I loved the guy. We hung out all the time. What happened to him was wrong. He had his faults, you know, there's no getting around that. Kind of a narcissist and egomaniac, but he was funny...funny as hell. We joked a lot and women loved him, which didn't hurt me at all when we hung out. He could reel them in and, well, I'd kind of get the chicks he didn't want."

"Ah, the buddy system."

"Yeah, I guess."

"Speaking of women, what do you know about him and Lucia Sorvino?"

"Lucia? She's a kid. He toyed with her a little, but Juliet suspected something was going on and he dropped it."

"I'm sure that didn't make Lucia happy."

Tommy shrugged. "I wouldn't know. I don't know her too well. Like I said, she's young, and I actually told Sterling to leave her alone. Her brother is a hothead."

"Hot enough to kill Sterling?"

"Maybe, I suppose. I know he can lose it, though, because I saw him yelling at his sister just last week. He laid into her real good. She was in tears."

"Where was this at, and when?"

"I had to pick up some menus for Ed because he's planning a shindig at his place next month and Pepe always does the catering. When I swung by, Mario had his sister cornered and cowering like a dog. I don't know what it was about. They stopped, and Mario turned into Mr. Suave when he spotted me and that's pretty much it."

"Do you think they could've been arguing over Sterling?"

"It's possible. I don't trust Mario, though. He kinda looks mean, if you ask me."

"Yeah."

"Why all the questions about this?" Tommy asked.

"I'm sorry. You have to realize that I am under a lot of stress with all of the scrutiny. The police don't seem to be listening to all the people out there insisting that I didn't do it. I'm trying to do what I can to find out on my own. I'm trying to clear my name."

He nodded. "I understand."

"Thanks. I was wondering if maybe you could tell me about last summer?"

"What do you mean?"

"Last summer Sterling went to see his family in Santa Barbara, and you went?"

Tommy nodded. "I went with him for a couple of weeks. Zach came down for a few days, too. We had a great time, but his family...a bunch of uptight jerks, if you want my opinion. We didn't hang out much at their place. That brother of his runs the show. His dad passed away not that long ago and their mom is pretty ill, I heard."

"How about Carolyn Taber? Did you meet her?"

"Sterling's sister-in-law? Briefly. She was a snob, too."

"Did Sterling ever say anything about her to you?"

"No. He couldn't stand Carolyn or his brother."

"Really?"

"Yes. Why?"

"I have reasons to think that maybe there was more to Carolyn and Sterling's relationship than what he might've let on."

"No way. He thought she was a total bitch."

"He never said anything to the contrary, like maybe he wanted to sleep with her? I wasn't born yesterday. I know guys talk like that, and she's an attractive woman. I saw her at the funeral yesterday and, I don't know, there was something that I picked up on that made me think she had more than just a sisterly type of interest toward him."

Michaela didn't want to tell him about the tapes. She wasn't sure she could trust him yet and she thought she'd let the police see them before she said anything.

He laughed. "Look, Sterling liked women. He liked a lot of women, but I can guarantee that his sister-in-law was not one of them."

This line of questioning was getting her nowhere. Obviously Sterling hadn't found Carolyn too off-putting, but he hadn't let on to Tommy that he was involved with her. Or maybe they hadn't gotten together until after the summer, when Sterling's stipend had been cut in half. "How about Rebecca Woodson?"

"You read some old papers." Tommy frowned. "I met her." He shook his head. "Talk about a wild one. Once she hooked into Sterling, man, she wasn't about to let go."

"She was not from a well-to-do family?"

"Not that I was aware of. My impression was that she'd gotten connected with a group of rich kids out there and glommed on to the party scene with them. The rumor was she had some old guy who was keeping her in the cash as long as she was keeping him happy. He was supposedly married, so he didn't have much say as to what she did on her own time."

"Did you ever get the name of that guy?"

"No, why would I? I really didn't care. She was a party girl, a kind of...you know...how do you say it nicely? I mean, she put out pretty easily."

"So Sterling wasn't really dating her?"

He laughed. "Like I said, she put out. Sterling was a guy. She was hot. Problem was, as soon as they connected and she found out how loaded his family was, I think she saw a better deal than having to pay homage to the old guy. You know, I shouldn't be talking about her like that. It's not cool. If you read the paper, then you know that the poor girl died, too. She drowned."

"I heard that. Sterling was there that night, wasn't he?"

"We both were. It was a crazy party out at some mansion on the beach. Tons of people."

"What happened?"

"Like I said, it was crazy, you know, like out of the movies. Rebecca and Sterling...well, everyone was drinking a lot. I was super buzzed. There were a lot of drugs, too. I'm not into that, but I had my share of booze. They got into a fight. He wanted her to back off and leave him alone. It was a pretty nasty scene. She left the party, and the next thing we know the police are at Sterling's house the next morning because they found Rebecca washed up on the beach near the party house."

"Was it an accident?"

Tommy shrugged. "I think it probably was. She had a bump on her head, they said. Her body was found right off the pier. It looked as though she'd leaned against some old railing, it broke, she fell, hit her head, and rolled into the water off the embankment, then drowned."

"But the cops thought there might have been foul play?"

"I know you're trying to clear your name, but why all the questions about Rebecca and Sterling and what happened in Santa Barbara? The police finally closed that case, said that it was an accident."

"But there's still speculation that it wasn't. And Zach told me that Sterling's family nearly disowned him after this took place, because the girl's relatives brought a civil suit against Sterling, and his folks didn't want the media attention or bad publicity."

"That's true. But still, why are you asking? I mean, are you going anywhere with this?"

"Honestly, I'm not real sure. But I have to wonder if maybe someone in Rebecca's family or even Sterling's own family didn't have something to do with his murder, and if it doesn't all lead back to the night that she died. Or is it even possible that the older guy who was paying for her company might not have sought revenge?"

"Oh. Wow. That's a good point." He nodded. "Yeah, Rebecca's family went berserk. Like I said, I never knew who the old man was that she hung out with. I'm sure some of the kids we partied with might know."

"Do you know anyone that I might be able to call?"

"Jeez, I don't know. I'd have to check my book. You know, that was just a party scene. It wasn't like I was making lifelong friends out there. I might, though. I met a couple of girls out there and took their numbers. I can call you if I find them."

"That would be great."

"What about Rebecca's family?"

"I wouldn't know how to get a hold of them. I know that she had a brother who came over a few days after they found Rebecca and tried to beat on Sterling, but he was arrested. I think his name was Ryan. Not sure. It was an ugly scene and I went home that afternoon, actually. Once Sterling was cleared by the police he came back here, and we never talked about it."

"Excuse me," the woman on the sofa called out. "I think we want to look at the first ring again."

"I'll be right there," Tommy said. "Hey, sorry, I've got to help these guys out. And then Ed wants me to run some errands."

"No problem."

"Hope I helped."

"You did. Thanks."

Tommy nodded and went back to assist the customers. As Michaela started to leave the store, her eye noticed a display of bracelets. She peered in through the glass and spotted what looked to be an exact replica of the tennis bracelet she'd found. She needed to ask Camden if anyone had come forward to claim it. It seemed odd that no one had. She could turn it over to the police—to Jude. Maybe not her best option, albeit logical, if she wasn't already in over her head.

She decided to wait around a few more minutes for Tommy. She wanted to ask him the price of the bracelet.

A saleswoman approached. "Can I help you with anything?"

Michaela looked at Tommy. He and the couple were engrossed in their business. She didn't know how long he might be. "Yeah, sure, you could help me. That tennis bracelet: How much is it?"

"This one?"

She nodded and the gal pulled it out. "Eight grand. Gorgeous, isn't it? I would love to have one of these."

"It is beautiful." Michaela reached into her purse and pulled out the bracelet. She'd hadn't gotten a chance to ask Tommy about it, but maybe the woman could help her. "I had no idea they cost that much. Can you take a look at this for me? I'm curious what it's worth."

"Let me take a look," the woman said. She held it up to the light and then placed it on a black velvet fold and studied it through a jeweler's loupe. "This is a great fake. Excellent really."

"What do you mean, fake?"

The woman looked again and nodded. "Yes. These are high-quality CZs. Cubic zirconium. Really nice, though. Didn't you know they weren't real?"

"No, I didn't. They look like the ones there in the case. I found the bracelet, so no, I didn't know. I placed a classified because I was sure someone would be missing it."

"I would think that someone would claim it, though. I know they're not real, but they still aren't cheap. Like I said, it's a great fake. That's what is so cool about good CZs. No one would ever know that they're not real, unless you have a trained eye." The woman handed the bracelet back to Michaela.

"Mitchell's doesn't carry cubic zirconium jewelry then?"

The woman smiled. "Are you kidding? Have you ever met Ed Mitchell? The man is super particular. Only the best of everything. Best for his store, best food, best clothes, best cars, best for his family."

The buzzer rang and an older, elegant-looking woman walked in. "Good luck with that," the saleswoman said and turned her attention to the new customer.

"Thanks." Michaela looked back at Tommy to say good-bye, but he was still busy with the couple.

THIRTY-THREE

"I DON'T THINK REBECCA WOODSON'S DROWNING was an accident," Michaela said. She'd called Camden to see if they could meet in town for a late lunch. "Have you found out anything on your end? Did you get a hold of anyone you know in that Santa Barbara jet-set circle?"

Camden nodded and set her iced tea down. "I talked with this gal whose family owns a big winery up there. She knows a lot of the gossip. She told me that the Tabers are real secretive."

"No kidding. But there must be someone who knows what they're about."

"She knew a few things. The scoop is that Charles, Sterling's brother, is a control freak and runs the entire family. After the dad passed away, Charles took over. They are filthy rich and everyone knew that Sterling was the black sheep of the family. Always has been. The thing with Rebecca Woodson was a big deal there last summer, but the Tabers have paid a lot of cash to keep things as low-key as they could. This friend of mine said that the rumor is they even paid off someone in the police department. When her family filed the civil suit, the Tabers settled with them out of court. Sterling came back here, and word was the family didn't want him around ever again, and they stopped giving him money to live on."

"Ten grand a month, though; he was still getting that. They didn't cut him out completely," Michaela said.

"When you're talking about a family with the kind of status and money the Tabers have, then I can see where Sterling was coming from, why he might have been disgruntled."

"This I have to hear."

"Think about it: Here's a guy who has been spoiled and has a sense of entitlement. Take it away from him, even if he'd done something to cause it, and he throws a temper tantrum."

"Imagine that." Michaela clucked her tongue.

"There's more." Camden rubbed her palms together briskly.

"You're scaring me. I think you're enjoying this in some perverse way."

"As if you aren't."

"Trust me, I'm not. It's a necessity. You like the gossip angle of it."

"Maybe a little…but listen, so there's been talk that Sterling had been in trouble with the law when he was a kid. He even spent some time at juvenile hall. His dad couldn't get him out of that one and his brother wasn't running the show at the time."

"What did he do?"

"I don't know this for a fact, only what my friend told me. She said that he was a thief. He stole. He would hang out at friends' houses and take any money lying around, that kind of thing. But he got popped supposedly for stealing some rare emerald off someone's nightstand."

"Seriously? Why would a kid with that kind of money need to steal?"

"For the same reason any kid does anything negative: attention. His parents were busy jet-setting, his brother was the golden boy, and Sterling had to lash out to get noticed. So he did it by becoming a petty thief…but it wasn't so petty."

"He was really screwed up. It's a shame." Michaela shook her head.

"You think he killed Rebecca Woodson? You know, it's so weird, because I knew him, and I never figured him for the pathological type."

"Your hormones knew him."

Camden shrugged. "You're right. What do we do now?"

"I don't know. I need to talk to Joe. He seems to know how to dig and get direct answers."

"What are you looking for exactly with this Rebecca Woodson thing?"

She frowned. "I can't pinpoint it, but I think Sterling's murder goes back to his past. There are people here who didn't like him and aren't sad to see him gone, but I can't help feeling like either he was killed because someone here was afraid of his past, or of him directly. I wish I could find out more about Rebecca Woodson. Or Carolyn Taber."

"Oh yeah, her. I wanted to tell you this, too. She's a manipulative one. She wormed her way into Charles's life. I guess she doesn't come from big money and she's been the one dark spot for Charles. The parents weren't keen on her, and she had to become Miss Perfect to get her hooks into him."

"She also got her hooks into Sterling. I guess he wanted to cement her situation all the way around. But it looked like it backfired on her."

Camden nodded. "I hate to run, Mick, but I've got to get back to the store. By the way, that necklace you wanted to give Joe's daughter for her birthday came in."

"Oh good. I'll be by to get it. Thanks for helping me with all of this."

"No problem. See you at home."

Michaela paid the bill and looked at her watch. She needed to go and work horses for a while. If she was going to get any further with finding out who'd done Sterling in, she knew she'd need some help. There were tons of loose ends; she just wasn't sure how to tie them up.

The fresh air, and working with her animals, might help clear her mind, but when she pulled onto the ranch, she knew that wasn't going to happen. To her dismay, another visitor had shown up. Detective Peters leaned against his car, waiting for her.

THIRTY-FOUR

"HELLO, DETECTIVE. I'M SURPRISED TO SEE YOU." Michaela hoped he wasn't here to arrest her for breaking into Sterling's place. What if Jude had told him the truth about how he had come into possession of the tapes? Would he do that to her? Especially after yesterday? She didn't think so, but she also didn't like the mere fact that she was questioning it."

Good afternoon, Ms. Bancroft." He crossed his arms and shifted from leaning against his car.

Oh no. What was this all about?

"Some new evidence has come to light in our investigation regarding Mr. Taber."

"New evidence?" she asked. He *was* here about the tapes then.

He nodded. "I'm here to let you know that Carolyn Taber, Sterling's sister-in-law, committed suicide this afternoon and left behind a set of incriminating tapes, along with a letter that has led us to believe she was involved in her brother-in-law's murder. I'm afraid that you were a victim of circumstance. My apologies."

"Suicide?" She shook her head. No, that didn't add up at all. Carolyn Taber was off—that much was a given—but she hadn't appeared suicidal. Michaela could buy into the possibility that she'd murdered Sterling, but not that she'd kill herself. The tapes. She rubbed her forehead. "Um, you said tapes? What do you mean?"

"Ms. Bancroft, this is an ongoing investigation and I'm not permitted to discuss it with you." He leaned back against his cruiser.

Rage suddenly boiled under the surface, overtaking her sense of shock. "*You can't discuss this with me?* After all the grief you've caused me in the past week, going after me like a pit bull, and you can't at least let me in on what you've found?"

"That is correct. The case against you was shaping up to be circumstantial, and it would appear after our forensics team went over the polo mallet again that there is another set of partial prints on there. I do apologize for any inconvenience this has caused you."

"*Inconvenience?* All I have to say, *Detective*, is that if I were a vengeful person, I'd have a lawsuit smacked down on the police department and you personally so fast that you wouldn't have time to shove another donut down your throat! This has been the most poorly conducted investigation." She shook her head. "I think it would be best for you to leave now."

She stormed off toward the barn as Peters drove away. *Now* they found partial prints other than hers on her mallet? Of course: Because she'd handed over the tapes, the investigation took a different turn. She kicked the dirt with her foot. "Damn!" She went into her office, grabbed a bottle of water out of the fridge, and sat down at her desk. The tapes. Peters had said that Carolyn had a set of tapes with her when she killed herself. But she'd pleaded with Michaela for *her* tapes. Sterling had told Carolyn that he'd destroy the tapes, or at least that had been her story. He hadn't destroyed his set, that much was for certain. Michaela had turned that set over to Jude. And Carolyn had presumably destroyed the set that Sterling had sent her. He told her on the tape not to bother destroying her set because there were others. Someone had another set of those videos. But who? Had Carolyn killed herself because she felt there was no hope? Maybe she thought that if her husband found out, things would be over between them and the gravy train would stop running. Again, though, how had she acquired a set of the tapes? Where was she when she'd supposedly taken her life?

Michaela wanted answers, because she wasn't buying the idea that Carolyn had killed herself. Women like

Carolyn Taber bounced back, even after ugly divorces and scandal.

She needed to talk to Jude. Would he give her the information she wanted? Or would he tell her to go and do what she was best at—train horses and teach kids? Wasn't that what he'd told her? She hit her desk. Here she should be thrilled. She was off the hook. No one suspected her of any wrongdoing and she was free to get her life back on track. But still, what good would it do if she felt in her gut that Sterling Taber's killer wasn't dead but still out there? Sure, Sterling and even Carolyn weren't exactly pillars of society, but they *were* people, and they didn't deserve to be murdered. And Michaela knew that Carolyn Taber had been murdered. She just knew it.

She got up from her desk and headed into the house. She had withheld one of the tapes from Jude, the one with another woman in it—which she'd assumed was a one-night stand. She hadn't thought it mattered the other night when she'd seen it, and then she really didn't think it mattered when she connected Carolyn to the other tapes. But *did* it matter, though? Could the mystery woman have had a set of the tapes, too?

As much as she hated to do it, Michaela put in the other tape. She watched all forty minutes of it and was thoroughly sick to her stomach when it was over. She saw nothing. Well, she saw something all right, but she couldn't find anything odd. The sound effects consisted of some grunts and moans and Sterling finally yelling out the woman's name—Sheila! Yuck.

Nothing there. Michaela paced inside the family room—usually a place of comfort and warmth, it now felt like four walls closing in on her. There were holes in all of this, and she was going to take them one by one and plug them up. She called Jude but he was out of the office, so she left a message. She was determined to learn what he knew about Carolyn Taber's apparent suicide. Since she couldn't start with Carolyn, she'd begin with Rebecca Woodson's fall from the pier in Santa Barbara last summer and her subsequent death. Everything about what had happened last summer smelled foul to her. She didn't believe the story that Rebecca had fallen by accident. She'd seen Sterling in action. The man had an anger management problem, plus he was a narcissist and complete egomaniac. He'd do anything to cover his ass. Both Zach and Tommy had witnessed Sterling and Rebecca drinking, then arguing, and that was all they knew until the next morning when the police questioned Sterling. Then, Rebecca's brother came by to beat *the truth* out of Sterling about what had happened to his sister. Then, the Woodsons filed a wrongful death suit that Charles Taber quietly made go away with a large sum of cash to the Woodsons. After that he'd cut down his brother's share of the family fortune and suggested that he leave for good; thus, Carolyn Taber and Sterling's desire to get back into his wealthy family's deep pockets.

Michaela got on the Internet, hoping to see if she could find out any more information about Rebecca Woodson. After about an hour of skimming articles and scouring phone information pages, she found the man she believed to be Rebecca's brother. She had to speak with him and find out what the family thought happened that fateful night. She picked up the phone and hit pay dirt.

Rebecca's brother, Ryan, hesitated to say anything at first. "Who is this? What do you want? You from the paper?"

"No. I'm not from the paper." Michaela explained who she was. She told him about Sterling's murder, the investigation over the past week, and why she felt the need to talk to him. Amazingly, the man didn't hang up on her.

"I'm not surprised that bastard is dead. You know, Becky was my baby sister. A good kid. Sure, she was a little wild sometimes. She liked to party, and if she hadn't gotten all caught up in that rich-kid crowd, she'd still be here. But that Sterling dude, he was no good, you know? Strung Becky along like he was dangling a carrot in front of a rabbit. Creep. I hear he done that with lots of girls. Liked to give them jewelry and things, you know, make sure they believe he was into them. Crazy, too, 'cause a guy like that didn't need to do no convincing girls to be with him, you know? A guy like that only needed to snap his fingers and there you go, the girls come runnin'."

"He liked to give women jewelry?"

"Oh yeah. Gave Becky a diamond ring, like he was gonna marry her or sumthin'. Please. That ring, she had it on when they found her." He started to choke up. "I know this is gonna sound real awful of me, but I needed money to investigate those people. Them Tabers are loaded and when Becky was killed—and she was killed, I know—it broke my mother's heart. I made a vow to get those people. I took that ring to hock it and get some cash to pay this guy I know who's a private eye, and the ring was a fake. Fake fucking diamond."

"Fake?"

"Huh. Yep, fake. Just like that guy was."

Michaela asked him about what he thought happened the night his sister died.

"I think Becky and what's his name, can't even say it, got into it. My sister was feisty and I think she figured out what he was all about, and they started in and he pushed her off the pier. He ran home and hid behind his family's dough. Money talks."

"I hate to ask you this, but what about the rumor that Becky had a sugar daddy?"

"That's bull! I never heard that. She wouldn't do that."

"What about the wrongful death suit your family filed?"

"I can't talk about that. The Tabers did pay my mother some cash and we decided to leave the situation alone. Too painful."

"Did you ever talk with Sterling again? After your sister's death?"

"Once. Dude actually called me three weeks ago. He had the gall to call me and tell me that he wanted to talk to me about Becky and what happened that night. I told him that unless he planned to admit that he murdered my sister, we had nothing to talk about."

"What did he say?"

"I didn't let him say nothing. I hung up on him. He came into my work a few days later but I wasn't there. I don't know what the hell he wanted. It's probably a good thing for him I wasn't here. But looks like I won't need to be worrying about Sterling Taber dropping in on me ever again."

Michaela talked a few minutes more with Ryan, thanked him, and hung up. Tommy was pretty certain that Rebecca had a wealthy older man keeping her in diamonds and pearls and that she played him on the side, but her brother claimed he had no knowledge of it. Was it pure rumor started by a group of wealthy, spoiled young people, or was there a secret life to Rebecca that her brother either didn't know about or denied? Either way, as far as she was concerned, she'd acquired two interesting pieces of information from Ryan Woodson. The first tidbit was that Sterling had gone to see Ryan when he was in Santa Barbara. Why? What was it that he wanted to tell Ryan about his sister's death? He surely wasn't going to admit any wrongdoing. The visit itself was a mystery, but could it be tied into Sterling's own demise?

The other fascinating thing she'd learned was about the ring that Sterling had given to Rebecca—a fake. It caused Michaela to think about the tennis bracelet she'd found, and Sterling's juvie stint for stealing an expensive jewel.

Before she had time to explore that train of thought, her doorbell rang—repeatedly. Oh God, don't let it be Peters with a change of heart about things.

"Okay, I'm coming!" she yelled. Whoever was on the other side of the door certainly wanted her to open it.

She was surprised when she opened the door and came face-to-face with Ethan's wife, Summer, holding Josh. It took Michaela a moment to even register who it was. She immediately recognized little Joshy, but—hold the horses—Summer was not in her usual state of yuppydom with carefully applied makeup and perfect outfit. "Summer?"

She handed Josh to her. "I have an appointment and I couldn't find anyone to watch him and I knew you'd probably be here and it's important, and you are his godmother, so watch him for me for a little bit, okay?"

Michaela nodded. "Sure. Are you okay? Is everything all right?" Was this for real, Summer asking her to help with the baby? Never in a million years would she have thought this would happen. Something had to be wrong. "I'm…well…uh…are you sure?"

"Yes, I'm sure," she snapped. "I don't have a choice. Are you going to help me out here or what?"

"Yes, of course, I'll watch Josh. Everything is okay, right?" she said again.

"Everything is perfect." Summer took a step back and stood up straight, brushing her hands across her tight, black satin pencil skirt and lacy white blouse cut down to…well, pretty low, and the hair—no longer the pretty copper that Michaela was slightly jealous of. No, it was magenta almost, and not pulled back, but down, long and wavy. If Michaela didn't know better, she might think that Summer and Ethan had some kind of hot date planned, because she looked every bit the seductress. "There's formula in here." She handed her a blue diaper bag. "And diapers, wipes, and a jar of food. Actually there's a few jars of food. He likes the sweet potatoes."

How long did she plan to be gone? Not that Michaela minded. She loved being able to spend time with her godson. "What time will you be back?"

"I left a message for Ethan, letting him know to pick him up here. My appointment could run late, so Ethan will be by."

"Okay." So they didn't have some afternoon delight thing planned. Strange, but Michaela was relieved, which was stupid, because it wasn't as if Summer and Ethan didn't sleep together. And now she herself seemed to have a sex life again. Sort of.

"Bye. Thanks." She gave Josh a kiss on the cheek. The baby smiled at his mom but didn't reach out for her as he leaned his head against Michaela's chest. Her heart quickened. She couldn't deny her desire for a baby, especially while holding Josh.

Summer rushed toward her Mercedes. She turned around at one point and seemed to hesitate, but then waved again. Odd. Actually beyond odd, but Michaela wasn't going to fight it. She was going to spend some time with Josh and she couldn't be happier to see his cherubic face and big blue eyes. "Hey, little babe, what are you doing?"

He cooed and smiled at her and she thought her heart would melt right there. To have a child—amazing. If she could feel this much love while holding her godson, then what would it be like to have her own baby? That thought brought her back to Jude and made her wonder if she should consider taking their relationship further. She knew that he wanted to. Could she allow herself to fall for him, completely and totally? He also had told her that he desired more children and he didn't mind that it looked as if she couldn't conceive. That if they ever did commit to each other then adoption might be a good option. They'd only briefly discussed it when he'd asked her about kids. She'd told him that she hadn't been able to get pregnant while married to her ex-husband, Brad. She'd endured a series of fertility treatments, which her insurance didn't cover, and at the time had caused her to go deeply in debt—this right after Brad took off with an ex–rodeo queen.

Michaela laid out Josh's blankie and some of his toys, then took each stuffed animal and made voices and faces to go along with it. The baby laughed and it was probably the sweetest sound Michaela had ever heard. They made silly voices, endured one diaper change, and then they lay on their backs and stuck their feet in the air, grabbing their toes—well, Joshy was able to grab his toes. Michaela wasn't quite so limber and wound up twisting and falling over to the side, laughing at herself. She hadn't had this much fun in ages.

Josh started to wind down and fuss. "I bet you're hungry. Auntie Mickey will fix you a bottle." She got up and took his bag into the kitchen.

As she started back from the kitchen she heard a noise. What was that? She came around the corner to see that Josh had pulled her purse onto the floor, spilling all of its contents. This quickly reminded her how disorganized she was, seeing everything from receipts, gum wrappers, and even an empty raisin box on the floor. She cringed and ran over to where the baby was putting a business card in his mouth. He'd just started rolling over and he must've pulled on the purse strap. Dammit, she should've moved her purse off the chair. "Oh no, no, you cutie-patootie. What do you have there?" She took the card from his mouth and shoved it in her back pocket while quickly cleaning up the mess on the floor so Josh couldn't get into anything else. She laid him back down on the blanket and handed him his bottle. She watched him for a minute, then reached into her back pocket to see if the card he'd had in his mouth was important, like her coffee card from the Honeybear. She was only one stamp away from a free cup.

The card *was* important, but not because it entitled her to a free cup of java; it was Erin Hornersberg's card. The card had the makeup artist's name on it with her title, but it also had the name of the shop—The Sanctuary—and beneath that it read, *OWNER: SHEILA ADDISON*. Sheila! The tape. Michaela turned the card over and her jaw fell. She remembered what Erin had said to her when she gave her the card. "Sorry, there's an address written on the back here, but I don't need it anymore."

Michaela had blown it off. No biggie. But looking at the back side of the card for the first time, she realized something: She recognized the address. She'd even been there. It was Sterling Taber's.

THIRTY-FIVE

AFTER JOSH SUCKED DOWN HIS BOTTLE HE started to fuss, forcing Michaela, for the moment, to forget about her questions regarding Erin Hornersberg and Sheila. She knew that she should drop the whole thing. Move on. She was clear of any wrongdoing. Her life was hers again. Why did she feel the need to pursue this? Maybe because she knew that there was still a killer among them. She had to get it off her mind.

Josh started to whine. "All right, little love, what's the problem? You've been changed, played with, fed..." He rubbed his eyes. "Ah, but you haven't been cuddled to sleep." She picked him up and wrapped a thin blanket around him, deciding to take him out to the back patio, where she had a wooden rocker next to the pool. Maybe the waterfall that flowed into the pool would soothe him. Nothing she'd ever experienced before was more comfortable than rocking and cooing to the baby.

She watched crystalline droplets of water flow into the black-bottom pool, which Uncle Lou had built to look like a lagoon. She sure did miss him. Green foliage surrounded the pool and area, along with an array of tropical flowers that flourished in the desert heat and dry air.

The beauty surrounding her and the baby in her lap brought a deep sense of contentment, despite everything else on her mind. She twirled Josh's fine brown curls in her fingers. His hair smelled of baby shampoo. He looked so much like his daddy. Ethan and Summer were lucky to have him. She couldn't help but nod off.

She didn't know how long they napped like that, but she was awakened by the touch of a hand on her head. She blinked several times.

"Hey, sleepyheads," Ethan said.

"Hi." She looked down at the top of Josh's head. He was still asleep. "How long have you been there?"

"Long enough to know this was the most peaceful that I've ever seen you."

She didn't know how to respond, but she knew that she didn't want him to lift Josh off her lap. "Summer call you?"

He nodded. "Left me a message. Did she say where she was going?"

"No. I thought that maybe she was meeting you."

"Uh-uh. I had a full day. I've tried calling her but I keep getting her voice mail."

"I don't know."

Josh stirred and as soon as he realized his dad was there, his mouth grew into a wide toothless grin. "Hey, buddy," Ethan said.

Josh reached his arms out for him. Michaela handed the baby over. "You are such a good dad."

"Thanks, Mick. I know you'll be a mom one day. I know it. You'll be awesome."

She didn't reply.

"I better get going. I've got horses to feed and this guy to take care of."

"Hey, Ethan, everything okay at home?"

"Sure. Everything is fine."

Something in his voice made her wonder if he were telling the truth. "Yeah?"

"Yes. Why?"

"I don't know, I guess I found it odd that Summer would drop Josh off with me and…well, you seem kind of distant; I don't know."

"I'm tired, that's all. Summer dropping the baby here…well, you're his godmother and I'm always suggesting that we have you watch him. Looks like she took my suggestion."

"Yeah. Okay." She gave Josh a kiss on the cheek.

Ethan took her hand and squeezed it. "Thanks, Mick."

"Anytime. I love having him here. Hey, did you hear? I've been cleared of the murder charges against me."

He grinned and hugged her with his free arm. "I knew you would be. No way in hell were you going to jail." He thought a moment. "Hell, you probably *could* get away with murder. Everyone loves you and people know you wouldn't hurt a soul."

She smiled at him, helped pack up Josh's bag, and walked them to the door. She was sad to see them go. Did Summer have a clue as to how good she had it?

THIRTY-SIX

EVENING WAS SETTLING IN AS A FULL MOON started to rise over the mountains and waves of pink and orange floated through the desert sky. Dwayne would've fed the horses tonight. Michaela contemplated making a drive over to the shop where Erin and her girlfriend worked. She wasn't going alone, though. She gave Joe a ring.

"Oh hey, Mick, Camden give you my message? Why didn't you call me and tell me that the cops are off your back? My cousin Anthony got a call from Peters today about it. That's great. You probably wanted to tell me about it tonight, right? Do you need any help getting all that stuff over here?"

Michaela smacked herself upside the head. How could she have forgotten Gen's birthday? They'd even talked about it when they'd gone over to break into Sterling's place. "Of course I'm coming. I told you that I wouldn't miss it. And, yes, I did plan to tell you about the case, but there are a few unanswered questions."

"Drop it, Mick."

"I'll tell you about it when I see you." She looked at her watch. She was supposed to be at Joe's in less than an hour. "I've got to go by the tack shop and get Gen's gifts loaded. Sorry for the delay. Nothing is wrapped."

"No, no. You been under a lot of pressure. I was gonna come by earlier today and grab them, but Marianne needed my help around the house. I got a few minutes to spare now; why don't I meet you down there and I'll help you get everything together. I appreciate you ordering all that stuff on short notice."

"I can do it, Joe, don't worry about it."

"I'll see you in, what, a half hour?"

"Okay." She sighed, knowing that it was no use arguing with him. She changed her blouse because the other had wound up streaked with baby spit, ran a brush through her hair, and darted out the door. She wanted to get to the shop before Joe did and see if she couldn't get a few things wrapped. Thank goodness Camden had thought of everything when she stocked the tack shop—including horse-themed wrapping paper.

When she pulled into the parking lot, it was obvious Camden had already locked up and gone home for the day. She stood in front of the double doors and unlocked them. Joe hadn't arrived yet.

She flipped a light on and punched in the code on the security alarm. Suddenly she felt anxious about being there. It was nearly dark. She turned back to lock the front door and as she did she stopped. Her heart raced and fear coursed through her as she stared into the eyes of someone in a mask, dressed in black. Blood rushed through her ears.

"Wh-what...do you want?" she stammered. "The money is in a safe. It's...it's not much, but you can have it."

The figure started toward her and she knew that whoever was behind the ski mask was not there for any money, but rather for her. She darted toward the door and he lunged in front of her, reaching out to grab her. She pulled back and raced in the other direction, toward the rear door. She could hear steps close behind her. Running between a row of English saddles, she turned to push a set of them down as hard as she could. The intruder tripped over them and grunted, then rose and started after her again. She was at the door, her hands shaking, and turning the dead bolt, when she felt something hard hit the side of her face. She screamed as she fell to the ground. Her assailant pulled her by the arm and dragged her away from the door. Michaela knew that her life was about to end. She looked up and saw evil in the eyes behind the mask. Then she saw a polo mallet in the one free hand. It rose above her. She screamed and twisted away as a voice from the front called out her name. The intruder turned, dropped the mallet, and ran out the back door.

"Joe! *Joe!* He's getting away!"

"What?" Joe approached her, clearly aware that something horrible had just happened. He sprinted past her and out the back door. Michaela stood, rubbing the side of her head. She could now see what the killer had initially swung to knock her down—a twisted snaffle bit. Her hands shook and her body felt numb. She tried to get up but could only sink back to the floor, stunned.

A minute later, Joe came back in and knelt by her. "You okay?"

"I...think so. What happened? Did you see him?"

"I'm sorry, Mick. The bastard got away."

THIRTY-SEVEN

"LET ME GET YOU SOME ICE." JOE BENT DOWN. "Looks like you got a bruise there across your cheek. That ain't so good. You got some in the freezer, don't you?"

"Yes—wait, don't leave me!" Oh no. Michaela didn't like sounding so needy. She prided herself on her independence and, yes, even courage. But right now the last thing she felt was courageous.

"Don't worry, Mick. No one is gonna hurt you. I'll kick the shit out of 'em."

She smiled at his retort. He was right. One look at Joey P. and the bad guy would be off and running.

A minute later, Joe brought back a small bag of ice and placed it on the rapidly swelling lump on her face. "That jerk say anything? Take any money? Anything?"

"No. He was here to kill me."

"What?"

"Yeah. I offered cash, but he chased me through the store, swung that metal bit at my face, and then tried to bash my head in with the mallet. Thank God you showed up when you did."

"You sure it was a man?"

"Seemed like it, I mean whoever it was, was pretty athletic."

"Yeah, but not a big guy. I got a good look at the physique; we can't assume it was a guy yet, but we gotta call the police, Mickey."

"What? No way, Joe. The last thing I want to do is call the police. I've had enough of them. I don't want to answer any more of their questions."

"What about Jude?"

"Not even Jude." She didn't want to say *especially* Jude. He was the real reason she didn't want to call the police. She knew that he'd come unglued.

"Don't be stupid here. Someone tried to swing that thing at you and you don't want to bring in the police?" He pointed to the mallet.

She shook her head. "Okay, okay, but look, you've got to go and be with your family. Next thing I know it'll be Marianne swinging a mallet at me and I wouldn't blame her."

"Ah, Marianne knows you're like a sister to me. She loves what you do for our kid. Don't go worrying about that. Let's call the police."

"Okay."

Joe made the call and within ten minutes a black-and-white arrived. Shortly after, Jude rolled in, his face strained with worry.

Michaela sat on the sofa in her office drinking the water Joe had gotten her. After Joe told the police what had happened from his perspective, Michaela insisted that he go on home. She told him where Gen's gifts were, and one of the officers helped him carry them to the minivan, while Jude sat down next to her. "You're going to give me an ulcer," he said.

"It's not as if I ask for this stuff to happen."

"I know." He reached for her hand. "Let me ask you, what do you think this was all about? You say it wasn't a robbery. Do you think this was some kind of copycat killer?"

"What do you mean?"

"Like Sterling Taber's killer."

"That was no copycat killer. That was *the* killer."

He shook his head. "No, Michaela. Peters is certain that Carolyn Taber hired someone to murder Sterling, if she didn't do it herself. She was found at the Marriott. She hung herself. She left a note for her husband, apologizing for the grief she'd caused, and for Sterling. Her husband says that last Saturday she told him she was going to a weekend yoga retreat, but we checked, and she never went there."

"I don't think Carolyn killed him. She came to see me about the tapes."

"What? You didn't tell me this." He let go of her hand.

"I know I didn't."

"Why?"

"I didn't think it was important. I gave you the tapes and I figured that was enough."

"No. That's *not* enough. That's you keeping important information from the police. From me. When are you going to stop playing detective? When are you going to trust me?"

She didn't reply.

He sighed. "What else? Is there anything you want to tell me about when Carolyn Taber came to see you about the tapes?"

"She tried to pay me for them. I told her that the police had them."

"Did you ever think that might be why she killed herself?"

Michaela sat up. "Wait a minute. You're not blaming me for Carolyn Taber's death, are you? I had nothing to do with that. She…she tried to threaten me. That woman didn't kill herself. There was another set of tapes somewhere, and whoever had them, that's your killer."

He stood and again reached for her hand. She didn't take it. "Come on, let me take you home," he said.

"No. I have a little girl's birthday party to go to. Do you need anything else from me?"

"Yes, I do. I need you to be honest with me. I need you to be a civilian, not a cop. I'm the cop. My guys are still dusting for prints. Now, let me take you home."

She tossed him the keys to the shop. "Lock it up for me. I have to go." She reached her truck and brushed away tears, wincing at the bruise on her cheek.

THIRTY-EIGHT

JOE'S FAMILY DOTED ON MICHAELA. MARIANNE and Joe had five kids, and they weren't without their tribulations—Gen dealt with autism, little Joe with anger management issues. Vincent, who was thirteen, seemed well behaved and mild mannered, and the twins, Giorgio and Isabel, were rambunctious toddlers who kept their mother hopping. But there was a lot of love inside this home, and Michaela enjoyed being there eating birthday cake with them while Gen opened her presents.

Gen smiled widely when Vincent took out the therapeutic riding saddle for her. "That's your very own saddle," Michaela said.

"It's just for you." Marianne stood behind Gen, placed her hands on her daughter's shoulders, and winked at Michaela.

Marianne mouthed "thank you" to her. Michaela nodded and smiled. Her head still ached, but being around the Pellegrino family helped. Their house was one of the newer tract homes and had that Southern California feel combined with Mediterranean flair that so many contractors were trying to emulate in the area. It looked like Marianne probably needed help with the housecleaning. There were toys pretty much everywhere, and the twins appeared to be messy marvins, as they were busy strewing the wrapping paper all over the floSor.

The adults steered clear of discussing Sterling's murder and anything related to it while the kids were around and instead talked about horses, TV shows they liked, and even the weather—anything light. They took special care in avoiding what had happened earlier. Marianne had taken Michaela into the kitchen and given her an earful when she arrived.

"You and Joe been getting into some trouble. He's worried about you. I'm worried about you. He told me what happened and that's not good. Are you okay?" Marianne rested her hands on her hips. She was a thin, petite woman, but Michaela knew that when Marianne Pellegrino meant business, she wasn't one to mess with.

"I'm fine. I'm sorry. I know I've been a pain, and I'll leave Joe out of this from now on."

"Oh no you won't. You'll get yourself killed if Joey isn't around. But I don't need my Joey getting himself killed either. Promise me you'll start carrying some pepper spray or something. Joey makes me carry it. No more dead bodies either. This business of you and murder...well, it's not good for anyone. You need to be teaching my kid and the other kids how to ride, and settling down."

"You're right." As if she really enjoyed coming across dead bodies. But she wasn't about to argue with Marianne, who at that moment played the part of a perfect mother hen.

"Of course I'm right. Now go and have some cake."

But once Marianne suggested that the kids get ready for bed and they all told her good night, Joe clapped his hands together and said, "What do you think? Should we put our heads together on this?"

"What do you mean?" Michaela asked.

"I mean, you know and I know the cops don't have this thing figured out. Someone tried to kill you tonight and we gotta find out who it was."

"I don't think that's such a great idea," Michaela replied.

"Why not?"

"Marianne had a little talk with me and I don't want to step on any toes."

He waved a hand at her. "Mare is all bark, no bite. I gotta help you and she knows it."

"No, you don't. Why do you want to anyway?"

He yawned and stretched. "Makes me feel kind of like that dude on that old TV show—*Magnum P.I.*"

Michaela laughed. It made her head hurt, but she couldn't help it. "Tom Selleck? Oh Joe, you'd have to lose some weight and grow some more hair."

He touched the top of his head. "You cut so low sometimes. You noticed I'm losing hair, too, huh? Marianne said something about it the other day. Used to have a ton of it only what, last year or so. Shit, this getting old stuff sucks."

"I'm sorry. So, if you're Magnum, that means I must be the pain in the butt Higgins."

He pointed at her. "Ain't that the truth. Wanna beer?"

"No. I have to get home."

"Uh-uh. Marianne and I talked and you need to stay the night until we get this all resolved."

"I can't do that. The horses need me and your family doesn't need the intrusion."

"Mickey, you *are* family and you got Dwayne and Camden to take care of the animals."

"That's right, which means they're there with me and I'll be fine."

Joe smiled. "Them two are too busy these days from what you say, being holed up in the love shack."

"True."

"So you'll stay."

Marianne walked into the family room. "Of course she'll stay. And I know you two are up to no good, so you are going to deal me in. If you're going to do your little private investigating then you better include me."

"Ah, Mare, come on. You wouldn't be any good at this."

She shook a finger at him. "Joey, I'm in and there's nothing you can do about it. I think three heads are better than two, so you two start from square one and fill me in. It's obvious by the bruise on your face, Michaela, that you're in trouble. So talk."

She looked from Marianne to Joe and nodded. Joe shook his head. "Women."

"I don't think you're going to win this one, Joe."

"I never win."

Michaela started from the beginning, going over the day of the match, what happened before it, after, and then the days following.

Marianne raised her brows when she revealed that she and Joe had broken into Sterling's place. She shot her husband a dirty look. He shrugged and looked chagrined. "You think that maybe this makeup artist had a set of tapes? Or that her friend Sheila had the tape she was in?" Marianne asked.

"It's possible, but it doesn't make sense that she would kill Carolyn Taber," Michaela replied.

"No, but we don't know for sure that the woman didn't kill herself," Joe said.

"She didn't."

"You still got that bracelet you mentioned?" Marianne asked.

"Yes, it's in my purse. No one's claimed it yet." She took out the bracelet and handed it to Marianne.

"Pretty. Looks real. I have some of these fake diamonds, the cubic zirconium like this, and no one knows the difference. You mentioned the Sorvinos." She looked at Joe. "You know that the Sorvinos are related to Diamante Pizzini."

"The Pez?" Joe asked.

Marianne nodded.

"Where did you hear that?"

"You're not the only one who has cousins." She smiled.

"Can I ask who the Pez is?" Michaela said.

"He's a low-life thug. He's been in and out of jail for stolen goods. Last time he got out, I heard he went into business with some wealthy guy in Palm Springs. He runs that Sinners and Saints club."

"The place that Lucia likes to hang out at?" Michaela asked.

"That's the one, but I didn't know they were related. You sure about that, Mare?" Joe asked.

"Sure I'm sure. I ran into my cousin Nancy last year who knows Diamante's ex-wife's brother and she said that the Pez is a bastard son of Pepe Sorvino's brother."

"Pepe has kept that one under wraps, hasn't he?" Joe said. "Not surprised. Pepe likes to act like he's all about being on the up and up, and as far as I know he is, but I do find it interesting that he's related to this guy and that his daughter hangs out at that club."

"If you want my two cents," Marianne said, "I'm betting that Lucia and her brother, Mario, had something to do with the murders and now tonight with Michaela."

"But why go after Carolyn Taber?" Michaela asked.

"That's a good point, and I don't know why, but we need to trap that little brat and get her to talk," Marianne said.

"And how do you plan to do that?" Joe asked.

Marianne thought for a few seconds, and then a smile spread across her face. "I got an idea."

THIRTY-NINE

THEY STAYED UP LATE INTO THE NIGHT TALKING and planning. Marianne had a good idea to get Lucia to talk, but it also involved some delinquency on everyone's part. Joe was surprised by his wife's sneaky side and by the way Joe patted her on the butt when they finally went to bed, she got the feeling that Joe wasn't only surprised by his wife, but that it also had ignited something else in him.

Michaela camped out on the couch. She awoke the next morning to four big, round brown eyes staring at her. The twins were up early. It wasn't quite seven and Isabel was touching the side of Michaela's mouth, which was open, and she realized that she'd been drooling. Oh, thank God they were only two. She swallowed and realized how badly she needed to brush her teeth. Instead of waking Joe and Marianne, she found bowls and some cereal and gave the twins breakfast. Vincent came padding out as she brewed a pot of coffee.

"Thanks," he said.

"For what?"

"Making the twins something to eat."

He was a good-looking boy with dark hair like his dad, and light green eyes like his mom. "It didn't take much. Just poured some Frosted Flakes into a bowl."

"I know." He smiled. "But it's still cool. My mom is tired a lot and it's good she's sleeping in. My dad, too."

Michaela felt a nudge of guilt. Had Joe spent too much time trying to help her? And now Marianne was involved. "You know what? Why don't you and me surprise the two of them? Your dad mentioned something about their wedding anniversary coming up. Why don't we send them away for a weekend and I can stay with you guys?"

"Really?"

"Yes."

"Are you sure you'd want to do that? The twins are crazy and Gen is a lot to handle sometimes. And have you ever seen little Joe throw a tantrum? It's ugly."

Michaela touched Vincent's shoulder. "And what about you? You look like trouble."

He smiled sheepishly. "I try to be good."

"I think you've got it handled. So I'll make some plans for them and then we can surprise them on their anniversary."

"I think that's cool."

"I think you're cool. Listen, I've got some things to do. Will you let your mom and dad know that I'll call?"

"Sure."

Michaela cleaned up and left Vincent with the twins. What a good kid…and spending a weekend with Joe and Marianne's family was the least she could do, given all they'd done for her.

She made a quick trip home, where she fed the animals, cleaned up, and got back on the road. This morning she was going to find out what the truth was between Erin Hornersberg, her girlfriend, Sheila, and Sterling Taber. She wanted to be sure all of the bases were covered before the planned attack on Lucia Sorvino went down.

FORTY

MICHAELA FOUND THE SALON THAT ERIN HORNERSBERG worked at and Sheila owned. It was definitely one of those posh spa places where all beauty services were rendered. The sound of ocean waves played over the speaker system, and the scents of patchouli and rose filled the air. Camden would love this place. Off to the right of the beige marbled flooring and peach faux-finished walls were a couple of manicurists and their clients. They spoke in hushed tones as they lacquered the nails of their cucumber eye-patched patrons, who sat in neck-massaging chairs.

A receptionist dressed in a white lab coat, as if she were a doctor of some sort, eyed Michaela as she walked up to the desk and asked for Erin.

"Oh, Erin hasn't been in for a few days. She must've quit."

"Did she call?"

"No." Another woman slid in next to the receptionist and looked at the appointment book. She had long golden hair, which cascaded down her back, a flawless complexion, and bright blue eyes. Her nametag read SHEILA.

"Sheila?" Michaela asked.

The young woman looked up. "Yes? Are you my next client?"

"No."

"She's looking for Erin," the receptionist said.

"Funny. Me, too."

"Oh?" Michaela wasn't sure what to say.

"Can I ask why *you're* looking for her?"

She leaned in and lowered her voice. "It has to do with a murder investigation."

"Are you a cop?"

"No, I'm not. Erin did a job for me last weekend. I'm sure you've heard about Sterling Taber's murder in the papers?"

The receptionist looked up. Sheila grabbed Michaela's arm. "Tell my client when she shows up that I'll be back in a few minutes. Come on."

"What?"

"Come on. I'll get you some tea."

"I don't want any tea."

The girl practically dragged her into a rear storeroom. She closed the door and crossed her arms. "What the hell do you want?"

"I told you that I wanted to talk to Erin. Can we keep the door open?"

"No. This is a place of business and I run a professional operation. I don't appreciate you coming in here asking nosy questions about Erin."

She should've brought Joe with her like she initially planned; she hadn't expected to be dragged off into a storage room. She didn't like this one bit.

"Wait a minute." Sheila snapped her fingers. "Did you and some other woman stop by Erin's the other night?"

"Yes."

She nodded. "Uh-huh, then you're the reason she took off."

"What? I have no idea what you're talking about. I'm here because a man was killed and she might know something about it. She had his address written on the back of her business card, and now another woman associated with Sterling is dead. I know that Erin was probably jealous of what happened between you and Sterling."

Sheila played dumb. "What do you mean?"

"Come on. Erin even told me that you went home with him."

"Who are you?"

"I am the woman who was accused of murdering Sterling. He was killed in my office."

"Oh, I see, and you think that Erin did him in because she was jealous of me and him."

Michaela shrugged. "Why don't you tell me?"

Sheila shook her head. "Erin had that address because the morning after I was with that jerk, I needed a ride home. Yes, it bugged her what I did, but we got through it."

"Did you know that Erin was looking for Sterling the morning of the polo match?"

"I told her not to bother. Look, the guy was calling and harassing me. He made up lame stuff like he had me on video and he was going to show his friends and anyone else who wanted to see. Erin wanted to track him down and tell him to leave me alone. She found out he was going to be in that match, so she went looking for him. Then she wigged out when she realized that she would have to do his makeup."

"She told you all of this?"

"Yes, she did. We don't keep things from each other."

"What if I told you that Sterling wasn't lying to you about you being on tape?"

"What?" Sheila looked truly horrified. "How do you know this? Are you sure?"

"I'm sure, and it's a long story," Michaela replied.

"Oh my God. I thought he was only trying to get me to come back over to his place. He was such an ass. Oh jeez. I never in a million years thought he was that sick."

"Do you think Erin knew about the tape?"

"No way. How would she?"

"I don't know, maybe Sterling said something to her about it at the show. You know, she came really unglued because he was harassing her about you."

"No, and you know what? Contrary to what people think about Erin, she's not a bad person. She's had some rough experiences and she's pulled through them."

"But you're looking for her?"

"Yeah," Sheila replied. "After you and your friend stopped by to talk to her the other night, she kind of freaked out. She called me and said that you were asking a lot of questions, and she was afraid that after the argument she and Sterling had on Sunday that the cops would come back and press her about it. Cops aren't exactly Erin's favorite people. She spent nine months in jail for a crime that she didn't commit. So she packed up and split, and I've been calling around looking for her ever since."

"I'm sorry." Michaela could understand how Erin might've felt. The police had been on her back since Sterling's murder, and even though she had nothing to do with it, Peters had been relentless. "You mentioned something about Sterling and his harassment. You figured that it was all just talk."

"I guess I was wrong."

"Do you know who his friends might be?"

She sighed. "No. I only spent one night with the guy, but I remember who he was partying with the night I went home with him."

"Who?"

"This one guy, middle-aged Italian dude, thought he was Al Pacino or something. I think he runs that club—Sinners and Saints. What a jerk—but Sterling told me that he did business with him. There was this little chicky there, too. I never caught her name, but she didn't like me hanging around with Sterling. I got the feeling she was hot for him. She looked kind of stupid, though. I'd seen her before."

"Stupid?"

"A wannabe. I know she had a wig on. Too dark a complexion for blonde hair. I don't know, maybe she dyed it, but it looked like a wig to me because she had one of those Britney Spears kind of beret hats on and she just looked dumb. I think she knew the Italian guy, too, because he kept whispering something to her."

"Were they there as a couple?"

"I don't think so. I think they could've been related. Then this other kid came in. Kind of a cute boy-next-door type with dimples, but trying to be a bad boy, you know. He wore a tank, looked like he had a new tattoo, and wore earrings."

"Earrings? What kind?"

"Diamonds. Big freaking ones, too."

"What was his name?"

"I don't know. I know they talked about playing polo."

"Was it Zach or Tommy?"

"Like I said, I don't know. I wasn't paying attention. Look, that's all I know. I went home with Sterling. He was an ass at about five in the morning, kicking me out. That's when I called Erin to come rescue me."

"Thanks. Hey, I'm sorry about Erin," Michaela said.

"Sometimes she likes to spend time in Big Bear, when she needs to think. She'll be back. We've had our issues before, but we always get past it. I might drive up there if she's not home in a day or two."

The receptionist tapped on the door. "Sheila, your client is here."

"Thanks. I better go."

Michaela eased out of the storage room and headed to her truck.

So, Sterling, a middle-aged Italian guy, and a younger Italian woman with a blonde wig had hung out. It hadn't been Mario wearing the wig after all, but more likely Lucia Sorvino, hanging out with her cousin Diamante Pizzini. What kind of craziness had they all been up to together? And the other guy? It had to be either Tommy or Zach. They both were good-looking and played polo. Michaela was banking that it was Tommy hanging out with them that night.

It was time to talk with Lucia Sorvino.

Her cell phone rang, snapping her out of her thoughts. Joe said, "Hey, thanks for feeding the twins and hanging with Vince this morning. Me and Marianne were kind of beat, I guess."

"No, thank *you*. I should've waited until you woke up, but I wanted to try and question Erin Hornersberg some more. It looks like she's skipped town."

"Interesting. Well, I may have something on the Sorvino girl. Can you meet me? I've got to take little Joe to soccer practice. Wanna come to the field?"

"Definitely. I'll be there in twenty. I found out some other things, too."

"Can you bring me a soda and maybe a bag of chips or something? I'm kind of hungry."

"Who do you think I am, the errand girl?"

"I'm your Magnum P.I., remember? Yeah, you must be the errand girl."

"I thought I was Higgins."

"Same diff. That dude always catered to Magnum."

"Ha! I'm not getting in any trouble with your wife. She told me about your blood pressure."

"She did? Damn."

"I'll bring you a bottled water and some fruit."

"Some friend."

"You'll thank me when you lose that extra fifty pounds and maybe start to resemble Tom Selleck."

"Fine."

Twenty-five minutes later she parked her truck next to Joe's minivan. "Hey, Magnum."

Joe waved her over to the soccer field, where a group of boys chased the ball up and down the field, with parents on the sidelines screaming their brains out as to how the game should be played. She never did understand the whole soccer-parent mentality. It seemed like a form of cruel and unusual punishment for the kids, or at least emotional abuse.

"I wish I'd never made that remark about Magnum. You're never going to let me live it down, are you? You know I love that show? I got all of 'em on DVD."

"I am not surprised. Okay, so tell me what you found out about Lucia Sorvino."

"It's not so much her, but it's her cousin the Pez."

"Yeah?"

"Yeah. Check this. You know how Marianne and I told you that he's spent time in and out of jail for theft. Well, some years back, one of the guys who works for him went to the big house on charges that he was taking real jewels like rubies, emeralds, diamonds, the good stuff, and replacing them with fakes, which he was selling to a high-end jewelry store."

"No kidding?"

"No, but it gets better: The jewelry store was in Santa Barbara. And Diamante was using rich kids in the area to steal for him as well—on the side. Didn't you tell me that Sterling got popped as a teen for stealing jewels and spent time in juvie?"

"I sure did."

"Uh-huh. Well, it's all connected. Sterling knew Diamante for the last eight years or so, and who knows how long and who they've been scamming. Sterling did his short stint in juvie, got out, and moved here soon after. His folks didn't send him away. He was a delinquent. He followed Diamante and I bet lived his life conning and stealing and soaking it all up. The guy in jail for the initial crime won't talk. Word is he knows that Diamante is connected and he got framed for the crime, 'cause it's really Diamante dealing in switching out fakes."

"You think that maybe the bracelet I found in the stall—which we know is a fake—is connected to this Diamante character and somehow connected to Lucia, who may have been involved with Sterling?" Michaela said.

She filled him in about what Sheila had told her about the Sinners and Saints club and who Sterling had been with. "I think Marianne was right last night when she said that Lucia has the answers. I had to try and talk to Erin to satisfy all my theories, but this really does come down to Pepe's daughter. Lucia is looking like she's a big part of this, and now I know why she told the cops that I was screwing around with Sterling: It's because she knew that people had seen him with a blonde woman, and because I refused Sterling's advances. She might have murdered him and framed me because it was easy to do. But still, why did Lucia need to go out with the disguise?"

"Pepe Sorvino. He wants his sweet little daughter to save her *virginal* self for marriage, and if he had an inkling that she's the little tramp that she is, he'd blow a gasket. I bet she was driving her brother's car the other day when she followed you. She was trying to figure out your next play."

"Why?"

"She's a dumb-ass kid, that's why. They do stupid things. Maybe she thought you suspected her of being involved and wanted to know what you were up to."

"I can buy that, I guess," Michaela replied. "But Lucia is not the mastermind behind all of this. She didn't come after me in the tack shop last night. What should we do next?"

He shook his head. "I don't know."

"Let's backtrack. Lucia's uncle could be trading out real jewels for fakes, turning around and selling them on the black market. Where is he getting the jewels, and how is Sterling connected?" Michaela said.

"Beats me—"

"Wait! You know what, I think I might know who is behind all of this and why, and also why Carolyn Taber was murdered as well."

"You do?"

"Yes. You ready to catch a killer?"

"Do you have to ask?"

FORTY-ONE

THE NEXT DAY MICHAELA, JOE, HIS COUSIN ANTHONY, and Marianne all met at Joe's house. Camden and Dwayne had agreed to watch the Pellegrino kids, which Michaela was sure would prove interesting, while they put their plan of attack into action.

Phase one began as they pulled up to Sorvino's with Anthony driving and Marianne in the passenger seat. Michaela was in the back covered by a blanket. Joe had called to find out if Lucia would be working, and what her schedule was. He'd asked the hostess these questions under the guise that he was a friend who needed to drop something off for her.

Joe was also in the backseat and made sure that Michaela couldn't be seen. Michaela didn't really need to be there for the plan to work, but she knew she had to be for her own sanity. She'd dragged her good friends into this and wouldn't miss it for the world. She knew that it was likely going to be through Lucia that they would catch a killer—one who had possibly framed Michaela and then attempted to kill her as well.

They waited for Lucia to end her shift, which luckily was the lunch shift, because there was still much to be done, and the first thing they needed was to get Lucia Sorvino to cooperate with them.

When she emerged, she headed toward the black Explorer. "You ready?" Joe asked Marianne and Anthony.

They nodded and got out of the car. The night before, they'd all rehearsed how this was going to go down. Anthony was as eager as Marianne as they'd sat around the kitchen table.

"With the attorney general's office, eh?" Anthony had asked. "Don't you think when she looks at my card, she might ask why it don't say nothing about being employed by the attorney general?"

"It says attorney on it, doesn't it?" Joe said.

"Yeah, it says *tax* attorney, though."

"That's fine," Michaela said. "If she asks about it, then tell her that stealing jewels is not only considered theft, it's tax evasion."

"She's going to deny it," Marianne added.

"Of course she will, and that's where you come in," Joe said. "You are an undercover police officer and you're there to help her. If she goes with the two of you, then her father or brother will have to know about it."

"I like it," Marianne replied. "Playing a cop. Cool. Do I get to carry a gun?"

"No," Joe said. "No guns."

Marianne had frowned.

Now, Michaela and Joe watched as they approached Lucia. Would their plan work? They saw Lucia take Anthony's card, then look back and forth between him and Marianne. "Do you think she's buying it?" Michaela asked.

"We'll see."

Marianne then slipped her hand around Lucia's arm and escorted her to the minivan. "Nice move," Michaela said.

"That's my girl," Joe replied. "I knew she could do this."

Michaela ducked down in the backseat. Joe had moved up front, behind the wheel, and as Anthony and Marianne opened the side door to the van, Marianne got in first. and Lucia sat between her and Anthony. Joe started the car and locked the doors.

"Who's that guy?" Lucia asked.

"The driver," Anthony said.

"Driver? Do I need a lawyer?"

"I am a lawyer," Anthony said.

"I didn't do anything wrong. I didn't," the girl protested.

"We want to help you," Marianne said. "Here is what we know. We know that your cousin Diamante Pizzini, also known as the Pez, has been trading out valuable jewels for fake ones."

"I don't know nothing about that," Lucia said.

"Really?"

It was all Michaela could do to lie in the back and stay quiet. They needed Lucia to talk. They didn't want her to know that Michaela was there—not yet.

"Yeah, really."

"Huh, well that's not what Diamante told the feds."

Marianne was good at this.

"Diamante? What do you mean, he told the feds? What did he say?"

"He said that you're the one who gives him the real jewels and sells them direct to the jewelers."

"That's not true! No. I don't do that. Sterling did that, not me."

"Sterling who?" Anthony asked.

"Taber."

"The man who was murdered last weekend?" Marianne asked.

"Yes. Him."

"So he was trading your cousin real jewels, swapping them out for the fakes, but who was cashing in? Who was Sterling selling them to?" Anthony asked. Joe kept on driving and Michaela laid low.

Lucia didn't say anything for a while.

"Lucia, it's your word against your cousin's, and we can help you if you talk to us. We may even be able to keep your father out of this," Marianne told her.

"And Mario, my brother? If he knew, he'd be so ashamed of me," Lucia said.

"I think we can arrange that," Marianne said.

"Fine, I'll tell you what I know if you promise me that my dad and brother don't need to know."

Marianne opened her cell phone and dialed. Michaela had no idea what she was doing until she spoke into it.

"Okay, Miss Sorvino has agreed to work with us. Yes. On the condition that her family is not made aware of the situation. Yes. Okay. Sure. I'll tell her. Yes, sir. Good-bye."

"Who was that?" Lucia asked.

"The attorney general. He says he'll do what he can for you, but he can't control what your cousin might say or do. However, I'm sure that whatever your cousin may say, you can convince your family that he's a lunatic. Especially if you have my help."

Priceless! Michaela wanted to nominate Marianne for an Academy Award.

And then Lucia spilled her guts.

FORTY-TWO

AN HOUR LATER, AFTER ANTHONY AND MARIANNE had versed Lucia on her role, they were ready to go. Michaela's back hurt from being driven all over town in such an uncomfortable position. She'd wanted to whip back the blanket covering her, jump over the backseat, and strangle the brat when she'd said that she only told the police Sterling said he was sleeping with Michaela because she was afraid that, if she didn't say something, the cops would find out about the jewelry scam.

"I had nothing to do with his murder," Lucia protested. "I was scared because I knew what we were doing was wrong. Looks like the police found out anyway."

"That's our job," Marianne said. "We think we know who murdered Sterling and why, and because it involves the jewels, it's up to you to get a taped confession. That is, if you want to stay out of jail."

"Wait, no. I can't do that! I don't know how to do that," Lucia said.

"So I'm going to tell you." Marianne went over everything that she and the others had concocted. "Make the call."

"Okay," Lucia replied, sounding shaken.

She dialed a number. "It's me. I need you to meet me at the club. Diamante called and needs us there. No, I don't know why. But you need to be there. Now. I'm on my way. I'll see you there." She hung up the phone. "The club won't be open right now, you know."

"We know. Everything can take place outside the club. You'll be wired and we'll park around the corner."

"Wired?"

"There's nothing to be afraid of," Marianne said. "We do it all the time."

"Fine, but you better not let me go to jail and you better be right about this."

"We are."

Michaela crossed her fingers. What if her theory was wrong? No harm, no foul, other than one irate Lucia Sorvino. It was a risk, but she figured that if they didn't take it, she might eventually wind up dead. Sterling's murderer was ruthless, and after the other night, Michaela feared that the killer still intended to see her wind up the same way.

The car stopped. Michaela heard everyone get out. Joe helped Marianne wire Lucia. "Play by the book, Miss Sorvino. We'd hate for this to all go wrong for you. Pretty girls like you don't last long in jail," Marianne said. Oh, she was good!

A minute later, Joe opened the back hatch. "She's around the corner."

Michaela pulled off her blanket and blew a piece of hair out of her face. "Oh my, you are so brilliant, Marianne. I could kiss you."

"I *was* good, wasn't I?" Marianne replied.

"What about me?" Anthony asked.

Michaela patted him on the shoulder. "Excellent, all of you."

"Yeah, well, it ain't over yet," Joe said. "C'mon, get back in the car, let's see what we can hear."

"Do you think she'll run?" Michaela asked.

"No. Her family is here, and we've got her on tape now. We've got plenty of leverage on her, and my wife scared her witless. She won't run. Shh, here she is. Listen."

"Hi."

"What's this all about? I don't like this. Where's your car?"

"I parked around the corner. I don't know what it's about. Diamante just wanted to see us."

Michaela and the others exchanged looks. Joe turned up the volume on the scanner. Michaela was wondering, as she was sure they all were, if Lucia would blow it, or if Tommy would press her about where she'd parked.

"It better be good. I had to make up some lame excuse why I had to leave work. Ed Mitchell gets a whiff of it, we may not have a jewelry store to use for this stuff. And I need this. We haven't reached our goals. Mitchell thinks I'm so dependable, that's why he likes me. If he knew I was robbing him blind...oh God." Tommy's laughter rang through the scanner.

Michaela winced. She had no idea the man was so completely calculating and coldhearted.

"I'm going to tell Diamante that I don't want to do this any longer," Lucia said.

"What? Why? You're kidding. How much money have we made at this in the past few months? What, a hundred grand each? Come on. Don't be stupid. What's all this about?"

"Sterling."

"Honey, we've talked, and even though he's not here any longer we can still go forward with our plans. Come on, you're being ridiculous."

"No. I'm scared," Lucia replied.

"Why? There's nothing to be scared of. We have dreams, and this is the way to get them."

"What about Michaela Bancroft? I followed her, you know, and she's been talking to everyone about Sterling and I don't think she did it."

"Of course she didn't. Haven't you heard the news? The cops are saying that Sterling's sister-in-law did. We've got nothing to worry about. Michaela Bancroft won't be snooping around any longer."

"What if she does? She might find out about the jewels."

"She's not going with the script," Michaela whispered. "What's the deal? I thought she was only supposed to focus on Sterling."

Marianne shrugged. "I don't know. Maybe she knows what she's doing. She better."

"You know she found my bracelet," they heard Lucia say.

"What?" Tommy asked. "That was *your* bracelet? You're an idiot."

"What do you mean?"

"She came into the store the other day and the other salesperson looked at it and told her it was a phony. Luckily, she told me about it. Quit worrying about her. I'll take care of Michaela."

"What does that mean?" Lucia asked.

Joe raised his eyebrows.

"Nothing. You need to quit worrying so much and do what you're told. Now, where the hell is Diamante? I don't have time for this shit!"

"I'm out. I can't do this anymore. I just can't. I'm gonna tell Diamante when he gets here. You and Sterling had dreams and I went along with all of this because you told me that you could convince Sterling to be with me and that he'd fall in love with me."

Joe and Michaela eyed each other. "I thought so," Michaela said. "I figured there was something going on between those two. Ed Mitchell indicated it as well."

"Shh!" Joe said. "They're still talking."

"Oh babe, love is overrated. Plus, you and I have had some fun together. We got enough cash stored away right now to run off to some Caribbean island and have a party."

"I don't want to party with you. I want Sterling back!"

"That isn't going to happen. Now what the hell is wrong with you? You didn't seem all broken up about Sterling after it happened."

"How could I be? Of course I was, but I couldn't show it. I had to think quick. I was afraid the police would think that I did it."

"Well, you didn't."

"Like I just told you, Sterling's sister-in-law looks like the bad guy now after killing herself. They think she hired someone to kill him. We can still make our deals, and like I said, we can go have some fun in the sun. And if that's not your thing...well, no problem, babe. I'll take my share and go have some fun. Don't be so fucking stupid!"

"You know what scares me is that I still think there's a killer out there. What if it's Ed Mitchell? He could have found out what was going on, and he'll take each of us out one by one. Or that daughter of his."

"Juliet? Please. The cops think it was a hired gun, and they don't go after people like us. They get paid, they do the job, and they take off." Tommy laughed. "Look, neither Ed nor Juliet had anything to do with it."

"How do you know? I don't like this. I don't believe that Carolyn Taber hired anyone. How do I know that it's not someone we know? Maybe it's even you."

"You are acting like a sick little bitch! You're gonna do what you're told to do because that's the way it is! We brought you in on this because we needed you to convince your cousin to work with us. After what happened with Sterling in Santa Barbara when he was a kid, Diamante wasn't too keen on working with him again, but you helped with that, and now you're the middleman since Sterling is fucking dead."

There was a rustling noise.

"What are you doing?" Lucia exclaimed.

"Get in the car!"

"No!" she screamed.

"I said, get the hell in the car. I don't like where this is going, and I don't think Diamante is on his way. I don't know what you're up to, Lucia, but get the hell in the car and start talking because we're going for a drive."

"No! Let go of me!"

"I should have killed you, too. Dammit. I knew you were trouble."

"What do you mean...ow!"

It sounded as if Tommy was hurting her. They heard a car door slam.

Joe cranked the engine on the minivan as Lucia screamed, *"No!"* again.

They squealed around the corner. Marianne and Anthony fell on Michaela as they scrambled for seat belts.

"Joey!" Marianne yelled.

"Get my piece from the glove compartment," he said.

Marianne did as he said.

"Anthony, you know how to use a weapon?"

"Hell no, Joe. I'm a tax attorney."

"You're also a Pellegrino!"

"I can use it, honey, I know how," Marianne said.

"No, Michaela knows how to as well. I need you to drive. Here, trade."

Michaela watched in awe as Marianne slid under Joe, who moved over to the passenger seat while keeping his hands on the wheel and foot on the gas until Marianne could take over. "You two are scaring me. You're like a regular Bonnie and Clyde," Michaela said.

"In my bag, in the back, grab the other gun. You remember how to use it?"

"Yes," Michaela replied. Joe had taken her to the shooting range several times over the past year after her uncle had been killed.

Marianne spun into the parking lot as Tommy and Lucia took off in his jeep. They all heard Tommy say, "What the hell? Who is that, Lucia? Who the fuck is that?"

"I swear I don't know. I don't!"

"Should have never trusted you. You should've kept your questions to yourself!" Tommy screamed. "I'll kill you just like I did Sterling and that stupid sister-in-law of his!"

"What? No!"

"Oh my God," Michaela said. "He's spilling it all."

"She hasn't lost the wire yet," Joe said. "This isn't good. Are you willing to use the gun, Mick?"

"I...don't know," Michaela said.

"No time for 'I don't know.' I think this guy plans to kill her," Joe said.

Marianne punched the accelerator.

"Lucia!' Tommy screamed. "Tell me! Who is following us?"

"I don't know," she cried.

"I'm going to kill you, Lucia, just like I did Rebecca Woodson! And frigging Sterling got all greedy on me and was gonna tell that stupid chick's family that I did it, all because he wanted all the cash from the jewels. Know what? He probably would've figured a way to have ousted you, too. He was a snake, Lucia, and you're being a moron! I'm willing to share with you and now you go and rat me out. Didn't you?"

"No! No! Diamante did!"

"He did kill Rebecca," Michaela said.

"What! What the..." Tommy turned down a one-way street, his tires screaming around the corner.

Marianne stayed right behind him. Tommy emerged on the other end, but just before Marianne got there, a huge semi started to pull in front of them.

"Oh shit!" Joe exclaimed.

Michaela held onto her seat belt.

"Oh Mary, Mother of God," Anthony muttered.

Marianne floored the gas and circled around the semi's cab, barely missing it.

"Around that way!" Joe yelled.

She followed his directions and they again got behind Tommy's gray jeep. "Now, Mick, now! Can you take out that left rear wheel?" Joe yelled.

"I don't know."

"Try!"

They rolled down their windows. Joe stuck his gun out the front window, Michaela the back, pointing it as best as she could at the tire. They were heading toward the freeway and traffic increased as they weaved between cars. The last thing Michaela wanted was for anyone to get hurt.

Anthony had his phone out. Michaela heard him calling the police, which at this point was an excellent idea. He reported an abduction and gave a description of the car. Tommy went down another street, away from the freeway and toward suburbia.

"Take the shot, Mick! You've got a better vantage!" Joe said.

She aimed and fired. The jeep squirreled out and then zipped around a light post, finally straightening out. "I think I got him!"

The jeep started to slow. Michaela watched as Tommy leaped out. "Stop the car!" Joe yelled.

When Marianne did, Joe scrambled out and started after Tommy. Michaela followed. What happened next seemed like it took place in slow motion. No one figured Tommy had a weapon on him, but he turned around and fired, and Joe went down. Michaela sprinted to him as Tommy ran off.

"Asshole got me in the knee." Joe winced. Marianne was by Joe's side in seconds, with Anthony behind. "Go check the girl. Make sure she's okay," Joe told Anthony.

"Oh no, Joey, Joey!" Marianne cried.

He reached a hand out for her. "I'm fine, sweetie. It hurts, but I'll be okay. Now, where did that SOB go?" Joe said, his face paling as the pain hit him hard.

"He got away. Again," Michaela said and took Joe's other hand.

FORTY-THREE

MICHAELA LEANED AGAINST THE COLD, HARD wall of the hospital corridor, coffee in hand and thoughts racing through her mind. Joe was in surgery, having a bullet removed from his knee. This was not how it was supposed to happen. Detectives were questioning Lucia, and Michaela was afraid that all of them would be facing some sort of criminal charges.

Marianne was in the waiting room; Anthony had gone down to the cafeteria. Michaela had no idea what Lucia would tell the police. If she told them what Marianne and Anthony had said, then, yes, they would all be in a lot of trouble. She didn't know if Lucia was even aware of her involvement in the car chase. Once the police had been called and emergency crews arrived, it all happened so quickly. The area had been sealed off and a manhunt for Tommy ensued, with no results. He had definitely eluded the authorities.

She turned to see Anthony walking down the hall. He held out a cookie for her.

"No thanks," she said. "What do you think will happen?"

"Joe is gonna be fine. He's tough."

Michaela nodded. She prayed that his knee would be okay. "How about Lucia? What do you think she'll tell the police?"

"She's not going to tell them anything. That's why I was looking for you. I just got a call from her and she has refused to talk until she sees me. She told the police that I'm her attorney." He smiled. "I better get on downtown. Don't worry, I'll handle everything."

Michaela had no idea what Anthony had up his sleeve. But the one thing she'd come to know about the Pellegrino family was that if anyone could get out of a sticky situation, it was them.

After Anthony left, she went into the waiting area and joined Marianne. She took her small hand. "I'm sorry, Mare."

Marianne turned and looked at her, her eyes red from crying. "Sorry? Sorry? Oh honey, don't be sorry. Are you kidding me? Joey is gonna be fine and we all knew what we were signing up for with this deal. You don't need to be sorry. I have to tell you, that was the best damn time I've had in years. Please don't apologize. The only reason I'm upset is that I know for the next however long it takes for Joey to heal, I've got to play nursemaid." She started to laugh. "Okay, so maybe I'm a little worried, but honestly, Joe is not a good patient."

"I imagine not." They both laughed. "I really do hope you know how sorry I am about all of this."

"Dammit, Michaela, you say that one more time and I'm gonna knock you across the room. Just stop it."

Michaela gave her a hug. When she pulled away she looked up and saw Jude heading toward them. Her stomach sank.

"Hello, ladies. Michaela, I think we need to talk."

She nodded. Marianne excused herself and Jude asked her not to go far, as he planned to question her as well. When she left the room, he turned to Michaela. "Do you want to tell me why you and your friends were chasing a car that Tommy Liggett was driving with Lucia Sorvino inside it? Oh, and don't leave anything out, especially the part where you shot out Tommy's tire."

He wasn't happy with her and she didn't know how she was going to get out of this. "We spotted Lucia being dragged into a car by Tommy and it didn't look good, so we followed them and could tell she was in trouble. I shot out the tire because I was afraid he was going to kill her."

"And why would you think that?"

"Because I found out that Sterling and Tommy were dealing in stolen jewels. Lucia had connected them with her cousin Diamante Pizzini, and then Tommy murdered Sterling, because last summer the two of them were involved in the death of a woman in Santa Barbara."

Jude placed his head in his hands. "Oh God. Go on."

"While Detective Peters was busy pointing the finger at me, and you were off on your cruise, I didn't have much choice but to try and figure out who really murdered Sterling Taber." She told him everything she'd found out about Rebecca Woodson and what she surmised had happened last summer on the pier. "I think Tommy was there, and whether or not it was an accident, either Tommy or Sterling pushed her. Then, I think they agreed to cover for each other. I spoke with Rebecca's brother this week and he said that Sterling had tried to get him to meet with him. He told him that he had information about his sister's death. I believe that Sterling was greedy and planned to tell Rebecca's family that Tommy had killed her. Tommy found out about this and so he killed Sterling—because Sterling was about to betray him and also because of the jewels they were dealing in. Sterling wanted all the profit. He wasn't the type to share."

"Interesting. If you have that all figured out, then why don't you tell me what part Carolyn Taber played in all of this."

"I think Tommy killed her. I think he had a set of tapes that Sterling probably gave him. When he saw that there might be holes in the case against me, he knew he'd need another fall guy and he chose Carolyn. She was easy to frame. I bet that if you run a handwriting analysis on the suicide note, it won't match Carolyn Taber's handwriting."

"Maybe you should become a cop."

"Funny." She smiled at him but he didn't return the smile.

"You know that Anthony Pellegrino, who is your friend Joe's cousin and who was in the minivan with you and the others, is now downtown with Lucia Sorvino, *representing her*."

"He's a good lawyer."

"He's a *tax attorney*, Michaela. I know there are blanks to fill in here. You haven't been forthright from the get-go. But honestly, I don't think I want to know everything anymore, because I've got a bad feeling that if I did know, I'd have to arrest you. And I don't want to do that. You better hope that the holes in your story don't get bigger and that none of your partners fill in the blanks.

"Yep." She took a sip of coffee. It was all she could say. A minute later, Jude stood. She asked him, "Have they found Tommy?"

"Not yet. But we will. I've got to get back to the station. Tell Mrs. Pellegrino that I hope her husband is better."

"You aren't going to talk with her? I thought you said…"

He held up a hand. "Like I said, I don't think I want to know. I've got enough to file a report and keep you out of jail. But we do need to talk. We really do. Just not now."

She nodded. Jude left the room and she watched him walk down the hall to the exit. She got up and paced the hall. A few minutes later Marianne came back and said, "Where's the cop?"

"Gone. He says he hopes Joe feels better and he changed his mind about talking with you."

"Huh. Okay. Well, Joey is out of surgery and the doctor says it looks good."

"That's great. Can we see him?"

"They say he's in recovery and it'll be a while. You know, why don't you go on home and I'll call you. I'm kinda worried about the kids anyway. I'm sure Camden and Dwayne have their hands full."

"Of course. Sure. Yes, call me."

Michaela headed home with an empty feeling inside. Her friend was hurt, and she'd done a dumb thing by trying to take down a madman. Jude was right: She needed to stop playing detective. She didn't have the skills for it.

It was getting dark and all the lights were on at Dwayne and Camden's place. She walked in and was pleasantly surprised by what she saw. On Camden's lap sat a sleeping Isabel; Dwayne was playing Monopoly with Vincent and little Joe. Gen was drawing and Giorgio was watching a TV show. Wow.

"Hi, Michaela," Dwayne said. Camden smiled at her and brought a finger to her lips. Who knew that Camden could be...domestic? A wave of comfort came over her and she wanted to sit down and start crying, but she knew that would raise too many questions, and the last thing she wanted to do was break up the peaceful scene. She went over to the table where the Monopoly game was going on. "Sorry guys, it took us a little longer than we thought. Um, and I think the kids will probably stay for a little while more. I'll go out and feed the horses and then take the kids off your hands and give them dinner."

"No, no. I be making some burgers for them. I got the grill fired up already and Cammy girl made the patties earlier for us," Dwayne said. "We all be good. You sure 'bout the horses? I can feed 'em."

"No. You look like you're having a good time." She glanced at Camden and smiled. "Look at you," she whispered.

"I know," she whispered back so as not to wake the toddler. "I know." She smiled.

Michaela left them and headed to the barn. She piled flakes of hay onto the wheelbarrow and began her rounds. She fought back all of the emotion that ate at her, which ranged from anger, frustration, sadness, and fear to the other end of the spectrum after seeing Camden and Dwayne with the kids—which had given her a sense of peace and happiness. She'd had her doubts about those two getting married, but any lingering questions had been wiped away in the last few minutes. They were going to be married and start a family and Michaela wanted all of that and more for them, because it was her strongest desire to have a family, too. If she couldn't have one then her best friend should, and she could share in their joy.

Her stallion, Rocky, snorted as she passed. Here was her family. He tossed his head as she started to open his stall door. "Okay, okay, easy. I'm getting it," she said.

Rocky pawed the ground. He was always eager when it came to dinnertime, but there was something off about him tonight. She pushed the stall door open a little farther as Rocky sent a shrill whinny echoing through the breezeway. It all happened in seconds, but Michaela felt something go around her neck. She reached her fingers up, clawing at the object. Someone was strangling her. Rocky reared up inside his stall. She could see the whites of his eyes and his nostrils flare, fear emanating from him. She kicked and struggled. She knew who had her: Tommy Liggett had come to her ranch and hidden out, waiting to strike.

As she felt the lead rope tighten further, she heard Tommy telling her what a stupid bitch she was. "You didn't have to keep snooping around. I killed Carolyn Taber for you. I actually liked you. I didn't want you to go to jail. Then I thought Carolyn would be a perfect killer to pin this all on and you'd be free. But no, you had to keep after me, send in Lucia and the troops. What the hell is wrong with you?"

Michaela, still struggling, grew dizzy. She knew she was losing the fight. And as she faded, Rocky shoved his stall all the way open with his head and charged at Tommy, who dropped the rope. Now on the ground, Michaela rolled quickly to her side. Rocky reared up again and came crashing down, knocking Tommy onto his back. He screamed, but it was too late; Rocky's hooves came down on Tommy's chest. Michaela sat up. Her horse had just saved her life.

FORTY-FOUR

IT WAS OVER. IT HAD BEEN A WEEK SINCE TOMMY Liggett was taken away in a body bag from Michaela's ranch. The police closed the investigation after running the handwriting analysis, as Michaela suggested. Lucia worked with the police in fingering her cousin in the jewelry scam and told them what Tommy had said to her in the car about killing Sterling. She did not, thankfully, tell the police about Marianne's and Anthony's role in any of it. Anthony was able to get her a deal if she cooperated with the cops, and no one was the wiser about how things had really occurred the day they chased Tommy down.

Jude and Michaela finally had that talk, and both came to the conclusion that maybe they weren't right for each other. She knew that Jude had been hurt by her dishonesty with him, and she'd been hurt by his lack of faith in her. She had to wonder if she'd ever find the right man and start a family. Joe was back home with his brood, and she'd taken food over for them several times and run errands for Marianne, wanting to help out as much as she could.

Dwayne and Camden had gone back to putting all their efforts into planning their wedding and running the tack shop.

Rocky was her hero, and every day she'd gone out to see him with an extra handful of carrots. As horrible as Tommy's death had been, Rocky had saved her life and she was grateful.

Michaela sat out back, her eyes closed, listening to the waterfall pour into the pool. She thought about Ethan and wondered how everything was going with him. He'd called when he heard what had happened, and wanted to come over. She'd insisted it wasn't necessary. She knew that the two of them needed to have some space between them. Summer was not her favorite person in the world, but Michaela knew her feelings for Ethan were wrong, and she needed him to stay away. She needed to move on with her life, and thankfully tomorrow would be the beginning of that as she went back to giving riding lessons. She got up and went inside to make herself some dinner. Camden and Dwayne had gone out for the evening, and although she thought she'd relish having time to herself after all she'd been through, she felt pretty alone.

She seasoned a chicken breast and put it in the oven to bake. As she started fixing herself a salad, the doorbell rang. *Who could that be?*

Ethan stood on the other side of the door, little Josh in his arms. He looked distraught. "Ethan? What is it? What's wrong?"

He walked past her, put Josh down on her family room floor, and handed him a set of plastic keys to play with. He grabbed her arm and took her into the kitchen, where in a lowered voice he said, "She left."

"What?"

"Can you believe it? Summer. She just left us. I was at work. The baby was at day care. I had to go down to the Rocovich Center in San Diego yesterday. Then, I got this call from the day-care lady, who said that Summer never picked him up. She'd called yesterday and asked her to keep him overnight, but then she didn't show up today."

"What?"

"Yeah, so I raced home and picked him up and came home to an empty house. She even took her horses."

"No, Ethan. No! That's not true."

He handed her a letter. "Read this."

Michaela took it. Summer's letter detailed how she couldn't handle being a mother, that she thought she'd loved Ethan but now she didn't think so, and she didn't want the life. She wanted a different life. The words were crazy and unfathomable. *How could a woman leave her baby?* The letter further stated that she'd met someone, and for Ethan to expect divorce papers and that she wouldn't fight him in a custody battle.

"Oh my God, Ethan. No. Look, you have to find her. Maybe she's going through some type of postpartum depression like we talked about, and she needs help. Women don't just leave their children. They don't do it, and I know she loves Josh. I've seen her with him."

"Find her? No way. She left her son and me. You read the letter. And you don't know the half of it. I didn't want to say anything. You've had so much going on," Ethan said.

"I don't understand."

He took her hands. "Summer. She has not been a mother to our son. I'm so exhausted. I come home from work and he's either hungry or needs to be changed. I don't know what to think. I'm the one who found the day care because I was so worried about him. I tried talking to her and she would scream at me and tell me that she was fine."

Michaela shook her head. "I had no idea. This is all wrong. She'll be back. This is crazy."

"No *she's* crazy. I don't want her to come back. She's found another man, and you know what, the whole way over here, Michaela, I kept running it through my mind. The day she left me at the altar and then wormed her way back into my life, and the way she has tried to keep us from being friends, and I know why. It's because she's seen all along what the two of us haven't, and as far as I'm concerned this is a blessing."

"What?"

He leaned in and kissed her hard, wrapping his arms around her. The world, her life, all of it swirled into a blur, as if she was in a dream. But it was real. And it was more than nice and more than special. It was a connection so profound that it brought tears to her eyes, and although she was confused by all of it, at the same time, she felt more clarity in those seconds than she'd ever known. He pulled away from her and said, "It's been you, Mick. Always has.

It's that simple. It has always been you and I'm tired of pretending or denying it. I won't do it anymore. Will you? I mean, we want to be in your life and I think there's a future here for us." He looked at Josh and then back at her. "The three of us. Don't you?"

Emotion caught in the back of her throat and she couldn't respond for a second. Ethan didn't take his eyes off of her. When she was finally able to express herself, she replied, "You don't even have to ask that. I think you already know the answer." She wiped her tears and kissed him back.

Excerpt from *Three Days to Die* due out 2013

CHAPTER ONE

Michaela Bancroft had to be crazy. What in the world had she been thinking? Who decides to get married during the holidays?! Oh yeah, she *and* Ethan, that's who. "Let's get married on New Year's Eve," she'd said. "It'll be like starting over, with a clean slate." He'd happily agreed, and the rest, as they say, is history. But now, just a few weeks before Christmas and up to her neck in holiday planning, it didn't seem like such a great idea. Michaela smacked herself in the head. *Brilliant, Michaela. Just brilliant.*

The baby monitor suddenly crackled to life as Josh whimpered softly in his crib. She set the box of Christmas ornaments aside and headed toward the nursery. "I'm coming, little man."

Truth be told, her best friend Camden was to blame for this whole mess. If she hadn't insisted on having a mai tai bar for her Hawaiian wedding and if Michaela hadn't caught the bouquet…although in retrospect, she was damn glad she had and even happier at the grin on Ethan's face when she turned to look at him. Then there was the slow dancing and the kissing, and the passionate interlude back in their suite at the resort. Well, after all that, a New Year's wedding seemed to make perfect sense. Until now. Why hadn't she suggested a good old-fashioned elopement? To Vegas? But Ethan had already been there, done that with Summer, his ex-wife and Josh's mother. And that ended with Summer ditching Ethan and her infant son for another man. Apparently being a wife and mother wasn't her forte.

Michaela opened the nursery curtains and lifted Josh from his crib, cuddling the toddler to her chest. As hard as it had been to watch Ethan deal with Summer's abandonment, she couldn't help but be glad things turned out the way they did. She now had Ethan—her childhood friend and lifelong crush—and Josh, who was by every standard (except biological) her son. Life was good. So, in reality, when she thought about it, a New Year's wedding wasn't such a bad idea after all. The holiday trappings would go along nicely. Everything would be perfect. *Sure.*

"Hello? I'm here," Camden's voice rang out from below. "Where's my god son?"

Michaela carried the drowsy, blue-eyed boy down towards the open arms of his godmother. Camden's latest hair color was bleached blonde and she'd pulled it straight back into a high, tight ponytail. She'd taken to wearing Wranglers, cowboy boots, and a silver belt buckle. Being married to Dwayne, Michaela's right hand man at the ranch, had obviously turned haute couture Camden into a true blue cowgirl. She even rode on a regular basis—something Michaela never expected to see.

Josh adored Camden as much as she did him. He reached his pudgy arms out to her as she cooed his name, "Joshy, Joshy boy, come to Auntie Cam." The little boy almost leapt into his godmother's arms and snuggled into her soft denim shirt.

It never ceased to amaze Michaela just how much Camden loved Josh. Yes, he was an adorable little guy, but Camden wasn't exactly known for her maternal ways. Her idea of a home cooked meal was Hamburger Helper, packaged salad, and a frozen margarita. All Michaela could figure is Dwayne had something to do with it. Since she'd married him, Camden had started cooking (real, albeit not gourmet, food) and had fallen hard for little Josh.

"I'm feeling a little second fiddle here," Michaela said wryly.

"Don't be silly. He knows who his mommy is." Camden's eyes locked on Michaela's. Neither one said what they were both thinking. Michaela was hoping to adopt Josh after she and Ethan married. It was clear to all involved that Summer didn't want to be his mother. She'd abandoned him as completely as she'd abandoned Ethan. But all the same, when it came to signing away any rights to the little boy, Michaela wondered if Summer would go through with it.

"He knows *exactly* who his mommy is." Camden tickled Josh's tummy and he let out a squeal of delight.

Michaela smiled and glanced down at her watch. "Okay, I should be home by lunch time. I'm going to run over to Winsor and take a look at that horse Devon called me about, and then swing by the florist. If I have time afterwards, I may try to squeeze in some more Christmas shopping."

"Oh honey, it's eight already. You're going to need more than four hours to do all that!"

Michaela raised an eyebrow. "I thought you knew me better than that. I don't need four hours to decide whether or not a horse will fit in my program or choose flowers for my wedding. As far as Christmas shopping goes, I already know what I'm buying everyone. I'll be in and out in a jif." She snapped her fingers. "Now if it was you, it'd be a whole 'nother story."

Camden shrugged. "What can I say? Auntie Cam likes to shop. Josh doesn't think it's a problem. Do you Joshy?"

The little boy giggled.

Michaela kissed him on the cheek. "Okay, be back in a bit. And remember, do NOT let him watch those reality TV shows."

"Oh come on, he loves The Housewives of OC! Those L.A. broads are crazy!" She circled her index finger by the side of her head.

"No. I mean yes, they'd have to be crazy to be on that show. But no, I don't want him watching that stuff," Michaela replied. "Nick Jr. or Discovery Kids if you have to. Actually, I'd prefer no TV time. Play with him."

Camden rolled her eyes. "You know I will."

"Ok, ok. Be back soon!"

Michaela headed out and did a quick walk through the breezeway of the barn. Her three-year-old, Leo, had cast himself the other night in his stall. She'd had to poultice and wrap him to help sweat out the swelling. Dwayne would have already checked him and likely rewrapped him when he fed Leo that morning, but it was rare for Michaela to leave the house without a quick hello to her horses. Today was Monday—a day off for everyone: the horses, Michaela's students, and herself.

Michaela trained horses with an emphasis on reining, but she'd ventured out her comfort zone recently when one of her clients had brought over an appendix filly she wanted trained as a hunter jumper. Michaela had done some jumping throughout the years but explained that it wasn't her strong suit. The owner didn't care. She'd heard wonderful things about Michaela, going so far as to call her a *horse whisperer*. Michaela still cringed a little when she thought about that. She just did what she did best—train using empathy and kindness, setting boundaries where needed.

Leo stuck his head out of the stall as he heard his "mom" approaching. "Yes, I have a treat for you." She rubbed his face and kissed his nose, his hot breath puffing on her face and hands as he sniffed for the treat. Michaela reached into the front of her jeans pocket and took out a handful of carrots. He nuzzled the palm of her hand as he sucked them up. "You're not a horse. You're a vacuum cleaner." She undid the latch on his stall and went inside. The woodsy smell of shavings mixed with earth and horse smelled better to her than any perfume ever could. She bent down and checked Leo's wraps. As suspected, Dwayne had beat her to the job.

Speaking of Dwayne, he was probably back in bed. He also took Mondays off and, according to Camden, typically spent them watching reruns of old shows like Gilligan's Island, Three's Company, and I Love Lucy.

Michaela closed Leo's stall door behind her and continued down the breezeway. Immediately the young horse started banging against the door of his stall with his hoof. "No more. Knock it off," she scolded him. His ears pricked forward and his eyes widened. She shook a finger at him. "You heard me."

There were twelve more horses to kiss and hand treats to. Some were there for training and some for her lesson program. Michaela gave lessons to kids. She'd also developed a program for autistic children. Nothing gave her more joy than the moment when a kid had a breakthrough because of a horse. Horses were gentle souls who, for the most part, seemed to understand how to help a person grow, heal, and be nurtured.

After her brief visit with the horses, she headed out to Winsor. Winsor Riding Academy was a nearby high school prep academy and riding school that educated both local and out-of-state kids. It definitely wasn't for families short on cash. Most of the kids at the school trained in three-day eventing, which Michaela loved to watch, especially the cross-country jumping. Those riders had some serious cajones! Galloping through a course, jumping over stationary obstacles—usually wooden logs that jarred both horse and rider if they hit.

Devon Winsor, one of the owners, was an acquaintance and had given Michaela a call the other day about an older gelding in their stable. Apparently he was also an appendix—half Quarter horse, half Thoroughbred—and although he'd been an excellent eventer and a good school master, he was at an age where he needed to be taken off the jumps. Devon felt the horse would be a perfect fit for Michaela's program. Michaela liked the idea of adding a gentle soul to the barn, one who could teach the beginners and also be great for her special needs kids. This horse sounded like a good fit, but she wanted to see him up close and personal—preferably without Devon hovering—to make sure. She didn't know Devon that well and before Michaela plunked down a few thousand dollars on a lesson horse, she needed to take a peek at him. His name was Silverado and per Devon, he was stabled in barn three. The horses had name tags on their stall doors, so she figured it wouldn't be a problem finding this one.

Cruising slowly down the long driveway leading up to the academy, Michaela noticed how empty the place was. Most of the kids had gone home for the holiday break. And while there were a few local boarders around, the place was pretty deserted.

Michaela smiled as she pulled up in front of the barns. Dr. Grace's truck was parked out front. Grace Morgan was Ethan's business partner. He'd recently bought into her veterinary practice when he'd decided to make a move from his old partnership. Ethan's former partner wasn't willing to learn new techniques and his bedside manner was far from pleasant. That was enough for him to buy the guy out and find a new partner. When Dr. Grace mentioned an opening at her practice, Ethan jumped at the opportunity.

Grace was well respected and renowned for her veterinary skills in Indio and beyond. She was cutting edge and did a lot of lab work and looked deeper than most to get to the bottom of a number of horse ailments. She cared deeply for the animals and it showed.

Maybe Grace could vet Silverado for her. She called out the doctor's name as she entered barn three. No answer. She called again into each of the barns. Still no response. Maybe Grace was up at the main house with Devon? Michaela checked her watch and realized she only had a few minutes left to check out Silverado.

She found the grey gelding down the aisle of barn three. He stuck his nose out to greet her. "Oh you are a cute guy, aren't you?"

The horse in the opposite stall banged against the door just like Leo had done earlier that morning. "Ah, another begger," she said, turning around to see what she guessed was a Dutch Warmblood. He was huge. At least seventeen hands, and had a wild look in his eye. He snorted, weaving his great head back and forth.

Michaela turned back to the grey gelding. "Looks like your friend has some issues to work through. But you, on the other hand look very sweet." She liked his soft, kind eyes. Devon said he was eighteen, but there was no sway to his back. He had great muscle tone and a very pretty face. She'd have to ride him to see how his disposition was. But so far, so good.

The wild guy across the way though—he was something else entirely. He became more agitated as she stood there talking to the other horse. She finally took a step toward the large animal and spoke in calm tones. "Hey, hey there." She squinted to read his name plate. Geronimo. Should've known. "Hey Geronimo. It's okay. It's alright, bud."

The horse blew out another snort and held his head high and out of reach as she went to try and stroke him on the neck. It was then that she caught a glimpse of what was making him crazy. She took a step closer and the horse backed away. She closed her eyes and shook her head. This could not be happening. She swallowed hard.

"Oh my God." Her voice came out in a croak. It didn't sound like her at all. She stared down at a sight she was certain she'd never, ever forget. Dr. Grace lay sprawled on the floor of Geronimo's stall—dark patches of dried blood all around her.

Made in the USA
Lexington, KY
12 February 2018